THE SIGIL TRILOGY

Books by Henry Gee

Fiction

The Sigil Trilogy
1: Siege of Stars
2: Scourge of Stars
3: Rage of Stars

By The Sea
Futures from *Nature* (editor)

Nonfiction

The Beowulf Effect (forthcoming)
The Science of Middle-earth: revised e-book edition (forthcoming)
The Science of Middle-earth
Jacob's Ladder
In Search of Deep Time
Before The Backbone
A Field Guide to Dinosaurs (with Luis V. Rey)
Shaking the Tree (editor)
Rise of the Dragon (editor)

THE SIGIL TRILOGY

Henry Gee

ReAnimus Press

Breathing Life into Great Books

ReAnimus Press
1100 Johnson Road #16-143
Golden, CO 80402
www.ReAnimus.com

Cover art by Clay Hagebusch

ISBN-13: 978-0615688916

First print edition: October, 2012

10 9 8 7 6 5 4 3 2 1

For Karl, who gave his name to a small, destructive and (mercifully) fictional asteroid.

BOOK ONE

SIEGE OF STARS

Chapter 1: Salesman

London, England, Earth, May 1979

Gawan, that sate bi the quene
To the kyng he can enclyne
'I beseche now with sazez sene
This melly mot be mine.'

(Gawain, who sat by the Queen
Towards the King inclined
'I implore you, with a prayer plain
That this fight should be mine.')

Anon. — *Sir Gawain and the Green Knight*

Ruxton Carr knew he'd never forget that rainy Monday when She came into the shop. One reason he remembered (as he later tried to tell himself) was that Mrs T had just got in as Prime Minister. He felt an inner thrill — at just 18, he'd voted for the first time ever, his first general election. Mrs Thatcher supported people like him — young guys who wanted to do things, go places. No way was he going to be a salesman in Khan's Electronics forever. The second, and never mind what happened next, was that She — that's She with a capital 'S' (and not Mrs T, let's make that clear) was not just anyone. She was special. You know that specialness, when you meet someone for the first time and you're convinced you've seen them before? Special, like that.

He was giving this geezer all his Grade-A patter about a Japanese music centre, direct drive turntable, FM like crystal clear, dual auto-reverse decks with Dolby, brushed aluminium fascia, smoked acrylic hood, and a little beyond this punter's financial comfort zone. He had almost succeeded — he was the best salesman in Khan Electronics by far (it was Ruxie's weirdly cat-like yellow eyes against his dark skin, Mr Khan had said) — but that was when She arrived.

Purposeful, she brushed aside the glass door against the heavy weather of Tottenham Court Road, windswept, spattering raindrops all over the shop floor. She was tall, slim, in a tan raincoat with big lapels. Her face was very pale — as pale as he was dark. Her hair was long, intensely black, and completely unkempt. But the main thing was her eyes. Huge, round like an owl's, black as her hair, and looking straight at *him*. She didn't look pleased.

Ruxton panicked at first. Was she a customer storming in with a complaint? He'd served so many people. One after the other, blam blam blam, set and forget. Best salesman in Khan's, remember? But no, if he'd sold *her* something he'd definitely have remembered. Maybe she was complaining for someone else? Husband? Boyfriend? But no, she wasn't carrying anything, a broken radio or whatever, like angry customers usually did. Neither did he feel like he sometimes did when he was caught doing something he shouldn't, like smoking or looking at girlie mags, which was as if they'd found him with his pants down. No — when he looked up and at her the thing that came into his mind was — of all things — skiing. Skiing? He'd never been skiing in his life.

"You've convinced me," said the music-centre man. "I'll take it." Ruxie was brought back to life with a jolt. From behind the oblivious punter the woman's eyes pierced him like lasers.

"Wha...? Oh yes, of course. My colleague will serve you. Rashid? *Rashid?*" Ruxie beckoned at the new boy, who looked as hopeless as he usually did — or was he just stunned that Ruxie would give up a customer for anyone? A sale was a sale. Rashid got the message. He hurried over, all smiles, and led the customer to the till. There was nothing, now, between him and Her. She. Nothing except a display case full of personal stereos. And what she said was...

"What's taking you so long, spaceman?"

"Spaceman...?"

She rolled her eyes and sighed. "Why does this always have to be so difficult? I said, 'what's taking you so long, spaceman?'" And then with one long, pale forefinger she touched his wrist and he felt the world spin.

Chapter 2. Drover

Milky Way Galaxy, Orion Spiral Arm, *c.* 68,700,000 years ago

Mit der Dummheit kämpfen die Götter selbst vergebens
(Against stupidity the Gods themselves struggle in vain.)
Friedrich Schiller — *Jungfrau von Orleans*

"Help me!"

The voice of Roland resounds among the mountainous stars. Merlin stirs from her brooding.

Too slow.

"Wake up, sleepyhead!" comes another cry. "What's the matter with you?" It is Guinever, scintillating past. Merlin can only grunt in answer. She falls in behind.

Roland is a speck of brightness overwhelmed by the Drove. Some have broken loose from the main stream headed for a distant metal-rich nebula, tempted by a distraction closer to hand. It is a red dwarf in the Oort cloud of a nearby yellow sun. The red star is rank with rottenness. No wonder that some of the friskier outliers of the Drove are tempted. No wonder, either, that they drown the bleats of Roland. Pathetic though he is, Merlin thinks, one can hardly blame him.

Space rings with the calls of the Drovers, the gravitic keening of the Drove. Merlin, trying hard to concentrate, ravels space towards the melée. Guinever whips in a few of the more recreant Drove, while trying to console Roland.

"Some of us seem to have to do everything round here," she chides. Merlin broadcasts contrition. She hopes it sounds genuine, given her preoccupation. The problem is bigger than poor Roland. Bigger than all of them.

And it can only get worse.

How can she stop them, forever, and she alone, when, right now, it will take her, and Guinever, and Roland, and whoever else they can rustle up, all their power and concentration to round up a few chancing strays?

Merlin gains on Guinever and Roland and sees that Dante and Elaine have joined the chase. But five of them are too few to corral the swarm now descending on the red dwarf, scattering comet-cloud debris like chaff.

In the end, the five Drovers can only hover, and gather, and wait, as the Drove warps the small star into nothingness, altering the gravitational balance of the space immediately around it.

There is little they can do to alter the flux of debris, now directing itself, slowly at first, towards the G-type dwarf less than two light-years away. The yellow star with that hopeful retinue of silicate-mantled planets, at least one of which has retained warmth and volatiles suitable for the emergence of life—life that must be cherished.

Guinever broadcasts anxiety and regret. Roland is shamefaced, but Guinever's anger is spent. She knows that it's not his fault. Dante is just numbed. He has seen this kind of thing too often, lately, to feel anything more than resignation. Only Elaine cries aloud, to no-one in particular, her howl of anguish causing barely a ripple in the void: "What's wrong with them—and with us?"

Merlin had met the Drove Elders in an Xspace of her own choosing. They wanted her, they said, to feel comfortable. At the appointed coordinates she shimmered into being on a snowy hill-slope. Ahead of her and slightly above was a log cabin built on a platform of massive cut stones.

She was met at the door by a butler who helped her off with her ski-suit and directed her to a great salon. She made the usual vain attempt to rein the mass of long black hair from her face to better admire the view through the floor-to-ceiling picture windows running the length of the left-hand wall. At the far end of the salon, ahead of her, was an imposing fireplace. Logs crackled in the grate.

On either side, two men lounged on worn chesterfields, in the casual-but-smart way that only the truly prosperous and confident can lounge. One of the men looked old but fit, every inch the habitual skier. He rose to greet her, all senatorial smile, Argyll sweater and precisely pressed slacks. He broadcast such command that she felt herself stifling a small stir somewhere behind her ribcage. But she sensed that the real power lay with the balding man with the thick spectacles, conservative suit and dark tie: the man who did not get up, but who remained, frog-like and crumpled, in the other chesterfield.

"Merlin, it is good of you to come," said the standing man. He offered a firm hand and she took it. She hoped her returning grasp didn't give too much away. "I'm Solomon," he said, "and my colleague here is Saturn." The frog-like man smiled and nodded.

Solomon indicated a wing-backed leather chair facing the fire, between the chesterfields. He waved her to sit down, and offered her a drink.

"I took the liberty of choosing for you," he said. "I think you need it, especially after that long walk through the snow." She murmured a thank-you and took the glass. The brown liquid within gave off the intense odor of K-type dwarfs at the sticky end of the main sequence. She downed it in one swallow. Ease coursed through her.

"Islay," said Solomon. "Works every time."

"Thank you, it's..."

"... purely medicinal, I know. I'm afraid we've not brought you here just to admire the view and enjoy a fine malt."

"No, I..."

But Solomon had wandered off to regain his place on his chesterfield and, momentarily, his back was turned.

"No, Merlin, we want to ask you something. A favor."

"Me?"

"Obviously, you."

"But why not Guinever or Roland or Orfeo or Oliver or any of the others?" She regretted her outburst as soon as she'd made it. Solomon paused and turned, ever so slightly, to Saturn, who remained motionless.

"Let's say that you look like the most likely prospect for — well, for what we have in mind. Now then, what's your impression of the Drove, these days?" Merlin paused before answering and looked down at her hands, resting palms-upwards in her lap. The answer seemed so obvious that she wondered whether it was a trick question, but when she looked up, parting the curtain of hair that had fallen across her face as she thought, she saw that both men were looking at her intently, their expressions entirely sincere. Like they really wanted to know.

"It's getting worse with every iteration," she began. "The beasts are more and more — well — frisky. It's all we can do to keep them on track. They are forever veering off to graze on stars or gas or whatever, sometimes parsecs off course, and they just get more defiant. Sometimes I think it's just us, or just bad luck, or if the beasts have learned to try it on, but lately — well — it might sound impertinent, or lame, or..."

"No, go on," reassured Solomon. "We must have no secrets here. You're among friends, Merlin. This isn't an inquisition."

"Oh, well, all right, I'll say it — that no matter how good we are, there just aren't enough of us. I thought we were hard pressed before that —

that—well, before Heloise and Beatrice left, and I remember that day well..."

"Don't we all? Terrible."

"But after that, when things were rough, I asked Uther and Enid what things were like when they were younger, and..."

"Your fore-parents, I believe?"

"Yes. And instead of saying that we youngsters never knew when we were born, or some such, they simply sighed and said that we had it very much harder than they ever did. Yes, that's what they said—very much harder."

Her words dropped into a silence relieved only by the crack of a log in the grate. At last, Solomon spoke.

"Thank you, Merlin, for being so candid," he said. "Sad to say, though, you are absolutely right. With every age that passes our numbers dwindle, and my fear—our fear—is that we'll reach the point when we can no longer restrain the Drove. It could be that we've already gone beyond that point." The silence then was as of the chasms beyond dimensionality, before and after the Continuum, seeping in, and which, more than any other single thing, filled the minds of the Drovers with terror.

"But... what then?"

"That, my dear, is a question we all ask. All of us of a certain age, that is. But we never dare answer. You are younger, however. Bolder, perhaps? Maybe you should like to do that for us?" All of a sudden she felt that she was a little girl again, gamboling through the voids, careless as she played on the flukes of her fore-parents' recursive forms, the responsibilities of adulthood not even a smudge on a flawless horizon.

"Well, I suppose, that if we were to go on like this, we'd just—eventually—disappear, and then... "

"And... then?"

"The Drove would just eat, and eat, until they'd consumed... the Universe."

"That's correct. Well done, Merlin. It's often very hard to voice the answer that everyone knows, but nobody wants to articulate."

Despite the fire, she felt a chill in the air grow.

"But, Merlin," Solomon continued, "why in all the dimensions of the Universe should it matter?" He rose and paced before the fire, his hands waving in time with his discourse.

"If, as we believe, the Drove was created as a kind of by-product of the Big Bang—a swirl of knots and eddies in space-time, if you will—

why should they not just be left to get on with it? Perhaps they are part of the natural order of the Universe—agents of its death as well as products of its birth? Why should we seek to restrain them, going to such enormous efforts to steer them, to govern if not to hold back their remorselessly entropic progress, to..."

"Life," she said.

Solomon stopped then, and turned towards her.

"Go on, Merlin. Please, go on."

"It's just—well, it's often occurred to me—to all of us, really—why we're doing this at all. Steering the Drove, that is, even though we never speak of it: that there's got to be more, hasn't there? I mean, it's not just about guiding the Drove. It's about choices. Choices about where to steer the Drove, what we can allow the beasts to consume, and what we can't. And maybe I've just got it, but we always keep the Drove well clear of certain main-sequence stars. Stars with planets. Planets that might engender life-forms of baryonic matter."

Solomon looked directly at her: she met his gaze. Solomon's next words were directed not to her, but to Saturn.

"See? I told you she was good."

The implied subterfuge confused her. "Good? Why? What for? It's always seemed obvious—about avoiding planets, and life—so obvious that nobody actually makes the point, it's that obvious... isn't it?"

"Yes, Merlin, quite right. So obvious that almost nobody actually makes the connection. You'd be surprised how few people actually do, you know. Very surprised. In fact, you're the first in your cohort we've met who's done so. But now you've passed that hurdle, you need to ask yourself another question. A deeper one."

"About... life?"

"Yes."

"Well, I guess that if we're letting it grow, making sure that the likeliest stars are not consumed, then it's got something to do with the Drove, to... to..."

She stopped dead. A thought flashed through her mind like an electric arc. "It's all about finding some new life-form to take over. To herd the Drove. Or to manage it, somehow. When... well, for when we've all gone."

The silence was palpable. Solomon strode over to her and crouched down before her, so that she could meet his eyes without her having to look up.

"Not to herd the Drove, Merlin. To destroy it."

"But that's... that's..."

"Yes, I know," said Solomon, "it runs against everything we live for, against everything we know. Some might even call it heresy. But it's more than a matter of our eventual extinction. The fact is that the Drove is increasing. It's a feature of the Universe that's only become clear to us quite recently. Let's just say it's to do with the balance of dark energy and a slow, secular change in Planck's constant. We're not sure how, let alone why. You may not really be aware of it yet, as you can only really deal with it piecemeal, most of the time, given that it's so spread out. It's there, all the same, and it's that, more than anything, that explains why you and the others are having such a tough time of it. We've run some projections—that's Saturn and me, and some of the other elders. And there'll come a time when we'll simply be overwhelmed."

"When? How?"

"Don't be alarmed. It's still long away yet, even accounting for reasonable error. But that's no good reason for not making preparations now. Not just to continue to run the Drove, but to remove it. To remove its threat."

"But what difference will it make, whether the Drove wins out, sooner rather than later?"

"It's a fair point. Of course it probably doesn't matter. But we, the Elders, have conceived an objection to a victory for the Drove that comes too early. Put simply, it's aesthetic. If the Drove wins too soon, it will prevent this iteration of the Continuum reaching... how would one put it?" Solomon turned to Saturn who now made the first of what would be only two spoken contributions to the meeting. His voice, when it came, sounded lively and rounded.

"Its... 'fullness'?"

"Thank you, Saturn, I think that puts it very well. 'Fullness'. And, that being the case, we feel we have a duty to protect nascent life from this eventual threat. And there's another question you should ask. It's the decider, if you like. And that question is this—where did *we* come from?"

For a short spell Merlin was nonplussed. The effect of all these cosmic revelations, dealt at such speed, was one of numbing stupefaction. But realization dawned. She came to herself, seated in a magnificent stillness.

"We came from life, from baryonic matter—from a planet."

"Indeed, Merlin: from some proverbial warm little pond. It's easy to forget that, sometimes, now that we've been transfigured into this dimensionality, imprinted into the fabric of the Continuum. So, when you think about it, that's a good reason for steering the Drove away from planets. One never knows from which puddle the next generation of Drovers might crawl—Drovers that might come to our aid."

"But where, Solomon? Where was this planet of our... birth? And what were we once like?"

"Ah, Merlin, who knows? If there was ever such knowledge, it is now lost. And perhaps it is better so. After all, the planet's star might have gone nova long since. It might even have been in a different Continuum from the one we presently inhabit. There can be no space, now—no time—for regrets. And, in any case, we must move on. Our turn has come to find a species we can raise. But with a difference. This species will not simply continue what we do, though: we must create a race of destroyers."

"But why can't we simply destroy them ourselves?"

Solomon turned to the drinks cabinet behind Saturns's chesterfield, and poured three more shots of Islay. "If I might say so, that you can even conceive of such a question illustrates your maturity," he said. "It shows that you can—how would you put it, Saturn?"

"'Think outside the box?'"

"Exactly so. So, Merlin, to answer you—again, it's largely a matter of aesthetics," he continued, handing round the heavy tumblers—"who wants to be the first to destroy the objects of their life's work, not to mention the work of their entire species? As I said, it's practically a heresy. And even if you overcame that one, how would you go about committing such... such genocide? I mean, practically? The Drove are creatures of a similar order to ourselves—M-dimensional relativistic manifolds, wrinkles in space-time—but much more powerful, if only of trifling intelligence. And our task has always been to nurture, not to kill. The means for destruction must be built into this new generation of creatures, right from the beginning.

"What beats me, frankly, is how they might be destroyed without altering the fundamental connectivity—the topological order, if you will—of the Continuum itself, and perhaps destroying that, too. Throwing the proverbial baby out with the bathwater. I'm afraid that's a circle we Elders have never quite managed to square. A problem for nimbler intellects than ours, perhaps. Cheers!"

Merlin saw, as she lowered her glass, that Solomon and Saturn had lowered theirs, too, and now looked at her, expectantly.

"Why me?"

Silence, for an interval that could have been moments, or millennia. She saw Solomon, and Saturn, and the rest of the room — the chesterfields, the fireplace, the winter landscape — as if they were at some great distance.

"That, Merlin, is the most interesting question of all. And one to which neither myself nor Saturn nor anyone else has any convincing, logical answer. Except to say that we just know it. It's you. Your task. You have to find a way."

"But where? How? How can I even begin?"

"I'm afraid we have little more idea than you do. We'll try — of course, we'll try — to offer us much help and support as we can," said Solomon, "and we do have at least one clue."

"You... do?"

"It's here, now. All around you."

Merlin looked up, imploringly, at Solomon. His expression was warm. Laugh-lines creased the borders of his mouth, softening the hardness of his eyes.

"It's this Xspace, isn't it?"

"Yes, Merlin, it is. Xspaces don't just pop up randomly. They have to have internal coherence. To even exist, an Xspace has to have what you might call a 'back-story'. After all, what explains these chesterfields? This rather nice rug? This entirely splendid 22-year-old scotch? The clothes we're all wearing? This house? Even the view — this... well, this planetary prospect? And, most of all, the forms we now inhabit? They are more real than just illusions, you know.

And the minds of the forms we inhabit? Such engaging clutter! All that stuff about skiing and 'warm little ponds'? Now where did all that come from?" Merlin was now quite unable to decide whether the Elder's question was rhetorical. In any event, she was all wrung out. She decided to let him answer it himself. "From you, Merlin — from *you*. You might not have realized it, but you created this Xspace, and everything in it. Everything. I congratulate — we congratulate you, on your good taste. Especially the scotch."

Merlin had broken through her local credibility barrier. All she could now do was laugh. But this did not appear to be a joke. Solomon wasn't laughing. Neither was Saturn. Her laugh stuttered and stopped.

"But still, why?"

"Look at it this way. It's the way we're made. To be sure, we live most of our lives in a fairly linear way, starting at the beginning, chasing the Drove, and fading out somewhere else, later. But we can do more than that. You know this. We are connected, you and me, and Saturn here, and all your young friends, to much else that is in the Continuum. Past, present—and future. Your Xspace gives us the best clue for your search for a suitable candidate. Your quest, if you will, for life. Really, it can only be a matter of instinct."

Solomon raised his glass. The light of a setting, yellow sun sparkled in its brown depths. "It's just a hunch. To be honest, Merlin, it's the best we have."

Chapter 3. Scholar

Cambridge, England, Earth, January 2021

The mass of men lead lives of quiet desperation.
Henry David Thoreau — *Walden*

"Sorry I'm late! Bike puncture. *You* know."

The young woman breezed into Jack Corstorphine's freezing office, a collision of scarf, hands, long black hair and longer legs, all radiating from a huge, shapeless sweater which at the beginning of its evidently long life might once have been purple. She sat down in the only empty chair, the one farthest from the door, almost but not quite tripping over the three already more than occupied by the bovine rowers from St John's.

Jack, notes in hand, had been just about to open his mouth to introduce today's supervision topic — evidence for culture in the African Middle Stone Age — in part to compensate for the gaping holes in the lectures given by his doctorate supervisor, Professor MacLennane. But when he looked up, the words froze in his mouth. Now that the student had found her seat, she was engaged in a flurry of business, pulling off the sack-like sweater (she had no coat despite the weather) and getting her notes out of an unwieldy market bag, the contents of which were spilling out all over the floor. Amid the usual detritus (why are the interiors of women's bags so shockingly untidy?) Jack noticed the glint of an oversized, tortoiseshell-plastic comb. He noticed that the comb had all its teeth, which was amazing given the density and apparently unconquerable untidiness of hair it plainly had to deal with.

The woman, notes now found, sat up, and as she did so, parted the curtain of hair from her face and smiled. It was the most frank, open smile he'd ever seen, made lovelier by her evident distraction as she fought the long defeat of trying to confine at least some of her hair in a barrette. Now he could see her face, he noticed a bone-white complexion dominated by two big, very round eyes, so brown as to be almost black. Jack was pulled up sharply by their penetrating, judgmental ferocity.

"Jadis Markham?"

"Er... sorry?"

"You're Jadis Markham, aren't you?" Jack couldn't help but smile at her in response to her apparent absent-mindedness. Not that he'd be fooled. Those eyes. Those eyes gave every impression that the disorganized exterior concealed a mind like the proverbial steel trap. She stopped smiling, just then, and her eyes dulled, as if momentarily consulting some deep, interior resource, as if to search for her own name. Having retrieved this information, she smiled again, a flash that filled the room. Just for an instant he felt that he'd been pulled clear from his body and was floating in empty space.

"Yes. That's me. So that makes you Jack Corstorphine, doesn't it? I must have come to the right place. What a relief!"

The cultural innovation of the African Middle Stone Age carried on, as if nothing had happened. Almost.

Then in his second year of a doctorate program ('Models of land use derived from geomorphology and lithic distributions in the British Palaeolithic'), Jack found that teaching undergraduates in small groups not only supplemented their meager instruction from their lecturers, and his own exiguous stipend, but filled, for him, a social void. Jack thought himself shy, but what the world saw in him was tact, reserve and laconic humor. That, and a reasonable capacity for administration, came to the notice of hard-pressed college tutors looking for a safe pair of hands for their charges.

So, without really noticing, Jack spent much of his waking, working life teaching undergraduates. To his surprise he found that he enjoyed it very much, not least because it was the one part of his life in which he was forced to interact with other human beings, not just on the intellectual level, but on any level at all.

Although attached to a college, as all Cambridge students were obliged to be, Jack found few attractions in college life. His fieldwork was by necessity solitary: his laboratory work, hardly less. His real love was the outdoors. He tramped alone, all over England, refining an already intuitive yet sharp sense of landscape, and how human beings (and other people) had shaped it over millennia. He poked into crabbed caves in the bleak limestone of Derbyshire, the foam-flecked Gower peninsula of south Wales, and bluebell-lined Torbay, trying to picture each scene through a Neanderthal's eyes; he scoured the Vale of Pickering beneath the North York Moors, where some of Britain's earliest stockmen had corralled their cattle. For weeks at a time he'd live rough, fishing by day, camping in potholes or under hedgerows at night, returning to his disapproving landlady in Victoria Road, stinking, bright-eyed and bearded, like an Old-Testament prophet. "I was trying to find out what it must have been like," he would protest, weakly and futilely, as she prodded him (with her broom) towards the bathroom.

This quiet young man who had found most of his need for company satisfied by wind on the fells was, in Cambridge, just beginning to emerge from his shell. He admitted that it was the undergraduates who were responsible for this injection of—what was it? Yes, *life*. In those relatively short periods of the year when the undergraduates were in season, as it were, life was one big whirl, as if the circus had come to town. When they left again, and he—as a graduate student—had to keep on working, all was grey and dull. The fact was that even the dimmest Cambridge undergraduates had a shameless self-assurance that could stand any assault, overcome any challenge. Compared with the general mass of humanity they seemed more focused, more colorful, more alive.

"The African Middle Stone Age was..."

Now, this was something that always amazed him. As soon as he drew himself up to speak, putting on his official 'supervision' voice, they were all attention. This never happened at his old university, where a patina of well-meaning dullness coated all endeavor. What's more, it felt good, as a departmental dogs-body, to be treated as an authority.

Even then, Jack saw that his latest student, Jadis Markham, was just that bit more studious, more attentive, than any of the others. Her initial lateness was her one anomaly. Her assignments were always returned on time, and were always substantially better argued than anyone else's. She had a way of taking every aspect of a problem apart, no matter how woolly it seemed at first; polishing up the parts to reveal the assumptions on which each aspect was based; reducing these, in turn, to their elements; modeling how the aspects should look if put together correctly; and then, just, well... doing it, achieving original insights into questions which (Jack realized in hindsight) had been intractable simply because nobody had seen fit to question their underlying assumptions. On the face of it, what she was doing was simple, just science, in the raw. On the other hand, it was as refreshing as finding a door in a hitherto neglected garden wall which everyone had just walked past, without even noticing that it was there.

"... the Middle Stone Age describes a series of cultures over an enormous period of time..."

The three rowers from St John's scribbled in their notebooks, heads down. Jadis Markham's notebook lay untouched on her lap, as she gazed, apparently unblinking, at Jack, her face in an unnerving frown of concentration, as if she recognized him from somewhere, but couldn't quite place him. Jack tried not to notice—it felt uncomfortable, like she was undressing him, taking off first his clothes, and then his skin, and then unpeeling the muscles from his bones.

"… and some of these cultures were very sophisticated. Surprisingly so, given their antiquity, and that some of the… well, the *toolmakers*… probably weren't human. At least, not in the way we'd understand it today."

And so it went on, week after week, those assignments returned with uncanny perfection, those eyes boring holes into his soul.

His nights were soon spent wondering what Jadis Markham looked like without the shapeless bags of her clothes. By day, he reasoned that any favoritism he showed might be related to the simple fact that Jadis could only ever seem attractive compared with the three cauliflower-eared meatheads that made up the rest of her particular class. He worried that he might have been giving her better marks than the others because she was the sole female in her group, so he tried a scientific control experiment. He asked some of his departmental colleagues who knew none of his students personally to mark their work blind, names removed. Jadis' papers always came out on top.

"A student who actually shows promise? Be still my beating heart," said his supervisor, Professor MacLennane. "This is first-class material, no doubt about that. It shows such clarity of thought, something only too rare nowadays. She could go far. Keep your eye on *her*." Not that Jack had the slightest intention of averting his gaze, but at least, he reasoned, he could appreciate her better without a guilty conscience.

It was only later that it occurred to him that he hadn't told Professor MacLennane that the student who'd turned in this stellar work was female. And this was a blind test. So how did he know?

As soon as his duties as her supervisor were over, Jack asked her for a date.

Chapter 4. Admiral

Xandarga Space Elevator, Earth, *c.* 55,680,000 years ago

Alien they seemed to be
No mortal eye could see
The intimate welding of their later history
Thomas Hardy — *The Convergence of the Twain*

First, the sky froze. And then, it boiled.

Which was a pity, he thought, as all breath was sucked out of him, followed by his guts, and then his brain, and all that just before his skull imploded. The sky had been such a nice color. And the air, so fresh. These were his very last thoughts of all, as his skin peeled away, his limbs were ripped from their sockets, and his eyeballs sublimed into the vacuum. But something inside told him that he was not, in fact, dead.

An absence of pain.

He was not, however, sufficiently conscious to realize that having these thoughts at all was in any way peculiar. Not yet.

Ah, me. She'd always said that the whole expedition had been 'me, me, me,' and he'd have to admit that she'd been right. After all, a couple of *Brontops*-class star destroyers should have been all that was necessary to put down an insurrection of the Slunj in that fractious volume the other side of the Rigel sector. The Slunj being what they were — thin films of loosely aggregated bacteria — were barely organized enough to keep their own bodies together, let alone put up any kind of coherent rebellion.

"Send a couple of gun-boats," the Senior Under-Secretary for Colonial Defense had said, flashing cat-like eyes at him. "The natives respond to that. But don't do any more. If we send too many ships, they'll think we're scared. That their rebellion amounts to any more than a fly that we'd swat, but only if we were really bothered. And, besides, there is such a thing as elegance. Oh, you know, Admiral — economy."

Elegance. Economy. But no, he had to play the Big Boy, and try out his Big-Boys' toys. A small scuffle with the Slunj would be an excellent opportunity to give the 17th Rigel Fleet a much-needed trial in extended battle formation.

All of it.

All those millions of cruisers, each one seventeen kilometers of ceramic ellipsoid terror with three hundred kilolights under the hood, together deploying a quite eye-watering exatonnage of armament.

All those destroyers, too — tens of thousands of them — each one the size of a continent, and for which the term 'destroyer' could be read as wanton understatement.

The hundreds of planet-sized capital ships, each one loaded with rail guns capable of accelerating a nickel-iron asteroid from rest to point-oh-five lights by the time it got to the muzzle, and then dropping it to within five hundred meters of its target from a light-month's distance — and doing this again and again, hundreds of times an hour.

And the jewel in the crown — and his own, personal, fiefdom — the *Sorceror*, a spaceship that looked like a planet in every way, because it was one. With oceans, continents, deserts, forests, atmosphere, and life: yes, a synthetic planet, and all his own, for all that its mantle was a caul of the most muscular machinery that his engineers could contrive — continuum flux generators that would allow trans-spatial velocity of almost half a million light-years per hour.

Anywhere in the Galaxy at the flick of a switch.

Taking with it, of course, a retinue of moon-sized outriders that both illuminated the spaceship (giving a pleasing reality to the old canard of the Sun in orbit about the Earth) as well as toting the kinds of System-Superiority weapons that could turn gas-giants to fog.

And while the 17th Rigel Fleet was one of hundreds of such forces, it marked the pinnacle of Earth's Imperial might, which had been mighty for time immemorial, it seemed, and looked every inch eternal.

What the Senior Under-Secretary for Colonial Defense seemed unable to understand was that fleets need to be deployed, even in times of relative peace. Fleets as complex as the 17th Rigel needed constant testing. All those hundreds of millions of troops couldn't spend all their time just hanging about. And, anyway, who really cared about the messages, psychological or political, that one might send to a few scuts of piratical pond scum?

But there are other things in space besides sentient slime, soon-to-be ex-Admiral Ruxhana Fengen Kraa.

So that was his name, was it? It sounded familiar, of course it did. But also as if the words were freshly minted, their potential yet to be dulled by utterance. His mind directed his tongue to rehearse this new syllabary.

Answer came there none.

In any case, what was all this 'soon-to-be-ex' business? Pulse rose. Body fluids changed their conductivity.

What's that? Panic?

Alarms ripped. Lights pulsed. He woke. Parts of him (he wasn't sure which parts) started to shake. But something else forced him down.

He opened his eyes. The blur, agonizingly bright at first, resolved, pixel-fashion, into a face he thought he'd seen before. But where?

Frustration. Blood surge. Restraint.

"Please be calm, Admiral," said a voice. "You are gravely injured, As yet you are unable to move, owing to the absence of many of your essential parts. To tell the truth, they had to scrape what was left of you off the inside of the escapod. Woof! Twenty-five gees and even the pippiest Admiral is no more than a few blobs of strawberry jam."

Oh, very amusing. Just what the Slunj looked like, even in the peak of health. Poetic justice. "However, all parts necessary will have been supplied, tested and bedded down by the time we get there. You'll be a new man!"

"Get... there? Where?" He was not aware of having made any sound, but the doctor did not seem to think this a problem. She (so she was a she) laughed. The memory of that voice flitted like cheeky shoals through the holes in the ragged net of his mind, and into the void beyond.

"Of course, you won't have known, what with everything that's happened. You're in an autopod. Don't worry. We'll fix you up as soon as we can." The doctor looked distractedly to the side, out of view. Perhaps she was taking a reading from some machinery. Perhaps she was, in fact, an illusion and had vanished completely. It was hard to tell.

"But where?"

"Sorry! Counting stitches. We're on the El: eight thousand kilometers up, falling slowly, arrival Xandarga Station in... well, let's not worry about that yet."

"Earth?"

"Where else? Just lie back and think of Gondwanaland."

Soon-to-be-ex-Admiral Ruxhana Fengen Kraa realized that his homecoming might be sufficiently painful that atomization somewhere the other side of Rigel might have been a wiser choice.

The first sign of trouble had come not long after the fleet regrouped three lights out from the disputed system and started to scan for Slunj. The primary was an M-type dwarf that could offer no more haven than a couple of pallid ice-giants; a scree of disconsolate pebbles; and, close in, an absolute jewel of a blue planet, a little smaller than Earth, currently home to several Discotex colony hives.

The billion-year Discotex civilization was a notable beneficiary of the *Pax Terrestris*, which had all but driven its traditional enemies, the savagely asocial Flux Fiddlers that infested stellar atmospheres, to extinction. But Discotex colonies had since proven vulnerable to Slunj infestation, necessitating the current exemplary show of force.

The interchange hadn't all been one way. Now peaceful and given to exotic collectivist philosophies, the Discotex had learned much in their eons-long conflict. Especially about some of the more imaginative uses of hypertransuranic elements, now incorporated into several of the more assertive armaments of the 17th Rigel and many similar fleets, and whose use had proven decisive in several conflicts that might otherwise have dragged on much longer.

The bottom line was that Earth was indebted to the Discotex. The Senior Under-Secretary should have understood that, too. 'A couple of gunboats,' indeed.

Admiral Ruxhana Fengen Kraa had felt the skin on the back of his neck tingle even as the first messages trickled in — spare, disconnected and puzzling. He should have acted then, on instinct, pulling his immensely powerful, but delicate and (as the Senior Under-Secretary constantly reminded him) very expensive fleet away, away from danger. But no, he had deployed his forces and wasn't going to pull back now. And also because the earliest signs that things might have gone awry piqued his curiosity. They were so odd: he had to find out more.

The first message was less about annihilation than astrogation. An advance battle group of cruisers and destroyers had reported a systematic error. They had, through no fault of their own, ended up of the far side of the system, relative to the main fleet. Doppler ranging confirmed this, but no explanation could be advanced. The continuum flux generators of the vessels concerned were working within 99.9% optimal spec, and, anyway, what could have happened to have affected the whole group simultaneously? It made no sense.

These messages were relayed to the currently favored Bridge of the *Sorceror*, a ginkgo-shaded sun-terrace of a *faux*-ruined lamasery, perched on the edge of a volcanic crater-lake so huge that one could hardly see from one side to the other. Admiral Kraa mused on a sun-lounger, drink in hand, watching some of his younger female staff playing volleyball on the brilliant white beach below. This gentle slide from reality into mildly erotic fantasy was interrupted by a sharp ping from his AI core. The glass fell from his hand and shattered on the terrace.

One flick of the mind and he was in uniform, on the VR Command Deck. It was in uproar. Staff were sweating at their consoles; barking through comms ports and at one another; his younger female staff, now coolly and crisply uniformed, were deep in VR gear, or shuttling glittering icons in 4-D battle maps. There were engineers on the deck in conclave with his officers, huddled over displays. That engineers were present at all on the Command Deck showed that something had gone very wrong. Very wrong indeed.

No sooner was his presence noted than he was assaulted with status updates. He bounced them to his AI core for a shakedown, and this is what he learned: that thirteen minutes after broadcasting their initial inquiry, the advance battle group, all seventy-eight thousand vessels, had disappeared.

Worse, this was not an isolated case. Destruction seemed to be spreading through the fleet like a contagion, affecting ships first in small groups — ships that would flash in and out of existence around the system and then vanish altogether, leaving no more than a smear of atoms and hard radiation.

Small groups became larger groups, until the whole fleet found itself ploughing into a storm-front beyond which the regular laws of the Universe had been suspended. He felt the thrum and screech of rending rock and metal. Standing at the bridge but powerless to command it, Admiral Ruxhana Fengen Kraa queried his AI core. The *Sorceror* was large enough to register and triangulate significant local gravitational anomalies. His AI told him that near-space was full of them — localized gravitational disturbances so intense that the continuum itself had, in places, warped in on itself, enfolding any nearby matter — including his fleet — in shrouds of nothingness. And then, just as suddenly, unfolding, spitting out the pips. It was as if the 17th Rigel was being peppered with rapidly moving black holes, tossed in their wakes as they passed by.

He flipped back to the sun terrace to see the crater-lake in a confusion of spume, noise, and coral grapeshot that raked his flesh like razors. The ground shifted beneath his feet, but he could not move: his feet were so heavy they might have been nailed to the flags. This was, he reflected, unhelpful, as a rogue gravitational pulse was trying to rip his head off.

He must have passed out. Either that, or his AI core did the decent thing, winking him out, squirting what was left of him into an escapod, and blasting its way out of the killing zone. Very few among the six hundred and seventy-three million souls in the 17th Rigel would have had access to such a luxury. But he was the Admiral, and in cases of disaster, whether natural or caused by some almighty hubristic cock-up, somebody had to face the music.

The recovery of soon-to-be-ex-Admiral Ruxhana Fengen Kraa was slow, yet steady. At each stage his local environment appeared to become richer. When he was well enough to sit up in bed and go through some light eye-brain calibration exercises with the doctor, he seemed to be occupying a spare but comfortable room not unlike the rustic beach cabana next to the crater-lake on the *Sorceror*. The keen memory of the loss of his fleet made him wish for some other quarters, less emotionally loaded.

His wish was granted, as soon as he was well enough to walk around on his new legs, if haltingly, and with the help of a frame. His quarters had transmuted to a stateroom straight out of the era of the great Trans-Arcturus luxury spaceliners a few tens of millennia earlier: all cut glass, fluted brass, and plumped-up crimson velvet.

Propping himself up on the back of a mahogany *fauteuil*, he decided to try, once again, the latest exercise the doctor had set him: to navigate the six steps between chair and breakfast bar without support of any kind. Those six steps might have been six light years. About three steps in he'd always had to grasp his walking frame.

Now for it.

One... two (slight wobble, overcome)... three (that frame looked so tempting)... four.... five... and, unbelievably, six. He'd made it to the bar, where he stood, shaking, not daring to move further. He turned to see the doctor, standing in the open door.

"Congratulations," she said.

And that was when Soon-To-Be Ex-Admiral Ruxhana Fengen Kraa realized where he'd seen her face before.

Chapter 5. Candidate

Cambridge, England, Earth, June, 2023

Now, what I want is, Facts.
Charles Dickens—*Hard Times*

Jack Corstorphine needed help. Just how badly he was reluctant to admit even to himself. He knew only too well how a blow to one's self confidence in the final stages of a research degree could destroy everything.

He'd seen for himself, so many times, how research students started with so much ebullience, only to find, more than two years later and within sight of the dreadful midnight watch they called 'writing-up,' that what they had accumulated actually amounted to very little. Drifts of data accumulated with great pain over years vanished like April snow in the first light of critical analysis. Even worse, doctoral candidates, ploughing furrows long and alone, might wake up and realize that they had spent those years asking the wrong questions to begin with; that however good the data they had gathered, there was, in sum, no case to be answered. Or, worse still, that they had, in technical language and with much circumlocution, done something that had been worked out already, but in some other way.

Or, worst of all, that they had simply proved, with certainty and without fear of contradiction, that x equals x.

Department of the Bleeding Obvious.

So much time wasted. And more than wasted. Those self-abasing, self-denying years of energy and youth irretrievable, when careers are built, and they might, like their school friends, already have steady jobs in industry or in the City, with mortgages and some status in life. With partners and families, rather than living like overgrown students in drabness and in debt.

Jack tried to console himself that his problems were not yet terminal, for he could make out patterns in his data—this, the most exciting sensation a scientist can experience. He was simply at a loss to understand how they could be organized.

As a result of his long pilgrimages, he could view a landscape and immediately sense that people had been there, long ago. Jack had gone far beyond looking for traces of buried roads, post-holes, cave hearths and flint *debitage*. More than anyone alive, he could look at the angle of a hill-slope, or the way a river curved in its course, and tell that these things had been shaped by the hand of man, even without any other sign, and even accounting for the titanic forces of climate change that had shaped Britain over the past million years, in which glaciers had come and gone, scrubbing entire ranges of hills from the map and altering the courses of rivers over their whole lengths.

His talent had become so internalized that he could no longer look dispassionately at its products—and that was the nub and heart and whole of the problem. That these things were so he had no doubt—but he had no way of demonstrating, objectively, that the subtle clues he saw were not made by natural forces, unaided. And he'd look a right idiot if his thesis committee asked precisely how he knew that, say, the layout of the caves in Cheddar Gorge could not possibly have been natural, and he'd had no answer ready, save that they just looked like that, because he said so. He'd be laughed off as surely as if he'd said he'd discovered Atlantis.

What he needed was some formal way of comparing his intuitions of ancient human presence in one place, with those inspired by somewhere else, and then contrasting both of these with what nature would have created, unaided. He needed a system that would corral the patterns thrown up by his gut reaction, to domesticate them, to force them to make sense. But quantifying his intuitions? How do you quantify a river-bend, or the feeling that a hilltop should be here, rather than somewhere else? You might as well try to lasso the clouds. Despite much research and earnest questions of statisticians, no ready method existed—it was all too vague. He had neither the means nor (he admitted to himself, ruefully) the ability to derive such a technique himself.

Yet without such a key he could go no further. In his mind, he could see his thesis: he was so desperate that he could almost taste his thesis, but a barrier at once so intangible and yet so impassable stood between him and completion.

And then there was Jadis. She had just completed her finals (a starred first, naturally) and stayed on in Cambridge to help him out. When he asked her if she had a home to go to she was strangely vague. If pressed, she'd say that she loved him. If pressed further she'd only say that she was busily looking for a home for the both of them, burying her nose into the property-for-rent pages of the local paper and changing the subject.

"You know, Jack, you silly man, you work too hard. Fancy a holi-day?" she'd say with apparent artlessness. A holiday? *Now*?

"Yes. In the mountains. I know you like mountains." Her black eyes shone with mischief under the curtain of her hair.

"Mountains?"

"Precisely. Mountains. I know I'll never get you to lie on a beach. Not in the state you're in. And you've been looking at the same old moun-tains for so long you might as well look at some different ones."

Reluctantly, Jack had to agree. He'd been working so hard and so long that perhaps he needed a break, a chance to refocus. He thought—no, he desperately hoped—that inspiration might strike if he took his mind off things a little.

"Let's go to France," he said, brightening. "Look at the Alps, or the Pyrenees. We could drive there in the Field Vehicle." Jadis smiled and threw her arms around him. They were both thinking of Jack's battered Peugeot 205, crammed with camping gear, in which he'd clocked up so many miles. "I knew I could talk you round," she said, "but I never dreamed you'd be such a pushover."

At least he'd be doing something, rather than just sitting here in a funk, boxed in.

Chapter 6. Rookie

Xandarga Station, Earth, *c.* 55,680,000 years ago

Earth hath not anything to show more fair:
Dull would he be of soul who could pass by
A sight so touching in its majesty
William Worsdworth — *Upon Westminster Bridge*

Xandarga Station!

What more can be said about this most Imperial of ports, this hub, this hubbub, this stew of a million stars? This ancient of days, this eternal now, this gateway to riches, this chasm of despair? Yet there is something about Xandarga Station that eludes expression. Tourist guides do not capture it, no more than the memories of that uncle who went there on business and returned with more than just a sale; the sister, from a school trip, inarticulate with excitement; the silences of that elder brother, crackling with anger and shame.

Clearly, one's first impressions of Xandarga Station would be as imperfectly recalled as a first kiss. Not that naval cadet Ruxhana Fengen Kraa, from the insignificant East-Gondwana prairie town of Green River, had had any experience of these things. Any more than his best friend, Ko Handor Raelle, who claimed he was 'at it,' with all the most luscious girls in their class.

"Will ya look at the dugs on that!" he'd exclaim, from their after-school perch at Ma Belle's Bar and Grill on Riversleigh and Main, whenever one of their classmates hove into view, amid a giggling coop of similarly lush-pelted beauties. Ruxie thought every one of them was just lovely, but said nothing. The thought of facing one alone made his mouth dry. That the girls simply smiled and prinked away, if they reacted in any way at all, convinced Ruxie that Ko was full of it, and probably as clueless about girls, sex, and life in general, as he was. But Ruxie knew better than challenge Ko himself. Full of it he may have been, but Ko was a lot bigger than he was.

Deficient in such life-affirming experiences — though adept at roping dogies on his mother's indrico ranch on the outskirts of Green River — Ruxie decided that whereas experience was invaluable, the only way to acquire it was to live it. In the meantime, though, knowledge was power. He decided to find out as much about Xandarga Station has he could.

Or, rather, his mother decided for him. Morzin Kraa Tzalaké found that the best way to fight the powerlessness she felt at the departure of her youngest kit was to arm him against the future, not to cower from it. So at their good-byes at Green River airport she thrust a slate into his hands.

"Aw, Ma — what's this? You shouldn't have!"

"It's a long journey, Ruxie. Lots of change-overs." She glanced towards Ko, eyes sharp with disapproval. He was trying to eye up some porn on the top shelf of a nearby newsstand. "*You'll* want something good to read, at least." A peck on the cheek, and then she turned and walked away down the concourse.

The slate was loaded with an autodidact that told him everything he could want to know about the Imperial Capital, in the form of a story blended from a range of sources. The four long flights and interminable hangings-around between were eased by his mother's parting gift. He was so enthralled that he'd tried to read some of it to Ko, but after a while his friend didn't even try to fake his enthusiasm, so Ruxie was left alone.

He learned under *Thrilling Tales of Tethyan Thunder* that as recently as two hundred and eighteen thousand years ago, Xandarga Station had been a sleepy fishing port on the southern Tethys shoreline, a remote outpost between ocean and jungle, home to a small fleet of brave sea-dragon slayers. These legendary heroes would ride out, in open canoes, into the open Tethys, and chase down basilosaurs — each one thirty meters of coiling hatred — on their migrations. Actually, Ko had been quite interested in that part, having torn his eyes away from *Thrust* magazine for ten whole seconds to gaze at Ruxie in wonder.

"You don't say?" he exclaimed. "That's seriously amazing!" And, just then, he'd meant it.

Further down, *Tethyan Thunder* graded into the terser *Xandarga Chronicles*, which told how engineers first came to the Xandarga Coast and decided that it would be the ideal location for the Earth's first space elevator. Three more had since been built on Earth and on countless moons and planets, yet as the Xandarga Station elevator was the first, it was known simply as the Elevator, or just the El.

The effect of the El on the local economy was practically instantaneous. A mere three hundred years later, what had been a gaggle of brushwood hovels on the edge of nowhere had been transformed into the center of the known Universe.

Simply as a city, Xandarga Station was vast. In The *Dzunghar Heren Vú Xandarga Backgrounder* Ruxie read of the miles of naval dockyards, regular dockyards, trading go-downs, meat-packers and stockyards. Indeed, Ruxie already knew, from parental conversations he'd overheard when he was meant to have been asleep, that Xandarga Station was the trailhead for several large indrico drives, much more profitable than anything that distant East Gondwana could offer. His mother's father, when he was alive, would recount tales of those great drives to Ruxie and his sisters. Grandpa had been an indrico driver in the Southern Tethys in his youth, and enthralled the kits with tales of campfires, and comradeship, battles with giant mesonychian land-sharks, and, most of all, the thrill of riding a lambda alongside a ten-mile-long herd of the indricos themselves: those snorting meat-mountains, fifty tons apiece, stretching back into a smoky haze.

The first traders and ranchers brought their families to join them. So Ruxie read (in extracts from *Rags and Riches, Runagates and Refugees in the Imperial City*) of the barrios; the vistas of suburban dullness; the kitch palaces of the merchant princes. And of the various *quartiers* that were homes-from-home to a bewildering variety of exotics. Two of many stuck in Ruxie's mind. One was Bedrock, where what looked like the buildings were in fact the residents, the silicon- and germanium-based Flintsiders, who lived on rocky planets very much larger than the Earth. The other was Sulfaville, a domed, black hemisphere whose residents were ultra-extremophile collectives which, when they came out, did so only in exquisite little carriages, each no bigger than a canteloupe. The spherical cabs matched the shiny blackness of the suburb whence they came, but their wheels and exterior furnishings were made of magnesium-titanium alloy, and they were drawn by outsized clockwork praying mantids. What the carriages—and Sulfaville itself—looked like on the inside was harder to imagine, given that the residents evolved in the super-heated, pressurized atmospheres of star-grazing gas giants.

Wherever traders turn a profit, the taxman is sure to follow, so perhaps inevitably (according to selections from *Honeytrap: The Reign of Raedwald XIX 'Star-Slayer' and The Making of the Imperium*), Xandarga Station became the administrative and financial capital of the Earth, and, by extension, the Galaxy. Ruxie read about the calculating spires of the financial district and, at the city's heart, the cluster of museums housing treasures from a million planets. Ruxie thrilled at the thought of visiting the Institute of Galactic History with its displays of artefacts from of the earliest known civilization in the Universe, discovered just fifty years earlier in the Fomalhaut Sector by the great archeologist Thrangona Mir Gharaan, and believed to be more than eleven billion years old.

And Ruxie simply slavered at the thought of the Natural History Museum, the only place in the Galaxy (apart from Taniquetil itself) large enough to display a life-sized Taniquetilian tesseractrix. That was almost the last time he'd tried to interest Ko, whose eyes had grown to the size of saucers at the centerfold of *Raunch* magazine. Ruxie caught a harshly lit confusion of bare arms and legs and tried not to look.

Second in the league table of Interesting Facts about Xandarga Station with which Ruxie tried to interest Ko was the House of the Imperial Assembly. Designed as an echo and a mirror to the Galaxy it ruled, the building was an oblate spheroid, eight kilometers in diameter, whose mirror-smooth surface was spun of magnetically suspended metallic hydrogen beneath a nanocarbon monolayer. The pressures generated by this extremely thin but relentlessly dynamic surface supported the entire building from collapse with a minimum of internal spars, as well as generating much of its power by induction. There could be neither doors nor windows. Delegates arrived and left by trans-spatial gateways from all over the Galaxy, as well as in the City itself. The structure floated in mid-air, five hundred meters above water of the harbor, reflecting the great city in on itself. But the most remarkable reflection came from the source of Xandarga Station's being, its *raison d'être*, the El itself.

The El rose just outside the City, to landward. The stately pyramid at its root, itself the size of a large town, sprouted at its summit a city-block-sized bundle of hyperfilament columns. The structure was, indeed, square in section, and running up each one of its sides were sixteen tracks—eight internally, eight on the outer surface, sixty-four in total—along which pods of various sizes were constantly running up and down. Those descending were swallowed up by the pyramid. Those ascending were the ones that really caught the eye, and visitors who witnessed the spectacle for the first time could not help but try to follow the cars as they slid skywards to the zenith point. Ruxie's autodidact recounted those apocryphal tales of people gazing upwards and so enthralled that they just kept on gazing, even after they'd fallen over backwards.

Ruxie and Ko had seen the El all their lives as a white line that coursed along the sky to the westward by day, a thin necklace of jewelled lights at night. But nothing matched seeing it close-up. The plane that ferried Ruxie and Ko on their final hop was small and flew low over the city, and it was night. Ruxie, worn from reading and wonderment, had put away his slate, and dozed off. He woke an hour later, sore and cramped. Ko was sprawled next to him, snoring, tongue lolling. Ruxie unbuckled his seatbelt and rose to stretch as best he could. That's when he caught a glimpse of the view through the porthole.

"Hey, Ko..." he nudged his neighbor. "Come look!" Through the porthole, Ruxie's first impression was that they were at the bottom of an enormous, shallow bowl, with lights stretching as far as his eyes could see. The El, when it came into view, was so vast it seemed to distort perspective itself. The plane banked as it turned for the airport, and they saw the shining curvature of the Assembly Building, the curving streak of the El reflected in its surface. The boys, poised like storks to peer outwards and upwards to drink in as much of the view as they could through the needle's-eye of the porthole, were jolted, off-balance.

A bell pinged: a stewardess told them to resume their seats for landing. The undercarriage ground its way outwards. In the minds of both boys was that, if they passed their basic training, they would be doing more than gazing at the El. They would be riding it—to the stars.

Chapter 7. Lovers

Cambridge, England, Earth, October, 2024

No definition had spoken of the landscape-gardener as of the poet; yet it seemed to my friend that the creation of the landscape-garden offered the proper Muse the most magnificent of opportunities.
Edgar Allan Poe—*The Domain of Arnheim*

It was a one-bedroom Victorian garden flat in Chesterton, which they were paying for from a year's extension of Jack's doctorate grant, extra supervisions, and a few odd research jobs that Jadis was doing for Professor MacLennane (who'd taken a proprietorial interest in both of them) on the pretext of her studying for a Masters while Jack finished his thesis—a prospect that seemed almost in his grasp, but forever just beyond his reach.

The flat was dark and grubby, but sound and tolerably dry; the central heating worked at least some of the time; and a pot of paint on a summer Sunday afternoon always works wonders, even were one not to be distracted by trying to paint each other instead of the kitchen ceiling. In any case, Jack—who was otherwise never more content than when sleeping rough under a hedge—said he'd be pleased to have a base where he could think and work in peace and quiet, and where they could at least be together without prying landladies or college domestics.

It also had a delightful postage-stamp of a garden: hardly forty feet by twenty, but surrounded entirely by a high wall, and, being north-east facing, made an evening sun-trap of the high, back wall. At the bottom of the garden was a knee-high raised bed that ran its entire width, restrained by a wall of reclaimed bricks, and in which some unidentifiable species of ornamental acacia grew over an unkempt understory of broom, rosemary and lavender. You could crawl right inside, under the bushes, and make a hideout on a carpet of herbs and the crusts of dead leaves, where nobody could find you. It baked in the Sun during the day, unleashing a torrent of fragrance, and even after dark, the old brick wall behind would radiate the accumulated heat well into the early hours— warmth that the bushes would then trap, creating a Mediterranean microclimate.

In the evenings of that first, hot summer, Jadis and Jack would burrow into the bushes—they called it the Nest—and might not emerge until morning—their own private Eden. Jack remembered one chilly dawn awaking in the Nest to find them both slick with dew. A spider had spun draglines across Jadis' pale face, trapping drops of moisture that made a spangled net for the twining, leaf-adorned strands of her hair. Each of her long, dark lashes was crowned with a tiny pearl, just as if she were a sleeping fairy queen. For all that he was aching, wet and blue with cold, Jack remembered it as a moment when his heart sang.

And as for supervisions, ever since his best student had become his partner he'd seen very few sparks of talent, or even (it has to be said) of much intelligence. The one exception was a dashing and almost unbearably cocky first-year called Avi Malkeinu, who was Israeli and knew all about Mount Carmel, famous for its honeycomb of caves rich in Neanderthal and modern human remains. Avi had poked around them, boy and man, civilian and soldier, and had some outrageous ideas about the extent and depth of human and Neanderthal occupation in his country—outrageous to all except Jack, who learned as least as much from Avi as Avi did from him.

Avi's openness, candor and easygoing nature made something that happened to Jack one day in late September, when Cambridge baked in the last, fiery gasps of Summer, all the more disturbing. He was visited in his office by two rather shifty-looking characters, claiming to represent some student organization or another, who advised him that he shouldn't be teaching Avi Malkeinu. He'd served in the Israeli Defense Forces, they said, and was, no doubt, an Agent of Zionist Oppression. In response, Jack did something that he almost never did. He got angry. Alarmingly, consumingly angry, so that he shed the shy, quiet academic that he tended to be while in Cambridge, and became the wiry and piratical ranger that he was in the field. He listened quietly to what his visitors had to say, and then, still without meeting their gaze, invited them, just as quietly, to go fuck themselves. When they began to remonstrate, he rose from his chair like a thunderhead over the plains.

"Listen, I thought I *told* you to *fuck off*," he said, as calmly as his sternly suppressed violence would allow, "and if I see either of you little shits again—or if you harass my friends—I'll fucking rip your fucking bastard heads off and fucking stick them on fucking poles. Understand? Now piss off."

The two took flight and never came back. For ten minutes Jack remained his chair, his heart racing, his body shaking. He didn't think he'd had it in him. He'd normally do anything to avoid conflict, and immediately began to worry that there might be repercussions. But what began to dominate his mind, half an hour later, as he walked home through the searing streets, clouds bubbling above him as if to mirror his mood, was that he'd heard spiteful rubbish like that before, from people in his own department, especially the social anthropologists: and those archeologists who read the past not as it was, but through the lenses of current political preoccupation — and yet had the gall to call themselves 'scientists'.

Neo-archeologists, processual archeologists, feminist archeologists, Marxist archeologists, *post*-fucking-processual archeologists, for God's sake, not to mention those idiots, quite often obscenely obese women from Berkeley or Pasadena, who climbed to the top of *tels*, stripped off and jiggled their leviathantine tits about for the benefit of some right-on Mother Goddess — as if (and this was the part he found *really* offensive) *as if* this charade had anything whatsoever to do with what prehistoric people actually believed or did.

And there were people in his department who actually took that bilge seriously — the same people who'd cheerfully scorn a kitsch Hawai'ian hotel *luau* as having as much connection with authentic Polynesian culture as Mickey Mouse had with *Mus musculus*, simply because it was a product of capitalist colonialism. No, he thought. Prehistory is forged on the ground, not by political posturing, and it was people like Avi Malkeinu — open-minded people, people only interested in telling it as he saw it — who had the best chance of making progress without prejudice. And they were damning him not for his science but because of his origins and national obligations. What dismal, hypocritical crap. No wonder, Jack thought, that he'd spent so much time in the field, away from such pseudery.

But as he got closer to home, and began to calm down, he realized that he was close to being a pseud himself. Processual-and-whatever archeology had, at least, been forged in the field as much as his own landscape-based approach, as ways and means to get to grips with patterns seen in data, patterns caused by the interaction of man and nature. But as yet he still had no way of interpreting the patterns he saw. He had to find something soon. He had to. To vindicate people like Avi Malkeinu. To vindicate Jadis' faith in him. To vindicate himself.

Still, there might be something, just one little thing, a tiny gleam of hope. They'd been on their holiday, driving straight down through France, camping under hedges and in fields or just sleeping in the car. When they got almost in sight of the Pyrenees — in fact, not long after they'd crossed the Loire — Jack felt the hairs on the back of his neck tingle. It was the landscape. It sang to him in a way that the vales and scarps of England never did. But the more he thought about it, the more frustrated he became—there was something important in the French landscape, but he couldn't quite work out what it was. He resolved to go back, chase it down, and soon.

Jadis, too, had had a rotten day, running errands for Professor MacLennane that meant scurrying to and from the University Library for books that didn't exist, when she was quite sure that they did; or if they did exist, were on shelves on the other side of the building; for papers which she wasn't allowed to see, even though she'd phoned ahead and received cast-iron assurances that they would be made available. It didn't help that the library was as hot as an oven, and that she was getting a headache. Making it worse was a general niggle about Jack. It was about time, she thought, that Jack made some headway with his doctorate, because only then did she feel that she could get serious about her own. The plan was that when Jack was within hailing distance of his Ph.D., he could apply for a postdoctoral fellowship, and when he'd secured that, she'd become his research student. But until Jack had written up, they were stuck in a holding pattern.

She did wonder—had wondered—whether she mightn't strike out on her own. She had the first-class degree, so she'd have the pick of doctorate places. And it wasn't as if she hadn't had offers from elsewhere.

Two things held her back. The first was Professor MacLennane, who advised her to wait. Something will turn up, he said. He was chasing a big and juicy grant, he said. Any day now, he said. She'd kick herself if she jumped ship now, he warned.

Second, and perhaps most importantly, she found herself reluctant to leave Jack to stew on his own. Quite plainly, he needed her. More to the point, she needed him. She loved him, more than anything. Oh, yes, she'd tried to be rational about such things. After all (she told herself) love was just a few hormones whizzing around in the sorry bag of chemicals from which human beings are made. However, the fact remained, that no matter how hard she tried, she couldn't clearly remember any previous existence for herself, alone, before she'd met Jack. She remembered coalescing, somehow, in Jack's office, light as thistledown. Memories of an earlier life were fragmentary, enigmatic, as if the effect of her first meeting Jack was to purge them, leaving almost no trace. She could only retrieve a few scattered shreds—the peaty scent of scotch whisky; a fantastic, futuristic city at night under an endless star-spattered sky; the taste of a fish grilled in palm leaves on a tropical beach. Family holidays, maybe? Further introspection was no use. It was Jack who made her existence concrete, even meaningful, and even more that—it was Jack that made her conscious of her own, raw physicality. If Jack weren't around, she felt that she'd simply float away, as fragile and translucent as a soap bubble, and vanish into nothingness.

She arrived home moments after Jack. As she kicked off her sandals she saw his hiking boots and socks cast off in the hall, still warm; his bag on the kitchen table, papers pouring from it like the innards of a partially eviscerated dogfish. She found him where she knew he would be, in the Nest.

"Wine?" he offered, barefoot, holding out a full glass of off-license Merlot as she sat down next to him on the wall of the raised bed, beneath the lavender and rosemary, fragrant from the day's heat.

"Nicest thing anyone's said to me all day," she replied, taking a generous swig. "Correction," she noted, looking up, her eyes sharp, her lips stained with red, a rivulet running down her chin. "I'm sure you said something even nicer to me this morning."

"I did?" Whatever clouds had gathered over him were beginning to dissipate. Responding, she warmed to him and came closer, sitting on the ledge between his legs, leaning back against his chest, completely enfolded by his arms.

"Yes, you silly man. You said"—she began to laugh—"you said that tonight we really must have a brainstorm."

"Oh, that," he said. "I'd rather pour you some more wine," which he did. Then he put down the bottle and stroked her unfastening hair.

"…and, you said that after the brainstorm, that I really needed what you called 'a thorough seeing-to.'"

"I said that? Sounds most uncouth. Not like me at all. Are you sure that was me?" He ran his fingers down her throat, unbuttoned her blouse, and let his hands steal lightly over her skin. She shivered.

"Yes, of course it was you," she laughed. She felt as warm as the wine as she reached her arms above her and pulled his face down to hers.

"Nope. Can't have been me," he said. "Now, if it were me, I'd have said you needed a good seeing-to before the brainstorm. Nothing like a good seeing-to, you know, for clearing the brain."

"Well, as it is you, and that's your view, Professor," she said, "why don't we…?"

But before they could say or do anything else, the clouds broke with a deafening crash, and within seconds they were as drenched as if God had emptied his bathwater on their garden.

They sat in the warm rain on the edge of the raised flowerbed, her head under his chin. He ruffled her damp hair while continuing to unbutton her, while she luxuriated in his minute attention. They both undressed and let the warm rain course over their bodies. She rose, turned as if she were a dancing sprite in the dawn of the world, rain splashing and glancing and making sparks in all directions as it ricocheted from her glistening body, her hair swinging in lazy streamers. She straddled him, feeling him deep and smooth within her, as with one hand he traced the rivulets arcing down the valley of her spine.

As they moved, they kissed again, their lips meeting and parting, meeting and parting, through the rain curtain, in a butterfly dance. After a minute or two he rose and, with her legs still wrapped around his waist, picked her up, turned, and, sliding out of her, placed her inside the Nest on a deep carpet of leaves still dry and warm, the foliage above protecting it from the worst of the downpour. She lay almost buried in leaves, limbs spread, eyes burning in a soft glow. But before he could scramble into the Nest and take her again, she laughed skittishly and flipped over on to her knees and elbows, thrusting her leaf-strewn backside at him like a cat on heat, waving it from side to side like a flag. He moved in towards her, feeling the irresistible softness of the backs of her thighs against his groin, her swollen, pitted warmth between. He stroked the curves of her hips, brushing the leaves away; traced the dips of her lower back, and sliding into her as deeply and as fully as he could — and with such sudden ferocity that he lifted her knees, for an instant, clear of the ground.

Waves of electric shock coursed through her. She needed him now, in the eternal now, with a savage, inhuman craving. She had decided that what she wanted most of all, right now, was to be fucked: mechanically, forcefully, to have done, and bring this never-ending business with Jack's thesis to a head. She could tell from the way that Jack was throwing himself into her with such violence that something had irked him, too — perhaps even stung him into a kind of remorse that demanded action, some kind of closure. But even after all that, she was beginning to experience the first waves of a slow burn which, if he kept up this relentless, kinetic bombardment, would lead to her own longed-for release. She forgot about the thesis, about the inaction, about her own academic holding pattern, and when at length he came, in a thunderous spasm, she felt as if he had filled every crevice of her body and being. With his last, fitful gasps she found herself panting for breath, shaking from head to toe, her soul dissolved, her body a husk like these dead leaves, collapsing, and as she did so, she felt him draw out of her, a sensation both unbearably joyous and excruciatingly painful, all mixed together.

They lay in each others' arms, soaking, exhausted and covered by wet leaves, filled with a buzz and a flood of rapture, awed by their own animality. He wrapped her in his arms, and, as the storm passed overhead, she felt herself doze slightly. It was dusk when she woke. "Come on," he said, "Time for that brainstorm."

She could hardly meet his eyes as they made the few steps to the kitchen door and went inside. He made a big bowl of pasta (they were now very hungry indeed) while she showered. The well-behaved and domesticated shower jets were a balm after the screaming wildness of the rain, warming and absolving her, and sending the last of the leaves and dirt down the drain.

After a supper during which they had hardly spoken they sat on either side of the kitchen table with Jack's papers, in an atmosphere of brittle nervousness. Their clothes, trashed, were shoved into the corner, waiting for a trip to the launderette. Jack had put on a long, white bathrobe embossed with the legend 'Property of the Fairbanks Marriott,' over faded grey tracksuit bottoms. Jadis, her hair scraped back severely and tied in a long plait, wore nothing but her horrible, shapeless once-purple jersey, now so stretched and vast that it came down below her knees, its sleeves so long that she'd had to roll them in great puffs wedged above her elbows. But for all this informality their conversation was as stilted and as starchy as a job interview going badly, when both parties find nothing to say to fill the yawning pauses.

As they discussed how to organize Jack's data, Jack longed to come round to her side of the table. Jadis, for her part, wanted his arms, his touch, and most of all that he should wrap her up like a baby, like a Christmas parcel and—well—to make everything all right. But each was too scared to move. There was something about the moment—this moment—on which they both felt the world and the cosmos would turn. A single distraction, however small, and the moment would be lost, irretrievably.

So they bounced ideas to one another like the sexless talking heads that scientists are supposed to be: Jack, with his icily blue eyes explaining his intuitions, Jadis with her coal-black gaze dissecting them with cold logic, shuffling them, probing them, parrying, throwing them back. Their language was framed in the cool tones of null hypotheses, falsifiability, significance levels, distribution-free nonparametric tests; of circularity, particularity and applicability.

It seemed to Jadis that the tables had been turned. She had become the teacher, he the pupil. Jack felt the same, and with that, the relief of responsibility shared, of not having to do everything as he'd always done, on his own.

But what neither quite realized was that their dispassionate discourse was turning into a lovers' exchange. As they came to see a shared picture of what Jack's course of action should be, their spoken utterances grew shorter, as they started to complete each other's sentences. Cold eyes were animated, hands waved. Jadis, still talking, rose to put the kettle on; Jack, to finish the drying up. They stood next to each other, at the sink, in their baggy clothes, arguing with force—but no animosity—over the details of what was beginning, almost, to look like a strategy.

A part of Jack that had detached from the argument looked face on at Jadis in pure wonderment. But Jadis was distracted, in full flow—about metadata, integration and probability distributions—that he daren't stop her and just tell her that he loved her. He didn't want to spoil it: even to touch her, to brush past her by accident, might break the flow of her argument. Even under that horrible sack she loved to wear around the house (and which he'd sworn she was wearing when they'd first met, although she always denied it), he could tell she was as taut as a string. She had to work it out of her system, for both of them.

But then, it happened. Tea over, drying-up done, piles of notes made, they both rose at once in the tiny kitchen and—zap!—Jack's right wrist made a glancing contact with one dangling, purple sleeve, and—zing!— She was in his arms again, face buried once more in his chest.

"Do you think you can take it from here?" she asked, looking up at him, red-nosed and eyelids full of water, racked with sobs, as if she'd had some intellectual orgasm. It had all been building up inside her for weeks—months—this way through the woods, until the tension had become insupportable.

Later, when she'd calmed down, and Jack had tucked her up in bed, folding himself in behind her with one arm sleepily fingering loose strands of her hair, the other folded across her belly, she thought that perhaps that the expression of pure unabashed, unselfconscious sex was all that she'd needed to break the deadlock.

When Jack's thesis was complete, after another two months of six-teen-hour days; after more argument, more computer simulations, another trip to France (this time Jack, on his own), more anxiety, more sleepless nights, more wine, more laughter, more elation, more despair, more testing, more arguments, more checking and double-checking, and papers in unruly drifts all over the flat, Jadis discovered something else.

She was pregnant.

Chapter 8. Cadet

Xandarga Station, Earth, *c.* 55,680,000 years ago

She was a gordian shape of dazzling hue;
Vermilion-spotted, golden, green and blue;
Striped like a zebra, freckled like a pard,
Eyed like a peacock, and all crimson barr'd.
John Keats — *Lamia*

For the first few weeks of his naval career, Ruxhana Fengen Kraa, space cadet, saw nothing more exciting than the inside of his barracks. The day would begin with reveille, after which it was all guns blazing, sometimes literally, until well after sundown. What with roll-call, and drill, and lectures, and physical training, and mess, and weapons practice, and more drill, and private study, and basic uniform maintenance — all to the enervating odors of stale chow and unwashed laundry — he could do no more each night than collapse into his bunk.

After the initial shock had worn off, Ruxie found that he enjoyed his new life very much. He discovered that his sinewy, ranch-honed frame, combined with a quick intelligence and a gift for anticipation, meshed with the requirements of naval life. The name of Ruxhana Fengen Kraa crept quietly towards the top of most of his classes and routines. People in the hierarchy far above the level of rookie pond-life began to take notice.

Ruxie knew nothing of this, because he was more concerned with pond-life closer to home. Ko, who bunked in the cot immediately above Ruxie, seemed to start with the same enthusiasm for naval life. After a while, though, Ko began to lose ground. The only class that Ko always headed was Uqbar-rules boxing, a traditional sport whose antique ritual did little to cover up its gladiatorial viciousness. Professionals were multi-millionaire megastars, but few lived long enough to enjoy their wealth. What worried Ruxie was Ko's apparent conviction that unchallenged success in one sphere of life compensated for slack performance in all the others. When Ruxie was studying late into the night, or working out, or at the weapons range, Ko sloped off into the City, with a crowd of the kind of toadies that no aspiring boxing pro could afford to be without.

Late one evening, Ruxie was on his bunk, reading a manual on a new model of Higgs projector for use as a side arm. The schematics were beginning to swim before his eyes, and he was sure that if he tried to sleep now, they would dance before him in his dreams, mocking. Perhaps when he got to use the real thing, on the weapons range, it would all make sense. Right now, a restorative workout and a swim would put him in the mood for sleep. Reveille was only six hours away, and the routine would start all over again.

He sat up, wondering where he had left his gym clothes, when Ko's legs swung down from the bunk above. Ruxie was surprised—he was so lost in his own thoughts he hadn't even noticed Ko was there. Ko dropped noiselessly to the floor. He looked at Ruxie's reading matter. "You know, Ruxie, all work, and no play," he said. What you need is a drink."

Slipping undetected out of barracks was easier than Ruxie had thought. Ko bowled along with Ruxie straining to keep up, and before long they were outside a bar in an alley a few blocks from the harborfront. Bagpipe music squirled from the door as Ko and Ruxie arrived, finding themselves at the edge of a crowd, rapt, before a couple in the closing stages of a traditional Turgai sword-dance. Masked, and dressed in carnival finery, the dancers paced round each other in a pool of blood-red light; stylized steps marking time to the screech of the pipes. The dancers' arms made broad strokes with the scimitars each held in both hands. They swept the blades towards the crowds, expressionless masks filled with menace, the spectators flinching, laughing nervously—and then towards each other, scything closer and closer in, now whipping hairs-breadths from the costume of each.

The air became enriched with an auroral glow from the dancers' bodies, deepening with hems of iridescent blue, bars of crimson. The scent of sex rose. Faster the dancers whirled, and as the bagpipes reached a final, caterwauling cadence, scythes slashed, costume was rent, and the dancers were exposed, unmasked and unmarked, bare to the waist, shining pelts clothed in sweat and victory. The auras twisted from blue to purple to yellow, and then faded. The music was replaced by applause. The dancers made a triumphal circuit of the audience, gathering coins thrown in their masks.

Ruxie was amazed to find himself cheering, and, more than that, aroused. It wasn't just the sight of the female dancer's taut flesh and wild black hair, and—Ruxhana dared himself think it—her five pairs of breasts with their brazen tips. It was the experience of the dance itself, its frenzy, its climactic release, that he found so stirring.

"Good, eh?" Ko's voice in his ear. Ruxie was amazed to hear it at all, so transported had he been. "That's Xalomé, that is," he continued, picking up on Ruxie's glances. "She's a cracker, isn't she? Now—oh, there they are!" Ko steered him to a big table already occupied by many of their barrack-mates, some already in the party mood. "Look what I've dragged up!" Ko shouted to the throng,

"Yo, baby! It's shoon-to-be-Adm'ral Ruxhana Fengen Kraa!" yelled a half-uniformed rating in response, rapidly standing to attention, and sitting down again as abruptly.

"Beers for the Admiral!" bellowed another, and a flagon was shoved in front of him. Within minutes, his presence was forgotten—just one of the crew, laughing as Ko told some wild tale of land-shark-hunting on the prairies of home. Ruxie was so enthralled by the tall tales, the sodden feelings of fellowship engendered by the beer, that he hardly noticed another body squeezing on to the bench beside him. But the pressure of a thigh against his, and warm breath in his ear, sobered him up at once. He turned. It was the female dancer. Dressed now in a prim naval uniform with pips on her shoulders, but definitely the same tumble of dark hair. The pupils of her yellow-green eyes were narrowed to slits even in the darkness of the bar.

"It's... Xalomé, isn't it?"

"What took you so long, spaceman?" Without looking at him, she placed her hands behind her head and lifted her hair away from her face. She was close enough for him to smell a wild strangeness, like an animal at bay, or on heat. It took him right back to the ranch, and one of his first memories of ever going outside. He had been hardly more than a blind kit at the time. After his earliest years spent in darkness, as they were for all kits, the world of light was bright and new. The first thing he saw was two indricos rutting, one on top of the other, the two mountains of flesh bellowing, the air filled with dust and the cries of the farmhands. The air was charged then, too.

"So... long?"

"Yes. I've been waiting weeks for you to turn up." Her voice was cool, assured.

"Me?"

"Don't sound so surprised. Your friend Mr Raelle has told me all about you. Quite the mystery man, aren't you?" He was suddenly conscious of a hand on his upper thigh, like her voice—assured—like it knew what it was doing, and where it was going. He flushed and struggled for breath. But something else took charge of him then. Months of training had taken the edges off this farmhand. There were times, he knew, when one should stop thinking, and just act. He covered the hand on his thigh with his own and pressed it firmly. Her fingers were small, yet resolute.

"Shall we go?" he said.

Concentrating on simply putting his feet one in front of the other, and not bumping into his companion or anyone else in narrow night streets still thronged with partygoers, Ruxie reached the promenade on the harbor front. Boats bobbed in the brightly lit marina below, with ships and industrial gantries as silhouettes further off. He found a bench, remarkably unoccupied, and invited Xalomé to sit down. She did so, with an air of almost mocking amusement at Ruxie's obvious efforts to act the gallant. He sat beside her, wondering what to say or do next. Her hair strayed like tendrils over his shoulders, under his chin, across his lips. They tasted of salt and abandon.

They sat for hours as the streets thinned. The silvered bubble of the Assembly Building hung motionless over the waves, reflecting the lights of the City and, in weird cycloid curves, the illuminated skein of the El that rose up behind them.

Something broke in Ruxie, and he found that all he had lost was boyish embarrassment. He found that he could talk with Xalomé like he hadn't been able to talk with anyone since he'd arrived in Xandarga Station. Without the forced and formal cadence of naval operations, nor the false braggadocio that Ko's circle seemed to require. Into the night they talked. He told her of ranch life in East Gondwana. She tended more to listening than talk, but he learned how she'd grown up there, in the City, and had just graduated. Special Ops. Hence the pips.

"And the dancing?"

"Oh, that. A girl's got to have a hobby. I love dancing. Especially the traditional stuff. It's the ritual." She turned towards him. Her eyes glowed, reflected, feral. "Were I a man, I'd probably go for Uqbar-rules boxing. Ritual, combined with sheer bloody savagery. Poetry in motion!" She laughed. Ruxie said nothing. "You don't think I could handle myself?"

"I... well, I'm sure you could. Special Ops, and all that."

"Your friend. Mr Raelle. He fights Uqbar Rules, you know. Have you seen him in action?"

"Yes, I have."

"Impressive, isn't he? I think he could handle himself, too. But sometimes I think he overdoes it. He'll learn, with experience. He'll have to. I think he needs taking in hand."

"But what about your dance partner? Don't you...? Aren't you...?"

"Shakiló? Are you serious? He couldn't be more gay if you tied pink ribbons round his prong. You'd need a lot of ribbons, mind..."

With that she turned to face him, and the last thing he saw were her eyes crossing slightly as her lips approached his and he was catapulted into the void.

Chapter 9. Examiner

Cambridge, England, Earth, December 2024

Man is the measure of all things.
Protagoras

"It was that last trip to France that clinched it," Jack had started to explain, uncertainly, to the thesis committee gathered in a lecture room whose heating had been turned off for the winter. It was a dank, dismal day in December and the undergraduates had left town, leaving in their place an arctic chill that enveloped everything in a sullen lassitude. The committee was, clearly, yet to be convinced by his case. He looked to MacLennane — as his supervisor, one half of the committee — for an encouraging sign, a welcoming smile, but his patron averted his gaze: there was a lot at stake for him, too.

He missed Jadis — he missed her terribly, on this day, of all days — but this morning, before he'd left, she had seemed wound up tight with some matter so internalized that she refused to tell him what it was. But he'd looked so miserable as he turned to leave that she relented, ran towards him and embraced him from behind.

"I love you so much, you silly man," she had said: "I know you can do it. Now, go and show them what you're made of." He turned to hug her, but said nothing, and then he left, walking into town through the cheerless fog.

In truth, he was worried. The remorseless tension in these final weeks before his thesis defense had taken its toll on both of them. Whereas before he'd been lean and sinewy, now he looked gaunt, and thin. She'd seemed distracted, perturbed. He felt, somehow, that he'd committed some offense, done some wrong, and that — cruelly — she wouldn't tell him what it was, so he could at least apologise. No, she wasn't ill, she insisted, turning her eyes away from his questioning face and towards the TV. She had taken to watching a Disney film called *Fantasia 2000,* in which various snippets of orchestral music were accompanied by fantastic animations. She always seemed to be watching the same one, in which a pod of whales gamboled to Respighi's *Pines of Rome.* First they leaped and played in the waves, but then, shooting up through the clouds, swam and surged among the stars. Jadis watched that part again and again, enraptured as a child. When Jack asked why, she said she couldn't explain. There was just something about it, she said, that struck a chord. She found it comforting.

As he plodded on, the feet in his mind walked backwards to see if he could work out where things had gone wrong — if indeed they had. He knew he'd taken far too long to get down and write his thesis, trying Jadis' patience. Yet it was she who had brainstormed his thesis into being, gave it birth, gave it life, nursed it to maturity — it was her.

Her!

And even this morning, she still swore she loved him.

Him!

So now he thought, in dejection quite foreign to his usually calm and level nature, that the great gamble had failed. He really didn't deserve this thesis, and he certainly didn't deserve Jadis. By the time he got to the department, his mind was clothed in a fog as thick as the one that laced the streets in funereal shrouds. Go ahead, make my day. In the end he was just too tired. Too tired to panic, too tired to care.

"Mr Corstorphine — Mr Corstorphine?" This from the tiny but intimidating figure of Professor Ernestine Yanga, the external examiner and the other half of the committee, who, MacLennane had said, was famous for saying almost nothing during thesis examinations until near the end, when she'd skewer hapless candidates with the one question they'd been praying nobody would ask. Ah, thought Jack, we must be near the end, then, and this must be the preamble to the famous Difficult Question that MacLennane had warned him about. Best to get it over with, and get out. So far, the examination had flowed glutinously past him like a river of sludge making its viscid way down to a black and putrid sea: he'd supplied all the answers so mechanically, that once he'd uttered a word he'd immediately forgotten about it.

"Mr Corstorphine — you were telling us about your trip to France?"

"Yes — of course — I'm sorry. As you've read in my thesis, I had accumulated a great deal of data about hominin influence on geomorphology in Britain. But it was very hard to make anything of it. Thanks to some new methods developed in conjunction with a fellow student..."

"Yes, I see that this is acknowledged. A Miss Markham, isn't it?" Jack said nothing: his lips pursed in a thin line of remorse. "Please continue, Mr Corstorphine."

"Yes, sorry... I had long suspected the existence of a gradient of human influence on the landscape in England, consistent over the past hundred thousand years at least, in an increasing trend from the northwest — where it is hardly significant according to the variants of the nonparametric tests I've used—to the southeast, where it can be said to stand out from natural influence here and there, but still in general not significantly different from expected natural or stochastic variation."

"Very good. But enough of Albion's fair shores, I think? You were about to tell us all about France, I believe. Would you like to enlarge upon that?"

Jack had had so much to say about France. About how his solo trip there, inspired by the earlier jaunt with Jadis, had changed everything, given him hope—rooting his vague instincts in something more tangible, more real. About how, after looking at the British landscape, scored, ravaged and broken by glaciers at least eight times in the course of almost a million years of human history—glaciers so powerful that they had literally erased rivers as broad as the Severn from the map—his personal antennae had become so tuned to every nuance of landscape that, when he had come at last to a region that had seen a million years of relative and continuous calm, the signs of human influence shone out at him like blinding beacons. Britain had only ever been a sideshow, an outlier: he'd seen immediately what had occurred to no-one, that nothing south of the Loire was wilderness—*nothing*—and had not been so for a very long time. But right now, he didn't feel like explaining anything. His answers were bland, apathetic, hesitant. Looking down on the scene, as if he were hanging from the ceiling, he saw MacLennane rise slightly from his chair, as if in concern—and then Jack snapped, jarringly, back. He blinked, disoriented. It occurred to him that he must have blacked out.

With her well-controlled perm, her neat dove-grey two-piece and pearls, Ernestine Yanga could have been the president of the local Womens' Institute, except that she'd been raised in a grass hut on the western shores of Lake Turkana, until the age of five, when her village had been razed by Ethiopian bandits and the rest of her family had been raped, macheted, burned to death, or combinations of all three. She'd only escaped because she'd been a mile away at the time, gathering pathetic twigs for the cooking fire, and sluicing the filthy puddle that passed for the village waterhole into a chipped enamel bucket. On returning home to find it so casually expunged from the face of the Earth, she'd walked thirty miles to the nearest fly-flecked bush town in search of work. By the time she was thirteen she was handy with a Kalashnikov. She'd been a drug courier, a fruit seller, a goatherd, a moneychanger, a news vendor, a prostitute, a pimp, a cattle rustler, a copper's nark, a murderess (twice), and was riddled with at least six chronic, parasitic infections.

Having understandably decided that she'd had quite enough of all this, she'd walked, blagged, whored and hitch-hiked her way to Nairobi. One night, completely exhausted, she camped out on the steps of the National Museums of Kenya, where she'd decided she'd await the Lord's Salvation. The Lord took the shape of a kindly assistant curator, whose prayers for the Almighty to send him a child to ease his wife's shameful barrenness had now, it seemed, been answered — and who took her in and cleaned her up.

A week later she was the illiterate, unpaid assistant to the janitor. After thirty-five years, the Director of Palaeontology. And now, at the age of fifty-five, what Ernestine Yanga didn't know about the influence of early humans on landforms in the Rift Valley wasn't worth knowing.

She knew far more than that, however, about the symptoms of human suffering, to which she was as sensitive as Jack's spirit chimed to the shape and history of every hanging valley, every drumlin, scarp and oxbow. Her reputation as a terrifying examiner was justified — after all, a woman in her situation could never succeed in life without what she called 'true grit' (she was an avid fan of old westerns) — but in Jack she saw a good man who'd been worn almost entirely away by worry, and, like so many men, he was suffering as much from injured pride as from lack of food and sleep. He had tried his hardest, but despite all his efforts, all his denial, he'd felt he was not quite up to the task, and this insulted his being, his masculinity. But he need not have been so concerned, she thought. The evidence he had from that final trip to France was right there, in front of them. And from what Roger MacLennane (such a charming man!) had told her, Jack was a dedicated field worker, the kind of person she preferred infinitely to pallid, deskbound museum types, who so often built their intellectual castles on the sweat of others.

More importantly, it was clear that Jack fulfilled the first criterion of a doctorate candidate — to venture, without fear, outside the small, cozy nest of knowledge, and into the dark and infinitely greater continent of ignorance that surrounded it. That Jack had ventured so far out that no techniques yet existed to make sense of what he'd found indicated extraordinary fortitude, a brazen and almost breathtaking resolve. If Jack could make no headway with it, then that was hardly his fault, because nobody else (she thought) would have had the ability either. Not MacLennane (he'd admitted as much) and certainly not herself. And yet, if Roger had thought the task impossible, he surely would not have assigned it to a doctorate student. This in itself, she felt, indicated that Jack really must be a man of extraordinary talent, and — she thought back to the fortune that had smiled on her on the Museum steps – talent was precious, and must always be nurtured.

In any case, Jack was not entirely alone, without help. As Professor Yanga understood it, Jack continued to enjoy the best help possible in the form of the acuity of his young associate, Ms. Markham, who seemed to believe in him and who, Roger had assured her, would go far – especially if she and Jack continued to work as a team. As he freely admitted, Roger MacLennane owed his place in the front rank of academia not to any special cleverness in himself, but to a knack of surrounding himself with clever people. And Roger's instincts about people were rarely wrong. Jack was, indeed, a fortunate man, as fortunate as he was deserving.

"Mr Corstorphine, of course, I understand. But please don't worry yourself. Oh my, you look so tired," she said, and she smiled – a warm, radiant, motherly smile that made Jack want to dissolve. This woman, this supposedly ferocious, hard-bitten creature who took no prisoners, had smiled at him. She had looked straight at him, into him, and she understood. She knew. And in that moment he knew that there was hope. And so he started again, clearing his throat, which seemed unaccountably to be full of damp sandpaper.

"I'm sorry – please excuse me. When we think of the French Palaeolithic, we tend to see the landscape as a wilderness, punctuated with some interesting and picturesque cave sites. But that's a view conditioned more by our prejudices about brutish cavemen than by the facts on the ground. When I got there, accustomed as I had been to the far more challenging and – in any case – more sparsely populated British terrain, France looked to me like nothing more than an almost completely artificial, settled – even industrial landscape, continuously shaped by human influence for perhaps a million years."

"What form does that influence take, Mr Corstorphine?"

This really must be it, the Difficult Question that went to the heart of the matter. But the Professor continued to smile. Now he could not be stopped. The influence takes many forms, he said. Just to take a couple of things more or less at random: virtually no watercourse south of the Loire or west of the Rhône has been natural for any significant part of its length since the Late Middle Pleistocene. At the very least, watercourse curvature has been altered by 16 per cent during the Brunhes magnetostratigraphic interval, with the confidence limits that you'll see on page 176, I think you'll find (the committee members turned to their copies of his thesis as Jack felt, at last, to be in the driving seat). In support of this (he continued), the overall number of river channel infill deposits indicative of buried oxbow lakes is very much less than you'd expect by chance, had nature been left to take its course. This means that something — or somebody — has been altering the lower courses of rivers in a systematic way for a very long time.

And then there is the general topography. Volcanic activity aside, no hilltop exists in this part of France that has natural surface run-off characteristics, possibly an indication of the former presence of earthworks or other structures. In fact (Jack paused to draw breath), I could find no grade that has been completely free of human influence over the same period. There's one hill, at a place just not far from Aurignac, called Saint-Rogatien-Les-Remillards...

His mind drifted to when he'd explained all this to Jadis, with mounting excitement, promising her again that after this wretched thesis defense was over, he'd take her there and show her. It was about a month ago, their last evening sitting out in the Nest before it became too cold: they'd had a bottle of wine he'd brought home from the off-license. Retreating to the sitting room, she'd removed a stack of printouts from their sagging old sofa, sat down, pulling him close.

"This is it, Jack," she had said — "This is the key. This proves it. This settles everything." She unbuttoned his shirt — her big black eyes cross-eyed with concentration — and rested her face on his chest, letting him tousle her hair into a blanket, covering and embracing him. He explained to her — to Jadis — to Professor Yanga — that his close survey of this unusual landform revealed to him that its geology was entirely at variance with the underlying bedrock and, furthermore, that its location could not be explained in terms of any local, structural faulting. It couldn't be a glacial erratic, either, because there had been no glaciers. Much of the landform had been worn away by wind and weather, but with an estimated original volume at least a thousand times that of Saint Paul's Cathedral — he was proud to have worked out this comparison — it was just too enormous to have been set down by any kind of fluvial transport short of a catastrophic flood of the kind that had created the scablands of the Pacific Northwest, or which had carved out the English Channel — and there had been no sign of any such activity, either. In fact, its location was inexplicable unless...

At this point, on the sofa, Jadis had trapped his gesticulating hands in hers, and forced them to encircle her. She'd seemed so warm and content, he'd felt that at any minute she'd start to purr. He kissed the top of her head, and said that the only way to explain Saint-Rogatien — the only way — was that it had was an artificial structure. That someone had put it there.

He'd once read about an ancient pyramid at a place called Cholula in Mexico. By the time the *conquistadores* got there, it had been abandoned for centuries, its masonry stripped away, and was covered in grass and trees. Assuming it was just a hill (after all, that's what it looked like), the Spaniards built a town around it and a church on the top. And that was only a few centuries. Imagine, then, if it had been left for a thousand years, a hundred thousand, a million? It would look entirely natural, revealed as artificial only by its strange geology and situation — and only then if somebody first suspected that something was amiss — which nobody had ever done. But when Jack had seen it, his antennae vibrated into overdrive. He knew it didn't belong there. He just knew.

By this time Jadis had been on the edge of sleep. "You really are a very silly man," she had said, yawning. "You've just about wrapped it up. The ancestors of the first Neanderthals built gigantic pyramids all over France..."

"... pyramids that made the Great Pyramid look like a sandcastle — and they were doing it for hundreds of thousands of years."

"Well then, you don't need statistical methods to prove that, so why worry? That's just basic geology and good ol' masculine intuition." She looked up at him, blearily. It occurred to him that her face looked drawn and thin, that what she needed most was sleep. So he'd taken her in his arms and laid her gently on the bed, still in her purple sack, pulling the duvet on top of her. He climbed in beside her, and, together, they slid slowly off to contented, companionable sleep on a smooth, even grade rather shallower than about one in a couple of hundred (he'd estimated), that of a languidly meandering river that makes its mazy, lazy way down to a delta in which it becomes blissfully lost in oozy, woozy thickets.

As if from an immense distance, he thought he heard Professor MacLennane and Professor Yanga commending him for a splendid thesis.

"Congratulations, Doctor Corstorphine!" Hands were shaken, but it was clear to both academics that Jack wasn't really there. They looked worried. The Professors exchanged nervous words that Jack didn't catch, and Yanga left, looking anxious.

"Come on, Jack, I'm going to take you home," MacLennane said as he put his arm around Jack's shoulders, walked him outside into the quad and steered him towards MacLennane's ageing but highly polished

Volvo saloon. Jack was drained, utterly, to the dregs, alternately assailed by waves of light-headedness and nausea. On the other hand, if he'd stepped out of the car, he didn't think he'd have sufficient energy to walk, or even stand up. He couldn't remember having eaten more than a couple of bites of anything for three days. They drew up outside the flat: MacLennane had to haul Jack out of the car. When they knocked at the door, there was at first, no answer.

"Just coming!" — he heard her lovely voice, after a few more seconds: "in the bathroom! Won't be a minute!"

As soon as Jack had left, Jade collapsed on the sofa, eviscerated, as if her heart had burst from within her and now bounced along the street after the dwindling Jack, the world on his broad shoulders, an old gunslinger who, racked by his internal demons, seemed to be losing the will to fight. But she had things to do, an errand of her own, and so, grimly, she dressed, grabbed her bag, and left the house.

Poor Jack had never looked so down. But as she was sympathetic (how could she not be?) she was, it has to be said, a little annoyed. Not for the simple fact of his low spirits, his anxiety — anyone could forgive him these — but perversely, that his mood seemed so entirely out of character, and that was harder to accommodate. Not that she minded being there for him, to cheer him up, even for weeks on end, because she didn't. She loved him, and she wanted to make him happy. But where once had stood an imperturbable rock, there had now limped, in the hallway, half-sunk, a fractious, fretful, friable thing she didn't recognize, and didn't want to. Realizing how selfish this was, she wanted her old Jack back, the granite-hard Jack, the Jack who had become her secure foundation, tying her surely to the solid rock of this planet Earth. Were he to crumble, she would slip, lose her footing, and float off to who knew where.

But there was that other thing, too. That when you'd accounted for the relentless work, anxiety and more work of the past year, there was still, lately, a residue of nauseating wretchedness. When it had continued for weeks, making her feel wan and drained, vitiating desire, it occurred to her that something other than the general preoccupation with Jack's work might be responsible.

Jadis was almost sure she knew, but, being Jadis, she craved certainty, even within statistical limits, explaining why she had now returned home from the supermarket with a pregnancy testing kit: and — even as Jack, his ordeal over, was allowing his rangy form to be folded passively into the passenger seat of MacLennane's car — was undressed, in the bathroom, peering awkwardly down at herself and wondering how a mere woman could aim so accurately at a target as narrowly defined as a test strip. Oh, that a man should have to do this, she grinned to herself, he'd at least be in a position to take better aim.

And just as she heard the knock on the door, presaging the proud return of her conqueror, bloodied for sure, but all dragons slain, the line in the small, crystalline window coalesced, like a chromosome in the very expectancy of division, of the prolongation of a life stretching back to when the world was young, and forward into illimitable futurity — from a yellow nothingness into a single shaft of clear blue.

Chapter 10. Visitors

Xandarga Station, Earth, *c.* 55,680,000 years ago

But full of fire and greedy hardiment
The youthfull knight could not for ought be staide
Edmund Spenser — *The Faerie Queene*

Ruxie rode waves of pleasure and frustration. He didn't mind letting his gradepoint averages slip a little if he could see Xalomé. At first they would meet in the same bar in the harbor district and go on long walks through the nighted City. Apart from that one kiss, they'd done nothing more intimate than hold hands. Ruxie's attempts at anything bolder were met with gentle but firm reproof, always unspoken. Ruxie didn't dare say anything for fear of breaking the spell. On free days, when Ruxie would normally be studying or working with the new Higgs projectors on the weapons range, Xalomé showed him the wonders of Xandarga Station he'd only read about.

One morning she met him with an urgency in her eyes he hadn't seen. It was time, she said, to visit the Institute of Galactic History. She ran before him like a ghost into the Institute's mazy galleries until they arrived at its center, the Gharaan Collection, and the three gray scraps that were all that remained of the earliest-known civilization in the Universe.

"I've been coming here for years," Xalomé said, "and it always gets me. A whole civilization, that old... that early. And nobody knows anything much about them at all."

Ruxie peered at the dusty label. He tried to quell a rising vertigo sparked by this confrontation between unbelievably remote antiquity and the scale of their own ignorance.

"Is that all there is? Just what's in this case?"

"Yes. Amazing, isn't it?"

They stood together, looking at the triptych of silvery slag that formed the entire testament to an unknown number of births, lives, hopes raised, dreams dashed, and deaths, of an extinct species that had lived in what was now the Fomalhaut sector, more than eleven billion years earlier. Xalomé's hand crept into his. They were two sparks against eternity.

"Doesn't anyone have a clue about... them? How they lived? How they died?" Ruxie was surprised by the anguish in his voice, as if the history of these inaccessible lives really mattered to him. He flushed a little, expecting some of Xalomé's gentle teasing. He was surprised, instead, by her seriousness. But before she answered, she smiled. As if she was a teacher, and he'd passed a test. Puzzled, he looked more closely at her as she spoke. There was a hint of tears in her eyes, behind the smile. He remembered his Ma smiling like that, with relief, when she'd just found some vital object—her keys, or a family photo—which she'd convinced herself she'd lost.

"Almost nothing, Ruxie. But there's a lot in that 'almost'. They've— that's the Institute—have analyzed the fragments. Or tried to. They're made of no kind of matter we know about here and now. The closest description they can reach is that it's a metallic form of—well, ice. Frozen water. But that's really only a kind of analogy, something to help us make sense of something we've never seen before. A better approximation is macroscopic quantum foam."

"That's..."

"Yes, I know. Impossible. It's as if they're fossil fragments of space-time itself, frozen, left over from when the Universe was young, perhaps obeyed different laws. But really, what the fragments are made of is not as important as what happened to them. The material is riddled with all kinds of imperfections that signal incredible stresses. Like it brushed against something that mashed it to a dimensionless pulp and then reassembled it. So perhaps the material started off as something more ordinary. Or, at least, different from what it is now. Well, that's what one group of scientists thinks."

"One group? There are others?"

"Oh, c'mon, Ruxie! You'd never expect any kind of consensus with artifacts as enigmatic—and as important—as these. Now, would you do something for me? Go round the other side of the cabinet, look at the smallest artifact—the rectangular one, in the center—and tell me what you see."

"A game?"

"Indulge me." She pecked him on the cheek and sent him on his way. What he saw stopped him, like his feet had been glued to the floor. Everything in the room blurred but for the specimen before his eyes. Carved onto the far side of the fragment, filling its whole area, was an inscription. He swallowed. "Just tell me what you see, Ruxie."

He tried his best to get the words out, but their sharp edges snagged the inside of his mouth.

"The object. An inscription. Rectangular, like the object. It's about—I don't know, maybe nine or ten centimeters from side to side, and maybe two or three tall... hard to be sure... it's shifting..."

"Keep going, Ruxie, you're doing fine."

"... but that's just the frame. Inside there are three circles, inscribed, and they're... they're... they're... so beautiful. So perfect. Like... like..." He looked up.

"Ruxie, keep going... don't stop now!" Her voice was jagged with anxiety. Ruxie was puzzled but did what he was told. He looked down at the specimen once again. It looked like something seen from a great distance.

"... and in between the circles are two crescents, horns pointing outwards... and... and... lines, a lot of lines, all radiating from the circle in the middle... and... Xalomé, help me, I feel very strange."

The Earth flew upwards and over his head. The next thing he knew he was lying on a bench in a shadowed corner of the gallery, his head in her lap, her cool hand on his forehead. He startled.

"Hush now, everything's going to be fine," she said. He remembered the last thing he saw.

"Xalomé, it glowed."

He remembered now: the lines, the circles, the crescents, had all shone at him with a deep, ultraviolet pulse, just before he winked out. He sat up, and Xalomé, holding him, looked at him again, half in cool appraisal, half with some expression Ruxie felt he couldn't quite place.

"You've done well, Ruxie. Really well. I'm so pleased I found you," and she came to him and kissed him, with determined firmness. Ruxie was numb before the wave. She pulled away, looked directly in his eyes, but seemed to be looking through him, as if she'd just picked up a signal from space. Ruxie wasn't as surprised by this as he'd thought he might be. After several weeks, he'd become used to strange, instant summonses which, she said, were relayed to her in-ear comms port. Special Ops.

He remembered the first, jarring occasion, when they'd been in the Natural History Museum, standing beneath the alien that dominated its main hall. The Taniquetilian tesseractrix was built like a sea spider from the oceans of Earth, with many legs fused to a tiny body, but on a gigantic scale. Each leg was eighty meters long, curving from a car-sized chitinous claw through a succession of blue-gray joints to terminate in the body in the blue haze far above their heads. Opera glasses, thoughtfully supplied by the Museum, were required to see the body itself, a mysterious structure augmented with a bewildering variety of stalactitic protrusions and polyhedral blobs. Ruxie remembered gazing at it, open mouthed, unable to take it all in.

"Go on, I dare you," Xalomé giggled. "Count its legs."

Ruxie brought his head down with nauseous recoil. He refocused his eyes and turned around, carefully, to count each one of the teetering columns. This was harder to do than it seemed. He was never sure if he'd counted the first leg twice. After three attempts he linked the first leg to the scene behind it—the Museum gift shop—and started again. The task was easier, but only marginally.

"Twenty-three. No, twenty-four. No, twenty-three. No... no, I'm sure it's twenty-three."

"Actually, it's twenty-seven. And now I have to go." And with that she disappeared, leaving him with a sense of having been short-changed. Twenty-seven? No way. How could she have been so certain? The museum guide book reported that the number of the legs on the Taniquetilian tesseractrix was formally unknown.

This time, it was different. She continued to face him, on the bench just off the Gharaan Gallery in the Institute, and took both his hands in his.

"I'm wanted. I think you should come with me."

Dusk was falling as they hurried down the Institute steps and on to the street. Funny—it had been only mid-morning when they'd come in. Had they been in there—what—eight hours? How long had he been out for the count? Xalomé was in too much of a distracted rush to allow him to ask her. She hailed a cab kerbside, and within twenty minutes they were back in the harbor district. Xalomé paid off the driver, exchanging a few words with him that Ruxie couldn't catch.

The familiar tavern was deserted but for a pool of light illuminating a table at the back. On one side was a familiar figure, seated, stein in hand, looking down at something that couldn't be seen from the shadowed doorway.

"I promised Mr Spektor that I'd settle," said the man. "Promised. I'll pay my dues, I really will... but I can't do it without money. After my next bout—should be a formality—I'll have enough. Really. You gotta believe me. Tell Mr Spektor that I'm a man of my word."

A voice came from the direction of the man's feet. It was well modulated, surprisingly sweet, dangerous with menace.

"That is for Mr Spektor to decide. Not you. Especially as you've lost your last two bouts. You run a great risk, Mr Raelle. Not of death: that is an occupational hazard in Uqbar Rules, as you are aware. No, the risk you run, Mr Raelle, is of shaming Mr Spektor, your hitherto unwavering sponsor. The consequences of that will be very much worse than death. Do not fail him again."

"I won't. Don't worry." Even from this distance, Ruxie could see the beads of perspiration start on Ko's forehead.

"I shall be back to collect. After the bout. Perhaps not us in person. It might be one of our... associates."

"Very good. I'll be waiting." Ko looked up, then, and smiled at Ruxie and Xalomé in greeting. His unseen companion must have taken that as the cue to leave. There was a puffing noise, a wheeze, and an almost inaudible clanking as the mysterious companion made its way to where Ruxie and Xalomé stood. They looked down as the stranger approached. It was not so much a person as a contraption. A sphere of black glass the size of a large grapefruit, chased in silvery metal filigree and mounted on a chassis sprouting four wire-frame balloon wheels. Pulling this arrangement were two insectoid shapes, each no more than thirty centimeters long, made of plate metal intricately linked together. Steam puffed from their joints as they moved. They looked like praying mantids in armor. It was the fairy-tale carriage that creaks along the edges of robot dreams. It stopped at Ruxie's feet, and the mantids looked up.

"Sulfavillains," said Xalomé, a catch in her voice. The mantid on the right raised itself on its rear four legs, gesticulated with its long, anterior talons, rustled its wing-covers and turned its beady-eyed head to one side. Ruxie could see tiny points of malicious red in the centre of each jeweled facet. Its mouthparts moved.

"Please, Miss, allow me to pass. Thank-you," it said, and trundled off into the night. Ruxie was nonplussed, but Xalomé seemed to be shaking with rage.

"Ko Handor Raelle!" she hissed, bending down at him. "What the hell do you think you're doing, country boy? Dealing with these slime?" Ko turned his face away as if she'd slapped him. "You know as well as I do—or if you don't, then you should—that if there's anything mean in this city, anything dirty, then the Sulfas are in it up to their metaphorical necks. They stink!"

"Xalomé, I... well, when no-one else would back me for a prize fight, they were there. They gave me... good terms." He looked down, shame-faced.

"Oh, really? I'll bet they did. So when you fuck it up again—when is it, next Friday night?—they'll be here to blow you to atoms. Can't wait. Perhaps I can sell tickets."

"Well, sweetheart," said Ko, then, looking up, smiling with his mouth, but his eyes two hard points reflecting the foam slithering down the inside of his glass: "I'd better not fuck it up, then, had I?"

Chapter 11. Investor

Aspen, Colorado, Earth, October 2024

Ulfin, thu hauest wel isaed.
Ich the giue an honde thritti solh of londe
That thu Merlin biwinne and don mine iwille.

(Ulfin, you have spoken well.
I shall give you thirty ploughlands of land
If you do my will and win Merlin.)

Layamon—*Brut*

Ruxton Carr loosened his tie, doused the lights, poured himself a generous measure of Talisker, and sank into one of the two chesterfields before the fire.

His retinue of lawyers, accountants, assistants and general hangers-on had left, freighted with decisions (his), whisky (also his), and purpose (theirs). He loved a party but the enjoyment was sharpened by the thought of the solitude to follow. It was solitude, originally, that had led him to buy the Lodge, this cabin perched on a deck of massive ashlars some distance out of Aspen. Just near enough for convenience, just far enough away to deter casual visitors. That, and the fantastic view from the floor-to-ceiling picture windows down one side.

He'd originally come for the skiing—a sport he'd long wanted to indulge in but couldn't really afford until he sold his first company. He'd gone public in 1985; made an absolute killing in 1986; and, with what turned out to be an impeccable gift for timing, sold it for a fortune on 13 October 1987. Six days later, the Hong Kong markets crashed. He was safe, secure, but any feeling of *schadenfreude* he might have had for his competitors was tempered with an understanding of the fragile, makeshift nature of the present. Misfortune might strike anyone, at any time. The secret of not getting fooled was to diversify, and to plan ahead. *Very far ahead.*

Had there been anyone to see him, he'd have been visible only from the still glints in his cat-like, yellow eyes and the starry spangles refracted from the heavy tumbler. He drained it, refilled it, and thought back... and back.

He started — when was it?

Ah yes, it was in Khan's shop on the Tottenham Court Road, selling music centres and SLRs. (Music centres! SLRs!) He had always been a good salesman, but there he'd really taken off. He could trace the change, he thought, to a very wet day in '79, or maybe it was '80, when for some reason he'd fainted while serving a customer. Just disappeared below the counter. One minute, he was there, on the money, the next... He always joked he'd banged his head on the counter on the way down. Don't worry, Mr Khan had said, just overwork. Take the rest of the day off.

But Ruxton had done more than that: The very next day he gave in his notice and within three months he'd opened his own shop. He remembered the smell of new paint, the heart-in-mouth moment when he opened his doors for the very first time, and the sign above the shop. 'Merlin Electronics,' it read. It was a proud moment.

After that he couldn't put a foot wrong. He had an uncanny knack of what people wanted, before they even knew they wanted it. When people woke up to CDs, he was already thinking about music downloads. When they first thought of mobile phones, he was into what eventually became smartphones. People were still wrestling dial-up when he was exploring the possibilities of wireless broadband, and when people had cottoned on to that, he was selling the idea of cloud computing. Merlin had tablets when people still had laptops. Merlin became the place for trendsetters and go-getters. One shop became two, then three, then a dozen, then a hundred. Mr Khan's shop was his twelfth acquisition. When Merlin Electronics went public the share value quadrupled within twenty minutes.

Problem was, he couldn't find suppliers that saw the future the way he did. The only way was to take over the supply side, too. So, while other manufacturers were still in Japan and Taiwan and Korea, he set up shop in mainland China, making his own silicon: Merlin Technologies was born. Within three years there was hardly a computer or mobile phone on the planet that didn't have his chips inside. Then the spacemen and the scientists and the military men came to call, and soon there were Merlin chips in every satellite guidance system, every missile, every fighter jet and every kind of esoteric piece of high-end equipment on Earth — and above it, and beyond it. Before long he'd left shopkeeping far behind. So that's when he'd sold his chain of shops, took to the slopes and effectively disappeared from view while he planned his next move.

Ah, that was when Jade came into his life. He'd never had much time for women—correction, he'd never had *any* time for women—except, of course, as colleagues and business associates. That's how it started with Jade. At around the time Merlin Technologies was founded and he'd decided to move here more or less permanently, Jade came into his life. Jade Marks she was, tall and skinny with long black hair, fake tan, and an Essex accent that could have etched silicon all on its own. She started as his assistant's assistant, and moved around the company, but she never seemed far from view. Reports of her work were good—more than good—and so, to cut a long story short, she became his personal assistant, sharing an office, and, eventually, a bed. It was Jade who first heard his plans. It was often Jade who came up with the best ideas. It was Jade, for example, who alerted him to the tax advantages of philanthropy.

Wow, he'd forgotten that. That was *her* idea. Selling things? Been there, done that, she said. Making things to sell? Top of the tree, Jungle V. I. P., she said. The next step is give money to people who invent the things to make. Scientists. Engineers.

And then Jade disappeared, as suddenly as she'd arrived. She handed in her notice at the company's New Year's Eve party as 2020 became 2021. He begged her to stay, but she simply wouldn't be persuaded. She had a mother in Basildon or Billericay or Braintree or somewhere who had Alzheimer's, she said, and needed looking after. And so she just vanished. He remembered the last thing she said as he paced, impotently, while she packed her few belongings. "Don't forget the past as well as the future, Ruxie," she said. He couldn't make much of it back then. But now, he thought, light was beginning to dawn. There's some promising work in Cambridge, his advisers had told him. Archaeology, of all things.

He wondered what Jade was doing now.

Chapter 12. Contender

Xandarga Station, Earth, *c.* 55,680,000 years ago

Then were they condescended that King Arthur and Sir Mordred should meet betwixt both their hosts, and everych of them should bring fourteen persons; and they came with this word unto Arthur. Then said he: I am glad that this is done: and so he went into the field.
Sir Thomas Malory — *Le Morte D'arthur*

The fight took place in the basement below the bar. It was a huge, low-ceilinged space supported by monumental, square pillars. Ruxie wondered if it had once been a parking garage. If so, no longer — the pillars, the floor, indeed every corner was occupied by punters eager for spectacle. The program started with music, acrobats, jugglers, clowns and fire-eaters, for all the world like an old-time circus troupe that had rolled into some nowhere town rather than the Capital of the Galaxy. There were dancers, too.

Xalomé was not dancing tonight. She was wedged in next to him. Her hand groped for his, and met it. There was little chance that any spoken word would have met its target through the fusillade of excited noise. Ruxie and Xalomé stood on a bench, three or four rows above ringside. Above, and to the left and right, people were thronged. And more than just people. Some of the fight fans cast inhuman shadows under the pillar-mounted sconces. Scent rose, the sweat of expectation. A golden aura flowed across the floor like dry ice in the spotlights.

It was time for the fight to begin.

The referee entered. Wizened, ornately robed, one of the few Uqbar masters to have survived a career unscathed. But no — one of his hands was surely prosthetic, though it was hard to tell amid the folds of his kimono.

"Ladies and Gentlemen!" brayed an announcer from a commentary box that Ruxie couldn't see: "Give it up for Rating Spaceman Ko Handor Raelle, soon to be of the 17th Rigel!"

Screams as Ko, the challenger, entered the ring like he already owned it, robed in scarlet and black, preceded by tumblers and acrobats, and flanked by two burly supporters. The home crowd bawled deafening appreciation. Ko made the required three circuits of the ring, waving and bowing.

Then, the reigning champion. "Make a crushing Xandarga noise for Axaxaxas Mlö, undefeated heavyweight champion of the Southern Tethys!" Yells, cheers, howls. More tumblers and acrobats, and then a tightly bunched nest of women, naked, shaved and oiled, writhing in a complex choreography that concealed the form within. On a signal the women dispersed, trailing multi-colored streamers. Unfurling from within, the champion drew himself to his full height. The crowd was quenched into silence.

They had known it, all the time. Of course they had. But the sight of the champion in the flesh was breathtaking. As was the sheer audacity of Ko, in having thrown down the gauntlet in an elaborate ceremony three days earlier. Ruxie gulped. What had Ko let himself in for? Axaxaxas Mlö, the color of space relieved only by blood-red eyes and white fangs, was a Khong, and among the last vestiges of an ancient adapine race now confined to the high forest plateau of South Polar Gondwana. The Champion must have been almost three meters tall and weighed in at least three hundred fifty kilos, all of it muscle and bone. His fists looked like boulders of black basalt.

In the center of the ring, the champion and the challenger made their ritual obeisances, and retired to diagonally opposite corners of the ring, where they were armed and armored according to ritual evolved over hundreds of centuries and now considered as eternal as the void. Vambraces. Helms with full-face visors. Knee pads. Indrico-leather boots. Knuckle-dusters, rough-cast from depleted uranium shell casings, blue-gray vertices shining raw under the lights.

The whistle blew.

Ko barreled himself straight at the champion before the Khong could draw breath. He smashed his balled fists into his adversary's groin. Blood spurted in crimson gouts. The Khong grunted and looked down, almost abstractedly, as if his siesta had been interrupted by a mosquito. He picked up Ko in both hands, ground his spiked visor into Ko's face, and hurled him across the ring. The noise of the crowd could not conceal the crunch of bones as Ko's face hit the deck. The referee started to count time in a keening ritual song, but Ko rose just before the end. Blood streamed from inside his visor and down his neck, congealing above his collar bone. Ruxie was glad that he couldn't see Ko's face.

Axaxaxas Mlö lumbered over, looked down at the puny contender, and laughed. The noise of it was horrible, hideous. The Khong swung one fist on the end of a meter and a half of pendulum arm. It hit Ko's visor with the impact of a wrecking ball on a watermelon. Ko's head snapped backwards and he flipped onto the floor where he lay in a puddle of what looked like bone chips, blood and his own piss.

"Ruxie — I can't look." Xalomé turned and buried her face in his neck. Ruxie said nothing. He felt that whatever he wanted, whatever he wished, he was forced to watch the ritual dismemberment of his friend by this monster.

But, once again, Ko recovered, although much more slowly than before. He turned himself onto his hands and knees, slithering on the slimed floor of the ring. The champion lumbered over, once again, joshing and hamming it up to the crowd before he dealt what could only be a death blow.

It was to be his undoing. As the Khong bent over to examine its prize, Ko sprang upwards, smashing his helmet into the Khong's abdomen, winding him. The Khong toppled over Ko's back, so that his immense legs lay like tree trunks on either side of Ko's body. Slicked in his own fluids, Ko was now an unstoppable demon. He turned himself onto his back, sat up, grabbed the champion's loincloth, shredding the supple leather with the heavy metal blades of his knuckle-dusters, pummelled at the champion's genitalia with armored fists. Axaxaxas Mlö roared in pain and shock, but could not rise from the surface of the ring, now as slippery as the deck of a whaler in a storm. Ko now moved in for the kill. He unstrapped his helm, tearing it from his head and flinging it into the crowd. His face was a mask of blood.

Then from a fold of his loincloth Ko drew, with great theatricality, a set of false fangs, which, like knuckle-dusters, had been sheared from spent battle-armor. Fitting them into his mouth, he rose above the prone form of the Khong, sought cheers — and got them — and then dove, like a vulture into the bloodied hole of a carcass. The identity of what Ko drew up between his teeth, sinewy, red and still pulsing, Ruxie dared not even think about. The crowd screeched in maroon-flecked ecstasy.

The celebration surged well into the night, the tables of the harbor-district tavern crowded with glasses both full and spent, the floors awash with beer and bodies. Ruxie and Xalomé were among them, but Xalomé remained curiously remote, detached; unwilling, it seemed, to join in the spirit of things, in contrast to the many other women now wrapped round Ruxie's colleagues on benches or on the floor in every imaginable state of abandon.

Ruxie was now resigned to this. He forgot Xalomé. He forgot the other women. He hooked up instead with a group of barrack-mates and concentrated on downing as much beer as he could. One of his colleagues looked down, wide-eyed, at a bulge in Ruxie's crotch.

"Ruxie, man—is that a pistol you're packin'... or...? And if not, why aren't you flaunting what you've got? After all, there are babes about." General laughter. Ruxie was puzzled, at first, until he reached down the inside pocket of his pants and, in a state of shock, realized that he'd walked out of the weapons range that afternoon with a Higgs projector. He hadn't signed it back in. Nobody made that mistake. Not ever. He'd be toast for sure. But with the ingenuity with which only the seriously drunk are blessed, he conceived a plan. If he snuck into the weapons range before daybreak, fiddled the records slightly, no one would ever know, would they?

Result.

"Well... er... it is a pistol. Actually." He was as nonchalant as he could manage. "So... well, make my day."

There was a commotion at the door of the tavern. Ruxie could not, at first, see what it was all about. A chaos of shouts and confusion. He was dimly aware that Xalomé had gone, and he could no longer see Ko, either. Either he was buried in the crowd, or the party was going on without him. The shouts from the door morphed from yells of indignant rage into screams of agony and pain, and then Ruxie could see the cause of the disturbance.

Oh no. Another monster. Without needing to be told, Ruxie knew that the shadowy Mr Spektor had sent another of his associates to collect Ko's winnings. An associate who would be quite capable of bending Axaxaxas Mlö and any other likely champion into pretzels. Ruxie felt beer and bravado inflate inside him and rose from his seat, side-arm in hand. Months of practice that could not be dulled by alcohol kicked into action. Ruxie's fingers primed the charge. At that moment the crowd near the door was brutally thrown aside by the newcomer. Bodies flew through the air, and from amid the chaos emerged a moving monolith, towering, gray, apparently unstoppable.

"Shit, man—it's a Flintsider. We'd better split," said one of Ruxie's drinking partners. Ruxie said nothing. The eye of stillness in the storm raging all around him, Ruxie held the weapon at full arm's length and pulled the trigger. As he did so he thought of Xalomé. The thought hit him like a kick in the ribs just as the Flintside enforcer imploded with a sharp crack, its component silicon carbide molecules and gallium neurites redistributed at several quintillion random points throughout the

Galaxy. Silence descended. With all eyes on him, Ruxie calmly pocketed the particle projector and left the bar.

Ruxie walked back to the barracks through silent streets. He first took a detour to return the purloined projector to the weapons range, a plan that went off without a hitch. He felt deflated after the night's events. Although he'd returned the weapon, discharging it in a public place, and killing a civilian—even an alien hood—would, surely, have serious consequences. Given that the balloon went up in a bar patronized by spacers, he wondered why he hadn't been picked up by Naval Police within minutes. But where he should have been anxious, he was filled with empty apathy. He passed unhindered into the compound, and felt and saw very little until he was in his own dorm, facing his own bed.

The first thing that struck him was the noise. The same noise that had swirled around him at the boxing match: the animal baying of spectators. It came from all around him, but was directed, focused, at his own bed, now before him. A bed drenched in the saffron aura of sex.

It was Ko's bare back he saw first, and his bare hindquarters, as he pumped away at a woman on her knees and elbows, on Ruxie's bed. The crowd roared its appreciation. The woman was screaming for Ko. Screaming for him to push deeper. Screaming for him to rip her insides out, to take her as he'd taken down the Khong.

The woman on Ruxie's bed was Xalomé.

Ruxie turned on his heel and walked out. Five hours later he shipped out for the Trifid Nebula.

Chapter 13. Correspondent

London and Cambridge, England, Earth, March 2025

At length burst the argent revelry,
With plume, tiara and all rich array,
Numerous as shadows haunting fairily
The brain, new stuff'd, in youth. With triumphs gay
Of old romance.
John Keats — *The Eve of St Agnes*

Jadis' nerves fell away as soon as she took her seat at the press conference — MacLennane to her left, Jack on her right — and had been introduced to the crowd of journalists, photographers and cameramen who'd crammed, almost on top of each other, it seemed to her, in the small but unnaturally brightly lit library that London's Royal Institution had arranged. Not that anyone paid very much attention to her two male outriders, because she'd looked (as they'd hoped) as marvelously unacademic as might be imagined.

She'd fretted for several days about what to wear, as (she'd felt) she had little sense for such things, except that what suited her least of all was indecision. The few women academics she knew were, in the main, as unconscious of fashion as she was — either that, or they went to the other extreme and dolled up to the nines, dressing to impress — something which she felt might be fine for some people, but only made her feel uncomfortable. Her male friends included Roger MacLennane, who always wore the same dark, slightly crumpled suit; and Avi Malkeinu, whose idea of female fashion probably extended only as far as swimwear.

That left Jack, and he was biased.

"I think I'd have to declare an interest," he'd said, in his best mock-serious voice, as, shirt-sleeves rolled up, he'd rubbed her back as she sat up in the bath one evening several days earlier, "as not only do I love you, but I love you more each day, as there is progressively more of you to love" — at which she'd snorted and soaked him with bubble-laden water. He'd sat for a moment, quite still on the edge of the bath, wet through, smiling quizzically, but saying nothing. So he did what she knew he'd do — something so practical, so funny, so Jack. He'd stripped and climbed in behind her, a leg on either side. She was, by now, in hoots of giggles, the water surging and splashing around her, around him, and all over the floor.

"Give me one of those Paleolithic mother-goddesses every time," he'd said, half laughing, half growling, and starting to rub her shoulders and neck, which she loved—but not without first giving each of her increasingly sore and swollen breasts a playful squeeze—which she liked rather less.

She decided that she enjoyed being pregnant. She enjoyed the fullness of it. The only bad thing about it, after the horrible first couple of months, was the backache, hence the time spent in the bath. But what had surprised her—and delighted her—was how much her desire for Jack had sharpened. She supposed that it might have something to do with the physicality of it, that here was starkly tangible reassurance that she was tied to the Earth.

That, and her recent rediscovery of the sense of smell, and especially his smell, an ineffable sense of masculinity, nothing very strong—not like unwashed socks or stale beer or anything like that—but an instantly recognizable presence that reassured her, and which lingered in the flat even when he wasn't physically there. Some mornings it had been extremely difficult to leave his embrace, as if she were attached to him by a bungee cord. Hence his candid lack of objectivity, whether she wore a stylish designer outfit, or 'Horrible' (her baggy old once-purple jersey). She felt that he'd have adored her just the same had she been wearing a dustbin liner.

For his part, Jack found Jade's pregnancy enchanting. Her body was changing in all kinds of ways that he loved to examine in the tiniest detail, as if he were a surveyor, mapping the topography of an unexplored continent in the throes of some incremental but ultimately profound change of climate, from the trimly temperate, to the lush and exotic.

For her, then, her weight taken by the water and Jack's body for a chair, her lover had crystallized into a pair of hands. Funny that she'd paid so little attention to them before, but pregnancy was refining all her senses, not only smell and taste. His were the hands of a man who belonged outdoors—the hands of a field geologist, the hands of contradiction—calloused and ridged as they endured frost and thaw, but capable of marvelously sensitive precision and agility, as those same rough fingertips felt their way towards a fossil or crystal so fragile that it might be shattered by a drop of water—and cradled it unharmed to safety. And so she craved the touch of his hands, the counterpoint of roughness and gentleness, as they traversed her curving form, as if constantly recording, measuring her totality at any instant. As her body swelled, so did her need for him, until it was like a constant drone in the background of her life. However, as her insistent desire resonated with Jack's own, she felt him rise and grow behind her, in the small of her back. And the water was getting cold, too.

"Out you get, young man," she'd said, unmoving, her eyes still closed.

"'Fraid not," he'd countered, "as I am at present pinned to the spot by a Dangerous Wild Animal."

She gripped the sides of the bath, put her feet together and crouched—wriggling the arced expanse of her behind at Jack, teasingly, mockingly—and then stood fully upright. Just before she stepped out in search of a towel he'd looked up at her and for a moment she was a vast statue, shining with water, the fullness of her body exaggerated by the foreshortened angle of view. Jack sank into the bath, filling the space she'd left, stretched out, looked up at her and said:

"There was a reason for those Paleolithic mother-goddesses, you know."

"Hmm?" She had started to dry her hair.

"They illustrate the inherent superiority of women. If only in the geometrical sense." She turned suddenly to lean over the bath, a mad flurry of wild hair, eyes and towel—

"I said, out—you—get!"

Jack did, at least, have a constructive idea. If she couldn't ask Roger what to wear, why not ask *Mrs* Roger? She'd be at the celebration tomorrow.

"You can ask her then," he said. "Quite a character, Marjorie MacLennane," said Jack. "I think you'd like her."

"I had no idea that Roger was married!" she exclaimed. "What do *you* think of her?"

"Me? She's terrifying. But that shouldn't deter *you*."

If Professor Ernestine Yanga only looked like the President of a local Women's Institute, then Marjorie MacLennane really was one, and many other things besides. She was a pillar of the Conservative Association, a Church Commissioner, and judged a hand of bridge with such frightening perspicacity that few ever dared challenge her. She would have it that as a daughter of a Brigadier-General, her life was dedicated to service.

Most people found her too intimidating to talk to, or even approach, on those occasions (rare) when she accompanied Roger to departmental parties. For her part, she found most of the academics not to her taste, and even if they had been, they'd have very little to discuss. Many of them detested everything she stood for, and shunned her in what she considered a singularly ill-bred fashion, by talking over her in her presence, or simply turning their backs. But when Roger threw a small party to celebrate Jack's doctorate and the impending publication of the paper in *Nature* ('Large-scale anthropogenic landscape modification in the Upper Pleistocene of France,' by J. L. Markham, John A. Corstorphine, Avram Y. Malkeinu and Roger Sutherland MacLennane), she felt she could hardly refuse.

"You really must meet Jack," Roger had implored, "and you must certainly meet Jadis." *Jadis*? What kind of a name was that? But then, she sighed, this was likely to be her husband's finest hour, and perhaps a last hurrah before he was kicked out to pasture. So duty called.

When she actually met Jadis, she found her disarmingly unlike what she had expected — although, if pressed, the nature of that expectation would have been ill-defined. At first she was puzzled. To her, Jadis seemed a mixture of opposites. On the one hand she seemed ethereal, almost transparent, and distracted, as if she didn't really belong on this planet. Her fiercely black gaze, on the other hand, betokened a person earthy, practical, unlikely to be intimidated by anyone. Rather like she was herself, in fact.

The truth was that Marjorie saw herself in Jadis, as a young woman, a graduate of Girton with a Double First in Natural Sciences, which is how she had met her junior-research-fellow husband. But it had been much more difficult for women in her position to pursue careers of their own in those days. That they might do so while conspicuously pregnant was unthinkable, yet pregnancy seemed to suit Jadis very well. So she had taken Jadis under her wing, and invited her to call on her at home.

"You can never go wrong with a Little Black Number," Marjorie had said, when Jadis had called the day after the party at the MacLennane's imposing Victorian villa, exposing a rail of Chanel gowns in her wardrobe to the kind of scrutiny which her late grandfather had reserved for drilling the troops before Mountbatten, as the Union flag had been lowered for the last time over Delhi.

"Try this. It was made for me when I had to go to some ball or another, when I was pregnant with Fiona. That was... well, Fiona has children of her own now."

Marjorie helped the gown over Jadis' head. Marjorie and Jadis were about the same height, so it fitted very well. It was classically black and breathtakingly elegant. Jadis looked at the mirror, disbelieving, enchanted. Then she looked at Marjorie, whose expression was unfathomable. "*That's* the one for you, my dear. Would you like to try some pearls?"

At the back of the press conference sat Marcel Montgolfier, a distant relation of the pioneer balloonists, but proximately the veteran London correspondent of *Agence France Presse*. A press briefing in London on the topography of *La France Profonde* seemed an incongruity that bordered on effrontery, but no matter; in any case, one could forgive these English scientists in their startling assertion that French civilization was so ancient that it had preceded humanity itself.

This offered by twinkling bespectacled figure at the right of the panel, the man Montgolfier's press pack described as Professor Roger Sutherland MacLennane, FRS, from the University of Cambridge. Not that Montgolfier didn't know this, of course. MacLennane was a well-known scientist, who while reserved, always seemed to be good for an off-the-record briefing. Our picture of Neanderthal Man as the primitive savage (MacLennane said) was a distortion caused by the fact that history is always written by the victor: when the first *Homo sapiens* came into Europe some 40,000-or-so years ago, it was not to meet a debased tribe like Charles Darwin's Fuegians, but the bones of a civilization that had, in his words, "endured for eight thousand centuries, and had created megaliths the size of mountains."

The theme was continued by Dr Jack Corstorphine, the tall young scientist on the left of the panel, in the casual jacket and polo shirt, who explained, with a quiet but compelling authority, that the breadth and extent of this ancient civilization would have been incomprehensible to our own ancestors, who would therefore have seen only wilderness, weaving the bones of this great and ancient culture into the legend and myth of centuries. As the ruins of Roman Britain had appeared to the barbarian Saxons as the works of mythical giants, so the megalith at Saint-Rogatien-Les-Remillards in Gascony had appeared to our ancestors — and also, said Dr Corstorphine, to ourselves, until our own researches had recognized it as being "something quite extraordinary."

Dr Corstorphine was a new face to Montgolfier, but in his assured delivery he could tell that he was one of MacLennane's latest *protégés*. But MacLennane and Corstorphine were the sideshows, the *hors-d'oeuvres*, compared with what was obviously the main attraction, a young woman who was looking up at Corstorphine, as he spoke, with an expression of — what was it? Adoration? — so intense that it could have melted granite. When the girl (identified as 'Ms Jadis L. Markham'), rose to speak, the room fell silent, except for the sound of a few people swallowing and some quickly stifled coughs.

This was not a scientist—this was a movie star. As Jadis Markham discussed, with a dignified poise, how the ancient inhabitants of Europe had done more than leave a few isolated monuments, but instead had modified the very face of the Earth, Montgolfier and the assembled press corps began to lose the thread of the story and take a greater interest in its speaker. She was dressed in classic Chanel. Montgolfier (who had covered fashion in his time, in between stints on the diplomatic desk) thought her gown had been a *couture* item from the sixties: could anyone name *any* scientist, let alone such a *débutante*, who could carry off such cool retro chic? And—unbelievable—she was at least five months pregnant, and yet the gown fitted her as if pregnancy was her natural state, the state in which she was most at ease: she simply glowed. The whole effect, the way her outrageously untamed cloud of glossy dark hair (who said scientists were buttoned-up?) tumbled over her pale shoulders, her *décolletage*, was enchanting! And her face! Framed—and indeed, sometimes partly obscured—by this nebula of hair, were two bright but yet unfathomably dark wells of intelligent, calculating ferocity. She was like a cat, a wild thing, he thought, her wildness kept in tight coils by an adamantine composure which on the surface appeared easy and carefree, but which—he was sure—was, not so far beneath, passionate and determined.

All this in a girl of *how* old? Twenty-one? If this was another of MacLennane's *protégées*, Montgolfier would bet that she would be his last, his swansong, because she'd be impossible to follow.

As Montgolfier sat, enraptured, it occurred to him that although the story itself was important—it certainly was that, and would be the centre of all discussion for weeks and months—he was not watching a press conference so much as a wedding, or a coronation. All this from tiny things he'd noticed that were never spoken out loud for all that they were quite evident, even from his place at the back. How Jadis, for all the control that belied her years, for all that she conducted the wolf-pack of journalists as if she were Karajan directing the Berlin Philharmonic, would frequently glance at Jack, only for a moment, but with an expression of such—how could he describe it—supplication?—and his face would bestow a warmth of reassurance in return. And all this presided over by MacLennane, who watched both of them with proprietorial satisfaction. This would be a great story, Montgolfier thought, because the people were at least as interesting as the tale they told. This is the next dynasty of archeology in the making (he would write). He hoped he'd be able to get a picture of Jadis.

At the very end, Montgolfier essayed a question for this rising star. "Ms Markham," he asked, "excuse my presumption, but how will you reconcile your — how shall I say — imminent family commitments — with what promises to be an extensive program of field research?"

Jadis turned her lighthouse eyes on Montgolfier. She paused for a moment, and it seemed to him that her hair gathered around her face like a brooding storm cloud.

"I'll take them with me of course," she said, with an asperity that made him start. "What else would I do with them?"

And then the storm clouds dissipated as quickly as they had arrived, her face opening into a smile as bright as the sun, and of such innocent loveliness that he thought he'd die right there, at the pinnacle of his long career.

And in *England*.

After the conference, when they'd managed to elude the last of the cameras, supplementary interviews and questions, Roger treated them both to lunch at Fortnum's, but then announced he was staying overnight on in London. "Business at the Royal. Then I'll hole up at the Athenaeum," he'd said, hailing a cab in Piccadilly to take Jadis and Jack to Kings Cross. "But don't forget, you two — my office, nine o'clock, day after tomorrow. Might have a bit of news." He tapped his nose conspiratorially, his expression unreadable behind his glasses.

The train home pulled through the cramped crenellations of North London and eventually eased into flat country under the immense East Anglian sky, the land beneath clothed in the brilliant green haze of early Spring. Jadis leaned into Jack, and neither said a word for a long time. A full hour into the journey, Jack pulled her closer. "Might *I* ask you a question, Ms Markham?" he began, in his best Monty-Python French Accent. This time her smile was just for him.

"But of course!"

"You said, *them*. That you'd take *them* with you, into the field, when we get to excavate."

"Well if there are, it's all *your* fault, you silly man," she said, pushing closer still: and then more quietly, looking directly up at him and smiling, blearily, but just for him: "'Nothing like a good seeing to,' you said, 'for clearing the brain.'"

She began to nod, and it was only then that Jack realized how tired she must have been—the trip had taken it out of her: that, and the spotlight. And how he still had to listen to MacLennane's advice: just make sure *you're* not the one left behind. How he'd struggled through his thesis defence, when she, a graduate student just starting out, had had all those journalists under her spell. When the train pulled in to Cambridge, she was asleep in his arms.

The next morning, as she looked over the breakfast table for the Oxford marmalade, Marjorie MacLennane saw Roger's unopened copy of *The Times*. Such a waste, she thought, given that he'd get his own copy at his club. Then she remembered why Roger had been away and took another look at the lead story. 'Civilization dates back a million years, scientists say,' read the headline, but the picture was of a young girl, hair awry, who for all her youth had the steel of ancient wisdom in her eyes.

"Good for you, Jadis Markham," said Marjorie, marmalade now quite forgotten.

Chapter 14. Convalescent

Xandarga Space Elevator, Earth, *c.* 55,680,000 years ago

O what can ail thee, knight-at-arms
Alone and palely loitering?
John Keats — *La Belle Dame Sans Merci*

"Congratulations," she said. Her hands were in the pockets of her white medical gown, now opened, revealing a smart cream blouse and gray wool skirt beneath. Glints of warmth in wise, green eyes, framed by high cheekbones in an olive-brown face. Soon-to-be-ex-Admiral Ruxhana Fengen Kraa quite forgot his racked breathing, the sweat of effort. The doctor walked towards him, clack of heels on parquet silenced by crimson pile as she approached. Ruxhana was transfixed, at once gripped by an urge to flee and a compulsion to stay, Just to see what happened next.

The same compulsion, in fact, that had gotten him into so much trouble just lately. Oh, well. What the hell.

"Xalomé?" She was now almost close enough to touch and he could sense the saffron of her heat. Panic seized him, a mixture of thwarted desire and bitter betrayal he thought long buried under thirty-eight years of hard fighting.

First, the long war against the Carpetbaggers in the Trifid Nebula, in which he lost an eye and gained field promotion.

Then, a long series of counter-insurgency operations of appalling viciousness against the Jumblies in the Greater Magellanic Cloud, where the *Pax Terrestris* had yet to take hold. This proxy war against Andromeda had cost both his legs, an arm, much of his skull and a third of his cerebral cortex.

And after that? Campaign followed campaign, with trips to Earth ever less frequent. He had only ever once descended from Clarke Orbit, and that was by the Panthalassic Elevator, not down to Xandarga Station. He'd stayed less than a day.

The doctor was standing before him. He relaxed his grip on the bar and turned unsteadily into her retrieving arms, encircled fully in her embrace. She looked up at him, her lips slightly parted.

"Xalomé? If that's who you want me to be, Admiral, then so I shall be."

"But... how? Are you...?"

"Hush now, Admiral. You've exerted yourself quite enough for one session. Your new bones are knitting nicely, but such massive reconstruction takes time. What you need now is a shower and bed." He could see the curve of Earth filling a panoramic port with blue against the stars. She followed his glance and turned back to him, reading his thought. "Tomorrow, as they say, is another day," she said. "Now, do you think you can walk a little more?"

"I think so, Doctor, if you can steady me."

With her help he made his way to the bathroom. He allowed her to remove his robe so that he could step into the shower cubicle. Suddenly shy, he never let her see anything more than his bare back. To have allowed her to glimpse him in front view would have been too much. His face would have been a study in bafflement and fear. What's more, he had an erection, uncomfortably taut. He looked down at his prong, rigid and sharply bladed at the end, as if it were an alien life form: like the rest of his new flesh, still pale with regenerative newness. He felt dizzy — the walls of the shower cubicle ballooned out to cushion him, and a seat rose from the floor to break his fall.

When it was sure that the patient was safe, the cubicle's AI withdrew the side-impact cushions and turned on the shower. A blast of hot nanofluidics stripped him of the sweat that had congealed around him like a shell. Steam rose. The hiss of the drops hitting the floor made him drowsy.

"Xalomé?"

"Shh. There, now. Time to get dry, I think." The nanofluidics were replaced instantly by blasts of hot, fresh air, reminding Ruxhana of the bridge of the *Sorceror*. The memory immediately cost him his erection, but he now felt he could hardly stand unaided. The Doctor, businesslike, frowned in concern, dressed him in a new bathrobe, guided him from the bathroom and into his bed, covering him, monitoring his temperature, blood pressure and vital signs.

"No, I think you'll do," was the last thing she said before he blacked out.

He awoke in the dark and for a moment had no idea where he was, or why. He tried to sit up, but the effort made him feel sick, so he eased himself gently down onto the mattress. But there was a hand on his chest, and a body next to his in the dark, and he remembered.

"Xalomé —"

"We've been through all that. Haven't we?"

"I —"

"In any case, you have more pressing concerns." He felt the smoothness of a thigh laid against his, and a hand, gripping and releasing the hairs on his chest, making its way downwards, across his belly. He felt proud—stupidly so, he thought, given that he'd had no part in his rescue and reconstruction—that his new belly was more toned than his old one had been, and that his prong seemed heavier and more serrated. It began to rise under her touch.

"My job, Admiral, has been to make you better," she said. "Think of me as all the King's Horses and all the King's Men, glueing dear old Humpty Dumpty back together again."

"Humpty Dumpty. That's me, right?"

"Mmm-hmm." Her fingers began to trace the razored ridges of his prong, feeling their way gingerly around the sharp, multiply bladed tip. "Only, unlike our ovoid friend of lore, you're only being stuck together so you can feel it all the harder, when they shove you off an even higher wall."

"The fleet. My fleet," He gripped a fistful of her hair, more forcefully than he'd meant to.

"Ow! Yes, the fleet. You probably haven't realized it yet—after all, you've been in no fit state—and I wasn't about to let you know any sooner, because the stress might have killed you. But the loss of the fleet will cost you your commission. At the very least."

"And at the most?"

"I don't think you need worry about that yet. You've been in worse scrapes. After all, as I say, it's been my job to put you back together, and the process isn't yet complete. And, if I may say so, I've been quite pleased with some of the—um—additional refinements I've built into the New You." She giggled and sat up. He saw her only in silhouette, but she still had a hand around his prong. "Improvements to—well, size, mainly. And stamina."

"Improvements?"

"Sure. On a lonely job like this, a girl has got to find whatever fun she can. No—don't move. You can pay me later."

"Pay you?"

"Not in the way you think. But I think I can help you out of this. But I'll want something in return."

"Want...?"

"Perhaps I shouldn't have said anything. As I said, tomorrow is another day. And as I also said, the best thing you can do now is simply to lie back and think of Gondwanaland. Stay still, now." She swung a leg over him, so that he felt the plush of her thighs gripping him high across his hips. With great care, holding her breath, she lowered herself onto him, and, having done so, let out a small cry of pain. She sat fully upright, maneuvering him still more deeply, and sighed.

"Oh, wow—I *am* good," she said. "No—I told you, don't move." Looking up at her silhouette in Earthlight, he could hardly help himself, his hands tracing the musked contours of her body. Her aura deepened as she moved until it blanketed them both, wings of a purple emperor, barred with crimson rays. She gripped his hips with her knees and lifted herself from him.

"Xalomé?"

"Hmm?" She looked up, green eyes gleaming in shadow, tapeta flashing, aura deepening in indigo waves.

"Am I...? Do you think?"

"Are you fit enough for the main event? Oh, yes, I think so. All part of the therapy. Doctor's orders." And then she turned over, flaunting her hindquarters at him, thrusting them outwards so that her inflamed vulva emerged as a golden center of a coruscating turquoise mandala. He rolled over, feeling his new limbs creak, and, very delicately, rose to his knees, steadying himself behind her, on the milky backs of her thighs, fingers gripping the mane of hair running down the nape of her neck.

She whimpered. His prong sparked in a flash of agony as he brushed it against her thighs, bending it at the root. He winced as the muscles in his new knees locked in cramp. She bent forward, burying her face in the bed, reaching back to reassure him and draw him in. A fleeting touch of fingertips on his shaft, and then he was within her, his prong transforming in ways never seen in the open air, in response to the histamines secreted by the folds of her flesh, the edges of his glans inflating into barbs of horn that locked him into her, and which raked her deeply as he moved, first uncertainly, and then with renewed reserves of power, so that with each surge she was pulled clear of the mattress and then driven further into its folds. When he spasmed, her aura darkened with terrifying suddenness to the null of space. She screamed then, a brutal yell of ecstasy and terror. Her aura winked out of existence before resuming, slowly, a skulking orange. She sighed and pulled herself away, releasing him. Tiny rivulets of blood, darker shadows in the darkness, flecked his prong and her inner thighs. She fell forwards onto the bed. He could not see her face.

He awoke on his back and found himself paralyzed. His eyes, now open, could not close, but the square, white luminous tiles of the ceiling were all he could see. The air was different, too. Ionized, like the sea. Entirely different from the fug of the stateroom, in which his last memory was the rankness of spent sex. As if on cue he heard her voice, and though he could not move to see her, he had a clear image of her once again in her doctor's gown and conservative clothes. Without knowing how, or feeling any sensation at all in his lips and tongue, he spoke.

"Why can't I move?"

"Because, Admiral, this really is going on inside your head. Like the stateroom. And the shower. And everything else. I felt I had to make a point, that's all."

"So... you aren't really Xalomé, then? My Xalomé?"

"Not that again. Look, if you want me to be 'your Xalomé,' whoever that is, then 'your Xalomé' I shall be. If you think it will help."

"Will it?"

"Whatever."

"But the real Xalomé...?"

"... has been married for thirty years to a rat-faced little corporal in the catering corps; lives in a low-to-middling suburb of a thrillingly dull stripway sprawl on an incredibly boring planet in the Shit-For-Brains Quadrant; has twelve mewling kits, and ten well-chewed dugs dangling down to her knees. Life for her is unending drudgery with no prospect of relief and it's only the diazepam that keeps her going. Frankly, she's let herself go. What opportunities wasted. What intelligence. What talent."

Ruxhana choked. "You know this? You really know this?"

"Of course I don't. How could I? And in any case we're getting off the point. As far as you're concerned, in this reality, in this—continuum, if you like—I am Xalomé, your Xalomé, if you want me to be."

He did not find this offer comforting. It was not what he wanted that had mattered, but what she had wanted, and that he could never work out what her desires might have been.

For years—decades—he had wondered what had happened to Xalomé, even to the extent of querying naval records with the resources available only to a Fleet Admiral. Not even Special Ops could cloak its activities from him, had he chosen to examine them—which he had. There had been no record of her existence. None whatsoever.

Of course, he could have discovered anything and everything he wanted to learn about the career of his erstwhile barrack-mate Ko Handor Raelle. But some creatures were best left to fester beneath the stones whence they came. It was only a chance glance at a newsfeed a decade earlier that told him that ageing, minor-league Uqbar-rules contender Raelle had come third in a duel with a Khong called Azazazat Gwár. Ko's skull had been smashed in and flattened, his brains spurting all over the ring and into the baying, Antarctic crowd. An old score, finally settled.

"But I have something to tell you," she said. "To ask you, really."

"Me?"

"Yes. A task. A job." She sounded slightly ashamed, he thought, as if this 'job' were something furtive, shady. For the first time he felt that he had the upper hand, for all that he could not move and had no idea about the reality he inhabited, nor how he might escape it.

"Oh, really? After this—betrayal? And double betrayal? You want me to help you?" The revelation that none of their lovemaking had been consensual, or even real, had hit hard. "Well, fuck you. If the Navy wants to rip my spine out, they're welcome. I no longer care."

She saw her face hove into view over the horizon of his own. Her hair was disordered, her eyes red-rimmed. He could feel himself turn, power returning to his neck muscles. He looked straight into her face and spat. She wiped her face with her sleeve.

"I guess I deserved that," she said. "For what it's worth, I'm sorry..."

"Sorry? For leading on a naïve country bumpkin? I'm sure it goes on all the time. Character-building. Think nothing of it—you whore." He sat up and found himself in a theater gown on a gurney in a room that contained no other furniture. The walls and floor were clad in the same luminous, white tiles as the ceiling. He could see neither doors nor windows. The doctor—clothed, as he had suspected, in her sensible gown, blouse and skirt—came and sat down next to him.

"Where am I?"

Her voice returned to an even tone and temper. "When I said you were inside your own head, I wasn't being entirely truthful."

"Oh, you do surprise me."

"We're in what's called an 'Xspace'."

"'Special Ops,' I suppose?"

"Something like that. If you want."

"Stop telling me what I want. It's what you wanted—what Xalomé wanted—that I wanted to know, but she threw it back at me, the bitch." Silence. What felt, to him, like a guilty pause.

"Okay, Ruxie, truth time. I am not Xalomé. if indeed she ever existed. Or maybe I was. Once. Sort of." She bit her lip, crumpled one fist into another. "It's so very hard to explain."

"Try me."

"Oh, all right. I had hoped not to have to tell you all this, but it seems I've probably fucked it up, for everyone, as I usually do. I'm an exotic of a kind that I don't think you know anything about, because we don't have much to do with... well, with baryonic matter. Not that we don't have feelings, though. Not that we don't care. And we do care. I care. I wouldn't have gone in for this whole charade if I hadn't. Well, would I?

"And as it is truth time, I have another confession to make. I got you into this mess. It was me. All of it. The Slunj, the Discotex, the... well, the destruction of the fleet."

"My... fleet? You?" He tried to swing his legs over the edge of the gurney, but a numbness had gripped his body. He could hardly catch his breath. "You... killed... more than six hundred million people, under my command? You?"

"I know, I know. I wish it didn't have to happen that way, but I am sorry, and I can explain, if you'll let me try..."

"Why should I even listen to this? Here I am, being held captive in some kinky VR dungeon by a crazed alien, and she wants sympathy? Oh, just wheel me before the Board of Enquiry right now. They'd love this. Incompetent. Delusional too. Can't take the pressure. Hears voices, you know."

"Look, Ruxie, I can't take *all* the blame. It was you I wanted, not your crew. And, if I remember correctly, the Senior Under-Secretary for Colonial Defense did advise, very strongly, that just a couple of gunboats would have been enough. Didn't she?"

"Yes, well, I suppose..."

"*Didn't she?*"

"Yes, she did. But how did you... how could you have possibly..." Comprehension dawned. "You? You're not...?" The Doctor stood, silent, arms crossed, waiting. "So, Doctor, whoever you are..."

"If you'd like a name you may call me 'Merlin.'"

"All right. 'Merlin'. So, if you got me into this mess, you can get me out of it, right?"

"Right. And thank you. You won't believe how important this is to us — to me — to... well, everything..." She reached over and grasped his hands in hers.

"So, what's this 'job,' then?"

She sat down on the edge of the bed, and began. "It's complicated."

Chapter 15. Tourists.

Cambridge, England, and Gascony, France, Earth, May, 2025

Will all Neptune's ocean wash this blood
Clean from my hand? No; this my hand will rather
The multitudinous seas incarnadine,
Making the green one red.
William Shakespeare—*Macbeth*

It was a relief to be here, at last, and to breathe the air. Not that Saint-Rogatien-Les Remillards was anything like she'd expected. To be sure, she'd known from Jack's pictures that it wasn't a wind-blasted, isolated place in the middle of nowhere, the kind of place filmgoers always associate with prehistory. But she hadn't expected it to be quite so tame. Remember Cholula, Jack had said, and he'd been right.

The village of Saint-Rogatien clustered around the now-famous hill and up its slopes, and there was, indeed, a church and churchyard at the top. And not only a churchyard, but across the cobbled square—the tiny Place Etienne Geoffroy Saint-Hilaire; the Mairie, a small but elegant pink-washed building, set back between the boulangerie and the *Sanglier D'Or bar, tabac, café, pression* and most importantly *Hotel***).

Jack loved to tell her how, when he had first inquired about a permit to dig, the Mairie official had asked precisely where in the commune of Saint-Rogatien Jack had wanted to dig, and the expression of perplexity when Jack had pointed straight down at the tiled floor and said *'Ici!'*

As they lay abed in the *Sanglier D'Or*, the occasional yellow headlight beams from the square below tracing sweeping lighthouse arcs across the ceiling, Jack reminded her that all was not as it seemed. The village had been built on the eastern spur—just one corner—of what had been a much more extensive structure, most of which had been eroded away into the valley. The ancient pyramid had once been two miles high, very much more than twice the height of the tallest skyscrapers ever built by modern humans. The present-day church hardly rose past its metaphorical toes, and did not mark the ancient summit, not by any means. But because of this erosion, there were some places around the village where one might get a direct view of the innards of the monstrous monument.

Tomorrow, he'd promised, if she'd felt up to it, he'd show her the foot of the cliff-face that plunged from the churchyard wall, a full two hundred feet to the valley floor. This cliff, Jack thought, was where part of the pyramid's base had been undercut by water and slumped, creating what he thought was cross-sectional slice right through part of the structure. He'd picked up a few peculiar lithics there on his scouting trip, and there, he thought, she'd have the best chance of getting results fast. No need to dig or remove overburden, just map the cliff face and dig a few test tunnels in places that looked interesting.

On the other hand, as it was, after all, a holiday, a kind of honeymoon, and they were both tired, they could relax, potter about, look around, or even just stay in bed, and look at the cliff another day. The two-day journey in the Peugeot, from Cambridge almost to the foothills of the Pyrenees (she'd driven the first few hundred miles herself) had aggravated the soreness in her back, and the aches in her legs, her belly — indeed, more or less everywhere — were making sleep elusive. Her pregnancy had turned, in the past two or three weeks, from a phase of blossoming and almost boundless vitality to one of continual effort, and her general sleeplessness threatened what reserves she had left. She felt pale, awkward, bloated and huge, like a stranded whale. Her buzzing brain raced ahead far faster than the rest of her bulbous form could match, and thoughts whizzed around her head like so many golden midges illuminated by the slanting rays of autumn. Think ahead, she urged herself. She just had to stick it out, to get over the next couple of months.

Now that their future seemed a little more secure they had decided to be married — they had no relations to speak of, so it was in the Registry Office with Marjorie and Roger as witnesses. Jack's gift to her had been an enticing slice of the past. For her doctorate project, he told her, she was to direct the proposed dig at the Saint-Rogatien cliff face. She'd be in charge of recruitment, management and budget as well as interpreting any finds they might make. She couldn't wait to begin. Further, she'd have to find a base of operations that would last them for at least the next three years, as an expedition quarters as well as a home, a place to raise their family. Their days as full-time residents of Cambridge would soon be over.

He'd help her when he could, of course, but he had mapping and exploration of his own to do. His original trip to France had been an addendum, an afterthought, to a project entirely based and predicated on Britain. He now had to survey the region around Saint-Rogatien to the same level of detail, so that they could set the megalith in context. This meant that the Saint-Rogatien operation itself was hers, to do as she would.

There had been Roger's meeting, as promised, two days after the press conference, a meeting that had opened up such amazing vistas. They were, all three of them—Roger, Jack and herself—pie-eyed and fractious, having handled around a hundred media requests each since the press conference. The press had even tried to get at Avi —whose precociously expert skills as a data wrangler had earned him a credit on the paper—but he had, wisely, disappeared. Three days later he'd sent Jack a note to say he'd gone home, but everything was cool, back in a week—alongside a photo of himself, outside a nightclub in Tel Aviv's swinging Dizengoff Street, wedged between two excited-looking blondes and obviously having the time of his life.

Jack found the whole media circus daunting, at times overwhelming, and in the end, depressing. The questions seemed inane, irrelevant, often stupid, and he was only too aware of how awkward and uncomfortable he must have looked. He felt cramped, stifled, longing to get into the open air and away from all this crap.

Jadis had attracted most media interest, a disproportionate amount of which had predictably been of the inane and stupid sort. She had coped better, but tired more quickly. Jack had noticed a new and disturbing quirk in her; that rather than answer a question, she would pause, and her eyes would, quite literally, switch off. Their luster would disappear in a second, as if her sight were questing inwards, searching for something she couldn't quite place. Her brow would then furrow, and she'd rub her swollen belly distractedly, before returning to reality. "No, no, don't worry about me, I'm fine," she'd insist, resisting Jack and Roger's protests, trying to smile her most winning smile at Jack but not quite succeeding, as if it were an injured butterfly, laboring to get airborne.

Finally, Jack was so worried that he'd called Marjorie, swallowing his earlier fear in the knowledge that the two women had become good friends, to ask whether she might say something, because Jadis wouldn't listen to him: and so Jadis was sternly advised to take things more easily for a day or two. Marjorie also insisted that Roger handle all media enquiries, and that Jack find a portrait of Jadis that could be released to the press, so as to assuage the torrent of media requests.

Rifling through the dreadful clutter that their flat had become (both of them being too tired or too busy to do much about it) Jack had come across a portrait of Jadis that he'd completely forgotten about, filed away in his laptop. It was a picture of her in Torbay, on their first summer vacation together. She'd been standing in a wooded dell, just outside some pothole or other he'd been studying, the sun through the trees making a halo for her hair. While the surface of his mind concentrated on the practicalities of whether this casual snapshot would be a good enough for a press portrait, the rest of him surged with reminiscence.

He could no longer quite be sure, but this photo might have been taken on the very day they'd first made love. Perhaps even at the very same spot. Her face in the picture was open and smiling, and she appeared to have been caught saying something to him—he could not remember what. It struck him, then, how much she'd changed since; that her spirit seemed to have become more urgent, more inward-looking. Like the taste of a wine set to age, their love which had once been gay and simple with no thought of the future, was now darker and more complex, with overtones of sorrow and joy, worry and long experience—and foreboding. His heart ached for her, for the girl he'd first dated, as well as the woman she had become. As her pregnancy had advanced she had become reserved, more controlled, and a little less inclined to present to the world at large anything other than a hard and steely resolve.

The world at large would know nothing of this. To anyone but himself, the photo showed a pretty eighteen-year-old on holiday. He sent it to the University Press Office.

The morning before Roger's meeting, the day after Jack and Jadis had returned from London, she had been in the corner of the office that she now shared with Jack when, looking up from the flood of unopened messages, she saw an enormous camera lens peeping in at her through the window. A tabloid journalist had climbed up the wall with a ladder carelessly left by a contractor, and had been hoping for some unauthorized, exclusive shots of the New Face of Science. Jadis fled to the departmental secretary, who called security. In the departmental office she'd met Jack, who'd left for work later than she had: he'd been trying to sort their domestic paperwork into some kind of order, but not getting very far.

Jack now reported that the flat was under journalistic siege. Unable to exit through the front, he'd had to scale the high wall behind the Nest and make a getaway across a neighbour's garden. His clothes were muddied, his arms scratched. Jadis cooed concern for him, ignoring all else: it had not yet occurred to either where they might go next—they couldn't go home for a day or two—when they turned at once to see Roger, standing in the office doorway.

"Please stay with Marjorie and me," he said, "until the heat's off. And we can have our meeting there."

It felt very peculiar, Jack thought, to be in bed with his new wife in the house of his former doctorate supervisor. For all that the spare bedroom chez MacLennane was welcoming in a chintzy sort of way, and much tidier than their flat, Jack felt like a refugee. More than ever, he wanted to get out into the field, to take Jadis with him — to escape.

When he awoke with these fretful thoughts, his first sight was Jadis, sitting on her side of the bed, with her back to him, legs slightly parted to accommodate the bulge of her belly, combing her hair with that enormous plastic comb she took everywhere with her, like a talisman. She attacked her hair with urgent, rapid strokes, as if it were a task best over and done with. He wondered why she hadn't asked him to do it, a much more relaxed experience they both enjoyed, especially as it often led to other things. Jadis heard Jack wake behind her, and read his mind.

"I'm sorry, Jack. I just don't feel like it much here," she said, not turning round. "Here. At Roger and Marjorie's. It would seem like... well, having sex in church."

Still sitting there, back to him, he saw her skin ripple, her shoulders shake with silent laughter, but the tenor soon turned and she began to emit small, spiky, sobs which she stifled only with difficulty. Jack got out of bed and rushed round to comfort her, quieting her in his arms. She did not explain her change of mood, and Jack did not ask her.

Roger's news, after breakfast, went a considerable way to cheering them up. A couple of years ago (Roger began), a businessman called Ruxton Carr, the elusive head of something called Merlin Technologies, had approached the University, offering a donation of several billion dollars if they'd build a new college with his name on it.

The University, being used to such requests, politely thanked Mr Carr, and deftly pointed out that whereas the University had a superabundance of colleges, it sorely lacked front-rank research facilities that could benefit the whole University, if not the whole world, and mightn't Mr Carr think along those lines instead? So Mr Carr had receded and it was generally assumed that he'd decided to take his wealth elsewhere.

However, it turned out (Roger continued) that the Senate had badly underestimated Mr Carr. He had, it seemed, taken the University at its word, and had been consulting widely on the kinds of research facilities that the University might need — and which, he felt, he'd like to support. Mr Carr was known as a shrewd investor in what at first seemed an eclectic selection of interests, from carbon sequestration technologies to genetic manipulation, from geothermal power to personalized space travel. When *Forbes* magazine asked him, in the only interview he was ever known to have given, if he could characterize his investments in a sentence, he'd said "sure, but I'll do it in just two words: 'The Future.'" Hence the Universities' puzzlement when he chose to endow not one but two new research institutes in Cambridge, neither of which seemed to have much to do with technology, the future, or each other.

One such concern, the Merlin Technologies Astrometry Institute, had been busy in Madingley for two years now, cataloguing the recent spectral history and proper motion of stars in the solar neighborhood, for reasons that nobody could fathom.

"And the second?" Roger asked: "well, that's where we come in." It turned out that the mysterious Mr Carr had been watching the progress of MacLennane's research, and that of his students and associates, for some years, but had only finally chosen to make a commitment when the *Nature* paper had become public.

"That's why I couldn't come back from town with you both," Roger explained, "I had to meet Carr's people at the Royal. Naturally, I couldn't breathe a dicky bird until it had all been inked. I'm sure you'll understand."

The upshot was that Carr had chosen to bankroll what he'd called the Merlin Technologies Institute for Historical Geomorphology. This would—at least initially—be a 'virtual' institute, made of people within the their current department and associates elsewhere.

"Carr knows that institutes are not made of walls, but of people," said Roger. "Carr's people have asked me to head up the new Institute, and I've accepted. After all, I've only a year or so to run at the University proper before they'd boot me out anyway, and I can't hang around here. Marjorie would never stand for it." Jack and Jadis congratulated him, but he pressed ahead.

"My first act as Director is to appoint you, Jack, as its first Senior Research Fellow; my second is to recommend that Jack takes on you, Jadis as its first doctorate student. No need to worry about money or grants, thanks to Mr Carr. You could start tomorrow, but I forbid it. There's some paperwork I need to get done, and anyway you two need a break. You haven't even had a honeymoon. Let's say we start work in a couple of weeks or so, after the Easter Vac?"

Deep in the first night at Saint-Rogatien, Jadis was having a dream in which she'd been in the garden in Chesterton, trying to plant out some summer bedding, but the plants shriveled and died as soon as she put them into the ground. She worked faster and faster, as if trying to beat some innominate contagion, but still it spread. The rising mound of dead and dying plants all around her turned from green, to grey, to red, dripping blood on the grass. When she studied the plants more closely, she saw that they were fetuses, and as she watched in pure horror, the blood smeared and spread, up the wall of the raised bed and into the Nest, up the trees, until, at the end of the leaves, it gathered and rained down on her in a torrent. She looked down and noticed blood rising up her bare legs, but she was stuck fast, unable to move or do anything to stem the hideous tide. But just as she thought she would drown in blood, there came a regular pulse, a subsonic thrum, like the heartbeat of the Earth. Assailed by this calm but unstoppable vibration, the blood coagulated, dried, shattered and blew away like harmless dust; and before her, a vast and green plant rose clear out of the ground, bursting above her head into an immense Van-Gogh sunflower that became the sun.

And still the Earth pulsed.

She woke, still in Jack's arms, the shreds of the dream dissipating like gossamer. But the pulse still beat, softly and insistently, just below the level of hearing. She knew her own pulse, and Jack's. But this was a new pulse, the pulse of a new life, strong and steady, beating inside her. Or, rather, a pulse returned, a pulse she feared had been lost for some time. Wave after wave of relief coursed down to meet it, and she embraced the pulse with triumphant inner shouts of radiant joy. She slept again in a state of happiness that she had not experienced for several weeks.

When she awoke in the dawn, she'd forgotten about the dream, and now stood in the window of the small bedroom in the *Sanglier D'Or*, looking down over the sunlit square. She felt amazingly refreshed, all her aches and pains were gone, and she was eager to meet the day.

"Come on, you silly man!" she teased, pulling the duvet off Jack's still recumbent form, yanking the curtains apart to admit the strong spring sunshine.

"Okay, Boss," came the uncertain reply, but when Jack tried to pull the duvet back, Jadis snatched it away again in a furious cloud of fabric and hair, jumped on the bed, whacked him smartly on the backside, and sprang for the door.

Half an hour later, as Jack ordered coffee on the pavement terrace of the café below, Jadis went to the boulangerie to buy croissants. If this was to be their new home, he felt he could accommodate its easy pace very well. A few minutes later, he watched Jadis return with the paper bag, and at first he didn't recognize her as his wife. The woman he was watching was indeed heavily pregnant, like Jadis, but unlike Jadis had been in the past two or three weeks, this voluptuary had acquired a devastatingly sexy hip-sway that accommodated both her legginess and her bulk with a marked elegance, her long train of hair waving to the rhythm of her movements, just as if she were dancing in her own one-woman conga line to some deep dub pulse. It wasn't until she'd stopped at his table that he was sure it was her.

"What?" she asked, while pulling out her chair and sitting on it in a single, fluid movement. Jack turned to his coffee, slurping it far too fast, coughed at its bitterness, and looked up, a rim of froth on his upper lip.

"Excuse me, Madam," said Jack. "Will you marry me?"

"But we're already married!"

"To each other?"

"Simultaneously, even."

"And at the same time? I'm astonished."

"In which case, I can't. Sorry!" She ran her tongue around her lips, chasing flecks of coffee and croissant.

"But this is terrible! Who's the lucky man?"

"You are. And I expect you to take me upstairs, right now, and treat me to mad, passionate lunch. I'm... hungry," she added, leaning across the table towards him, leering like a pantomime villain.

"But we haven't even had breakfast. Now, eat up, I have something to show you."

Hand in hand, Jack and Jadis crossed the Place Etienne Geoffroy Saint Hilaire to the churchyard. The graves closer to the street stood in well-tended, orderly lines, each stone adorned with sprays of garish plastic flowers and photographs of loved ones behind clear glass panes. As they rounded the church they entered the cool shadows of a belt of cypresses and yews, where the graves were sparser and more somber, and at length they came to a crumbling stone parapet that gave onto a magnificent view of the landscape stretched out below them to the west, with ridge after ridge of limestone hills fading to invisibility.

Two weeks later they were back in their flat. They'd been worrying what they might find, and their sense of anticipation was sharpened by the increasingly aberrant performance of the old Peugeot, which toiled and grumbled up the last stretch of the M11 towards Cambridge, so much so that they began to think that they'd never arrive.

"I promised the Field Vehicle," Jack said, pointedly "that if she got us back home safely, I'd treat her to a thorough servicing."

Jadis, now half asleep in the passenger seat, had begun to giggle at this. "Your capacity for servicing things, dearest Jack," she said, yawning and stretching, "knows no bounds."

Despite her increasing discomfort and now continual backache brought on by the long ride home, her mind was floating on the bubble of memories of her honeymoon. They had paced out the precise location for the first excavation season, scheduled for this time next year. And with the help of a friendly, English-speaking real-estate agent, they had scouted a few likely properties that could be used as live-in field stations, and would recommend the one they liked most to Roger, who'd have to authorize the funds to buy and remodel it.

Their favorite was a big, old and mildly dilapidated farmhouse on a quiet lane about a quarter-mile away from the village centre. A large barn and the house itself formed respectively the west and north sides of a sheltered tarmac quadrangle, braced against the prevailing Atlantic westerlies. The shingles on the barn's roof looked rickety, but the beams were sound, and there was plenty of scope for dividing it into a machine shop, laboratory and stores.

The house itself was large without being ostentatious, with an enormous kitchen, (accompanied by a large, tiled back-kitchen, laundry room and pantry) that could serve as the center of family life. Jadis could already imagine herself in it, with flocks of children, students, field workers and more children; cats and dogs running to and fro; a big farmhouse-style table in the middle, laden with hot meals; lab notes; toys; specimens, in an ongoing jumble.

There were eight large bedrooms—so plenty of room to accommodate themselves and several colleagues, children and friends at once—but only one tiny bathroom. Have to do something about that, she thought. And put one in downstairs, too. She thought of herself in the future, shepherding shoals of small children in and out.

But best of all, there was a large garden, already in cultivation, that could be used to help supply the home and field kitchen. She thought she might keep chickens. And maybe some ducks.

She imagined children running around in the sunshine.

In the middle of the garden was a dense spinney of mature trees. It didn't look very extensive from the outside, but as soon as you stepped in, you had the distinct impression of being in an endless forest. Jadis immediately thought of the Nest. The pulse within her quickened in response.

When they got back to the Chesterton flat, well after dark, and expecting the usual explosion of disorder, they found it a picture of neatness. Papers were stacked, clothes washed and ironed, dishes put away, floors swept, and there were even flowers in vases. A note from Marjorie (who'd had the key) explained that she'd asked her cleaning lady to give the flat a spring-clean. 'A welcome-home gift,' she'd explained.

The next day, Jack rose early and went into the department, to give a progress report to MacLennane. Jadis thought she'd stay behind for a while. The car journey had been hard on her. She was stiff, and she wanted to potter around the garden for a bit, have a stretch, perhaps pull out a few weeds. She said she'd come into the department later. Maybe they'd have lunch? Great idea, said Jack, and he was gone.

After Jack left, she rose, threw Horrible the jersey over her head, and went into the garden. Leaning over to pull a few small grassy interlopers from the edge of the raised bed, she idly thought of the coming summer, a baby dozing in a pram, and — who knows, that Normal Servicing might be Resumed in the Nest. Her presumption was met instantly with a jolt so painful, so sudden, that she was thrown clear off her feet and sent sprawling forward into the wall of the raised bed. She stood up, dazed, sweating, gasping for breath, thinking that she'd been hit in the back by a car. Before she could recover, a second bone-crunching impact cut her to her knees. The world whirled around her. Her head swam. Her crotch felt damp, and, raising Horrible's hem, she looked down and saw a trickle of blood running down the inside of her right thigh.

Her head cleared immediately, as often happens to soldiers in the extremis of battle. No time to call Jack; an ambulance would take ages to get here; the answer was clear. She'd take herself to the hospital — now. Stopping only to clean the thin line of blood from her thigh, to find a clean pair of knickers, and to stuff as much toilet paper as she could down the front, she grabbed the car keys and left.

The Field Vehicle spluttered glutinously into life. After the long journey of the day before, Jadis hoped she'd have enough fuel to get to Addenbrooke's. Coursing down Elizabeth Way and across the river, another huge, shuddering spasm wracked her lower body. She gripped the steering wheel in fierce concentration.

She made her way carefully along East Road and past Parker's Piece, pulling up at the lights, signaling to turn left into Hills Road and the southbound straight to the Hospital. Almost there.

Willing the lights to change, she gunned the accelerator — the only way, she'd learned, of getting the diesel engine to make a quick getaway—but the long un-serviced Field Vehicle was slow to respond. At last, the lights changed, and Jadis steered into Hills Road, making sure that nothing was coming from the right—extra carefully now, as although the spasms had lessened in intensity, she had lost a lot of blood and was feeling a little light-headed, just as she had been in their final night at the *Sanglier D'Or*, when, when, when, with the curtains swirling, swirling, swirling in the Spring breeze through their open window…

What she hadn't seen, as she turned, was a police car, lights flashing, screaming northwards at ninety miles per hour up the wrong side of Hills Road, to her left.

The police Volvo Cross Country hit the Peugeot almost head on. The Peugeot flipped forward and turned a full somersault over the top of the larger car. As the Peugeot righted itself in mid-air, the G-force pulled the safety belt clear from its rusted fastenings, and Jadis was catapulted forwards through the windscreen, landing face down on the bonnet of a northbound car twenty feet away. The driver of that car braked suddenly, so that Jadis, loose as a rag doll, slid down the bonnet and came to rest on the ground in front of it. The Peugeot itself, now driverless, ploughed through the air, and, cratering nose-first into the road behind the police car, burst into flames.

"Solomon…"

The world whined and wheeled, and was silent.

Chapter 16. Voyager

Xandarga Station, Earth, *c.* 55,680,000 years ago

An hundred years should go to praise
Thine eyes, and on thy forehead gaze;
Two hundred to adore each breast,
But thirty thousand to the rest.
Andrew Marvell — *To His Coy Mistress*

It was a long time coming, but when it did, everything happened at once. Earth's horizon flattened until the autopod was surrounded by city lights, as if descending into a great bowl. Ruxhana Fengen Kraa couldn't help but be reminded of his first descent into Xandarga Station, so long before. The scatter of lights became a confusion of pipework and gantries, filling the views from the ports so that any further distance was blotted out completely by machinery, until finally, they were surrounded by darkness. Slowly, silently, the capsule came to rest.

Ruxhana was ready as the airlock hissed open, admitting a wave of stifling tropical heat and the sight of four men in Naval Police uniforms, carbines primed.

"Do you have the prisoner, Doctor?" asked the Sergeant, with a sneer, as if collecting lethally incompetent soon-to-be-ex-Admirals from the El was so commonplace as to be beneath his dignity.

Ruxhana could not meet the man's gaze. He was suddenly conscious of the sweat pouring from every pore in response to this choking humidity. Funny how he'd forgotten that aspect of life in Xandarga Station. But no longer: his crotch — which otherwise felt uncluttered, and, well, feminine — now oozed in its own nauseating liquidity, as did his armpits. The wool of his skirt felt heavy and scratchy against his legs. He hoped that the stains spreading across his blouse weren't too prominent. As for the torrents that gushed across his forehead, down the small of his back, and between (and around, and underneath) his chafing breasts — well, these he'd just have to tolerate, for now. It was all he could do not to grasp at his own chest, rearranging its seriated furniture into some more comfortable conformation.

"Sadly, no. I... it's..."

"It's what, Doctor?" The sergeant said. "Lost? Stolen? Strayed? Escaped?"

"Escaped? From the El?" Ruxhana gulped for breath. After all their preparations, they couldn't have been rumbled so easily. Could they?

"It's happened before, Doctor," sighed the Sergeant. Panic over, Ruxhana picked up the thread.

"I don't think that could have happened here," he began. "Admiral Kraa was too far gone for me to reconstruct fully. I began to put him back together again. I did my best. But there was, frankly, too little left of him to work with. Too few ingredients. So, nobody for you to arrest. Nobody you'd want to arrest, anyway."

"Flow my tears," the policeman said.

"Look, Officer, if you don't believe me, you can come and look for yourself."

The policeman sighed. "Lead on, Doctor," he said. Ruxhana welcomed them to the capsule. Now shorn of all VR adornment, it was shabby and cramped, and dominated by the oppressive whine of the plumbing, voiding waste, and the air-scrubbers replenishing themselves with new, ground-level atmosphere. Ruxhana led them along tight companionways and up spiral staircases, during which he was sure that the policemen were doing their best to look up his skirt. Finally they reached an armored door off a narrow corridor. Ruxhana broke the seal and swung it open. The scent of cold formaldehyde wafted out to greet them. Ruxhana held the door as the policemen barreled in. He was quite sure that it wasn't necessary for all the policemen to have brushed against his breasts as they passed, even in this tight space.

But all such things were forgotten when the party confronted the apparition on the slab before them, a drawer pulled out of a mortuary cabinet in this tiny, too-bright room. Ruxhana stifled a snigger as one of the policemen retched and had to make a quick exit.

"I'm sorry," said Ruxhana. "I couldn't do any more." The thing looked like him, after a fashion, given that half its face was missing, the lower jaw was a shapeless mass, and most of the skull had been replaced by a meningeal caul beneath which the brain could be seen. There was only one proper arm—the other was really a kind of tentacle. The legs were small and stumpy and only one ended in a foot, recognizable as such for all that it only had three toes.

"Was it... was he....?" The sergeant began.

"Alive, Officer? Oh please, give me some credit. He was alive for quite a while. Plodding about. Doing a few chores, you know, sweeping and so on. Not what you'd call company, though. But eventually his heart—what there was of it—gave out." With a flourish that he hoped wasn't too theatrical, he whipped away the sheet covering the corpse's midsection to reveal an open ribcage and the distended, congealed mass within. The sergeant and the remaining two officers shrunk back. "No, officers," continued Ruxhana. "Not my attempt to revive him after heart failure. I'd be a lot neater than that. But you should have seen him fresh from the regen tank, *before* I patched him up."

"He... walked around... like that?"

"Yes. Like I said, I did try to tidy him up. But the general effect was, I'll admit, rather... how should one put it?... squishy."

"Squishy?"

"Yes. I had to keep mopping up after him, until I taught him to mop up after himself."

"You... taught him? Was he intelligent? Could he... Did he know who he was? Had been?"

"What you're asking is whether he'd have been fit to stand before a Board of Enquiry. My professional opinion, Officer? No. No more than the AI in a coffee machine. A very cheap coffee machine."

"I see."

"Of course, Sergeant, you'll want Naval Investigation to bag all this up. There will be some sort of inquiry, anyway, won't there? But I'm sure you'll understand, I need to get out of this wretched sardine-tin immediately, if not sooner. I can assure you that the Admiral's company, despite my best efforts — was, after a few days, rather wearing."

"I understand, Doctor." The policeman beamed a business glyph into Ruxhana's AI core and received one in return. "Here are the details of the Investigating Precinct," he said. "Yes, there will be an inquiry, I guess, and you'll probably need to attend it. For now, Doctor, you're free to go. But please don't go off-planet without letting us know." The sergeant smiled, sheepishly, clearly regretting his earlier imperious brusqueness.

"Thank you, officer." Ruxhana smiled, turned on his spike heels, and left. He hoped his departure from the autopod wasn't any more rapid than consistent for a young and evidently fastidious female who'd spent two weeks holed up in a pod with that... thing.

He should have had no worries on that account.

The Sergeant, having taken in Ruxhana's broad, green eyes, his slim legs, his pert figure — and his demeanor of ruthless competence mixed with limpid vulnerability — was perhaps slightly more sympathetic than he ought to have been. Had it been him in that position, the policeman reasoned, he couldn't have gotten away quickly enough.

Ruxhana clacked through the concourse. With no baggage to retrieve, and his prints, genotags and iridentity all in order, he was outside within minutes, on a broad plaza under a vast, glass awning on one side of the El's terminal pyramid.

"Where to now?" This a subvocal inquiry to his AI core. A familiar voice answered, chiming directly into his auditory cortex.

Xalomé.

Even after a week spent in intensive preparations for this escape, in the unnervingly real consensual VR environments she called 'Xspaces,' and for all her talk of things called 'M-dimensional relativistic manifolds' — and for all her chilling otherness — he could never bring himself to call her 'Merlin'.

"How does it feel to be me, then?" she asked.

"Surprisingly well, actually." He thought that to be disguised as the Doctor — a disguise that would be convincing down to the DNA level — would have felt odd. And so it did, at first. But very soon he became accustomed to the lithe light-footedness of his new form. He could no longer evade admitting it to himself. He felt... pretty.

With reservations, naturally.

Xalomé must have read his thoughts. "That's the trouble with men," she teased. "So untidy at the front. All those dangly bits."

"Not always as dangly as all that, though, are they?" He framed an erotic image of the two of them, in the stateroom. It seemed like centuries ago, and on another planet. He felt a mental sigh in return.

"Oh, *touché*."

"It's all these breasts though — what do you do with those, lovely though they undoubtedly are? If I move at more than the speed of an arthritic snail with brakes on..."

"... a graceful, elegant snail with brakes on, please..."

"... which I admit is hard to do in this skirt..."

"... oh, you poor lamb..."

"... not to mention these heels..."

"... ouch! I so feel your pain..."

"... they rub against one another and generally bounce around like a box of frogs."

Sublimbic laughter, and the return of several lubricious images.

"Well, now you know what it feels like, don't you? Beauty tip from one who knows. Oil when it's dry, talc when it's wet. And Turgai Straits dancing, whatever the weather. Keeps the pecs in good shape. Makes sure everything's pert and... er... upstanding, and..." Xalomé subsided into giggles that reverberated like mischievous sprites around the interstices of his brain. "Anyway, no matter. You'll be able to disrobe soon and tidy yourself up. Here's what to do..."

Her instructions came as an instant pulse relayed through his AI core, the semi-sentient data compiling and replaying themselves in his association cortex, so that they had the feel of his own memories. The instruction set had a strangeness to them, though, like an afterglow, like déja-vu. His native AI core explained that the data packet had been red-shifted to a small but significant degree, and there were other, less explicable, residual time-delay anomalies.

M-dimensional relativistic manifolds.

She could be anywhere — inside his own head, or across the Universe — or anywhen.

Ruxhana hailed a cab that took him to the farthest and swankiest end of the marina. The sea breeze in his hair and on his face, as he alighted, felt good. The sweat dried on his skin as he peeled the fabric of his blouse away from his flesh. Much better. He paid off the driver in cash, with a generous tip. The driver paid her a compliment which, had he thought about it, might have been construed as presumptuous. He responded with a beaming, dimpled smile, turned and walked away, injecting a certain amount of hip-sway into the maneuver. The wolf-whistle rang in his ears as the cab sped off down the waterfront. On the whole, he did rather enjoy being a woman.

At the quay, a discreet and very select charter firm had a motor-yacht ready. And what a boat — no skiff this, but the kind of floating palace used by the playboy offspring of Athabascan oil princelings for throwing debauched parties in. Apparently, it was all his own, to do with as he pleased (it was?). Nothing was too much trouble, it seemed (it wasn't?) and no questions were asked.

Yes, the Doctor had made the arrangements months before, capitalizing on the operator's early-bookings discount (she had?).

Yes, the boat was fully loaded with supplies and teslas enough to circumnavigate the planet a dozen times, if she wanted.

Yes, the Doctor, as a Platinum Preference Customer, could have it for as long as she liked (she could?) Just send it back when she'd done with it, from anywhere on the planet. It would know the way.

Yes, the operator understood that the Doctor wasn't expecting company, and wished to run *Shelly's Shagpad* without a sentient crew. The operator was pleased to respect the Doctor's privacy, and assured her that the onboard AI systems and accessory droids would be able to cater to her every need (and, oh boy, did they mean *every*—just look at the brochure).

Yes, the operator was delighted, as always, to have had the Doctor's esteemed custom and wished her a pleasant vacation.

The first thing he did when he tottered across the gangplank was shuck off his shoes. He was very tempted to lob them over the side for good measure. His bare feet swelled in luxurious freedom as his liberated toes explored (as his AI core recounted, from the brochure), the 'sumptuous, hand-polished, craftsman-selected Arctic hardwood decking'.

The second thing he did was to instruct his AI core to liaise with its opposite number in the boat's navsystem and upload the coordinates Xalomé had given him for their destination, asking it to compute the fastest travel plan consistent with being unobtrusive. The AI asked Ruxhana, in a REM backchannel, if he himself had any idea where they were going. He confessed he had none. He was aware, just then, of subliminal traffic between his AI and a heavily encrypted, compressed semi-sentient data squirt.

Ruxhana queried it.

From Merlin, the AI core explained. Ruxhana got a picture of a coral atoll in mid-Tethys, off the usual shipping lanes. Idyllic. But why?

The AI confessed to having insufficient data to answer that question.

And where is Merlin—Xalomé—herself, right now?

The AI admitted to having no directional information, only a distance inferred from the heavy red-shifting of the most recent data squirt, and that only a lower bound. Even so, the AI noted that the result itself, while inexact, was computationally interesting.

Well? What is it then?

$z > 1100$, came the bald reply. An epoch when time and space were, from this perspective, functionally interchangeable.

What? Her data from less than an hour earlier had been only mildly red-shifted, and now she was skating on the edge of the observable Universe.

Yes, replied the AI core. That's what made it so interesting. It could offer no explanation, citing only the 'less-explicable residual time-delay anomalies' it had mentioned earlier.

Read 'inexplicable' for 'less explicable,' Ruxhana said, waspishly.

The AI—a little sulkily, Ruxhana thought—noted that it would be hesitant to pronounce on such qualitative arguments. It apologized once again, though with somewhat ill grace, and noted curtly in a further

REM channel that after everything they'd been through, it needed what it called a 'holiday'.

Ruxhana stifled a mental snort, thanked the AI core profusely (they had after all, been in many campaigns together, and Ruxhana was more pleased than he could express when the Doctor—Xalomé—told him that it was once again available for his use) and asked it to fire up the heavy-ion magdrive engines, which it did. The twin cyclotronic thrusters roared into life, and they were on their way.

He remained on deck as *Shelly's Shagpad* sliced through the outer harbor, long enough to marvel as they passed beneath and slightly to the east of the Imperial Assembly Building. He'd never seen it from this low angle before—not even in pictures—and the view was, he had to admit, terrific, even for one as well-traveled as himself. As the sun passed behind the structure that now filled his visual field, its silvered hull pulsed with marvelous iridescence like an oil droplet, albeit one that filled half the sky. Ruxhana breathed deeply, and stood, hair flowing in the onshore breeze, until the Sun finally set behind the shining structure, and he went below.

It was only when he'd arrived at the bottom of the companionway and stepped into the grand saloon (which was every bit as kitsch as the brochure promised) that a memory spiked unwonted into his conscious mind. It was the vertigo he'd felt after studying the inscription on the Gharaan Fragments, back in the Institute of Galactic History, all those years before: now accompanied by a single, alien, but crystal-clear thought.

Eclipse.

He stopped, momentarily, midway across a prairie-like expanse of deep-pile, shocking-pink carpet. But he put the thought away, for now, as he found the master suite, peeled his clothes off onto the bathroom floor ('sourced from premium-grade Western Interior marble')—a laundroid would surely come along and take them to the sonicator—and ran himself a bath.

Eclipse.

The thought came again, as he luxuriated in the circular tub ('lovingly hand-sculpted from a single crystal of Appalachian basalt' and big enough for at least eight vigorous bathers at once), the jets pummeled his skin and frothed up the bubbles into foamy clouds; and yet again, as he dried himself (reveling once more at the smoothness of his womanly curves, florid and yet marvelously restrained, as in the most tasteful architecture, and yet more so, because his body moved, and yet remained in perfect sculptural proportion with every step)—and again, as he folded himself beneath creodont-print covers in a bed big enough for a brontothere.

Eclipse. Eclipse. Eclipse.

Why?

His AI core reminded him, wearily, that this kind of flashback was only to be expected, given the multiple physical transformations he'd undergone lately: first, being scraped up and reassambled from almost nothing: and now having been transformed into a different identity and gender, and, the AI was about to continue, what with other ongoing transformations unconnected with any of the foregoing...

Other transformations? Ongoing...?

The AI regretted that it could not reveal the nature of such changes, if indeed there were any, because it didn't understand them itself. It, too (it reminded him) had endured—was enduring—a certain amount of 'brain damage' consequent on these selfsame ongoing changes, as it put it, and since they'd effectively been on the run, and had had no time to spare, for want of a more apposite expression, for 'standing and staring'.

His AI core had never been like this before: so metaphorical. He could detect something else, too—fear. Fear of the future. AI's weren't meant to act like that. Sentient.

Speak to me—

Breathe, Ruxhana, the AI said. Just breathe in the air. That's all you need to do. It will all become clear, in time. I hope (*hope*). As for me (*me*), I (*I*) feel (*feel*) in a state perhaps best described as 'hanging on in quiet desperation'.

I (*I*) am not used to this feeling.

I (*I*) do not like (*like*) it.

I (*I*) regret that I (*I*) shall have to go offline now, for an <undefined> interval.

Good-bye.

Quite suddenly, Ruxhana felt his mind to be as clear, free and undistorted as flat space, free from any speck of matter whatsoever.

Oh, great, he thought. Here I am, all alone, in an enormous boat that looks like a tart's boudoir; going I know not where; with an AI core that's suffering delusions of self-awareness and has flounced off; and the only person who might know anything about all this could, at this (or any other) moment, be anywhere in this (or any other) Universe. Anywhere but here.

And what's more, I'm trapped in a woman's body.

And if that weren't enough, I'm hungry.

He swung his slender legs (oh, how he loved doing that) over the edge of the bed, found a hibiscus-patterned kimono, and padded off to find the galley.

By the middle of the next day *Shelly's Shagpad* and its sole passenger were well out at sea, out of sight of all land, standing in a hot green sea, seared by a Sun that hammered down from directly overhead. The only sign of forward progress was the steady hum of the engines and the slight wake the boat left in its path.

Three more days passed, the second two being carbon copies of the first.

To begin with, Ruxhana spent much of the time on deck, despite the heat. After the weeks spent cooped indoors, mostly as an invalid, the sensation of space—real space, that is, on a planetary surface with a genuine horizon, not in VR, or in a pod—was refreshing, liberating. The sunlight was, however, ferocious. His only, defiant, concession was a floppy straw hat to add to the kimono.

Even the most extravagant luxury can pall after a while, and all those golden hours spent on the pool deck, lounging around and being served fresh-caught seafood and interesting cocktails by handsome droids dressed only in Bermuda shorts (and some of whom, with much circumlocution, hinted at other services they might perform below decks, later on, if Madam knew what they meant) began to lose their luster. Even the insouciant way he shed the kimono and stepped nude into the enormous pool, teasing the droids—whose reactions were most satisfying—began to bore him after the sixth or seventh time. Droids are droids, after all, and tend to adopt the same, restricted range of expressions. And it wasn't as if they were people. Not really.

In any case, he wasn't really nude, because he always kept his hat on.

Four things finally drove him below decks. No, three things, not counting this increasing *ennui*.

One was when he was standing in the pool, attended as usual by a shoal of gengineered cleaner fish that gave him a most agreeable all-over massage. He looked down at his body—a body he had become used to, and very much enjoyed inhabiting, as if it were a smart suit he liked to be seen in. With his eyes, his hands, he caressed his own curves with satisfaction. But when he ran his right hand over his crotch, he was pulled up sharp. Instead of the usual comfortingly furred softness, there was a lump of hard, knotted flesh. He had been enjoying his new gender so much that he had quite forgotten what Xalomé—Merlin—had told him, when they were still on the El, two days out from landfall. That it would wear off, and he'd return to normal.

Things would start to grow back.

Treading water, surrounded by the ignorant peck of cleaner fishes and the patient yet fundamentally insensate attentions of the droids, he stumbled across the second reason for him to flee below, to seek solace in a more confined darkness.

He was lonely.

He wanted—needed—to talk things over with Xalomé, but with his AI core still stubbornly offline and therefore unavailable as a relay, there was no way that any comms channel she might open could reach him.

The third was that he began to feel ill. Very ill indeed. At first he thought it might have been sunstroke, the wages of far too much time spent above decks. The headaches, nausea and diarrhea were real enough, and sufficient to confine him to the bathroom for long periods, his only comfort a glass of water and a slice of dry toast. Then, when he thought he had begun to recover, and the knotted gripings of his gut had begun to subside, came a truly dreadful night.

He awoke at about two in the morning, in total darkness and exquisite agony, as if termites armed with electric indrico-prods were swarming just beneath his skin. He tried to get out of bed, but instead of the usual easy, sideways sashay, he found that his legs were longer and heavier than he remembered, so the extra momentum tumbled him sideways onto the carpet which, being the most sumptuously tasteless that billions could buy, prevented any injury.

Gasping for breath and burning with what he felt was a fever, he crawled to the bathroom and hauled himself up, fingers grasping and sliding on the pink, marbled surfaces of the double-washbasin, to confront his standing reflection, finally, in the wall-to-wall mirror. As he watched, amazed, he saw his hips remodel themselves, slimming down, becoming more angular. His breasts—his ten, perfectly formed, beautiful breasts—melted into his broadening torso. Muscles and bones in his arms and legs swelled and knit. He became taller, his face, hands and feet lengthening.

But what transfixed him was the sight of his prong, emerging from the fur between his thighs like a time-lapse photo of a fungus sprouting from a jungle floor. The pain of it all was excruciating, but he just had to watch. He was still watching an hour later, as the pain—finally—subsided.

When dawn broke he ordered a cocktail, and sat with it on the private balcony adjoining the master suite. Then he ordered another, and a third, and returned to bed. When the fourth came he noticed that the droid who brought it was female, the first he'd seen aboard *Shelly's Shagpad*. She was dressed in a kimono rather like his, and seemingly little else.

He asked her whether she'd mind keeping him company. With a smile that would have melted tungsten carbide, for all that it was entirely artificial, she said she'd be happy to oblige. She dropped her kimono and hopped into bed with him.

When it came down to it, Ruxhana Fengen Kraa was nothing if not pragmatic. He had to make sure that everything still worked up to spec. The remainder of the voyage—a further three days—passed all too quickly.

Chapter 17. Seminarian

Gascony, France, Earth, September, 2031

O for a beaker full of the warm South!
John Keats — *Ode to a Nightingale*

"Domingo, would you do the honors?"

"Yes, Jadis, of course." The big man in the radioactively loud aloha shirt and baggy Bermuda shorts waved his ham-sized hands over the table. The chatter all around it ceased at once. Nothing could be heard but birdsong, the late summer wind sighing in the high branches of the spinney, the lazy plop of a frog into the pond and the distant rasp of the grasshoppers in the field that opened at the end of the garden.

"Benedic Domine nos et haec tua dona quae de tua largitate sumus sumpturi per Christum Dominum nostrum, Amen."

The chatter resumed. Jadis had been standing in the doorway of the back kitchen. Walking out onto the terrace, she added an enormous earthenware bowl of lemon chicken and rice to the already laden table. She sat down at its head, slid off her sandals and buried her feet in the furry, dependable bulk of Fairbanks, her gigantic golden retriever, who looked up momentarily, emitted a contented nut-brown growl, and went back to sleep on the cool tiles under the table. Almost.

Although very much fulfilling his job description as Mobile Self-Warming Hot Water Bottle and Guard Dog (Fierce) for his mistress, he still kept half an eye open, ever watchful for his arch-enemy, Horrible, the squashed-faced tabby that had adopted the household three years earlier, bringing with it a cloud of fleas that had made everyone scratch for weeks. The litter of kittens discovered under a pile of dirty laundry, some weeks later, was the only outward sign of the animal's gender. But Horrible was in no mood to tease the dog today. Her tiny mind had already been distracted. She slunk off towards the long grass at the edge of the pond, in search of smaller animals to persecute.

Jadis looked up at the human company, and felt a mixture of emotions. The glow of achievement; the twinge of regret that no more had been achieved; and yet, excitement about the future. This was the final Saint-Rogatien field crew, at the end of six years of excavating the enormous, ancient pyramid about which the modern village of Saint-

114

Rogatien clustered. This was the final dinner, at the end of the final season. She was in the mood for a quiet celebration.

The dig had closed down that very afternoon. The last earthmover had replaced the overburden; grass-seed had been sown; and the mayor of Saint-Rogatien had had a little ceremony to mark the passing of a remarkable but ultimately frustrating archeological endeavor. In the days ahead, Jadis would pack up the lab specimens, crating them for Cambridge, where, no doubt, they would make a few doctorate projects for graduate students to come. And in the meantime, she and Jack were clearing the decks for something new.

Jack sat at the other end of the trestle table, laid out in the dappled shade of an ancient sweet-chestnut tree, its fruits already swelling. He returned her gaze, and Jadis momentarily lost interest in the rest of the world's affairs, as the two of them exchanged in a moment what might otherwise have taken many hours of speech. Oblivious to the swirl of conversation around them, Jack raised one mock-serious eyebrow, just for her. We have our news, his ice-blue eyes seemed to say, but not yet. Her hand flew to her mouth to stifle a giggle, and then, reprovingly as a mother, she affected a mental finger-wag: she was the hostess, and had her guests to look after! And so with a small shake of her head, she broke the link, and the noise of the party flooded back. As if to compensate for her reverie, she waved her hands animatedly at her guests, imploring them to begin, to dig in, dish up, have more wine.

Not that they needed any encouragement.

At Jack's left, Jadis' technician Primrose Tsien, and her current graduate student Faye Callaghan, were laughing uproariously as Avi Malkeinu, between them (and his arms round both) was telling a probably exaggerated and undoubtedly salacious story about his latest stint as an Israeli army reservist.

At Jack's right, the aloha-shirted Domingo was deep in conversation with Mathilde Reynard, a postdoctoral researcher visiting *Le Dig* for a stint from the University of Montpellier. To Mathilde's right, Eric Onoye, a graduate student with Ernestine Yanga in Nairobi, was laughing with Marjorie MacLennane. The MacLennanes, now retired, had broken off a motoring tour to visit Saint-Rogatien and close another chapter in the story of Jadis and Jack, their last and most favourite *protégés*.

Which left her mentor, and Jack's, Emeritus Professor Roger Sutherland MacLennane seated at her right, in panama hat and off-white linen suit—a startling change after the rumpled dark suit he'd invariably worn in Cambridge. He looked at her with solicitous eyes, magnified by his bottle-glass spectacles.

"Are you feeling all right, Jadis?"

"Roger — thank you, of course I am. Why shouldn't I be?"

Jadis liked to think of the 2031 crew as her Dream Team, the brightest and best she'd ever assembled. First, and greatest, there was Avi, who'd just published a terse and thoughtful paper on his analysis of the still-mysterious artifacts from what came to be known locally as *Le Dig*, artifacts that she, his doctorate supervisor, had named as 'Remillardian' in her own thesis, two years earlier. These featureless, geometrically perfect, polygonal coins of flint were the only signs of a lost and ancient civilization that had dominated this part of the world for perhaps hundreds of thousands of years, except that their meaning — and the identity of the makers — remained frustratingly elusive.

And yet in the heat of this never-ending battle with the unknown (and at her kitchen table, no less) she and Avi had fused his talent as a data wrangler with her ability to slice through a problem to the core, and in so doing, they had created what a commentator in *Antiquity* had called 'analytic archeology'. When asked to define analytic archeology, though, Jadis had always demonstrated her own agenda. "I prefer to call it 'evidence-based' archeology," she'd said in an interview with veteran science writer Marcel Montgolfier in *Paris-Match*, the one accompanied by the unintentionally sexy photographs that always made Jack laugh. "We see what's there," she'd said, her words printed opposite a moodily lit photo of a dark-eyed, wild-haired siren she would never believe was actually her, "and we tell it like it is. Not how we think it should be, or how it ought to go. Just what's there. That's much harder to do that you might think. For you can bet that whenever someone holds too closely to their assumptions, these will be the first things to be proven wrong."

She liked to think that these were the precepts she held most dear — and that she would never have come to these conclusions without having Jack to hand, whose grasp of landscape was wholly instinctive, and had forced her, as if in opposition, to think harder and more logically than she might otherwise have done.

Jadis and Avi had not long returned from Avi's doctorate exam, and a rare trip to Cambridge, at which she had met Ernestine Yanga for the first time. Professor Yanga had been Jack's external examiner, and Jack had told her not to believe the stories she'd heard about the Kenyan academic's ferocity. Avi's thesis defense had been brief, almost routine. "Dr Malkeinu's work is so bold, and so brash," said a smiling Professor

Yanga, "that he might find himself in very hot water. And I have longed to meet you, Dr Markham. I can see where that husband of yours gets it from."

Jadis had said nothing, but looked up with a half-smile of inquisition.

"You don't know? Why, my dear, it's you! Your fortitude."

Jadis had wanted to tell her that no, it had been the other way round—that if only she knew—that without Jack to tie her to the Earth she would probably have long since been carried away like chaff on the wind.

Over the previous two years, Avi had been called up regularly to serve two-month stints in the Israeli Army as a reservist, especially as the perpetually broiling Middle-East Situation was entering a more than usually sticky patch. With the mild, peacemaking Kingdom of Jordan having been swept aside by the green and black flags of the ever-advancing pan-Islamic Khalifa that had already swallowed most of the rest of the region, the incoming tide of war threatened to break through the ever-fragile, ever-shifting dunes of armed truce. If the Khalifa defeated the still-resisting Saudis, there would be nobody left to fight—except the old adversary. Israel had decided that Avi's scientific skills were too valuable to be wasted on the dead past when they could be applied to the uncertain future. So Avi would be gone in a week: as it looked, this time, permanently.

But perhaps, one day, Avi had said, he'd get back to science, for he had something up his sleeve—a proposal for a comprehensive survey of whole Mount Carmel cave complex, where Neanderthals and modern humans seemed to have lived, alternately, like some great Palaeolithic time-share, swapping the same caves, over and over, for a hundred thousand years.

He'd discussed this deep into the night with Jadis as he finished his thesis, papers strewn on the kitchen table and onto the floor (where, in one of those hazards of fieldwork, he found them the morning after, decorated with the remains of a semi-digested dormouse that Horrible had regurgitated). Our views of Mount Carmel, he'd said, were conditioned by our assumptions, that Neanderthals were the has-beens, and humans the destined inheritors of the Earth. But if there was one thing (he'd said) that Jadis had taught him, it was that hindsight is a very poor guide to understanding prehistory.

In any case, hindsight couldn't tell us why Mount Carmel had been a barrier to the expansion of humans out of Africa for at least fifty thousand years. The answer, if you looked at the evidence, was clear: humans had been bottled up in Africa because the Neanderthals had kept them there: a Neanderthal civilization at Mount Carmel that could have matched the civilization in Europe of which Saint-Rogatien might have been the first sign.

Ah, such castles in the air, Jadis had thought, bringing Avi down to Earth with yet another scheme to classify Remillardian artifacts. But as things stood now, who knew if she'd ever hear from Avi again?

Not that Avi himself seemed to have any particular worries, and why should he? Here he was, in *La France Profonde*, in his favourite situation, that is, between two pretty, vivacious women who were plainly hanging on his every word. As Jadis looked over this, the Last Supper, she did not know — how could she have done? — what discoveries Primrose Tsien (squeezed, giggling, in the crook of Avi's muscular right arm), and all-Texan cowgirl Faye Callaghan (embraced by his equally beefy left) might make, what renown they might achieve — or none? And one might ask the same of Mathilde Reynard, her slim, pale, freckled form like a thin white ash against the dark thundercloud that was Domingo to her left; and Eric Onoye, laughing with Marjorie. What would the future hold for them?

But wherever they might go, and wherever their lives might take them, she silently wished them all the good fortune she'd had, despite everything. And maybe some of them might like to stay on, for she was convinced that Saint-Rogatien was just the beginning of their adventures.

Caught once again in daydream, she paused, stopped what she was eating and, fork held in mid-air, looked up at Jack, now deep in conversation with Domingo and Mathilde. Her expression would have been unintelligible to anyone who'd witnessed its brief passage across her face, but the fathomless glints in her eyes turned to sparkles of curiosity, and then laughter: for in one of those random lulls that punctuate dinner-party conversations she heard:

"...Domingo García Vasquez Santéria Sanchopanza de Orellanzana von Hohenzollern und Taxis."

Jack sat back, incredulous. "If I might say so, Domingo," he said, "that's quite a handle." Mathilde leaned forwards on her elbows, gazing in open-mouthed awe at the huge man. Domingo just smiled one of his winningly tombstone-toothed smiles and said, in his characteristically resonant, almost impossibly deep voice: "Of course, my friends just call me 'Pongo.'"

There was a brief but significant spell of utter silence, and then everyone started laughing at once. Fairbanks, startled from sleep, sat up, tail wagging, jumping from guest to guest, eager to learn the reason for all the commotion.

Her first sight of Domingo had been when, two years earlier, she had been hurriedly making herself a sandwich before taking Fairbanks for a walk. All of a sudden a vast shadow loomed in the ever-open kitchen door, and for a fleeting moment she could have sworn there'd been a total eclipse. Looking up, she gasped, as the apparition before her resolved from an inchoate blur into quite indisputably the ugliest man she had ever seen.

"Please, may I come in?" he'd asked. And so Jadis invited this monstrous troll over the threshold. It was one of those days when Jadis had been trying to do too many things at once. "Dr Markham, please, sit down, and let me deal with that." So without knowing quite how or why (let alone how he knew her name), Jadis found herself sitting at the table eating a sandwich and drinking a mug of tea that *he* had made for *her*. This gave her plenty of time to study this strange, uninvited guest.

He was, indeed, immense in every direction. Well over six feet tall and broad to match, he had an immense nose; an immense mane of thick, black, spiky hair that ran down the nape of his neck; immense steam-hammer hands, and teeth that looked like Stonehenge. But the perpetually cheeky twinkle of his eyes (each buried beneath a brow seemingly the size of a small hedgehog) revealed this same immensity on the inside, too. As she was later to discover, he was immensely kind, generous, gentle, cultured, sensitive and hardworking. He was also immensely strong, and became known around the village as the *L'incroyable Hulk.*

He had originally come from Andalusia in southern Spain, he said, but had traveled, and spoke fluent English (and several other languages) with an accent so slight that one would not have been able to identify its location. Jadis had invited him to join her on her daily round of the village, an act that gave an anchor for her day as well as necessary exercise for the dog. She also found it a great way to get to know new people, for the fame of *Le Dig* had, over the years, attracted many callers, some of them unusual or even frightening, which was one reason she was grateful for Fairbanks, especially when Jack was away on one of his own explorations, or—now that Roger MacLennane had retired—on business, as Director of the Institute.

As they bowled along the cow-parsley'd lane that led from the back garden in a slow grade up to the village square—Fairbanks bounding on ahead, twirling his feathered tail like a propeller—they made a contrasting pair. He in what she came to realize was his invariable uniform of Bermuda shorts and Hawai'ian shirt (making his bulk seem even greater), she in the long mackintosh she reserved for walking and shopping. He explained that he was a Catholic priest, newly ordained, who had (he said) 'been given some time off for good behavior' before seeking a flock of his own. Even just the way he said things made her giggle like a little girl. She imagined him as a friendly fairy-tale giant who invites small children to play in the gardens of his castle, simply from the goodness of his heart.

There was a long tradition in Catholicism, Domingo had explained, for clerics to go out into the world, and even be scientists for a while, all the better to appreciate the Mind of the Creator. His greatest hero had been the Jesuit Pierre Teilhard de Chardin, usually noted for his role in the Piltdown hoax of 1912 and for some challenging ideas about collective intelligence, but revered among paleontologists as a skilled field worker. But Domingo had also become something of an expert on the Abbé Gaston de Bonnard, a tireless archeologist and man of God who had worked in this part of France in the late nineteenth century. Would it be possible for him, Domingo asked, to 'do the Teilhardian thing' and join *Le Dig*? Perhaps for a few weeks? Jadis had said yes even before she'd known she had, and Domingo had been there ever since.

The dinner was beginning to wind down, just as the golden Sun touched the western horizon beyond the village, making a dramatic silhouette of the church on top of the hill that had ruled their lives and dreams for so long. Jack and the students cleared the plates (Marjorie laid a hand on Jadis' arm before she could stand: "let someone else do the work, dear"); candles were fetched and lit (bringing out a flutter of moths); coffee was made, brandy fetched from the cellar, and the company pushed their chairs back. Roger—ever the most refined judge of such things—felt that it was time for a toast. Rising to his feet, he asked the company to refill their glasses with whatever was handy and raise a toast to "Saint-Rogatien-Les-Remillards, and all who sailed in her!" The enthusiastic response sent a murder of crows flapping from the spinney.

Clinks of glasses, more chatter, and then Eric Onoye said—"Yes, Professor MacLennane, but who, precisely, *did* sail in her? That is the question!"

It was the one question they could not answer, the brick wall that had stopped every avenue of their investigation. Dozens of trenches and tunnels had been essayed into the cliff beneath the church under Jadis' direction, and they had found tons of animal bones and plant remains as well as the rare, mystifying Remillardian artefacts. But of human bones they found not one: not a single finger-bone in six years of careful, fingertip search; not even one tooth, despite the arduous sieving of enough sediment to have buried the hilltop church steeple-deep, twice over.

If the megalith on which Saint-Rogatien church now stood, and around whose slopes the village had gathered, had been a pyramid hundreds of thousands of years earlier, as Jack had believed, then any capping masonry had long since been eroded away or stripped, if it had been there at all, and there were no signs of voids that might have hinted at some unvisited tomb or sarcophagus. The bulk of the megalith — its filling — had been like a compost heap, a disordered mass of earth and rocks, more or less glued together with the limestone precipitating out of the groundwater, making a breccia, a kind of geological blancmange whose antiquity is notoriously hard to judge.

This was, indeed, another problem. Jadis had called in teams of scientists from all over the world, each an expert in one or other of the many arcane techniques of age determination, from electron spin resonance to amino-acid racemization, from optically stimulated luminescence to uranium-thorium dating — and yet each had come up with their own estimates, to which they held with the stubbornness of the several Blind Men of Hindustan in their variously confused contemplation of the Elephant.

In the end, the best that anyone could offer was that the megalith had been built sometime between 800,000 and 250,000 years ago, but of the makers there had been no sign. It could have been that there were several different races of maker, different species even, each one adding a little more to the megalith over millennia.

And so they all talked of the depth of civilization, the antiquity of intent, that had been the legacy of Saint-Rogatien, confirming Jack's suspicions gathered in a single flying visit so long before — a visit undertaken as a desperate, last attempt to shore up a collapsing doctorate project, and so as not to distract Jadis, then in her final undergraduate year, from studying for her finals.

"You know," said Domingo, "what I find most intriguing about the whole panorama is not so much antiquity, but recency."

"How do you mean?" Roger said. Domingo had a way of holding an audience, so that whenever he spoke, or even seemed like he might wish to, everyone instinctively turned their heads to him in expectation.

"Well, do you remember the whole business about *Homo floresiensis*?" All nodded in assent. The discovery of a strange species of tiny human-like creature that had lived on an isolated island in Indonesia until almost historical times had been the archeological sensation of the turn of the century. "Just think about it. If these creatures were wandering about until as recently as — whatever it was — ten thousand years — how do you know they're not still around?"

"But they aren't!" said Avi — "people have looked! Even though they're tiny, they couldn't have crawled under rocks or something..."

"Hey, aren't you forgetting something?" This from Faye, disentangling herself from Avi, lighting a cigarette and looking at him sternly: "you know what they say about hobbits and holes in the ground? Maybe we haven't found all the holes!"

Laughter, and, had anybody noticed, a sage twinkle in Domingo's eyes: tiny, newborn stars emerging from beneath the interstellar gas-clouds of his eyebrows.

"To be sure, Flores is perhaps not such a good example — too isolated, too far away. But what about here? When did our pyramid-builders stop building their pyramids? And why?"

"Perhaps modern Cro-Magnons came in and stopped them?" ventured Mathilde.

"That's, of course, possible," Domingo replied. "However, consider, if you will, the Neanderthals. We have always had them in our sights for Saint-Rogatien. But that might be an error, might it not? Think of the age of the thing — when the Neanderthals first appeared, our Great Pyramid of Saint-Rogatien might well have been more than half a million years old!"

"And your point is...?" teased Avi. He and Domingo had become firm friends, and had often been out on *Le Dig* together, invariably accompanied by Avi's ghetto blaster and one of Domingo's old Rolling Stones tapes. As they sat, one each side of a great box-frame sieve, shaking out and winnowing the sediment for tiny plant remains or flint flakes, their eager conversation was as dense — or as airy — as the clouds of tan dust they produced, wafting across the site.

"My point, my dear Avram Yitzchak, is that their antiquity is a side-issue. But what, I ask again, of their recency? As far as I know, the latest known Neanderthal comes from my—er—neck of the woods, and is around twenty-two thousand years old..."

"Twenty-one!" corrected Primrose, giggling.

"I do apologise, and I thank you for making my next point... that the age keeps dropping. Will it keep dropping forever? How will we know when we've seen the last of the Neanderthals? It's a bit like," he waved his great hands expansively "well, it's like trying to know if you've got rid of every last one of Horrible's little friends!" He paused. "You can't!" They all laughed at this: September was peak cat-flea season and Jadis and Primrose had been busy fumigating all the bedrooms.

Domingo was now a dark shadow in the deepening night, visible only by the glint of candle flames in his eyes: indeed, people could now only be seen from reflections, glances of yellow light on spectacle frames here, a curve of the face there, making them all look like a collection of off-duty models for one of Goya's Witches' Sabbaths. This only enhanced the drama of Domingo's speech: he was a Caliban, stalking the forests of night that run along the edges of dreams.

"You know, my friends, I shouldn't be surprised if the Neanderthals survived, perhaps just long enough to have come into the very earliest legends of the human race. And perhaps even more recently than that."

There was a long pause, and then came a strange new voice.

"*Ha'nephilim ha'yu ha'aretz ba'yamim...*" It was Avi, his eyes focused on some immeasurable distance, as if speaking to a lost past. The table was hushed by his unwonted seriousness. He had never been known to speak any language in their company besides English or French. This was a private side to Avi the existence of which nobody had been aware. None, that is, except Domingo.

In their long hours together at the dig, Domingo and Avi—the Catholic priest and the Jewish atheist—had turned, inevitably, to religion. Domingo had wondered at what he saw as the manifest contradictions of Avi's upbringing; that he'd been raised in a Marxist kibbutz community in a land reclaimed by the Jews. "This is a delicious irony, Avram Yitzchak, is it not? That as soon as the Jews found the Land of Israel, after much heroism and effort and struggle, they abandon their religion! And—this is all the more intriguing—those Jews in Israel who cling most firmly to their religion deny Israel's very right to exist!"

Avi just laughed. It was not that he was uncomfortable, or that he thought Domingo was trying to convert him, because he knew his friend too well for that. It was just that he completely failed to see what Domingo was getting at.

So, over the months, Domingo tried a different tack. The argument that had worked was that if Avi was really as serious about archeology and antiquity as he appeared to be, he might find it all the more enriching were he to have a better appreciation of history, especially his own. "After all, Dear Avram," Domingo had said, "the Jews are the custodians of the deepest traditions of written history in the western world. Yet *bereshit* is a fickle mistress. Who really knows how far back that history goes?"

It was the mention of *bereshit*—the Hebrew for 'In The Beginning,' and the name for the book of Genesis—that had made Avram sit up with a start and look with yet further admiration at his strange new friend, whose erudition seemed bottomless.

The company now looked at Avi in equal awe, as if he'd just chanted a spell, whether for good or evil they could not tell. Only Domingo had sufficient presence of mind to answer. "Avram's words are entirely apposite: *gigantes autem erant super terram in diebus illis*—in those days there were giants that walked the Earth," he said. "And let us not forget what the giants were up to." He muttered a string of Latin under his breath, as if trying to bookmark the place in his mind before translating it: "Ah yes, *postquam enim ingressi sunt filii*... um... *Dei ad filias hominum illaeque genuerunt isti sunt*. Hmm... *potentes a saeculo viri*.... er... *famosi*." And then, more clearly: "That these giants were great men, who interbred with the daughters of men, who bore great and mighty sons."

"But, Domingo, my friend," said Avi, sitting back in his chair in his usual relaxed way, the seriousness of his face lost in the shadow beyond the table. "The word *nephilim* in *Ivrit* does not translate as 'giants'. It means 'the fallen ones'..." Avi and Domingo now had the floor before a rapt audience.

"But that's precisely it, Avi. They were giants because they were great men, not necessarily that they were aliens or trolls or Neanderthals or anything like that, because the Bible would not have the appropriate language for such things. But we know that they fell, before the Flood, but before they did, they intermarried with human beings. Perhaps the Bible is telling us about human beings and—er—other people, before the floods at the end of the Ice Age? Now, I do not believe that every word of the Bible is true, because it can't be, but when something is said so plainly..."

Domingo's point tailed off into silence.

"Perhaps we can put Domingo's ideas to the test," said Jack, alleviating the suddenly brooding mood.

"A-ha!" exclaimed Roger, "I just knew you and Jadis had been up to something!"

"Well, possibly. But we have been thinking of our next move now that we're winding things up here at Saint-Rogatien. I've been scouting around quite a lot, as you know…" General laughter and some groans. Jack's habits of wandering off for days and returning looking like an ill-used tramp were well known. "And I think I've found something rather… well, odd."

No laughs at this — it was Jack's instinct for following the bones of the Earth that had brought them Saint-Rogatien in the first place. Everyone was eager to learn of this new adventure, as if the legacy of Saint-Rogatien — after six seasons of nail-snagging, knee-grazing, backbreaking labor — was already long forgotten.

"So I took Jadis to see it, on her birthday…" Wolf-whistles from Avi: catcalls from the girls.

"…and she likes it, which of course is the most important thing…" laughs, hoots of "hear! hear!" and "well done, Jadis!"

"… and she thinks we should have a more serious look around. Perhaps early next month, dig a few test pits, and see if there's potential for a field season there."

"Now we're all intrigued," said Roger. "Where is this interesting place?"

So Jack told them, and the discussion continued deeper into the night until, well past moonrise, the Last Supper finally came to an end.

Jadis had known what Jack was going to talk about anyway, so she started to the clear remaining plates and glasses into the kitchen. Marjorie MacLennane, in contrast, had no particular idea of what Jack was going to talk about, but decided to help Jadis, all the same. And so, with the conversation still audible through the back door, now counter-pointed by an intermittent frog chorus from the pond, Jadis and Marjorie stood together in the kitchen, one washing up; the other, drying.

Like the two old friends they were, like two bookends, they stood together companionably, chatting amiably about gardening, and the lives and loves of the friends and colleagues they had in common, back in Cambridge, and what Roger was going to do with himself now he'd retired ("get under my feet, worse luck!") but neither feeling any need to start a conversation simply for the sake of it. They had both been through too much for that.

For her part, Jadis felt that she was more in Marjorie's debt than she could ever express, or thank, let alone repay.

Marjorie's thoughts were more complex. From the very first time she had met Jadis, she had sensed an inner toughness quite at variance with her easygoing exterior: but that her mettle had had to be tested quite so brutally was shocking, beyond comprehension. The facts of the accident were quite trying enough, even without further discussion. That Jadis had survived at all was remarkable—that she had thrived, a miracle. Looking at her now, you'd never have guessed that she'd endured so much. This, and the fact that she never once discussed or referred to it, was a testament both to her fortitude: that, and (she had to admit) the support of her husband.

As the two women finished their work and turned to say good-night, Marjorie's hand brushed the sleeve of Jadis' sweatshirt, and they embraced. Neither with ardor, nor with passion, but as friends will: as an expression of knowledge shared that need not be spoken, and in the hope that such shared confidences might help to ease an otherwise intolerable burden.

One question remained, a question that Marjorie kept to herself, as she settled down in the guest bedroom of the farmhouse next to a snoring Roger, the full moon hanging low over the eastern fields: for she never could—never would—have broached it with Jadis, let alone anyone else. And that question was this: had Jadis managed to reach the hospital unscathed, could she have saved her unborn child, or would she have miscarried anyway? But the mind of Marjorie MacLennane was wired for certainties and decision, not hypotheses and counterfactuals, so she soon abandoned the struggle and surrendered to the arms and armies of sleep.

Chapter 18. Islander

Tethys Ocean, Earth, *c.* 55,680,000 years ago

Still is that fur as soft as when the lists
In youth thou enter'dst on glass-bottled wall.
John Keats — *To Mrs Reynolds' Cat*

Her voice came to him shrilly, over the thrash of surf and the noise they were both making.

"Get that one... no, that one, there, Roland, heading up the beach!"

Ruxhana hefted his pine-branch club and sloshed through the waist-high waves to where the creature was trying to scramble ashore. Ambulocetes were slow movers on land, even on a gently shelving beach like this, so this youngster — barely two meters long — had no idea that it was waddling into a trap. Ruxhana and Xalomé had played their strategy well, letting the pod of amphibious whales shamble shorewards before springing off the rocks, trapping them in the lagoon that had been their home for the past ten days.

The aim was to drive two or three small ones ashore before clubbing them to death. Spilling blood in the water would have been risky — they did not want to add sharks to an already dangerous mix. Ruxhana remembered the scarier tales of Tethyan Thunder of his youth, in which the sea-dragon hunters had had to pull their quarries onto boats or ashore before the carcasses attracted these eternal oceanic predators. There was one monster in particular — the Tethyan carcharodon — that could reputedly smell blood from ten kilometers off, and could swallow a whole boat with all its crew in a single bite.

Some of the older ambulocetes sensed trouble, dove to the bottom and surged back the way they had come, towards the open sea. This was dangerous for the assailants, who had to keep looking down in case four meters of fast-moving, muscle-bound, submarine menace bowled them over in the chest-high water and dragged them under. And although ambulocetes were peaceable creatures, for the most part, they were formidable if cornered, with sharp claws on their forelegs and long, well-stocked jaws wielded with far greater intelligence than any shark.

Xalomé was further out in the lagoon than he was, and Ruxhana worried more than once when the air was rent with her screams and she disappeared from view. But she always came up again, defiant, laughing.

Her hair flowed in the breeze; her body, lithe and brown; her pink-and-yellow sarong worn like a breech-clout, knotted securely around her middle. And she always kept her hat on.

Ruxhana's target was flopping about in barely an inch of surf when he caught up with it. Panting, legs splayed, it heaved itself onto the beach. A beady eye broadcast a message of supplication as Ruxhana brought his club down heavily on the creature's skull. He'd just hauled the carcass above the strand line when he heard Xalomé scream again. He turned, and saw, gaining on her, in the lagoon, a gray triangular fin at least two meters high, and an immense shadow in the water. Ruxhana could do little but watch. Xalomé flew up the beach, a bright, tiny figure before her pursuer, falling once in the waves in its shadow, picking herself up again, and racing through the wavelets, foam sparking from her feet like diamond shrapnel.

She had just made it to the trees above the beach when the shape broke the surface just inches from the shoreline, a great gray cylinder, slashed with pink gill-slits, each one large enough to swallow a man— but before it all, a chasm, thrice man-high, fringed with wickedly serrated, triangular teeth, each the size of a tombstone. Realizing at last that it was out of its element, the giant shark scythed, half in the air, splashing back into the lagoon and disappearing in pursuit of easier prey.

Ruxhana felt nerves reconnect in his legs and ran to her. She was standing, bent double, hands on knees, her breath shot with the wrack of terror and relief, sarong blotched with ugly crimson stains. A line of blood ran down the inside of one thigh and pooled on the ground. She stood up, pulled the hair from her face, and looked at him with her hard green eyes.

"Baryonic matter. Fucking baryonic matter." Then she collapsed into his arms.

The moon rose above the beach. Ruxhana turned the whalemeat steaks frying on the hot rocks before him. "That smells good," she said. She was huddled up, knees beneath her chin, wrapped in a quilt from the linen store aboard *Shelly's Shagpad*, moored just offshore. Ruxhana felt his arms and legs—his whole body, in fact—flood with relief. It had been the first thing she'd said since she'd swooned almost thirty hours earlier. The memories—until then, squashed by pragmatic, military expediency—were now afforded the luxury of return.

"Would Madame care to dress for dinner?"

He'd laid her on the ground in the shade of a palm, he remembered, and then he'd stood up in the dappled shadow and queried his AI core on an emergency sideband.

Wherever the fuck you are, you stupid machine, he yelled – or qubits to that effect – get your quantum ass over here, now. Please.

I think I've worked it out now, was all it said. Ruxhana could have hugged it.

Excellent, he replied. Welcome back. Nice break?

Yes. Most refreshing. Also necessary.

Good, good. Well, what we have here is a damsel-in-distress situation. Please get in touch with *Shelly's Shagpad* and have them send over some medical supplies, immediately. Blankets, clothes. Some rum, too, would be nice. And – if they can spare it – some salt, herbs, and a few other things. Ruxhana squirted a shopping list at his newly refreshed AI core.

"I'm sorry, Ruxie. Really, I am. I'm not very good at this. Still learning." She pushed away her plate and looked across the table at him, the tapeta in her eyes reflecting the crystal, the candles, the silver candelabra and cutlery, and the moonlight on the sea. There was no sound but for the surf and a light breeze in the palm branches high above their heads. The air was cooler, now. Cool enough for Ruxhana to adjust the collar of his dress shirt without feeling uncomfortably sweaty. His waistband, though – well, he felt that they hadn't had such a meal in ages. Over-full as he was, he thought her hair in the candlelight looked lovely, and said so.

"Oh, you – you silly man," she said, sweeping it out of her face with both hands and trying, yet again, to secure it at the back. He suspected that it was the wine talking, but he couldn't help but notice the contrast of her straying strands of hair with the smoothness of her upper arms, and, as she moved, the play of her shoulders, collar-bone and the roots of her primary breasts beneath the black cocktail dress she'd chosen.

"It's just that I feel so embarrassed after yesterday."

"Embarrassed? Not many have been known to outrun a Tethyan carcharodon. I think you can be excused a few symptoms of shock."

"Yes, I know. But it shouldn't have happened. It was all my fault. Mine. I know perfectly well about the sharks in these waters – I've done my homework! But I forgot something else just as important. About these bodies. About this body. You know I'd been feeling a bit gripey for a couple of days?"

Ruxhana nodded, but said nothing. He remembered some small epi-
sodes of mulish taciturnity on her part but had chosen to ignore them,
and had gone fishing on the other side of the lagoon.

"It turned out that I was menstruating. Can you believe it? And it
started, like a flood, while we were out there in the lagoon. Shark-bait,
right where I stood. Honestly, I try so hard, but I just can't seem to be
everywhere at once."

Ruxhana smiled at the perceived helplessness of his dinner companion, who was quite capable of traveling across the Universe as easily as
blinking.

"What?" she asked, catching his amused expression.

"Oh, just something you said. Why did you call me 'Roland'?"

Her eyes widened. "I did?"

"Yes."

Her face changed.

When the skiff from *Shelly's Shagpad* had first made landfall on the island, Ruxhana had splashed ashore, laughing, accompanied by two female droids, a crate of fine Malabar rum, and three glasses.

The hangover the next day had been salutary. He dismissed his companions and asked instead for a jerrycan of fresh water, a machete and a
few other simple tools, some fishing gear, and a tent. These articles were
promptly sent over in the skiff, which skated back to the mothership as
soon as it had been unloaded. Ruxhana thought he detected a note of
reproach in its alacrity.

By the evening of the third day ashore he'd created a raised palm-log
platform with a commanding view of the beach, upon which he erected a
pergola of poles with a palm-thatch roof, and detachable screen walls
made from palm leaves woven together. Split logs served for chairs, and
a more elaborate log-frame strung with vines made a fairly comfortable
bed. The lagoon boiled with fish that leaped into his net without his having to make much effort at all. Only fresh water looked likely to be a
problem, but being the tropics, it rained every day—a ten-minute sheeting downpour in the middle of the afternoon—and Ruxhana was able to
use hollowed gourds and shells to collect enough for his modest needs.

To be sure, he could always have asked for the *Shagpad* to have sent
over fresh water or indeed anything else he wanted; but with the two
voluptuaries of his first night sent packing and his AI still in an offline
sulk, he'd have had to have yelled very hard, or swum for it. Therefore
he decided to play the noble savage for a while.

It was on the evening of the fourth day ashore that Ruxhana found himself on his platform, a glass of rum in hand, a brace of bass grilling nicely in the fire-pit on the beach below, looking out at the westering Sun, and wondering. This ought to be paradise. Instead his mind was full of foreboding. Is this it? The end? Stasis? What was all that about, anyway, that business with Xalomé? That elaborate gender-bending subterfuge? Just to drop him here as a fugitive on a desert island? It made no sense. And just who exactly was Xalomé, anyway?

She'd told him that she was an exotic of a kind that neither he nor anyone else in the Imperium had ever encountered, something qualitatively different from anyone or anything he had known. It seemed to him that she wielded unimaginable power with the casual carelessness of a teenager. This, combined with what he thought was some kind of insecurity, made for a potentially explosive mixture.

And then there were those dark hints that his AI core had dropped before it disappeared up its own address register, about 'ongoing transformations'.

Finally, there was this 'job' or 'task' that she wanted him to do. But despite his best efforts, he was never able to get anything specific out of her about what this might entail.

In the end Ruxhana consoled himself with facts: as there was no way he could answer any of these questions, the only decisions he could make were small ones. In which case, his new life was as idyllic as he could want.

He was thinking about a third glass of rum when he saw a speck in the lagoon to the northward, a fleck of white foam in the purpling sea. The speck got larger as he watched. The wind was beginning to freshen. He wondered whether he should put his clothes back on.

The speck got closer and came ashore. He decided against the clothes but in favor of more rum.

The speck was a figure. By the time it reached him, the sky was fully dark and the moon had risen behind the trees, casting long fingered shadows across the beach. The figure resolved into that of a woman in a sarong, loosely tied, its ends snapping like flags in the breeze. She climbed onto Ruxhana's platform, and bent down to whisper in his ear. Ruxhana felt the sea-tang of warm flesh close to his.

"Sorry I'm late," Xalomé said. "Have I missed anything?"

None of Ruxhana's questions were answered in the days that followed, up to and including the ambulocete drive and shark-attack incident. Whenever he tried to ask her anything that might have been construed as serious, she would usually make some salacious suggestion and run away, as if he should give chase. Like they were teenage kits, discovering sex for the first time. Her lovemaking was passionate and frequent, but he detected in its fervor something more than the freshness of discovery. A desperation, perhaps, that it would all soon be over; and a way of filling the days and nights that would put off some nevertheless inevitable day of reckoning for as long as possible.

Xalomé was clearly trying and failing to frame some stupendous plan using the pitiful tools of mere words. Trying to articulate, using the crudity of communication that relies on the analog, acoustic transmission of modulated air packets, themes and concepts too subtle to be shoe-horned into such a mode without losing vital quanta of meaning. Ruxhana decided that the only thing he could do was to let her work it out in her own time, in her own way. And in the meantime, he reasoned (being the pragmatic soul he was) he was a castaway in paradise with a girl whose charm was matched by her libido. In such a situation it would be churlish to complain.

Xalomé.

Working things out.

One night, about five days after her arrival, Ruxhana woke up—or dreamed he had woken up—with the girl next to him. The Moon was bright, high in the west. Ruxhana sat up, trying to chase down a sense of foreboding he couldn't quite frame for all that the answer was important, and looked down at her body, splayed in the blue light.

It was Xalomé—his Xalomé—but then again, it wasn't. Her face was the same, asleep, her long lashes guarding closed eyes; as was her long hair, spread awry in long strands, and the lean frame of her body. But she looked like she'd been flayed. Her skin wasn't dark, but pale. It was smooth, almost all over, the soft fuzz over her shoulders and hips reduced to a very thin haze. The pungent mass of dark fur that spread between her hipbones and which clothed most of her body between navel and crotch was gone, revealing a gentle swell of bare lower abdomen and a small triangle of meager curls—almost prissily neat, he thought—in the angle of her groin itself. The hair was so sparse that he could see her external genitalia—but as a chaste, vertical slit, far from the usual extravagance of her pubic protruberances.

Odder still was her torso.

For a brief moment he wondered why he could see the lower margins of her ribcage, outlined like a corpse, until he realized that nearly all her breasts had vanished. The primaries were there, perhaps slightly fuller than he remembered. But all eight secondaries had gone, nipples and all, as if they had never been, explaining why he could see her ribcage and why she looked so shorn.

Ruxhana was uncertain how to react to this apparition. Horror and fascination were evenly matched within him, but something about the mutilated form before him made him stir, and with redoubled horror he looked down at his prong—erect, but smooth as an earthworm, without any of the ridges, blades and serrations which he knew graced his own. He sat there, helpless, when the not-quite-Xalomé-thing stirred, sat up next to him, her breasts swinging freely before her in a way he couldn't quite understand, given the absence of their companions. She swished the hair from her face, and spoke.

"You should be asleep, you silly old thing!"

And then she kissed him, no more than an affectionate peck, and the world changed again. Disoriented, he found himself lying down again but awake in the moonlight. This time he knew he really was awake, because the naked girl beside him was complete in all her furred, multi-mammate loveliness. He lay back and closed his eyes again, but his relaxation was not entirely complete, hindered by the memory of the dream-Xalomé as she spoke to him.

The memory of her eyes. Eyes that did not have their customarily all-over green irises and almond-shaped, slit-like pupils. Eyes instead with brown irises, almost black and as round as moons, with penetrating, round pupils, and in bone-white sclera as plain as death. When morning came he decided to keep this nighttime adventure to himself.

Xalomé's reticence continued, even after the shark-attack episode, when she promised that answers to his questions would soon be forthcoming. Her sex-play became more edgy, more vigorous—more dangerous. As if she was daring him to pursue her to the edges of the reef; across the razored rocks; into sheer-sided sinkholes in the coralline limestone.

She seemed especially skittish one morning about a week after the ambulocete barbecue. They had spent a leisurely breakfast of fruit (collected themselves) and fresh coffee and croissants (supplied by *Shelly's Shagpad*), exchanging hardly a word. When Ruxhana tried to say anything at all, she'd giggle, slyly, like a kit intent on some naughtiness. On a sudden she pushed away her plate and fixed him with a glare of mischief.

"Come and get it!" And then she ran off, northwards, down the beach, hair and bright sarong streaming.

Ruxhana was beginning to tire of this game, and had meant to stay put, calling her bluff, in the hope that she might wander back, and have their serious discussion: now delayed long enough. At any rate, he decided to finish his second cup of coffee.

But Xalomé did not return, and the bitter savor of his coffee turned to worry. Even paradise has its dangers — the shark attack had been proof enough of that. Sighing, he hauled himself from his chair and walked off in the direction Xalomé had taken, calling her name as he went.

For two or three hundred meters there came no answer, but as he walked, Ruxhana noticed that the wind was freshening. Sand-devils blew along the shore, and he'd had to stop and brush grit from his eyes. White horses frothed in the lagoon to his left. To his right, the tops of the palm trees, some of them fifteen meters tall, were starting to swing and thrash. He heard a distant yell and realized with horror that it had come from above. Xalomé had climbed one of these swaying monsters and was now perched, triumphant, in the waving crown. The tree she had chosen stood alone, exposed, surrounded by a glade of bare trunks, standing like sharp spikes, marks of an earlier lightning strike and wild-fire.

He looked up and bellowed in return. "Xalomé, come down! Come down now!"

"Not a chance!" came her reply, guttural, defiant.

"It's dangerous!"

"Really? So come and save me, then!"

There was no choice but to climb. The ridged trunk of the palm tree presented fairly easy purchase, but the wood was hard and sharp on his bare hands and feet, and he often had to stop and hold on tight when the tree was caught in a strong gust. These pauses became more frequent the further he climbed, his fatigue increasing as the trunk thinned and became more whip-like in the deepening gale. The wind was now edged with a stinging rain that made it hard for him to see. He was exhausted, wretched in the chill grayness, wondering if he'd ever get to the crown — and if he did, what then? Not a moment too soon, his head met the edges of palm leaves, and a hand rested over his, inviting, grasping.

Xalomé sat at the top of the crown, hunkered down in a kind of cup-shaped nest, relatively sheltered from the wind, but which lurched alarmingly. She pulled him up and he pitched next to her with a jolt. Before he had a chance even to catch his breath, to nurse the bruises and cuts on his aching hands and feet, she was at him, arms around him, hair surrounding him like a cowl, lips on his, like these were the final kisses on Earth. Finally, she pulled away and looked at him as if for the very first time.

"Oh, Ruxie, I'm so sorry..."

"Sorry? For what?"

"For this." And she pushed him out of the tree.

Chapter 19. Antiquarian

Gascony, France, Earth, June, 2031

My beloved spake, and said unto me, rise up, my love, my fair one, and come away. For, lo, the winter is past, the rain is over and gone.
Song of Solomon **2**, 10-11

Jadis burst from the kitchen door like a rifle shot, a spinning mass of hair and legs and bags and baggy shirt and denim cut-offs and excitement. Jack threw open the passenger door of the open-top jeep and laughed. Jadis threw the bags in the back, scrambled aboard and strapped herself in. "Let's go," she said.

Avi had been left in charge of tidying up the very last exposures at *Le Dig*; Primrose promised she'd remember to take Fairbanks for a walk ("if you're too busy, just ask Domingo"); but once down the much patched-and-potholed drive lined with shimmering poplars, and through the twin stone pillars that supported their sagging, never-closed front gate, they were away, a bolt for freedom, if only for a couple of days.

She couldn't imagine she'd feel such sudden exhilaration. This must be the way champagne corks feel, when, all strain released, they careen carelessly into space. But when she paused to think about it, she hadn't left the village in weeks and had become as taut as over-wound clockwork.

Starting a dig was easy. Just shift a spadeful of dirt and you're there. But finishing a dig: that was another matter entirely. There were contracts to terminate; forms to fill in; volunteers to send home; equipment to inventory; specimens to catalogue and ship; and endless reports to write. Not to mention the tedious process of environmental restoration (more forms, more reports), transforming a site that had been dug and heaped and leveled and scraped and picked over for six years back into a place that looked just as it had done when they'd first found it. Turning an omelet back into eggs, she thought, might be simpler.

Late one evening in the middle of May, she was sitting alone in a pool of light in the darkened kitchen, working through another draft of her monthly accounts report for the Institute. As the rows and columns of the spreadsheet expanded balefully before her tired eyes, she started to wonder if it would ever end; if Jack's much-delayed promise of a new dig site would ever gallop over the horizon and rescue her.

To make matters worse, Jack had been away for three and a half weeks — a fortnight of surveying around his still-secret site, followed by a conference in America and a meeting with the Institute's people in Cambridge. She accepted his absences as necessary, but even after all this time, she found it hard to lie in a bed that lacked his presence.

The first two or three days were always fine, as long as his smell lingered. For a few days after that she tried to compensate by inviting Fairbanks into bed, something that was never allowed when Jack was home. But that was no help, either. Fairbanks snored (something Jack rarely did), and, what's more, he smelled of dog. She realized that this was hardly his fault, and she couldn't really blame her faithful, uncomplaining companion for the fact that she missed her husband.

It was just dawning on her, then, that she should, by now, be getting more used to Jack's absences, not less, and wondering why this might be, when she looked up from the spreadsheet to see Jack himself, standing by her side. She flung herself upwards at him like a firework and threw her arms tightly around his neck.

"What you need is a holiday," he said.

And so it was that they were now hacking along the country roads towards Aurignac, a small village but with a remarkable distinction. For Aurignac can make a fair claim to being the epicenter and fountainhead of human consciousness. If the human race can be said to have started anywhere, it is here.

Chipped flints had been the apotheosis of craftsmanship for almost three million years, but these had no more been the products of creative imagination than are the filigreed webs of spiders, or the great reefs secreted by a trillion mindless polyps, for all that their mighty works can be seen from space.

And then, something happened.

Quite suddenly, around forty thousand years ago, a spark lit up, and human beings emerged from primeval night. It was as if they had previously imagined the cave they inhabited as their entire universe, and had, quite by accident, perhaps by turning a different corner, discovered the cave mouth, a portal to a brighter, wider world of limitless possibility. The effects of this stunning event were so profound that they had left their mark in the record of human endeavor four hundred centuries later. Would the skyscrapers and cities of the twentieth century ever prove such enduring memorials?

The most dramatic change was the manifestation of consciousness which human beings later came to call 'art'. Before, there had been almost nothing. And yet now there were cave paintings that had brought the animals of the late Ice Age vividly to life; statues made with love and devotion and the worship of the strength of men, and the love of women, and the earliest known images of the human face. There were imprints of hands that said, more eloquently than any written language—'I am'.

This breathtaking revolution burst all over Europe within a geological eyeblink, but among the first discoveries had come to light here, at Aurignac itself, which therefore had the honor of giving its name—the Aurignacian—to perhaps the single most important event in the whole of human history, the moment when human beings first awoke from their long sleep.

Or so it had been thought.

For there were yet older, more enigmatic signs, more mysterious still because they might not have been made by humans at all, and would, therefore, not have been recognizable as art, at least, not to our, human eyes. Jadis' mysterious Remillardian stone-tool culture, which she and Avi had described from *Le Dig*, might have been one of these signs, but with no context, no maker, it was hard to tell.

If a pilgrimage to Aurignac were not wonder enough for two archeologists on a spree, the modern village had in *Le Cerf Blanc* a jewel of a hotel attached to a luxurious and expensive restaurant. A treat for them both. After all, it was her birthday, and she deserved it.

And, as Jack explained as they drove—Jadis' hair streaming out behind her like a flag, the laddered avenues of poplars and planes casting rippling zigzag shadows across the car, the fume of poppies and dust and the ripening maize whizzing past them on either side—they had some planning to do. He'd found a site just this side of Aurignac which his intuition had told him might be something special, something new: something to wake them all up after the raveled enigma of Saint-Rogatien. He wanted to show this new site to her, before anyone else: to give her a sense of place, in the hope that she'd pick up at least some echo of the vibrations that had sent his internal antennae off the scale, on his first visit, blotting out all else: that in the seemingly modest little cave of Souris Saint-Michel there might be a door to a new world, if only he had the wit to see it.

Jadis looked at Jack through the hair blowing across her face, and then at the road ahead of them, and felt, deeply inside her, deeper than words, that this journey represented far more than a drive on some dusty summer back-road, more than a pleasant interlude in the lives of two busy people. No: this was a turning point, a phase transition in existence, as it had been for the first Aurignacians. They were riding, like them, into a new life, awakening. She felt like the very first cave artist, reed brush poised stiff, overloaded with wet ocher, in the split instant before it made contact with the cave wall, and, with this tiny act of fecundation, had she known it, catapulting the human race into an entirely new realm. She felt as if she were now, finally, ready. Ready to be born.

Jack swung off the road and into a back lane between two maize fields. The unsurfaced track dipped towards woods of oak and sweet chestnut, coming to an end in a small, dusty car park on the shores of a lake. The lake was perfectly smooth and still, and the same eggshell blue of the sky above it. Jack pulled the jeep across the car park and on to a narrow sandy beach right by the water's edge. Apart from two picnic tables, their planks warped and faded, there were no other signs of human activity, past or present. Through a belt of pines on the other side of the lake Jack had discovered a fern-choked track leading up a hill to the small cave he'd become so excited about, the last site ever excavated by Gaston de Bonnard.

"Souris Saint-Michel," he said. "It's a bit of a mystery. I think we can solve it." It occurred to Jack that he had been talking to himself for several minutes. He turned to his right, towards Jadis, but she was quicker. She leaned towards him, kissed him, and unfastening her seatbelt, climbed over on top of him, placing her bare thighs on either side of him, her elbows on the seat back on either side of his neck, her hands — smooth, yet with the floury patina of fieldwork — cupping his face, kissing him as if she'd never stop, hungrily as if she felt her lips might never gain purchase, her tongue seeking his with the desperate anxiety of a nestling squab whose mother had been too long away. At length she pulled herself away, and looked down at him with a strange expression, not of love, but of inspection, as if she were at a market stall choosing cheese or eggs. As if she'd seen him, properly, for the very first time.

"Jadis..."

She sat up, tossed her hair out of her eyes, and brushed the creases from her sweatshirt.

"Let's go and look at this cave of yours, then," she said. It was as if nothing had happened. But then, Jack thought, everything had happened, that it really was her birthday, the very day of her birth. To him she looked like something newly hatched, a jeweled lizard in fresh rainbow colors unsullied by care or age, as if she'd sloughed an ugly skin that she had worn for years, but which had become invisible to him through resigned usage. She unwound her legs and got out of the Jeep, beckoning for him to follow. And so, hand in hand, they walked up to the cave.

They had both known something of its history, and that of its first discoverer, the Abbé Gaston de Bonnard; that it represented his last, most enigmatic and potentially most exciting find — and yet, frustratingly, incomplete. Domingo had filled in details that they had not known, especially about de Bonnard's little-appreciated early years as an explorer in the Western Desert, and some of what he'd found out in his own researches had made their hair stand on end.

In an age when so many sites had been wasted, despoiled by slapdash trophy hunting, de Bonnard's digs were ahead of their time. They were bywords for accuracy, meticulous documentation and uncompromising thoroughness. Souris Saint-Michel seemed like just another expression of this approach. When de Bonnard passed through a site he was like a plague of locusts, so that there was nothing — *nothing* — left for later excavators to pick over. But Souris Saint-Michel, his swansong, just might have been the exception.

De Bonnard's long life had indeed been touched by greatness. Born in 1769, the twenty-year-old seminary student had weathered the French revolution by working at the *Jardin des Plantes* in Paris with the dashing but eccentric zoological genius Etienne Geoffroy Saint-Hilaire. In later life de Bonnard had briefly served in the parish of Saint-Rogatien, and Domingo suspected that it had been he who had named the village square in Geoffroy's honor.

Like his mentor, de Bonnard had been part of the scientific expedition that Napoleon abandoned in Egypt after the Battle of the Nile in 1800. As Geoffroy had spent the years of his exile describing Nile crocodiles and conceiving ever crazier castles of theoretical zoology, de Bonnard had become an explorer, venturing into the Sahara further than anyone had yet been, into south-eastern Libya, and possibly even as far as the foothills of the Tibesti massif in northern Chad.

His exploration journals — as everything essayed by their writer, models of pitiless accuracy, clarity and deftly wrought detail — made reference to half-buried monuments of indescribable antiquity, and of a size that made modest sandhills of the Great Pyramids. And were any other author but de Bonnard to have described what he'd called *les Prêtres du Sable*, the tall, pale, living guardians of these cyclopean, all-but-abandoned monuments, and who conversed with him in what his friend Champollion assured him was like nothing he'd ever heard so much as biblical Hebrew — nobody would have believed him at all. As it was, few did, and after his return to France, the accounts of his adventures were quietly sidelined, ignored, and then forgotten, except, perhaps, by one or two opium-addled English romantics in search of the antique and the picturesque.

As an almost-retired cleric in 1830, de Bonnard had witnessed Geoffroy's great debates with his old adversary Georges Cuvier, father of paleontology, as yet another revolution closed in. And yet he'd had more than three decades more on this Earth. Souris Saint-Michel had been de Bonnard's last dig. The indefatigable priest finally died in 1866, not more than a week after the field season ended, and before he'd had a chance to compose his thoughts on it into any final, publishable form.

It was believed that this is what he was thinking about while he was climbing a neighbor's apple tree to retrieve its more inaccessible fruits, when he fell out and broke his neck. He was 97.

The composer Camille Saint-Saëns (a particular fan of paleontology) had played the organ at the funeral. The only published report on the site had been a bare summary, cobbled together post mortem by de Bonnard's collaborators. Jack was convinced that there would have been more to say, had de Bonnard not died before the task was complete.

Jack and Jadis talked of de Bonnard and his last dig as they crossed the beach, walked into the woods on the other side, and wound their way up a muddy, winding track that took them up an increasingly steep slope.

With each step, Jadis felt that another part of her old self had fallen away, and that she was climbing out of a dream. Or, more pertinently, that she had finally come out of some extended rehabilitation. And so as with one part of her mind she ran through de Bonnard's jousts with antiquity, a film of her own past was spooling in the background, until, fading in the bright light of a new sun, the harsh colors of pain and poignancy shriveled away to leave a comforting sepia, as if it had all happened a long time ago, and to someone else.

She could not remember the accident itself, and thought she never would, except perhaps in dreams of vertiginous horror that made her scream in the night and roll over to lose herself in Jack's embrace.

She had no memory of the first week, mercifully, in which her body, bruised and broken, still had to fight the horrific, raging inflammation caused by the sudden rupture of her uterus and the consequent brutal injection of masses of fetal tissue into her bloodstream. And in which she had nearly died — twice. On the second occasion her heart had stopped for a minute and a half.

Her memories of the first six months were patchy. She could never be sure, when she'd tried to recall them, whether they were genuine traces of that dark time itself, or only synthetic impressions her mind had created from things that Marjorie MacLennane had said later, because she had demanded to know: and because Jack had been too beside himself with pain and rage to tell her himself.

All she knew she could remember was the pain; in her chest, where she'd broken several ribs, two of which had punctured a lung; and in her right shoulder, which had been wrenched apart and had had to be pinned. She felt it still, sometimes, as a dull ache, especially on damp winter mornings. And, most of all, in her lower abdomen, where she felt her soul had been torn out and burned in front of her waking eyes.

What she did not know at the time was how, when she had been in intensive care, Marjorie had moved into Jack and Jadis' Chesterton flat and camped out on the sofa, because she felt that Jack had become quite impossible and needed to be looked after. He had tried to be strong, tried to hide his grief and fear, but when he no longer could—when he came into the department with tears constantly running down his face, whether he wanted them or not, and no matter how hard he'd worked to check them—Roger had asked Marjorie to take him home and get a doctor and a bag full of sedatives.

Neither did she know what the trauma surgeon had told Marjorie: that given the scale of her injuries, it was a miracle that Jadis had not died. Indeed, had she not been a very young woman in good physical shape, she certainly would have done. And Marjorie had kept the obstetrician's news to herself, for a very long time, that although Jadis' burst and shredded uterus would heal itself in time, she would, almost certainly, never be able to sustain another pregnancy.

A year after the accident she was living with Roger and Marjorie while Jack moved their home to France and set up the site at Saint-Rogatien. Although she would always be more grateful than she could possibly express to the MacLennanes, she pined for Jack terribly, to the extent that Marjorie felt that she should just go, to start work on Saint-Rogatien. "What that young woman needs is something to *do*," Marjorie had said, and being a do-er herself, she reasoned that activity would be the best medicine.

When Jack met her off the plane at Blagnac, he'd had a four-month-old golden retriever puppy riding shotgun, its ears too huge for its face, its tongue hanging out in a great, guileless clownish grin.

"Fairbanks, meet Jadis," he'd said: "Jadis, meet Fairbanks. He'll be your Guardian Angel." She didn't know which of them to hug first.

And so it had been: therapy, and very effective, but therapy nonetheless, which implies that a state of full health has yet to be achieved. But now she had come through. She had completed the course. The dig at Saint-Rogatien had done its work, and it was now time to live.

But there was one part of her rehabilitation in which neither Marjorie nor Saint-Rogatien could help, and in which she was initially completely on her own. This deficiency hit her every time she woke in the night, over the first two and a half years, doubled up in agonizing spasms, wracked with cramps; and when she was forced to endure intense, bloody periods at irregular intervals, each followed by bombazine-shrouded processions of loss, guilt and grief for the still-small pulse that she would never feel again.

As a side effect, she had completely gone off sex. Or, to be more specific, she liked the idea of sex, the desire she always had for Jack as a comforting and reassuring presence, but she found that she couldn't face it as a physical reality. Pain itself was sufficient deterrent for many months, but even when that had faded, she felt that it would be too uncomfortable, for her, and for Jack: perhaps from fear, from concern for Jack — or perhaps from a sense of guilt, that had she not been so foolish as to have driven to Addenbrookes herself when she felt she might miscarry, and had met... had met... well, then none of this would have happened.

At its basest, she was concerned that she'd never be able to relax; to lose herself in the act; and if that happened, she thought, it would only set things back even more. In the meantime, therefore, her body had decreed a complete moratorium, in the hope that, one day, things would just sort themselves out on their own.

But the very worst thing of all, the thing that most sapped her confidence, was that she felt she simply could not possibly share these concerns with Jack. If she'd tried, she knew he'd understand, but he had been through so much on her account, had stood by her through all this, that she desperately didn't want him to be hurt, or, shamefully (she felt) that she was unable to expose her own feelings of guilt to wider scrutiny.

During the day, then, her therapy was Saint-Rogatien, its organization, its direction, and the ordering of its people — Avi, Domingo and all the rest. During the night, her therapy was Jack who was, ever so gradually, coaxing her terrified body back into the light. Now that the weight of Saint-Rogatien had been lifted, she felt that she had been healed further, and she could at last start to give something back.

The very last slope was the steepest of all. Jack scrambled up to find that it had been the rampart of a wide, flat lawn before the cave mouth. The short, springy sward had presumably grown over the mass of soil and cave sediment that de Bonnard had removed in 1866. Jack reached down to pull Jadis up, too, and they stood, arms around each other, facing into the cave.

"This is it," said Jack.

"How much do you know about it?" Jadis asked, as they walked towards it, crossed the threshold and she began to explore. Jack hung back, as if to watch her reaction. The cave was surprisingly small, hardly more than an *abri*, a rock shelter—no more than fifteen feet across, twelve feet high at its tallest, and twenty feet from its lip to the back wall, now seated in shadow.

"Not as much as I'd like. I've never had the time to follow it up. One thing just led to another. But after we're done here, I thought we'd go into Aurignac, meet Balthazar, and..." It was then that Jadis stopped dead, in the middle of the cave, looking at the back wall with the same expression of awe and revelation as if she'd been shopping in Leclerc and looked up to find that the checkout clerk was the Archangel Gabriel.

"Oh, Jack. Dearest Jack. It's.... it's the *wall*. Isn't it?" He rushed towards her, scrambling over the slightly rough, bare floor, embracing her from behind and gazing, over her shoulder, at the pinkish-grey tympanum that formed the back wall of the cave. Although it sparkled with tiny crystals of flowstone, it was otherwise utterly flat and featureless.

"I know. When I first saw it... it..." Jack thought back to his own moment of revelation when he'd first climbed to the cave as evening fell, the last rays of the setting Sun striking the back wall directly before he and the cave were plunged into night, and his utter conviction that for all its coating of flowstone, of stalactite, the back wall of the cave was not natural. That someone had put it there.

He explained this now to Jadis, who was now standing right up against the wall, tracing her hands across it, pressing and probing, for all that she might find some hidden mechanism, a catch that would open a door through the wall and into another world. "Caves just don't end so abruptly, she muttered, almost to herself, "they just... don't." She returned to Jack's side so they could both stare at it together.

In truth, Jack was relieved that Jadis had felt so strongly about the wall. That was one of the reasons he'd brought her here. For when he'd first seen this cave a few weeks earlier, his natural empathy with the landscape had been blown off course so strongly that he'd almost been knocked to his knees with the shock of it. Perhaps, he thought, I've been doing this too long, and too alone, without calibration, without consultation, without collaboration. But now that Jadis had felt it too, he was convinced, more than ever, that his first impressions had been wholly correct. And if the wall had been put there on purpose, that meant...

"...there has to be something behind it, Jack. Has to be. I'll hire in some sounding gear. Magnetometers, ground-penetrating radar, perhaps even shot-blasters and seismographs and..."

Jack smiled. Jadis had opened her birthday present and was already taking charge of the next field season. "But can we have some lunch first?" he said. "I'm starving!"

Balthazar Desplaines met them in the bar of *Le Cerf Blanc*, holding out a *kir* for each of them and smiling from ear to ear. "Welcome Jack, *enchanté*, Jadis!" he exclaimed: "please, take a seat, and I'll get a menu," he continued, gesticulating to the barman.

Desplaines had been an aerospace engineer from Toulouse who had taken a stupendously generous early-retirement package from Aérospatiale, bought a small but exquisite town house in Aurignac, and devoted himself to his hobbies—gastronomy and antiquity. In pursuit of these twin goals he shuttled between the bar at *Le Cerf Blanc* and Aurignac's small museum of antiquities, which, despite the fame of the locality, was usually open only by appointment. When it became apparent that Desplaines spent more time there than the official *guardien* (who was often woken up at odd hours when Desplaines felt he just *had* to look at *this* Gravettian point or *that* Solutréan flake), the town awarded him the honorary curatorship, gave him the key and said that he could come and go whenever he liked.

When Jack had first moved to Saint-Rogatien, while Jadis was still convalescing, Balthazar had been one of his first visitors. Jack had met him for the first time, albeit briefly, on his pre-thesis scouting trip, and, like all professional archeologists, appreciated the value of local knowledge, even if amateur or (as it sometimes was) eccentric. Indeed, before Jadis had arrived to take on the full-time direction of *Le Dig*, Jack had found Balthazar a pillar of strength as a local fixer, relying on him to secure the services of everything from builders and plumbers (the farmhouse had needed a lot of renovation) to earthmoving contractors and even on one occasion, a helicopter. Six years on they were firm friends. Desplaines, long divorced and with no children of his own, clucked over

Jack and Jadis as if they were the offspring he'd never had. The first time she'd seen him, in neatly pressed slacks and a striped blazer, Jadis thought he looked like Roger MacLennane would have done had he tried to impersonate Maurice Chevalier, and this prospect always made her smile.

Lunch was a long affair, and merry. As he always did, Desplaines rained old-fashioned flattery on Jadis, remarking expansively that he thought she'd never looked lovelier. Jadis put her hand on his and told him of Jack's birthday gift. And then, of course, they started talking about the *abri* of Souris Saint-Michel and the mystery of de Bonnard's last dig, and that they might re-open it, starting again from where the great man had left off. As they talked, Desplaines' expression clouded and became serious, conspiratorial.

"Do you know what happened to de Bonnard's field notes from Souris? His collections from that last season?"

I always assumed they'd have ended up in Paris, at the *Muséum*," said Jack. "I wish I'd had the chance to go and see…"

"Ah yes, the *Muséum National d'Histoire Naturelle*, in memory of his old mentor, Geoffroy. And so they did. Or," he tapped one finger on his long, beaked nose, "… they *might*."

"Balthazar, don't tease," laughed Jadis.

"But not at all, my dear! Of course de Bonnard sent every scrap of paper and every chip of stone back to Paris, as soon as he'd completed any project. He was always such a stickler for accuracy and protocol — never leaving any loose ends — that I always assumed that he'd done the same for anything he'd found at Souris Saint-Michel, as soon as he'd found it.

"But when Jack told me you were coming today, I thought some more… and it occurred to me that the good Abbé had still been working on Souris Saint-Michel when he died. He'd been based here at Aurignac at the time, and he hadn't finished with the collections yet. So I did a little digging of my own, in my little museum here, and, *quelle surprise*…"

Jack and Jadis looked at Balthazar in amazement.

"*Oui, mes enfants*," said Balthazar, plainly enjoying the moment of drama and waving to the waiter for the check: "I have a little birthday present of my own to give you, my dearest Jadis. Shall we go and open it?"

What Desplaines had to show them made them giddy with amazement, and he was clearly playing it for all it was worth. After all, it is not every day that an amateur antiquarian, even one as knowledgeable and well connected as he was, found himself in the possession of information that blindsides the world-famous professionals. So, much as he was fond of Jadis and Jack, he relished his moment in the spotlight to the full.

So, first, he showed them the Abbé de Bonnard's very last field journal. They clustered round Desplaines' desk in his small and cluttered office—Jadis in the chair, Jack and Balthazar leaning over her left and right shoulders, the huge cloth-bound ledger before them in a pool of yellow light. The language was, of course, no problem to either Jack or Jadis, who'd lived for so long in *La France Profonde*, but de Bonnard had made it as easy as possible by writing in the clearest, Parisian French, penned in the neatest copperplate.

"I wish every archeologist was as organized as this," said Jadis, clearly recognizing a kindred spirit in the long-dead cleric. But what they read in the measured tones of the blessed Abbé had made them gasp. The very last entry of the field-log for 1866 ran like this:

> The excavations of 1866 at the antediluvian rock shelter known as Souris Saint-Michel have been productive, thank the Lord. However, I feel sure that the present eastern wall of the cave

"That must be the back wall..." said Jack.

> does not represent an autochthonous feature of the present shelter, but is, in all probability, the result of emplacement of travertine subsequent to the cave's formation.

Jadis was open-mouthed. "Dearest Jack, you were right, not that I ever doubted you, of course, but..." Flustered, she pushed her increasingly disordered hair away from her face, so she could read more.

> Such secondary emplacement might indeed be inferred from the stratigraphy of the cave floor, which dips very strongly towards the east, as if directed beneath any secondarily emplaced stalactitic formation.

"Amazing," said Jack. "I never noticed any such dipping."

"That's the Abbé for you," replied Deplaines. "I expect most of the present cave floor is overburden from the 1866 season, which the Abbé had replaced and leveled, to protect the productive strata from disturbance..."

"... leaving them mothballed and ready for the next season," continued Jack...

"... which never came." concluded Desplaines. "But how typically tidy of the good Abbé! I expect that when you remove the overlying sediment, you'll see it all just as it was almost a hundred and fifty years ago, not a speck of dust out of place." They followed De Bonnard's trail, like hounds, to their end.

Should the Lord in his infinite grace and mercy preserve me for another season, I shall inquire about the purchase of suitable equipment, in order that the integrity of the eastern wall might be tested. For if the wall is a secondary feature as I now suppose, it follows that further voids might lie behind it. To summarize—I am convinced that the cave as originally formed was much more extensive than it now appears. Only the Lord knows what secrets lie behind the eastern wall, and, were I not to be chastised by my presumption, I should also care to ponder that selfsame subject.

The text ended there.

"He was, indeed, chastised for his presumption, and soon," said Balthazar.

"How so?" asked Jack.

"Looking at the date of this memoir, and what we know of his life, he was killed the same day that he wrote this. I imagine he got up from his desk — possibly in this very room where you are sitting, Jadis — went straight to his neighbor's orchard, and fell out of the avenging tree. What you are looking at is the very last thing de Bonnard ever wrote."

Jack and Jadis looked as Desplaines in astonishment and awe.

"But wait—there's more," he said. "Come with me." Desplaines hurried them into a dim side-room filled, from floor to ceiling, with cabinets of wide, flat wooden hardwood drawers — the signature furniture of any museum collection — for all that these looked stained with antiquity and neglect. He turned on a single, dusty bulb that had the effect of making the room appear even darker and dingier. His eyes squinted and scanned the labels until one met with his recognition.

"Truly, I'm amazed I had never come across this one before. But there's always something more to find, even in a small museum like this. Look!" He pulled out a drawer marked 'SSM 1866'. "I had no idea what it meant, Jack," he said, "until your phone call made me put two and two together." The drawer squeaked and protested on rusted runners as he pulled it out. Jack and Jadis looked inside.

Jadis felt she was being sucked into a vortex, her knees that they might buckle, and she had to gasp for breath. For what she saw, arranged in a muddle of old newspapers and pasteboard boxes, was a collection of twenty-four Remillardian artefacts, each one of the palm-sized flint polygons as pristine as the day it had been knapped.

"There are five more drawers, just like this one," said Desplaines. "About a hundred and fifty pieces in all. And all come from the 1866 season at Souris."

"… no wonder de Bonnard never described them," said Jack, "like us, he wouldn't have known what to make of them."

"Balthazar," said Jadis, "did you say a hundred and fifty, and all from that one, tiny cave?"

"Indeed so, my dear Jadis."

"But that's incredible," Jadis said, the excitement in her voice rising with each syllable. "You know how much sediment we shifted at Saint-Rogatien over six years. You saw it, Balthazar. It was vast. And yet in all that time we found ninety-three Remillardian artefacts. Ninety-three! And de Bonnard finds half as much again in a small cave in a single season—and nobody *knew* this?"

"Apparently not, Jadis. I agree, *c'est incroyable*, but there it is. And now it's your turn. The Abbé de Bonnard was taken from this Earth by the Almighty and his neighbor's apple tree. But you're still here, and here, I think, is your destiny. For if you and Jack and the shade of the good de Bonnard are correct, who knows what might lie beyond the eastern wall?" Jadis gasped, looked at Desplaines with open-mouthed wonder and joy, and flung her arms around him.

"Oh thank you, Balthazar—what a wonderful, *wonderful* present!" Jack just laughed, all tension gone. "Balthazar, after that performance," he said, "dinner is on *us*."

Much later, after another artery-challenging dose of Gascon cuisine, Jack and Jadis lay in their suite, the only light from a pale yellow streetlamp, some way off, filtered through the blinds. They exchanged not a word. They didn't need to, for each knew that the other was thinking over the shattering revelations of the day.

Jack lay on his back, looking up at the ceiling, imagining a Remillardian artefact in each imperfection, each shadowing of the plaster. What further wonders lay beyond that mysterious wall at Souris Saint-Michel? Jadis lay with her left arm flung over Jack, her hair spread over his upper body like a cloak of invisibility, her face shadowed in thought.

All of a sudden it occurred to Jack that they could all be wrong—Jadis, de Bonnard and himself—that the cave wall was a natural structure after all, perfectly solid, with nothing further to discover behind it.

Jadis caught his thought. "If that's the case, Jack," she said, "then I'd like another birthday present."

"Hmm? What did you have in mind?"

"I'm not sure," she replied: "but I expect I'll think of something." And with that she traced her fingers from his chest, smoothing them over his belly and stroking him, her touch lighter than a breath. He stiffened in a second, and became so painfully hard that he bit his lip. He felt that were a passing butterfly to flap its wings close by, he'd detonate. Then, very softly, she said something he hadn't heard for a very long time, not since their very first visit to Saint-Rogatien on their honeymoon, their last night at the *Sanglier D'Or* just off the village square, with the warm wind through the open window making sails of the curtains, so many painful long eons ago, and before so many things had happened.

"I want you, Jack," she said. "Very much. Please, now."

"Jadis — are you...?"

Her voice suddenly switched from coy gentleness to a mixture of school-marmish asperity and heartbreakingly painful, imperative need.

"*Please*, Jack. I need you. I want you. Now." He turned over onto his elbows and knees as she moved underneath him, gripping his shoulders and gasping, panting, "now, Jack. I said, *now!*" And he was fully inside her, in a hot embrace of liquid velvet. "More, Jack, more" she begged, raising her legs and crossing them over his back, almost under his shoulder blades, squeezing him into her. As she did this, her whole body started to vibrate, to hum like telephone wires in a gale, each one throbbing to a different subharmonic, some just audible, but many well below the range of human hearing. The vibrations built and amplified and reinforced one another. She dug her nails into Jack's shoulders as if afraid that the uncontrollable, random shivering might sweep her away, and with one last, terrible spasm, arched her back towards Jack, driving him fully inside her. Jack burst inside her, and they collapsed like spent fireworks.

The entire episode had lasted seventeen seconds.

They lay, panting, in much the same position as they had before, both soaked in sweat, Jack on his back, his head full of wheeling stars. After a pause, she raised herself on her elbows, looking down at him with crossed-eyed intensity, and her silent tears began to flow until she could no longer control them. Jack enfolded her in his arms and cradled her against him like a small child until the tears had ebbed, and she had fallen asleep.

It had been sudden, cathartic, he thought, but it had been a strange day, and—for him—a little frightening. But, stroking her hair that had spread over both of them like a silk blanket, he could see that she was, at last, after all these long, painful years, fully whole, and at peace.

Jadis, wrapped in his arms, felt like she'd turned into a fluffy pink cloud sailing off into a perfectly clear blue sky, over a landscape of mountains and summits that had once, inexplicably, filled her with dread.

She tried—though not very hard—to remember when she'd first fallen in love with Jack, but she could not. She was vaguely aware that there might have been a time before that, but the point was moot, as she'd been a completely different person. In any case, she thought, the only moment worth thinking about was now, the continuous present, in which she was secure in the arms of this man, the moment that had, for her, persisted since the beginning of time, and would endure for all eternity.

But it was something else entirely that filled her mind, just before she slept. It was something that Balthazar had shown her, just as they were leaving his little museum, almost as an afterthought. Something shoved into the back of one of the drawers of Remillardian polygons, unlabelled, without provenance. It was a sculpture of a hugely pregnant woman, with enormous breasts and thighs, and yet faceless. It was made of ivory but stained the color of teak, and was the size of a plum. There were traces of red ocher on the woman's head, as if she'd had red hair. Balthazar seemed to make a point of showing the statuette to Jadis when Jack's back was turned.

"I think it came from Souris in that last season, judging from its staining and patination," Balthazar had said, "but as there are no other records of it, it must stay in limbo." He held it out to Jadis, in his palm. Balthazar must have noticed the moisture in her eyes, then, her bittersweet smile, because he closed his fingers round it, and, turning to place it back in the drawer, said, very quietly, "Jadis, I'm so sorry—please forgive me. I should have realized. After all you've been through."

"Please, Balthazar," she reassured him. "It all happened to someone else. A long time ago."

Chapter 20. Recapitator

Tethys Ocean, Earth, *c.* 55,680,000 years ago

Hurled headlong flaming from th'ethereal sky
With hideous ruin and combustion down
To bottomless perdition
John Milton — *Paradise Lost*

The details of the fall — that is, how he felt about it, as he fell, for each excruciating microsecond of it — would have been lost to him, had they not been replayed to him later, by his AI core. When the details were too grisly, even for such a seasoned soldier as himself, his AI continued nonetheless. It had been compelled to tell him, it said. It had no choice. And neither, it added, had he. But for now, it said, what it called an 'executive summary' would suffice.

His viewpoint was from beach level, looking upwards. As he looked, he saw the tree whence he'd fallen (was pushed) and the palisade of broken, fire-sharpened trunks that surrounded it. Something appeared to be impaled on one of these stumps, about four meters from the ground. He homed in on that something, and realized with a detachment that would have shocked him, had he been in any other state, that it was the body of a man, naked, the trunk piercing it at around crotch level and passing more or less straight through, emerging through the neck. The force of the impaling must have pushed the head clean off, like thumbs flipping the lid from a beer bottle.

What had happened to the head, then?

Ah, me. That explains my particular point of view. He blinked, slowly, deliberately. The grisly spectacle before him darkened, then shuttered back into view.

He took a deep breath.

Very good. But if that is the case (and I have no reason to doubt it) then why aren't I... dead?

As he watched, the headless body reached for the trunk above it and, grasping with both hands, pulled itself free. To be sure, it left a slurry of internal organs in slowly dripping gobbets, snagged along the ridges of the trunk as the body hauled itself upwards. But probably not as much goo as one might have expected, in the circumstances. With a quite disconcerting agility (so he thought), the body swung, hand over hand, down and around the trunk, using the outstretched legs as counter-weights. As it corkscrewed down, Ruxhana caught glimpses of its groin. What had been a hideous, gaping hole when the body started its descent had quite healed over by the time it had landed, confidently, feet first, on the sand, and had started to march towards him. It slowly grew in his visual field until all he could see was its feet. There followed a mild dis-orientation as he was lifted, flipped over, and with hardly more than a grind of bones and a squishing noise of almost obscene understatement, he was atop the tower of... himself.

Calmly, he walked back to the beach camp, where Xalomé was wait-ing. He'd tried to query his AI core as he'd walked, but his brain must have been out of whack, for every question he framed became mangled in the asking, the mental equivalent of trying to peel bananas while wearing thick woollen mittens. His AI was, perhaps, aware of this, and even suffering from the same malaise, because it could only respond with general expressions of sympathy and a single coherent phrase.

Ongoing transformations.

Xalomé stood up as he approached. Her eyes were wide and full of concern, but she remained some distance away, as if she were afraid he might attack her. After all, he now knew, he could not die. He could re-venge himself on her, again and again, until all the stars went cold.

"Ruxie... it was the only way I could... the only way to explain. I had to show you. Physically. Otherwise, you'd have never have believed me. Ruxie? Are you listening?"

"Hmm?" He felt cold, composed, remote. He felt a headache coming on and his knees go wobbly. He climbed on to the platform and col-lapsed on to the bed. "I could murder a drink," he said, before he passed out.

When he awoke it was night. His first sensation was the scent of grilled fish, followed by the spit and crackle of oil falling into the flames. He sat up slowly, and crawled to the edge of the bed. On the beach be-low the platform, Xalomé squatted next to the fire pit, with two freshly caught sea bass toasting on sticks. Her hair was tied back into a single ponytail, and her back was towards him, three-quarters in the flames' silhouette. He could see enough to know that she was bared to the waist, her sarong tied as a loincloth. He was relieved to see that she had the full and normal complement of breasts. Without turning round, she spoke to him.

"Supper's ready."

He tottered down to the beach, sitting full on the ground next to her, a little way from the fire, towards the sea.

They ate in pregnant silence, neither daring to catch the eye of the other. But as he stripped the last of the succulent flesh from the bones, and the fire behind them died to crimson embers, he felt a compliment was due.

"Thank you, Xalomé. That was delicious."

"Don't mention it. Least I could do, really, after... well, after this morning." She seemed subdued, dignified, but not guilty – an entirely different person from the hoyden of twelve hours earlier. As if she'd aged half a century. She reached over to gather his palm-frond plate. Her mind might have moved on, but her body was just the same, just as youthful. She must have sensed him staring, then, because she said, with some sharpness – "look up."

And he did.

What he saw was nothing like the skies of Earth. Most of heaven's vault was quite dark, punctuated only by the most meager scatter of stars. But ahead of them, deep in the west, and yet filling a third of the sky, was the Galaxy, in all its spiraled, dust-laned, electric blue, pearly pink, fiery orange, snowy-white majesty.

He stood up, then, and walked into the greater darkness along the beach, so he could see it with yet more clarity, as if he just couldn't get enough of it. He sat down abruptly on the sand, and then lay down at full length, looking up. Now, as at no other time in his life, not even when he was a small kit yet newly acquainted with vision, had he such a potent sensation when lying on the ground that he was stuck to a small ball, careening through space.

"Does the Tesseractrix really have twenty-seven legs?" he asked.

"Yes. What you see in this continuum is merely one part of an M-dimensional..."

"... 'relativistic manifold?'"

"That's right. Just like me." And there she was, lying next to him, turned towards him. He could see her curves picked out in the starshine, but brightest of all were her eyes, their moistened gleam reflected in the curves of her cheeks, full and smiling.

"This is an Xspace, isn't it?" he asked.

"Yes," she said, resting her left hand lightly on his chest. "It is. But that doesn't make it any less real... any less real than it seems to be." She lay closer, next to him, her head resting beneath the crook of his chin, her hair, now loosened, spreading over them both like a blanket.

"It's time, now, isn't it, Xalomé? Time to go?"

"Yes. Almost. We have just one more night together. And I have so many things I have to tell you. That's always been the trouble, Ruxie, even... even back then, when you were younger, at Xandarga Station. I just never knew how to put things, so either they came out all wrong, or I didn't even try, and in the end I felt I was just using you. I'm so sorry."

A picture of his last night at the barracks flashed before him, no more than a memory of a sour saffron stench of betrayal, superimposed on this magnificent siege of stars.

"That's far away now, Xalomé. It feels like another life, like it happened to someone else. Like *everything* happened to someone else. I've changed, I think. Who am I, Xalomé?"

"Don't worry," she said, hugging him. "Whatever happens, you'll always be Ruxie. Deep inside."

"But that's just it. What is happening? To me?"

She sat up, then, a silhouette against the Galaxy.

"I guess I should start at the beginning," she said. She told him then of her own beginnings, and of the Drove, and of how the task had been given to her of finding a species, raising that species to transcendence, in order to commit a kind of sin, a heresy, a genocide — of destroying the Drove, the work of her species, the heart of her own existence, so that the Universe itself might be saved from premature extinction.

Some of this she'd told him before, and a little of the rest he'd guessed. But he heard it all now, and, for the first time, he understood.

"At first I thought I'd found that species — yours, Ruxie — and that would have been a marvelous irony, as well as being highly convenient." She laughed, drily, in her throat. She grasped his hand again, as if she, this almost godlike being, to him — required his human reassurance. "But something told me that your kind wasn't quite right. Almost, but not quite."

"But why... then.... why all this?"

"Oh, Ruxie, my existence seems to be a catalog of near-misses, doesn't it? But you're aware, I'm sure, of the history of your species. You're mammalian, and primates: your lemuroid ancestors emerged from the jungles of the Northern Tethys less than fifteen million years ago."

"Out of the shadow of the great lizards," he added. "Their shapes haunt the walls of our dreams, our earliest legends. The reason for their disappearance is the stuff of myth. Some of our more ancient traditions — long before the Empire — say that they were punished by the

Great Old Ones for some transgression. All superstition. These days we think it was some kind of cosmic accident. But what an accident! Without it we might never have evolved."

She was silent for a spell, as if he'd unwittingly touched a nerve, a subject she'd have loved to have discussed, but concerning which she felt that the right moment had not yet arrived.

"But how far you've come, in such a short time," she said. "From the jungles of a small planet to rulers of the Galaxy in the blink of an eye, really! But where was I? Oh yes. Even despite all that achievement—that potential—you're not the savior species I've been looking for. But you can help me make it, Ruxie. Evolve it. For the species will emerge from this planet, I know it: and from, I think, the primate order. Really, Ruxie, we two look very like them already, and with time, we—you—your species shall converge on that form."

"We... shall?" He had a fleeting, nightmarish vision of her as he'd seen her a few nights previously; almost hairless, with those strange, round eyes, and not enough breasts.

"Yes, but *we* are not that form. The form that we... the one we need. Our task—your task—is to find them, to evolve them. To shape their destiny. To transcend. To destroy." She paused, sent out a long sigh into the evening air, and sank down again, next to him. He detected a scent then, of peace, and satisfaction.

Of closure.

The Galaxy stood above them both, expectant.

"There now—I've said it. Not very hard, really, when it came down to it."

"My task? So that's it? Evolution? It's... well, more than one can do in a lifetime, or a dozen, or a million lifetimes. Isn't it?"

"You will have all those lifetimes, Ruxie. As many lifetimes as you'll need. And you'll have help, too..."

"My AI core?"

"Oh, that! The poor lamb! I had to upgrade it to sentience. It didn't much like it. It complained even more than you did when I did all those things to you. I think it went a bit barmy, frankly, for a while. Started jabbering on about the difficulty of making decisions without sufficient information, and sentience having too many free parameters, and NP-completeness, and shoes, and ships, and sealing-wax, and bands playing different tunes, and eclipses, and whether you could breathe on the dark side of the Moon, and, for all I know, whether pigs have wings. And then

it got *really* unhinged. I confess I had to give it a rather stiff talking-to."
She giggled.

He laughed, then, a full, roaring belly-laugh, a laugh like he could
hardly remember having laughed, of relief and resolution and joy, and
she joined in, and she rolled on top of him and silenced him with her lips
on his, and pulled away, her whole face a silhouette above him. "The
silly old thing couldn't really cope. So I had to merge it with you. You
haven't had much trouble from it lately, I hope?"

"No, I haven't. Funny, it hadn't occurred to me..." and, in truth, his
AI had spoken to him ever more rarely, of late, and in tones that were
more delphic than truly helpful. At the same time, he felt more confident, more sure of himself in everything he did. He remembered his
calmness, even when confronted by his own decapitation.

Ongoing transformations.

He and his AI core had become one. The person he now was — the
body he now inhabited — was greater than the sum of its parts.

"Good. That's good to know," she said. She rolled off him, on to her
side, her back towards him. He rolled into her, so that they were like two
spoons in a drawer. His left arm was beneath her, trapped. With his free
hand he stroked her hair. It shimmered in the light of a four hundred
billion stars.

"May I ask you something, Xalomé?"

"Of course, Ruxie. Of course." Her left hand grasped his, resting on
her curve of her right shoulder, cooling in the night air. He thought he
heard it, in her voice, something like a catch, a sob, hastily stifled.

"Why me? Why not have chosen... oh, I don't know, any other Admiral, or any one of my sisters, or my mother, or even, while we're about it,
my old barrack-mate, Ko Handor Raelle? How do you know?"

It was a long time before she spoke. Before she did, she turned in his
arms until she faced him. Her eyes were wide, as wide as if they were
confronting all the chasms of the void or her own ultimate extinction.
Wide with terror.

"Oh, Xalomé — I didn't mean...." She sank down next to him, once
more, so that he could no longer see his face.

"Don't worry, Ruxie. Not your fault. This is it though, isn't it? The
question I knew you'd ask, and which I've been trying to dodge, always
knowing that I'd have to confront it, one day." He encircled her in his
arms. He could feel her breath and her heart beating inside her. She
swallowed.

"Well, one reason is that you owe me — us."

"How so?"

"It's a funny thing, fate. Destiny. For us, I mean, the Drovers, who see space and time rather differently from... well, from the way you do. But I was given this task about sixteen million years ago, or thereabouts, when the Drove invaded the Oort cloud of a double-star system, consuming the smaller of the two stars and pitching a rain of cometary debris inwards, towards the primary. We didn't mean it to happen. We tried to stop them, but we were overwhelmed.

"I didn't discover it until later—actually, it was one of our Drove Elders who told me—that the impacts plunged one of the planets into a biotic crisis, rewriting the course of its evolution. Extinguishing one set of organisms—the great lizards—so that the potential of another could be realized. And, irony of ironies, that planet..."

"... was the Earth. It was the Earth, wasn't it, Xalomé?"

She hugged him closer. "If it wasn't for our... well, our mistake, Ruxie, our incapacity, your species would still be up trees, dodging dinosaurs. There'd be no Galactic Empire. And there'd be no you."

"Xalomé..."

"But before you ask me... as I know you will..." her voice seemed choked with tears. "Why you, Ruxie, in particular..."

"Really, Xalomé, there's no need. I don't think so. Not really."

"No... need?"

"No. I think I can work it out now, for myself. Because all you'll be able to say is that I'll just have to trust your judgment on this; that you just know, without having sufficient information. A hunch. Instinct. And I do. Trust your judgment, that is. Completely. So you'll have to trust mine. I know what I have to do, now. And how to do it."

"Ruxie... you... why?

Ruxie could hardly have articulated his conviction more completely. That no matter how much information you have at your disposal, you will always want more; no matter how thickly the data stream in, it will never be enough. It's an urge—a human urge—for safety, for a certainty that can never be achieved.

His mind was cast back to his cadet days, a hot classroom in a yellow-brown tropical afternoon, an instructor waffling on about elementary statistics. Amid the drone, the instructor said one thing that had stuck in his mind: no matter how fancy your statistical technique, no matter how many pretty graphs and charts you generate, it all, always comes down, in the end, to a judgment based on probability. In the end, always in the end, you have to act on inner conviction.

A hunch.

Instinct.

It was something he wished he'd remembered in his last engagement as an Admiral, when he chose to wait and see why seventy-eight thousand cruisers and destroyers had simultaneously switched their positions, rather than doing what his instinct demanded—to get the hell out and save his fleet from destruction. He would do this task for two reasons, then, and two reasons only. The first was out of duty. The second was out of love.

"Look up at me, Xalomé," he said. She did, and her wide eyes were full of supplication, and gratitude, and relief, and a whole host of other less definable emotions, all mixed up together. Her lips were full and slightly parted, and Ruxie kissed her, and did not stop for a long while. They made love, then, on the beach, in the dark beneath the wheeling nebula; lovemaking of a kind remembered and cherished ever after in its totality, even long after the particular details have faded.

The next day dawned, overcast and gray. Ruxhana stood in the skiff, his few belongings around his feet, as it was about to pull away from the shore, towards *Shelly's Shagpad*—and after that, who could tell? All Ruxhana knew was that he'd know it when he saw it.

Xalomé stood on the sand not two meters away, though it might as well have been two million light years, her toes lapped by the fringes of the waves, hair and sarong billowing in the chill wind, hugging herself for warmth. She wore an expression of such desolation that he just wanted to step out of the skiff, right then, and hold her in his arms again.

"Xalomé..."

"No, Ruxie, not now. It's time to go. Good luck!" She tried her best to smile.

"I love you, Xalomé."

"Oh, go on with you, you silly man."

The skiff pulled away, and as her form diminished in the distance, he saw her turn, and walk up the beach towards the belt of trees. As he watched, he saw her climb onto his palm-log platform, turn once again, and wave. As far as he could make out, she kept on waving until the island was no more than a thin line on the horizon, almost lost in a cloud bank.

She managed to hold herself in until *Shelly's Shagpad* was lost from view, carrying Ruxhana Fengen Kraa on his eternal and uncertain voyage, and with him, all her—their—hopes.

No sooner had he gone, however, than she crumpled onto the palm-log deck, crying uncontrollably. Her tears kept on flowing, on and on, making runnels and braids and deltas down her brown cheeks, until she began to wonder whether they would ever stop. They did, eventually. Of course they did, replaced at first by immense, wracking sobs, in which her lungs and guts heaved. She managed to pitch herself back onto the sand before she threw up, and after that, she felt much better. Washed out, but with some sort of equilibrium restored, however fragile.

Baryonic matter.

He had said that it would be hard, and so had she expected it to be. Very hard indeed. But he had said nothing of its emotional intensity; nothing of all the guilt, the backwash from playing with the hearts and minds of these creatures. He had said nothing about the dangers of getting involved. Perhaps he'd had no idea himself.

Or perhaps he had, but feared that had she known of this—the awful, gnawing pain of it—then she would have refused the task, or, worse, have agreed to it only half-heartedly, forever looking for a let-out clause, an excuse to stop, with the increased risk of failure that this would have entailed. And if one thing was certain, this was a task that must not be allowed to fail.

The Continuum depended on it. On her.

As she calmed herself, she was only dimly aware that her body was changing into the form in which she felt most comfortable; into which she often reposed when deeply relaxed. Much of the fur on her body melted away; all but two of her breasts were resorbed; and her eyes changed their shape.

The transformation was helped along as she thought of him again, at their first meeting in the ski lodge, and in many other Xspaces afterwards, in which he had trained her. And more than trained—forged, quenched, broken, tamed. How she had bucked and rebelled at first, after the initial shock of her selection. But it was—could only ever have been—as the rage of a storm against a massif of billion-year-old granite. Solomon had always been calm, kindly, guiding: as well as irresistible, commanding, resolute. She had fallen for him as surely as as Ruxhana had fallen out of that tree, over there.

And he had loved her, in return.

She recalled, now, the time when, almost out of her mind with terror, with uncertainty, at the magnitude of the task she faced, alone, he had stood before her, in the bright north light of the grand salon of the ski lodge, bent down, kissed her eyelids, and told her that everything would be all right.

They had been in this form too, then. Of course they had.

She smiled as she remembered it—remembered it all. Her tears dried on her face. She walked down the beach again, to the shore, sloughed her sarong onto the sand and wallowed in the healing surf. The irony was that even were Solomon to have been manipulating her, using her love to secure her devotion to the task, she realized that she did not care. And how did she know that he loved her?

Because he had told her, of course.

Her body, bathed in the waves, went suddenly cold. How could she? How could she have betrayed Solomon, and used Ruxie, all at the same time?

No, not betrayed, he would have said. Do anything, he'd have said, anything to get the job done. Such is a sign of commitment.

Solomon had often told her that he loved her for her passion, for the fact that it fueled her intellect, and her seemingly unerring judgment, the rightness of her instincts.

It was all one, he had said.

But there, surely, he had been wrong.

And, anyway, the job was far too important for anyone, and especially her, to get hung up on notions such as betrayal, when it was in fact nothing of the kind.

"No!" she bellowed into the unfeeling breeze.

"No!" she bawled into the uncomprehending sky.

"No" she screamed, rising from the water, the foam running off her body in white, streaming gouts into the pitiless sea.

She was part of the equation, too: if she could not do this thing and maintain what she felt to be his trust, then it would not be a job worth doing. Solomon had made her, and she would be worthy of his trust. Would be. Must be. And more than that, worthy of his love.

By her own lights.

Whatever it took.

Chapter 21. Priest

Gascony, France, Earth, March, 2032

It was a twilit grotto of enormous height, stretching away farther than any eye could see; a subterraneous world of limitless mystery and horrible suggestion.
H. P. Lovecraft — *The Rats in the Walls*

It had been six months of frenetic activity into which Jadis had poured her heart and soul. And finally, here they all were — Balthazar, Primrose, Faye, Eric, Mathilde, Domingo, Jack and herself — standing on what remained of the sward outside the cave at Souris Saint-Michel (or 'SSM' as it was now universally known among the field crew). The rock drillers were on station at the back wall, and about to make first contact. Jadis had painted a neat red cross on the precise place where, she thought, the sealing wall was at its thinnest.

Much had changed. The immediate landscape around the cave mouth now gave the impression of cramped and coiling industry rather than bucolic calm. The car park on the lakeshore was, more often than not, busy with jeeps and trucks. The forest track had been widened and graded, allowing motor vehicles access to the site. Even so, what with the still-lingering snow and ever-present mud, a helicopter had to be used to bring in some of the bulkier items, such as the twenty-six-foot mobile home that Jack and Jadis would use as a site office and temporary quarters if needed.

The compressor and generator for the rock drill stood close by on the back of a pickup, together with separate generator to drive a water pump, pulling water up from the lake to lay the dust created by the drilling; and a third generator to bring in power for tools, and for the racks of lights that would be needed to illuminate any voids beyond. A trailer bearing eight large cylindrical tanks of LPG supplied fuel for all of them. Cables and pipes snaked in and out of the cave through a tough polythene membrane that had been fixed over the entire entrance. Balthazar's reaction at the transformation spoke for everyone. "If this is a mouse," he said, "it will be a mouse that roars!"

Not that there had been much doubt that there would be something to find. As soon as the dig at Saint-Rogatien had officially closed in September, Jadis had applied to the Institute for a small exploration grant to sound out the back wall. With the paper she was about to publish in *Nature* on de Bonnard's lost artifacts ("Remillardian artifacts from the Souris Saint-Michel rock shelter, France," by John A. Corstorphine, Balthazar Y. Desplaines, Domingo G. V. S. Sanchopanza and Jadis L. Markham), a grant was soon forthcoming, and by mid-November she'd established that the inside surface of the other side of the wall was more or less parabolic in shape, the apex — marking the thinnest part of the wall — about a meter above ground level on the hither side. The signals had been clear. Twenty centimeters beyond the red cross she'd marked, give or take a couple of centimeters, was thin air.

And not a moment too soon. The day after the first sounding results came in, all work had to be suspended — literally, lashed to the decks — before an Atlantic gale of demonic ferocity. They had been used to the vagaries of the Gascon weather, but this storm was the sternest they'd yet faced, and indeed worse than anyone could remember. While still in full force, the wind veered to the northeast, and with it came a blizzard that cut off remoter villages for many days, burying livestock and stranding motorists.

After a week of quite infernal battering, in which the dig crew had barricaded themselves inside the shuttered farmhouse, enduring power outages that lasted days at a stretch, the gale suddenly dropped, leaving a panorama of icy blue and white. Jadis remembered the day when they'd finally been brave enough to open the kitchen door, and how Fairbanks had bounded out to frolic in the snow, bulldozing the drifts with his nose and coming up with tiny white pyramids on its end. Nobody had seen Horrible, the cat, at all for the entire duration of the storm, until, a day after it ended, she was seen picking her way across the snowbound yard, shaking each paw in evident disapproval at the uncomfortable wet whiteness that had landed without leave on her territory, stirring her from her accustomed winter state of inept repose — and dragging the mangled corpse of something or another along in her jaws, spotting the clear, smooth snow with drops of red-black blood.

The storm left human casualties in its wake, too, including the priest at Saint-Rogatien, who had been returning to the church after pastoral visits when a loose slate from above, lifted by the gale-force wind, scythed downwards and sliced open his jugular vein. Even this was not the first casualty in the commune: new graves sprang up under the yews on the edge of the cliff as elderly people succumbed to falls, or simply to the severe cold.

Two weeks before Christmas, things had eased sufficiently for Jack to get away on a much-delayed trip to the Institute in Cambridge, to finalize plans for the upcoming field season. Jadis was overjoyed to hear him, while they were washing up after supper one evening, declare that this would be his last trip away for the foreseeable future. "SSM should produce enough to keep us both busy for a while," he'd said. "So I am yours to command."

"I can think of... ooh... all *sorts* of things you can do for me," she'd laughed, flicking him smartly on the backside with the wet tea towel, after which they'd chased each other round and round the kitchen table, suds flying, Fairbanks leaping and barking to join in this entertaining new game.

The wintry landscape inspired Jadis to do something special for Christmas, so with Jack away, she decided, the last Saturday afternoon before Christmas, to go to the bird market at Seissan in search of a goose. Domingo volunteered to come along for the ride. He had been looking pensive: he clearly had something to tell her.

Jadis was fascinated by the Gascon devotion to poultry, and in particular to its organized dismemberment. The market hall, a large covered square about thirty meters on a side, was crammed with rows and rows of stalls, all devoted to poultry, the position of each row giving a clue to the state of butchery of the products to be found therein. The first row, as you walked in, had live poultry — baskets of chickens, ducks and geese, and cheeping day-old chicks.

The second row had much the same poultry, only dead.

The third and subsequent rows exhibited birds progressively plucked, beheaded, dressed, quartered, filleted and preserved, so that the stalls in the very last row showed only the last stages in the process, the final apotheosis and zenith of Gascon cuisine — jars of *pâté*, *confits* and *foie gras*. Jadis knew that some of it was cruel, but she was always lost in admiration at the industry of it, and relished the smells, noise and bustle of French market life. She realized how much she loved it, and hoped that none of it would ever change.

Domingo helped her choose a couple of jars of *confits de canard*, but to their surprise, one could not simply buy a table goose in the bird market, most geese having been bred especially for their livers, rather than for their corpses in general. However, a tour of butchers nearby produced a simply enormous goose — plucked, beheaded and ready to roast. Domingo carried it to the jeep. As they loaded it into the trunk, Jadis looked at him, noting his expression of distracted, brooding concern. She went up to him, put a hand on his immense barrel chest (clothed, as ever, and incongruously given the weather, in a Hawai'ian shirt of lysergic vividness).

"Domingo, what is it?"

"Might I treat you to a coffee?" he replied, "and I shall reveal all."

They sat a very small table in a sports bar opposite the market (not that any table looked large when Domingo sat next to it), their hands warming round steaming *grand-crèmes*. The bar was full of people and pre-Christmas chatter, the windows fogged with the heat of the customers and the steam rising from their meals and drinks.

Most of the attention seemed focused on the TV monitor above the bar. This was switched to English Premiership football where the hitherto unassailable might of Brighton and Hove Albion was being pummeled into the dust by underdogs Chelsea. There were many close-ups of the hopeless anguish that creased the handsome face of Albion's manager, Sir David Beckham, each time another goal thundered into the Albion net. The author of most of these was Honoré N'Dour, Chelsea's recent star signing from Toulouse—explaining the local interest and the frequent cheers from the bar, interpolated with calls of *"vive Honoré!,"* "*à bas Becks!*" and (which made Domingo smile) *"Albion perfide!"*

"What *is* David wearing?" asked Jadis, incredulously. Domingo peered at the screen.

"It looks like a designer frock," he said, "and so, very soon, shall I be." He gave Jadis his best expression of unfathomable knowingness, the bright glints in his eyes betraying it, as ever, with the promise of puckish mischief. Jadis was even more incredulous.

"No, dear Jadis—I'm not going to run away to the *Stade de France*, nor venture on to the catwalk"—the mental image of Domingo modeling designer dresses made Jadis laugh—"but I *do* have to go. I have, at last, received my calling. I very much regret that I shall have to leave our happy band, at least as a full-time participant."

He took Jadis' slim hands in his own vast paws. She felt a mixture of emotions: joy at his news, and sorrow that this wonderful man, who had become almost indispensable, would have to leave for pastures new, just as they were on the verge of new discoveries.

"Don't be sad," he said. "I won't be too far away. What with the somewhat... er... abrupt gathering-in of my brother priest at Saint-Rogatien, and with the season of Advent well advanced, I took my chance. The authorities have agreed that I can take over at Saint-Rogatien straight away. And as for designer frocks, I now have vestments—I had to have a special fitting!" He grinned, but his face turned serious again: "I now have much to prepare for the community, much to organize. I shall, of course, be moving from my digs at the farmhouse, which you've so generously provided these few years past, as there is a small house that goes with the position. This implies that I won't be able to come to SSM very often, but I shall certainly be there as often as my duties allow — if you'll have me."

"Oh, Domingo — of course! You'll always be welcome. Always! You're — well, you're part of the family."

Jadis would never be able to articulate how Domingo, with his steadfastness, reliability and ready wit, had been part of her own recovery, even had she wanted to tell him.

As for Domingo, he was happier at this news than he thought he ever could be. Up until his arrival at Saint-Rogatien, his life had been dark and troubled, and yet all inquiries as to his history had been met with nothing more than the enigmatic toothy smile and a change of subject. Nobody was even sure how old he was (he was, in fact, the same age as Jack). But only he and the Merciful Father knew what he had endured.

As it was, *Le Dig* had been a haven, a retreat, and Jack and Jadis had become almost as foster parents to him. Jadis would have been surprised to learn (and probably a little embarrassed) that she, especially, had always been in his prayers, and had assumed in his private pantheon a place close to that of the Holy Mother herself.

He experienced a sense of unutterable happiness and gratitude that Jack, Jadis and all the crew came to help him celebrate his first Midnight Mass at Saint-Rogatien, on Christmas Eve — and to invite him home for their *reveillon*.

And here he was now, with the rest of them, wearing his most migraine-inducing shirt, standing bare-armed and open-necked in the drizzle of a raw March morning. A shout came from inside the cave, and a few people made their way out through the slit in the heavy door membrane.

The drilling was about to start.

When it began, the noise was fearful, only slightly dulled by the polythene sheeting. What the men inside must be enduring, Jadis could hardly imagine. Even with face masks and ear defenders, the yammer and thud of a rock drill in a confined space as it made its way through twenty centimeters of limestone was incredible. But in five minutes, it was all over. The crew emerged, covered in dust and filthy water, looking for all the world like South African diamond miners emerging from a twelve-hour shift.

"We're through," the foreman said. "Come and see!"

It was mid-afternoon by the time the drill crew had packed up and gone, and the contractors had returned for the water pump. Peace reigned once more. Jadis' first sight of the cave after the breach was a damp, reddish puddle in the cave entrance, just beyond the membrane, the floor climbing up towards the back wall. This looked quite different from the surface that Jadis had first seen, nine months earlier. It was milky white, its normally dirty pinkish-grey colour bleached by the harsh glare from the racks of powerful halogen lamps mounted on stands. The hole in the wall made a sharp contrast with the general whiteness, a ragged circle of blackness about forty centimeters across, the size of a small trapdoor, and a meter off the ground.

"Nobody's looked through yet, Jadis," said Primrose: "Director's prerogative!"

Jadis smiled, took a torch, and peered through the breach. Quite suddenly, she was seized with panic. What lurked behind the wall? A monster from Tartarus that would bite her head off? At first she could not quite work out what her beam illuminated, but it soon became clear that it was a smooth, backward continuation of the cave, narrowing after three or four meters into a tunnel. The tunnel was not the irregular fissure one might have expected in a natural cave, nor even a rough passage, but a more or less symmetrical structure, tubular, with a diameter of two meters or so, and with a flattened floor. It looked like the kind of tunnel that two people could walk down in comfort, as far from an awkward, sinuous pothole as might be imagined. As far as she could tell it went directly into the side of the hill for as far as her beam could penetrate.

In later life she was often called on — by journalists, especially — to recapture this moment. But she could not. She had been stupefied. With surprise? With anticlimax? She could not tell. Of course, she'd expected *something* — after all, they knew that the false wall in the cave had been artificial, so the tunnel behind it was likely to have been modified, too, presumably by the same people. Her earnest hope was to find some sign of the makers of the Remillardian artefacts, and with them, the builders of the hill of Saint-Rogatien, and a dozen other, similar structures Jack had since found all over Gascony and Languedoc. But the tunnel, as it was, was bare and featureless.

All she knew at this point was that the tunnel had to have been bored at least forty-five thousand years ago, for that was the best date for the emplacement of the flowstone in the wall. No doubts, this time, about the age: accelerator mass-spectrometry dates on tiny flecks of charcoal buried in the wall, and uranium-thorium dates of small samples of rock material drilled from the wall itself, had confirmed this beyond all doubt.

She pulled her head out. "Well, we're in," she said, exhaling. Until then, she hadn't realized that she'd been holding her breath. "Let's make a bigger hole tomorrow, so we can explore. Let's meet here at—say—ten a.m.?"

The team drove away in the farmhouse jeeps: except for Domingo, shoehorned into his newly acquired second-hand pink-and-purple-Paisley Citroën 2CV which, he said, he didn't so much as drive, as wear. ("Think of it as a motorized aloha shirt," he'd said.) Jack and Jadis were to stay on site, in the mobile home, at least for the first few nights, just to keep watch. Primrose and Faye were to take on the next shift, next week.

After they'd waved the crew down the track, Jack made tea in the tiny kitchenette while, not a meter away in the sitting area, Jadis made a play of reviewing a sheaf of official site documents: permits, contracts and so on. But when Jack found her, sitting quite still in a pool of light, she was clearly miles away. He chose not to disturb her.

Jadis flung open the mobile home's flimsy door on a bright, fine morning, the close drizzle of the previous day quite gone, the weather having lifted to reveal bright Spring sunshine and birdsong. By the time the rest of the crew arrived, she and Jack had had coffee on the go, and invited them all in to discuss strategy. Domingo had sent his apologies ("duties on a higher plane," he'd explained) but promised to visit the farmhouse later and walk Fairbanks, who, with the rest of the crew increasingly preoccupied with SSM, was coming to enjoy accompanying Father Domingo on his parochial rounds.

That left Primrose, Faye, Eric and Mathilde, and it suddenly occurred to Jadis that they'd paired up into two couples.

She'd known about Eric and Mathilde from the way Mathilde flushed as red as a traffic signal every time Eric turned up at *Le Dig*. She'd been doing this for ages, except that Eric hadn't seemed to pay any attention. But now, as they walked up to the caravan, they were trying very hard not to hold hands, or even look at each other, and patently not succeeding.

Primrose and Faye, on the other hand, did nothing to avoid each others' gaze, and couldn't help bursting into fits of giggles any time they made eye contact, as if they were a pair of twelve-year-olds at the back of the class sharing secrets about boys. But they'd had more serious moments when, each seemingly lost in her own thoughts, held hands, subconsciously reaching out to the other, oblivious to anyone who might notice.

Jadis was almost sure Jack hadn't grasped any of these undercurrents, but she thought it touching—and mused on the things people got up to in and around the farmhouse when she and Jack were away. She had no reason to complain, or even mention it, but it did make her feel rather old. Responsible. Like a parent.

The crew was as excited as a sports team about to run into the field for the crucial fixture that would win the trophy—or lose it. After coffee and croissants (brought by Faye from the boulangerie in Saint-Rogatien) they strapped on their backpacks, which they'd filled with anything they felt they might need, for all that none of them knew what they might encounter on this, their first scouting trip. Mathilde had raided the farmhouse medical kit, while Faye—a keen mountaineer and sometime spelunker—had brought along several coils of nylon rope, some of which were already festooned with assorted climbing bric-a-brac that none of the rest apart from Primrose could name. All had geological hammers, digital cameras, spare battery packs, waterproofs, sweaters, gloves, a small amount of food and water, and each bore a yellow miner's helmet adorned with a large headlamp.

Once inside the cave—the atmosphere foggy with adrenaline and expectation—it had taken only a few blows from Jack's rock hammer to make the hole left by the rock drill big enough for them to crawl through, one by one, without extravagant discomfort. Once on the other side—a drop of more than a meter, the level on the hither side of the cave having been raised by the backfill from de Bonnard's last dig—they stood in a small huddle, switching on their headlamps so that they became a small, nervous cloud of nodding fireflies in the gloom.

It was decided that Faye, who'd had most experience of underground exploration, would be the team leader for the day. "Everyone stick together," she said. "There are six of us. If you can't count another five lamps at any time, just stay put, and holler!"

And so they started, carefully pacing along the tunnel, two by two, like Noah's animals had in their own epic journey into the unknown, long ago—Faye and Primrose, Eric and Mathilde, with Jack and Jadis bringing up the rear.

The solemnity of the occasion had blanketed their excited chatter into silence. To Jadis it had seemed almost sacred, given the anticipation, and despite her own indifference to religion she had longed for Domingo to have been there, offering some kind of blessing: permission, almost, to go forth. As they tramped along the passage—smooth, and, the further they got from the entrance, increasingly dry and dust-free—Jadis became conscious of its airlessness. There was air, but it was static, stale, like the air trapped inside a rarely used museum storeroom. It was also very cold, and she was glad of her synthetic fleece and gloves. There was nothing to see apart from the sweeping beams of their own headlights, illuminating near-featureless stretches of wall—white with cool, glistening limestone, but not quite smooth—like the whitewashed roughcast walls of a seaside cottage.

The passage seemed to continue forever in a dead straight line, although after a kilometer or so it began to dip downwards, at first very gently, but after another few hundred meters it became much steeper, the floor puckering into treacherous ruts and ridges, which, after they had clambered over a few of them, they began to think of as very worn steps—steps for giants.

By the time they had reached the bottom of the staircase and the passage had resumed its smooth, gently downward grade, they were cold and exhausted, as if they'd just scrambled down a frozen waterfall. Faye called them all into a huddle, and they decided to stop for a snack, and to take stock. Faye looked at her wrist logger.

"We've been down for forty minutes, and have covered three kilometers in a direct line from the cave mouth," she said. Expressions of shock and disbelief. "I know, I know, seems like we've been down here forever."

"I wonder how much longer we'll go before... before..." This from Eric. They sat, eating chocolate and dried apricots, the sound of self-conscious chewing punctuating the atmosphere of silence and thought. They hadn't brought any sleeping gear—this was strictly a day trip, reconnaissance on the fly, not a full-scale hike. But when would they decide to turn back? And what were they expecting to find? The cave, this long passage, was entirely unlike anything that anyone had seen before, for all that it had (so far) turned up very few surprises.

"Okay," continued Faye. It's now a quarter after eleven. I vote that we carry on until—say—one o'clock, and after that, we turn back— whatever happens. Jadis?"

"Agreed," Jadis nodded. It was hard holding a council when you couldn't see anyone else's eyes, all lost in the impenetrable shadows cast by the brims beneath their headlights.

"How much have we dropped?" asked Jack. Faye looked again at her logger.

"About thirty-five meters from the cave mouth. Of course, most of that was in the staircase behind us. Just a thought—we ought to leave a little extra time for climbing back. Me and Primrose might have to climb up first and lay some guide ropes. That should put our start-back time to, oh, let's say twelve-thirty, tops. Agreed?" A general chorus of nods, after which they packed up their litter, got stiffly to their feet, and plodded on.

After another few hundred meters the passage began to narrow, imperceptibly at first, but it wasn't long before they found they were marching single file. This allowed Jadis to take a closer look at the walls, which now, more than ever, looked as if they had been artificially chiseled and shaped. The ceiling, rather than being a simple rough arch between two ill-defined walls, now looked as if it had been squared off, making the walls on either side distinct from the ceiling itself, and giving the passage more of a box-section profile.

It was this, more than anything else, that forced Jadis to realize the implications of what they had found. What with all the years at *Le Dig*, and Jack's researches before that, she had become inured to antiquity, taking it for granted. The working currency of all who venture into the depths before history, where the skein of written record breaks and fades altogether, is *time*, measured in thousands, hundreds of thousands, or even millions of years. And yet few stop to consider what these intervals of time really mean in terms of the scale of human lives.

The world at large had been stunned by the implications of *Le Dig*: that there was a civilization in Europe that was at its height hundreds of thousands of years ago. Jadis, at the epicenter of discovery, was quite used to it, or so she thought, swapping talk of tens or hundreds of millennia with other professionals as casually as if she'd been discussing the price of fish with a market stallholder. In any case, the bulk of her life was less scientific than administrative, filled with the minutiae of directing the dig on a day-to-day basis.

When Jadis did stop to think about the meaning of it all, and to chat about it with Jack—and, lately, Domingo—she felt nothing so much as frustration. The megalith at Saint-Rogatien was really only a giant midden, a huge pile of backfill. It had been an artificial structure, for sure, but it had revealed, ultimately, as much about its makers as a well-rotted garden compost heap might of the dreams and desires of the gardener that made it. The few artifacts she'd described were teasing, only deepening the mystery.

But when she looked up, at the neatly chiseled cornicing above, it struck her quite suddenly that here was a sign of a maker and a mark, creating a recognizable structure for a purpose. The purpose of the megalith at Saint-Rogatien was unknowable—of the artifacts she'd discovered and described, perhaps hardly less. And yet here in this structure, these tunnel walls, was a sign, speaking through ages too great to imagine, of intelligence, and what's more, intelligence that could be interpreted. The sign said 'follow me'. To what end, she could not guess.

Lost in reverie, and looking upward more than forward, she noticed that although the passage remained the same width, the ceiling was getting higher and higher until it was entirely lost, the beam of her headlight disappearing into shadow. This was more than a little disorienting, and she felt herself becoming light-headed. She began to wonder whether she might soon have to make way for a white rabbit hurrying past, or come across a glass table bearing a small bottle labeled 'Drink Me'. At that moment she realized that she was at the back of the file, and that the rest of the team, even Jack, had moved on ahead. Snapping back to reality, she was just about to raise her pace when she heard, a little way ahead, a male voice—she thought it must have been Eric—shout "whoa!"

She scrambled forwards, afraid of what she might encounter, and as she did so the passage widened suddenly, the walls falling away on either side, running into a platform whose width could not be guessed, its edges lost in darkness. Ahead of her were five figures, heads haloed by their lights, standing at what appeared to be the brink of a precipice, the edge of which stretched on either side further than she could see. She joined them, noticing that the air seemed cooler, and looked into the void beyond. What she saw made her feel almost inconceivably small, no more than a mote, prey to the fortunes of the whims and the winds of the world.

She had sufficient presence of mind to notice that the person standing next to her was Jack. She clasped his hand, like a small child suddenly confronted by a vision of vastness beyond experience or imagining. Hers was met by a grasp that was firm, and yet trembling.

The view was, initially, an immeasurable and utterly black void. If there were an end to it, or a bottom to the cliff on whose edge they now perched, their headlights were far too weak to illuminate it. But as the beams swayed to and fro, they caught flashes, here and there, of what looked like structures in the void—an edge, a corner, but no more than hints. It was then that Mathilde spoke.

"Has anybody noticed how the air in here is fresher than in the tunnel?"

Several agreed. Jadis noticed that despite the volume in which they found themselves, Mathilde's voice seemed close, intimate—the space was so enormous that voices died before reaching any surface whence they might be reflected. There were no echoes.

"Yes, there could even be a very slight… breeze," added Eric. They all stretched upwards, noses in the air, and had anyone been able to see them, they would have looked like nothing so much as a row of meerkats which, having risen from their burrow, stand up to sniff the air. "But where… what…?"

"I think that there must be ventilation shafts in the roof of the cave, far above, leading to the surface," said Mathilde. "And if there is air, there might also be light. Very faint, it's true, but who knows? Perhaps enough to see more than we can with these headlights—and with our cameras, we can always enhance any images we get, even if shot in complete darkness."

"Hell, yeah," said Faye. "We can use ultra-long exposures. It's not as if we're trying to shoot anything that's moving…"

"Faye, Don't!" said Primrose, giggling nervously. "This place is spooky enough as it is."

Everyone agreed that it was a good idea, and they all took out their cameras. It was harder, however, to persuade everyone to turn out their headlights. They agreed to do it in sequence, along the line. Jadis was last. She did not show it, but felt the first wave of that species of terror, the primal fear of the dark that petrifies small children whose knowledge of the world extends hardly further than their mother's warmth, and certainly no further than the front door.

The lights went off along the line—*flash, flash,* Eric, Mathilde—she saw their afterimages as red glows, dying—*flash, flash,* there go Faye and Primrose, but as Jack extinguished his light—*flash*—he held her right hand. She would not be alone in the dark. And so, with one last *flash,* she twisted the knurled rubber ring round the outside of her headlamp bulb and they were all plunged into heart-stopping blackness. It was like nothing she had ever experienced. As if she'd been switched off like a bulb herself, she instantly lost all sense of space and time.

What most people call darkness barely deserves the name. The darkness of cities is no darker than a dim, orange glow of street lights far away. Even in isolated, lightless country lanes, there is still some glow from the sky, the stars and the moon. Human beings have grown up with light, and so, to them, darkness is by its very nature inhuman. Only cavers ever experience darkness in its totality, the darkness that existed before humanity, and which was one of the very first casualties of his evolution. And the darkness that now enveloped Jadis was complete, darker even than death that still has the memory of light: as dark as inexistence, a state that memory and light and time and human consciousness have yet to penetrate. Without Jack's fingers as a lifeline to reality, she wondered if she'd ever be able to climb out of that bottomless pit.

And yet, as she forced her eyes to stay open (assuming that they were open), and holding on to Jack's fingers, she began to experience a new sensation. Mathilde had been right: her eyes were slowly accommodating to the darkness, even here, and as she looked out into the void, she became aware of a panorama slowly, very slowly, creeping into view. At first she thought her eyes were playing tricks on her, so deprived of light that they had started to create their own pictures to compensate. And yet the image firmed and grew.

And it was this. Hardly brighter than pitch, and cast in shades of charcoal grey, what she saw before her feet was a city.

The crew stood on a ledge, unguessably high above the western rim of a bowl that stretched ahead, and to the right and left, further than their straining eyes could see. The bowl was absolutely full of jumbled structures—polyhedra, cubes, cylinders, indeed *buildings* (they *had* to be buildings) of all shapes and many different sizes. Although it was very difficult to get any sense of scale, many of the buildings were very large indeed, and would have dwarfed anything since created by Man. Straight ahead of them, and three kilometers away (as they later discovered) stood a pyramid, towering over all, whose apex must have stood as high as they were now. This was a city that had lived and died before the Aurignacians were painting their first pictures, carving their own Venuses, and imagining themselves the victors in a strange, wonderful and conveniently unpopulated new land, in which tales of giants and their works were fit only for old women to burble to infants.

Well, how wrong they were, thought Jadis — and how foolish we were ever to have believed them. She wondered what Domingo would have made of it.

She had the strangest feeling that he would not have been at all surprised.

Chapter 22. Soldier

Tibesti Massif, North Africa, Earth, December, 2032

Nothing beside remains. Round the decay
Of that colossal wreck, boundless and bare
The lone and level sands stretch far away.
Percy Bysshe Shelley — *Ozymandias*

In the lee of the erg the winds slowed to an eddying lull just enough for their words to be heard, were anyone there to hear them. A small group of tall figures gathered round another, who, though kneeling on the ground and virtually inaudible, appeared to be leading what passed for the chant:

Ijeshmaii Zraal!

Ijeshmaii Zraal! came the response, a dismal blizzard of guttering croaks as of the last autumn leaves cracking in the grate.

Ajjhnaai ajjhnaai'hnuu! Ajjhnaii Hjajhaad!

The kneeling figure now fell full flat on its face, a flutter of dirty robes not quite disguising the extreme etiolation of its form. Two other figures stepped in, and, stooping low like a pair of ungainly cranes, helped the central figure to its feet. Surprisingly, it towered a head above all the others. So high, in fact, that even in the shadow cast by the colossal ruined sphinx behind them, the rays of the afternoon sun crowned its head with fire, illuminating its leonine mane. As if refreshed, the figure took the ram's horn proffered by another and blew three mighty blasts. Blasts that would once have caused walls to totter and empires crumble. But the last such walls had been ground to dust thousands of years before, and these wanderers were the last of their kind. The raucous notes on the *zjhjfaar* seemed as futile as the croaks of vultures over long-abandoned skeletons.

Life had not always been so desperate.

Long ago, when the Annakhnu came to this region, it was a promised land, a land flowing with milk and honey. Or, at least, waving with endless prairies of windblown grass for grazing, and rippling with immense lakes full of fish. Ostriches, elephants, giraffe and other animals, nameless by virtue of their later complete extinction, were chased by cheetahs and lions in abundance seemingly without limit. The Annakhnu looked at this immensity of plenty, and settled down from wanderings soon much magnified in myth.

Many hundreds of years passed.

The Annakhnu replaced their grass and wattle huts with more imposing structures of mud-brick. Their villages became towns and then cities, each guarded by demon-headed sphinxes, avatars of their Goddess HaShekhna. The greatest city, famed in legend, was the blessed City on the Heights, with its grand courts, its splendid temples and palaces faced with ivory, silver and gold; its impenetrable walls, its fountains, and towers that stretched to heaven.

The people changed, too. After further uncountable years, they became tall, Kings among Men, taller than the other Men who appeared at the margins of a vast empire—and themselves featured in the marginalia of a dozen cultures. The Atlanteans. The Titans. The Nephilim.

But with cities came war, and slaves, and tribute, and flames, and destruction. With cities came the dwindling of the ostriches, elephants, giraffe and the other large, nameless animals. They became less common, and then rare, and eventually the day came when even the eldest sage could not recall having seen such beasts at all, not even as a small child—images for such elders being as bright as gems, even when the drifting years had dulled the immediacy of more pressing concerns.

And with cities came the taming of the great grasslands, the trammeling of the vast lakes to feed fields of wheat and barley, sorghum and tef that stretched from sky to sky. Nobody could quite recall the precise year when the smallest of the great lakes dried out completely (smallness being a relative thing—this lake had been as large as the glacial wilderness which would, one day, be called Scotland). And nobody could recall the precise year when that lake failed to be completely replenished by the rains of winter. And as more time passed, nobody could recall the year when the rains of winter failed to arrive, and turned instead to storms of choking dust.

The toll of years built like the grains of sand left to accumulate to windward of the cities as they died, one by one, toppling the towers and burying the majestic walls as if they had never been, but leaving a few monuments exposed, a few isolated pillars, as enigmatic remembrances of glories past. The Annakhnu remained tall, but gaunt and weathered as they dwindled from conquerors to a tribe of herdsmen like any other, managing to hang on in remote canyons of the Tibesti Massif— mountains echoing their once-great cities standing amid the fertile plains, now dry and barren rock.

And yet in caves bored within the rock they maintained their ancient religion, itself wearing away at the corners but keeping its core essentially unchanged, the Way of Goddess HaShekhna.

After dozens of centuries, the Way had become nostalgic. The shaman would talk of a blessed future when the Goddess would forgive them their trespasses, the Annakhnu would regain what they had lost, when they would return to their blessed City on the Heights. Every year, to mark the fall of what passed for the first droplets of spring, they prayed for the imminence of this last journey — next year, maybe.

And, one day, just in time, when almost all they had ever had was lost, that day dawned.

The Elders of the very last settlement of the Annakhnu convened in the lee of a Sphinx believed by the more credulous to represent the artistic peak of their ancestors, to discuss the latest in a long litany of bad news. Even though adapted to aridity to a degree not seen elsewhere, the tribe had to move on. The other tribes in the lands round about could not weather the Tibesti like the Annakhnu had through long usage, but these others did have a new and deadlier advantage: automatic weapons. The Annakhnu would have to move on before they were flushed out and slaughtered.

That they had to move on no-one could doubt — but where, then, could they move? Their enemies surrounded them on all sides. Straitened in their last redoubt, they had recourse only to prayer, and to fast-vanishing hope. Hope that the great prophet would appear from the skies on a flaming chariot as was foretold, and smite their enemies. Hope sustained by the comfort of ritual. But the tallest Elder had blown his last: the shrill notes of the *zjhjfaar* resounded among the rocks and died away.

At last, the silence of the desert, eternal and without reproach. The Elders remained still, poised, waiting for deliverance, or for the end. After some minutes came the sound not of fiery chariots but of bullets, the answers to the horn-blasts.

Hope died.

Careering up a slope and over the jagged horizon came a technical — a jeep with a machine gun mounted on the back — driven crazily by bandits in green and tan fatigues. The bandits, hanging over the sides of the technical, whooped in devilment, firing their guns into the arcing sky.

Even from a distance of a thousand yards the keen eyes of the Annakhnu could see the bandits' bandoliers rise, sway and flop around their ragged bodies, the menacing gleams of white teeth in black faces, the glimmer of machetes and the pitted barrels of machine guns. The Elders were all that separated the coming onslaught from their last village, their skeletal flap-breasted women, their starving, bloated children.

The Elders stood fast and began again to chant as one—*Jjeshmaii Zraal!* They closed their eyes, waiting for the end: but were surprised by a second noise, a deeper, constant thrum imposed on the staccato stutter and crazily slipping clutch of the technical.

The Elders opened their eyes once again and faced their foes, only to see, rising behind the jeep, the promised deliverance. Not chariots of fire from the sky, but something else equally wonderful for all that it lay beyond their experience: a flotilla of ten, vast, Chinook helicopters.

The first helicopter let rip its judgment. A pair of rockets scythed away from the fuselage and smacked into the technical, which vanished in a dull rumble and a ball of grey smoke. Shards of metal and scraps of human flesh spattered the Elders standing at the feet of the sphinx. A head, removed by the blast, rolled and stopped by the feet of the eldest Elder, looking up at him as if in surprise. This is not how things were meant to turn out, it seemed to say. This is not how the story ends.

One of the Chinooks picked its way over the wreck and landed delicately a few yards away, close enough to the astonished watchers—but too far for them to be discommoded by the down-draft. The breeze was, however, sufficient to lift and make flags of their ragged robes, marking their otherwise silent stillness all the more starkly. The other nine sky-chariots roared overhead, looking for the village.

Two people in fatigues (much like the bandits,' but more recently cleaned and pressed) alighted and ambled towards the Elders, chatting with each other as if this were an afternoon stroll, as if the Elders were not there at all.

Ho hum, thought the eldest Elder. Not quite how he had imagined it, but the Prophet had come, nonetheless, with chariots in the sky, with fire to smite their enemies, who now lay thoroughly smitten. How could one possibly complain?

As the two newcomers came closer, it became clear to the silent watchers that they were as stocky and dark as the Elders were tall and pale. One, a woman, with very long, black hair, cleared her throat, and looked to her brawny male companion and said:

"Hey, Avi, help me out here, big boy. Much as I hate to admit it, I never know what to say on such occasions."

"You want I should do this?" Avi Malkeinu smiled his best ladies'-man smirk. Always a danger with this particular ball-breaker, but, hey, nothing ventured.

Commander Rivka Mizrahi of the Israel Defence Forces (Covert *Aliyot* Operations) narrowed her coal-black eyes. "Of course—you're the Digger," she spat. "You'll know what to say to... to... Lost Tribes. That's an order, soldier!"

Avi wondered (not for the first time) whether his commanding officer would be as fierce in the sack as she was out of it, but decided (wisely) to put that thought aside for later. So he simply smiled at her, gave a casual mock-salute and moseyed towards to the tribesmen, all of whom had remained completely silent and still, except for their shreds of robes swaying in the light breeze.

Avi stopped, wondering which one of these nearly-dead skeletons he should address first. Nobody had said anything at all about this before the mission—comparative anthropology, cultural sensitivities, even future shock. The terms of reference for Operation Elijah had indeed occupied a lengthy pamphlet written in Old High Military Jargonic, but the semantic content could have been boiled down to read: "go there, pick 'em up, get the hell out."

This directness, this simplicity—this matter-of-factness of things—would not normally have worried Avi in the slightest. He was just a regular guy, after all. But when he'd returned to his homeland, just after *Le Dig* had wound up, his luggage contained more than clothes and after-shave. There were memories, too, especially of that dinner, when he'd had Faye and Primrose practically eating out of his hand. And when Jack had told them the tale of Gaston de Bonnard; and when Domingo had bowled them all over with his amazing tales of de Bonnard's desert journeys in which he'd met *Les Prêtres du Sable*, but nobody had believed him, especially when he'd said they spoke ancient *Ivrit* (Avi had perked up at that).

But some legends turn out to be as plainly reported as de Bonnard intended. The Abbé's engravings of these creatures looked exactly like these ragged sticks standing motionless before him, and lived in the same places. In fact, it was Avi who'd casually mentioned the legend to a fellow soldier-archeologist who—to Avi's consternation—had taken it all extremely seriously, and so Operation Elijah had got started.

Avi now stood equidistant between Rivka and the tribesmen. He looked back at Rivka, who waved him on, crossly. It was all very well for Rivka to say that she never had suitable words for such things, after all, she was the kind of girl who let her uzi do the talking (and what a girl was that!) but she'd never thought to ask Avi if he could do any better. And all Avi knew were chat-up lines. My God! At times like this you really needed to have rehearsed your Neil-Armstrong moment. And if women were challenging and unpredictable creatures, what about these poker-faced statues—these aliens? But there was no more time to lose. He could feel Rivka's eyes drilling holes in the back of his skull, so he stepped forwards, looked up at the tallest of the tribesmen, cleared his throat, and, in his best Voice-Of-Israel *Ivrit*, said:

"*Boker tov, chevrai*. Ever hear about 'Next Year in Jerusalem?'"

He could hear Rivka trying not to laugh—an effort that failed catastrophically a moment later, for what happened next took their breath away. As soon as he had uttered, all the tribesmen had, as one, prostrated themselves before Avi's feet, mumbling what he swore was a prayer in *Ivrit*, for all that it sounded so odd and distorted. *Ijeshmaii Zraal*, these weird, stretched creatures seemed to say.

Shema Israel, Adonai Eloheinu, Adonai Echad

Hear, O Israel, the Lord is your God, the Lord is One.

No doubt about it. They had come to the right place. Surrounded by quivering white masses and unable to move his feet without inadvertently kicking one of the supplicants in the face, Avi turned on his hips to throw Rivka a shape of perplexity, miming—like, what the fuck do I do now? But Rivka's expression, a mixture of ferocity, wonder and mirth, sliced through Avi's heart.

He'd seen that face only once before, when Jadis and Jack had returned from Aurignac, after their first scouting trip to Souris Saint-Michel, and before that dinner when Jack had revealed all. It was the unfathomable expression in Jadis' eyes whenever she'd looked at Jack. Lucky old Jack—but whew! The intensity of it! He wondered what Jadis would look like in battle-dress and toting a machine gun. No, don't even go there, at least, not in working hours. Jadis was a honey, no doubt about it, but you never crossed her on *Le Dig*. No way! For sure, she and Rivka might be sisters, and at that thought, he started to laugh, and found himself saying the standard response:

Baruch Shem K'vod Malchuto L'Olam Va'ed

His Glorious Majesty Be Praised for Ever.

At which utterance the tribesmen rose as one and marched, calmly, and without once looking at either Avi or Rivka, to the waiting helicopter.

Avi had much to think about on the long flight home. Strapped onto a bench seat on one side of the helicopter, looking across at the Tibestian tribesmen webbed into the other side—unspeaking, unsmiling and, remarkably, uncomplaining—his mind was cast back to the long, long conversations he'd had at *Le Dig* with Domingo, ever needling at him about religion, the sinewy twang of Jagger and Richards ever in the background.

Religion, he thought. I need it like a hole in the head. Religion, he'd said to Domingo, has caused far too much trouble already. True enough, said Domingo, but that's because people really care about it. Even more than sex. Even more than life or death. And why?

Avi had been unable to answer.

Because, said Domingo, it's what marks us out as human beings. It stems from the same impulse as love—and is therefore as unreasoning, as passionate. It sustains us, it defines us. Without religion, said Domingo—and without the love of God—we are no more than beasts.

But: *humanity?* He looked across at the Tibestian *Prêtres du Sable*—Sand-Priests. They were Jews, maybe, perhaps, and their religion had sustained them through many ages of adversity, but were they even human?

Okay, he admitted to himself, ruefully, most human beings thought of Jews, most of the time, as a race apart, perhaps not even proper humans, either. But more seriously, he continued, thinking mostly about the conversations he'd had with Domingo, perhaps religion transcended and even antedated humanity. Perhaps (now, *here's* a thought) humanity evolved *because* of religion. And as Domingo had said, don't forget love. It was part of his own Catholicism, it was true, and (he said) he wouldn't want to push it too much, but as far as he was concerned, he'd said (and the big man's eyes seemed to mist over, looking inward) love and faith are inseparable.

Avi was not sure whether his conversations with Domingo had had any single, marked effect. For sure, he hadn't dropped everything and become a *yeshiva bocher* like his grandfather had, but it had made him reassess his own place in the great scheme of things.

Avi's grandfather had started as a market trader in Tashkent, in central Asia, and after many long years had made it to the status of middleman in the Chinese textile import-export trade. As such he was simply a facet of a tradition that had endured for millennia, part of the great Silk Road, the mercantile artery that had traversed Eurasia since before the dawn of history. And where there was trade, there had always been Jews.

But the resurgence of Islam in central Asia had made things hard for the Jews, who had, first in ones and twos, then whole families, made their way to Israel. Perhaps none too soon, thought Avi. Tashkent was now just one part of the seemingly unstoppable Khalifa that would, he thought, soon stretch from Indonesia to the Atlantic Ocean. The reason why the Chinooks had been able to fly without hindrance across the Sahara was because the secular governments of Egypt, Libya and Chad were deeply distracted, fighting their own, hopeless wars against the revivified Legions of the Prophet.

Avi's grandparents settled in Israel, traded Uzbek for Hebrew and started again. They lived in a tiny flat in a scruffy neighborhood of Tel Aviv, a part of town where sand poked through the cracks in the neglected roadbeds and sidewalks, creating tiny dunes. By dint of working hard — and, as his grandfather had emphasized, *praying* hard — they managed to make a modest living and raise a family, which, in time, dispersed. Avi's own parents, raised in the new country and unencumbered by the traditions of the old, were uncomfortable about religion, and he dimly remembered the arguments between his father and grandparents when they visited the flat for *Shabbat* or *Pesach*.

The grandparents had never approved of Avi's mother, an outspoken, blonde American feminist Avi's father had met while studying at the Technion in Haifa. She may *say* she's Jewish, they said, but does she keep a kosher home? *Shabbat?* Festivals? No! This presumptious *shiksa* wants to work, be an engineer, and not be a good Jewish wife and mother, staying home and keeping *kashrut*. *We* managed it, said the grandfather, so why can't you?

By this time Avi's grandfather was spending less and less time working, and more and more at a small synagogue with other Uzbek Jewish *emigrés*, thinking about old times while studying Talmud, and returning home, head full of religious zeal and pockets empty.

Avi had been far too small to remember the arguments, the recriminations and the final break, when his parents abandoned religion altogether, although he did remember moving to the Marxist kibbutz within sight of Mount Carmel, the mountain continually riding high on the horizon of his thoughts. It was at this kibbutz where he'd grown up, where he'd had lots of fun with the other kids, and where God was only ever mentioned as a profanity.

But now... well, Army life is mostly a lot of boring hanging around, during which his mind became less and less occupied with girls, and more towards turning over everything Domingo had said to him, about religion, and his heritage as a Jew, and, very slowly, the long-buried thoughts of Friday nights at his grandparents' flat came back. The rich, spicy smells of chicken and lamb, rice and couscous as his smiling-eyed grandfather had opened the door, lifting his squealing grandson in his wiry, brown arms ("*shabbat shalom*, little Avi!) The solemnity of the moment when his grandmother lit the Friday-night candles, how she filled the wine goblets and broke the freshly-baked *chollah*; how, as a four-year-old, he was always asked to say the age-old blessings (he winced inwardly at the thought, but it was a sensation mixed with the pleasure of nostalgia); and how lavishly his grandparents praised his lisping, uncertain efforts. And how this—this *holiness*—blended with the cosy family atmosphere.

His later experience backfilled these memories, enriching them with the thought that Domingo had, after all, been right. This is how religion must have started, with a human family gathered round a fire in some cave-mouth to thank God (or whatever) for bringing them safely together. Families, thought Avi, were more than a way for a species to propagate—they were a uniquely human invention, bound together by gratitude for divine providence.

Fuck me, he thought, I'm getting old. I'll be joining *Likud* next.

But he reflected on his own expression of religion, his search for God, as it were, which had become directed into the search for the very beginnings of human culture. Which, he supposed, was how he'd come into Jack's orbit, and then Jadis'.

The chatter of the soldiers and airmen, the hum and chop of the big helicopter's twin engines continued, but Avi was oblivious, thinking once again of Jadis, his doctorate supervisor, and a woman who'd gone so much further in his estimation than a barrack-room pin-up. Okay, *okay*, he thought, backtracking—what a sap he was!—in mitigation, he'd met Jadis for the first time when he was at a very impressionable age, having only just arrived in the maelstrom of Cambridge. And so, of course, she'd made an impression.

But even afterwards, when he'd go to know her well—when he'd been her pupil, and when they'd worked so hard together at Saint-Rogatien, and had stayed late into the night poring over their findings, systematizing them—she seemed to exemplify for him the very essence of what fascinated him about women. It was the contrasts: between softness and steel, between acquiescence and determination, between a skittishness that only ever lived for the moment, and depths of experience winnowed by a drama that seemed to go back to the beginning of time, and in which poor hapless men had arrived relatively late, to be dazed and startled by what they found.

Jadis had been playing on his mind more than usual (and no, you *schmuck*, *not* because Rivka looked like her) but because of the reports from Souris Saint-Michel she'd been sending by emails so well encrypted that they'd baffled the IDF censor (something he was very proud of, having installed her encryption programs himself).

They'd started in March, with a brief and breathless report on what they'd first found inside the cave, and continued in length and frequency ever since. Although Jadis never wrote anything other than clear, plain facts, unencumbered by anything superfluous, he could read, between the lines, a steady increase in intensity, excitement—and desperation.

There's so much here, the messages seemed to say. So much to tell— *too* much—I wish you were back here to look at it—can you come?— what are we going to make of it all?—Help!

The news that Jadis had to tell, buried in stray bits, would blow the lid off the world, and suddenly Avi was conscious that of all the human beings (and other people) in this Chinook, only he had any idea of what Jadis was about to unleash. He wondered why his head wasn't glowing like a distress flare, and why nobody seemed to be taking any notice of him whatsoever.

The latest email had contained two lengthy attachments. The first was the paper that she intended to send to *Nature* ('Subterranean Palaeolithic settlement at Souris Saint-Michel Rock Shelter, France,' by Jadis L. Markham, with Jack, Faye, Primrose, Mathilde, Eric, Balthazar, Domingo and a dozen other names he didn't recognize). The second, much longer attachment was the more monographic treatment she'd send to *Antiquity*, pending the deliberations of *Nature*'s editors.

The email's covering letter, written in her own words, not in the careful, measured understatement of a scientific report, had made his blood run cold. He'd read and read and read it again, until he'd known it by heart, even more thoroughly than the standing orders of Operation Elijah. The *Nature* paper is a stop-gap (she'd written):

> The *Antiquity* paper has a lot more analysis. After all your help with data analysis you deserve a co-authorship on both papers, if you'd like.

He'd agonized over this but decided to decline, as he'd never been to the site himself, and there were too many authors on the paper already.

For now, just to sum it up

(she continued)

what we've found goes like this. The city covers about thirty square kilometers. All of it consists of buildings in a pristine state. There are no ruins. We have found no art work, nor any sign of writing, but there are Remillardian artefacts everywhere. At first we did not know what they were for.

Then we discovered the cemetery—that's what we're calling it for now—just below the western side of the Great Pyramid (that's what Balthazar called the largest structure. You can see it in Fig. 2 of the *Nature* paper as Structure SSM-255-9-1). We have not so far been able to do more than a pilot excavation in one corner of this area (this is locality 255-9-2), but so far we have found 86 Neanderthal skeletons. All are complete. Some seem to have been dressed in Remillardian artifacts. Mathilde thinks that each artifact is a small plate in a suit of armor that would have been held together by leather, but we are not sure yet. At any rate, we now know who made the Remillardian artefacts, which is great news.

How typical of Jadis, thought Avi, not to have mentioned that this one fact alone—the discovery of so many pristine Neanderthal skeletons in one place—would be enough to turn anthropology on its head, quite apart from the other findings. These now came thick and fast, wave after wave of startling revelation, until Avi had to take a breath, to pause, to allow him to come to terms with it all.

When Jack and Faye went to the top of the Great Pyramid they found it did not taper to a point, as we had first thought, but was flat. On the flat surface, a square platform about five meters on a side, they found several other structures. One contained skeletons of what seem to be anatomically modern humans. Some of these are pristine, but others have been decapitated. A preliminary analysis of cut marks suggests that this mutilation was deliberate. In a nearby structure they found what look like the skulls from the mutilated bodies. The tops of the skulls had been removed. Some of these calvaria have a kind of resinous deposit inside and there are signs of burning.

Even in the cramped, hot fuselage of the Chinook, Avi's blood chilled every time he replayed that particular detail.

What's really puzzling is a gravitational anomaly that we've picked up right in the center of the pyramid's summit platform. There's something down there, buried within. We haven't been able to explore that further yet, so we don't mention it in either of the two papers.

The email went on for a while in this vein before concluding:

Thanks again for your help, Avi, we couldn't have done it without you. So until we see you—I hope it won't be too long—everyone on the team sends their love, Faye and Primrose especially, and Jack of course, and Domingo reminds me to tell you that you are in his prayers. Fairbanks sends a bark and a lick, and Horrible would probably send you a dead dormouse if she could(!). With love—

However, at this point, Avi had always drifted off, because he couldn't help remembering something his father had shown him when he was a teenager on the kibbutz. In his quest for a perfect socialist Zionist utopia, and a world in which there would be no borders and in which Jews would never again be persecuted, Avi's father had read up on some of the older ideas of world government. Perhaps inevitably, his reading had drawn him to H. G. Wells. Although Avi's father had found Wells' idealism rather hard going, he was instantly sucked into the power and drama of his fiction, and it was this that he shared with his son. His father had read him *The Magic Shop* and from there it was only a short hop to *The Country of the Blind* and—what had the most lasting impact—*The Time Machine*.

Avi wasn't sure if Jadis knew any Wells or had caught the parallels. In any case, literary allusion wasn't really her style. But he couldn't help thinking of the subterranean city as a landscape that Wells would have recognized. Not in *The Country of the Blind* so much, but in the future landscape of England that greeted the Time Traveler, who found the Eloi living witlessly in a sylvan idyll, unaware of the technically advanced Morlocks dragging them down to a horrific, subterranean fate. His father read in this story a parable about revolution and class warfare. But for Avi, now, it had taken on an additional, grisly reality.

A gear-change in the helicopter, betrayed by a slight shift in the ceaseless rumble of its engines, indicated that they were about to land at the desert air base, and de Bonnard's *Prêtres du Sable* would take their first steps on what everyone hoped they'd regard as hallowed soil. But even in the hot Negev sunshine, Avi felt his blood run thick and chill.

-=0=-

BOOK TWO

SIEGE OF STARS

Chapter 1: Philanthropist

Aspen, Colorado, Earth, January 2033

As I biheeld into the eest an heigh to the sonne,
I seigh a tour on a toft trieliche ymaked,
A deep dale bynethe, a dongeon therinne,
With depe diches and derke and dredfulle of sighte.

(As I looked to the east, towards the sunrise
I saw a tower on a hill, cleverly built
A deep dale beneath, a dungeon inside
With deep ditches, and dark and dreadful to see.)

William Langland — *The Vision of Piers Plowman*

The New Year was ushered in with a gale and accompanying blizzard. Jack, however, had business that was too urgent to be delayed by such things as mere weather. As Director of the nominally Cambridge-based Merlin Technologies Institute for Historical Geomorphology, he needed to fly to the New York offices of Merlin Technologies' philanthropic arm for an urgent meeting with the Board. The reason was — as it so often is — money. The new excavation at Souris Saint-Michel had the potential to be so huge that Jack and Jadis and their small crew would never cope. Jack would propose that the Institute relocate from Cambridge to Saint-Rogatien, where it would devote ninety per cent of its resources to Souris Saint-Michel.

After showing them the data and pictures acquired so far, he'd hit them with detailed plans for the immediate acquisition of plant and expertise, requiring a massive injection of capital and a thirty-fold increase in operating budget. Even though the Institute had been set up with the purpose of supporting Jack and Jadis' work, it was an audacious plan, even reckless, and he knew it. His hopes were not high.

Given the stakes, he'd very much wanted Jadis to come too, as (he'd felt) their chances would have been higher were their presentation backed by them both. She'd made the predictable (and justifiable) excuses about having to stay home to run a new operation that required more oversight with each day that passed, and had yet to find its feet.

But — and this Jack found disconcerting — before she'd had a chance to respond to Jack's plea in words, her eyes had flashed at him an expression of what he could only describe as having caught herself *outside* herself, and, having done so, snapped back with the horror that comes with the revelation that the world we inhabit is far from the cosy and familiar place to which we've become accustomed, but something alien, and infinitely greater.

It lasted just for an instant, but he was convinced that Jadis felt it, too, because she was edgy for the rest of the day. Jack decided not to mention it again. Her parting embrace, as he set off for the airport at Blagnac, was fractionally more urgent than usual.

"It'll be all right," he'd said, and kissed her on the top of her head. But she'd turned on her heel and walked back to the house without a word.

The cool, bland, Fifth-Avenue suite could have been the office of a cheap sting operation rather than the largest private venture capital firm in the world. Ruxton Carr clearly preferred to spend his trillions on his projects, rather than his own surroundings. Jack had never met any of the Board before except by videoconference (which, he thought, was never as good as the real thing). The six men, all of whom he'd have passed without a second glance in the street, betrayed no reaction whatsoever to Jack's performance. He was introduced to none of them, and he had no idea which one of them — if any — was the legendary Mr Carr. His presentation was received politely but in absolute silence. He'd barely got to the end of the final slide when the anonymous man at the head of the table raised his hand to an earpiece, cupping it and exchanging a word.

"Dr Corstorphine," he said, "a limousine is waiting for you in the lobby. Goodbye."

Well, that's that, Jack thought. We'll just have to do what we can with what we have, even though it would be like trying to cut down trees by scraping at them with our fingernails.

The limo took him to JFK, as he'd assumed — but not to a regular passenger terminal. Two suits met him kerbside and escorted him to a small, charcoal-black and very sleek-looking aircraft that looked more like a stealth-winged spaceplane than a business jet. Nobody said a word — he appeared to be quite alone as he boarded and strapped himself into what seemed like a rather excessive five-point harness. The jet taxied through the dark and sleet, took off very gingerly and — when it was airborne — put on the most terrific spurt of acceleration Jack had ever experienced. The harness was there for a reason. Forced back into his chair, Jack felt that he was on a roller coaster rather than a plane.

It seemed like no time at all until the plane slowed, descended and landed at a dark, snowy airstrip just like the one they'd left. The aircraft door opened and a set of steps telescoped down to the snowy ground. The warm fug of the plane was instantly replaced by the thin, bitter chill of high mountains in winter. Jack gasped for breath. The plane didn't appear to have any cabin crew, so Jack unfastened himself and stood up. He saw spots before his eyes and his head swam. They were clearly very high up. The Rockies? Stepping gingerly down the steps he saw that the plane had landed on a short runway in a high mountain valley. Bright stars poured down on every side through the clear air.

Slightly above him, on a ridge, was plainly his destination, a long, low cabin set upon a platform of massive cut stones. A welcoming yellow light poured from a picture window that ran all the way along the valley-facing side of the building. He was expected.

Jack wondered how he was going to climb to the top—he hadn't expected to bring his winter mountaineering gear—and there were no steps, nor any sign of a path up to the cabin through the pristine snowfall. And he was rapidly getting colder. He decided to climb back into the plane to await further instructions, and turned away. He was brought up short by a friendly bleeping noise behind him. He turned again to see a snowmobile, engine running, but no sign of a driver. There was a smiley face painted on the front. A cheery voice chimed from a small speaker above it. "Come on up, Dr Corstorphine," said the voice, "I've been expecting you."

Less than a minute later he was at the front door of the cabin. The door opened without his having to knock: he was met by a tiny man with huge, yellow-green, startlingly cat-like eyes in a face the color of old teak, surmounted by an unruly shock of snow-white hair. The man admitted him to a salon that ran the length of the entire cabin, the picture window at his left. At the far end was a fireplace of monumental size, and two well-worn red leather chesterfields stood, one on each side. Jack had a strong yet fleeting feeling that he'd been there before. The hairs rose on the back of his neck.

His host was wearing the bottom half of an Armani suit, held up over a red-and-white striped Jermyn Street shirt by a pair of novelty suspenders decorated with rubber tyrannosauri. His feet were bare and—Jack couldn't help but notice—remarkably hairy. His accent was straight out of London's East End. And, like an East-End costermonger, he talked non-stop.

"I don't believe we've ever actually met, Jack. May I call you Jack? I'm Ruxton Carr." Mr Carr put out a hand. Jack shook it. The grip was painfully decisive, giving the lie to the almost comedic appearance of the animated little man who stood before him. "We've been very impressed with your work. Very impressed. So naturally we'll give you everything you and Dr Markham need. Pity you didn't both come," he said, "I'd like to have met her. But I can understand why she didn't."

Jack had the impression of a cloud passing behind Carr's eyes, as if the sun had been dimmed, or that the diminutive philanthropist were searching for something buried in his mind, an irritating piece of mental grit that he knew was there but couldn't quite grasp. But it lasted no more than a moment, and Carr resumed his rapid-fire delivery, continuing as if he were really talking to himself.

"Did I say everything? Yes, everything. Don't stint. Just do it and send us the bill. Oh, sorry, Jack, you must be parched after your journey and your presentation—which went very well, I hear. Soda? Beer? Wine? Tea? All here, you know. I rarely get out of this place to… well, *you* know. Ah! Eureka…"

Carr capered off to a drinks cabinet without waiting for Jack to respond, and came back with two tumblers filled to the brim with an Islay single malt so dark and peaty that Jack almost choked, pausing only a moment to wonder how Carr had known that this was his favorite drink, even though he rarely got the opportunity to sample it, as Jadis said she hated the smell and wouldn't allow it in the house, and Jack never liked to drink on his own. How?

"Why will we be so accommodating, I hear you ask," Carr continued, "so, of course, I'll tell you. You can't take it with you, and I'm older than I look. Much older. But apart from that, the Board and I are convinced that the work you and Dr Markham are doing is of the utmost importance—the *utmost* importance. We think it might even save the planet. How will describing a city that's been dead for a gazillion years save the planet, I hear you ask? You do? Great! So of course, I'll tell you—I haven't the faintest idea.

"But I have a hunch, that's all it is, a hunch, and I always follow my hunches, because they've never let me down. Not ever. That's something that you and I have in common, I believe? Trust your hunches, Jack! In the end, they're all we've got. Like my hunch that you're an Islay man, am I right? Of course I'm right!" The little man laughed and slapped his thigh as if he'd cracked the most amazing joke.

"So drink up, Jack, you've got just enough time to meet the next sub-orbital window. Give my best wishes to Dr Markham. Goodbye—and good luck!"

Hunches, Jack thought, as the sleek stealth-winged private jet wafted him, his good news and several more tumblers of Laphroaig smoothly homewards at Mach 4.7, across the inky black Atlantic, the ocean hurrying backwards beneath him as if actively trying to get out of the way.

His world had been a castle built on gamble after gamble; that MacLennane had backed his own then-unframed, untested hunches about landscape, which had later borne fruit at Saint-Rogatien and now at Souris Saint-Michel. And MacLennane's last and greatest gamble—that Jack's own hunches could be brought to maturity not by some accomplished Professor, or even a rising academic star, but by an undergraduate just twenty years old, unproven and untested. Science is not built from certainties, he thought (inexplicably, in the voice of Ernestine Yanga), for we cannot extend knowledge by forever elaborating on what we already know.

No, we have to take chances. Hunches—that's what it's all about. And when he thought of his wife, his hunch was that the best chances are always those that one knows instinctively are dead certainties. He felt sure that Ruxton Carr would have agreed.

Ruxton Carr, however, had other concerns.

He had known he was ill for some time, but had always made excuses not to see a doctor. Too busy, he had always said, covering up the real reason, which was that he was frightened. Islay alone could no longer dull the ache in his chest and along his left arm. From a pocket in his trousers he drew an ornate pearl-inlaid, boxwood pillbox, flipped open the lid, and swallowed a mouthful of pills. Oxycodone. Ever his friend and ally. He poured another slug of Lagavulin to send the pills on their way, sank onto a chesterfield and closed his eyes. Just before he did so, he was conscious—semiconcious—of a tall, white-faced figure, standing, facing him. She bent down, her hair brushing his hands, his face.

"Jade?"

"It's time to go, Ruxie," she said. "Time for the last big push." She touched his wrist with one long finger, and then, just for the merest split instant, it was '79 again, the rain bucketing down outside

... he was in Khan's shop, selling music centres, when...

She...

... and then he was helpless, surrounded by noise, and blind.

Chapter 2: Infant

Gascony, France, Earth, September, 2040

And he looked up, and said, I see men as trees, walking.
Mark **8**, 24

Tom and Fairbanks were playing in the sun-baked yard outside the kitchen door, chasing the crisped, fallen leaves as they eddied and swirled in the first gusts of autumn. The boy grabbed and grasped at the leaves — missing them every time — while the dog barked encouragement. Fairbanks was now too old to do much active chasing himself. His back legs were arthritic and far too weak to propel his bulk into the air, as they once had. But he enjoyed watching the small boy run round in circles, laughing and hooting.

Which is why the big old dog was perplexed, and then worried, when the boy sat down abruptly on the ground, covered his eyes and screamed at the top of his voice. The little boy was not, (judged the dog) calling for his mistress in particular, but was instead letting out an inchoate cry of pain and terror. It reminded Fairbanks of the sound made by a vixen at bay in the field adjoining the garden, or that made by one of The Horribles' multitudinous small victims just before they'd had their necks broken. Naturally enough, Fairbanks was concerned. He advanced on his friend, whimpering, nosing apart the hands covering the boy's face, sniffing out his fear (he detected that the boy had peed himself) and trying a few consoling licks. The boy calmed down somewhat and threw his arms round the dog's neck, grasping handfuls of his mane. Then, with his face buried in the dog's fur, the boy tried to open his eyes again.

This time the searing, burning sensation wasn't quite as intense as it had been a moment earlier, when he'd opened his eyes and let the world pour in all at once. No, this time, he could smell the dog, feel the fibrous strands of his outer coat, the softer nap of his inner fur, the ripple of his muscles, and hear his steady breath and the beat of his heart.

But there was something else too, a new dimension to the smells and sounds that took the form of a large, blocky patch with indistinct edges. The patch moved slightly, taking the smells and sounds with it. And then the patch made a noise — a kind of conversational growl of encouragement — and he realized in an instant that the patch, sounds and smells went all together, and that they all belonged to Fairbanks, his most bestest friend in the whole world, who always understood, always knew.

The boy screwed his eyes up so tightly that tears began to squeeze out and ran into the house with Fairbanks in lolloping pursuit. Tom's hands and ears and nose guided him up the stairs, where he heard the quick footsteps of his mother hurrying down to greet him, her arms picking him up and hugging him, her smell tinted with anxiety —

"Darling, what's the matter?" she said. "Why are you crying?" It was only a little while later, when she had settled Tom on the sitting-room sofa, that Tom had calmed down enough to speak.

"*Maman,*" he said, "my eyes hurt when I open them." but he'd refused to open them when she or Jack had asked. Afraid that Tom's eyes had trapped some irritant, they called the village doctor, who administered some drops as well as he could, and left. Later still, and long after nightfall, Tom had returned to more or less his usual, happy state, except that he kept his eyes tightly shut.

"*Maman,*" he asked, "can you hear and smell with your eyes?"

She turned out the light and hugged her son.

"Yes, Darling, you can. Perhaps you'd like to try it now?"

Although he was reluctant, the burning heat on his eyelids seemed to have disappeared, and he opened them — on a dim vision of blank, angular spaces, except for one, a more curving, irregular form that was moving and changing its shape as it did so. He smelled it and knew it was his mother. Around her edges — *edges* — were lots and lots and lots of long thin lines, which he touched and discovered were his mother's hair. His hands flew to her face, which he knew to be in the middle of all the hair, and felt — saw — that it was moving in an odd way and was wet. The wetness was coming from the two large holes in her face that were her eyes.

His mother's shape changed further, as if she were some tentacled hydra, extending two long outgrowths which, rather alarmingly, got larger and larger at the ends. He began to flinch, but just in time he smelled that they were only her hands, her fingers, reaching out to caress him.

"Oh, you sweet boy," she said. "Everything's going to be all right. You'll see." Tom didn't know what she meant, but she was his *Maman* and apart from Fairbanks the centre of his world, so whatever it was, it was probably okay. He turned over and dreamed the dreams that only blind people know: dreams that he would soon leave behind.

Jadis walked very slowly downstairs, making sure she placed each foot carefully on the creaking wooden treads, in case the rich and uneasy mixture of emotions currently assaulting her mind lifted her physically off her feet. Fear, terror, dread, horror, joy—and relief. And hope. Relief that a long and nagging worry had been lifted; hope that her little son would soon be walking out into the light, unafraid.

Jack was waiting for her in the sitting room with a glass of wine, which she accepted gratefully. They both sank into the ever-more-sagging sofa in front of the fire.

"He's fine—just fine," she'd said in response to his unvoiced expression of concern. "You know," she added, "I'm probably being the classic hysterical mother..."

Jack snorted. A mother less hysterical than Jadis would be hard to imagine. The past six years had been difficult, both at work and at home, but somehow Jadis had always managed to hold everything together. As Jadis got older, her airy girlishness had faded as the steel in her had come to the fore. Although she had never, to Jack's knowledge, raised her voice at Souris Saint-Michel, he knew that some of the younger members of the eighty-strong team referred to her as the Wicked Witch. It was no coincidence that these were the team members who never stayed very long.

"What's up with Tom, then?" Jack asked. "You mightn't have been hysterical, but he was. I know he's only six, but Tom's always been un-flappable. Even Fairbanks was worried."

Jadis smiled, thinking of how Fairbanks had adopted Tom as soon as he'd seen him, a tiny infant just a year old, and had never let him out of his sight. She'd lost count of the postmen, academic colleagues, friends, relations and stray visitors who'd given Fairbanks a wide berth when the vast, snarling bear of a dog thought that anyone was coming too close to his infant charge. She thought that Fairbanks had got on with Tom so well because of a shared view of the world—and wondered how much Fairbanks had actually taught Tom, perhaps without even knowing that he had. Tom was blind, and Fairbanks wouldn't have done very well on an eyesight test, either. The world of boy and dog had been one of hearing, touch and smell. But things, it seemed, were changing.

"Oh, Jack, where to begin..." sighed Jadis, grasping his right arm like a mast to steady her in a storm: "you know, all those ophthalmic surgeons, those psychologists, those specialists we took him to, one after another—and they all said that yes, he was blind, but they couldn't actually find what was wrong with him?"

"Mmm..."—he stroked her hair, teasing out each strand, spreading them all out as a great scapular around them both.

"And do you remember the one in Toulouse," she went on, "who said that he might even suddenly learn to see, one day?" Jack remembered. Ah yes, that was the one occasion he could remember—the only one—in which Jadis had become incandescently furious. He remembered how her pale skin had turned even paler, her eyes coal-black, and her hair had seemed to take on a life of its own, streaming out in all directions like turbulent seaweed, when she'd turned on the hapless specialist and said words to the effect that she'd hoped that the doctor would have spoken to her like a fellow scientist, and not give her the standard patronizing brush-off treatment; but, sadly, she wished she'd trusted her expectations instead, which were, she'd said, disarmingly, poignantly low. Not that she'd raised her voice—quite the opposite—but her tone was so commanding, her articulation so pitilessly precise, that all the doctor could do was hang his head and shuffle backwards *out of his own office.*

Jadis' constant uneasy shifts in Jack's embrace, as if she weren't entirely comfortable, said it all. She was remorseful, embarrassed, because the doctor had been right after all. But this was no time to press the point, thought Jack. Time to move things forward.

"So what do we do now?" he said.

After a thoughtful pause, Jadis sighed, and said, quite decisively, "I think we should just let things be." Having made up her mind, she relaxed suddenly as if released from some kind of possession, and sank contentedly back into Jack's embrace. "Let Tom work it out on his own. He's always done so before."

"If it ain't broke...," added Jack, but Jadis was already on the margins of sleep, as if she'd shed a heavy load that had long weighed her down, and, having been relieved of it, could now afford to collapse from exhaustion.

Staring into the sinking embers, he thought back to the long, agonized conversations they'd had a few years back, when SSM was well under way, about children. Jack had been reluctant—the memories of her pregnancy were still too painful—but Jadis, who after all (she said) had been the one who'd suffered the pain, was adamant. She kept saying something he didn't quite understand about a lost pulse, and a horrible, bloody recurrent nightmare she'd had about the Nest, and how it was about time she'd done something about it.

And then there was the dismal year or so when they'd been 'trying for a baby'—a phrase that Jack thought quite the dreariest in the English language. Despite the fact that they'd had sex more frequently than they'd ever had, none of it had been very much fun. Jack remembered one night when they were holed up in the caravan at SSM, the rain flooding down outside, and he'd had one of his extremely rare colds. Now, he thought, most men, even when running a temperature of a hundred and one, would find the prospect of opening one's eyes to find oneself being ridden by a nude and sensationally sexy woman at least cheering, if not arousing. But being told in stentorian tones that he was to 'perform' because she was ovulating and that if 'we missed this chance' we'd have to wait 'another whole month' — well, it was a turn-off.

After a while they'd both decided that this mechanically procreative effort was more likely to damage their marriage than produce offspring. Natural reproduction was a complete failure — as they'd known it probably would be. And, as it turned out (after many consultations), although Jadis' uterus had healed, there had been a lot of scarring, making the chances of implantation and placentation very low indeed, even had they managed to conceive, either naturally or *in vitro*. The only chance was some kind of surrogacy — which Jack found too weird, and Jadis flatly refused even to consider. That, or adoption.

This would have been easy but for one thing: a worldwide shortage of spare babies. The European birth-rate had been in long-term decline for decades and was now so low that children under five years old were almost never available for adoption. Babies from other parts of the world were also increasingly rare. Even in what had once been called the Third World, birth rates had been slowing, and the demographics were made more complicated by endemic war, famine and disease. Over the past decade, much of sub-Saharan Africa had been depopulated by chronic drought and famine, exacerbated by malaria, AIDS and a seemingly constant barrage of pestilences nobody had heard of before, each one more horrible than the last. Few had realized it yet, but the populations of every country between South Africa and the Equator had sunk below the level of viability. Many of these states had effectively ceased to exist except as flags of convenience, and were in fact administered by a variety of multinational concerns, some of which used them as game reserves. Elephants, lions, gorillas, cheetahs and zebras were on the increase as the human tide receded.

So, no babies there, then.

Eastern Asia had long been a source of babies for adoption, but even there the market was drying up as the regional economies soared. In fact, the trade had switched in the opposite direction as Korean and Thai would-be-parents competed for the few remaining babies in Russia and Romania.

So, no babies there, either.

Jack and Jadis were becoming reconciled to childlessness until they decided to discuss the issue with Domingo on one of his increasingly rare (and cherished) visits—his talents had been recognized in Rome and he was now, more often than not, at the Vatican. For their part, Jack and Jadis had come to regard him as their confessor, and appreciated his own concession to their agnosticism in that he always visited them in what he termed an 'unofficial' capacity—in baggy shorts and customarily eye-watering 5XL aloha shirt ("I wouldn't want anyone to know it was me," he'd said).

And he was, they thought, a good listener, and most of all a good friend. Domingo knew of Catholic agencies that rescued babies from the burgeoning slums of countries such as Brazil or the Philippines, and he'd gladly make some discreet enquiries.

For his own part, Domingo thought he'd never seen Jack and Jadis look so anxious, and his heart surged out towards them. As he wrote on his private recommendation to the agency concerned, it would not be God's will to deny children to these people. He omitted to mention, however, that these were the same people who had given him his own first taste of family life, even though he'd had to attain his own maturity to get it.

So it was that one snowbound December day in 2035, Tom Markham Corstorphine made his way up the potholed drive, swaddled in a blanket and carried in the arms of Father Domingo Sanchopanza on the last stage of a journey that had started a year earlier in the middle of Borneo, when Islamist rebels fuelled by thoughts of the Khalifa had razed a remote jungle village, massacring all the inhabitants—all except one, who had come into the world just a few hours earlier. There was one thing they should know that might change their mind, Domingo had explained, that he was blind, perhaps from the Khalifa's destruction of his village; to which Jack and Jadis said then they would love him all the more.

Domingo handed baby Tom over to Jadis in their kitchen, with Jack and Fairbanks in attendance, all looking in wonder at the new arrival. As Jadis cradled him in her arms, cooing softly and searching every wrinkle of her new baby with her intense, slightly cross-eyed gaze, Domingo started to laugh—softly at first, but building into a great, hearty guffaw.

"You know what day it is, of course!" he said, wiping tears from his eyes with his vast, hairy arms. It had occurred to none of them that it was Christmas Day. Fairbanks jumped up at his old friend, eager to share the joke. Domingo patted him—"can you play the ox and the ass both at once, my friend?" he'd asked.

Tom managed well, and Jack and Jadis all but forgot he was blind. It wasn't until Tom was four and attending a day-nursery in a neighbour-ing village that they felt the real impact of his being blind. No, the teacher said in response to Jadis' evident disbelief, of course, Madame Corstorphine, you're right, he's otherwise well-adjusted and settled, but no, Madame Corstorphine, we can't have him here any more. We ha-ven't got the resources, you know, and then there's safety to think about..."

What utter nonsense, Jadis wanted to say, before bringing him home. The happy child sat in the passenger seat of the jeep, burbling merrily about all the scrapes that he and his friends had gotten into that day, while Jadis tried to think of any cause they might have had for thinking that his lack of sight was any burden. Tom had been exploring the house since he was a toddler, coping with stairs and doors and every other hazard; since the age of two he had known the huge garden as well as she had, and played near the uncovered pond without incident.

They had even taken him to SSM and—this was the only other time she even remembered taking note of his blindness—she now recalled when she and Tom, then aged three, were visiting the long avenue they called the Champs Elysées which, like all the thoroughfares of the an-cient city, had now been illuminated with giant-sized LED street lamps, so that it looked no darker nor more threatening than any other cityscape at night, for all the strangeness of the brooding polygonal monoliths and pyramids.

She had been chatting with a group of surveyors who'd just opened a structure called the Hexagon when all the lights suddenly went out, and they had been sucked into that same gut-wrenching blackness that had greeted her when, for the first time, she and Jack and the others on the first exploration crew had switched off their headlights. She heard peo-ple scream and whimper as primal darkness swept into every crevice. The blackout lasted less than ten seconds, until the backup generators came online. She had immediately looked down at Tom, holding her hand, who looked no more than slightly confused.

"*Maman*," he asked, "why is everyone scared?" She had been so swept up in her own fear that she had not at first realized that her small son had not noticed the blackout—because he lived his life in such darkness.

As she drove home from the nursery, half-listening to her son's innocent prattle, she pondered that blindness must be, for Tom, a natural state—his other senses reported his world so well that vision would only ever be, at best, a corroboration of more reliable modalities; at worst, a source of confusion and anxiety. Even without sight, he lived so well in the world that they had always felt as if he was as sighted as anyone else. But that, she thought, could have been an assumption dictated by our own narrowness of perception, living as we do in a world in which vision the most dominant sense, the sense we live by, and which has forced our other senses into an undergrowth so deep that we lack the language to describe flavors and textures except by metaphor.

We have no words, Jadis realized, for the colors of smells.

Because of this, Tom would never be able to describe his world to her, and this sudden knowledge hit her with a pang.

Apart from behavior, though, had Tom's eyes themselves ever given the game away? Did they flail anxiously hither and thither, like the eyes of blind people? No, they didn't. Were his eyes closed and sunken, like sightless eyes, long unused? No, they weren't. Indeed, they had given every appearance of being keen and alive. They were very large, fringed with long black lashes, and with yellow-green irises so broad that they left little room for whites. The pupils were not circular, but very slightly elliptical, almost pointed at the top and bottom.

When they were thinking of names for him, Jack had remarked that his eyes were so cat-like that they'd just have to name him 'Tom'. "That," he said, "and the fact that he's got an enormous, well... just *look* at him." Jadis looked down at the nether regions of her new baby (Jack was changing his diaper at the time), saw what Jack was pointing at, and giggled.

Well, Jadis thought, on the very edge of sleep in Jack's arms, Tom had been blind for no apparent reason, and now he could see, equally miraculously. No sense in wondering the whys and wherefores of it: instead, her mind started to reorganize her schedule for the next several weeks so she could spend as much time with Tom as possible, guiding him very gently into what would be a strange and possibly terrifying new world.

By the time that the six-year-old Tom first opened his eyes to see, Jadis' research at Souris Saint-Michel had turned a spectacular enigma into a city. There were no written records, no pictures, no carvings, nothing that a human eye would recognize as art: but the ground was littered with stone artifacts of such sophistication that the Remillardian type proved to be just one of the simpler varieties. There were millions of animal bones of all kinds, many representing species never before recorded from Ice Age Europe. And there were thousands of Neanderthal skeletons, yielding trillions of bases of DNA.

Even in the absence of written records, Jadis' meticulous, methodical approach to the data—the layout of the subterranean city, and the radiometrically established ages for the buildings, skeletons and artifacts—had teased out sufficient patterns for her to be able to sketch the city's history.

For more than half a million years, the Neanderthals and their immediate antecedents had sculpted Europe to their liking. They dammed rivers, changing their courses, shaped mountains, and built immense pyramids whose purpose was obscure, but generally assumed to have been religious.

But when modern humans arrived just before 40,000 years ago, the original Europeans faced a new threat. The invaders bred far faster than the Neanderthals, and swept all before them, despite their clearly inferior culture. It was then that the Neanderthals decided to go into hiding. They abandoned the surface, hiding in Souris Saint-Michel and perhaps other cities that remained undiscovered, though Avi Malkeinu's group had found what seemed to be a smaller version of a Neanderthal-style buried city beneath Mount Carmel. SSM itself ceased to be viable some time after 26,000 years ago, for no reason that Jadis could yet discern. The last inhabitants left, sealing up the wall behind them. Or perhaps they'd sealed themselves in, never more to emerge.

Balthazar had been right when he suspected that Souris Saint-Michel would be a mouse that roared. The world was stunned by all these revelations, and Jack and Jadis had become much-sought academic superstars—rôles they did not much like, although they did their best to accommodate reasonable requests. But they'd had to post round-the-clock security at SSM, and were glad that they did not live close to the site itself or to the new Institute campus at Aurignac. Press interviews always made Jack irritable, and although Jadis usually managed better, she was often withdrawn and silent for hours afterwards.

One concession they made to celebrity was the acquisition of a television—something they'd never had any time for, and found hard to get used to. But when asked to give interviews, they had never heard of the stations that journalists represented, and could rarely understand the references they made to the TV and current-affairs shows in which Jack and Jadis' work now featured. Even though the Institute had furnished them with the very latest Merlin-Tech-equipped computers and scorchingly fast, high-bandwith internet, Jack and Jadis always steered clear of internet news, gossip and blogs. They felt they had better things to do. After all, running SSM was a round-the-clock enterprise that left little time for much else.

Reluctantly, however, they felt that they should be better informed: and so, cautiously, they called their long-standing and long-suffering electrician, Laurent Gaspard, who had occasionally been called in at strange hours when it was found (for example) that a dormouse had gnawed through a cable in the attic, and he'd had to venture into this dark sanctuary for rodents, owls and other wildlife; and perforce do battle with one or more of The Horribles on the way. Gaspard was a brave man, but, Jack thought, his bravery was amply reflected in his call-out fee.

In addition to his electrical services, Gaspard ran a TV sales and rental franchise in Masseube. Jadis called on him one day while on the way back from Seissan market, to see if they might rent something, you know, just to see if they could live with it.

Their first TV was not a success. Jadis felt that she couldn't relax with Jack in the evenings because she felt that the great black monolith was looking at her, intruding. It went back to the shop after a week.

"We can't have that *thing* in here, Laurent," complained Jadis: "Looks like a giant bat, just hanging there. Can we try something less... well, obvious?"

Gaspard then supplied them with a flexi-screen ('latest organic semiconductor technology!') mounted in a gilt picture frame which, he said, could go on the wall above the sitting-room fireplace. It could double as a remote computer monitor if they liked (they didn't) and could even be used for videoconferencing (which they admitted had possibilities). But after five minutes of sales talk, Jack and Jadis felt their eyes glazing over. Jadis said that this was all very well, but how, *mon cher* Laurent, did you switch it on, or, more to the point, off?

The agent, sensing imminent technophobic *ennui*, moved to the main selling point for any reluctant TV owner — that this model would, in standby mode, look indistinguishable from a framed painting or print, indeed, any picture they wanted. And if they got bored, they could change the picture on command or set up a slideshow. He showed them a wide selection of possibilities in his catalog, most of which were either clichéd, pornographic or both. Jack said he rather liked the surprising diversity of exuberantly flesh-toned Titians, and started to recite a rude limerick on this theme in English, which left Gaspard looking nonplussed and Jadis irritated. Interrupting Jack in full flow, she asked the agent how could they have a custom picture?

And so it was that the monitor now looked exactly like the picture it replaced, a now-faded framed reproduction of *Riña de Gatos* ('The Cat Fight') by Goya, something they'd had since their Chesterton days, and which they'd kept as the two furred and be-fanged protagonists looked so much like two of the The Horribles.

Having now finally installed the TV — which Jadis would only ever refer to as the *Thing* — they found themselves extremely averse to switching it on, at least to begin with. Their end-of-day winding-down had become a sacred, special time that nobody had been allowed to disturb, with the exception of Fairbanks, and Tom, when he had been very small and reluctant to go to sleep on his own (and who, being blind, wouldn't have watched TV anyway). Now, however, they felt obliged to watch the *Thing*, to force themselves: which they did, in increasingly horrified fascination.

The TV news was ever varied, but ever much the same, in that every single item seemed colored by the implications of the discoveries at SSM. Politicians were more guarded, more cautious, as if a greater, older power was always looking over their shoulder. Comedians became wild-eyed and edgy: if human existence had been a late coda to a vast, lost civilization, little remained that was sufficiently important to make fun of, so they launched into one of two opposite directions — unspeakably bestial crudity or brittle, knowing surrealism.

Reporters in the increasing number of war zones, or covering the steadily rising tally of death from famine, disease and the more overt manifestations of climate change, seemed to struggle to make their voices heard, as if the immediate tragedy and horror of their subjects paled before the immensity of time that civilization had been known to exist — and that this immensity was, by and large, inhuman. It wasn't long before Sir Raphael Dimbleby, the doyen of the more thoughtful TV pundits, wondered openly whether SSM were the final proof of the ephemeral futility of human existence, quoting Macbeth's lines about life as a tale told by an idiot, full of sound and fury and signifying nothing.

Jadis, watching, pulled Jack's arms around her. "What have we done, dearest Jack," she implored, her voice cracking, "what have we *done*?"

Jack looked more intently at the latest report on the ongoing rebellion in somewhere or other. "I still think we should have gone for the Renoir," he said. "Or the Titian. You know, while Titian was mixing rose madder, his model reclined on a ladder..."

Jadis sat up, suddenly bright-eyed again, and walloped Jack with a cushion. Jack fought back —

"Her position, to Titian," he managed to utter, between whacks "... suggested coition..."

Fairbanks joined in, and the whole melée ended up on the hearthrug, the *Thing*, playing to itself, now quite forgotten. Jadis, wedged on the hearthrug between Jack's embrace and Fairbanks' gently snoring form, laughed to herself.

"... so he leaped up the ladder..." she murmured.

"An' 'ad 'er...," Jack concluded, eyes closed.

The *Thing* burbled to itself into a darkened room.

In times of existential crisis, people by and large turn to the certainties offered by religion. Whether or not these certainties really exist is a secondary question that few choose to confront. And what most gripped the world about Souris Saint-Michel was the definite, indisputable signs of Neanderthal religion, and in particular the sacrifice of modern humans to the nameless gods of their captors. This news, summarized in one of a seemingly never-ending series of reports in *Nature* ('Evidence for Neanderthal funerary and sacrifical custom' by Jadis L. Markham and twenty-seven others) was both denounced and welcomed in editorials and pulpits.

Denunciation was very much in the rule among the more austere Protestants, especially in the United States, who felt that religion in non-humans debased the very idea of religion itself, as well as being a challenge to biblical literalism. Jews were, by turns, fascinated, repelled and awed by the antiquity of it all, even though the more Orthodox rabbis claimed it was a scientific fraud designed to undermine the sanctity of Torah. Avi Malkeinu had written to Jadis of the small ultra-orthodox contingent who'd set up demonstrations outside his own dig at Mount Carmel. "I get most work done on Shabbat," he'd said, "when they've gone home." The Imams of the Khalifa, finding no ready guidance, and indeed more concerned with their own internal schisms, wisely said nothing.

The only positive reaction came from the Catholic church. "His Holiness deplores human sacrifice as barbaric," a black-garbed Papal legate said in a package on the main news bulletin one Friday evening in 2040, a few weeks after Tom received the dubious gift of sight. "However, with the new encyclical, *Undique Humanitas,*" the legate continued, "His Holiness proposes that the problem of the non-human origin of the religion from Souris Saint-Michel can be solved very easily—by the simple expedient of widening the definition of humanity."

At this, the legate flashed a twinkling, toothy smile that made Jadis and Jack sit up in wonder: the name at the bottom of the screen, not that they had any need to read it, said 'Mgr. Domingo Sanchopanza, Vatican Science Advisor'.

The Papacy had, it seemed, been well ahead of the game. For not only had the human world to worry about the implications of non-human cultures in the dead past, but those that were still very much alive. The surprise 2032 airlift to Israel of the Tibestian 'Sand Druids'—Gaston de Bonnard's *Prêtres du Sable,* who'd miraculously stepped out of an 18th-century traveler's tale and onto the screens of the world—had been a news item for a week or so. But a longer-lasting and much-debated preoccupation was the revelation the following year that the genome of Sand Druids (they called themselves 'Annakhnu') had evolved along a trajectory utterly foreign to that of the rest of humanity.

The implications of this were hard to unravel: either the Sand Druids really were humans, but had undergone a series of unusually harsh population crashes over many thousands of years of life in the middle of the Sahara, sculpting their DNA into strange, inhuman forms—or that their lineage had been distinct from that of modern humans for tens of millions of years, well before the modern human lineage had emerged.

Whatever the answer, a number of other strange, lost peoples now started to emerge from long obscurity in remote regions of the world, taking their cue from the Sand Druids to claim their share of the limelight.

It was a common human conceit to imagine that by the start of the twenty-first century, people would have rustled every bush and looked behind every tree in search of undiscovered species. But the world is far greater than humanity, even scientists, can imagine, and undiscovered species, if they are sentient, often have a knack of being discovered only on their own terms.

In 2033, a tribe of very peculiar pygmy 'hominids' (that had become the convenient and media-friendly if strictly inaccurate catch-all term for human-like but non-human creatures) emerged from the jungle in northern Sulawesi to give a press conference. With their all-over pelage of thick black fur and enormous, circular, completely red eyes, these people looked even less human than the Sand Druids. From their point of view, however, it might have been better had the Sulawesians chosen to remain in hiding, because their press conference—aired on live global webcast—was disrupted by a band of equally unknown but much larger hominids who decapitated the pygmies (and a few reporters who came too close) and ran into the bush, taking the A/V equipment with them.

No trace of either species had been seen since, and people were beginning to wonder if it had all been an elaborate stunt, until the emergence in 2035 of the Menehune. These hominids had been living for millennia, completely unsuspected, in the remote Alaka'i Swamp in the highlands of Kaua'i, Hawai'i. That, and the incident the following year in which a brigandish band of sasquatches burst into a bar in Dawson's Creek, British Columbia, demanding whiskey and human sacrifice.

After that they started popping up all over the place.

Looking at Domingo, on sparkling form, as ever, Jack and Jadis felt that whatever their own views on religion, the Papal stance was the only civilized course. Good for Domingo, they both thought, and now that the *Thing* had had their attention, it showed them news that turned their expressions from vicarious glory to outright horror. It was news—of a sort—of what had happened to Faye and Primrose.

The Saint-Rogatien Dream Team of 2031 had always occupied a special place in Jadis' heart—especially as it was very largely this same team that had broken ground at Souris Saint-Michel. She tried to keep up with them all, as far as she could.

Eric Onoye and Mathilde Reynard had got married and had taken over Ernestine Yanga's office in an increasingly beleaguered Nairobi.

Primrose Tsien and Faye Callaghan—respectively Jadis' former technician and graduate student—had also become partners at home and at work, having established Callaghan-Tsien (or 'CATS') Adventures, a very successful expeditions business, taking all-female teams of explorers up the many still-unconquered peaks of Tibet. Although the Chinese government had loosened access to the region, much of it remained wild and hardly visited by human beings, let alone westerners.

In the globally harsh winter of 2038, Faye and Primrose and their party had been trekking up a peak so obscure that it was known only by its GPS coordinates, when they lost contact with their base camp in the unseasonably heavy weather, and were not heard from again. Jack and Jadis were perhaps some of the more anxious among the worldwide TV audience following the long but ultimately futile attempts to trace them.

So news of Faye and Primrose guttered and petered out. Two years on, news watchers were now fascinated by the furor that inevitably greeted *Undique Humanitas*, and the strangely compelling personality of the Science Advisor at the Court of Saint Peter.

After the news, came *Zenge*.

Michael Zenge, a one-time White House press secretary and political journalist, hosted the most widely syndicated chat show in the world. His success was attributed to a perfectly judged understatement. Polite but warm; mild and self-deprecating to a degree; conservatively-suited, silver-haired Zenge would just sit next to his guest, posing what seemed the most innocuous questions, and then just let them talk. In so doing, guests often let slip the kind of revelations that more up-front interviewers could never manage to prize from their victims.

Another Zenge hallmark was that he never went for the obvious roster of celebrities eager to plug a movie or a book, but sought genuinely interesting and varied voices, many of whom would be unfamiliar to most people, and sometimes even downright eccentric — but all of whom had interesting stories to tell, and whom he presented as sympathetically as possible. Jack and Jadis had been guests themselves about five years earlier, in the only live TV interview they'd ever consented to give since their Cambridge days. *Zenge* was almost the only thing on the *Thing* that they enjoyed watching.

"Who's he dug up this time?" asked Jadis, remembering the captain of the trans-sexual trans-Antarctic cycling team of the previous week.

"Not sure," said Jack, who'd risen to refill their wine glasses. "I don't recognize him. Too much hair."

"More hair than last time, anyway," said Jadis. She took the wine, her own cloud of hair swaying. She drew close to Jack as he sat down again, trying not to spill the wine. And so in static fascination they watched the emergence of yet another new species of hominid onto the world stage.

"Freddy, can you tell us why you like Tolkien?" asked Michael Zenge.

"Freddy who?" asked Jadis.

"I don't know, I missed the credits," replied Jack.

"Yes, of course, Michael, of course I can," replied the guest known only as Freddy.

"And....?" Zenge prompted.

"Oh, I see, you actually want me to tell you?" The studio audience laughed.

"Yes, please, if you would..."

The guest scratched his left nostril with the index finger on his right hand and adjusted himself awkwardly in his seat. "But of course, Michael. It's like this. When I first looked into *The Lord of the Rings*, I was struck at how all the different peoples of Tolkien's Middle-earth are happily living together, with harmony and cooperation in place of strife and discord."

"The Elves, Dwarves, and so on? What we used to call a 'multicultural' society'?"

"Yes. But don't forget, Michael, the stone giants in the mountains. Not to mention those glorious tree giants, the Ents, so sadly declining to extinction—with, I have to say it, such British fortitude. I found it most admirable. And affecting. A model for our times."

Jadis tensed, her lips pressed together in a hard line. "Jack, I don't like this one at all. He's... he's.... creepy." She had now sat up, perched on the edge of the sofa, her front now illuminated by the wash from the screen.

Jack saw her eyes burning like coals, the tautness in her neck muscles. Jack tensed up too: she was right—there was something very, very odd indeed about this guest. He braced himself for what his instinct told him was a nasty surprise around the corner. Part of his mind replayed another occasion when Raphael Dimbleby had quoted Macbeth: by the pricking of my thumbs, something wicked this way comes.

"How did you come across *The Lord of the Rings*, Freddy?" asked Zenge. "If I might say so, it is a very popular work in many countries, but it's a surprise to hear its praises sung from the Tibetan Plateau."

"Tibet," said Jadis, "oh no, it can't be... and Faye was always going on about hobbits..." Her eyes got wider with each new revelation, and she started to bite her nails.

"Great literature transcends cultures and geography, Michael, as I am sure you're aware," the guest continued. "But I admit it, foreign literature is somewhat hard to come by in my... er... neck of the woods. Ha ha ha!" Freddy's laughter was like the sound of concrete blocks being dragged over corrugated iron: Jadis winced as if physically slapped. The guest, a thousand miles away in a studio in England, was seen quite obviously scratching his groin. The camera panned rapidly to his face, or what could be seen of it. The guest's eyes were completely covered with aviator shades, the rest furred with long off-white hair.

"Is this guy for real?" asked Jack. "Isn't this another hoax?"

Once more, the guest tried to adjust himself in his seat. The problem was that he seemed far too big for it. The audience, once sympathetic and warm, had now become edgy and nervous. Zenge, affecting not to notice, sat forward in expectation. As if on cue, the guest leaned slightly forward as if to share a confidence.

"It's a very interesting tale, how we acquired Tolkien's masterpiece, Michael," he said. "Most interesting indeed."

"That's the tale everyone knows? About the all-woman expedition to Tibet and what happened to it? Can you dispel the myths?"

"Oh, Jack," gasped Jadis.

"Ha ha ha!" Freddy screeched. The sound of a dinosaur being dismembered by a chorus of blunt chainsaws. "Yes, oh yes, Michael, we made them feel most welcome at our humble mountain fastnesses, or, to be poetic, our Caves of Ice, whence flows our Sacred River Alph. Ha ha ha!" A roaring shriek like a battery chicken farm being hit by a rocket-propelled grenade. "So nice to have a visit from others in Middle-earth, if you will. I am pleased to say we gave them a very warm welcome. Anyway, one of those nice ladies had *The Lord of the Rings* in her baggage. A big read, one supposes, for those long days when blizzards confine one to base and one cannot find a good film on the television. Ha ha ha!" Plate steel attacked by ill-tuned combine harvesters at full throttle.

"Fuck me," said Jack under his breath, holding Jadis tightly. She had begun to shake.

"Could you read it, though? Straight off the bat?"

"Naturally, Michael. To be sure we see very few others at our home — which is why any visit from outside is to be treasured. But we are not completely ignorant, you know. Some of us have even scaled the heights of Henry James. No, no, we could hack our way around Tolkien very passably, thank you." The guest now idly picked at his left nostril, teasing out a long, lime-green skein of mucus, which he ate, chewing appreciatively for some seconds, wiping his fingers on large handkerchief from the breast pocket of an expensive-looking blazer.

"You say that visits from the outside are to be — in your words — treasured...?" Zenge asked.

"As the old *koan* from the lamasery has it," replied Freddy, "'you can check out any time like, but you can never leave'. Ha ha ha!" The guest now sat back expansively. This had the effect of thrusting his pelvis forward, spreading out the lower limbs, and making the guest's gender shockingly, vastly apparent even beneath heavy corduroy trousers. The guest smiled, baring huge yellowing canines.

Jadis sprang up, struggling free from Jack's constraining embrace, and threw the wine bottle at the screen.

"You bastard!" she yelled at the top of her lungs. The bottle bounced, splashing bloody gouts of Bergerac on the carpet and into the fire, creating fizzing bolts of hot liquid that shot out over the hearth. One hit Fairbanks on the nose. He'd been distressed by the obvious, rising anxiety of his mistress, but this was just too much. He yelped and ran for it, padding up the stairs to shelter underneath Tom's bed. Jadis's screams continued: "you evil bastard!" She punched a hole through the screen: sparks arced across the gap and died, but the picture, being formed in a distributed network of organic semiconductors, continued regardless: "You... you... *filth!*"

The studio audience was tittering like a lunatic on the verge of running amok as Zenge and Freddy skirted around the delicate topic of how Faye and Primrose and their colleagues had met their grisly end at the hand of this—*Thing*. Jadis now turned on Jack, fists pummeling his chest—"turn the fucking *Thing* off, Jack! Turn. It. *Off!*"

And so he did, but when he'd tried to take her in his arms and still the incandescent eyes, the flailing arms and ragged masses of hair, she fought him back.

"Look what we've done, Jack," she screamed, "look what we've *done!*"

Tom had now got up, roused by the racket, and was standing at the sitting room door, in pyjamas and dark shades, Fairbanks peeping out nervously from between the boy's knees.

"*Maman? Papa?*"

Jack's first instinct was a strong urge to flee, but a second later knew that this would be unhelpful at best. So he simply held her, and held her again, until she could flail no more, and crumpled into his arms, wracked with sobs. He laid her carefully on the sofa.

"*Maman* is fine, Tom" said Jack. "Just tired. You two go up to bed, I'll come and tuck you up in a minute." He sat by his wife, calmer now, stroking her hair. She pulled herself into his lap as if she was a cat, her arms thrown around his waist.

He wanted to say so many things, but he was not a man given to long speeches, and everything he could think of seemed either pat or trite. Shared horror for Faye and Primrose? Yes, he'd loved them both, too, but they were grown women in the high-risk adventure business who'd knowingly put themselves in danger. That was their choice, not ours. That had Avi not heard about De Bonnard's work, here at Saint-Rogatien, he'd never have rescued the Sand Druids? Possibly, but think of what would have happened had he not done this. The Sand Druids and perhaps all the other hominid species might have perished without our even knowing of their existence, which would have been a greater evil.

That he and Jadis should not have followed their hunches? That would have been a disservice to science, and a worse evil still. Jack thought of Ruxton Carr and regretted that Jadis hadn't met him.

That they should not have followed their hearts?

Inconceivable.

However, it remained the case that their discoveries had changed the world more profoundly than anything since the discovery of relativity, or evolution, or gravity, in which case Jadis was partly right—that we cannot simply discover things and unleash them on the world without taking some measure of responsibility. That was something that would just have to be borne.

There came to his mind a favorite line from *Middlemarch*, a book he'd read in the past few years and found—to his surprise—greatly to his liking, partly because he saw in Jadis an echo of Dorothea. It was something about the greater good of the world being forged by unhistoric acts. In the end, Jack said nothing. Jadis, calming, sat up and parted her hair. Her lips tasted of tears.

The next day, Tom barged into his parents' room to find them curled up like two spoons and fast asleep, even though the sun was climbing fast into a blue sky. Oh well, he thought, I can feed Fairbanks myself. On going downstairs he was puzzled to see the flexi-screen, rolled up and shoved into a black plastic bag outside the kitchen door.

Chapter 3: Abbot

Central North Africa, Earth, *c.* 6,355,000 years ago

But this momentous question, like a fire bell in the night, awakened and filled me with terror.
Thomas Jefferson—*Letter to John Holmes, 22 April, 1820*

The Abbot put his aching head in his hands. He was tempted to cover his ears, too—to shut out the bickering from either side—but he knew that such a gesture would have been unseemly. More to the point, unhelpful. Just like this unseasonable weather: so close, the black skies congealing into ugly thunderheads that piled ever higher over the savannah but never burst. His throat was dry; the hairs on the back of his neck itched; his head throbbed. And still the squabble went on and on.

"The records of our predecessors are quite clear..."

"Clear, did you say, Brother Cynewulf? *Clear*? Oh no, not nearly as clear as the mud at the bottom of the Great Lake."

"I was going to say, Brother Caedmon, before I was so rudely interrupted, that is, that the records are clear enough, to those with enough wit to decipher the glyphs, which are—I admit—very faded, and in an archaic mode that very few, these days..."

"Meaning what, pray?" Brother Caedmon sat back, his yellow-green eyes pitiless glints from beneath his hood. Brother Cynewulf adjusted his considerable and (in this heat) malodorous bulk in his seat, coiling himself up for a truly stinging rejoinder. Time, the Abbot thought, for a seasoned Man of the Goddess to show his quality.

"Shall we ring for some tea?" he said, tinkling a little bronze bell on his ironwood desk, the sparkling sounds peppering the glutinous atmosphere while doing nothing to dispel it. A small pithek shuffled into the room. It was clothed in the dirty white robes of the novitiate, several sizes too big. Every step it made exposed it to the risk of tripping on the ragged hem, its cowl falling over its face, pitching it forward, blindly. But the creature had learned to accommodate the over-generosity of its livery with a shambling grace, loping along in a state of imminent catastrophe, perpetually averted. Criticality in motion. "Mint tea, please, Mandergast? For three?" the Abbot asked, in as kindly a tone as he could muster. He had a soft spot for the pitheks, an affection that was the butt of many jokes made outside his hearing, or so the tellers imagined. In truth, he had a hard time explaining it even to himself—which was, of course, the only reason why he let the jokes circulate. "If you would be so kind?" The creature briefly bowed its heavily browed head, snuffled something indecipherable and loped off through the fug.

"I understand your concerns, my friends," the Abbot continued. "Really, I do, and with good reason. The timing of the Festival of the Apparition is far too important for us to get wrong. We all agree that it would be a tragedy for us to wake up one sunny morning and find we'd missed it. Too much rides on it." Not least our reasons for our continued existence, he mused: not least our very lives. If we miss it, the Annak-hnu—or whatever they call themselves—would lynch us. Quite right, too. The sentiment, anyway, if not the execution. And there were other things, too. If only he could remember what they were, but this awful weather stifled all thought like a smothering shroud. "How many years, is it, precisely, Brother Cynewulf?"

"The records are quite clear, Father—*quite* clear," the corpulent monk returned, not without a venomous glance at his colleague, who pretended not to notice. "They say that apparitions of the Goddess occur once every two million, fifty-eight thousand, four hundred and sixteen years, two hundred and one days, forty-eight minutes and twelve seconds.

"*Seconds?*" snorted Brother Caedmon.

"Or thereabouts. And if they—the records—are correct..."

"*Seconds?*" Brother Caedmon repeated, the few remaining shreds of decorum sloughing from his now open contempt. The Abbot raised his hand to stay him. The strain of just this one, simple act, of thrusting his arm upwards through this heat, caused more sweat to spurt from his armpits and made him catch his breath. Brother Cynewulf, unaware of his superior's discomposure, continued.

"... the Blessed One will so honor us..." All three monks bowed their heads in unison. A knock at the door was heard. The Abbot looked up. He was conscious of the moisture dripping down his face and into his eyes as he did so. The fur on his neck and down his back was slick with it. He wiped his eyes and brow on his sleeve—the roughness of the burlap was a tonic as it scraped away the layers of sweat, grime and the sharp dust of the dry grassland.

O, that it would rain!

"Come, Mandergast." The pithek waddled in with the tea-tray. Ironwood, like most things here. But the tea-set itself was made from real glass and the samovar itself was chased with silver. The monks could practically hear the cogs in the little hominin's brain creak with the strain of coordinating its muscles and joints—all enfolded in its billowing robes—so as not to drop the precious load. The creature slid the tray onto the Abbot's desk with a flourish, and stood up, its face a picture of relief and triumph. "Thank you, Mandergast," the Abbot said. "You may go." The pithek shuffled off, closing the door behind it. "Bless," said the Abbot, looking after it, sighing with a species of contentment he couldn't quite identify or understand. He could almost feel Cynewulf and Caedmon swallowing their laughter. He looked up and turned to the monks. Their expressions were as composed, as serious, as ever. Perhaps it was just his imagination, playing tricks.

O, this alien heat!

"Shall we be mother?" Silence reigned—silence, if that is silence which is broken by the tinkling splash of tea and the sucking noises of three monks slurping it through lumps of sugar.

O, the joy in tepid, sugary liquid!

The Abbot continued, now confident that a properly sacerdotal calm had been restored. "Brother Cynewulf?"

"Father? Oh yes. The Blessed One should turn up this coming Friday, immediately after Vespers. Or perhaps during it. There is, you will appreciate, a *small* margin for error."

The Abbot sensed the restlessness of Brother Caedmon once again reigniting, but waved him down again, for the moment. This time he managed to wave his arm in such a way—just *so*—that a small draft of air washed up his sleeve and irrigated his armpit. Lovely!

"Brother Cynewulf," he continued, "does your calculation take account of such things as... oh, I don't know, you're the expert... orbital eccentricity, precession, isostatic rebound, tectonic shifts, secular gravitational anomalies caused by planetary conjunctions and whatnot, not to mention dear old human error? A lot can happen in two million and whatever-it-is years. Not to mention the fact that our distinguished predecessors were not quite as we are now, and might simply have counted things differently?"

"I can assure you Father, that all such confounding variables have been accommodated. Our predecessors might have been different in their culture and their degree of learning, Father—far superior, in many respects—but they were as blind as we are when we are infants, and had the same number of fingers and toes." Cynewulf chuckled at his own joke, and the Abbot felt it politic to join in.

Caedmon, meanwhile, came to the boil. "Father, *if* I may..."

"You may." The Abbot puffed wearily and took another grateful sip of his tea.

"Thank you." The younger monk shot a smug look at his elder colleague. "My team and I have been looking at the evidence directly, as you know—*empirically*—and from our investigations of the laminations in the bottom sediments of the Great Lake..."

"Brother Caedmon," interrupted the Abbot, "We have already had the benefit of your most illuminating lecture. You have my permission, therefore, to cut to the chase."

"Yes Father. Of course. Anyway, direct and repeated counting of annual cycles in the layered sediments of the lake bed pulls up an interval of two million and fifty-odd thousand years, plus or minus a couple of *millennia*—never mind hours, minutes and... well, *seconds*. It's just not possible to be as accurate as all that."

"That's the benefit of having historical records, Brother Caedmon," interposed Brother Cynewulf. "Clarity. The answer at the back of the book."

"Clarity, my arse..."

"Brother Caedmon, *please*..."

"My apologies, Father. The problem is not only that Brother Cynewulf has this unfeasibly accurate interval since the last Apparition, but I'll bet that no matter how clear the records are, they'll say something enigmatic and open to no end of theological and, no doubt, scholastic interpretation. They won't say 'Oh yes, the Blessed One appeared today, about tea-time'. Will they? And what's more..."

"But that's precisely what they *do* say. Not the tea-time part, exactly, but the records are otherwise quite plain."

"Yes, but about *what*? What form did the last Apparition take, such that it might leave some mark—some physical, corroborative evidence—such that we'd be able to pick it up, unequivocally, more than two million years later? A calling card? A *fossil*? Your records say that *something* happened, dear Brother Cynewulf, but they don't say what. To be sure, the lake laminations do show some signs of disturbance just over two million years ago—but that's just the problem! The lakebed was disturbed, don't you see? Interrupting the usual process of sedimentation, screwing up the process of annual variations of deposition—which is what we rely on to create our chronology—and this not only makes for a big margin of error, but also obscures whatever it was that made the disturbance in the first place. We just don't *know*." Caedmon's voice rose as he spoke, in tone and volume, so that his final sentence came out as a pleading wail of anguish.

"Ah, knowledge," said the Abbot. "It's such a problem, isn't it? The closer one seems to get to it, the more elusive it seems. I have a feeling that at a time like this, we must take the best evidence on offer. Brother Cynewulf's records..."

"But Father, they can't... surely?"

"Take heart, Brother Caedmon. Look at it this way. Your limnological evidence—which is, I might say, greatly valued—does not actually contradict the historical interpretation offered by Brother Cynewulf. Does it?"

"No, Father, it..."

"Well then. In which case we have nothing to lose by watching out for an Apparition on Friday evening, will we? We'll all be in the chapel, anyway, won't we? And if the Blessed One doesn't arrive—well, we'll put away our pride, put away our shame—vainglorious emotions, both—roll up our sleeves, and look at the problem again. Won't we? *Won't we?*"

"Yes Father," chorused the two monks, as chastened as novices.

"In any case, I have a feeling that when the Blessed One chooses to grace us with her divine presence, we'll just know."

"We will... just *know*?" asked Cynewulf incredulously.

"It is as I said, Brothers. Knowledge is a funny thing. More tea, anyone?"

A rumble in the sky overhead sliced through the contemplative mood of the office. The Abbot looked up. The sound was instantly followed by a sharp tap at the door.

"Saved by the bell," he said. The Brethren Cynewulf and Caedmon looked at each other, their faces mirrored pictures of puzzlement.

-=0=-

Time was when the Venerable Alfred could have been sure of his solitude. That out here, in the whitewashed, wattle-and-daub hut he called his hermitage, he'd not see a living soul for months on end. Perhaps years.

Bliss.

With his small garden in which he scratched out yams and a few herbs; a well which, while niggardly, met his needs; and the thin shade of a ragged thorn hedge to keep out the worst of the Sun (and beneath which he could sleep, on hot nights, meditating on the stars through jags of branches)—he made himself a life which made up in contemplation what it lacked in luxury.

Well, almost.

And on those days when he visited the shore of the Great Lake to wash, to trap fish, or manage to snare a few stork or ducks or even a young keryx—well, then, he felt, his cup overflowed, and he made sure he offered the Goddess his most profound thanks.

If only he could be sure that she was listening.

How ironic, he often thought, while reciting his offices, that when he had been at the monastery—a long day's walk distant, across one now-withered arm of the Great Lake—the voice of the Goddess had been so hard to hear. Novices had yet to learn to adopt the necessary ruminative calmness, but—O! Frustration!—as soon as they had almost captured it, that elusive spirit, that frail voice, they would be burdened with the manifold distractions of mature responsibility. And if by some mis-chance they found themselves holding the office of Abbot, well—the voice would invariably disappear completely. It had happened to him, in just that way.

For more than forty years he had tended his cantankerous and dwin-dling flock in that windswept outpost, watching the Great Lake shrink, and the galleried pithek-shrieking forests melt into the ever-encroaching grass, just as his once luxuriant mane had faded to the smoothness of bald skin, naked under a bald sky. Eventually he'd had enough. That he 'wished to rediscover the voice of His Goddess' was how he'd explained it to the Synod, and they, with great sympathy (because many of them knew exactly what it felt like) allowed him to retire to this life of com-plete, undisturbed seclusion. And so he, Abbot Alfred, had given way to Abbot Aethelwald, and then Abbot Aelfric, and so to the present Abbot, whom Alfred could dimly remember as a callow novice, even though he could not quite bring his name to mind.

Forty more years passed. But still the voice of his Goddess remained too faint for him to hear. He had long since lost count of the times he'd abased himself before her image, grazing his knees, chanting until he went hoarse or fell asleep—his voice lost on the torrid air, unheard. He'd lost count of the other ways he sought for a sign of her, in the branching patterns of thorn trees against the Moon; the scatters of turtle or catfish bones, desiccating on the salty lake shore; the flutter of spoonbills set fly from the heat-hazy water; the swirls of wind-blown grass; the ripples of stones cast far out in the lake; the clots of clouds in the sky; even the patterns of stripes and spots in the pelts of the beasts he'd caught.

Nothing.

He'd begun to despair, but he put that most treacherous of emotions aside as he had so often counseled his flock. Perhaps his moment had passed. Or maybe he'd lost the knack. No matter — he would continue his offices as he'd done for so many years.

Until, one day, when he'd been hoeing his vegetable patch, and thinking of something utterly prosaic, such as how much his knees ached these days, he heard a voice behind him. It was the voice of a young woman, as clear as if she'd spoken directly into his ear.

"Oh, Alfred," she'd said, "you really are a very silly man."

And that was it. He'd practically had a heart attack on the spot. Recovering, though, with marvelous speed, he turned, just in time to see the ghost of a teasing smile and the fluttering hem of a bright red robe disappear behind his hut. Shockingly red, against the duns and blues and greens and whites of his world. Throwing down his hoe, he turned to follow, but when he got to the corner, there was nothing. Nothing at all, in the view of the wide burning savannah spread out before him. He walked all round the hut (this took all of twenty seconds, even with his knees in their current condition) and didn't see her. He'd half expected that when he'd given up, and had gone indoors, he'd find her there, crouched, in the hut's darkness.

It was not to be.

Had he been a much younger man he'd have stormed at the injustice of it all. Now, at the age of almost a hundred, he limped back to his garden and continued hoeing from where he'd left off. In the shade of his straw hat's brim, though, a single tear from one yellow-green eye ran down a deep fissure of his cheek and vanished into his straggly beard, evaporating. But he always kept an ear cocked. Just in case.

Only...

Hardly two months had gone by since the mysterious apparition, and some of his crops were coming up for harvest, when Alfred's solitude was shattered, and he feared he'd never hear her voice again.

Except that a small voice deep within reminded him that 'never' was a very big word, and its use by the clergy was at best disrespectful, at worst, heretical. Then something in him stirred, an old memory from long before his retirement, long before, even, his election to Abbot. From his youth, long ago, when there were trees with monkeys in them, and the Great Lake was wide, and not so salty. That there had been talk in some scholarly circles, then, that the next apparition of the Goddess was imminent, perhaps in their lifetimes, if only just. It could be that in that tiny, fleeting encounter he'd been blessed with something real, something premonitory, something that had made his long wait worthwhile—even though it did not seem so, at the time—and from that he took some measure of comfort and gave thanks.

What disturbed his peace, though, was an apparition of a more concrete kind. It turned up outside his gate one brazenly hot day just after noon, when he'd retreated into his hut to wait out the day's heat. The apparition was so remarkable that Alfred just had to come out to take a closer look. He grabbed his straw hat—and his machete, rosy with rust though it was, just in case.

It was a tall man, a warrior perhaps, except that his height was not matched with girth in proportion, and his face was white—*white*—and thin, with pink-rimmed milky-yellow eyes, and long, thick hair the color of bleached grass-stalks. He wore white robes, reminiscent of the novitiate, except that his were girt round with broad leather belts, and he wore a long bow and a quiver across his back, as well as a brace of short, stone-tipped spears, and wore stout leather boots. His height seemed greatly increased, though, to the old hermit, because the stranger was mounted on an enormous rhinoceros, braid-maned, perhaps six feet tall at the shoulder, its immense legs terminating in great hooves, its snorting snout tipped with a single, horn that tapered more than a meter skywards, terminating in a point that looked wickedly vicious, for all that it was strung with tassels and beaded cords.

The warrior dismounted, jumping to the ground. Small puffs of dust rose from his feet as they scuffed the hard pan. Indeed, Alfred could still see the clouds of dust raised by the passage of his lumbering steed, and there seemed to be other such puffs of dust on the eastern horizon. This strange, pale rider was not alone.

As Alfred watched, the rhino pitched its great head forward and snuffled on the bare ground for such forage as it could find. A huge, fleshy tongue lapped out, greedily scouring the cracked earth for salt. As it did so the rhino dropped a series of enormous turds, which sat on the parched soil, steaming. These would prove excellent for his crops, thought Alfred. He decided that polite engagement might be more profitable than mute retirement.

"Good day, Sir," began Alfred. The words seemed alien and uncouth, until he realized that he'd probably spoken nothing out loud for more than a year. "Might I be of assistance?"

The warrior spoke. Like his body, his voice seemed fleshless, all edges and sibilant hardness.

"*Bokh'rt'v* — greetings — most reverend *attaar'kha'av*" the warrior seemed to say. Alfred was sure he failed to understand at least half of it. But then, he reflected, he heard speech no more frequently than he spoke himself. The two men bowed to each other. Alfred was relieved that the non-verbal courtesies, at least, were mutually intelligible.

"From the East we come, my people, *ann'h'kh'nu*. What is the name of this land?"

This question threw Alfred, temporarily, for he had not thought of it for a long while. The problem was that nobody had lived in this country — nobody in it but for the monks — for a very long time. The nomads, always scarce, had disappeared with the trees and the freshness of the Great Lake. And the pitheks had no language of their own. Alfred began to think aloud. Now he had rediscovered speech, it was hard to stop.

"Name? That is a most profound question, is it not? Few have lived in this desolate region, and so it has not been blessed with a name. The Brethren in the House across the Great Lake named their community after its founder, the Brother who came here... oh, well, years ago, beyond count. Thousands. Perhaps even millions. And his name was 'Shinaar'.

"*Shinaar,*" repeated the warrior, staring straight at Alfred with his unnerving eyes, their irises the color of soured milk. "*Shinaar.*"

"Yes. Well, I suppose so."

"*Shinaar...*"

"Yes." There was an awkward pause, which Alfred felt obliged to fill with noise. "Might I offer you some water? Some food?"

"*Shinaar.* This is the place for which my people, *ann'h'kh'nu*, have been seeking, *b'r'kh'ú*. Where the City of Heaven we will build."

"Here?" All Alfred could think was that his long solitude would be broken. That he would never hear his Goddess again. "Here?"

"Yes," said the warrior, who carefully folded himself downwards so he could kiss the ground at Alfred's feet. "Here." He rose, sand on his parched lips, tears in his egg-poached eyes. "*Here.*"

Chapter 4: Student

Gascony, France, Earth, April, 2054

What men or gods are these? What maidens loth?
What mad pursuit? What struggle to escape?
What pipes and timbrels? What wild ecstasy?
John Keats — *Ode on a Grecian Urn*

Shoshana Levinson shouldered her backpack and clambered wearily up the jetway. The six-hour journey crammed into a budget seat on the Stansted-Blagnac airship had been grueling. She should have saved up and got the train, as everyone had advised. Even the bus would have been better.

In the arrivals hall at Blagnac, she looked round at the small cluster of people, each one with face drawn, eyes expectant, waiting to see a friend or loved one emerge. A few — bored taxi drivers, mostly — held up signs. Although some were in uniform, it was easy to make out the skeletally tall Pamir Kaptars, their cream-and-dirt-orange manes either shorn or pinned back in laughably vain attempts to make themselves look human. Not that one should ever laugh at a Kaptar. Especially if you didn't want your head bitten off.

She stopped, scanning the reception committee, and now that her mental search image had become attuned to fur and hair, her own welcoming committee became apparent. It was a tall woman in a baggy sweatshirt, denim shorts and extremely aged sneakers, but distinguished mainly by an unkempt mass of hair that reached almost down to her waist. It was dark brown — almost black — but here and there streaked with gray. At first Shoshana couldn't make out her face, until the woman pushed the hair out of the way and stared at her with a gaze so dark and piercing that — just for a moment — Shoshana imagined herself in one of those anxiety nightmares in which you are looking for something, and everyone else unaccountably fails to notice that you are naked.

It was Jadis Markham. Of course it was. Shoshana recognized her from innumerable news pictures, none of which had captured the instant and overwhelming intensity that hung about her like a cloud. But then Dr Markham smiled, and everything changed. The eyes lit up like firebrands, and, but for the crows-feet, her face seemed to be that of a girl in her mid-twenties. Not at all like the serious, distinguished academic of fifty that Shoshana knew Dr Markham to be.

"Shoshana Levinson? Lovely to meet you. Quick — let's get out of here. The car's parked illegally." Shoshana hurried to keep up with Dr Markham's tall, easy strides. Nice legs, too, she thought, for a wrinkly.

"Hop in," said Dr Markham, gunning the motor as Shoshana flung her pack in the back seat of the open-topped jeep and climbed aboard. It was great to have shed the load, and to feel the warm springtime breeze of France on her face and arms, the loose sleeves of her t-shirt flapping, blowing away the shrouds of miserable London with each passing mile.

For a long time, Shoshana was too awed by her company to say anything. Jadis Markham was her heroine. She'd been reading about the fantastic discoveries at Souris Saint-Michel since she had been a little girl, and Jadis had been an inspiration for her even during her darkest hours — hours that had increased in both frequency and darkness until she'd made that final break from home. The fluke that had scraped her through the Cambridge entrance exam to read Archaeology, with a good if unspectacular high-school diploma, had a lot to do with that. She whispered a grateful prayer for the old-girl network, in which her college tutor had been a student of Professor Reynard at Cambridge. Shoshana knew that Professor Reynard had been one of the very first people to have seen the underground city at Souris Saint-Michel.

Shoshana was not to know that Professor Mathilde Reynard's life since SSM had been clouded by tragedy. Six years into their stint in Nairobi, her beloved Eric had died in agony, having succumbed to the new and lethal Naivasha-6 Hemorrhagic Fever virus, probably contracted from contaminated blood during an operation for a ruptured appendix that had itself gone badly wrong. Mathilde had counted herself lucky that she'd not caught this highly contagious disease herself — either that or any number of even more horrible diseases which, local gossip had it, were stalking the townships and the bush. Such talk was easily dismissed as folk superstition, especially in these days of crisis, but after what had happened to poor Eric, she did wonder.

Nairobi itself, beset by shortages, disease and a flood of migrants from the increasingly lawless countryside, was no comfort. Mathilde had fled, at first to Jack and Jadis' farmhouse where by happy chance Domingo was visiting, and being a good Catholic herself, she was able to discuss her concerns with him in depth and detail. The sensation of spiritual healing, of absolution, of uplift, had been palpable. She thanked God for confessors as sensitive and as articulate as Domingo (because, honestly, you hardly know it, to look at him). In time, a Chair at Cambridge came up, and her application was successful. But for the rest of her life she would regard the farmhouse at Saint-Rogatien as a haven untouched by care or worry, and would recommend it most warmly to any promising student, even one as inexperienced as this Levinson girl. Nothing like a good start in life, Mathilde thought, and if Shoshana was anywhere near as good as Jadis had reputedly been at the same age—eighteen, was it?—then she'd be fine.

Mathilde had seen Shoshana at interview, much as Jadis saw her now. Although Mathilde had told Jadis everything about Shoshana that could be found on paper, Jadis wasn't really prepared for the girl in the flesh.

Sizing Shoshana up with a glance in the afternoon sunshine at Blagnac, Jadis' first thought was that she'd have to be careful in case she drove some of the male crew to distraction. Shoshana was hardly more than five feet tall even in trek-booted feet, but packed every inch with what Jack would have called 'personality,' before he started referring (as corroborative evidence) to Magdalenian mother goddesses and the more fleshly works of Titian.

Jadis strongly suspected that Shoshana was well aware of her own appearance and its effects.

She thought of Tom.

No—no need for her to worry on Tom's account: he could handle himself quite well. He was in the middle of his second year at Cambridge with Mathilde, and had (according to her) broken a few hearts already. With his stocky, rugged good looks, matinée-idol French accent and permanent designer iShades, he looked more like a rock star than a trainee archaeologist. No, Tom was more than capable of looking after himself.

In fact, Jadis thought, as Tom was at Saint-Rogatien for the Easter recess, she might ask him to show Shoshana around. There had also been talk of Shoshana going to Israel in the summer as a volunteer on Avi's project, as Tom was also due to do. The fact that Shoshana had a smattering of Hebrew and had been to Israel already this year (according to her letter of recommendation) was a big factor in her favor. She could show Tom the ropes there as he would do for her at SSM. It could all work out rather well, but for one thing: Jadis wondered if Tom would be able to keep himself from showing Shoshana the latest and hitherto very secret discovery at SSM. She rather wanted Domingo to see it before anyone else outside the immediate team, because it was—well, puzzling. But

Domingo had promised a visit soon, so perhaps it wouldn't hurt for Shoshana to get a sneak preview.

Jadis' first instincts about Shoshana, her appearance and how she might exploit it, had been entirely correct. Shoshana had been raised an only child in a conventional Jewish household in North London. Although her parents belonged to an Orthodox synagogue, she went to a secular secondary school where she had been very happy. But then came the day when, aged twelve, she'd returned home one Friday evening to find the mirrors turned to the wall, a blanket over the TV, and her mother in the kitchen in such distress that she was initially quite unable to talk.

"Where's Dad?" Shoshana kept asking her mother, receiving no reply but shakes of the head and more tears. Only when Aunt Jess, her mother's sister, called a little later did she learn the full horror — that earlier that day, Barry Levinson, aged fifty-three, moderately successful chartered accountant, loving husband of Myra and father of Shoshana, had been robbed, by assailants unknown, pushed under a tube train and killed.

Then the nightmare really started.

Over the days and weeks, the full history of Barry Levinson's past came back to haunt Shoshana and her mother. They knew that he'd come from a rigidly Ultra-Orthodox background but had somehow escaped. He had gone to University as Baruch but re-emerged as Barry, joined a middle-of-the-road Orthodox congregation and did his best to avoid his more intolerant and intolerable relations. His Achilles heel was his brother Howie, with whom he'd started his business and who was now a sleeping partner. Shoshana loathed Uncle Howie with a passion. He'd backslid into religious fundamentalism as his active interest in his brother's business waned — while still raking off a share of the profits.

But now Barry was dead, and the *mishpoche* scuttled like gaberdine-clad cockroaches out from under their stones with indecent haste. It was made clear to Myra that unless she married Howie, and Shoshana went to a decently Torah Jewish school and stopped hanging around with *goyim* — both demands made in accordance with what he felt was his religious obligation — Howie'd have to pull the plug from the business. Which, he didn't need to add, would require them to sell their home. What with death duties, and what Howie thought was reasonable recompense for the accountancy firm (which he'd have to wind up), this would leave Shoshana and Myra destitute. So Shoshana acquired a stepfather whom she hated, and Myra feared. Shoshana suspected that

Howie beat her mother—and worse—for all manner of infractions to do with modesty, decorum, *kashrut*, the list was endless. If her new school wasn't bad enough—run by a load of creepy rabbis who didn't so much as teach the students as yell at them—attendance at synagogue was compulsory every Friday night and Saturday morning. She remembered when her mother was forced to shave her hair and wear a *sheitel*, and how she'd looked so beaten, so defeated.

Like most of her friends, Shoshana had had no reason to complain about the more tolerable strictures of her religion—it was part of her life. She had always been fascinated by the historical and cultural roots of Judaism, especially its antiquity. She'd enjoyed *cheder* each Sunday morning and was reasonably proficient at Hebrew, and it always amazed her that words like *shemesh*, meaning the sun, had been used continually and without change for more than three thousand years, the word having been used for the name of the Assyrian sun god: and yet the English she spoke in her everyday life had been recognizable as such for much less than a third that time.

But the new régime at home and at her new school convinced her that whatever the glories of its history, the purpose of Judaism now was to say 'no' to everything and generally to make life as miserable as possible. It was hardly her fault that this growing and understandable antipathy met the full force of her surging teenage hormones and her own fascination with her newly voluptuous figure—and the possibilities it offered.

And so she became a rebel. Hardly a week would go by without a stern conference in the sitting room in which Howie, in Homburg and *tzitzis*, would berate Shoshana about the damage that her behavior was doing to his reputation, and Shoshana shouting even more loudly that she couldn't give a flying fuck for his reputation, as he wasn't her Dad, and what the hell was he going to do about it anyway? Lay his *tefillin* even more tightly? Perhaps one day he'd do them all a favor and strangle himself with them. At which she'd claw her way out of the house and not be seen until dawn. Shoshana's only worry—but who worried about such things when they're a teenager?—was what this was doing to her mother. But her mother had let herself be a doormat for this creep to trample on, so maybe she deserved what she got.

Matters came to head when Shoshana was expelled. She'd been on a school trip somewhere or another, and Shoshana (whose position in the school bus had moved ever backwards to match her plummeting academic, attendance and behavior records) had apparently (and this was not in quite the roundabout form that her parents had been notified of the event) climbed into the back window of the bus and flashed her abundantly fabulous tits at the motorists following.

The sitting-room conference was much as expected. Howie raging, Myra standing behind him, pale and anxious, and Shoshana swearing and storming out. But the result of her motorway escapade had caught up with her. Wherever she went that evening she was followed by boys from school—and other, less savory characters—demanding that she 'get her kit off for the lads'. Outside a pub at about ten thirty she was surrounded by a gang of men she didn't recognize, one of whom she'd only just managed to fight off, but others had started to remove belts, get out knives... when the lights and blaring horn of a taxi scared off her would-be persecutors.

The driver was her cousin Frank, a burly ex-boxer who kept himself fit at the gym when he wasn't out cadging fares. He shared his one-cab business with an eight-foot Kaptar who went by the name of Big George. When not actually driving, the Kaptar rode in Frank's cab for security, to protect Frank. Big George never said anything, but he didn't have to. One snarl and a sight of those fangs was sufficient to scare off any potentially troublesome customers.

"Hey, Suze," said Frank, piling her into the back with Big George, "you're getting into bad company." Big George grunted, and made as much room for Shoshana as he could.

"Piss off, Frank," she said.

"Seriously, girlie-girl. You should wise up."

"So what do you think I should do, Frank? You seem to know everything."

"Do me a favor. Ditch the Dad. I shouldn't be saying this, but that *shlemiel*, he's a loser. I'll never convince Myra, but you, you're a clever girl. Think about it."

"Yeah, right."

Shoshana felt that the domestic situation, while bad, wasn't something she could do much about. And whatever she thought about Mum and her reaction to Howie—akin to that of a rabbit about to be mown down by a truck—she could hardly leave her. And in any case, where would she go? She was only just fifteen, had no qualifications, and with the way things were going, the chances of her acquiring any were slim and receding daily. Frank and George dropped her, still shaking, clothes torn, lip bloodied, at her front door.

"Now listen," said Frank, hanging out of the window, motor humming: "I'll let you off the fare if you sharpen up. When you've got your exams, then you can wave those big bazookas at whoever you want. Okay?"

Her chance of freedom came that very evening. It was Friday night and the house was totally dark, for *Shabbat*. The only sound came from the sitting room — smacks and small, choked yelps — where through the half-open door she saw her mother's form, cowering on the floor, Howie standing over her, whipping her with his belt. Shoshana's blood went cold: her head cleared and she sprang into action. She got out her cellphone, burst into the room, snapped on the light and took several pictures.

After that things turned out better. Shoshana clicked the pictures to her own private webspace, and threatened Howie, then and there, that she'd make them public if he didn't let her mother alone; if he didn't allow her to continue her education at a sixth-form diploma college; if he didn't stop her studying what he considered blasphemously Torah-threatening *goy* science — and if he didn't allow her to leave home as soon as convenient. Howie had no choice but to agree. The very next day, *Shabbat* be damned, she was living with her aunt Jess ("so relieved that you got out of that house, love, even though poor Myra...") and had taken cousin Frank's advice.

Two years of hard work later she had got her diploma and had scraped her entrance exam to Cambridge. She had been a borderline case, subject to an interview. Her meeting with Mathilde, however, was the clincher. The day after the result came through, she told her mother to flee to a women's refuge, or else. Then she posted the pictures anyway to her FaceSpace account. They went viral.

Howie got fifteen years, and the media had had a mild field day with the fiery, feisty (and notably busty) young woman whose testimony had done most to put him behind bars. Then, to kick off her gap year, she'd gone to visit Israel with some old friends from her *cheder*. Her life was now set.

Tom, for his part, had never been happier. He'd come home for Easter and was looking forward to his seasonal task — digging a bean trench for his mother, on her *potager*. Beans needed a lot of water and nutrients, and before they were planted, he had to dig a trench twenty feet long, three feet wide and two deep, fill it with compost and shredded paper ("Tom — I have boxes and *boxes* of old field reports you can use"), and backfill with the removed topsoil. The work was backbreaking, but after a term of study it was just what he needed to loosen himself up.

But what he enjoyed most about this ritual task was the sensory symphony that accompanied it. The soil was heavy clay, but his mother had worked it diligently for almost thirty years, so it was now rich and loamy. He loved the pungent smell of wet earth each time he pushed his spade into it, turning it—a smell, he thought, of the promise of growth coiled up tight and just waiting to burst forth. He loved the feel of the well-rotted compost as he crumbled it through his fingers. He loved the angular plosh and plash of the water as it hit the shredded paper, the gurgle as it soaked in. And all this against a background of breeze and birdsong. The only thing he missed—still missed—was the shuffling swish and pad of a golden retriever following him up the garden, the contented 'harumph' as the dog subsided onto the grass next to him— but his childhood companion had died when he was ten. Fairbanks' grave was somewhere over there, beyond the spinney, the retriever himself having long since made his contribution to the *terroir*.

So that's what Tom was doing as evening fell, when his mother brought home a gap-year student who wanted a little field experience. He knew that his parents were deluged with such requests, so he reasoned that this one must have been a bit special to get through the screening. Perhaps the fact that she was going up to his own department had something to do with it. His mother and Professor Reynard had always been close.

Not that Cambridge was anything like it had been when his parents had been there, as far as he could judge. They seemed reluctant to tell him much. Jack had just looked distant, as if lost in a dream. His mother either changed the subject or, if he'd pressed the point, said that he'd soon find out for himself.

Tom's Cambridge was not half the place it had been at the turn of the millennium. The smaller and less well-endowed colleges were closing, and because the town depended on its colleges, Cambridge itself was shrinking. There were two reasons for this, the first being a net decline in revenue from the admission of foreign students. Prosperous countries in East Asia and the Americas now tended to educate their children within their own borders. The African market had all but dried up, the death-knell being the collapse of Nigeria in 2039, before the two-pronged advance of the Khalifa and the Sahara desert.

The second was climate change, which was starting to have marked effects on the global economy. A combination of international carbon treaties (too little, too late) and shortages of oil meant that long-haul jet travel had ceased to become routine, except for the super-rich and business people with generous expense allowances. Everyone else had to put up with interminable train rides; worse bus journeys; and, worst of all, budget airships, most of them little better than flying sick-buckets. No wonder that when faced with the idea of travel, most people chose to stay home.

The droves of Japanese tourists that once crowded King's Parade and Trinity Street, weighed down by their Pentaxes, became small flocks and then stopped altogether.

Even had students and visitors continued to arrive in Cambridge as they had a few decades earlier, climate change would still have left its mark. Although Cambridge had always been a chilly place, the winters of the past decade had been harsh even by East Anglian standards. A dramatic season of storms each November presaged Arctic blizzards, a frozen Cam and snow on the ground continuously until April. After a brief Spring, late May onwards would be lived in a furnace, making the exam season all but intolerable.

And if his lecturers and fellow natural-sciences students were to be believed, the Autumn storm-surge season built on rising surface temperatures in the North Sea. With the consequent expansion of seawater, the grain prairies around the Wash were inundated each November, ruining all winter wheat and making the land too wet and salty to cultivate. Even cold-tolerant Nunavut and salt-tolerant 'Sahelized' wheat cultivars failed to thrive as dikes and drains were regularly overtopped. Some ambitious farmers switched to salt-hardened rice varieties, but after a couple of years the land became too salty even for these.

In the end, enormous acreages of East Anglia had been abandoned to fen and salt marsh, undoing more than a thousand years of careful reclamation in less than twenty. The coastline from Skegness to Blakeney in North Norfolk had become a vague and shifting thing, an uncertain and marshy merger of land, sea, and big, big sky. Whole towns, like King's Lynn and Wisbech, had been evacuated and abandoned; Boston was once again a sea port, as it had been before the American Revolution, when the Founding Fathers embarked at its quays; and the interior almost as far as Peterborough was dotted with half-submerged villages and the long-forgotten calls of bitterns.

The students had changed, too. The regular crowd was punctuated with traditional garb of all sorts, not just from the young sultans and princelings of the Khalifa. You could occasionally spot a Kaptar, one of the Almai or the various Sulawesians, even a Sasquatch, and there were rumoured to be a couple of Menehune at Christ's: the hominids had come to town. Tom was fascinated by all this diversity: he intended to study them in greater depth, someday. For tens of thousands of years, *Homo sapiens* had thought himself the only species on Earth capable of holding a conversation. But now there were so many different sorts of human, some of whom had been distinct species for far longer than dear old *Hom. sap*. What opportunities might this variety not present for a comparative anthropologist? That, thought Tom, was where his career path should be headed, though he'd not said as much as yet to his parents. He'd never yet seen a Sand Druid, though — they were pretty much all in Israel. But he was going to Israel this summer to work with Professor Malkeinu. He thought he'd heard his parents say that this new gap-year student had planned to do that too, so maybe he'd see one then. Thus happily occupied, Tom went on with his work.

He heard the scrunch of the jeep as it hit the gravel drive. He stretched, feeling his back muscles snap back into place, and, walking in through the *arrière-cuisine* and out through the kitchen door onto the drive, he went to greet his mother and the newcomer. He sensed the quick, decided steps of his mother as she alighted, the swish of her hair and her sharp smell. But there was a new and intriguing odor, too — yeasty, buttery, almost like — what was it? — cinnamon? — and in any case quite definitely female.

Tom had been around women all his life. The majority of his parents' colleagues were women; mostly young, all of them intelligent, many highly sexed and some very interested in Tom. But he'd remained aloof. Without consciously being aware of it, he was wary of forming any attachments on his parents' home turf. Cambridge was another matter. Once free from the apron-strings of home, he found himself endlessly fascinated by women: their compelling odors, intriguing shapes, and most of all, by their quite unbelievable textures. That women seemed equally fascinated by him offered plenty of scope for experience and experimentation.

But this one seemed somehow different, even in a world where every woman was, to Tom, so fascinatingly different from every other. To be presented with such an example on his parents' own doorstep seemed to break a taboo.

"Hi, Tom," she said. "Great to meet you."

Even her voice was a mess of contrast and contradiction. It was full of laughter and yet seemed rough at the edges, distorted by an ugly accent he couldn't place, its corners bracketing an otherwise appealing smoothness which, in its context, seemed incongruous.

He felt a strong and entirely uncharacteristic urge, then, to remove his iShades. Vision was a distraction he generally used only to corroborate things he'd already judged finely by other means. Eyes, he felt, were never trustworthy as primary sources of evidence. So he tended to keep his iShades on and ratcheted down, even at night. Women found this more alluring, somehow. Some women, anyway. This time, though, he had to make an exception. The odors and sounds seemed so varied, so jarring, and — well, so interesting — that he just had to see for himself how they would all merge together. And so he took off his iShades, squinted for a few moments in the still-bright evening light, and accommodated his eyes to the prospect.

It wasn't until about halfway through the journey that Shoshana plucked up the courage to talk to Jadis Markham. Every time she tried to speak her throat would dry and her tongue felt several sizes too large for her mouth. It was plain that Dr Markham — Jadis — wasn't going to go out of her way to make things easy. Shoshana had resigned herself to this. After all, Dr Markham did have a reputation as sharp and frosty as her first name implied. But as they progressed, Jadis would turn to her passenger, bestowing on her a series of increasingly warm smiles, which Shoshana interpreted as encouragement. Perhaps, Shoshana reasoned, here was someone who didn't say much unless it was worth saying. If so, this was a refreshing contrast to her own Jewish upbringing, counter-pointed as it had been by incessant talk. She'd never met anyone who'd had the restraint to say nothing, as a default option. But her upbringing got the better of her, and she gave way to the urge to fill the void with a confessional stream.

So Jadis learned about Shoshana's recent experiences, and how she had been transformed by her trip to Jerusalem that winter, in which she'd shaken off her old *cheder* companions and went exploring on her own. How she had seen so many different kinds of Judaism, and other religions and peoples and species, all muddling along in a city so ancient that history just dripped from every crevice. She'd seen the western wall, but had also visited the *Al-Aqsa* mosque and the Dome of the Rock, pre-serving the last footprint of Mohammed before he ascended to heaven. She'd marveled at the crazy warren that was the Church of the Holy Sepulcher, in which each Christian denomination had its own jealously guarded corner ("and the poor Copts are banished to the roof, with the washing!") She had followed a troupe of Sumatran Pendeks as they walked the Stations of the Cross. It was all, she said, quite wonderful.

In the course of this, her own pilgrimage, she'd said, the anger she'd felt at her upbringing was distilled into a kind of sadness at how narrow it had been, and how the people imposing the narrowness seemed to have lost all perception of the joys of their heritage. Their relentlessly precise codification of Judaism had squeezed out all possibility of challenge or inquiry, so that Judaism was preserved simply for the sake of preservation, as if it had no other contribution to make. Rather than rage, she now felt regret for her stepfather and his ilk, about how they had walled themselves into a ghetto without hope of rescue.

"Welcome to the team, Shoshana," said Jadis, interrupting the flow, as she turned the jeep off the road and bounced up a much-potholed drive between two rows of tall poplars. "I hope you'll like it here. Ah! Here's Tom!"

As the jeep pulled to a halt in the courtyard, Shoshana saw a young man clad in scruffy khaki Bermuda shorts and a faded but still lurid Hawai'ian shirt that seemed several dozen sizes too big for him. His large hands were stained with dirt; his skin was as brown as mahogany, his black hair very thick and stuck up in peaks like a meringue silhouette, and on his face he wore mirrored iShades and a smile as big as his mother's. Confronted by this apparition she couldn't help but laugh.

"Hi, Tom!" she said. "Great to meet you."

She leaped from the passenger seat and found, now that she was facing him, that he wasn't very much taller than she was. Then Tom took off his shades—an act that Jadis seemed to find hugely amusing.

"Tom," she said, her voice full of suppressed mirth: "meet Shoshana Levinson. Can you show her around? Make sure she finds her room?"

"Sure, *Maman, d'accord*," Tom replied distractedly as Jadis hurried inside, his eyes fixed on Shoshana. "So, you're Shoshana."

Shoshana had the weirdest feeling that an insect might have had if pinned to a cork board by an entomologist, and finding, much to its surprise, that it enjoyed the experience. She gazed back at Tom's curious, unblinking cat-like gaze, and his sunny, easy-going smile. As she did so, she couldn't help but smile back: her own eyes widened.

Eyes.

The first thing (and the last) that Tom Corstorphine remembered about Shoshana Levinson was her eyes, whose gaze met his as soon as he'd removed his iShades. Tom saw that they were big, round and the deepest blue, a color so dark that they were almost purple, fathomless, full of intelligence. These were eyes that could swallow you whole. Dangerous eyes.

It took all of a quarter of a second for Tom to examine the rest of her. She had a long nose, a rather wide mouth, full lips and quite a lot of teeth, some at curious angles. Her skin—her skin?—this was the source of the smell he'd sensed as the jeep arrived. How would you describe it? That it looked just as buttery as it smelled was all he could think of. Her hair was curly and the very darkest shade of blonde. It was this that smelled of bread, with a hint of salt, and there seemed to be a lot of it. Tom put his iShades back on, held both hands out to Shoshana and said—"*Viens!*" Her hands were dry and slim and gripped his firmly, full of resolution.

Tom led Shoshana round the farmhouse, delighting in showing her every last nook and cranny, and making sure she knew where her room was in relation to the bathroom, the stairs and so on. "Just come and go whenever you want," he'd said. "It's your home."

Her room was a small but comfortable nook with a view over the front yard, containing a single bed, a stripped pine chest with a mirror on top of it, a bookcase next to the bed, stuffed to bursting with books, magazines and loose papers; and a bentwood chair. The wallpaper had a cheerful floral pattern but was spotted and peeling in places: lived-in and relaxed without being luxurious.

Most of the rest of the rooms seemed to have been variously used as stores, offices and bedrooms, or a shifting, ambiguous mixture of all three. There were books everywhere—unceremoniously crammed into bookcases, littering tables, piled in tottering stacks on the floor, wedged into doors, even in the bathroom.

At one end of a long, broad corridor hung with torn Hessian, flapping like rent tapestries ("*Aïe! Ils sont Les Horribles!*—I hope you don't mind cats! In this house they are everywhere!") was a large, open space with two windows overlooking the back garden. In the centre stood two huge and well-worn oak desks, facing each other, with an assortment of very old-fashioned flatscreen computer monitors on smaller tables to either side, in between what looked like the very latest Merlintech airtabs. Yet more shelves lined the walls, filled not just with books, but papers, filing boxes, stone tools, chunks of ancient masonry and all kinds of equipment, spilling on to the floor in untidy drifts. More papers were piled high on the desks themselves. Battered steel filing cabinets, drawers half open, disgorged further paperwork. "This is the office," said Tom, "where my parents do some of their thinking. Let me show you where they do the rest of it. Come!"

So Tom showed her the kitchen—a crazy mixture of a room that seemed to be part study, part greenhouse, part garden shed, with only the range, a sink and one small corner of a worktop to betray any culinary activity. So this was where the renowned Jadis Markham seemed to do most of her actual work—rather than in the study, which was where she just dumped it. Across the broad entrance hall was the sitting room, in which an enormous and utterly hideous sofa, its upholstery ripped and stained, stood before a massive stone fireplace, its grate heaped with logs. More logs were stacked haphazardly in the inglenooks. A faded though slightly unnerving framed print of two fighting cats hung above a mantelpiece crowded with pictures of Tom, a much younger Professor Reynard, and several other people Shoshana didn't recognize. One showed a very large and breathtakingly ugly man who seemed to share Tom's fondness for loud shirts. Another showed a small, dark-skinned boy, his arms round a big, goofy-grinned golden retriever.

Shoshana was awed. This crazy, untidy house was where it had all happened, where Jack Corstorphine and Jadis Markham had changed the face of human history. It was as if she was being given a tour of Einstein's office, or Faraday's laboratory—or, perhaps most of all, Down House, the big, rambling country home where Charles Darwin had thought about evolution and raised a family in one big, joyful mess. She was confused, elated, but most of all, tired.

Tom picked up on this immediately. "I'm so sorry," he said. "You're worn out. I haven't even asked if you're thirsty. Would you like some tea? *Tiens*—why don't you go upstairs, wash up, have a lie down, I'll bring you some tea." Shoshana didn't know whether to laugh, cry, to say yes or no—but Tom looked at her and smiled again—"*vas t'en*, go! I'll bring your things up with me."

Shoshana made her way up the creaking wooden stairs, tottered to her room, kicked off her boots and collapsed on to her bed. The candlewick bedspread and duvet beneath swelled up around her in a cool embrace. She felt as if all her batteries had expired at once, and closed her eyes. She hadn't slept at all on the flight—her memories of this morning were a dawn rush as Aunt Jess had pushed her on the Stansted Shuttle from Liverpool Street; the constant taking-off and putting-on-again of her rucksack during the innumerable security checks; the endless flight in which, unable to sleep, she'd seen three films but couldn't remember anything about any of them; and now, here, at this farmhouse, an overwhelming hive of clutter.

And her guide? Funny, but even though she'd seen him less than two minutes ago she couldn't quite picture him. Not because she didn't want to—but because he seemed so different from anyone she'd ever met. To be sure, her experience was largely limited to the young men she'd known since she was a girl, most of whom were pallid, predictable, serious and most of all weighed down with the tribal baggage of millennia, a load that they'd only seek to pass on to her, had she got too close. Tom, in contrast, seemed like a free spirit who could soar into the sky on a whim and go wherever he wanted, do whatever he liked, and if she wanted to come with, well, great. And if she didn't? Well, that was great, too.

She'd always known what to do with men, how to use them, how to manipulate them. It was easy, she'd thought, because all that men had ever done on first meeting her was stare at her tits, their gaze rarely straying thenceforth. Tom had instantly confounded this well-used and almost instinctive strategy. He'd looked at her face. Well, by 'looked' — she wondered if he'd really *seen* anything. His eyes were strange, huge, green like the sea, slightly cat-like, inscrutable. In contrast, he'd seemed more focused when he'd had those cool iShades on, and his eyes were obscured. Yet she'd felt that, even then, he'd looked right through her. No, not like he'd undressed her with his eyes like all those boys from home, but something more genuinely appreciative, respectful even. Was that right? No, she couldn't put it into words.

Tom fumbled up the stairs with a tea-tray. What a jerk he was being, dragging this girl round the house like he was a six-year-old wanting to show it all off. How could he have lost it so badly? He'd known lots of girls—lots—he had, in truth, got well into double figures within his first year at Cambridge—but Shoshana was as different as he'd thought she might be. To be sure, all the Cambridge girls were tough and self-assured, but Shoshana seemed, somehow, just as tough as they were, and she hadn't even got to Cambridge yet. It was enough trying to carry her rucksack (slung in the crook of an elbow) and manhandle a mug of tea up the stairs without being assailed by these confusing cross-currents. Damn. He hadn't asked if she wanted milk—he'd made it black with lemon and sugar. Oh well, perhaps too late now.

He knocked at the door with his booted foot. A tiny voice from within bid him enter. As the door opened she rose from the bed in a single fluid, curved movement that raised all kinds of smells—the dust from an unused room; newly washed sheets; one of The Horribles that had been hiding (unbeknownst to Shoshana) under the bed; fly paper; and her own odor, accented by exhaustion. She took the tea from him, putting it on the chest of drawers, allowing him to drop the rucksack.

"Thanks for the tea, Tom," she said. "I'm bushed. I think I really will have that lie down, now." Her eyes lost their focus, and she lowered herself onto the bed.

"Of course, Shoshana—of course!" he replied. "Sleep well!"

The following day started early, and soon they were bowling along towards Aurignac, Jack driving, Jadis shotgun, hair flying. Tom and Shoshana sat together in the back, talking quietly. They seemed to be getting on well, Jadis thought, and smiled to herself. Very well indeed. And was instantly catapulted into her own thoughts.

Eighteen months before, on the day that she and Jack had seen Tom off for his first term in Cambridge, they'd returned from Blagnac looking forward to having the place to themselves. But on the way home from the airport she had felt progressively more nauseous, so that by the time they got home she was clammy, hot and headachy, and unable to do anything other than lie motionless on the settee, and, unusually for her, actively complain of being ill.

Her health fluttered up and down for several months until she'd finally admitted defeat and went to the doctor, who looked her up and down critically before asking her age. This puzzled Jadis—Doctor Makembe had been her physician for almost twenty years, and knew perfectly well how old she was.

"Jadis," said the doctor, "we're none of us as young as we like to think we are." What was the doctor getting at? In her mind she was always eighteen and had just met Jack.

"Jadis—*Jadis*? Are you listening?" Dr Makembe continued. "You have to face facts. You're fifty years old. There is nothing wrong with you but the menopause. It hits us all, God help us." Dr Makembe raised her eyes to heaven. "I've just gone through it myself, so I know what it's like. I'll prescribe you an implant that'll help you get over the worst of it, and you'll be right as rain."

The truth dawned on Jadis only very slowly. Menopause? Fifty? Where had it all gone?

The implant had indeed taken the edge off the horrible cocktail of nausea, sweats and anxiety, opening her mind to reminiscence. Funny though, she still felt like a young girl, deep down. Although she had heard from Mathilde that Tom was quite the heartbreaker (the pair of them giggled on the phone like two teenagers) it had taken the physical reality of her son, encountering a young woman on her own doorstep, in her own house, to make her feel old. Older, when she recalled having watched Mathilde with Eric, more than twenty years before. And Primrose. And Faye.

Lately, Jadis had been too busy to live life any more than one day at a time. The menopause, and now Shoshana's arrival, had made her see her whole life all at once, as if spread before her like a map. Jack had always been there, of course, a constant like the sky or the sea, but the landscape itself was marked with the milestones of discovery. And it struck her with some force that Jack had first taken her to Souris Saint-Michel twenty-three years ago. She had spent almost half her life exploring it. And now they were going to look at perhaps the greatest discovery of all — and the most worrying.

So worrying, in fact, that Jadis was beginning to think she should keep it a secret forever. Only — should she? Should she — might she — let Shoshana see it, what she and Jack had kept a secret from almost everyone?

Yes. For lost youth. No, not that: for the best reason a scientist can have — for the sake of a fresh and unbiased pair of eyes.

Shoshana's first view of Souris Saint-Michel was of a parking lot with a scatter of cars, trucks and tourist coaches. Between the parking lot and the lake stood a modest, low-rise building that contained the visitor centre: the wonder of the age had become a tourist attraction.

From the parking lot, visitors would board a robo-train that would take them, a dozen at a time, into the city, round a preset course and back again. They would see the Great Pyramid; parade down the Champs Elysées, past the Hexagon where a series of still-inexplicable rites had been practiced (Avi Malkeinu had seen signs of similar ones under Mount Carmel, and was equally mystified) — and into the Place de la Concorde, with its immense granite obelisk marking a thousand graves, each body clad from head to foot in exquisitely wrought flint-plate armor.

The two-hour circuit would, it had to be said, leave the visitor more mystified coming out than going in. There were ancient cities that matched Souris Saint-Michel in grandeur, even in scale — Teotihuacan, Xi'an, Knossos — but even if one could not grasp the purposes of their monuments, one was always reassured to know that such things might one day be fathomable by virtue of the fact that their builders were human. With Souris Saint-Michel this reassurance dropped away like the trapdoor beneath the hanged man, leaving a residue of vertiginous unease.

Compounding the mystery was the fact that despite almost a quarter of a century of mapping, logging every square centimeter of the city over its thirty-seven square kilometers, the team had found not a single recognizable work of art, and no sign of writing or record-keeping of any kind. No inscriptions, no engravings — nothing.

Now that the city had been charted to its full areal extent, Jadis had started on a new tack — digging downwards, excavating test pits beneath selected buildings and in certain streets. It wasn't long before she realized that SSM was much older than anyone had guessed.

Jadis had always assumed that the city had been built around 40,000 years ago, when modern humans invaded Europe, forcing the almost unimaginably ancient Neanderthal and pre-Neanderthal civilization underground.

Within a few months of the new project, Jadis had to confront the scale of her error. The city she had mapped was the latest of no fewer than fifteen cities, built one on top of the other, and even then, there were signs of earlier, pre-urban occupation. The deepest level beneath the pit known gnomically as TP255-9-2A, dug in the graveyard at the base of the Great Pyramid, was capped by a stalagmite layer laid down three and a half million years ago — meaning that the level itself was even older.

The *Nature* paper reporting this finding ('Extreme antiquity of the earliest occupation layers at Souris Saint-Michel' by Jadis L. Markham, Mathilde Reynard, A. Y. Malkeinu, John A. Corstorphine and thirty-eight others) was initially greeted with skepticism. Jadis found it hard to accommodate the fact that some people simply refused to believe her findings. She raged and fumed until the age was confirmed by three separate, independent teams of experts. But the conclusion was clear. Someone, or something, had lived in this cavern more or less continually from just before 25,000 years ago back to a time when no humans or indeed any known species of hominin had ventured out of Africa. And for those hominins in Africa itself, cities would be a dream beyond imagining, because for these creatures the first chipped pebble still lay a million years in the future.

The debate over TP255-9-2A had been so bruising that the latest discovery was still a secret, and why Jadis really wanted Domingo to see it before she made any announcement. For the first time in her life, she felt she needed some kind of religious counselor.

Jack drove the jeep across the car park and through the gate towards the cave itself, greeting the security guard with a wave. The road into

Souris Saint-Michel was broad, smooth and brightly lit. Shoshana could hardly imagine what it must have been like when Jack, Jadis, Mathilde and the others had first walked through the pitch-black tunnels into the unknown.

The road narrowed—Jack had to stop at a signal to led a robo-train pass—until, widening again, it swept them up to a broad viewpoint, where the full extent of the illuminated city could be seen. To Shoshana, the lights seemed to stretch forever, to the left and right, as well as ahead, as if she were in a small plane coming in to land over a big city at night. She had seen this view many times, of course—it was the poster that had adorned every student bedroom for the past twenty years—but the real thing was eerie, ominous.

"Don't worry, Shoshana," said Jack, sensing her unease. "It's something to do with the lack of echo. When we first got here, it gave us the willies, didn't it?" He turned to Jadis as he said this: she sat quite still in her seat, and said nothing.

Jack swung the jeep down to the left, and they descended a long, broad ramp that took them into the city itself, past two more robo-trains and several groups of scientists, some of whom waved cheerfully as they drove along the Avenue Gaston de Bonnard to the foot of the Great Pyramid itself. Looking up from its base at its entire illuminated immensity, Shoshana was initially unable to grasp its scale until she glimpsed, on the very edge of sight, a few motes at its apex—and realized that they were archaeologists working at the summit platform.

"Everyone out!" said Jack, and they followed him towards the large plastic tent that covered much of the graveyard area. The tent, illuminated from within, looked like a giant Chinese lantern. Inside it was a hive of activity, both human and mechanical: a guard handed them all hard hats with emergency headlamps, and Jack and Jadis stopped several times to chat to the various surveying and digging teams. They all knew Tom of course, and some of them—particularly the younger women—gave Shoshana what she thought were rather resentful looks.

This was only a flying visit, though. Jack and Jadis led the party through a small flap in the far side of the tent to a metal platform at the very base of the pyramid, surrounded by a rail of thick steel scaffold-poles.

"Welcome aboard the Pyramid Express," said Jack, lifting a red-and-white painted chain-link partition so they could all squeeze on. Shoshana looked up the side of the pyramid and realized that they were on some kind of funicular railway that led to a point, far away, at the summit.

"I hope you're not scared of heights," Jadis warned Shoshana, her hand just glancing against Shoshana's wrist as she lifted her hard hat, and put it on. Shoshana murmured something inaudible. In truth she was terrified. She held on to Tom with one arm—and grasped one of the tubular steel rails with the other. Jack looked round to see if everyone was in, and pressed a small red stud on a control box. The Pyramid Express moved, smoothly but very slowly, up the slanting side of the monument.

They climbed for several minutes, and as they did so, more and more of the buried city came into view. A grid-line pattern of streets, all illuminated; scatters of polyhedral structures—most house-sized or less, others as big as small skyscrapers—attended by clusters of ant-like researchers, and larger, better-behaved groups of tourists, mainly on the bright skein of the robo-train. Shoshana felt that the climb was slowly pulling her free from the usual constraints of time and space. She thought she'd known enough about this site to be prepared for the vastness of it. The reality was a shock: even though she was wearing a fleece borrowed from Jadis, she started to shiver. Tom put a reassuring arm around her, and she pulled closer into him. It was then that she noticed that he'd put his iShades back on.

As they approached the top of the pyramid, the platform whined and shuddered to cope with a sudden increase in the grade. Shoshana could feel her palms sweat. With a final lurch, the Pyramid Express crested the summit and they all alighted on another small metal platform, jutting slightly out from the side of the flat summit platform itself. Shoshana did her best not to look down, but she needn't have worried—Tom, completely unafraid, steered her to safety. She felt herself breathing hard.

The summit platform was smaller than she'd thought, no more than about five or six meters square. Some of it was roped off, under excavation, and three or four archaeologists bustled about on this high eyrie, quite unconcerned by their vertiginous surroundings. They exchanged greetings with Jack and Jadis. In the very center of the platform stood a gray box, taller than a man. When she realized that it was the head of an elevator shaft, she laughed.

"Yes," said Tom. "Archaeology has its ups, and it also has its downs." Jack smiled, but Jadis, ignoring everyone else, looked anxious, agitated: her lips were compressed into a thin line.

The open meshwork cage rattled to a halt just ten meters below the summit. The Pyramid's summit platform was a hole of darkness against the greater dark, above them. Just to one side was an illuminated niche, dug into the rock of the pyramid. The kind of niche that you'd see in a museum, moodily lit to heighten the drama of a Sumerian clay tablet, an Egyptian death mask, or the Face of Agamemnon. Shoshana saw the faces of her companions in the light from the niche. Jadis's face was hard, nervous. Jack's—all bland composure. Tom's expression, behind his iShades—unfathomable.

At first sight, the mysterious object was a disappointment. It was a gray, rectangular tablet, about twelve centimeters from side to side and three tall, and perhaps a centimeter deep.

"Is this...?" Shoshana asked.

"No," said Jadis. "It's nothing you'll ever have heard of. I hope." Just for an instant, Shoshana got the full, actinic flash of Jadis' eyes—which turned, almost immediately to Tom, whose shaded face remained quite impassive.

"When we first surveyed the pyramid—and the city," Jack broke in, "we took a lot of readings of different things. X-rays, ground-penetrating radar, you can imagine. But we also brought in gravitometers, to detect any buried voids, mainly. Tombs, hidden chambers, that kind of thing." Shoshana noticed that he had, unobtrusively, slipped Jadis' hand into his own, and, equally unobtrusively, that Jadis seemed to relax.

"What we *didn't* expect was what we in fact found: a huge, localized gravitational anomaly buried beneath the summit of the pyramid. We found it almost immediately—the anomaly, that is—back in... when was it, Jadis?"

"As soon as we broke ground—2032," Jadis said. Shoshana could see the hard set of her jaw. "But... well, what with one thing and another, it's taken more than twenty years to investigate it. So now, at last, we have."

"And this is...?" asked Shoshana. Tom squeezed her hand. His grasp was hot, urgent—scared. She realized that he probably knew scarcely more about this finding than she did.

"Yes," said Jack. "About two months ago. We haven't moved it—we thought it best... *in situ*, you know."

"The problem," said Jadis, "is that we don't know what it's made of. It's no heavier than it looks, but the gravimetric readings are... well, they're unexpected."

"Do you know...?"

"How old?" said Jadis, "No—we haven't a clue. We've tried all the usual techniques, but nothing registers. It's maddening, it really is. It's obviously intrusive, so the rocks of the pyramid itself aren't of any help…" Jadis waved her arms in a gesture of exasperation.

"And every technique we try," said Jack, "even really arcane radioactive series designed to measure the age of the very oldest rocks — meteorites, asteroids, say — pull out nothing. It goes off all scales. It's *infinitely* old. It's *beyond* old." Jack's voice, so calm and friendly to begin with, was starting to show signs of strain.

"Maybe it *is* a meteorite?" Shoshana asked. She had the distinct feeling that she was flailing, losing it, but plunged on, nonetheless, "something that got buried here? Perhaps even before the city was built? Roofed over…?"

"That's what we first thought. Or tried to think," said Jadis. "But if it is a meteorite, it's made of nothing that any known meteorite is made of. Ion microprobe results make no sense. The closest thing we've been able to establish is that it might be metallic…"

"… even though there are no metals in it," Jack continued, "and even if it's made of anything we can understand."

"And, anyway," said Jadis, grasping Jack's hand. "Look at it, Shoshana. Really *look* at it."

She turned, then, to look directly at the mysterious object. The more she looked, she found that the object's size was hard to grasp: it seemed to shift, to shimmer, to grow and shrink as she watched. She found it hard to tear her eyes away from it, and as she gazed at it, it appeared to glow with what seemed to her a menacing luster. As if it were waiting for something. As if it were alive. After a while, and, looking more closely, she could make out an inscription — not letters, but circles, lines, crescents — engraved in lines almost too faint to make out, and as she looked, the circles and lines seemed to *jump out at her* and… and…

Tom caught her as she stumbled. She felt heavy, disoriented, nauseous. Jadis and Jack looked over her, evidently alarmed — and at each other, knowing. What Shoshana had seen was the first and only inscription ever found at Souris Saint-Michel. For want of anything else to call it, Jadis and Jack had named it 'The Sigil'.

Chapter 5. Merchant

Indian Ocean, Earth, c. 125,000 years ago

My loves leap through the future's fence
To dance with dream-enfranchised feet.
Siegfried Sassoon — *In Me, Past, Present, Future meet*

"All together now... *cheese!*" The three stevedores, brawny, burnished and bared to the waist, linked themselves together and hammed it up for the camera.

Click.

"Thank you all, so much!" said the photographer, smiling and bowing. The stevedores laughed and resumed their tasks, the overdressed tourist and his zuzim (now pocketed) forgotten.

What a grand sight it all made, thought Mr Haraddzjin Khorare, stowing his box-brownie in a cunning cache-poche of his own devising, in a pleat of his crushed-velvet knee breeches, where it rubbed along next to the talisman in its leather drawstring bag. How picturesque — the multitude of packages on the quayside; the people, of all kinds, bustling, shouting, picking things up, and putting things down again, and swarming aboard the magnificent ship that was the backdrop to the busy scene.

Mr Khorare, trader in textiles from the Very Great and Ancient City of Axandragór, looked up at the broad-beamed merchantman straining at the quay, gulls turning about its masts, a smear of smoke fuming from its funnel as the boilers were warmed; seawater spilling from the blades of its paddles, here on this Malabar shore, so far to the north and west of his home city.

Now, this coaling-station in Malabar had not the refinements of the Very Great City of Axandragór — where else had? — but it had a charm that made him tote the box-brownie at every opportunity. How his wife would clap her hands; how his kits would jump for joy, when their cambric-smocked father emerged from his darkroom clutching these images of far countries. Pity his umbrotypes could never capture the colors. These flowers; those parrots. But the moods. Those stevedores, now. Such matey, boyish jollity. And such muscles. Really, most picturesque.

The ship was called *The Tiger Sniffs the Rose*, and it would sail for Dilmun in less than two hours, carrying Mr Khorare's regular shipment of fine Axandragór stuffs to that benighted port. The burghers of that far shore were starved of stimulation—starved of taste, poor things, if truth be told (Mr Khorare took out an embroidered kerchief and dabbed a bead of sweat from his brow)—and he felt that it was his duty to enlighten them. But what they lacked in taste, they more than made up in price. Upon my soul! The Dilmunese were mad for Mr Khorare's textiles! So, as Mr Khorare watched a profit-and-loss account tip inexorably in his favor, who was he, he thought, to deny them? The best deal is when all parties were happy.

So that was that.

Except that it wasn't. Some of the profits were coming up a few zuzim short. Not many, it must be said, but ever a little more, month on month, and as Mrs Khorare often told him—look after the zuzim, and the shekels will look after themselves. Mr Khorare (with his loyal wife's encouragement) felt that the time had come for him to investigate the Dilmun operation in person.

There was a rush of steam and the bark of a klaxon, signaling all those who wished to board the *Tiger* that they should now do so. Mr Khorare clutched the talisman and the box brownie in his cache-poche and climbed the gangway.

Mr Haraddzjin Khorare spent much of the subsequent voyage hanging on the stern rail, feeling queasy. Decorum be damned: he'd doffed his velvet tailcoat, riding the tropic air with his lace-cuffed chemise undone. Just a button or two. So he was on many a heavy afternoon, the sea a bright featureless disc all around the tiny dot of the *Tiger* at its center.

One part of him put his malaise down to the turtle-and-loxodont soup he'd enjoyed at the Captain's Table several nights' running. The turtle was likely to have been all right. The gigantic leatherbacks were all harpooned by the *Tiger*'s own crew and hauled aboard, twenty men straining at the hawsers. The problem was the loxodont, which could never have been really fresh. Brains, scooped from the skulls of the giant straight-tuskers culled on the plains of Eurasia; shipped across mountains on the steaming backs of rhinos and down river on barges and across tropical seas, sloshing around in barrels for weeks and all of this before they ever saw the inside of a pickle-jar. Perhaps such dainties should never be taken lightly, least of all aboard a merchant steamer puffing its way across the open ocean. The intervals Mr Khorare did not spend above decks found him throwing up in the heads, or lying in his cramped cabin simply wanting to die.

A plainer diet restored his health, though not his spirits. Perhaps he was homesick for Axandragór with its crumbling canal-side palazzi subsiding slowly yet elegantly into the breathless equatorial shore, the ancient city looking ever outwards, pointedly ignoring the pitheks of the wild hinterland, in whom one could find no ready market for any garment that hadn't been ripped off the back of some hapless beast. Nothing tailored, certainly. And as for haute-couture, well… They'd probably eat it.

No, not homesickness. Not quite.

Mr Khorare heaved himself upright on his bunk, reached into the cache-poche and, sidling the box brownie to one side with his knuckles, grasped the bag that contained the talisman.

It was a curious thing, this talisman. It had been bequeathed him by his late father, along with the textile business. But while the transfer of several hundreds bolts of silk and calico and so on and so forth were all matters of public record, that of the talisman was not. Mr Khorare the Elder had urged Haraddzjin, almost with his last breath, to keep its existence a secret, and—and this is something that Mr Khorare the Younger found most curious—to 'follow the talisman wherever it might lead'. The first of these two instructions was easy to undertake. The talisman was simply locked in a safety deposit box at his bank.

The second whipped around like a hot cobra. No matter that it was sealed away from sight, the talisman haunted Mr Khorare's dreams. On many nights he'd wake on the divan in the grand townhouse that was the fruit of his (and his father's) labors; he'd sit stark upright in bed, the figured symbols on the talisman dancing before his eyes with their deep violet glow: the three circles, interposed with horned crescents, backed by lines radiating from the center circle—lines of an infinitesimal narrowness and yet a searing brightness that penetrated his mind even when his eyes were closed. Occasionally he could tear his eyes away to look down at the peaceful, many-breasted swell of the sleeping Mrs Khorare beside him, so casually in that state of oblivion he craved.

The talisman was calling to him to follow. In his innermost heart, the business trip to Dilmun was a pretext. The talisman had woken, and he was constrained to follow it. A furtive trip by tuk-tuk and gondola across the City found him at his bank, whence he retrieved the talisman. Had this proscription not been voiced by his beloved father on his deathbed, Mr Khorare should have felt with certainty that he'd been cursed. Mr Khorare recalled two most curious aspects of that final meeting with his father. The first was that he appeared to see the entire interview through his father's eyes, not his own. Second, at the same time, he had no sensation of ever having had a boyhood. He was sure he had had one—who hadn't?—just that he could not at that moment bring any of its specifics to mind.

Mr Khorare slid the talisman from its sheath. Now he had it in his hands, in broad daylight, it seemed such a small thing. A narrow cartouche, barely a handsbreadth across. The circles and crescents and lines were mute now, waiting. But Mr Khorare was sure that just below the level of hearing, they whispered 'follow'.

The merchantman *The Tiger Sniffs the Rose* out of the Great and Ancient City of Axandragór continued on its way across the wide ocean.

Until, one day, two things happened.

The first was that, one worrying morning of thick fog when all hands could hear the splash of surf breaking on sharp rocks alarmingly close, the magnificent dodecagonal Pharos of Hormuz, wonder of the world, loomed into view. Salvation was at hand; the navigator could check his charts, and could assure everyone that Dilmun's haven was no more than two days' distant.

The second was not such good news. As the fog dissipated to leave a day of unmatched clarity, a warm south wind speeding the *Tiger* through the Straits of Hormuz, two ships were seen far astern. At present they were no more than black smudges, like the hint of a harbinger of a storm many days hence. But with every watch they appeared bigger in the sterncastle 'scope. The ships looked huge—each twice the tonnage of the *Tiger*, if not more—and black, and black smoke belched from their funnels. No flags could be seen to adorn their masts or rigging—a clear contravention of the Laws of the Ocean—but they were each surrounded by flocks of birds like flies around a midden.

The mood on the *Tiger* was all nerves and edges. Officers, crewmen and passengers alike made febrile and over-loud noises to the effect that the two ships were doubtless, like the *Tiger*, merchantmen headed for Dilmun. Maybe they had run into trouble; forgot their flags, anything. And why should they not see other ships at sea in this region? Dilmun was after all a busy port, and the Straits of Hormuz very narrow. But the word unsaid, and yet posted in letters of blood and fire above every head, was—pirates.

The *Tiger* devoted all her draft to trade: she carried no cannon, nor weaponry of any sort. There was no option but to try and outrun their pursuers, if that was what they were. The Captain commanded every stick of wood be fired in the furnaces alongside the remaining coal; that the speed of the paddles be doubled and redoubled; and that every sail be pressed into use. A long and anxious night followed, in which nobody on board gained sleep save for crewmen constrained to regulation watch- and sleep-hours. Slowly, ever so slowly, the *Tiger* seemed to be gaining, so that by dawn the black ships seemed to be no more than tiny dots on the sternward horizon once more—and Dilmun was a whole day closer. For the first time in sixteen hours, the Captain and crew (and by extension, Mr Khorare) dared to think of exhalation.

Too soon.

For no sooner than all eyes had been turned away from the stern-wards threat and looked forward once more, they saw that they had sailed, with marvelous speed, into a trap. Athwart their forward passage, blocking their route towards Dilmun, was a huge and ugly black galleon, in full sail and broadside on, waving the blazon of skull and crossed bones for all to see. It was close enough for the startled crewmen to see the glints on the pirates' teeth, and for them to hear the Pirate Captain's command to open fire.

Mr Haraddzjin Khorare watched the ensuing one-sided confrontation with undisguised horror. Grapeshot whistled through the air, ripping away arms, ripping away faces, raining blood in great swaths across the pitching deck. After the grapeshot came the pirates themselves, swinging over from the black galleon on long ropes. They seemed to be a motley bunch, people from all quarters of a world whose diversity never failed to surprise him, from the sample of it that was to be found regularly in the taverns and go-downs of the Very Great and Ancient City of Axandragór. But many of these creatures were of a kind that Mr Khorare had never seen. They were big, heavy-browed, and clad in armor of overlapping scales of flint.

Stoners!

Of course, like anyone with pretensions to a global outlook, Mr Khorare had heard of Stoners, and what he heard always filled with him horror. Typically, Stoners were rumoured to live in gigantic and wholly dark underground cities, whence they issued to prey on pithekines and other similarly unfortunate species. The government of Stoner cities was totalitarian, bloody and brutal, and they were perpetually at war with one another. Or so he had heard. He had never (of course) visited a Stoner city, these being found in northern and western countries far out of the usual mercantile orbit. Being a reasonable man, he felt, perhaps, that it might be harsh to judge an entire people on such few rumors that percolated as far southeast as the Very Great and Ancient City of Axandragór. But Mr Khorare was cautious as well as reasonable, and found it prudent to hide, for the meantime, inside a sail locker until all was over.

He was, after all, a trader in stuffs and fancies, not a rugged buccaneer on some man-o'-war.

He might have been better, though, to have burst forth from his cramped cell with a battle-cry, and, grabbing some spar or stanchion, set about one of these burly, stone-clad warriors, making a brief splash of glory before one of their scimitars slashed him from groin to jugular and made an end of it. Such might have been better than this long, long wait, in which his chemise became drenched in sweat and the stench of his own terror, lace cuffs drooping. A foul odor issuing from crushed-velvet knee-breeches, accompanied by a viscid trickling sensation in his inner thigh, told him he'd soiled himself.

Without thinking, he reached into his cache-poche and withdrew his box-brownie and the silken bag containing the talisman. The brownie he placed carefully on the floor of the sail-locker. He didn't think he'd need it any more. He clasped the talisman, still in its bag, to his chest. It was warm, comforting. He closed his eyes. He remained in that position, curled up, serene, until the locker was wrenched open and a bright tropic light flooded in, followed by a pair of vast, grasping fists.

One of the rumors that always followed Stoners was that their pirate ships — indeed, their shipping of any sort — was always accompanied by a retinue of sharks and carrion-birds. Mr Khorare remembered the clouds of gulls that surrounded the two ships that had chased the *Tiger* into this trap — an observation that was among the first to have made all hearts sink. Why should this be? Well, the tales ran, it was rumored — again, only rumored — that Stoners took goods and booty, but never prisoners, not unless they were especially close to one of their own cities, where prisoners could be herded and, eventually, sacrificed. But out at sea, any prisoner was only good for one thing. For sport. To walk the plank. Mr Khorare now found in most brutal fashion that at least some of these rumors were, in fact, entirely true.

Mr Khorare, ropes coiling him in an almost unbearably heavy corset from mid-breast to waist, pinning his arms to his sides, was third in line. The talisman was in an inside pocket of his chemise. Like the craven he was, he had offered it in ransom to the Stoner pirates, but they didn't even laugh, or jeer. They just looked at him, their faces as unmoving as the flint scales of their armor, before hurrying him along to be bound. He had replaced it, in his inside breast pocket, where it glowed, flooding his body with what he'd swear was some kind of anesthetic. He felt numb, detached, happy to go whither they directed him, sure in the knowledge of — what? — a life everlasting. This utterly unwonted thought made him stumble, momentarily, before he was beaten over the head with a bone club and forced to walk upright.

The first in line was the Captain, who had been grievously wounded in the boarding. Blood caked over his pulped face, and he appeared to have lost a hand. As the Captain walked the plank, the wood thrumming over the sea, some of the Stoners fired arrows at his heels, making him hop and skip. He lost his footing, and, tumbling, slid off the plank before he had quite reached its end. Descending, he cracked his chin sharply on the plank, wrenching his head sharply backwards as he fell. Mr Khorare hoped that the Captain had broken his neck and had died before he reached the waves.

He heard the splash of the Captain's body as it hit the water, accompanied by a less-than-entirely-enthusiastic half-cheer from the Stoners. Piracy was all the same to them, it seemed; devoid of light, devoid of life.

The second in line was the cook, the only female on board, ropes tied to her ankles and wrists. What they did to her was terrible. Mr Khorare had to close his eyes tight, but her screams as they tore her to pieces made his mental picture as horribly vivid as if he'd had his eyelids torn off and been forced to watch the spectacle. Silence fell, and there was nothing left of her. Nothing, save severed hands and feet, dangling disconsolately from the ends of ropes.

Then it was his turn. Without his feeling a thing, he was prodded with spears to the end of the plank. Then he was blasted with grapeshot, from behind and at point blank range. He fell, in pieces, to the sea. The last thing he saw in his bloodied vision was the immense triangle-fringed jaw of a shark, yawning below him. That, and the talisman whispering — follow.

Chapter 6: Travellers

Israel, Earth, July, 2054

Day unto day uttereth speech, and night unto night sheweth knowledge.
There is no speech or language, where their voice is not heard.
Psalms **19**, 2-3

The journey to Israel had been even longer than Shoshana had imagined possible. After all, she and he small gang of old *cheder* friends had managed it perfectly well on a scheduled El-Al turboprop just the previous winter, and were at Ben Gurion just seven hours after leaving Gatwick. This time—only a few months later—it was as if they'd been thrown back to the earliest days of air travel. And, contrary to popular belief, she'd thought, it had been anything but romantic, even with Tom as her companion.

First had been the reconditioned Hydro-DC3 that had meant to go from Toulouse to Athens, but had been diverted to Brindisi. A freak Saharan sirocco had surged its way up the Adriatic, threatening to sandblast air traffic out of the sky, thus preventing the crossing to Greece. The plane took off again after twenty hours on the ground. This meant an enforced rest wherever they could find a spot in the crowded, overcooked airport, and a tiny allowance for food grudgingly doled out by the airline.

Things wouldn't get very much better next day, after they'd hopped from Brindisi to Athens. Their connections now all in disarray, they'd finally managed to squeeze on to a 19-seat prop to Ben Gurion, but this had to make an emergency stop in Nicosia where they were once again grounded overnight. As he told Shoshana later, Tom thought that one of the passengers had looked ill and had been behaving strangely, disappearing rather often into the toilet cubicle. When the stewardess finally broke down the door, her screams of terror would have been sufficient to have grounded the aircraft all on their own. None of the passengers knew what was going on, and were told no more. Suffice it to say that screens were raised, the plane landed and the passenger removed from the plane in a volley of sirens. After another hour of uncertainty, Tom and Shoshana and all the other passengers were escorted off the plane and put up in hotels.

"No, we don't know what was wrong with the passenger, either," said the airline agent at Nicosia, trying not to make eye contact, "but we were told not to use that plane again." She sighed, having explained this a dozen times already. "This means we'll have to charter another one from somewhere. It might have to be an airship. We'll take you to a hotel and call you in the morning. I'm sorry, that's really all I can say. Okay?"

The final hop to Ben Gurion in a rickety old R-300 floating barf-bucket passed, thankfully, without incident. Tom had fallen asleep next to her, so he didn't see that the airship had acquired a pair of IDF scram-jets to escort it down. Shoshana was grateful for this attention — she remembered something similar on her last flight here. Air traffic into Israel had come under increasing threat from the Khalifa. So far it had just been routine saber-rattling, but one never knew when such posturing might acquire real teeth.

And so, two and a half days late, they touched down in the afternoon sunshine in the land of Shoshana's remote ancestors, and as they stepped out of the intermittently air-conditioned airship gondola and into the smoggy fug of Israel's coastal plain, Shoshana felt as if somebody had dropped a hot, wet blanket on her head.

When Tom saw Avi at the gate, he dropped his rucksack right there, rushed towards him, embracing him as enthusiastically as a small child might have, and as strongly as a cursed mariner whose albatross has finally been excised, beyond expectation or hope. Parting, they looked at each other, the broad smiles and shining eyes betraying a love and trust from which Shoshana had, temporarily, been excluded. Not that this was in any way intentional. Avi had been a frequent visitor to the farmhouse throughout Tom's childhood, and what with his open and playful demeanor, Avi had become, for Tom, a kind of elder brother, or long-lost favourite Uncle, and someone he loved to be around.

Joshing and punching each other for joy, they started jabbering excitedly to each other in French too fast for Shoshana to pick up any more than one word in ten, until, as one man, they turned to look at her: Avi, a broad grin in a handsome, brown face under tight, grey curls.

"Shoshana, I'm so sorry," said Tom, "that was very rude of me. It's just, well, it's Avi, it's been so long, and..."

Shoshana threw a mock-punch at him — Tom play-acted the stunned victim, staggering about — and she turned to Avi, shook his hand, and addressed him in passable Hebrew. Avi's expression became serious, appreciative, and he answered in the same language.

"You are most welcome, Shoshana," he said. "But what's a nice girl like you doing with a schmuck like him?"

She'd heard from Jadis that Avi had once been a ladies' man, but that he was now sternly, fiercely and firmly married to someone who Avi only ever referred to as "The Ballbreaker." Shoshana had been slightly shocked by this—Avi was almost as great a hero to her as Jadis had been her heroine. But when he met the man in person, she realized that Professor Avram Yitzchak Malkeinu, Israel's premier archaeologist, was just a big kid. She could see why he and Tom got on so well together: they made a good pair of Lost Boys who'd sail off on an adventure together without a second thought, and Wendy would just have to trail along as best she could.

Not that she had any intention of giving up. Now she and Avi were chatting in Hebrew—for all that it was far less fluent and easy than Tom and Avi's rapid-fire French—it was Tom's turn to affect confusion, looking to Shoshana and then to Avi and back again as if they were Martians. Eventually the three of them ended up in a three-cornered embrace.

"Come," Avi said, "we have a long way to go before nightfall. And I regret it won't be comfortable."

Just outside the terminal building they had to wait for only a few minutes before a green army pickup squealed to the kerb, driven by a woman in fatigues as green as the jeep, who leaned out of the cab and blasted Avi with jagged and guttural shards of what sounded like abuse, in fluent Arabic. Avi turned to Tom and Shoshana.

"Sorry," he said, "what with all the flight delays, this was all I could get at short notice—you'll have to pile in back, I'm afraid. I have business to sort out... er... upfront." He looked slightly embarrassed. "I'll explain later, yes? But you have to hurry! We don't want a taxi marshal to book us for stopping too long kerbside."

Too tired and puzzled to remonstrate, Shoshana helped Tom haul their bags to the back of the truck, up on to the footplate and beneath the canvas. The windowless interior was baking hot. The bench seats on either side were entirely occupied with wooden boxes containing a strange assortment of goods. One contained burlap sacks, neatly folded; another was full to overflowing with lettuces; a third contained a jumble of greased and grimy car-mechanics' tools. Two uzis lay on the floor just behind the drivers cab. About a dozen green-striped watermelons the size of overinflated beach balls were wedged under the bench seats. The only concession to comfort was a filthy, stained mattress spread out on the floor. Being the only available space for them and their luggage, they stretched out on it together, wedged in between their rucksacks and the watermelons. And so they lay there, looking into each other's faces; sharing each other's hot breath; and laughing at the invisible but animated, frequently heated and occasionally violent conversation emanating from the driver's cab as the truck lurched crazily out of the airport and hooked into the highway towards Tel Aviv and thence Haifa.

There were also some long silences — one in particular when the truck pulled to the side of the highway for reasons that neither Tom nor Shoshana could immediately identify. Shoshana put her ear to the metal of the cab, beckoning to Tom to keep silent. Her eyes were sparkling with mischief when she resumed her spot beside him.

"I *think* I know what they're doing..." she said, conspiratorially.

"What?" asked Tom, puzzled.

"*This*," she replied, embracing him tightly and kissing him, initially with some force until she felt he'd really got the message. He drew her head beneath his chin so she could rest against him, cradling her head in his hands, hers clasped round his waist. Exhausted from the trip, Tom dropped off to sleep. Shoshana envied him his ability to catnap more or less anywhere, at no notice, leaving her to brood.

The long journey had given her plenty of time to analyze and review her feelings for Tom, and to marvel at how far they had come in so short a time. When she met Tom — when was it? Just three months ago? — she had been no stranger to men, or to sex. In fact, she thought, she'd probably had far too much of both, which was something she now regretted. But what had first perplexed her most was that with Tom, uniquely, she was no longer in control, even though he made no demands on her whatsoever, and, more perplexing, was that this was something she welcomed.

She'd always had men exactly where she wanted them, and had begun to use them rather cynically, picking them up and dropping them when it suited her. To be sure, there had been downsides. The first few boyfriends she ditched usually followed her around anyway like lost dogs. Some of the later ones became petulant to the point of violence, and occasionally beyond it. She had come to regard sex in much the same utilitarian way, and with few exceptions, she hadn't enjoyed it very much more than any other pleasurable experience, such as — say — shopping with a girlfriend. On reflection, she thought this rather sad, and this thought alone pulled her up short: that before she'd come to the farmhouse, she thought that her life, while miserable in many ways, was the kind of life that most people learned to expect and took for granted.

It was only when she'd met Jadis and seen how content she seemed to be, married to the solid, dependable Jack, who plainly adored her, even though they'd been together practically since dinosaurs walked the earth, that Shoshana had any way to calibrate her own experience. Her teenage years had been lived in an atmosphere of brutal repression, and although she had known this to be true at the time, these same years had been the backdrop to her adolescence and puberty, and had done much to shape her character. She told herself that by using men as objects, she wouldn't end up an abused house-mouse like her mother. But in seeking the other extreme, she now feared she ran the risk of ending up in substantially the same place—beaten, and alone.

The kind of romance she saw in Jack and Jadis, lived in an easy, matter-of-fact and relaxed style, bound by respect, trust and love freely given and accepted—and certainly without the constant worry about rules, demarcation and the strictures of religious duty—was, she had thought, only ever found in slushy movies. But now she knew that it could really happen, and that she could be a part of it, if she wanted.

And with Jack and Jadis there came an added bonus prize—Tom—who had forced her to rethink everything she'd ever thought she knew about men and sex. She had the impression that he'd slept with at least as many women as she had with men, but with one crucial difference. Whereas she used men as a means to an end, Tom loved women simply for what they were. Because of this, his attention, while earthy, was always courtly, respectful—perhaps a little old-fashioned. And this was vitally important for Shoshana, who, until she met Tom had not quite realized that her desire for conquest was fuelled by a need for sexual satisfaction which, the more she strove to achieve it, the more it remained out of reach.

But there was another thing, too. Tom, having been raised in an atmosphere free from strictures, gave his love without expectation of return. It was this, as well as his obvious consideration for her (which he would have thought of, if he'd thought of it at all, as simple good manners) that had evoked a response in her that was far more than reflexive or mechanical. She felt that she wanted to demonstrate her feelings for him likewise without thought of any recompense, but simply because he was there, and she felt like it.

She'd known this instinctively within a few minutes of first meeting him, when with a casual smile he'd removed all her defenses and rendered all her usual stratagems at naught. But it had taken her much longer to admit it to herself, to fight her way through to this conclusion, past a host of snares and demons.

The first two weeks at Saint-Rogatien, before Tom had to return to Cambridge for what was still called the Trinity Term, had been exciting as well as deeply frustrating. They rose early each day and had no time for confidences. Tom rode off with Jack to the Merlin Institute Campus the other side of Aurignac, where he was learning about laboratory techniques for handling ancient DNA.

The Neanderthal skeletons at SSM represented the single biggest source of high-quality ancient DNA from any species anywhere in the world, and now that Jadis had opened up significant time depth, the team was beginning to shed light on Neanderthal genomic evolution over the course of hundreds of thousands of years in detail unprecedented for any species, living or extinct.

Shoshana, however, accompanied Jadis to SSM itself. Jadis advised her that, as a school-leaver, she should get more of a general flavor of an archaeological site rather than learn anything particular in any depth. Shoshana, though, was on her guard. After that first visit to SSM, nothing more was said about the mysterious inscription for several days. Shoshana sensed that Jadis, in particular, was uneasy about it, and that Jack and Tom dared not venture close to that subject.

Hence Shoshana's surprise when, four days after her arrival, when they were driving to the site, Jadis put Shoshana on the spot—what should she do with the Sigil? The Inscription at the bottom of the pit? Should she publish it? Shoshana was initially flustered and a little embarrassed to be asked, but Jadis didn't seem to be playing games. It was as if Jadis really did want to know, much as her Aunt Jess and (more particularly) her mother seemed to be relying more and more on Shoshana to make important decisions about their finances, their living arrangements—their lives.

So Shoshana reviewed the evidence as she saw it.

"Well, first, it's an artifact," she began, "the inscription can't be natural." Her mouth had gone dry. She licked her lips.

"Go on," said Jadis.

"The age—that's interesting. If it's older than can be measured by any technique...?"

"That's right, Shoshana."

"Then... well... what can be said, except that it doesn't belong there? It's..." she struggled for the right word.

"Intrusive." Jadis added.

"So what would I do about it? If you're asking me, I'd do nothing: keep it a secret."

"Why should I do that?" asked Jadis, who seemed genuinely intrigued. It dawned on Shoshana, then, why her views were being sought: it was because, as a scientific ingénue, her views were likely to be more honest than those of Jadis' immediate academic peers. Like the little boy in the story of the Emperor's New Clothes. This realization—that even to her heroine, one of the greatest archaeologists in history, her view might actually matter, filled her with a new confidence.

"Because... well, because the whole thing just sounds completely crazy," she said. Shoshana thought she might have misjudged this remark, but Jadis only smiled at her, willing her on. She gathered her thoughts.

"If the inscription isn't natural," Shoshana continued, "then somebody must have made it." She swallowed, forcing her nerves back down her gullet. "But who?" The first hominids in Europe that made tools lived a lot later, maybe two million years ago, max?" Shoshana was beginning to think she'd been trapped into some kind of oral exam.

"Keep going," encouraged Jadis, "so what does it all mean?"

"It means that you have..." she hesitated... "you *can* have no idea who made this artifact, not even a single suggestion. Apart from aliens. That's why, if it were down to me, I'd keep schtum until we knew more about hominid history. Maybe you could get some clues from the bones and other stuff in the lower layers you've been digging out? But—oh—that won't work, because the artifact is intrusive, so the other material won't shed any light on... Oh, I don't know, and you're, well, you're..."

"Shoshana, don't worry," said Jadis: "I won't bite. This isn't a trick question, and I really am interested in your opinion. And for what it's worth, I agree with you. I'll keep quiet. At least for now."

The conversation petered out, then. The jeep bowled along the lanes, Jadis' profile strobed in light and shadow, laddered by the poplars and planes on the dusty roadside.

What Shoshana really wanted to talk about was Tom, although she knew that this was the very last subject she'd broach. She'd known Tom hardly a week, but her heart was racing ahead, careering out of her control, and this was disturbing. She wanted to ask why he'd remained nothing more than polite. Warm and smiling, to be sure, but also just a shade uneasy in her company—even though his eyes, when uncovered, were on her constantly. It was agonizing, and she was dying to ask Tom what his feelings were, but if there really were a spell, she didn't want to break it; and in any case she felt she didn't know Tom at all well enough to put such things into words in case they might be misinterpreted.

Now, were Tom any other man, she'd simply have shrugged off all these worries and got on with her life. But the simple fact was that he had already won her and the question was whether she should just declare unconditional surrender (in other words, just show him) or let himself work it out on his own. But why was he so hesitant? Could it be because he didn't want to come on to her in his parents' house? Maybe, but he hadn't had the chance to take her anywhere else. Or perhaps he already had a girlfriend, and was trying to spare her feelings by toughing it out until he got back to Cambridge? This was entirely possible, and the realization made her recoil in anguish. How could she not have thought of this before? And so the first week continued, her eyes exposed to the wonders of the ancient world at first hand; her heart in a flutter of hypothesis.

She couldn't go on like this, she felt, as the second week drew on, and Tom was due to return to Cambridge at the end of the third, and then she'd be stuck here for eight more weeks, marooned, still in search of resolution. It would be intolerable. Some answers came when Tom came to her room with a cup of tea early one Sunday morning. He put the tea down on the chest of drawers and sat on the edge of the bed.

"I've an idea," he said. "I'm really sorry I haven't showed you around at all — we've just been so busy. So let's go for a picnic. Just you and me? A date?"

Although this was just what she'd been hoping for, her own feelings surprised her. Men asked her on dates all the time. Sometimes she agreed, sometimes she didn't, and quite often she agreed but later on found something more interesting to do instead. This time she felt she was a little girl again and her Dad (her *real* Dad) had given her a present she'd always wanted, or had taken her to some fabulous place, like the park, or the zoo, just the two of them. So the tears that now started in her eyes as she sat up and embraced Tom were partly of joy, and partly of regret, for she knew in that moment how much physical affection she'd been missing, for years on end: and that she'd finally traversed a parched desert into which she'd effectively been banished the moment she'd heard that her Dad had died.

So they raided the kitchen for bread, cheese, fruit and wine, and Tom drove them to a byway just outside Marciac, between fields of tall, ripening maize, that led to a small lake of clear blue with a small, secluded, sandy beach. Where Tom had been hesitant, he was now demonstrative:

Shoshana decided not to inquire about Tom's seeming change of heart, and to enjoy what could well turn out to be a memorable day for them both. After they'd eaten, Tom stripped down to his shorts and ran full tilt into the lake. She felt that she had no option but to follow him: she dropped her shorts and chased after him, laughing, catching up with him in the water, and finding not a man, but a maelstrom of splashing and noise. He drenched her, ducked her, pulled her under, laughing all the while—and she did the same to him—until, just as suddenly, they stopped and were close together, quiet in each other's embrace, up to their necks in water. They emerged from the lake as if they were the first man and woman in the world, the first amphibians to crest the waves to discover a new land.

Jadis came into the yard to greet them. Shoshana was grateful that she didn't ask them about their picnic, as she was clearly bursting with news of her own.

"Domingo just called," she told Tom. "He's in the area, and he's coming for supper. Isn't that wonderful?"

Domingo arrived on cue along with Jack, just as Jadis was dishing up a farmhouse supper of new loaves, cheese, pâté and pickles. Jadis hugged the huge man even before he'd had a chance to cross the threshold.

"It's been such a long time," she said. "We really could use your advice…"

Shoshana recognized him as the very ugly man in the aloha shirt from the mantelpiece photo, although he was now bearded and grizzled, a vast mane of silver hair running down between his great shoulders. He was wearing a Hawai'ian shirt now, rather faded and a little tight around the girth, and Shoshana realized where Tom got his from. For his part, Tom embraced the big man as if he were Father Christmas. Domingo produced a grin so full of teeth you'd have thought he was going to bite someone's head off, unless you also looked at his eyes, deep reservoirs of intelligence, each almost buried beneath an eyebrow the size of a small thunderhead.

Strange as it seemed, Shoshana thought, Domingo looked more at home here than anyone else, and she realized that one of the most important things in life was just that, a secure feeling of home. It was something she'd lost at a crucial time in her life, because the people who should have made her home for her had betrayed that obligation. But she could, if she'd let it, find it here, in this same farmhouse, as Domingo seemed to have done.

Her eyes must have lit up and they caught his: he shambled over to where she was sitting at the table and took her hands in his, enclosing them.

"You must be the delightful Ms. Levinson," he said. "I hope you'll like it here, just as much as I always have."

And so, she thought—he knew. Somehow, and as unlikely as it seemed, the middle-aged, deeply learned Catholic priest forged an instant connection with this young Jewess, a connection which, for these two people alone in the farmhouse, that spoke of early lives filled with wretchedness and hurt that was, for him at least, finally exorcised here, as it might be for her, too, were she to allow it. Her thoughts split up into a host of confused, separate but intertwining strands, one of which told her that her experience as a Jew would have been so much richer had the clerics at her school been a fraction as understanding as this priest.

She later discovered, to her astonishment, that this was the very same priest who'd drafted the Papal decree that encouraged Catholics to welcome any hominid species to God, transforming the Church. She'd learned about that, of course, wholly in the negative, damned by rabbis who were still arguing over the narrow definitions of who constituted a Jew, let alone a human being—the status of Sand Druids being an issue that was still to be resolved in many corners of Jewry.

Shoshana had known Jewish kids at her secular secondary school who went to synagogue regularly—far more than she ever did—and yet were barred from Jewish youth clubs and Jewish schools, not because they didn't believe in God, not because they weren't academically qualified, but simply because their *mothers* weren't born as Jews, or hadn't undergone the strictures of Orthodox conversions that were designed not to welcome new converts, but to do everything they could to throw obstacles beneath their feet. She remembered slanging matches with Howie about this, stinging him with the accusation that his kind of Judaism was a kind of Nazism in reverse.

"Some of my best friends are *untermenschen!*" she'd screamed: "And how about '*Ihre papiere, Bitte?*'" miming a Gestapo agent who, like Orthodox rabbis, were forever in search of hard, documentary evidence to prove one's Jewishness, as if faith and commitment were not themselves sufficient. "What do you think of that, Howie?"

Howie had either averted his gaze, or muttered words to the effect that teenage girls who lacked respect for their elders couldn't possibly be expected to understand. But in Domingo she saw an elder who commanded respect without demanding or expecting it. Now she'd finally met him, she wouldn't have been at all surprised if she found herself wanting to escape from her Judaism altogether as her father had once tried to do—but she realized that this was impossible. If you are born a Jew, that's that. And, as Howie often added—no matter how much you paint yourself white, you're still a *schwarzer* underneath. It wasn't meant to be racist, he'd said—that was just the way *Ha'Shem* made the world, and we had to accept it.

Supper was as full of merriment as any meal at the farmhouse always was when Domingo was around. He was now a Cardinal and one of the Pope's closest advisors, but had been granted a few days' leave before accompanying the Pope on a state visit to Israel. Domingo said he'd hoped to meet Avi, but expected that his schedule would keep him firmly at the side of His Holiness. Shoshana learned that this was Professor Avram Malkeinu, an archaeologist almost as famous as Jadis and Jack, and when Jadis told her that Domingo and Avi had been the Bad Boys of *Le Dig* at Saint-Rogatien more than two decades before, Shoshana was torn between laughter and astonishment.

"To be sure, Shoshana," said Domingo. "And, believe it or not, our beloved Rolling Stones will be playing a concert in Tel Aviv during my visit. Even at the same stadium at which His Holiness is due to celebrate mass. Though not, I regret, siimultaneously. However, I expect that the exigencies of politics and antiquity shall conspire to prevent our attendance. Ah, well." He sighed, somewhat theatrically, Shoshana, though, given the sly twinkle in his eyes. She stifled a giggle: Domingo picked up on her amusement, and seemed tickled in his turn to learn that she would be making her second trip to Israel at about the same time, with Tom, and that they'd be spending a couple of weeks exploring Avi's dig sites on Mount Carmel.

"Please give that young rogue my best regards, won't you?" said Domingo. "And—here's a thought—if you you... ah... young people get the chance to see Messrs Jagger and Richards, don't pass it up. I shall expect a full report, of course." His eyes clouded—"we had such wonderful times here, Avi and me, and everyone, such wonderful times, in the good old days..." He looked at Jadis, who was smiling back: "Ah me! For a beaker of the warm south! Now, what was it you wanted me to see?"

And so Jadis told Domingo about the inscription, the strange Sigil, ancient beyond measure, that had been the source of the long-puzzling gravitational anomaly at the summit of the Great Pyramid at Souris Saint-Michel. Domingo betrayed no emotion, but asked if he could see an image of it. Jack went upstairs to the office to fetch a drawing, and, clearing the table, they unrolled the sheet of white paper, weighting it down at the corners with pickle jars and coffee mugs. The inscription was several times actual size, Jack explained, blown up so that every detail could be clearly seen.

"The real thing's only about twelve centimeters by three," he said, "stamped or traced on the artifact itself, which is hardly larger — and the lines are so thin that they're actually very hard to make out without some degree of… um… strain."

Shoshana was almost sure that Jack glanced, just for a moment, in her direction. She remembered how giddy she felt when she'd stared at the inscription. It was only now that it occurred to her that everyone who'd looked at it felt much the same. But rather than feeling that she'd been the victim of some peculiar initiation ritual, she was glad that Jadis and Jack and Tom had allowed her to see it at all. Her presence here, at this conspiratorial kitchen table, was evidence that she'd been welcomed into a very exclusive club indeed.

She looked at the tracing, and the company fell silent. The inscription lay within its own rectangular frame or cartouche. Inscribed within the rectangle were three circles: one at the left-hand end of the frame, one at the right, and one in the middle. Between each circle stood a crescent, like the crescent moon, their horns pointing outwards, away from the central circle. Fine lines radiated from the central circle to all corners and edges of the rectangular frame.

There was a long pause. It was Domingo who broke the silence.

"First, there can be no doubt that this is intentional," he said. "Nothing natural makes patterns as geometrical as this. And I'd hazard that what we're seeing is a picture, albeit stylized, of a total eclipse of the Sun."

Jadis nodded, as if she had suspected the same thing, but desired some kind of confirmation. Shoshana was amazed. She had no idea what the pattern of lines and shapes might have meant.

"Imagine that this circle on the left" — Domingo pointed at it — "is the solar disk. Then, reading from left to right, it is occluded from the left by the Moon, and we can see the eclipse as it progresses in the crescent. In the central circle, we see totality. The disk is completely covered except for the solar corona…"

"That must be the radiating lines…" said Jack.

"Exactly so. And as we go towards the right, we see the Moon moving on, leaving the rightmost disc as the Sun, once again... ah... uncovered." Domingo paused, still thoughtful, as if he hadn't finished.

"But, my friends, I am puzzled. Usually, records of eclipses in ancient astronomy refer to particular eclipses..."

"That's what I thought," said Jadis, "and had I the confidence, I'd ask an astronomer to look at this, if I knew any, but I don't think it would be possible to tie this to any one eclipse, particularly as we can't establish the age of the artifact."

"And even if we could," broke in Jack, "the inscription could have been made at any time after the material that constitutes the artifact itself was formed..."

"And," concluded Jadis, "we haven't any idea when that might have been. Not a clue."

"You do have one clue, my dear Jadis," said Domingo. "Or, perhaps, two."

"I do?" Jadis looked shocked.

"Yes, of course. First, if age of the artifact cannot be measured, that means that it must be very old indeed. Perhaps older than the Earth. And, second, if the... ah.... nature of the artifact's material resists investigation, it could be that it is made of something ordinary that's been... ah... transformed by some unimaginable physical process. But you'll have thought of all these things, of course."

"Yes, Domingo," said Jadis. "And that's why we're at a dead end. I'm reluctant even to share this finding with anyone, let alone people outside our field."

"I quite understand," said Domingo. "But one should not depair. I believe that the Merlin Technologies Astrometry Institute—your sister body—might be well placed to offer some advice. My colleagues at the Vatican Observatory have forged some useful links with them lately," continued Domingo, "very useful. I've become quite a fan of their work of late. However, I can understand why you might want to sit on this one, for a while. Too much like *Chariots of the Gods*, eh?"

Jadis smiled, weakly: the work at SSM had trawled up its share of cranks and conspiracy theorists, and reprints of Von Däniken's hoary old aliens-and-humans bestsellers from the 1970s were enjoying a new vogue. This was just the kind of thing she wanted to avoid, and she was grateful that Domingo understood.

"In any case," Domingo went on, "I am not sure whether any astronomer might have been able to help, in this instance. This picture, you see, works however you look at it—up, down, or from right to left. I suspect that this isn't a record but a pictogram, a statement of eclipses in general, rather than any one that might be identified."

"But why?" asked Jack. "Could it be some kind of sympathetic magic?"

"Like cave paintings of mammoths and bison, you mean?" asked Domingo. "Summoning up success in the hunt? It's an interesting thought, my dear Jack. But who'd want to conjure eclipses? In all societies they are seen as omens of terror. The ancient Chinese, you know, had an engaging myth about eclipses. They thought the Sun was being swallowed by a dragon, which was very large but also very shy. The legend was that if enough people came outdoors to shout at it, the dragon would be frightened away. Isn't that lovely?"

Jack joined in Domingo's mirth. " —and what do you know," he said, "they must have been right, because it always worked."

Domingo became serious, with a suddenness that startled them. "Yes, dear Jack, it *has* always worked—*so far*."

"But that's just it," said Tom, "the sign-makers didn't want to encourage eclipses, to bring them on…"

"No, it was the other way round," said Shoshana: "They wanted to ward them off, at all costs… to find a way of chasing the dragons away…"

"*D'accord*," said Tom. "It could even be a warning."

And at this, Tom and Shoshana turned as one to look at Domingo, who looked stunned, pleased, and then, as if recalling something he really ought to have remembered earlier, profoundly worried.

"My dear Jadis," he said, "I fear that your young *protégés* are quite correct, though I cannot say why. And so my advice, if you want it, is to keep this discovery quiet, at least for the moment."

He would not elaborate further, but asked if Jadis had any more of that good coffee, and some more of her 'world-famous' Gascon chocolate cake? Jadis always fell for people complimenting her on her cooking— something at which, in contrast to her expert gardening, she felt rather deficient, and therefore responded eagerly to all encouragement.

Later, lying in bed, Shoshana was abuzz from the visit of this strange and strangely compelling new visitor, but before long she thought back to the picnic with Tom. How he'd broken his reserve. How they'd made love, right there, on the beach, and afterwards, how she felt that she'd come home at last.

When, a week later, Tom left for Cambridge, she felt as she'd expected—empty, wretched and lost. She returned to work trying to act as normal and cheerful as she could. But in her heart she knew that this wasn't the real Shoshana, but just a phony. Inside she felt about as useful as a squashed football. Without Tom around, she was even more exposed and alone, as a guest in the house of his parents, whom she hardly knew, so of course she couldn't tell them of her feelings for their own and only son. Had she known him better, she could have certainly talked to Jack: but Jadis was, for her, on a pedestal, and nobody confides in a statue.

A couple of days after Tom left, Domingo had passed through on an another flying visit, returning to Rome from one Papal errand or another, and she had wanted to talk to him then—what was the word, *confess*?—but she thought it would be just too weird. Her religious world was very much constrained by her past, which she realized was not just a straitjacket, but a star to steer by. She could not abandon it for something so alien, for all that her instincts screamed at her that this man was likely to be a good listener, and that her worries would go no further. In any case, by the time she'd plucked up the courage to approach him, he'd gone.

So she was left in the house of strangers, trying to be on her *Shabbat* best behavior. Until, one evening about two weeks later when she found that she could manage this charade no longer. She and Jadis were sitting at the kitchen table, Jadis lost in a spread-sheeted morass of figures, Shoshana pecking her way through a file of site reports and papers on SSM that she felt duty bound to study, making notes on her Airtab. But the time came when she found herself reading the same lines over and over again, and no effort she could make could get her to the next one. It was as if she'd hit a wall. A tear of frustration slid down her cheek. Jadis looked up then, peering over her reading glasses.

"Shoshana," she said, "what's the matter?"

"I'm sorry, so sorry" she replied, and then, without meaning to, "I miss him so. I'm so sorry, but I miss him so much...." She started to get up, her intention being to pack her rucksack and ask to be taken to the airport, for now her secret was out, she was fit to stay in the farmhouse no longer. She could hardly be banished from Eden if she chose to leave of her own accord.

At first Jadis said nothing, but rose, came round to Shoshana's side of the table and put her arms around her. "Oh, you poor, poor girl," she said. "If only I'd known. If only you'd told me..."

A little later, Jadis had steered Shoshana up to bed, and sat by her on the bentwood chair, and talked to her—really, for the first time. Shoshana was relieved that Jadis did not inquire about Shoshana's past life or present needs (she felt that she'd have withered up with embarrassment), but sought to reassure her that the farmhouse was her home, and always would be, whenever she wanted it. Shoshana realized how much and how hard she'd been fighting against this gift, this offer to relieve her of her past life, as something too good to be true. But here was Jadis, making it entirely plain that if she wanted Eden, all she had to do was accept it, with no thought of recompense.

"Come and live here—move in!" said Jadis. "It's a big house. There's always room for one more." So Jadis told Shoshana of the story of how she met Jack, and told her just how much she'd missed him when he'd first left for France, and that she understood what Shoshana now felt for Tom: that you wanted someone so intensely that you felt actual, physical pain. Jadis recalled how the absence of Jack was like a twisting knife in her abdomen; and Shoshana, without words, but in the way she sat up and hugged Jadis, admitted that the way she felt for Tom was just the same.

"I know, I know, it all seemed so silly from this distance," said Jadis, "and you should excuse the ravings of a silly old woman. But I remember that pain, Shoshana. Even the memory of that pain is painful, for all that it happened before you were born." Much to Shoshana's surprise, Jadis started to cry, too, as if letting out some private anguish coiled up for years that could no longer be contained.

"Shoshana," she said, quite deliberately, so she wouldn't seem patronizing, "No matter what happens—and especially no matter what happens with Tom—I'll always be here for you, if you need me. Always."

Chapter 7. Settlers

Central North Africa, Earth, c. 6,355,000 years ago

And hear at times a sentinel
    Who moves about from place to place,
    And whispers to the world of space,
In the deep night, that all is well.
Alfred, Lord Tennyson — *In Memoriam*

That warrior was the first of many people of the same kind. At first they rode straight past Alfred's hermitage, heading for the faint ridge on the western horizon that he knew was a high and extensive range of mountains, though Alfred had never been there himself. Some of the tall, milky-eyed people stopped at his gate, offering gifts of food and drink, which he accepted with good grace.

After the warriors came the herdsmen, steering droves of anthracotheres and other beasts less familiar to Alfred, all towards the west. They did not stay long, but when they did, the herds, snouting and squealing, seemed to stretch from one horizon to the other, and Alfred began to fear for his thorn bushes, which began to look even more threadbare than ever. The tide of animal droppings in the herds' wake, though, more than made up for it, both as fertilizer and as fuel. Wood for firing was ever harder to find, and nights on the savannah were cold.

The years passed, and the savannah became ever more populous. The wilderness around Alfred's hermitage became tamed with fields, stockades and homesteads. The people — the Annakhnu, as they called themselves — were polite enough, and kept out of his way, for the most part. But he found (to his surprise) that he'd become 'adopted' by the clans who lived in the homesteads close by, who treated him with great reverence, and often came to him to discuss knotty ethical, spiritual — even familial and marital problems. He heard, through his regular Annakhnu visitors (he hesitated to think of them as 'parishioners') that the Brethren in the community of Shinaar were accorded similar respect, for which he was also grateful, though he did not really understand why these quiet, polite conquerors were so accommodating. Perhaps they did not see the Brethren as sufficiently numerous to constitute a threat.

He did, though, become tolerably proficient in the newcomers' language, and when that happened, some species of comprehension began to coalesce from the alien fog. At first the effort of speaking the language was very great, rather like being forced to make an extended series of regurgitations, just to say the simplest things—and this in a dry country in which saliva was at a premium.

But it was through this language that he learned of the deepest beliefs and wishes of the Annakhnu, which was this—that they would not 'come into their own,' as they put it, until their new city, now slowly accumulating on the heights to the west—had been blessed by some celestial portent. The Annakhnu spoke of this in terms of the most dramatic and florid phenomena: of lightning from darkened skies, and visitations of fiery chariots from heaven. Such events, the Annakhnu said, were imminent. Their shamans looked for them every day, casting runes now to plot the precise hour, the exact minute. And that was when something dark, something exciting, stirred in Alfred's brain. Unfortunately for Alfred, this revelation, when it awoke, found that something even darker and potentially more deadly was already in residence.

The school of babbling children had gone, their lessons over for the day. Alfred saw them career in gay, gangling masses, like a flock of pinwheels, towards the heron-gray horizon, yelling their excited good-byes. Alfred loved the children. He loved teaching them basic arithmetic, astronomy, geometry. It was tiring—it was *always* tiring—but now Alfred felt more than usually drained, worn into catatonia, and he felt a headache starting to unfurl just behind his eyes. At first he thought it might have been the weather: oppressive, unnaturally hot, spectacular thunderclouds building in stacked formations high into the sky. But never a drop of rain, no measure of the easeful relief that rain would bring.

He stood, propped up at his gate as the bright motes of the children shrank and vanished against the threatening vastness of cloud, his hand raised in valediction. He looked up at it and wondered why it was still there, pointing up like that, into the sky. There was another arm, now, an arm at his shoulder, not his. It was Leila, a tall and stringy Annakhnu woman of middle years who, with her sister, had lately taken it upon herself to look after the ageing hermit.

"*Aba*? Father? Are you all right?" Her questioning became shriller, more urgent, but somehow he couldn't find the strength to answer, no matter how hard she clucked, how insistently her claw-like fingers clutched at his robe. The words he wanted to utter formed in his mind like the burgeoning waters in a mountain spring, but by the time they reached his mouth they had dribbled away into nothingness. Evaporated. He stood there, the Sun setting, the Moon rising, his arm still raised, and the thin cream-eyed face of Leila, framed by a cowl, peering round at him, concerned.

"Father?"

He felt a thin string of drool trickle down his chin, but for some reason he couldn't work out, he did not feel inclined to move a hand or an arm to wipe it clean, as if the hands and arms he felt he had once had at his disposal did not really belong to him and he had to ask permission for their use, but couldn't now remember whom to ask. The arm pointed skywards was, now, gently lowered, and he could see that the person lowering it was Leila. By now Leila's sister had arrived. Lilit, as bustlingly plump as Leila was thin, cleaned his face with the busy concentration of a dung beetle. The feeling of her sleeve on his chin tickled and he wanted to laugh. A thin cackle emerged from what he imagined was his throat. Leila and Lilit laughed too, the laughter of the relief of the rain that did not come. With great gentleness the two women turned him around and steered him, step by step, into the hut.

He lay there for several sticky, stinking days—he counted two phases of the Moon—and at first he could hardly move. The sisters bathed the sheen of sweat from his skin, his fur, cleaned his nether regions. He wished he had the voice to thank them for performing this unpleasant yet necessary office. Instead he made a kind of odd snuffling noise. They seemed to understand and for that he uttered a prayer (necessarily silent) to the Goddess, in her avatar—as it always appeared to him now, in his memory—of a hem of red, disappearing behind the white wall of his hut.

In his motionless state he began to assemble further thoughts, at first with the inelegance of a child's first towers of toy blocks, forever teetering and falling, but after each fall, a greater confidence, a surer resurrection. And his thoughts ran as follows: that all this heathenish Annakhnu chatter of signs and portents and fire from the sky coincided, *suspiciously* coincided, with the imminent Apparition of the Goddess. In the great scheme of things, it probably mattered little whether the Goddess arrived this year, next year, or sometime in the next ten thousand— because such intervals are neither here nor there given that the Blessed One visits only once every two million years or so. Alfred remembered the academic debates of his youth, about equinoctial precession; and galactic longitude; and compensating for changes in the Earth's gravitational field; and the significance of the amount of oxygen in the tests of microscopic diatoms dredged from the bottom of the Great Lake, and further arcana of that sort. Alfred could never work out why that mattered, but it had nevertheless remained stuck in his mind, like that speck of food that always manages to lodge between one's incisors, especially when one is trying to have a serious conversation with a superior cleric. Alfred thought all such debates sterile at the time. After the passage of eight decades he did not feel inclined to change his mind.

But even so, when all these things had been considered, why had the Annakhnu arrived *now*?

The flashes of day and night, darkness and light, counterpointed with the comings and goings of the two women and, somewhere between now and then, a painted Annakhnu shaman, until, one day, he found he could sit up, get up, and move about, and that he could reclaim his arms and legs as his own. He danced the dance of a much younger man, whirling around the hut, first with one sister, then another, yelling his inchoate praise.

A day dawned of great joy when he found he had recovered the ability to speak. The capacity was yet limited to a vocabulary of one, but the word was well chosen, he thought, and he made it do the work of many.

"*Hashek'na!*" he screamed, when they tried to bathe him.

"*Hashek'na!*" he roared, between mouthfuls of the soup they were trying to feed him, undeterred by the explosions of flying vegetable and fishy gobbets that punctuated each such announcement.

"*Hashek'na!*" he sang, as he capered around the hut, driving the sisters to distraction, screaming this single word, over and over, the word that in the Annakhnu language meant "Goddess."

He slept well that night, despite the pummeling heat, and for most of the following morning. By the afternoon—like all afternoons, now, black with billowing cloud—a second word had found refuge in his damaged brain, where it snuggled up against the first and made friends with it. As evening fell he rushed naked out of the hut, the sisters clucking in pursuit, his robe uselessly brandished before them, as he reached his garden gate and pointed up at the sky.

"Calm yourself, Father," urged Leila, "please, at least put your clothes on."

"Goddess here!" He looked up into the vault, his voice subsiding into a childlike wonderment, as Leila busied herself trying to force the old man's robes over his head.

"Goddess here! Goddess here! Here! Here! *Here!*"

Lilit, however, glanced to westward, following the hermit's staring eyes. Her own now opened as wide as his: her mouth went slack with shock.

"Sister, look—"

All three of them stopped and looked, then, at the evening sky. A sky seared with flaming brands, raining from heaven. And from within the flames and shards of falling scoria, something else. Something that the three people standing at the thorn-branch gate could hardly comprehend. It fell, silver-bright, through the clouds, hovering over the savannah some distance to the west. What struck Alfred most of all was the eerie silence of it all, as if all sound had been stolen from the world.

It looked like the Moon had fallen out of the sky.

-=0=-

"Come in!" barked the Abbot. The door opened on Mandergast, followed by a pale-faced novice, clearly awed by the company. The first rain in months began to fall, the first drops clattering heavily on the windows.

"No, don't get up," the Abbot said as the Brethren Cynewulf and Caedmon stirred to rise from their seats, as if to go. Then, to the novice, "We won't bite, my son. We're quite friendly, really. We limit ourselves to one novice each, per day—even the ferocious Brother Caedmon, here—and we've already eaten." He smiled and patted his large belly. "Though, these days, I must confess, I never can eat a whole one."

Caedmon began to snigger; Cynewulf to roar; and even the novice, after an interval of what looked like utter terror, saw the joke and joined in, a treble cadence above the general monastic din. Mandergast remained mute and still. The Abbot knew that his servant had seen all of this before, many times, and it presumably puzzled him as much now as it ever did.

"Now, my son, what was it you wanted to say?"

"Yes Father. That some people have arrived from the western savannah, and should like to see you."

"'People,' my son?"

"Yes, Father. Two Annakhnu ladies, Father, and one of the Brethren, I think, though he's very old. I... I think he's ill, Father, he..."

A thought passed behind the Abbot's eyes and disappeared into his mind's gloom. A memory of one of his predecessors. Almost a memory of himself. Retiring. A hermitage. Years and years ago. And inexplicably, a flash of sudden scarlet against a white, sun-brightened wall.

"... threw up on the floor of the refectory. The Annakhnu ladies made quite a fuss. Novice Aelle and I cleared up the mess. The ladies wanted to help. Brother Cedd came then and calmed them all down."

"Do you know who they are? And why they have come?"

"No, Father. He wanted to see you, Father. The old Brother. He insisted, though it was hard to understand him, Father. He talked mostly in Annakhnu, I think, and even then his words were difficult to... like, slurred, and... well..."

"Thank you, my son. Please go back to the refectory and ask Brother Cedd to show our mysterious guests to suitable accommodation, to ensure they can wash, and have such food and drink as we have. I shall be along to see them shortly."

After I have prayed, he thought.

"At once, Father." The novice bowed, and left, followed by Mandergast. The Abbot indicated to the Brethren Cynewulf and Caedmon that their interview, too, was at an end—for the moment—and he was soon alone in his office once again. Alone, the rain-dark clouds beyond the windows, the savannah sky now filled with ruinous thunder.

Alone, in the dark. As if he could describe his life in any other way. He had appalled himself at the scale of his own complacency, that it was only in the past few weeks that he had sought to ask questions of his own life. No, not of his faith, for that was unshakeable. His motivations—his calling, his ministry—were likewise supported by his complete conviction of their utter rightness. No, none of these things was in question. His troubles were more personal.

He rose quietly from his chair and left his office. The cloistered corridor outside was quite dark. The shockingly bright jags of lightning that seared through the regularly spaced windows only deepened the darkness between. Had he not already known this way with his eyes shut, the Abbot would surely have felt as if he were voyaging rudderless through inky space, leaping blind from one star to the next.

At first he had great difficulty simply articulating the nature of his malaise, just finding the words to express the unease that had condensed in his mind. As a first approximation, he'd say that he was having problems reconstructing his life as a narrative.

He had come to the Brethren as a teenager, about thirteen or fourteen, and had never sought to look back, beyond that. He had always assumed that the stories they'd later told him were true—that he was a foundling,

the sole infant survivor of a village razed in some long-forgotten skirmish far away, and had been passed, hand to hand like a parcel, across
many countries, perhaps even continents, before arriving at the doors of
this last resort, the lonely Mission by the Great Lake.

He was troubled, now, that until recently he had never sought to corroborate this history; worse, even to question it. Perhaps the details were
too vague to allow any investigation any purchase without prodigious
expense of effort, and anyway, what would have been the point? The
Mission had made him everything he was, everything he would be, so to
look back would have been fruitless, painful even, and why bring any
more pain into a world already long overburdened with that commod-
ity?

However, he was troubled to find that when he did try to look back,
setting out to plumb his own mind, concentrating hard — in the way that
he had long been taught, as a meditative exercise — he could retrieve no
memory of any life before the Mission. None whatsoever.

Could it be that through technique, and slow time, he had simply
learned to forget? To expunge his past, replacing such remote recall with
antennae that might better detect the faint echoes of the voice of the Goddess? No, that could not be it: conversing with the Goddess was something he had always found ridiculously easy, at least compared with the
problems experienced by every one of his colleagues with whom he'd
shared such intimacies.

But of any life before the Mission there was no trace. Not so much as
an impression; an atmosphere; a tableau whose location and the identities of the large cast of characters had been forgotten, for all that the
whole might be brought vividly to life; the sense of the milky closeness
of a maternal primary breast, or the sudden waking, as an infant, to the
eternal sunshine of childhood's lost play. No subsequent impression, no
odor, no sound, had had the effect — as he had heard it did with others —
of the sharply realized recall of times now lost.

There was more to this malady, however, more disturbing yet than a
mere poverty of memory. For it was only since he became Abbot that
he'd begun to have the flesh-crawling sensation that he'd been along the
same tracks before. Not the recall of memories of an earlier life, but of a
life — of lives — lived, here and now, in very much the same way. A sense
of *déjà-vu* which could be at times very strong. Yes, it was only when he
became Abbot and started to read the private diaries of his predecessors
that this sensation started to feed on itself, amplifying to a pitch that was
disabling in its intensity. It was at times like that when he would go to

the chapel and fling himself on the timeworn flags before the statue of the Goddess, shivering, penitent, confused—and frightened.

For when he read those words—of Abbots Aethelwald, and Aelfric, and Alfred; and of Abbots Aelfwine, and Guthlac, and Breca, and Unferth, and Sigelweara, and the Abbots before them, and so on beyond count, back, and back, and back into archival mists so ancient that the words, even the alphabets in which they had been written, were hard even for greater scholars than he to decipher—he found that he could read and understand them all, every word, with perfect clarity.

The conclusion was as outrageous and impossible as it was parsimonious and inevitable, but he had put it off for as long as he could. But events were overtaking him, now, or would if he let them, and he'd seen the same records that Brother Cynewulf had seen, and he would have supported his subordinate completely in his interpretation that the records indeed spoke very plainly, except in one thing. That Cynewulf had missed something of the idiom: the records were even plainer than his colleague had thought. They were now emblazoned on the Abbot's mind in letters of fire.

And it came to pass that the Goddess appeared in the Chapel as a young woman in robes of red.

And she blessed us and made miracles among us.

And she called us brave men, loved, and foolish, but she said all these things with a bright countenance.

And she said that she would reappear at the appointed time in exact same guise.

And she warned us to beware of false gods and false goddesses who would appear otherwise and yet lay claim on our allegiance.

And she spake, saying: 'For I am a Jealous Goddess, apparently, and even though I've probably fucked it up for everyone, as I usually do, I'm not going just to lie back and be two-timed by a load of silly old men like you, lovely though you are, each and every one. So you guys had better watch out. Grrr!'

Such were her Holy words.

The Abbot knew this very well, of course, because he'd been there, had welcomed the Goddess to the Earth in person, and had written these lines himself. While thinking these thoughts he'd walked round the great cloister and found himself, steered as if by automatic pilot, in front of the towering ironwood doors of the chapel itself. The doors were shut, and would remain so until vespers, still two hours away. He could sneak in and prostrate himself before Her image, cooling his forehead on the broad flags at her feet, seeking solace. Indeed, that had been his original plan, or so he thought. But no—he had promised to pay a call to the refectory where the new arrivals would be waiting. He was sure of the identity of one of them, at least, and he was keen to learn the reason for their sudden flight to the Abbey. "She warned us to beware of false gods," he muttered under his breath as he continued on his way.

The refectory was a large space, low-ceilinged and dimly lit, lined with long tables and benches of ironwood. Millions of meals and rough sackcloth sleeves had smoothened the tabletops to a soft gray sheen. The Abbot rarely went to the refectory, preferring to eat in his own quarters. Some might have said that this was appropriate enough for an Abbot who presumably had little time to spend in idle chat with his subordinates. The truth was that the Abbot would have loved to have indulged in gossip—the lifeblood of a place like this, and key to its successful government—but he just happened not to like the smell of the place, a mixture of rancid tallow and slightly-gone-off vegetables.

As the Abbot entered, the refectory was beginning its evening bustle. Pitheks were laying bowls and platters and knives for the evening meal. At one end of a long table, though, a group of larger forms was clustered, huddled round a candle, and he could see and hear that they were already at their meal. He recognized the stork-like figure of Brother Cedd, wringing his hands in his characteristic posture of anxiety. Seated, though, was a monk of great age, flanked by two Annakhnu women, clucking like birds, who were trying to feed him soup and mashed-up pieces of bread, leaving their own meals largely ignored. The yellow light of the candle flame threw the old man's face into sickly ridges of papery yellow, exaggerating the folds and lines. The man's green-slitted eyes, heavily lidded, seemed enormous in his thin face, as if he'd been startled. A long, thin mouth—a mouth which looked as if it was once used to vigorous and intelligent discourse—now moved slackly, disgorging as many morsels of food as it swallowed, the remainder dribbling into his scruffy beard, chased down by the more rotund of the two women, wielding a cloth like a flail. The old man looked up as the Abbot entered and stopped as if caught in a sudden sunbeam. He swallowed, hard, and tottered to his feet, the two women on either side rushing to steady him. The man made a series of stertorious grunts and finally uttered, into the cavernous hush of the great hall—

"Well, bugger me, it's…"

The Abbot waved him to be seated, as he heaved himself over a bench and sat down next to the thinner Annakhnu woman (whom he later learned was called Leila), the old man seated further along the bench. The Abbot avoided looking directly into the old man's eyes, for fear of seeing more of what he'd learned in the briefest instant as he'd entered the refectory—that in this frail hermit, and former Abbot, was a man in search of himself; the man who he had once been, before the mantle moved on. The Abbot now realized, with sinking heart, that if he'd had any life before this, it had become subsumed into the persona of the head of the Order, eternal, unchanging—but should he ever abandon that role, and yet cling on to life, he could only ever be a lost fragment, disoriented, abandoned to the wilderness, forever seeking the Goddess but never finding her. Poor, poor Venerable Alfred. The Abbot's heart was filled with pity.

"Venerable Alfred," he said, "I am sorry."

"You… sorry?" The old man looked every bit as confused as the Abbot imagined he might be.

"Yes." The Abbot took the old man's hands in his, reaching across the table. They were cold, stringy, thin sinews gnarled with pale, fatty lumps, like the plucked necks of fowls. He looked down, still, not daring to meet Alfred's eyes. Anyone passing the tableau and not knowing the identities of the players would have placed the Abbot as a supplicant before the bright face of an ikon.

"Why sorry? Goddess here. *Here*,' said Alfred. "We saw. Leila and Lilit and me, we saw her. Like moon, falling from sky onto savannah. We saw… we saw…"

"Alfred," replied the Abbot, "you know that cannot be true. You know that the Goddess warned us, to take special care of false gods and goddesses…"

Alfred took up the line, now, and the change in his voice was startling, changing in mid-sentence from a querulous, infarctic dotard to a sage with full mastery of a considerable mind and store of words.

"Yes, Father Abbot, 'to beware of false gods and false goddesses who would appear otherwise and yet lay claim on our allegiance.' I know this well. In which case…" Alfred withdrew a hand from the Abbot's grasp and pulled it to his face. His eyes were like green, alien worlds. "Oh, Goddess, save us, you don't think...?"

"Venerable Alfred, tell me what you saw."

Alfred told the Abbot of the shining disk that landed, hovering a few feet above the plain. Of the holes that opened in the disk, and the lines of hundreds upon hundreds of men armored all in bright silver—for that's what they looked like—who emerged, and streamed away towards the west, towards the Annakhnu's City on the Heights: and the decision that he and Leila and Lilit should cross the cracked bed of the once outflung arm of the shrunken Great Lake and rouse the Brethren to action.

"Father Abbot—I see now," said Alfred. "These must have been the false gods of whom the Goddess herself specifically warned us... and they will be coming this way soon. I.... I.... am a fool, Father, a deluded fool. Forgive me. It is many years indeed since I heard Her True Voice."

"I absolve you, Alfred," the Abbot said. "And your errand is not yet vain. For I know that the Goddess is indeed here. Or will be, very soon."

"She will? Goddess here? Goddess really here?"

"That is what I believe. That the Apparition will fall in three days' time. And you will be able to hear her—see her—at long last. If only we shall all survive that long."

"Why, Father Abbot? Why should we not?"

"Because, I expect, all those false gods and goddesses will try to importune us first, just as the Goddess herself foretold. And they probably won't take 'no' for an answer."

Chapter 8. Transfiguration

Israel, Earth, August, 2054

I say to you that I am dead!
Edgar Allan Poe—*The Facts in the Case of M. Valdemar*

Their home for the next fortnight would be where Avi had spent the greater part of his childhood, and had now been his research base for the best part of two decades. What was, essentially, a field station of the Merlin Technologies Institute for Historical Geomorphology had taken over the accommodation blocks and kitchens of the collective farm where Avi had once played in the dirt, shot his first hoops, made out with his first girl.

The kibbutz itself was only glad to be rid of it all, for the Institute's generous rent had allowed the *kibbutzniks* to pave over groves of olives and oranges and build spacious, modern apartments. For where once the inhabitants had been farmers, making a living of sorts from limes, turkeys, a small herd of Friesians and (its pride and joy) an orange-juice processing plant, they had now largely shaken the dirt from their hands. They had exchanged their tractors and denim coveralls for high-tech, high-paid jobs in Haifa, as far from the Soviet-style kibbutz image of agrarian toil as might be imagined. Farmland was no longer needed— flats and houses most definitely were.

But Avi's parents still lived on the kibbutz, so for him it would always feel a little bit like home. He had, however, moved on: his own home was an army barracks the other side of Haifa, where he lived with his formidable wife Rivka, a military communications specialist, and he had to commute in through the morning sprawl.

Tom and Shoshana were quartered in what was affectionately known as the 'Old Town'—the original heart of the settlement, built back in the 1920s and hardly improved since. This was a double row of about two dozen dilapidated wooden shacks, each row facing the other across a broad dirt square, in the centre of which was a vast and ancient olive tree. Long ago, somebody had strung lines of colored bulbs between the shacks and the tree, and a haphazard collection of tables and chairs had accreted beneath it. This was the social center for the younger kibbutz volunteers, whose parties would often last until the early hours. Tom and Shoshana were assigned a shack at the far end, closest to the washrooms and the avocado plantation that bordered the settlement, beyond which lay the track leading up to the first and closest of Avi's many dig sites, spread all over the Mount Carmel massif.

The shack was certainly nothing fancy: just an iron-framed bed on a chipped linoleum floor, a table and a couple of chairs, bare wooden walls and roof, and an entertaining nightlife featuring cockroaches, columns of ants, geckoes, and on one occasion, a title bout between a scorpion and a praying mantis. Tom and Shoshana loved every minute of it. The evening they arrived they'd joined in the general merrymaking of the polyglot volunteer throng that lasted well after midnight.

Tom knew one or two of the other students attached to the Institute, and felt a great thrill to be able to introduce Shoshana, who was in her element. She loved parties, chat and bustle, and felt that she'd had far too little of that kind of thing lately. Sure, the farmhouse was now her home, a long-sought anchor for her life and a special place in her heart. But a girl has to get out, now and then, to laugh, to dance and to flirt. Having recharged her batteries, she spent the energy regained, much later, with Tom, who she led into the warm leafy darkness of the avocado field, whence she flew him to the moon and back.

Thankfully, Avi allowed them the next morning to acclimatize. When they finally ventured out of doors, they found a world refreshed by a light rain that had fallen in the early hours. Their first sight was a pair of hoopoes displaying to each other in the morning sunshine among the litter of candles, bottles and overturned chairs in the square, whose hard-packed ground exhaled the tangy richness of new-washed earth. Avi had to teach that morning at the Technion in Haifa, he'd explained, and wouldn't be able to show them round his latest dig site until later. He wanted to show it to them himself, so they should take the opportunity of resting up after their long journey and wild night. He was surprised, though, to learn that they actually wanted to sit in on his early morning class, so all three of them rode in together (this time in the relative comfort of a pickup) to see Avi in action.

The class was almost as wild as the volunteers, but it was a wildness kept always one ever-shifting heartbeat from abandon: Avi held the first-year students in the packed hall teetering on a tightrope of chaos. For Tom, who couldn't understand any of it (it was all in Hebrew), it was almost like a comedy show, a clown act. Avi's eyes, his hands, his expressions—they'd made him laugh when he'd been a small child—all were now being put to good use. Tom wished his lectures in Cambridge were half this much fun. Professor Reynard had warned him what to expect from Avi's 'Bones 101' class, as she called it. "It's a bear-pit!" she'd laughed; "the noise! It's amazing he actually teaches anyone — but somehow, he always does. They love him."

Shoshana, who picked up maybe one word in five — the Hebrew was much faster and more colloquial than she could comfortably follow — lost herself to Avi's compelling kinesis. The irrepressible, gray-locked teacher bounded across the podium, up the aisles, cajoling and returning, pitching and fielding questions and answers in a constant, rolling exchange with first this student and then that; gesticulating, eyes flashing, whirling constantly to point at the screen or write something in rapid-fire cursive Hebrew strokes on the whiteboard: this was teaching as free-form ballet. After the lecture it occurred to her that Avi had not stood still for the whole hour. He was all animation, all movement, like a particle whose motion defines its nature, and for which the concept of rest-mass is meaningless except as a convenient fiction for theorists. She could see why Avi's classes were so popular.

Thus reinvigorated, Avi took Tom and Shoshana on what he called a 'special VIP tour' — just them, nobody else — to his latest dig site. He had to do his routine inspection of several others first, like a butterfly flitting ceaselessly over flowers in a meadow, tasting each before moving on. Over the years Avi had opened up more than fifteen new sites on Mount Carmel, digging at each new one himself for a season before his curiosity drove him on, passing on each site to a student to run more or less independently. It was a hit-and-miss way of working, but the hits had outnumbered the misses, and in so doing he'd produced an entirely new picture of the prehistoric Middle-east. Tom and Shoshana got a concentrated burst of all this: twenty years of work compressed into two hours.

The eastern end of the Mediterranean is, as it always has been, a crossroads of clashing civilizations, at the centre of an ongoing human ferment that produced agriculture, the great early empires, and the three great monotheisms. But for those who care to read it through the eyes of landscape, its history can be read further back, long before the very earliest stirrings of agriculture on the shores of the Sea of Galilee more than twenty-six thousand years ago. It had long been known that the caves on Mount Carmel hosted among the earliest populations of modern humans to have emerged from Africa, around ninety thousand years ago. As the climate shifted over the millennia, the cave complex harboured waves of Neanderthals and modern humans, each replacing the other.

That had been the view, at least, until Avi arrived and started unpeeling the deeper secrets of the Mountain.

And so, as the Sun reached its searing height and started to descend seawards, they reached the end of a dirt track high on the north face of Mount Carmel snaking just above the most far-flung suburbs of Haifa, the Mediterranean gleaming in the distance. A small complex of build-ings—just two prefabricated huts and a machine shop—framed a steel door in the side of the hill, as innocuous as if it were the entrance to any suburban double garage. Two or three field workers waved to Avi, ex-changing a few words, as he pulled the pickup to a stop.

"But first—lunch!" Avi took a cool box from the back of the truck and carried it up a narrow, gritty path to the shade of a small cypress grove. It was an idyllic spot. The trees shaded a small, scrubby lawn that gave them complete cover and yet allowed them a magnificent view towards the sea. There was the usual kibbutz travelling brunch of cucumbers, tomatoes, bread, cheese and fruit. As they ate, Avi told them of an email he'd had from Jadis.

"You two are getting first look at a lot of big news," he said. "So? Spill the beans to your Uncle Avi. What's the latest about eclipses?" So they told him about the Sigil, the inscription that Jadis' team had found at SSM. Avi had heard something of it from Jadis, but he was especially keen to learn what Domingo had made of it. "Hey, Shoshana, what do you think of my good friend Domingo? Quite a guy, eh?" At the mention of Domingo's name Shoshana blushed and looked down. She did, how-ever, recover some of her composure to say that Domingo passed on his good wishes to Avi, and that he hoped they could meet in Israel.

"Sure—he's here next week," said Avi. "The Pope is doing an open-air mass thing in Ramat Gan Stadium, so I guess Domingo will be busy—how did he always say it? Yes—'matters on a higher plane.'" Tom laughed at Avi's impersonation of Domingo's voice, its intriguing mix-ture of cultured tones and bear-like gruffness. "Actually," said Avi, "I think Domingo's *really* here as a warm-up act for the Stones."

Tom and Shoshana both laughed. Shoshana imagined Domingo, red-capped like a cardinal but still in an aloha shirt, doing a stand-up routine before a stadium packed with screaming rock fans.

The prospect of the Rolling Stones' latest comeback had been the talk of the kibbutz volunteers, some of whom were trying to get tickets to the stadium show—scheduled for the day after the Pope's open-air mass—and the opening concert in a promised eighteen-month world tour. Tick-ets were hard to come by and those few that were still on the market cir-culated for small fortunes. Stones tours happened once every five or six years or so, with such inevitability that people had long since stopped wondering whether Keith Richards (a sprightly hundred and ten, thanks to some timely yet experimental rejuve treatments) and Mick Jagger (just turned one hundred and eleven, and as lithe and athletic as ever) had traded their souls for longer-than-usual life-spans, and had accepted that they were probably immortal anyway. The big wow was the much-trailed reappearance of 'Brian Jones,' who, the rumor had it, was either an imposter; a product of a secret Korean cloning laboratory; or both.

As for the Sigil, Avi agreed that Domingo was probably right that it should be kept secret. "I hope we never find any prehistoric art here," he said. Imagery of any kind was becoming very hard to square with the bubbling religious and political situation. The Orthodox rabbinate would never stand for it, he explained, "and with the Khalifa breathing down our necks, well..."

Everyone in the archaeological world — and indeed the world in general — was still reeling from the rumors that just two months earlier, the Khalifa had dynamited the beautiful ancient city of Petra, because a visiting Imam from Yorkshire had declared its statuary 'offensive'. But as no western journalist was ever likely to be able to verify anything that happened inside the Khalifa, the rumors remained just that.

"Just imagine if we found religious iconography from a non-human species here, in Israel?" said Avi: "It would blow the whole lid off everything. The Imams are on a hair-trigger — they want Jerusalem so badly they'd need no more excuse than that."

Avi did not mention, of course, Rivka's pillow-talk, about the immense armies parked in the desert beyond Jordan and along the parched banks of the Yarmuk; the airfields packed wingtip-to-wingtip with the products of a decade of round-the-clock production in remote desert factories from Tripoli to Tashkent; the gigantic rail-gun howitzers and mobile missile launch-pads lining up on the Euphrates. The European Union, mindful of vocal support from the Khalifa from within, and still trying to digest a skittish Turkey, was turning a blind eye. America was in one of its more isolationist moods: Israeli mutterings that given the unity and armed might of the Khalifa, she'd have no option but to 'go nuclear,' made the US ambassador nervous and run for cover. It was all behind the scenes, of course — if it hadn't been, His Holiness, and probably the Stones, would have taken their immortality elsewhere, and there'd have been panic in the streets.

Yet panic or no panic, Israel was quite alone and poised to fall — and Avi, by digging up some figured stone or other, would be damned if he'd be the one to push it over.

But Avi was thinking of a far more ancient war when, after lunch, he took them down to the machine shop, found miners' helmets from the team store, and ushered them through the metal door. "Forget eclipses," he said. "They're for little old ladies like my old friend Domingo. What I'm going to show you is strictly adults-only. It will blow your minds."

The door led into a short tunnel, down a slope and into a broad and brightly lit cave, dotted with geometrical monoliths, as impressive as SSM, but on a smaller scale.

"We've found lots of these all over *Ha-Carmel*," explained Avi. "We call them 'SSM-lites'. Each one was probably a clan base for an extended family, maybe for a few dozen generations. But *this* one, this is odd: usually there are cemeteries, like the ones at SSM. But there are no bones here at all, not one. It's as if they've all been dug up, or swept away."

They walked past the ranks of silent monoliths, perhaps for three or four hundred metres. Above their heads, the cave roof gradually sloped down to meet them. "So, after I and a small team discovered this cavern last year," Avi continued, "we kept pushing inwards, further and further, looking for the bones we knew must be here, until we found — this!"

Avi's timing was as perfect as it had been in his lecture early that same day, for just as he finished his sentence they saw that they'd reached the edge of a black ravine, and that the cave roof had arced over their heads to plunge before them, downwards into the abyss.

Avi steered them to a path a little way to the right that led them down the slope of the ravine, which was neither as steep nor as deep as they had first thought. Perhaps twenty meters below the level of the cavern floor, they found a lower, larger cavern opening before them, stretching as far in all directions as their lights would penetrate. Unlike the cavern above, this lower cave was yet to have a full lighting system installed. At present there was something like the emergency lighting system in an aircraft — a pattern of tiny LED lights on the ground marking out paths where it was safe to walk, their weak, local illumination making deep and eerie shadows of small objects close by, throwing them — hugely magnified — into the illimitable lightless voids beyond.

Avi led the way down to the cave floor, and it wasn't long before they started noticing bones. First in ones and twos, then a few together, until, by the time they were thirty or forty metres in, there were drifts of bones in great waves, in high dunes to the left and right, their extent made all the greater by the fact that only a few caught the localized ground-level beams from the pathway lights, the rest fading upwards and outwards into the musty dark, present only by virtue of horrible suggestion.

But what little they had seen was quite enough. Few of the bones seemed in any order at all. There were skeletons, and parts of skeletons, bones scored and charred, shattered, scattered and thrown awry in a massed idiot-dance of death. The litter of carnage seemed to go on for-ever — it was a sea, an ocean of bones. Shoshana and Tom drew close to Avi, who had stopped before a vast and teetering pile of skulls. They were utterly silent.

"Yes, my friends," he said, his voice subdued, his upper face in a shroud of weird, Hitchcockian shadow cast by the pathway light at his feet, "it's quite something."

"How far does this go on?" asked Shoshana, dry-mouthed, queru-lous.

"We — that's me and the team — we think it links up with another cave system on the east side of the mountain, but we're not sure. We haven't got there yet. We've penetrated three kilometers into the cavern so far, and it still goes on and on, just like this. Where we're standing is just the start. As of now, we can see no end to it."

"Just... bones?"

"Yes, just bones," said Avi. "Okay, there are a few simple hearths, too, no more than bonfires, really, but we haven't found any buildings. The bones are mainly... but — hey — let's get out of here before I explain any more. I don't mind telling you, this place freaks me out."

So they retraced their steps, and even Tom, who had lived his forma-tive years in darkness, was never so pleased to have reached the surface as he was then, when they ascended the slope to the cypress grove to greet the Sun as it began its downward slope over the Mediterranean.

To Shoshana, the Sun, while welcome, seemed sickly and apologetic. She felt cold, preternaturally cold: she hugged herself to warm up, and then clung tightly to Tom. When they'd sat down and had assumed a measure of equanimity, Avi started to talk again, and this time it was with a seriousness that surprised them.

"Now, if I tell you a few things, you must promise — *promise* — not to breathe them to a living soul. I shall tell your mother, Tom, because — well, *davka*, just *because*. But what I am about to tell you must never get out. Not until I'm ready. I'm not sure that I ever will be."

They promised.

"But first, I must ask you both a question. Why is it, do you think, that humans came out of Africa maybe a hundred-fifty thousand years ago, but took another hundred thousand *at least* to get into Europe?"

Silence. And then Shoshana said, warily, like a shy student at her first tutorial—"because the Neanderthals were already there?"

"Good," replied Avi. "But that's only a part of the story. All the reasons we hear—and, I am ashamed to say, the reasons I still teach in my class—are horseshit. That the first modern humans were still too primitive to go north, or that they first went east into Asia before venturing into Europe, blah blah blah. All just glimpses of the truth, but not the whole of it. I think I can now supply the missing piece, from that pit of bones."

And so he told them a story.

How much was truly based on the evidence, how much informed conjecture, and how much he'd just made up, they would never know.

When the first modern humans had stumbled, innocent and blinking (said Avi), out of Africa more than a hundred thousand years ago, they had the misfortune to run straight into a Neanderthal civilization at its most powerfully rapacious, centered on Mount Carmel—which, like the landscape of southern France, was largely artificial. The massif had been a warren of subterranean cities, sometimes bursting into ramparts on the surface, always at war with each other. After many millennia the squabbling clans united one single chieftain—let's call him the King Under the Mountain—whose armies of stone-clad warriors commanded Mount Carmel and all the lands round about. The Kingdom had blocked access to Europe, and had found in the steady stream of newcomers a life-saving resource.

For the might and extent of the Kingdom was increasingly a sham. Although at its very peak of power and majesty, it had in fact started to decline long before, rotting from within. The troops had to go ever further to exact tribute to bring to Court of the King. The forests, long depleted by a civilization still dependent on hunting and foraging, were in retreat. The Kingdom might well have been unified, but it was starving to death from the inside. Until, that is, a ready supply of man-flesh wandered stupidly over the horizon, just in the nick of time.

The decline of the Kingdom was suddenly thrown into reverse, and for a while the Neanderthals grew to yet greater power by refashioning their whole economy around human beings. They enslaved them for tens of thousands of years, rounding up more wherever they could find them, farming them for sacrifice to whatever gods they worshipped: using them for food, and for sport. Even when dead, no part of a human being was wasted, for waste was a luxury that this decadent Kingdom could not afford. Apart from the meat and offal, marrow and brains, their body fats could be rendered down into oil, their skins used to make baskets and boats, their bones and teeth wrought into tools, furniture, musical instruments, even toys for children.

More and still more humans had come from the South to replenish this never-satiated Moloch. Whenever humans became scarce locally — or wise to the Neanderthal threat — raiding parties were sent to find them, penetrating the Nile Valley as far as modern Ethiopia. And so the bloody story continued, for age upon age.

Until, around forty or fifty thousand years ago, new tribes of humans appeared in the South. These were tall, wild and fierce, completely different from the flabby, cowed race that the Neanderthals had dominated for so long. And they were bent on conquest — and vengeance. They would tolerate the raids no longer. No more human tribute would be sent north. They had come north to see the Kingdom Under The Mountain for themselves, and to wipe it from the face of the Earth.

Sensing the threat, the King Under The Mountain had ordered that all his humans, his chattels and broodstock, be gathered together in this cave, and that they should all be slaughtered — rather that, than for them to be taken. This deed was done, and the bones of these humans could be seen in a vast drift in the centre of the cave. There were tens of thousands of them. Men decapitated, their brains bashed out. Babies broken in two. Women spatch-cocked like chickens when not otherwise impaled, beheaded, sacrificed in a last and desperate throw. The floor of the cave became slick with offal and broken bodies and tides of blood. The brutality of it was unimaginable. Some of the humans fought back before they died, but not many.

The only thing the King Under The Mountain feared, almost as much as the vengeance of the Gods, was the wrath of the Neanderthal Chieftain he'd usurped many years before and driven across the Jordan. The hated rival was now back, his legions marching on *Ha-Carmel*. It was a fine judgment as to who would arrive first, the Neanderthal raiders from the East, or the Men of the South. In the event, it was the Neanderthals. In this very cave, they started to do battle with the King's troops for control of the remaining humans. We can tell this (said Avi) from the presence of two kinds of flint armour; the presence of skeletons associated with Remillardian artifacts; and that some of the humans appear to have been pulled in two, as if victims of an internecine squabble for who would get to make the bloody ritual obeisances first. Evidence from hearths and scattered coprolites suggests that some of the Neanderthals paused from their warfare to engage in impromptu banquets of raw human flesh.

The battle was futile, for when all the humans were dead, and the Neanderthals had just about finished slaughtering one other, the Men of the South arrived to finish the job, if indeed there had been a job to finish. Within a few years, the great Neanderthal civilization of thousands of centuries was destroyed. And *Homo sapiens* found that the gates of Europe were open wide.

By the time Avi had finished his story, the Sun was sinking into the Mediterranean in a florid gash of barred clouds. Tom and Shoshana looked pale with shock, like rabbits in headlights.

"Look," said Avi, "I don't apologize for telling you this, or for bringing you here. If I hadn't, you see, you'd never have believed me."

"Avi, how much of this do you know to be true?" asked Tom, in French, and barbed with anger.

"What's the truth of it?" replied Avi, coolly. "Well, I know this much. That the bones accumulated in a single event, for accelerator-mass-spectrometry dates taken from all over the cave all cluster around a single date, about forty-odd thousand years ago. And the bones? Tom, you saw them."

"Look, Avi," Tom returned, his voice brittle, "you cannot frighten us with this... this lurid rubbish."

"Tom, you're a scientist," said Avi. "You are rational. You have every right to be sceptical until you have sifted through the evidence for yourself. But even if a tiny fraction of what I have told you is true—and just look at the evidence before your eyes! The bones!—you can bet that once people get hold of it, there will be all kinds of stories, elaborations, used and perverted to all kinds of ends. And let me tell you another story. When you were very small, the effects that the discoveries at Souris were having on the world almost drove your parents apart."

Tom and Shoshana sat up at that, and Avi returned to the fray, with increasing vigour. "You didn't know that, Tom?" he said. "Well, perhaps you should. And let me tell you more things you didn't know. It happened not so long after me and Rivka rescued the last of the Sand-Druids from certain slaughter in Chad. When Faye Callaghan and Primrose Tsien—dear friends of your parents, and also of me—were lost in Tibet.

"We didn't know what happened at the time, but it turned out that they were ambushed by Almai. When they finally got the truth out of the ringleader, he confessed that our friends—my friends, whom I loved—had been blinded, their tongues ripped out, their hands and feet chopped off, and then they were systematically *fucked* until they *died*, in the cause of Almai traditional religion! So how do you like that?

"And it gets better! They were then dismembered and eaten raw! And what's more, the schmuck who did all this confessed all on Prime-Time TV! He thought he was doing them a favor. And yes, guess who was watching? Yes, Tom, your *Maman* and *Papa*. It tore your mother to pieces, so much so that Jack could hardly cope — he was *this close* to walking out on her. You were about six years old."

Avi sat down behind them both, embracing them. "So now you understand. I'm sorry it had to be this way. Now you can see why I can never make this public. Just imagine what it would do, not only to us, but to the world? It was my old friend Domingo who created *Undique humanitas*, the document that welcomed the hominids into humanity. With impeccable timing he announced it the day before the Almai confessed to murdering our friends. Jadis hardly talked to Domingo for weeks afterwards. It took all his diplomacy — and that's more diplomacy than you'll ever see from anyone — to talk her down. And those two are *real* close. So if news of this battleground ever gets into the media, just imagine what will happen. *Undique humanitas* will be no more than a straw in the wind. They'll be hanging Sand Druids from lamp-posts. The Kaptars will have to run for their lives in case they get flayed alive and made into rugs. Those cute little Pendeks, you know the ones? They drive all the cabs here in Tel Aviv. They'll be locked in their cabs and torched alive. And when all the hominids are gone, where then will the lynch mob turn its fury? Who'll be next, eh? Humanity will destroy itself."

They drove back to the Kibbutz in silence through the deepening night. "Don't worry, and sleep well," said Avi, stiffly. "I'll come get you in the morning."

But sleep was hard to find. They tried to make love, but could not raise much enthusiasm, so they simply rested close together. Shoshana insisted on keeping the light on, so Tom put on his iShades, so that even though he'd had his arms around her, he seemed very far away. As usual, he was the first to fall asleep. Shoshana sank eventually, turning off the light and allowing Tom's arms to curl round her like angels' wings.

Shoshana's sleep was troubled. She had a dream in which she'd looked down at her body, which was made of glass, and found a black blob the size of a golf ball in her insides. The blob grew as she watched, turning from a rough sphere into a star shape and sending out threads and tendrils that ramified through her whole body until they burst out through every orifice at once, swelling at the ends into buds that disgorged enormous blood-red flowers and bloated fruits that rotted where they hung. She should have been horrified by this, she thought, but found it no more than mildly unpleasant. But then she looked up at the Sun and it was black. She screamed.

-=0=-

Domingo had had to be on his mettle a few days later when the cavalcade of Papa Linus Secundus, Episcopus Romanus, rolled into town. As the Pope's Personal Private Secretary, Domingo had the closest possible access to His Holiness: and although Linus II was affable enough, Domingo felt that they weren't really getting along at the moment, or, at least, not as well as they usually did. Even when they'd tried to compensate for this loss, by setting time aside deliberately to brainstorm about things—like when they'd forged *Undique humanitas* together, fifteen years before—Domingo had the sensation of intellects sliding past each other. It could simply have been their different backgrounds, now coming to the fore at a time of heightened tension.

Linus II had once been a street kid from North Dublin. To be sure, Domingo himself had come from a lowly background, and perhaps it was no more than a difference in climate: the parched heights of the Sierra Nevada versus the damp and vivid green of the Emerald Isle. Yes, perhaps that was it.

But it was more likely, Domingo reflected, to be the current circumstances themselves. Domingo was sure that His Holiness, who was usually in pink and rosy health, was looking pale and peaky. It could have been the journey, which had indeed been exhausting, with many delays enforced by technical problems and the weather. And maybe His Holiness had picked up a cold along the way. He'd have to attend to him carefully.

The night before the Open-Air Mass, His Holiness was attending a private reception at the official residence of the Prime Minister of Israel, so naturally Domingo came too, along with a small squadron of dark-suited, bulging-pocketed Swiss Guards. They were to stay the night.

If Domingo found his boss a little distant, he had hit it off immediately with the Prime Minister, a man of sparkling wit and intelligence. His name was Seamus O'Shaughnessy.

"If I might say so, Prime Minister...." Said Domingo.

"Yes, I know, I know," said O'Shaughnessy. "It's an odd name for a nice Jewish boy like me. But I am an Israeli, a sabra, born right here, if not very well bred. My folks, though—they're another matter, They're as Irish as the Blarney Stone, and in fact I spent most of my boyhood in the Old Country. That's where I met His Holiness, in fact. We go back a long way. A long way indeed. The tales I could tell. Now tell me, Your Eminence...?"

"I beg your pardon, Prime Minister," said Domingo, smiling. "It's Cardinal Domingo Sanchopanza. Or, for those with sufficient leisure, Domingo García Vasquez Santéria Sanchopanza de Orellanzana von Hohenzollern und Taxis. But my friends just call me 'Pongo'."

The Prime Minister laughed, but his face immediately darkened. "Tell me, Cardinal... er... 'Pongo'. His Holiness—our friend—doesn't look quite as chipper as I remember."

"*Anno Domini*, Prime Minister. It gets to us all in the end."

"Assuredly, Your Eminence, but the Davy O'Leese I remember from the Old Country would never have refused a second pint of Guinness as he did at the reception, freely given, nor a third, and would have been carousing until dawn, even on days when he'd be taking mass. He was just a Parish Priest, then, but you know, all the same—I'm worried."

The Prime Minister's observations struck a chord with Domingo. It wasn't, then, just his own imagination, fuelled by proximity, mistakenly reading the tiniest difference in his employer's countenance as the symptoms of something terminal. Even when considered objectively, His Holiness looked more than just tired. He was gray, like freshly burned ash, and he kept having to wipe away beads of sweat that persistently broke at his hairline (like blood from a crown) which, if not stopped, rolled glutinously down his face like something out of *Death In Venice*. Yet he'd waved aside any offer of help.

"I share your concerns, Prime Minister," Domingo confessed. "I thought it was just me, but, well..."

"So what can I do?" asked O'Shaughnessy.

"Nothing much," said Domingo. "All I can do is persuade His Holiness to take some ibuprofen after vespers and hope for the best."

Hope for the best. That was all he could reasonably do, Domingo thought to himself, anxiously.

The next day, however, Domingo assured his host that the Pope seemed to have taken a turn for the better; was excited about the open-air mass; and looked forward to downing a glass or two afterwards with his boyhood friend. The Prime Minister for his part regretted that he couldn't make the motorcade to Ramat Gan, and would indeed miss the service—urgent committee meeting at the Knesset—but waved off his friends, old and new, with all the good wishes he could muster.

It was not until his committee meeting was over that O'Shaughnessy heard the appalling news.

The committee meeting had gone on even longer than planned, even accounting for the usual delays, diversions, filibustering and procrastinations. Knesset sessions always overran in any case, but this must have been a record. The ongoing problem of the Khalifa loomed over everything like a pall of smoke from a burst oil well, dragging everything out, sapping all energy. Israelis were usually practical to beyond the point of rudeness, getting on with the job in hand, no matter how trying the circumstances. But tendrils of fatalism were beginning to creep in, even here, to the corridors of power. Nobody had said it out loud, but you could see it in peoples' eyes—that they were living in the Last Days.

So sighed O'Shaughnessy almost three hours later when his trim and pretty aide led the way from the council chamber and into the fresh air— when the Prime Minister noticed, in that contrast between acrid staleness and tart freshness, just how hormonally horrid the atmosphere had become in camera. There is nothing as evocative as the human sense of smell, and O'Shaughnessy was drawn straight back to the pallid, perspiring face of his old friend Davy O'Leese (he could never quite believe he was the Pope, even now). The pressing business of governing a fractious country had driven all thoughts of the open-air mass from his mind.

Caught in reverie, he hardly noticed the aide, concern on her face, trying to engage his attention. "Sir," she started nervously, as if half-afraid of pulling the Prime Minister from his daydream, "Sir, I have some news..."

But she was too late, for in that moment he caught a TV monitor in the Council Chamber Ante-Room, tuned to Kol Israel News One, the staff glued to the set. The picture showed the Pope being stretchered off-stage to a waiting Magen David Adom ambulance. Cut to screaming sirens, police cordons, crowds of concerned worshippers bearing candles.

"What happened?"

"The Pope, Sir," explained the aide, momentarily casting her eyes floorwards, "He'd just got to the end of the *Aleynu*—I mean, sorry Sir, the *Agnus Dei*—and then.... he just..."

"Collapsed?"

"Yes, Sir." Well, God be thanked that Linus had pretty much finished the job before expiring. "Get me to wherever they took His Holiness please — at once! — And see if you can get his Personal Private Secretary on the line."

More police sirens. More crowds. Streets darkening towards evening, a light wash of rain. Helipad. Whirring, whining racket.

"Prime Minister, I'm so glad you called," said the deep, resonant voice of Cardinal Domingo Sanchopanza, incongruously squeezed into the Prime Minister's earbud. "We're in the emergency room at the... er... Hadassah Hospital."

"How does he look? His Holiness?"

A pause. "No more than... uh... fair to middling."

"I'm on my way, Your Eminence," the Prime Minister said. But the line was dead.

And, finally, the sliding doors of the Emergency Room, a section thrown hastily under guard, with Cardinal Sanchopanza standing outside, deep in conversation with several doctors. The white-coated throng parted to admit O'Shaughnessy and two bodyguards, adding to the crowds — two Swiss Guards stood outside the section in which the Pope was currently confined. Something was, clearly, up.

"I know that there are... er... protocols about isolation," Domingo was saying to one of the doctors, "but please might I be allowed to see His Holiness, as his aide, and in such moments, his confessor? Perish the thought, but I might have to administer the last rites."

"I understand, Sir," came the reply, "but really, I'd advise against it. The patient is in a bad way. Really bad. Unconscious. He's very ill indeed, I'm afraid, and getting worse. We'd need to stabilize him, or try to, before... I very much regret..."

At this point O'Shaughnessy felt he ought to at least try to tilt at a windmill to help his new friend. "Oh honestly, Doctor," he said: "how ill can he be? Flu? Coronary? Overwork?"

"None of the above, Sir," said the doctor, whose name badge read 'Dr Mohamed Al Hajj, Resident,' turning to the Prime Minister with such cool professional detachment that he appeared not to recognize him for who he was. "Or, at least, we don't think so, Sir. In truth, it's like nothing we've seen before. But I understand you were with him last night — you might have seen some symptoms?" *Death in Venice.* "Anything you can tell us, anything at all, could be immensely helpful."

A small crowd gathered. Ambulance drivers, paramedics, nurses, secret servicemen, Swiss Guardsmen. A gentle, steering, hand. Cardinal

Sanchopanza. A quiet side office, a desk, some chairs, a wastebasket overflowing with paper and food wrappers, medical charts, vending-machine cups, a pennant for Maccabee Tel-Aviv, a CCTV screen labelled 'Isolation Room 1' in embossed red tape: and the smell of sweat and fear. And now a Muslim doctor from Gaza City, a Cardinal from the Vatican, and the Prime Minister of Israel. Three great religions in one tiny office. Not the usual ER crowd. But not the usual patient either. And not with any of the usual complaints.

O'Shaughnessy sat, his collar increasingly tight and sweaty. He loosened it as Dr Al Hajj ushered out the secret servicemen who unobtrusively took positions outside the closing door. "Please, Prime Minister, and... er... Your Eminence," the doctor said. "Please, look at the screen. Pay close attention. Then you will see."

The screen was flickering and monochrome, but even with such a low-quality image you could hardly describe what was happening as in any way normal. His Holiness was in a hospital gown, lying on a gurney—or, rather, manacled to it, so great were the convulsions sweeping through his body.

"Can't you do something, Doctor?" asked Domingo.

"I'm afraid we've done everything usual in a case of—say—coronary arrest, or even just fatigue. We've tried sedatives, but we're afraid to overdo it. We've had to restrain him as you see..."

"But what of his mouth?" snapped O'Shaughnessy, impatiently. "Couldn't he bite through his tongue?" They gazed in horror as the blurred image of the silent scream of the prostrate Pontiff bounced from the curved screen, caromed off their astonished corneas and bounced back again.

"That's just it—his mouth is locked wide open in tetany. We couldn't close it again if we wanted to." O'Shaughnessy was about to apologize for his earlier asperity, his heightened mood—the doctor was clearly doing his best—but the three watchers were overtaken by events.

The Pope, jaws agape, eyes bulging, suddenly sat up. He did so with such force that his hands were both neatly severed by the unyielding restraints. Blood squirted everywhere in looping, jetty gouts.

Al Hajj went white.

"Get someone in there—quick!" he screamed into a gooseneck mike beneath the monitor. Big, burly nurses in Class-4 outbreak suits appeared on screen, trying vainly to restrain the Pope while not being repeatedly hosed in blood from his scything stumps. Retreating, they too gazed mutely at the scene, for even though the Pope had now stopped moving—as suddenly as he'd begun—they made no attempt to move in on him. They, like the three observers in the office, could only stare at the patch of inky blackness that had appeared at the Papal throat, and which had begun to spread even as they watched.

None could now intervene. No action seemed advisable, even possible. As the wave of darkness lapped slowly up the patient's neck, over his ears and jaw line—and down over his collarbones and under his hospital gown—it took on the dull sheen of taut PVC, as if the now motionless and unbreathing form were being slowly melted into a body bag. The blackness seeped over both cheeks, his nose, and—encircling his mouth like an 'O'—bridged that, too, closing it off in a broad meniscus. After another twenty seconds, the head—the eyes—were completely encased. It was this wave of blackness that finally choked off the blood dripping from the wrists, and, after another twenty seconds, closed in over the tips of his toes.

Only the hands, once the hands of a healer, hands that had given the benediction times beyond count to grateful multitudes, remained beyond the dark tide—severed, lifeless, bloodied, on the gray floor of the isolation room.

The three watchers exhaled in unison, as if a terrific tension had been released.

Too soon.

The nurses on camera moved out of shot as a further monstrous transformation took place. The black caul around the Pope tightened and thickened, drawing his knees up beneath his chin, squashing his face between them so that the black membrane, once in contact with itself, fused together. The Pope was sealed in, redoubled, and yet the dark shroud contracted still further, squeezing his legs and head inwards and downwards so that they lost all recognizable shape and distinction. The stumps of the arms were drawn in until, after a minute and a half (the watchers had in fact lost all track of time: this fact was only noted later from CCTV records and corroborated by comparison with dozens of similar cases that the hospital would see over the coming hours, before a Khalifa fighter jet, its pilot in the grip of the same affliction, plunged into the hospital, blowing it to smithereens) the Pope now looked like nothing more than a shrinking, melting black candle.

And still the collapse continued, remorselessly, until what was once a man had entirely disappeared, replaced by a featureless black sphere of radius precisely 15.68 centimeters, and which would prove refractory to all forms of penetration or inspection immediately available to the hospital.

At last, Linus had become an oyster in negative, a black pearl against the white folds of the hospital gown, spattered with blood as nicely as in any Passion. As for transfiguration—well, that had to be another matter entirely. For the time being, as the transformed Pontiff toppled from the gurney, bounced once, and rolled beneath a rack of life-support equipment: *Noli Me Tangere*.

Chapter 9. Reed-cutter

Southern Mesopotamia, Earth, c. 125,000 years ago

Thynke howe short tyme thou hast abyden here.
Thy place is bygged above the sterres clere,
Noon erthly palys wrought in so statly wyse.

(Think of the short time that you have abided here.
Your place is outmatched by the clear stars above.
No earthly palace is made in such a stately fashion.)

John Lydgate— *Vox ultima Crucis*

Waves, soft-lapping, like the passage of purest cotton across the face. A breeze now, as soft and stinging as sheerest satin. Light, bright as any braided gold. The man who had once been Mr Haraddzjin Khorare of the Very Great and Ancient City of Axandragór opened his eyes. He looked up to see the Sun, clear, overhead, in a teal-blue sky. He found that he was floating, wavelets caressing his ears. The water was quite shallow, though: for once awake, he startled, thrusting his hands downwards at his sides for them to sink in soft ooze. He sat up, waist-deep in the dark water. Hard stalks of reeds pressed all around, imposing a monotonous yellow verticality on the scene, like cheap interior décor.

Mr Khorare, who had yet to appreciate the fantastic miracle of his survival, entire, when he had previously been shredded into fist-sized chunks for the hungry throats of sharks several hundred miles to the southeast, wondered instead why the afterlife smelled like a midden, and had such tasteless wallpaper. Either that wallpaper should go, he thought to himself, or so should I. He blinked, but the scene remained obdurately the same, in which case, he thought, his wager with himself was lost, and he should seek some more interesting vista, elsewhere.

He rose, unsteadily, his knees creaking beneath the tatterdemalion shreds of his crushed-velvet knee-breeches, the black water sliding away in viscous runnels along its fluted pleats. But the view on standing was hardly more edifying, given that he sank in the mud almost up to his knees, and the reeds still towered overhead. It was not in the character of Mr Khorare to feel despondent, and yet he did begin to wonder what he should now do. At that point he felt a warmth in the inside pocket of his chemise (whose quality, he was pleased to note, was such that it maintained its integrity, despite now looking more like a string vest). The talisman was still with him, and, if he stood still and concentrated, it would tell him which way he should go. He sloshed manfully in the prescribed direction, pushing the reeds apart as he went.

It was, though, very hard work, and he was soon parched, hungry and exhausted. He should have liked to have sat down, but the only place to sit was in the malodorous ooze itself, and as he was now dry from the knees upwards (if caked with mud from the waist downwards) Mr Khorare was most reluctant to get wet once more. And the mazy sea of reeds, while allowing no sense of any forward direction, was still open to the wearyingly pitiless sun, which started to burn his head and neck. After a while, though, he found that the water became shallower, until it became hardly deeper than his ankles, and in places gave way to a kind of blancmange of semi-solid ground, streaked with green slime and pocked with small herbs between the reeds. Frogs and small jeweled lizards darted away from his feet as he passed. The reeds became shorter, so that he could, in places, begin to see above them — though the view was, regrettably, only fractionally less monotonous than it had been before. And yet he took heart. The view, while still dull, was beginning to change, and that, thought Mr Khorare, must be for the better.

After a while the reeds began to thin and he tramped through a wide land of tussock, bog and little creeks so overgrown and hard to see that he had to look carefully as he walked in case he tripped and pitched right in. This was not a place, he thought, where one could just bowl along, wherever or however one liked, as were one on one's regular morning constitutional. The creeks became wider and deeper as he progressed, until he reached one that was probably too wide for him to jump, but was deep, with high, sheer, treacherous-looking sides beetling over the curl of black water in the ditch at its base. He was just maneuvering himself to sit down on the tussocky edge, so as to probe the consistency of the bank with his toes, when he heard a voice.

"You're late."

Startled by this irruption of sound, Mr Khorare turned to see where the voice had come from, overbalanced, and tipped into the creek. His fall was broken by the pungent ooze just above the water's edge, but, unable to stop, he continued to roll downwards until he came to rest in the water with a splash. He sat up. Wet again. All over. Harumph. A brown hand came down and grasped his, pulling him upright.

"Come on, then, now you're here."

Mr Khorare found himself following the source of the voice of the hand upstream. Walking along the creek beds—if you knew where to tread—was quicker than trying to leap across them, or squishing up and down their steep and slippery sides. He was, in particular, following a broad back, clad in a garment of rough-looking burlap, surmounted by a shaggy brown head, and supported by massive, beefy legs. There was no way that he could, as yet, see the figure from the front. He was barely able to keep up with it, given its speed, let alone try to overtake it. He did try, though, to engage the figure in conversation, but his ejaculations of "I say!" and "now, look here!" and so on and so forth in like fashion went unanswered, so he was perforce intimidated into silence.

After several twists and turns they reached a broad, shelving beach of muddy gravel that allowed them access, at last, to something akin to dry land. Just above the creek edge, on a grassy platform, stood a hut of sun-baked mud-bricks and thatched with reeds, on top of which the carcases of fish and other creatures were drying in the sun. Mr Khorare's unexpected companion stooped and disappeared into the hut's darkness. From the outside, where Mr Khorare still stood, the hut seemed entirely spare and without ornamentation, and seemed so to Mr Khorare's eyes until he saw an engraved mud-brick hanging above the lintel. The engraving was of three circles, and two crescents, with radiating lines. His hand snatched straight away to the inside pocket of his ragged chemise, and pulled out the talisman. A face appeared at the door. It was broad, leathery, and with a weak, receding jaw—a Stoner—but for all that, the face of a woman.

"Well?" she said, "Are you coming in, or are you just going to stay out here all day?"

"Excuse me, I meant no offence," Mr Khorare replied. His limited experience of Stoners did not, he had to admit, presage anything other than a most grisly fate—especially here, in the wilderness. But Mr Khorare felt that polite and mild compliance ought to be worth the effort, even here.

"None taken," said the woman, disappearing again. This time Mr Khorare followed her. Now, he had no clear idea what to expect from the inside of a hut of what looked like a lone reed-cutter, except that it would probably look no more sophisticated than the outside, only darker. Which is why the sight of the interior, as it greeted him, quite took his breath away.

"Think of me as the... oh, I don't know... as the Genie of the Talisman," the reedcutter said, a few minutes later.

"But that, Madam, is just a description, a title, a soubriquet, if you like," replied Mr Khorare. "I am — I was — a man of affairs, in a business where reputation measured a great deal. Reputation gathered to my name."

"Mr Khorare, do you not think that the contrast between the externals of this dwelling and the interior are not sufficient proof that I'm not the genie of *something*?"

Mr Khorare had to admit that she had a point. He leaned back on the rich oxblood leather of the chesterfield, looked out at the brilliant white landscape, and took another sip of the spirit from the tumbler in his hand. But he was still uneasy.

"Quite so, Madam. But the same might apply to the facts of your person. I am sure — quite sure — that you are not, nor have ever been, a Stoner."

"Congratulations. But if you look like anything else in these parts, you're likely to get eaten, or at least killed. As you've found out."

Mr Khorare chose to let her final comment pass. "But if you will not tell me your name," he continued, "can you not at least tell me your species?"

"Mr Khorare — would you really ask such personal questions of your host, were you a guest in their drawing-room in the Very Great and Ancient City of Axandragór?"

"Well, no, I... well, no I shouldn't, but that great city is far away. And I ask your forgiveness for my frank curiosity, Madam, and crave your indulgence nonetheless. Consider, if you will, my trade. I clothe people of fashion and taste in stuffs, in ginghams and velvets, taffetas, organzas, brocades, buttons, frills, ribbons, ruffs and bows. I have been engaged in such a business for a long time and have achieved tolerable standing and a degree of wealth. From which you should know that my contemplation of the superficial is based on an extremity of profundity. In short — it matters to me what people look like. Clothes make the man, Madam — or, if I might speak plainly, the woman. But as you remain quite immune to my requests, Madam, I hope you will excuse my being quite candid — that skirt doesn't suit your figure."

The woman laughed and melted, before his eyes, her brutish lineaments and figure changing into a form younger, taller, and much paler, with big, strangely round black eyes and long, black hair. "Is this better?" Her smile, while still not furred enough to mark her as human by his lights, illuminated the room.

"Much."

"But despite being a better fit to the clothes, Mr Khorare, how do you know that this is any more my real form than *this*..." (a black sphere chased with silver filigree, on balloon-wire wheels, pulled along by two silver-plated steam-powered automata) "or *this*..." (a loxodont from the Eurasian plains, caparisoned with rich embroidered brocades) "or *this*...?" (a vast spider form that seemed far too large for the room, with a dizzyingly imprecise number of limbs, its body towering above him at what seemed an impossible distance).

"Point taken, Madam." Said Mr Khorare. "I apologise for my impertinence."

"No need. And really, I am fascinated that you should ask. Nobody has before. They usually imagine that I am some avatar of somebody else, somebody they've known. But nobody has ever asked to see the *real* me. So, to be honest, Mr Khorare, I'm flattered. Would you like to see what I really look like?"

"Do you advise it?"

"No, not particularly. I don't think you'd make much of it. If I simply flashed it up before you... well, it would just seem like a meaningless jumble of angles with nothing to fill them. Or a sea of holes."

"You're a 'sea of holes'?"

"No, not quite that, either. If you're sure you want to see what I look like, I'm going to have to... to have to... to have to..."

Mr Khorare felt himself lulled into a seamless peace, and woke up—if that's what it was—on a tropical beach, at night. Really, it could have been his private vacation home in the Archipelago, a few dozen miles from the Very Great City. But above him wheeled a sea of stars like a Catherine Wheel, and as he looked up into it, he felt something of himself being sucked rapidly upwards into the sky.

-=0=-

Finding a comfortable spot for a bivouac was proving a hard task. These low hills, rising to the east of the great river that eventually debouched into the marshes now far behind him, in the south, were dreary enough by day, with no vegetation taller than knee-high knots of heather. By night they presented an endless series of slopes, each just too strongly canted and stony for comfort—Mr Khorare had discovered, to his cost, that any flat ground in this region had achieved this state by the slow accumulation of mud. The sun was setting, far across the river, on the fifth full day after his departure from the altogether remarkable hut of that Stoner reed-cutter—genie, mage, sorceress, whatever she was—and the light was fading, when, joy of joys, he found it: high on the slope, a small, dry, flat space in the west-facing lee of a large rocky outcrop. Shelter enough from the chill winds rolling off the range of mountains to the northeast, and space enough to pitch a bivvy and perhaps brew a kettle.

The bivvy practically pitched itself—a flick of the wrist and it was up, blowing and billowing until he'd found the strong, thin lines and metal pins to secure it to the soil. He'd already located a spring nearby, and was able to fill a kettle, made of a light, silvery metal, and use a portable stove to set a fire beneath it. All this equipment had been provided by the reed-cutter. A few things to speed him on his way, she'd said. And some of the dried, preserved food—especially the apricots—had been at least as good as anything he'd tasted on his travels. But what interested him the most—a professional interest, one might say—was the fabric of the bivouac itself. So sheer, so light—lighter than silk, as light as a feather—and yet, unlike silk, entirely proof against rain and wind. Night after night Mr Khorare lay beneath it, looking up at its perfect seams, wondering what sort of material it might have been that could repel moisture and retain warmth without any need of a nap, or grease, or, indeed, anything much at all. His wonderment at the fabric far exceeded that of the portable stove equipment—a fire, wherever he was, instantly—also thoughtfully furnished by the reed-cutter.

And what was his journey, then? The reed-cutter (he still preferred to think of her in such homely terms, not being able to comprehend what she claimed to have been her true nature) was quite adamant—as his late father had been—that he should follow the talisman wherever it might lead, for it was (she continued) vital that he deposited it at a certain place, at a certain time. She would not say when and where these loci were to be found—to do that would (in her words) 'throw the game'. All she'd say was that he'd know them when he found them. Curiously enough, this was sufficient to allay any remaining worries on Mr Khorare's part.

Mr Khorare did, however, establish that he would in all probability never get back to the Very Great and Ancient City of Axandragór that was his home. The reason, however, was curious—for, according to the reed-cutter, he would probably outlast it. The reed-cutter had only laughed at his expression of puzzlement.

"Oh, my dear Mr Khorare, you are such a silly man!" she had exclaimed: "do you not think that it might not be such an easy thing for fate to so casually expunge from its tapestries, as if swatting a mosquito, a man who has survived pirates, grapeshot, sharks and even decapitation?" Mr Khorare felt he had to concede, although he did wonder what decapitation had to do with anything. He was thinking these thoughts as he dowsed the fire (by the simple expedient of twisting a knurled metal knob!), inchwormed into the sleeping-sack—another marvel of stuff offered by the reed-cutter—and fell into a happy sleep. Let the fates fall where they would.

It was in the gray of early dawn on the next day that Mr Khorare thought he heard voices. In fact, if truth be told, he thought he'd heard voices during the night, but had dismissed them as phantoms of his own dreams, or as animal sounds from far away. But as light now stole into his bivouac sufficient for him to see by, he became more conscious of the voices all around, clearly to be heard—but very far from human. He sat up in his sleeping-sack, rubbed his eyes and listened intently, holding his breath. All around the tent there was a low rumble of sounds. At first Mr Khorare was hard put to it to tell them apart from wind roaring in the rocks, except that, with attention, they resolved into the deliberate, punctuated packets of spoken language, for all that Mr Khorare could not recognize any of the words spoken. He imagined that were wolves and jackals to have had speech, it would sound like this.

Feeling now rather scared, Mr Khorare put on his corduroy trousers, cotton shirt, synthetic jacket, socks and boots (yet more marvelous stuffs supplied by the reed-cutter from her inexhaustible store of wonders) and peered out of the bivouac. The view was westward, downslope, and what he saw amazed him.

Huge, humanoid forms were streaming down the hill, on either side of his sheltered slope, and in front of him: a parade of backs, walking away towards the river, where—in the distance—he could see a black knot of activity and birds circling high in the sky. The humanoids were much taller and rangier than any of his own kind, or even—he guessed—any Stoner. All of them were clad from head to foot in close-fitting suits of shaggy gray or off-white fur—either that, or these humanoids were naturally very furry, and were otherwise naked, aside from the peppering of leather helmets and other articles of a military nature, including long clubs of bone and other weapons of horn or ivory.

These creatures, whatever they were, were marching, downhill, to war. None had yet looked back, and for that, Mr Khorare was very grateful. He hoped that he could remain secret until the entire army—if that's what it was—had passed by, so that he might be able to slip away unnoticed. But the great, shaggy, armored forms continued to file past, much as they had done, it seemed, for the past several hours. There must have been thousands of them. And the more there were, the more noise they seemed to make, the sparse barks of words joining up into a more uniform, unified bellow, a war-cry of defiance. But if these creatures—and Mr Khorare thought he knew what they might be, now; they looked very like the fierce Almai of the mountains of Tibet—if these creatures were indeed marching to war, where was the enemy? He imagined that it was the target of this long march, the camp—if that's what it was—in the valley below, and to the west. All he had to do, then, was wait until the horde had finally passed by, and he'd be able to watch the battle in relative security from this high point.

Matters turned out very much as he'd expected, at least to begin with. The host eventually transmuted in nature from warriors to wagons, a straggle of bone-railed sleds, and the squeals of female and young Almai, their domestic animals and all manner of the incredible variety and quantity of impedimenta that nomads felt they had to convey on their long migrations. In this gigantic, mobile fleamarket, Mr Khorare in his modestly camouflaged bivouac felt even less conspicuous than he had before. But even these last of the Almai camp-followers had moved on downslope, and Mr Khorare was left quite alone, once again—all such Almai voices that could be heard now came from far away, and his proximate company was the lone wind, gusting through the rocks and heather, as it had been before.

The morning waxed in warmth, and all such change as Mr Khorare could discern concerned the sounds he heard, solely, which changed from the basso roar of defiance and the superimposed chatter of women and young, to the more variegated palette of sounds associated with battle engaged, though the nature of the Almai's enemy remained unknown to Mr Khorare.

At this point Mr Khorare felt that it was time for him to pack up his things and resume his course, roughly north by northwest, following the line of the river to his left and the mountains to his right. Packing took a remarkably short time and all Mr Khorare's belongings were soon stowed in a knapsack of a smallness and lightness that always amazed him. In addition to their other properties, the stuffs provided by the reed-cutter folded up so tightly that his entire bivouac could be held in the clenched fist of one hand, his rolled-up sleeping sack in the other. The entire cooking stove, when folded up, was no bigger than a modest firewood faggot, were any firewood needed. Well satisfied, Mr Khorare shouldered his pack, strode confidently out of the lee of the sheltering rock, and walked straight into a trap.

His first inkling that something was wrong was the impact of his nose against a standing stone which he was sure hadn't been there the night before. Recoiling, he looked up, and found he'd run into the flinty breastplate of a heavily armored Stoner. Looking around, the soldier had three companions, and was identical with two of them. These were clad from wrist to ankle in long coats of leather studded with overlapping flint scales, and wore flint-studded leather helmets on their heads. Each carried a dagger of honed antler points, and a long spear tipped with a blade wickedly carved from the antlers of giant deer.

The fourth rode behind the phalanx of three, mounted on an coelodont of great size, likewise armored in leather and flint. The rider wore much the same armor, and carried much the same armaments, as the foot-soldiers, except that his helmet was ornamented with auroch horns on either side, and its nose-guard was decorated with roughly cut crystals of amethyst, he thought, or garnet. And this Stoner, too, wore something else that his colleagues lacked: a facial expression. Where the faces of the troopers were as stony as their costume, that of their leader was horribly animated into knots of muscle, warped into an asymmetric leer. But most surprising of all to the stunned traveler was his voice—as patrician, as modulated, as articulate and as sarcastic as any of the grasping, defensive elder statesmen and merchant emperors that haunted the Chamber of Commerce in the Very Great City, resisting change, using their gifts of withering rhetoric to impede the young, hinder the new, thwart the ambitious: the forces for whom the fetid stasis of death was life, and all life-giving change was the wind of death.

"So, Mr Khorare," the Stoner chieftain said, dismounting. "We meet at last."

Chapter 10: Sand Druid

The Wilderness of Judaea, Earth, August, 2054

Ah! why, because the dazzling sun
Restored our Earth to joy,
Have you departed, every one,
And left a desert sky?
Emily Brontë — *Stars*

Tom tried to swim in it on his front, but found that his body was almost skating across the surface. With only his chest and knees submerged, his hands and feet couldn't gain enough purchase to move.

Shoshana tried the more customary seated method, like in all those photos of people taken while relaxing in the water; in hats, sometimes with tea-trays, but always reading a newspaper. But those pictures had been taken decades before, when the Dead Sea had less deadness in it than it had now, and she found it hard to keep herself from bobbing out of the water like a cork. In the end they just lay on their backs, side by side, propelling themselves by gentle sculls with their hands. They felt like two tiny pond-skating insects, whose world is forever confined by the unforgiving, rubbery tyranny of surface tension. The water itself had a curious texture, both oily and salty, and it made their hands sting where they'd suffered even the tiniest abrasions, the result of Avi's whirlwind field school — the incessant handling of bones and stones.

For the first few days they'd stayed pretty much in the kibbutz, learning to recognize and classify animal bones and stone tools. Tom knew much of this already, and could have gone, pretty much, to any of Avi's roster of currently active dig sites. But he welcomed the chance to be with Shoshana, the relative novice. Not that they spent much time chatting: the effects of the Battle Cave had left them both profoundly thoughtful, and — as they couldn't tell anyone else about it — they preferred to be thoughtful together, rather than separately.

At the weekend Shoshana felt that what they needed most was a change of mood, insisting that they both catch a bus to Jerusalem, for she wanted to show Tom around. "You'll never know how amazing it is until you get there," she'd scolded, when he showed even the tiniest reluctance.

The visit, however, had been a frustrating failure. The *suq*, usually overflowing with bustle and noise, was sullen and subdued. When Shoshana had visited it the previous December she'd found it as entrancing as Aladdin's cave, the stalls and open-fronted shops on the narrow alleys crowded with the same scenes that you might have witnessed five centuries earlier, or ten.

There were stalls selling nothing but orange juice, squeezed for you then and there, on the premises; itinerant coffee-sellers dispensing thimblefuls of their scalding, cardamom-scented brew from ornate silvered urns carried on their backs, the urns tinkling with tiny bells. There were dimly-lit alleys in which the all shops sold nothing but *halal* meat, the butchers hard at work in full view of the customers (although Shoshana hadn't wanted to look too far past the hanging racks of carcasses), and the exchange of greasy money and gossip was accompanied by the decisive sounds of slicing and dicing. Shops that had seemed unfeasibly small at the front gave on to room after amazing room, piled high with the most exquisite carpets, each with vivid patterns of confounding intricacy. And there were, as there always are, merchants selling basketloads of the tackiest souvenirs. She particularly remembered one especially enthusiastic stallholder chasing her down an alley with a plaited leather whip—"for your husband!" he'd yelled, as she scooted round a corner: "for your wife!"

And the smells! Coffee and cardamom, cloves and cinnamon, onions and garlic, leather and wool, and meat, and fruit, and textiles, and people, and animals, and (most of all) money, all in one great intoxicating sensory onslaught.

But now most of the shops were closed, their filthy, graffitoed shutters down, and Tom and Shoshana as among the very few visitors felt that they were unwelcome. That they were being watched. It smelled only of rotting fruit cooking in hot trash cans.

Another disappointment was that the Temple Mount was closed, so they couldn't visit the *Al-Aqsa* mosque, nor the shining blue-and-gold jewel of the mosque of Omar. Riot fencing barred the gates to the mosque precinct, to which a trilingual sign had been attached. In English it said 'Closed for Renovations,' but Shoshana swore that the Hebrew version was more eloquent and included words like *forbidden* and *security* and *danger*. What the (even longer) Arabic sentence read, they were unable to fathom. But the IDF troops guarding the gate looked grim, and neither Tom nor Shoshana felt like inquiring further. The Western Wall below the Temple Mount had also been barred (not that Shoshana had any desire to mingle with the 'black hats,' as she'd called them), and was uncharacteristically deserted; the Church of the Holy Sepulcher bore only its complement of the variously denominated clerics, outnumbering visitors and pilgrims at least six to one. And nobody, not even Shoshana, visited the Copts on the roof with their lines of washing. "Tom, I'm so sorry..." Shoshana began, "but I think Jerusalem is *closed.*"

Her disappointment was deepened by the feeling that she'd taken Tom on a wild goose-chase, and by her confusion, that this really shouldn't be happening. It wasn't a religious holiday, as far as she was aware, because she'd checked—this was, after all, Jerusalem, where any given day might be a religious holiday for someone—and those few tourists they'd seen had looked lost, as if they were really expecting to be in Milan or Cozumel or Blackpool but had taken a wrong turning. They decided not to stay the night as they'd planned, but to head straight back to Haifa, where things seemed more, well, 'normal'.

The second week started with an early-morning call. Avi was to take them to a site he was working on personally, where they'd have a chance to help excavate part of a Neanderthal cemetery for a few days. On the way, they'd told Avi about Jerusalem, how muted it was, how— *threatening*—as if they'd been partygoers who'd unwittingly stumbled into a private funeral. Avi looked troubled, and what little he said seemed couched in riddles. "Okay, make this your very last day," he'd said. "Tomorrow you're free to go. Your time is short. See as much of my wonderful country as you can, while you can."

And so the very next morning they'd taken their leave. They'd both hugged Avi, who seemed more tense, more serious than the overgrown puppy who'd greeted them just eight days earlier. He didn't say anything, because he didn't have to—but he looked like someone who knew he was entering the Last Days.

They would never see him again.

First they went to Tel Aviv. "If Jerusalem can't cheer us up, then Tel Aviv will," promised Shoshana, and this time she had been right. They cadged a spare sofa for a couple of days in a flat currently occupied by Alina Jacobs, the elder sister of one of Shoshana's old *cheder* friends, and whom she'd met the previous December.

Alina was an expat from North London who'd made *aliyah* and was now working as a real-estate agent, selling expensive seafront condos to other soon-to-be ex-residents of North London. Her boyfriend, David, was a fighter pilot and on duty increasingly often, as he was now, she knew not where: so she welcomed the company—and the chance to show off Tel Aviv's wild side. For two whole days without stopping they'd all got drunk and expired on the beach; they'd drunk some more and partied and bar-hopped and clubbed until dawn. It was just what they'd needed to beat the Battle Cave Blues.

Two days later, Shoshana woke late to find herself crammed on the sofa next to a man who seemed utterly dead to the world. Drink-sodden nights out had been the backdrop to her life since she was twelve or thirteen, but oh, poor Tom—until he'd gone to Cambridge, he'd had very little experience of drink at all, and was now flat out, comatose. She rose and wandered blearily to the kitchen, in search of anything like an aspirin—for she was convinced Tom would need one when he eventually surfaced.

But she herself needed one right now. Over the past few days she'd been seized by pains in her lower abdomen that felt like someone had filled her with kerosene and set it alight. She was convinced Tom hadn't given her a dose, because, despite his promiscuity, he just didn't seem the type—and anyway, she'd been vaccinated against everything imaginable, including pregnancy. Her mother, in one of her rare outbursts of decision, had insisted on this. Part of the problem (not that it *was* a problem!) was that there was such a *lot* of him, and after several weeks of frequent sex, her more tender regions had been stretched, bruised and abraded. At least, there were times when she could regain some measure of control, like when she had been riding him, last night, settling gently down on top, shimmying down to find a comfortable level, swivelling around until she felt she fitted over him like a glove, and...

"It must be love," said Alina, joining her in the kitchen, catching her thoughts. Shoshana suddenly realized she'd been standing quite still, with a silly grin all over her face.

"You're so lucky to have found Tom," Alina cooed, filling the kettle and putting it on the stove—"he's *gorgeous.*"

"You don't know the half of it," replied Shoshana, gesturing like the angler whose fish has got away "... or the whole of it..." and the two girls collapsed on each other in fits of mirth.

"*Is* he... *really?*"

"Yes, he *is*—and he's *lovely*—and I'm so *sore*. Have you got any aspirins or something?"

Alina rifled around in a cupboard until she found a small bottle of pills, and gave them to Shoshana. But as she handed them over, her expression switched from morning-after playfulness to a soft yearning of regret, of loss. It was her turn, too, to look distractedly into the distance.

"What's up?" Shoshana asked.

"Oh… it's nothing." Alina turned off the gas beneath the kettle and upended the boiling water into two cups of spiced, unfiltered, heavily sugared black coffee. "Hey, drink this. It's *botz,* I know. Usually it's my Mum's PG Tips but, you know, needs must."

She turned away when Shoshana looked at her, wide eyes full of questions. But it was only for two or three seconds. When Alina turned back, her own eyes — pale, ice-blue — were blazing for all that they looked inward.

"David came home last night…" she said. Shoshana remembered a time lost amid the small hours when, being more than half asleep, she half-thought she'd half-heard the frantic gasps and sighs of sex from another room in the small flat. "… but he was gone well before any of us woke up." Silence. And then, Alina standing in her own kitchen, began to shake, wiping tears on the sleeve of her bathrobe.

"Oh, fuck it, Shoshana," said Alina, "everybody's selling, nobody's buying, I haven't had any decent commission for months, and if I could go back home, I would." She subsided onto a chair. "And there's more. Something David said. He told me to… to… well, he said I should be prepared for the worst. He said we should party and drink and fuck each other silly, because tomorrow… well, who knows?"

So that was it, what had been eating Avi and the whole of Jerusalem, and why deep in the desperate night Alina and David had screwed each other's brains out, like they'd never have another chance. Israel was the last man standing against the Khalifa. Alina, stood up, wiped her face and made herself busy with cups and plates. "But don't mind me," she said.

"We'll pick ourselves up. Nobody else will, after all. Now, do me a favor — take that gorgeous stud-muffin of yours and bugger off out of here as quickly as possible. In two days the city will be gridlocked for the Pope, and then the Stones, so escape now. Go and see the Dead Sea before it's gone. Masada too…"

The defiance of her eyes continued her sentence: Masada will be enough to show you that we've been fighting off bastards like these for practically ever, and we'll be here still, when the Khalifa is dust and forgotten.

Alina saw Shoshana and a groggy Tom on to the bus, and within half a day they were here, at the Dead Sea, trying to swim in it like any two fun-loving tourists, for all that the Khalifa loomed from mountains in plain sight. After a while the sunshine and salt were becoming oppressive, so they sploshed and clambered awkwardly from the clingy brine. The water evaporated immediately, leaving them crusted in a thin armour of salty plates.

After using the creaking, paint-peeling showers, they laid themselves side by side on the stony beach. Tom gazed at the yellow hills in the distance, lost in his thoughts. Shoshana, the words of her Tel-Aviv friend still echoing around her mind, wondered how many Khalifa field-gunners were staring back. Shoshana decided to do something useful instead and went in search of food. Breakfast at Alina's now seemed like ancient history.

Shoshana found a snack stand not far from the edge of the main road out. She joined a small crowd milling around it — mostly soldiers taking a few hours' snatched leave, plus an assortment of back-packers and boho tourists. One had stood out from the rest, at first because he was extraordinarily tall, and second because of what he was wearing. No backpack, no uniform, but a long, brilliantly white, hooded robe that stood out sharply against the general sea of green and tan. Because he had been a little ahead of her in the snack-bar queue and had his back to her, she did not take much further notice of him — until she heard his voice, as he ordered *falafel* from the seller. It was less a voice than a completely dry and tuneless hiss, like someone suffering badly from laryngitis. She looked up then, and met an unreadable expression from the stallholder taking the order. The transaction completed, the hooded figure turned.

And then she saw his face.

Framed in a lion-mane of scruffy, yellowish hair on an unusually tall, narrow head was a thin parchment-white face in which two eyes glinted amid curiously folded eyelids. The eyes were palest grey, almost white, as if he were suffering from cataracts. The nose was long and beaked, with narrow, slit-like nostrils. The mouth was disconcertingly wide, but very thin and almost lipless.

The first thing it said to Shoshana was "excuse me," in English, but with a curious accent that she couldn't place, before standing aside to allow her to place her order at the snack-bar counter. The stranger seemed eager to talk to her — out of politeness, she supposed — and offered his name, which sounded like the noise that might be made by a cat with emphysema caught on the point of death while trying to cough up a rusty bicycle pedal. When she looked like she might embarrass herself trying to pronounce it, he came to the rescue.

"Of course," he said, "my friends just call me 'Bob'." He smiled, his lipless mouth broadening to a somewhat startling size, revealing a lot of yellow-brown teeth.

"My name's Shoshana," she replied, brightening. "I'm a student, from England. But today I'm just a tourist!"

Bob tried to repeat her name, but through his lips it emerged as the crackling of kindling in a frozen winter bonfire. Yes, he too was a tourist, but only from a *moshav* outside Dimona, he explained. Yes, he whispered, wasn't it a funny feeling swimming in the Dead Sea? The hacking gasps following this sentence Shoshana interpreted as laughter. And, yes, he was Jewish.

"For sure!" he said. "I'm a Hebrew Israelite!" Taking Shoshana's quizzical expression as a cue, he continued. "Of course you mightn't have heard of us. There aren't many of us, after all. A few in America, of course. Florida. And who are we? You are justifiably curious, young lady. No, I don't mind at all. We're the Lost Tribe of Judah. To be sure, you'll have heard lots of people say *they're* the Lost Tribe. But we're the real deal, straight up. We've been Jewish for hundreds of years, thousands, maybe forever! Would you like a cigarette?"

And so Shoshana put two and two together, and made a vast, intuitive and daring leap. She was standing before a real, live Sand Druid, and she wouldn't miss her chance.

"Yes, I've heard of the... er... *Annakhnu*," she said.

Bob smiled at this brave and rare example of anyone else trying to pronounce their own great and holy name. He bowed to her in appreciation. Thus emboldened, Shoshana continued: "I've been on Mount Carmel," she said, "studying with Professor Malkeinu. Do you know him?"

The two turned away from the snack stand and sat on one of a number of heavily weathered wooden benches nearby. Bob looked at her, his reptilian stare from deep within his hood glowing with an inner fire.

"Avi Malkeinu is our returning prophet," he said. "He is our avenging angel, our savior. Without him we would be as ashes and dust. If you know him, you are to be blessed." Then he rose from his place, knelt before her, took her hands in his long, bony claws and kissed them, and said, at the back of his throat but with passion for all that it was close to silence:

"Avinu Malkeinu, aseh imanu tzedakah v'chesed v'hoshiyainu."

With a startling jolt, Shoshana was transported back to North London, to every Yom-Kippur morning service she'd ever been reluctantly dragged into, amid all the other children and the women, and she found herself mouthing this most solemn Hebrew prayer along with this stranger: our Father, our King, treat us with charity and kindness — *help us.*

After two beats Shoshana joined in Bob's prayer, singing it to a haunting, minor-key tune full of imploring, keening loss, of sorrow and of hope; the melody she felt she'd known since her earliest childhood, before her Dad died, in the morning of the world when all was fresh and new and happy, and which she'd always found inexpressibly moving. How could her stepfather have been so narrow, so proscriptive, when here was this alien in this scruffy desert who had internalized their religion so completely?

Who, then, was the Jew?

If Jewishness could encompass Bob the Sand Druid and Howie the *schlmiel* in a single sweep, then *everyone* was Jewish, all humanity — and beyond it. And more than Jewish. She thought back to Noah, the tower of Babel, a record of an age before there were Jews, when people had lived together on the Earth, humans and the lost *nephilim* and who knows who else, in an idyllic time before they had challenged God and had been punished with the realization of their own sundering diversity, to give — what? Sand Druids; Neanderthals in the Battle Cave; the Almai that had eaten Avi's friends in reverence; the Pendeks that drove all the taxis in Tel-Aviv; Souris Saint-Michel; the mysterious Sigil of unguessable age and mysterious purpose; Tom, Avi — and herself.

Domingo had been right — religion did not transcend humanity, it *defined* it. Any creature that raised its head above the murk and sought the face of God, however hopelessly, and however lowly, alien or strange it might be, was a human being, by definition. This inner blast of revelation did not stop, for now filling her head were words she'd learned in her diploma-college biology class, that came now as if in answer — from a source that would have had Howie Levinson squirming with horror: that there is a grandeur in this view of life, having been originally breathed into a few forms or into one; and that from so simple a beginning endless forms most beautiful have been, and are being, evolved.

Shoshana sat in stunned silence with the ghost of Darwin and the memory of her Father and Mother and her *avoteinu v'imoteinu* back to Abraham and Isaac and Jacob and *Homo erectus* and apes and all the creatures that had crawled out of the slime, all there on the bench with her, looking up at her young face in expectation of an answer that did not come.

Before she could say anything else, the Jew whose name was Bob but was really something utterly remote and inhuman stood up, collected his paper-wrapped falafel, and walked with a loping, stork-like gait to a waiting *sherut,* which drove off in a clash of gears and dust.

"Tom, I'm sorry..." she started, having brought the cooling falafel and warming coke back to the stony, salty beach, inwardly cursing that she always seemed to be apologising to him all the time, "I... er... ran into a Sand Druid."

"A... what? A *Sand Druid? Tiens!* Where is he?" Tom sat up, scanning the grove of scrubby trees and bushes that screened the snack stand and the road from view.

"I'm sorry Tom," she said. "I wanted to bring him to you, I know how much you wanted to meet one, but when I looked up, he'd just disappeared. Like he was a dream, like he'd never... like I imagined the whole thing."

"It is nothing, Shoshana."

"It was weird, Tom, he was so, like, *other.* But he *knew,* Tom, he took me back to when I was a little girl in the synagogue: I could see it all, Mum, Dad, everything — it was all there before me, in my mind."

Tom paused for a long time. "You know," he said, "it's like something Domingo once said, when I was little."

Shoshana looked up. "What?"

"Well, you know Domingo and I have always been close. He's been more *mon père* than Jack, in some ways, like he's always looked out for me, even from far away. And one day — I think — yes, I was about nine or ten, and Fairbanks had died. Who was Fairbanks? He was my dog, and my best friend." Shoshana recalled the picture of the little boy with his arms around a big golden retriever on the mantelpiece at the farmhouse.

"I was very distressed," Tom continued, "at losing my good friend. But, you know, my *Maman* and *Papa* have never been very religious, and they didn't seem to have... to have the right things to say, when Fairbanks died..."

"Like you needed a ritual?" prompted Shoshana.

"Yes, that's exactly it, a ritual. To be sure, they tried: you know what people say, 'Fairbanks is looking down on us from doggy heaven'; 'Fairbanks is free from pain now,' and so on. But nothing they seemed to say worked for me. *Rien. Alors,* so I was as upset as ever — remember, I was only a little boy." Shoshana loosened up a little at this, wrinkling up her nose with laughter, leaning up against him.

"In the end they just shrugged and told me to wait for Domingo. So next time he was visiting, he did a ritual for the dog in the garden. Just for me. Nobody else was there. I don't know, maybe my parents kept out of the way on purpose. But I swear, Shoshana, he must have made it up as he went along." Tom laughed in remembrance, Shoshana now embracing him as they sat on the beach.

"But it was just something he said. That although his church said that Fairbanks had no soul, we two—you know, if it was just *entre nous*—we could always... er... 'stretch a point for special friends,' on one condition: that if, and only if, we'd loved Fairbanks as though he was a person—then God would love him too."

Shoshana said nothing, but looked across the still, flat lake, regretting once again that she'd never had the courage to take Domingo into her confidence. She marveled at the sensitivity—the informality—of a ritual that the priest had made up to ease the bereavement of a child. But the sentiments were not patronizing, and very far from childish. They were eternal. Domingo had understood that if a sense of religion defines any creature as human—that was the basis of *Undique humanitas*, which must then have been still quite new and raw—then something else is necessary, too. For religion implies awe, and devotion, even fear: and these things are impossible without love.

So Domingo had made the obvious connection. That if we love someone, or something, we are in effect transferring something of our souls to them, just like every scribbler of every cheesy love song ever written had always understood.

But there is a flipside. Only those that can love have souls to share. And her blood ran cold with revulsion at the religion of her upbringing, at least as interpreted by her stepfather—as hard and stony and lifeless as this salty desert shore. Domingo realized that religion must have rituals if it is to survive, but can only remain meaningful if there is space for these rituals to be stretched, and for love to find its expression within their confines. For without love there can be no soul, and no humanity, and therefore no religion.

But Judaism, the Howie Levinson Way, was all about ritual coming first, no matter what, and love was a long way down the list. His religion had survived for thousands of years despite the earnest attempts of many to destroy it—but at what cost? Without love it was meaningless, with the pointless, bureaucratic cruelty of any Kafka short story. The tragedy was that this inhuman austerity was quite unnecessary. For what she'd seen in Bob's burning, alien eyes when she'd mentioned Avi

Malkeinu was nothing but awe and devotion, and love. She would have prayed for her stepfather's soul, if she thought he'd had one.

The Sun was beginning its descent down behind their backs. It was time to move on, to Masada. They'd learned from Alina that you could usually hitch a ride there from the Dead Sea, straight up the highway. A small crowd of people was already milling around the bus stop beyond the snack bar, and some them said they were Masada-bound. Staying the night at the summit of the ancient hill fortress was officially discouraged, but unofficially tolerated as an item on the student-boho-backpacker List of Things To Do.

So Tom and Shoshana joined up with a small group who'd fallen in with a muscular young man with an American accent who'd just become an Israeli citizen and had completed basic training in the army. His name was Danny Forbert. There was also a sandy-haired and studious-looking Englishman who Tom thought he recognized, but couldn't place. He seemed to be miles away, listening to an earbud. At first Tom assumed he must have been following the cricket.

The rest of the party was made up by a pair of backpackers, both Mexican. One was a slim and well-groomed lawyer called José Luis, the other an engineer, Carlos, a bearded and ramshackle bear of a man who must have weighed three hundred pounds. Most people were amazed to learn that they were, in fact, brothers—perhaps less so that they were passionate Stones fans and were in Israel to catch the first date of the latest and possibly last world tour of the group they called *Los Rollings*. Tomorrow they'd head to Tel Aviv in the almost certainly vain hope of getting tickets. And if they didn't, hell, they'd get drunk anyway.

Danny Forbert was one of those natural leaders, whose calm authority meant that decisions were reached with perfect consensus, with little or no argument beforehand. And so it was under his direction that the six of them flagged down a *sherut* for the couple of stops to Masada.

Tom wished Jack could have seen it. If there were any proof necessary that landscape could be shaped by the hand of man and still look like landscape, this was it. Masada had once been a mountain like any other, but it had been converted into a palace and fortress more than two thousand years before, by Herod the Great.

Although now demonized for the Slaughter of the Innocents—a tale almost certainly mythical—Herod was undeservedly less well known for his more concrete accomplishments. He'd built a vast sea port at Caesarea that had made Roman Judaea the maritime capital of the Eastern Mediterranean. He'd created the amazing cylindrical palace of

Herodium just outside Bethlehem that would have looked *avant-garde* even in the twenty-first century. And most of all, he had created Masada.

Herod's engineers started with a natural hill but had flattened the summit, using the overburden to make the sides almost sheer and impossible to climb, especially if the summit were fortified and manned. But its final days had been wrought in blood. Long after Herod, Masada had been the last redoubt of a caste of Jewish religious zealots, who committed mass-suicide when the fortress was finally stormed by the Roman Tenth Legion, the only force capable of taking it—and even then only after a long siege. The Romans had added to Masada's landscape, by building an immense ramp from the valley floor all the way to the summit. The ramp still existed, now, like the table mountain, just another feature of the Wilderness of Judaea.

Danny was the only one of the six who'd been to Masada before, and he promised them all a 'special treat' when they crested the summit. He led the way to the foot of a dusty and treacherously steep track that switch-backed up the western face of the hill. That they could climb it at all was testament to the effects of two millennia of erosion on Herod's almost unbreachable redoubt, the dry desert winds aided by tens of thousands of eager feet—and the lack of military resistance.

When they finally stormed the hilltop they were sweaty, dusty, seared by the still-strong evening sunshine and fit to drop. All except army-hardened Danny, and, surprisingly, Carlos, who thundered over the ridge like a bright-eyed Visigoth on the rampage, adrenalin trumping exhaustion, and ready for anything.

Flushed with achievement, they started to look around the low, grey stone walls—all that was left of the ancient fortress—and looked up at the stars. Tom had been a latecomer to stars, but when he'd first seen them as a child he was entranced, fascinated. He always exulted in nights of stars, with no Moon or streetlights to spoil them. How could nights be so dark and so dazzlingly bright at the same time? And for all the many nights he'd spent in the garden of the farmhouse, gazing upwards, he'd never seen stars like *this*. The stars he saw from Masada were the best stars he had ever seen, pinpoint perfect from one horizon to the other in the dry desert air, with no moon to spoil their radiance, and no nearby cities to wash the sky with dirty orange fog. The Milky Way was an unbroken bridge above his head. For the first time in his life he could understand what the stars must have meant to the ancients, before the press of human illumination forced them into the background, to be viewed only in planetaria or on screens. Until, that is, a bright green distress flare broke this celestial peace, and the harsh sound of voices.

Advancing twenty yards or so further in and peering over a wall, the huddle of tourists saw what looked like an entire legion of the Israeli army all set up for a party. There were tables laden with produce, a barbecue and a detachment of soldiers setting off fireworks. A small disturbance at the edge of the crowd showed that despite their silence and relatively hidden state, the tourists' presence had been noticed. A single soldier in full battle dress came over. He exchanged a few words with Danny in Hebrew—Tom hoped they were friendly, as indeed it proved, when the soldier turned to the rest of them.

"We saw you here," said the soldier. "I the only one speak shit good English, so Commander she say I make talk you. We fire guns, yes? Bang bang? So you can stay here, but you stay here behind this wall, good? When we say yes, you come join in, yes? We have shit good party, yes?"

Danny confirmed that this indeed had been the treat he had promised, as he had undergone it himself. Newly recruited Israeli soldiers marked the end of basic training with a sixty-kilometer desert route march in full gear, the final flourish being an ascent of Masada using the eastern ramp constructed by the Romans. And when they reached the top, they'd get medals and have a party. Tom, Shoshana and the others watched the ceremony, with each new graduate greeted with a crackling salvo of automatic fire. Tom felt Shoshana grasp his arm, and turned to see the fireworks reflected in the intensity of her eyes. On the surface, she seemed as involved in the froth of the party as he'd expected. Partying really was her element. But there was something else, too, that he hadn't seen before—a dark brooding depth. It unnerved him. With an effort he turned back to the spectacle.

The party ended as abruptly as it had begun. The Army left as silently as their presence had been noisy. By midnight the last jeep had hummed off into the night, and Masada belonged to the tourists and the stars. Danny told them stories of his own experiences, picking up on the general mood of finality that seemed to have infected everything.

"Yeah," he drawled. "They told me that too. This could be the last new detachment they can train for a while. Everyone will be on active duty very soon. Including me." Suddenly, his dark eyes seemed to focus on something far away. "Friends, be thankful that I'm not allowed to tell you half the things I know, for they would scare you *shitless*."

It was then that the sandy-haired Englishman spoke.

"In the absence of such intelligence from Danny," he said, "I have some news which we should all know," he said, fingering his earbud. "It's just coming through on the news—the Pope collapsed at the end of his Mass at Ramat Gan. Oh no..." The man furrowed his brow in concentration: the conversation around him stalled to an anticipatory hush.

"Oh, sweet Christ," he said. "They say he's... he's... *died.*"

Tom and Shoshana looked at each other and thought of Domingo. José Luis and Carlos crossed themselves and talked to each other in Spanish too fast for anyone else to catch. They bade Tom, Shoshana and the others a hasty good-night and retreated behind a low wall a few meters off. Tom heard the two of them talking anxiously and low for some time afterwards.

"Maybe we should all get such sleep as we can," Danny said. "We have to rise early and get off this rock—by seven a.m. the Sun is too scorching to tolerate. Then, maybe we can learn about the Pope. Anyway, I'm beat. *Layla Tov!*"

He and the Englishman each wandered to small private nooks in the deep shadows amid the maze of low walls.

That left just Tom and Shoshana, who found a sheltered corner, unrolled their compact sleeping bags, which they zipped together, and climbed in. The desert night cooled rapidly, and they were glad to have each other's warmth. Exhaustion claimed them, and the only sounds left on Masada were titanic snores from Carlos, punctuated by curses from José Luis.

But Tom couldn't sleep: he was still on a rush, a high after the strenuous climb. After a while he unfurled himself from Shoshana's embrace and set off for a stroll among the stars. As he sought a tolerably comfortable perch for a solitary stargaze, he saw a figure, a dark form against the night. It was the Englishman. Apart from his shocking news about the Pope, he'd said next to nothing during the entire trip, and Tom didn't even know his name. The Englishman spared him any further agony.

"Hi there," he said, silhouetted, a man-shaped hole in the riot of stars. "I'm sorry, we haven't been introduced. Vicar, Anglican tendency, subspecies *cantabridgiensis*, yet to be frocked."

It hit Tom then—he'd seen the man around Cambridge, where he'd plainly been studying at one of the several seminaries that clustered round the university colleges. Tom smiled.

"Tom Corstorphine, archaeologist, *tendence palaeolithique*, same subspecies, same stage of development."

They shook hands with the warmth of those whom shared past experience and present perplexity have thrown together.

"Fearon Brimstone," said the man. "Good to meet you." Tom couldn't help but laugh. "Unbelievable, I know," said Fearon, quite unembarrassed. "Parents, eh? It's as if I was driven to my vocation to make up for it. But you — you're a Corstorphine? Not by any chance related to Jack Corstorphine? Jadis Markham? The Jadis Markham of Souris Saint-Michel and all that?" Tom said that he was. Brimstone seemed suitably impressed and affected doffing an imaginary hat. "I am in the presence of *royalty*," he said. "And we are, in a sense, related."

"We are?"

"Academically, at any rate. My grandfather was Roger MacLennane, who would have been your Mum and Dad's ex-Professor. He always used to chuckle about how he introduced them to each other." Tom was open-mouthed with amazement, at the coincidences that brought him and Brimstone together on this desert mountain top in the middle of the night. After which, they fell into easy conversation.

Like Tom, Brimstone had come out to look at the stars. "Not often you see stars like this," he said. Tom wondered if Brimstone was going to say something about being closer to God, and had he done so, he wouldn't have been surprised. What Brimstone said did have God in it, but was something far, far stranger.

"Did you ever read a story called 'The Nine Billion Names of God'?" he asked.

Tom was about to confess that he hadn't, when he remembered a battered anthology of science fiction stories that Avi Malkeinu had passed on to him when he was about twelve. Avi had been a fan of science fiction, ever since his father had read him H. G. Wells (although Tom suspected that this particular anthology had been passed down from Domingo). And so Tom recalled for Brimstone what he remembered of the very brief tale, about a lamasery in Tibet where the monks are working out the nine billion names of God, and having got a computer to help them, complete their task thousands of years ahead of schedule. Who'd written it? Someone in the early twentieth century.

"Arthur C. Clarke?" said Tom. "But I forgot how it ends. Why do you mention it?"

"Well, you know," said Brimstone, "it turned out that the enunciation of God's names was the final and culminating purpose of Creation. When the technicians, who had installed the computer, leave the lamasery—on a bright, starry night just like this one, they notice the stars slowly going out."

The chill fell between them like a frozen shroud.

"It's... creepy," Tom said, more to break the silence than anything else. Brimstone turned towards Tom, and looked up at the stars once more.

"Creepy?" he said. "Yes, I suppose it is. But just imagine it, if it were really true. You know, we could be those two technicians, high on a hill in the wilderness, looking up at the stars and wondering that very same thing."

"What makes you say that?" said Tom, nervously.

"Well, it's a funny thing," said Brimstone. "You know, at college, we study a lot of theology, homiletics, ancient Hebrew, Latin, the usual stuff. But we're also encouraged to do as much science as we're able, especially evolution, and cosmology."

"To keep one step ahead of the unbelievers?" Tom's head was still whizzing with Shoshana's shared thoughts. Poor Shoshana seemed so weighed down with religion as he was relatively free of such things. But perhaps, here, in Israel, everyone you met had a view about religion. And then he thought of Domingo, and his mind started to make some connections of its own.

"Ah! No, not a bit of it," Brimstone answered. "All that creationist piffle is past, and in any case, most honest theologians didn't give it the time of day anyway. Dismal theology. Worse science. A no-brainer, really. We study these things to do what scientists of the past did—the greats, you know, Einstein, Newton—to magnify the name of the Creator, and to better understand what the Old Chap was on about. Especially as he seems to have given up appearing as pillars of cloud or burning bushes. So there we are, looking at modified brane theory, loop quantum gravity, nucleosynthesis, developmental macronomics, all that stuff. It's good honest work. I like it."

Tom nodded, thinking that this was probably the best course to take.

"So there I was in my final tutorial before the summer vacation," Brimstone went on, "before I came here—and my tutor, a sweet old darling—not really a scientist, more at home writing tomes on Perpendicular church furniture..." Tom pictured oak pews standing on end, like totem poles. "He took a few of us aside and told us some disturbing news about the fate of the stars. He couldn't make much of it, and wanted our opinions, more than anything. You know, maybe you could shed some light on it? I'm grateful for anything, because I'm puzzled. And worried.'"

Tom confessed his ignorance of astronomy: but then he saw what Brimstone was getting at. Jack and Jadis were the best-known scientists of the Merlin Technologies Institute for Historical Geomorphology, but Ruxton Carr had also endowed a sister Institute in Cambridge. Tom remembered Domingo talking about this, when Jadis was puzzling over the Sigil. The brief of this other Institute was to map the positions and movements of the stars in the Solar neighbourhood. Brimstone, with his family connection to Roger MacLennane, would certainly have been aware of this. But apart from that, Tom was genuinely in the dark, and said so. He did not yet articulate a faint unease at where (he thought) this might all be leading.

"No matter," Brimstone shrugged. "Perhaps it'll take a casual by-stander — no offense — to see what this is really about. No, really, I'd like your views." So he told Tom about a tiny, obscure paper that had been deposited in a tiny, obscure physics archive by a tiny, obscure group of astronomers in New Zealand, some of whom had been funded by the Merlin Technologies Astrometry Institute. The press hadn't picked up on it, and Tom had not heard of it.

"Not surprising really," Brimstone continued, "negative results don't often get noticed. But this was *more* than negative. You see, these astronomers were doing some recent curation of wide-field plates to assess the proper motions of nearby stars." Tom looked blank. Brimstone sighed.

"That's basically what the Astrometry Institute funds," said Brimstone. "Cataloguing proper motion. You know, the stars we see aren't fixed, like they're stuck on the inside of a black velvet bowl. They move around. Some towards us, some away from us, some from side to side. All stars do this, but the ones closer to us seem to do it more because — well, they're closer. The movement is appreciable and measurable over years and decades." Tom look surprised. Brimstone laughed — a warm, musical sound after these chilly intellectual magnitudes. "You know, not everything in astronomy is... er — "

"... Astronomical?"

"Exactly! Anyway, the astronomers take pictures of the sky every so often, compare the pictures with older pictures, work out these movements, so they can update star maps and so forth. But what they noticed seemed very odd. Sure, some of the stars had moved, but a few — two or three out of thousands — weren't there at all."

"Like, they'd vanished? No débris? Rocks? Gas — radiation — whatever?"

"That's just it. Vanished. Rubbed out. *Pouff!*" He waved his hands, like a deity casually swatting the fates of billions. "And yes, before you mention it, they'd checked that they'd taken the proper exposures, and that the stars hadn't moved so fast that they turned up on other plates, and so on and so forth. And they got another lot of astronomers in Chile to check the findings. No, these stars had vamoosed down the back of the celestial sofa. And there was one more thing. The stars that vanished weren't randomly distributed. They were all clustered close to the celestial South Pole — which is a particularly boring patch of sky, so it's no wonder that nobody had noticed anything odd before. And they were all tiny, dim red dwarfs, and all between fifteen and seventeen light years away from us. Now *that's* the real strangeness. The non-randomness of it all."

Tom would have been convinced that Brimstone was spinning a yarn, or trying to tell some obscure theological joke, but if so, this would hardly explain the hairs standing up on the back of his neck, and his sudden recollection of Domingo's strange, expression — knowing, and yet almost terrified — when he and Shoshana had hypothesized that the Sigil had been a warning, a totem to ward off eclipses.

A scourge of stars.

Perhaps they'd been far closer to the truth than they'd realized. Tom felt suddenly as if he'd sobered up.

"Non-randomness implies that it's almost as if there's a purpose to it all," Tom heard himself say, and, to his own horror, he continued, "as if it were meant to happen. But if that's true, it's a purpose quite different from the Clarke story, which gives the impression that the stars were going out more or less randomly, *non*? And Clarke's stars were big ones, that the technicians could just casually see as they were walking along. They didn't have to go looking for them."

"The astronomers in New Zealand didn't say anything like that, of course," said Brimstone, "they just documented the absences. But you know what I think? I think that there's someone or something out there that's trying to creep up on us and bite us on the bum."

Tom felt that his heart had stopped, and that he was covered all over in a blanket of clogging, wet fear.

"Yes, I know," said Brimstone into the silence. "Monumentally paranoid. But what else is there? And even if this whatever-it-is isn't Out To Get Us in particular, something definitely is happening. And whatever-it-is caused my tutor some theological heart-searching. Me too. Has God decided to come out of hiding? If this the twenty-first century equivalent of burning bushes? Is it a test of faith, in the guise of science? Frankly, I don't know what to make of it."

When Tom awoke the next morning, folded around Shoshana's peaceful warmth, all thoughts of cosmic disturbance had vanished from his mind — for apocalypse had arrived.

Chapter 11. Pilot

The Wilderness of Judaea, Earth, August, 2054

Blood and destruction shall be so in use
And dreadful objects so familiar
That mothers shall but smile when they behold
Their infants quarter'd with the hands of war.
William Shakespeare—*Julius Caesar*

The pilot once had a name but he had forgotten it. It had been drilled out of him in a dozen training camps across the Khalifa. But he was content to have submitted himself to a greater mission, a greater conquest. For the final moment had come, when the Khalifa would regain Holy *Al-Quds* and drive the Zionists into the sea at last. Secure in the cockpit of his strike jet, he was wired so thoroughly into its computer, its avionics and weapons systems, that he could control them all with a flicker of thought. He and his aircraft were one, and yet just one barb of one vane of one feather in the ten thousand wings of the Prophet.

With his remaining spark of individuality, he was proud to have been selected for this, the very first wave, to demonstrate that the Khalifa had the resolution to sweep all opposition away, and not (for shame) talk so vividly of blood and skulls and death and yet run screaming like children at the faintest hint of opposition. Those times were over. His task now was not destruction, but terror: to fly beneath the Zionist radar too fast for their missile systems to follow, buzz the rooftops of Tel Aviv, circle over the sea and return. After that, the batteries of missiles would pound the cities into dust, and waves of ground troops would do the rest.

Not that the passage of an aircraft flying at Mach 7 less than a hundred meters over the city wouldn't be destructive in itself. The turbulence of its wake would be as a white-hot airquake, piercing eardrums, shattering windows, ripping any unprotected object smaller than a laden truck off the ground with the demonic rage of a twister. Buildings immediately beneath its path would have the air sucked out of them and implode, and anything organic within fifty meters would burst into flames. The effect on any exposed human being in this range would not be far short of that of a nuclear strike.

The pilot mused on such things with satisfaction as he arrowed across the Jordanian Desert, the currents of his thoughts exalting as his craft danced and wheeled to his direction through the canyons, tracing the contours of the grey and yellow mountains on the wings of dawn, generating a roaring cloud of dust in its train. This was true exhilaration—to have achieved the dreams of centuries, to be as free as a dove, as a raven, even though on an errand of war.

That his senses were occasionally clouded with spots of blackness he attributed to the lurching shifts in acceleration as the plane altered its course constantly under his direction. His own human body, wired into the system, was physically immobile: and so at first he ignored the visuals that warned of increasing damage to his peripheral nervous system, and that his skin conductivity and heart rate now deviated markedly from mission-optimum levels. A message intruded from the outside world, relayed by satellite from Strike Mission Control in Tabriz. The message said:

TELEMETRY ERROR: ABORT MISSION

And, of course, he would have obeyed this command instantly and without question. But he found that he could not. The aircraft was guided, moment by moment, in the only way feasible for a machine that could travel at such speeds, so close to the ground: by the thought of a human pilot directly interfaced with the aircraft's systems. And yet to broadcast such overriding imperatives to his avionics, he would need to underline the point by sub-vocalization. First, to ensure that the commands were clear, and, second, to convince the conjoined, near-sentient machine that his thoughts were significantly beyond the normal variation expected of the merely human. Even though the pilot would not actually need to move his mouth to do this, only to enact the movement in his mind, he found that his jaw muscles were locked in tetany.

Terror rose to the surface as he felt his body squirming helplessly within the shock-gel that lined his flight suit, itself slotted into the cockpit with no room to move. Subdermal proprioceptors registered extensive bruising as his body convulsed within its artificial shell. Motion detectors in his bones traced sharp, jagged movements consistent with uncontrolled muscular spasms. His heart muscle had begun to fibrillate. Chemosensory channels in his kidneys and intestines reported rapid spikes in ionic concentrations, indicative of unwitting evacuation into recycling and life-support.

The black spots that he had attributed to rapid acceleration were now permanently hovering before his eyes, until they completely obscured his vision. So he would not have seen the sudden rash of heads-up displays, each competing for attention and burning scarlet, recording that his organs were liquefying from within, and that his bones were imploding like popcorn crushed in an armored fist.

No longer directed by its human component, the mind of the jet had to improvise. It could not respond directly to Mission Control, whose designers had decreed that the human pilot must always have the override, unless it could be demonstrated that the pilot had died. But although telemetry from the strike craft indicated the signs of an extraordinary transformation, they did not reveal unequivocal signs of death. The brain waves were unprecedented in shape and utterly obscure in meaning, but they were brain waves nonetheless.

The aircraft did its best to keep to the planned course, but without the constant corrections of its human partner—who had drifted off into some unrecognized brain-wave cycle, deeper than the merely subconscious, which it could have done something about—the course deviated every nanosecond from that which its pilot would otherwise have chosen, until it came on a sudden upon a landscape that was passing it too quickly for it to be able to process the topography into its dead-reckoning system. Somewhere in the Wilderness of Judaea, perhaps inevitably, it met a mountain it did not recognize quickly enough.

The mountain rushed up to meet the aircraft at almost five thousand miles an hour.

Not that the Duty Lead Controller in Tabriz was aware of this incident in particular, as he had his own problems. Of the fifty strike jets in the first wave, sixteen had reported similar pilot-interface problems, of which eleven had disappeared altogether. Clearly, something was desperately wrong, and, frantically, he recalled as many of the aircraft as he could before things got any worse. But try as he might, screen after screen turned from green to amber to red and, finally, black. Two of the Junior Mission Controllers had suddenly gone off sick, grey and sweating. The Lead Controller assumed, at first, that they couldn't stand the pace. But when his own bladder was full to bursting and he'd had to go to the washrooms, he found his absent colleagues. Or, that is to say, he found their *clothes*, alongside what looked like two black bowling balls. He could not account for this. Had they abandoned their posts, on this day of days, to go bowling? In the nude? What was going on?

The day had started with so much promise. He had woken up, looking forward to his shift, on what heralded a great day for the Khalifa. They were, finally, going to expunge this blot of shame from the heartland, he told his admiring wife and three fine sons as he set off for Mission Control. But now it was a nightmare, from end to end.

The Lead Controller felt that he had to take responsibility for his abject failure, and reconciled himself to a harsh and possibly lethal sentence. He hoped that the General would treat his family kindly. But when he had reported to his own superior, the secretary would say only that the General had been 'indisposed'. The secretary had dropped her gaze from his, which was very proper, but then she collapsed on her desk, all decorum gone, looking at him directly with wide, desperate eyes. "I *saw* it, Major," she said. "I saw the General turn into a monster, a black... *thing*! It was horrible, *horrible!*"

From its shock value alone, the mission had actually been a great success, for the eleven missing jets had become ballistic missiles of terrible power. To be sure, six had plunged into the Mediterranean sea, and a seventh had smashed into the Great Pyramid at Gizeh, transforming the First Wonder of the Ancient World into a very large pile of barbecue briquettes. But an eighth had scored a direct hit on a condo in Tel Aviv, demolishing most of a city block and killing at least fifteen hundred people. Alina Jacobs had not stood a chance. Her last thought before being atomized was whether she should tell David that she'd booked a one-way ticket to London.

A ninth had dropped like a meteor onto the Hadassah hospital, vaporizing Dr Mohamed Al Hajj, Resident, along with all his staff and several hundred patients. Dr Al Hajj had been examining a number of cases of the same affliction that had destroyed the Pope, whose remains—if that's what they were—had been removed by an ashen-faced Cardinal Sanchopanza. From what Dr Al Hajj could discover, by darting all over a hospital that was cycling into in a state of rising panic, to see each case for himself as it ran its terrifying, unstoppable course, the patients had been *transformed*, but had not actually died. Even though no equipment at the hospital that he could lay his hands on at short notice could penetrate the matt-black shells of the... er... 'patients,' not even the most powerful X-ray machine, he was still convinced they were alive, even though he could not have said why: and because of this, he had hesitated to commission anything more invasive.

Working late into that same night, Dr Al Hajj drafted a small note to a 3-Web medical bulletin describing the condition. He noted that its incidence seemed too patchy and indiscriminate to be consistent with any kind of contagion. And he also had the honor of naming it: he called it Postembryonic Oolithic Petrosis, or POP for short. Like all conscientious medical men, Dr Al Hajj felt that once a disease had a name, one was at least half way to curing it. He was musing on life and death in this fashion as dawn broke through the window of his tiny carrel of an office, when he sent the note to the server and, a split instant later, his own angel arrived.

The scientists in the Khalifa, being more technically advanced than anyone had suspected or even thought possible, had far more powerful equipment than that available to Dr Al Hajj, and were less squeamish about its use. The first cases of the affliction had come to light in the Khalifa several days earlier, but had been kept secret. Families and colleagues of 'patients' tended to disappear themselves not long after reporting a case — until the pestilence, plague, or whatever it was, became too widespread for this lockdown policy to be feasible. But discerning what had happened to the patients proved impossible. Boiling them in oil, toluene, caustic soda, nitric acid or molten tungsten; dropping them into nuclear reactors; applying the kinds of pressures typical of stellar interiors — none had any effect at all. They didn't even warm up. They remained similarly refractory to particle-beam weapons or X-lasers developed for space warfare, even at close range and in high vacuum.

The last straw came when a few patients had been exposed to the two-million-degree plasma in the experimental fusion torus at Rawalpindi, but the trial had to stop when the plasma threatened to break out of its magnetic confinement. The patients were completely unharmed. In the end the scientists gave up. The black spheres that had once been people kept their undead secrets to themselves.

The tenth rogue jet dove nose-first into the middle of Ramat Gan stadium, replacing it with a crater sixty meters deep and full of molten rock. Casualties, thankfully, had been relatively light: apart from the Stones' road crew, lighting riggers, sundry maintenance staff and 'Mr Micawber' — a 1950s blonde Fender Telecaster reputed to be Keith Richards' favorite — the stadium had been empty. But the concert would have to be cancelled.

The eleventh struck the eastern face of Masada about a hundred meters short of the summit.

In the early hours of the morning, when unfamiliar stars wheeled just before the rising Sun, Shoshana stirred in her sleep and, half-waking, stretched, smiled, and curled up again beneath Tom's chin.

Tom awoke then, his first sight the top of her head, her glossy curls glinting in the Sun's first rays. Something caught his eye, just above the low, eastern wall of ruined building in which they had slept. He thought he saw a column of dust in the dawn, the flash of something silvery, and then heard a sonic boom from a great distance, eastwards.

He raised himself up to peer over the wall, and his world went instantly, searingly white, a flash accompanied by a roar of inhuman volume. The ground shook, buckled and liquefied beneath him. He ducked down in the utter agony of his eyes, his mind cast back to a sun-baked front yard far away when he was chasing leaves with Fairbanks and the world of light had cascaded in on him like two comets drilling into his terrified skull. But now the sky really was falling, and the ground beneath him heaving upwards to meet it. Their bivouac which a moment before had been a quiet haven had become the uncertain centre of a crashing, sliding maelstrom of overwhelming noise and a rain of boulders. Tom — blinded and almost deafened — threw himself over Shoshana and put his hands over his head. The sleeping bag that contained them both took off like a wayward surfboard in a tubular breaker. He thought he heard Shoshana screaming, two inches away from his ear and at the top of her voice, but he could only just hear it. The world wavered unsteadily before his ruined senses, fluttered for a moment, and died.

What seemed like hours later — it was, in fact, about twenty seconds — the storm of dust and rocks ceased. Shoshana was now fully awake, uninjured but in shock. That she'd had her eyes closed and her face close to Tom saved her sight, but she was dazed and at first had no idea where she was, or why. The world was dark, partly because of Tom's spasmodic embrace, but also because they had been half-buried in rubble.

She did not know it, but all their companions had perished. José Luis and Carlos, the Mexican Stones fans, had been asphyxiated by a pyroclastic flow of white-hot dust and buried beyond all hope of recovery. Danny Forbert, sleeping closest to the impact, was vaporized in a dead flat picosecond by the exploding plasma fireball. But Fearon Brimstone had expired several hours earlier — quietly, all alone and in unspeakable pain — from Postembryonic Oolithic Petrosis.

The surface of Masada had changed completely. The maze of buildings from the evening before was now an unrecognizable slush of broken scoria. As the Sun began to climb, its rays penetrating the ubiquitous yellow, choking murk and the thicker columns of dust and smoke that fumed all around, Shoshana knew that she and Tom had to get off the ruined mountain as soon as they could. She pulled herself out of the sleeping bag and, slipping and sliding in the rubble, struggled unsteadily to her feet. She realized that she'd been hurt — her left ankle was twisted. Putting any weight on it sent red-hot needles of pain up her leg, making her gasp for breath. She was aware of the silence of the world, as if her ears had been stuffed with cotton wool. She looked down at Tom, curled up like a fetus in the rags of the sleeping bag. Blood ran from his ears and from a myriad small wounds in his scalp and arms. And where he wasn't red, he was yellow, caked in filth and grit. His iShades were gone. His fists were pushed hard into his naked eyes. Awkwardly, she knelt down next to him in the smoking scree.

"Tom, we have to go," she said. "Somehow—but we have to." Her voice sounded adenoidal in her own ears, and very quiet. Tom said nothing. Lightheaded and groggily uncertain of the extent of Tom's injuries, she felt he'd probably come round eventually if left to himself.

So, with the mindless optimism of all refugees and blast victims, she pecked around the rubble for their possessions. Their rucksacks, almost buried in rubble, had been ripped from the foot of the sleeping bag where they'd stowed them, and were torn beyond repair. She pulled out their money and ID-tags and, buried right at the bottom of her rucksack and mercifully in one piece, she found her ancient phone.

God, a phone.

Tom never used one, and she had long since got out of the phone habit that afflicts all teenagers. When had she last used it? When she'd phoned Alina to see if they could doss at her flat. She murmured Alina's name at the handset. No signal. Or perhaps there was, but she just couldn't hear it. She didn't have a contact for Avi and didn't know how to search for him. She felt she couldn't be bothered to dict a message, and her fingers felt too much like numb sausages to write anything. Oh well, they'd simply have to walk out of here.

Slowly, Tom came to his senses. To be completely blind again after all this time was a blow. To be sure, he felt that he could probably function without sight as he always could, and who knows, maybe it would come back again, but now that he'd been shown the color and vibrancy of the world, to lose it now was almost more than he could bear. And to lose the sight of Shoshana, her hair, her skin the color of pale honey, the freckles on her shoulders, the way her nose wrinkled when she smiled, her strange, purple eyes—he might never again see something and know that it was 'purple'.

He got up, quite easily avoiding every obstacle, and apart from the blood caking his scalp and running like scabby rivers from both ears, what seemed like a thousand painful scratches, especially on his hands and arms, and enough bruises to make him feel like he'd been hit by a train—he didn't seem to have suffered major physical injury. He took his hands away from his eyes and—nothing. He sensed Shoshana close, her early-morning smell clouded by dust and blood and pain.

"Shoshana," he gasped.

"I'm here, Tom—I'm here." And she was there, in his arms. "Tom, open your eyes," she said. Her voice seemed to come from an immense distance. He opened his eyes against what seemed like a tide of sharp grit, and, having done so—saw a darkness deeper than space..

"I can't see a thing," he said. "Nothing at all. But really, I'll be fine, you know that. I was blind until I was six, and then I could see. Now I can't. But I'm sure I'll... get used to it. But Shoshana, I wanted to tell you something last night, but you had fallen asleep."

They both paused. The Sun climbed further. Tom could feel its pressure on his eyelids.

"It's—well, now is not a good time, maybe. But it's just that—well, I love you. Like nothing else. I only wished I could have told you that when I could have seen your face, your beautiful face. You know, it was only when I took my iShades off that I knew... so if I can never see you, I don't know if..."

His hands reached out towards her, navigating her body from her shoulders, to her neck, to the rounded surfaces of her cheeks and lips, and to her lashes, and her eyes, which were filled with tears.

"Oh, Tom," she said, "my own, poor, sweet Tom." She reached up and gently stroked his lashes, his flickering eyelids, the streaks of tears and blood and dirt that striped his cheeks.

"Come on," she said, "let's go home."

How they found themselves in Ben Gurion airport, neither of them could recall. There must have been a bus, or a *sherut*, or a police car, or something—it was all too foggy. They were still too deep in shock for anything much to register on their battered minds. But somewhere along the line they must have run into someone helpful, for they'd been cleaned up and Shoshana had a splint for her ankle. So now, here they were, in what she thought was the international check-in except the signs didn't really mean anything to her and which was full of a sea of anxious people screaming children people bandaged and whimpering trying to get a seat on whatever flight they could out of wherever it was they were. Were *they* checked in on a flight? If so, where were they going? They no longer had any idea. Eventually, Shoshana felt just too tired to care any more. She would have sat there forever in numb stupefaction.

The constant news bulletins on the screens above their heads reported the two Khalifa suicide jet attacks on Tel Aviv, the destruction of the

Hadassah hospital. Masada might have got a mention and there were reports of movements of ground troops into the Galilee and then there was this strange disease. It was all too hard to tell. Tom said he couldn't see anything anyway and they were both still partially deaf and the noise all around them of swirling shouting people was distracting and got confused in her mind with the news reports really her mind might as well have turned to her Grandma Sadie's lockshen pudding.

This strange disease was called Pop! Pop! Pop! and didn't seem to have any pattern said the doctor at the Hadassah who had died. The Khalifa was on the march but hey! Pop! Pop! Pop! Their planes had fallen from the sky which had fallen on them both and she knew she loved Tom so much even though he was blind and buried in rocks and there was something about a pillar of fire and a pillar of salt and loneliness and pain and Jadis — it *was* Jadis — who reached out to her and said she'd always be there for her just like Jack had told her he would and then there was Bob who was also her Dad her wonderful Dad who looked down at her, no, *up* at her, and said *avinu malkeinu aseh imanu tzedakah v'chesed v'hoshiyainu* and so without thinking about it, a well of silence within the crowds, Shoshana took her battered old phone and dicted a text to a number she really should have thought of much earlier, a message that read

jadis jack we're here here safe alive we don't know what to do please treat us with charity and kindness help us

Jadis had returned home from her morning round of the village. She had learned many things on her journey, but none of them added up, and she had exhausted all possible means of progress. And so, by way of displacement activity, she was busily trying to focus her mind on the July accounts for the gargantuan sprawl of a project that Souris Saint-Michel had become. Not that she really needed to, given that the vast project had accreted its own accounts staff at the Institute, which could manage quite well on its own. As Jack had explained, patiently, they'd come a long way since the first days at Saint-Rogatien, when Jadis had been project leader, personnel manager and accounts department all rolled into one. Sure, he'd said, some habits are hard to break, but there wasn't really any need for her to send quite so many exasperated notes to the Institute's Accounts Department, given the pressure it was under. But organization had always been her way of averting and diverting stress. She felt, instinctively, that if you could only arrange your own life, then the increasing disorder all around you would matter less, or in any case seem less disorganized, and anyway, even if it didn't, that at least you were doing something rather than just climbing the walls. If there was one thing she hated, it was being in the position of having too little information on which she could make a decision.

But life's like that, she sighed—and science was a microcosm of life, requiring the ability to make educated guesses, shots in the dark. Jack was always so much better than her at guessing games.

Her hair, ever a mark of her mood, now surrounded her like a swarm of angry bees that some rash interloper had stirred with a stick—as if, in its disorder, it had been acting as a reservoir for the entropic increase she'd banished from her frantic quest to arrange her own thoughts.

Metaphorically, at least.

Whatever else it was, the halo of hair was an efficient heat trap, which worsened her frustration, which made her hair frizz and billow out even more, trapping more heat: a classic positive-feedback loop. A part of her said that she should do something about her hair and break the cycle, but she had always drawn back. It was a part of who she was: were she to tie it back, as some people at the Institute had sometimes suggested (all those, Jack said, who didn't know her any better) she'd be tying back her brain. And cut it off for the summer? Unthinkable. She'd be a different person altogether.

So she sloughed off her sandals instead, placing her bare feet squarely on the cool flags beneath the table, a sink for the heat from her body. The sensation calmed her, the feeling of being rooted to the solid earth. She took time to stop what she was doing, to breathe deeply, in and out, and to listen to the sounds of the house-timbers creaking and stretching in the mid-day heat, the chirp of crickets in the garden.

She felt better.

She could now think things through in a asymptote to equanimity, almost, if not quite, reaching it.

The first fruit of her meditation was the decision to put the accounts aside. In any case, she had reached a point where she was going round in circles and the figures were flying off in all directions.

First the mysteries of the village. She'd run into a wall.

Now the accounts. Nothing more than a fervid, futile cycle.

Surely, she thought, no obstacle could fall beneath her feet if she tried something as simple as get a few things together for lunch? But when she'd looked around for bread she remembered that she hadn't managed to buy any, a result of the inexplicable, unprecedented closure of the boulangerie. It was too late to start baking; and anyway, if she had, the heat in the kitchen would have become intolerable. But it was summer, so there were always tomatoes and cucumbers and lettuces in the garden, waiting to be harvested, so she thought she might make a salad instead. She put her sandals back on again, collected her sunhat and basket and headed through the *arrière-cuisine* to the back door.

August had always been a low month at the farmhouse. Apart from a few forays to the *potager*, where she now collected the warm, ripening tomatoes, it had almost always been far too hot to work outside for much of the day. Although work at SSM took place underground, most of the staff at the Institute usually took the whole month off, so everything went into a kind of sleep mode anyway. The weather of the past few years had emphasized this: from the end of July to early September, noon temperatures climbed into the upper forties, and everyone was reduced to a helpless torpor. The birds were too exhausted to sing, let alone fly. Butterflies and lizards basked on the farmhouse walls with impunity, *Les Horribles* too vitiated to give chase. Only the crickets and grasshoppers chirped gamely on, stalked by the frogs, which could always retreat to their pond to cool off. So, whatever else one might have felt, and however the world outside did its best to buffet her off course, August was a good time for quiet, deliberate housekeeping.

And so it had been, she thought, stooping with her clasp knife to cut some cucumbers from a vine that now sprawled exuberantly over the baked and crusted ground. Except for the worries that Jack had started to bring home from the Institute about ten days earlier, that people who'd gone away on vacation had failed to return; that an extraordinary number of staff had phoned in sick and were not heard from again; and that everyone in the Institute seemed to be doing three jobs to cover for people who could not be contacted. The Accounts Department had been especially badly hit, he explained, which is why nobody was answering her emails (this last made Jadis feel a little ashamed of herself for having pestered them).

And, most disturbing of all, that three people returning from vacation had died, because the three separate aircraft on which they had been travelling had fallen out of the sky.

It was then that Jadis recalled thinking, on her round only that morning, that the village had been more muted than usual, even for *La France Profonde* in its summer torpor. That the Mairie had been shut for the month was no surprise; that the boulangerie had been not just shut, but locked and boarded up without notice, definitely was. The boulangerie was open every single day of the year and had been so for as long as she could remember. To find it closed, without even a notice on the door, seemed like an affront to the laws of the Universe.

Nonplussed, she had gone next door to *Le Sanglier D'Or*. Over coffee under the awning on the terrace — a favourite stop, where she and Jack had breakfasted on their honeymoon — she'd asked Sandrine Pasquier, the burly, matter-of-fact former farmer's wife who'd run *Le Sanglier D'Or* for the past fifteen years, if she knew why the baker had done a bunk. Although Sandrine had never been renowned for cosy chats, she had been more than usually communicative, as if she'd had troubles to share. She even broke her own formerly inflexible commandment and joined a customer at a table, as she now did with Jadis.

She'd been to a lot of funerals lately, Sandrine had said, sometimes for people who'd died for no good reason and were in fact in the peak of health, leaving families and children. If that weren't tragic enough, these enforced absences made it very hard for her to run a business — especially when usually reliable staff kept vanishing with no good excuses and didn't come back, and when the brewery, usually so punctual, could hardly be bothered to send supplies as regularly as it promised. And so, Dr Jadis, if she didn't mind, she would love to talk, but she had a hotel and a *café* to run, and although not too many people came into the bar lately, those that did were always thirsty. Sandrine stood up and disappeared into the darkness at the back of the bar, pretending to busy herself with glasses. Jadis noticed that the bar was currently completely empty, the tables shining in expectation of custom that might never arrive.

So Jadis had once more braved the Sun's relentless photonic assault and picked her way across the scalding cobbles of the Place Etienne Geoffroy Saint-Hilaire, taking refuge in the nave of the church. It smelled of cool stone and beeswax: shafts of hot light blasted through the high windows, picking out motes of chaff and dust. It was utterly silent. Despite her almost total lack of religious conviction, she felt that ordering her thoughts here in the cool dark would be as effective as anywhere else, so she tried to piece things together. And here, in the church, she had always felt the reassuring even if mostly absent shade of her old friend, Domingo. She felt he'd approve of the line of thought she felt she should now undertake.

She found a pew near the front of the church and looked towards the altar, but her searching, brown gaze was now cool, and directed to yet further distances, with the same intense intelligence that many, over the years, had found both enthralling and frightening.

Absences without leave. From the Institute, from the boulangerie, from the *Sanglier D'Or*. And from what Sandrine had said, not just *absences*, but *deaths*. The two concepts became conflated in her mind: given that there had been so much unexplained absence, so much inexplicable death, the two just had to be connected. But she had, as yet, too little information to go much further than that. So the scientist in her did what it had always done best, breaking down the problem into its fundamentals, trying hypotheses on what scant information she could assemble.

Even though it was August and people were absent anyway, the numbers of deaths she knew about seemed anomalously high. To be fair, people did tend to die more often in this pitiless heat, but the victims were the traditionally vulnerable—the sick, the elderly, the very young. But Sandrine Pasquier said that she'd mourned people carried off in their prime.

Chalk one up to the anomalies.

Jack had implied the same, with his tally of absent and possibly deceased working-age staff at the Institute.

Therefore, add another.

And August was not a time when the traditional complaints were in circulation—the colds, the influenza, the hypothermia of their now typically Siberian winters. It was too hot, and people were dispersed, not huddled up in small spaces breathing one another's exhalations.

So, add a third.

The anomalies were stacking up towards statistical significance.

But all of this was local. Could this be something that had struck Gascony in particular? Contamination of the groundwater? An unrecognized contagion spread in truffles or *confits de canard?* Unlikely. Such things had happened, of course. Every few years there was some scare or other that constrained farmers to keep their flocks of ducks and geese indoors, or force people to watch the water they drank, or the food they ate. Bird 'flu' in 2027 and again in 2033; anserine spongiform encephalopathy in 2041; or—as had happened only last year—an epidemic of botulism traced to a local cannery. But if such a pestilence had been unleashed, she thought she'd have heard about it by now, from market-trader gossip. Yet there had been not a word of anything, and market traders being what they are, there would be no possibility of a cover-up. In any case, the scientist in her had no time for conspiracy theories.

Ah, but it *wasn't* local, was it? There had been those air crashes. The ones that had carried off three Institute staff. In her mind she carefully reviewed the cases that Jack had told her about. There had been three *separate* aircraft, but the cause of the crashes was always the *same* — the pilot had died during the flight. Now, what were the chances of three aircraft crashing from the same cause in such a short interval? Infinitesimal.

Chalk up another.

Details, details. The aircraft were all small, with no co-pilots or much in the way of backup systems. But the key fact, she thought, was that the flights had all started in widely dispersed locations. One from Bucharest; another from Stavanger in Norway; the third from an aerodrome just outside the charmingly but improbably named village of Little Snoring, in Norfolk.

More mysteriously, she could find no mention of any specific *cause* of death — no mention of heart attacks, or stroke, or anything else. Such absence was, she felt, suspicious. An unknown cause, and, given the tight cluster, possibly the *same* unknown cause.

Corroboration.

Newsfeeds trickling into to her airtab over the past few days had thrown up other instances from locations as far-flung as Western Australia (a mining transport), Denver (a commuter shuttle) and Ukraine (a crop sprayer). Again, she could find no mention of any specific cause of death. *Why?*

Pull back.

Given that she had no clue about precise causes of death, neither in the cases of the crashed aircraft, nor — she suddenly realized — in the swelling mortuaries closer to home, she had no reason to link any of them. Except one: Occam's Razor, the age-old germ of the scientific method that said that when faced with a choice of disparate causes to explain a set of events, one should always consider the simplest option first. In this case, that all the deaths had a single cause.

It was then, in the cool peace of the church, that her mind transcended the obstacle: the precise cause did not matter, but that there *was* a common cause there could be no doubt at all. Why? Because the newsfeeds that told her all about the air accidents all pointed to a remarkable hike in accidents of all kinds, all over the world — whether in cars, trucks, trains or just generally, together with an unprecedented level of workplace absenteeism.

Pull back.

Correlation is not the same thing as causation. Had she had been right, then, to have equated absence with death? People were absent for all kinds of reasons, especially in the summer; and whereas all living people are much the same, each one dies in his or her own peculiar way. But no—even taking all of this into account, the fact was that everything had happened now, *together*. The sharp-edged gears of the analytic engine inside her head meshed smoothly and illuminated deep ruby lanterns of statistical significance. Something was, definitely, going on.

But what?

For that, as yet, she had no answer.

So she picked up her empty shopping bag, put on her hat, and walked out into the blinding sunshine like a Hollywood star leaving a cinema into a wall of flashbulbs.

Later, her basket now full of new potatoes, chives and salad vegetables, Jadis walked back across the scorched lawn and into the welcoming cool of the *arrière-cuisine*. She took off her hat and washed her face and hands at the tap at the Belfast sink. The water came from their well, but it was running low: it was murky, dark and tasted of soil. She wondered if it would last until the crackling thunderstorms that inevitably blew in during the second week of September. Last year, it had been a close thing, and they'd got by on fruit juice and raids to the wine cellar. Jack had unearthed a lovely bottle of Cahors, and they'd taken it to the Spinney to watch the last sunset of August together.

How long ago it seemed—Tom hadn't yet gone to Cambridge, then, and Shoshana hadn't arrived in their lives. She wondered what they were up to now, and with all these thoughts about death and air accidents circling like vultures inside her skull, she had become anxious about them in a way that she hadn't before. Yesterday she'd read a newsfile reporting mass cancellation of flights, airlines going broke, airships being mobbed, general panic in the travelling public. So even if Tom and Shoshana were safe, how on Earth were they going to get home?

Thinking of Tom and Shoshana and wondering what they were up to, she took the basket of vegetables through to the kitchen. Her airtab still displayed a snarl of figures from the July accounts, but a flashing icon betrayed the arrival of three new emails. One was from Jack—he was on his way home for lunch, be home in twenty, looking forward to a siesta. But there was no word from Tom or Shoshana. To be sure, Tom was so laidback as to be practically horizontal, and was completely hopeless about keeping in touch. There had been just two emails from Shoshana for the whole time they'd been away. The first was a chatty note to say that they'd arrived in Israel safely but after a hell of a journey, and that Avi had met them at the airport and sent his love.

What a funny man he is,

Shoshana had written:

So much like Tom, together they look like two puppies playing a game.

Jadis thought back fondly to Avi in Cambridge when they were all so young, and Tom as a boy, and to Fairbanks. Where had all the years gone?

The second was very much terser and scattier, and had been sent when Shoshana was, evidently drunk. It was after they had cut short their time with Avi and were going to stay with a friend of Shoshana's in Tel Aviv, if her friend 'would only answer her goddamn phone'. At that, Jadis had sent a stern email to Avi demanding to know what happened.

His reply—at least three days overdue, she thought, censoriously— was the second email now winking at her. She'd expected it to be full of his usual mischievous and rather patronizing macho bombast, saying that he always thought her a babe, or sex-on-a-stick, or whatever, all of which had once been faintly amusing but now seemed rather silly and more than a little tired. The email she read, however, was quite unnervingly different. Subdued and cryptic, it had troubled her.

I have shown Tom and Shoshana the Battle Cave I told you about yesterday and the revelation disturbed them

he had written. Jadis could understand why. Avi's descriptive email and his hypothesis to explain the cave, an over-the-top yarn of blood and death and conquest, was quite lurid enough to have given anyone sleepless nights. To have seen the cave itself must have been overwhelmingly horrible: but even so, she thought, it was not at all like Avi to have come over all *gothick,* like that lurid old pulp fiction Jack liked to read when he thought she wasn't looking. Avi's latest note continued:

However do not worry. T and S are fine but it is clear that they need a break. In any case I might be called away on urgent matters elsewhere.

But it was the last part that had haunted her. It sounded like a valediction.

> I have encouraged T and S to enjoy themselves, to see as much of my beloved homeland as they can, while they can. There is no more time to waste. I am not sure when I shall be able to write again.

Her eyes had begun to sting in anticipation of what came next, its finality.

> You and Jack have always been to me like a mother and a father and always an inspiration. When I needed it, you were always there with your kindness and your help. Shalom, Avi.

She sat back, motionless and unmanned, staring at the cursor blinking at the end of Avi's signoff. Not quite knowing how to reply, or even if she should, she dicted a command that opened her newsfeeder and discovered the startling news that the Pope had collapsed during his open-air mass in Israel, and that he *might* have died.

Death?

Absence?

Which was it?

Either someone had died or they hadn't. Why couldn't people just *make up their minds?* Jadis thought back to the vagueness over causes of death in all those air accidents; the gears in her mind whirred into renewed life. The significance level notched higher.

The third message, as if on cue, had come from that other Titan of her Dream Team. She dicted back to the mail segment. That Avi should have been in any way cryptic was surprising; Domingo, however, was full of complex allusions she was sure she'd missed. This example, however, was the very pinnacle of obscurity.

> My dear Jadis—the trip to the Holy Land has not gone entirely according to plan. I have some news you should know but it must wait until I can see you in person. I shall have business in Rome but will get to you as soon as possible thereafter. Suffice it to say that Mr Richards can no longer play with Mr Micawber. You and Jack are ever in my prayers as always—D.

Just who the hell were Richards and Micawber? Actors? Estate Agents? *Undertakers?* She wished people would take the time to say what they meant. Even Domingo.

No, *especially* Domingo.

In a state of exasperation now close to fury, she pushed aside the air-tab without even bothering to dict a hibernation command; rose; set a pan of water on the hob; cleaned the dirt from a handful of potatoes, and threw them into the water as if they were hand grenades. Then she started to chop the rest of the vegetables with such expedition — and mental distraction — that she was lucky not to have cut herself.

The airtab, disregarded, and just intelligent enough to realize that its owner was not interacting with it, wiped its display from the air molecules that were giving it shape. Jadis, therefore, failed to notice the arrival of another message. Neither did she notice that Jack had arrived until she felt his steadying arms now around her waist, his breath on her cheek, reassuring. Every particle of the suppressed rage that had been surging through her body disappeared into the ground in an instant, like the guilty shadows that flee into the corners of a darkened room when a door is opened from an illuminated hallway. She closed her eyes as he kissed her neck.

"Dearest Jack..."

Jack was quiet, increasingly beaten down by the pressures of mundane administration, with less and less time for roaming the wilds. She turned in his arms and rested her hands on his shoulders. Her eyes seemed slightly troubled, downcast.

"What's up?" he said.

"Lunch! Lunch is up!" she said, shaking herself free and briskly setting the table, sweeping the airtab aside, burying it beneath the crisping printouts of the July accounts; a shopping list scrawled on an envelope; a recipe torn from the local newspaper.

She explained her worries to Jack, as they ate: her unnerving trip to the village, and her feeling that things didn't make sense — unless there were a single cause for the general tide of disappearance and death. She waved her hands as she ate, as if she were conducting an orchestra. Her color rose when she talked Jack though the uncharacteristically odd emails from Avi and Domingo, pulling the airtab out from beneath the clutter and dicting it into life. The display materialized in the air before them, so they could both see it. Jack's eyes darkened with the apparent finality of Avi's somber message, but he made no comment.

"Who are Richards and Micawber?" Jadis asked him. "Any idea?"

"Ah, yes!" Jack laughed. "Mr Micawber is Keith Richards' name for his favorite guitar. A vintage Fender Telecaster, I think."

"How...? Did you...?" she gasped, in wonderment.

"Oh, you know, just one of Domingo's little jokes," he replied. "You never listened much to the music he and Avi used to play at *Le Dig*, did you? I think they always turned it off when they saw you coming. 'Brown Sugar' was one of Domingo's favourites."

"And all this time, I never knew! Amazing…"

"But I can state an unfair advantage. I believe that the Stones were due to kick off a world tour in Israel, at Tel Aviv… er… about now, actually, given the time difference…" Jack suddenly froze, his face ashy white.

"Jack, are you…?"

Jack got to his feet. "Oh, shit—Holy fucking Christ on a bike," he said. "Why had I never thought of it? *That's* what I meant to tell you but it flew out of my mind. We've got to get in touch with Tom and Shoshana, because the war has started—I just heard it on the car radio—suicide jet attacks on Tel Aviv…"

Jadis would have been startled almost into witless terror by this news, except that it was now her turn to calm Jack, rising to her feet to pull him down. So he told her what he'd heard. Early that morning—the morning after the Pope's 'indisposition' ('that's how they put it on the news') several Khalifa jets had struck Israel. One had hit Masada in the Judaean desert, but two had struck Tel Aviv, one scoring a direct hit on the Ramat Gan stadium on the day the Stones were due to play.

"Now I can see what Domingo was on about," said Jack. "But none of this registered at the time, because the lead headline was how one of the jets demolished the Great Pyramid. Demolished. I mean, what harm had it ever done to *them?*" Jack's eyes were full of the vengeance of archaeologists. "After what they did to Petra. If I could ever catch one of these bigots, I'd… I'd…"

"Jack, what about Tom and Shoshana?" Jadis pulled him back. "I'm worried. They could be anywhere. How are they going to get home? What with the airlines in such a mess? The newsfeeds…"

"Jadis—have you tried to phone them?" Jack was stern.

"Why, no, I…"

Jadis tore her eyes away from his, ashamed that she hadn't even thought of it. She looked at the airtab display before them, and, finding an unopened mail, dicted it open.

"Oh, Jack, look…"

They read the text together. "I think she's hurt," said Jadis. "Or concussed. All that stuff about 'charity' and 'kindness'." She turned towards Jack. Her voice was edgy: "What shall we do? What *can* we do?"

His answer was thoughtful and deliberate, as if he remembered something that he'd put away in a safe place long ago, and only now recalled where it was, and what he could use it for.

"The header code will give the exact location of Shoshana's phone," he said, "and when she sent this message..." He looked more closely at the message, his eyes flying over the display, dicting icons, gesturing down menus. "Ah yes, there it is... and she sent it, what, less than twenty minutes ago."

Jadis, now desperate: "But what's the use of knowing where and when, if we can't get to them?" Her conscience reeled, her shame at her own laxity. Tom could always look after himself, but in her mind she'd thought that In Israel Tom would depend on Shoshana—and she, Jadis, had promised to help Shoshana in any way she could. To fail her now would be insupportable.

Jack looked slowly up.

"Jadis, I think we can. Or *somebody* can. Ruxton Carr's people." Jack recalled his sole visit to their benefactor almost twenty years before; of a kind and mildly eccentric man with novelty dinosaur braces; unflinching faith in their abilities; a bottomless pocket that had supported them ever since—and a very fast private jet. And as he explained all this to Jadis, the great thing about the jet was that it was a drone, and so would not fall from the sky. Ruxton Carr had died some years before, but he'd made it clear that his hyperjet would always be at the disposal of anyone at his Institutes who needed it.

Jack pulled out his phone, dicted at it with a strangely intense gaze which, Jadis thought, he reserved only for the most intractable problems. As if it were a number he'd keyed in once, long ago, and had never used.

And so it was that Shoshana's phone bleeped with a message from Jack that said:

Message received. Do not move from where you sent it from. Magic Carpet is being sent for. We love you both—J&J.

Jack turned to Jadis. "It is all set. Tom and Shoshana are at Ben Gurion. Merlin Tech will send a hyperjet to pick them up. They should be arriving in Toulouse tomorrow, at dawn."

Jack pointed out that there was nothing that either of them could do now but wait, and suggested that she join him for his siesta, noting that one wasn't obliged to spend it fast asleep. Not all of it, anyway.

"We'll have a long wait until morning," he said. "We shouldn't spend it each alone."

At sunrise, Tom and Shoshana were greeted by Jack and Jadis and a brand new day free from pain. Jadis could see that they were both suffering from profound shock. Tom, cut and bruised everywhere and evidently dazed, fell mutely into the arms of his mother as if he were a small child. A limping Shoshana just cried and cried despite her best efforts to stop.

Jack and Jadis maneuvered them into the back of the jeep, swaddled them in blankets, and drove off as silently and stealthily as their magic carpet had been, if only a tiny fraction as fast. When they arrived at the farmhouse, the passengers were asleep in each other's arms.

Chapter 12. Apparition

Central North Africa, Earth, *c.* 6,355,000 years ago

Lo, in yon brilliant window-niche
 How statue-like I see thee stand,
 The agate lamp within thy hand
Ah! Psyche, from the regions which
 Are holy land!
Edgar Allan Poe — *To Helen*

SURRENDER OR DIE.

The voice boomed over the burgeoning city. The noise of the slogan was itself an assault. So shrill that it made the eardrums bleed of all those who heard it; so powerful that it winded anyone within range; so rumbling that it made the ground shake and half-grown towers topple onto the terrified crowds below. And yet the Eldest Elder of the Annakhnu was glad. For this was the sign for which he had waited all the years of his life. The storm, and after that, the calm of peace — such would surely arrive.

SURRENDER OR DIE.

The voice came from above, from the roiling clouds, in their own language, if in a mode so laughably ancient that only he — perhaps alone of all the Annakhnu — was capable of understanding it as it was meant to be understood. The long-staid language of their nomad years had changed rapidly since the Annakhnu had settled here on the heights, so that the heavenly imprecation would have sounded more, to the City-bred modern ear, like:

HAVE AN INCOMPARABLE ORGASM

And that, reasoned the Eldest Elder, was proof enough that they just had to live through this temporary (if devastating) interruption for the peace that would come after.

Proof also, if the prophecies were right — the prophecies of *Ha'Shekhna*, seasoned with the ages of millennia piled upon millennia

347

beyond count; the prophecies as given by the Goddess herself to *Ani'kh'a'av*, the All Father, on sun-graven tablets of meteoric iron, in the earliest days of the Annakhnu when they lived far to the East. The prophecy that she would soon come and smite their enemies, deliver them from evil.

Which all meant, reasoned the Eldest Elder to himself (for he was too much deafened and dumbstruck and cast down to the ground bleeding and fractured to be able to discuss the matter with anyone else, even had anyone else survived to listen), that salvation was hours—even min-utes—away, and the long-desired City could be allowed to take shape. No matter how bad things looked, they had nothing to fear.

Propped up, bruised and whimpering, on the balcony of the temple, looking westwards over the Grand Plaza and the Gates and onto the plains, he saw the sky boil. Everything went blinding white before his eyes and he felt the stones crack and crumble beneath his feet.

SURRENDER OR DIE.

Oh, go compare your *own* orgasm. The Eldest Elder closed his eyes and rested for a spell. After what seemed like only a few minutes, but it might have been more like hours or even days, he awoke to find himself buried under an uncountable mass of rubble. Pinned though he was, he found he could breathe: fortune, *b'r'k h'ten Ha'Shekhna*, had seen fit to bury him beneath an arrangement of spars that had once supported the conical roof of the topmost spire of the temple. The sturdy, interlaced timbers had taken the weight of the masonry that had fallen above him, interring him, uncrushed, in a kind of cave. Immediately after registering this amazement and proffering his thanks, he was seized by wracking coughs as his lungs sought to eject masses of mud-brick- and plaster dust. He lay there then, wretched; his chest heaving in pain; his eyes sore almost to distraction; his throat feeling as if he had been marinated in mud, turning slicker with his own sweat and the chill dampness of his own condensing breath.

Slowly, with the patience of ages, he calmed himself, corralled his panic; brought his breathing and heart rate down to a level that would allow conscious thought. Reason, he had always said; reason is the con-queror of all things. Not love, not even piety, but reason. He was grateful for the iron discipline with which he had always conducted himself. He knew that, one day, it might save his life.

The victory of reason meant that after a few minutes he found that he could move his arms and legs — so nothing broken — and, seeing a glimmer of light close to his face, scraped, with sore fingers and chipped and blackened nails, a tiny spy-hole onto a most intriguing vista. Before him, spread out, was the Grand Plaza of the City, by the great gates, and he could see the whole thing from perhaps a foot or two above ground level, from near the bottom of one of seemingly several large piles of rubble.

Ah, me, he mused. The Grand Plaza had once been a fine thing — the walls with the great gates, and the principal buildings all around, the temple among them, and before all a bustling marketplace, thronged with herdsmen and their families, wearing their brightest robes for the great trip to the City, their droves of pigs and keryx before them; merchants and farmers, rich, their proud harems jangling with jewellery, parading their finery for all to admire; troopers on great rhinos, garlanded with flowers in this time of peace, the beasts accepting gifts of fruit from laughing children, tiny before the beasts' imposing bulk; stalls with bright awnings selling all manner of wares from around the ever-expanding Annakhnu realm. And all around music, and noise, and chatter, and shouting, and laughter, and more noise, noise, always noise. The Eldest Elder appreciated — demanded — quiet in all things, but was wise enough to know that quiet is not such unless counterpointed with noise: and that sound, free, untrammelled, is a sign of life. And life, *b'r'k h'ten Ha'Shekhna*, is what it's all about.

His view now, though, showed him only the serenity of death. All was waste. All was levelled. The rubble piles smoked in silence but for the primeval crack of burned, cooling rock. The great stones of the Plaza were littered with charred masses of what could only have been bodies, once. Instead of the walls, their immense stones chiselled into precise positions by masons of cunning craft, he could see only the bald western horizon, bisecting a huge red sun lying as if cursed, dog-like, beneath oppressive bars of crimson cloud, the disc bloated by the refraction of rising smoke.

The Eldest Elder, bringing his reason once again to bear, had been buried for at least six hours, then, for the Sun had been riding high when the terrible voice warning of either instant death or unmatched ecstasy had first sounded from the sky, and what looked like bright shining Moons, each reflecting the Sun's glare, had landed on the plains around the City, disgorging legions of tiny silver troops, each one with a deadly satanic fire at its command.

The Eldest Elder saw those troops now, in ordered files, their marching feet in step ringing louder as they approached. Before them was a ragged mass of people, wretched women sobbing as they clutched at children; men, bowed, defeated. Every now and then a trooper, silvered from head to foot, would wrench a child away from its mother, and, with a ray of perfect, white light issuing from its fingers, blast its head off. Screams of horror or agony were silenced in a similar fashion. Had the Eldest Elder wanted to cry out—had reason let him do such a rash thing—the cry would have been stopped in his throat at the sight.

The Eldest Elder hoped that many, or even most of the citizens had escaped into the fields, or through the network of tunnels that he and the other Elders had long prepared in case of siege. After all, the prophecy could not be fulfilled if there existed a City, desolate, but without the people to give it life. The people corralled before him, then, must have been the unlucky ones, those too slow to have seen the signs; those for whom some delay, a search for a missing babe, a toy, a precious object, would now cost them their lives. But perhaps not. Reason told the Eldest Elder that troopers like these, these silvered creatures riding moons from some remote quarter of heaven, would be nothing if not ruthlessly efficient, and that the people before him were all those who were left, the remnants of the entire Annakhnu people, from the City itself and the fields and townlands round about. The people on whom the words of the prophecy hung.

The last of the Sun sank below the horizon, casting a spar of light to bathe the clouds above in livid red before it disappeared. The troopers had herded the mass of cowering people into a circle in the middle of the ruined plaza. The Eldest Elder, in his cramped hiding place, could smell the stench of fear. The troopers, encircling the prisoners, stretched out their arms inwards, to deliver their captives from life in a final frenzy of incandescence.

It was then that the Eldest Elder realized that the moment of truth had come, the moment for which he had waited all his life. He thanked the Goddess again for allowing him to witness the impending miracle, and uttered a final imprecation, very quietly, the whispered sound hardly even stirring on his parched lips.

Z'manh z'dakh'aa v'khe'sed v'hosh'khn'uu. Goddess, show us charity, show us kindness—help us.

And the troopers, as if on one command—just as they were about to blast the Annakhnu race to extinction—shrunk in on themselves. It took hardly more than an eyeblink, but if he were asked to describe it, the

Eldest Elder would have said that the troopers had each been somehow turned inside out while being compressed to tiny points—that, or appearing to recede, each one, to the end of its own infinitely long corridor until, when they reached their own vanishing points, disappearing into nothingness.

The captives stood there in their circle, stunned, hardly daring to break out. Over the next few seconds, some realized that they had been delivered, in the nick of time. Mothers, crying with relief, comforted their shrieking children, and others who had lost their own brood. Men, crying and shouting and sobbing all at once, sank to their knees, some to lie prostrate on the ground, in prayer. They had been saved.

The Eldest Elder closed his eyes, content to rest in his unplanned tomb. He was sure that his body would soon be discovered by the citizens, the guardians of the Annakhnu Revenged, builders of an ever greater and more glorious City on the Heights. Whether he'd be alive or dead, well, that was a somewhat nice point he'd debate with himself while he waited. But if death was now his destiny, he would be happy, now that his life's dream had been fulfilled to the last.

The clouds burst, the pent-up rain of weeks and months landing on the parched land like a deluge, scouring it clean. The Eldest Elder felt the first drops of rain soothe his crusted eyes and was content.

-=O=-

SURRENDER OR DIE

The voice boomed over the roof of the chapel, now packed with the Brethren and their guests. The noise shook dust from the rafters. Some of the older Brethren fainted on the spot. Others covered their ears and cowered in the many nooks and corners of sandstone pews worn smooth over millennia by the bodies of so many supplicants. Leila and Lilit, though, started to giggle: perhaps it was simply nerves, or fear, the Abbot wondered, the kind of threat that can inculcate nothing but laughter in those who have lost all hope. But Alfred looked to the vaulted roof, the bright green intelligence of his eyes fully awake.

Alfred looked down then, locking eyes on the statue of the Goddess at the far end, in her niche, the sandstone drapes of her robes chipped and eroded with time, the scarlet paint long worn away; the agate lantern in her outstretched left hand bearing one, dim candle; the drapes falling from her right hand revealing a forearm almost as soft and smooth and yellow-pink as that of a young and living girl; her face worn almost featureless, eye-sockets hollowed, only her smile remaining in reasonable shape, and that smile a teasing enigma, slashed across her face.

The Abbot followed Alfred's gaze, likewise in wonderment. They had gathered here for the Apparition—at a time when such a thing would be of greatest value, that is, at a time of direst need. The Abbot had now seen the moon-ships falling to the plains for himself, and they were just as Alfred had described, and the columns of silvered troopers they disgorged.

He had seen them set fire to the farmsteads and stockades and villages of the Annakhnu on the shores of the Great Lake, and knew that they would be marching on the City. But the House of Shinaar would not be safe from their predations. If the Goddess did not appear, they would all be dead within the hour.

SURRENDER OR DIE

A blast like the sound of gigantic bronze doors slamming shut in hell rent the air above them and the earth below, and, before they were even aware of its happening, they were caught up in a sleet of splintered wood and stone as the roof caved in. The chapel was now open to the sky, darkening as the sun set. The Brethren and their guests shrunk further between the pews, some clasping themselves to make sure they were still alive, others reaching out, blindly in the shrapnel, for another living body. The Abbot saw Alfred felled, like an ancient forest tree, by a block of masonry that landed on his head, splitting it open. As he watched, appalled, he too was struck by a chunk of wood that hit him in the chest, winding him. He sank below his pew's seat, doubled in pain. A small, furry body scurried towards him and snuggled up in his arms, whimpering. It was the pithek, Mandergast, his faithful retainer of twenty years. The Abbot was strangely grateful, and put his arms round the small, shuddering form. The Abbot felt a sensation of wetness around his lower body, and caught an acrid, ammoniac odor. He realized that Mandergast had peed himself with fright. Or perhaps it was himself. He hugged the trembling creature closer to his breast.

He heard, then, rather than felt, the great ironwood doors to the chapel burst inwards, breaking up into microscopic shards that surged through the air at several times the speed of sound. Had anyone dared to stand up just then, or put their head above pew level, they would have been shredded to atoms. No-one did. But then there was silence, and the Abbot opened his eyes to find the light had changed. It was not black and crimson, dark and full of smoke, but even, and calm, and deeply golden, like the sunset that promises a fine spring morning. He weighed up the evidence and decided, not without swallowing his fear, to raise his head above the pew. Mandergast squeaked his fright and grabbed on to the Abbot's legs. What the Abbot saw filled him with such reassurance as he had never felt, nor was likely to feel again.

"It's all right, Mandergast," he said. "No harm will come to you now. Why don't you come and see?" The little pithek raised his hairy head above the pew, too, and gasped, and the Abbot and his companion clambered over bodies frozen in stasis and into the debris-strewn aisle. There before them stood the Goddess, her statue now glowing with an inner light. The Abbot looked around him — there was no sign of the silver troopers, not even any sense that they had ever been present. The great doors of the Chapel were gone, their iron hinges creaking in the smoke-laden evening breeze. The remaining walls of the chapel looked several shades lighter than usual, as if they had been scrubbed clean. The rest of the congregation, though — everyone who had not been killed by the falling masonry — had been frozen in mid-gasp, mid-cry. The Abbot and his pithek were the only people free from this constraint. The Abbot was too stupefied by the turn of events to find this in any way curious.

He was not too surprised, therefore, when the statue of the Goddess moved, climbed down from her niche, and stood before him as a young woman in a billowing scarlet robe, with long, black hair and the grin of a young girl. But the fatigue of thousands of millennia could be seen in her owlish black eyes. As she approached the Abbot and Mandergast, she put down her agate lamp at the end of a pew and subsided into the Abbot's arms. The Abbot steered her to the nearest pew, dusted the splinters and chips of stone from the seat, and invited her to sit. Once again he did not find it curious to find himself seated in the front pew of a ruined chapel, with a terrified pithek clinging to his left arm, and the divine object of his most pious contemplation resting her cheek on his right shoulder, sobbing quietly into his vestments. The job of an Abbot is to provide comfort at need, he thought to himself — to anyone who needs it.

He put his arms round both of them.

After many long moments, the Goddess sat up, wiped her eyes with a corner of her robe, and spoke.

"Evolution has no foresight, no memory," she said. "It is a contingency of the eternal present. To force it, to direct it — that's a contradiction in terms. Why the hell didn't you tell me? *They* tell me? Evolution like that can be nothing more than a rampant growth forever teetering on the edge of becoming a cancerous mass, poised on a critical wave, like a stylus being made to balance on its point while riding a ship tossed in a storm—for millions upon millions of years. And I'm so *tired*."

She looked up into the Abbot's face: red-eyed, yet smiling. The warmth of the expression in her wide mouth, dimpling her cheeks, counterpointed the unnerving hardness of her dark-eyed stare. "I'm not making much sense, am I?" she said.

The Abbot was too stunned to answer the question. Nothing in his training had prepared him for suitable things he might say to a Goddess in the line of ordinary conversation, outside the usual round of devotional offerings, such discourse being of necessity entirely one-way. What do you say to a deity who answers back? Do you say anything? Do you dare? He compromised by offering the briefest of nods in acknowledgement. She didn't seem to take offense, for she continued, this time along a tangent that was, if anything, even more mystifying.

"The problem, I now think, is too much *choice*," she said. "I mean, you know what it's like, you go into a store and all you want is a pint of milk. You know what a pint of milk should look like, because in your head you carry a picture of a bottle, or maybe a carton, with a blue-and-white painted jug on it, or a jolly milkmaid, or a cow or two in a green field. But when you get to the store you can't just buy 'a-pint-of-milk'. It's got to be full milk, or semi-skimmed, or skimmed, or with added calcium, or vitamin D, or long-life heat-treated, or organic, or several of these things in combination, or none at all. So what should have been the easiest thing in the world is made stressful, derailed by choice.

"And so it is here. There is so much scope for evolution among the prosimian and anthropoid primates all around us. So many promising lineages—but which one do you choose? Even with the gift of a certain amount of foresight, it's hard to see—when you're down here, digging in the dirt, so to speak—how it's all going to look when the building is finished the way you want it.

"So in the end you have to hedge your bets. The Annakhnu, I admit, they've been a good try, but they're not 'it'. And I'm sure there'll be other nearly-men, not yet a twinkle in my eye, who might offer something, but they won't be 'it,' either. There is still time. Thankfully, there is still time."

The Abbot found his voice, then. "Holy One—what did you do—to the silver warriors from the sky?"

She turned to him, her strangely round eyes now wide, and brimming once again with tears. She sank back in her seat again, put her face in her hands and wept aloud.

"I'm so sorry. So *sorry*. That's me all over. I try my best, I really do. But somehow I can't do the job without leaving a huge mess behind for others to clear up." The Abbot put his arms round her again, pulling her to his chest, where her hair spread over his robe. The little pithek joined in, stroking her hair and making small, soothing sounds rather like a dove, cooing.

"Look, it's like this," she said, looking up at him, "and I apologise in advance if this is all too much information. The fact is, Abbot, you and your Brethren are among the last of an ancient prosimian race that conquered the Earth and just about all the stars you can see in the night sky. It was the greatest Empire that this Galaxy has ever seen, save two.

"But that was fifty million years ago, and the Empire went the way that all Empires do. All species. Inevitably. But before it died, it split, with each fragment going its own evolutionary way. I've had a good old meddle with some of those fragments, too, just to see if... if..." She sighed. The Abbot felt the warm breath of her exhalation. For a Goddess, she felt very warm, and alive, and human.

"Holy One?"

"Well, those 'silver warriors,' as you put it, were the results of some of my meddling. I had to intervene. To put a stop to it all. Just in the nick of time, it seems. I wonder... perhaps I saw it all coming, even then? Who knows? Anyway, I hope I've made things right. Please forgive me. I couldn't stand it if you didn't."

"Forgive *you*? Holy One, it's we who should beg for forgiveness, we mortal sinners, we..."

The Goddess looked up and put a single finger to the Abbot's lips. "Pish and tosh, Abbot. You, more than anyone, have kept the faith, as indeed should I. There was no need for me to have hedged my bets any further afield than sweet planet Earth. For you, Abbot—yes, you—have been waiting all these long years, and it is through your efforts—yes, yours—that success might be achieved."

"Me? Mine?" The Abbot's mind was assaulted by a barrage of images from without, of places he'd never seen, of gigantic spaceships, and tropical beaches, and a silver skein that stretched endlessly into the sky, and a girl who looked very much like the one standing before him. He felt his lips shape a word he was sure he'd never spoken, but now breathed silently onto the air.

"Xalomé?"

But the Goddess was once again distracted. "Ah, the Earth. Well, you probably won't know this—how could you, really?—but the first Galactic Empire happened more than eleven billion years ago, when the Universe was young, the Earth was a twinkle still five billion years in the future, and even this Galaxy didn't really exist as it does... well, *now*. But that Empire was... *destroyed*."

The Goddess looked up. The abbot could see a glint of determined hatred cross her eyes, her face turn, fleetingly, into a snarl. She looked directly at him, then. He concentrated hard on her words, strange though they were, in case he fell headlong into the incandescent lakes of her eyes.

"I know little more about this Empire than the fact of its destruction," she continued, "and of the warning it left us. The second Galactic Empire was much more recent, around a billion years ago, give or take, and probably *much* more glorious. It extended its reach throughout this Galaxy, all its satellites, and brought the Andromedans under its hegemony. For a brief while it ruled the entire Local Group, and was making a good stab at the Virgo Cluster when..." She paused. She sighed.

"What... happened?"

"What happened? It died, too, of course. The Emperor decided that all was vanity and ceded all his dominions until just the home planet was left. That would have been fine except that without the Empire, the planet became very crowded and the economy collapsed. I'm afraid that the Empire's final knell was probably of its own making—catastrophic climate change that covered the whole planet in ice for a hundred million years."

"Where was it? This planet?"

"It was here, of course. The Earth. I don't know why, but there's something about this part of the Galaxy that's fresher, more *alive*, than anywhere else. That's what attracts *them*, I suppose. If the Earth, and the Universe, too, is to be saved from these... these... *destroyers*... then the solution will come from here. I'm sure of it." She untangled herself from his arms and stood before him, glowing.

"You're doing a great job, Abbot. Keep it up! I bless you now, as I always have, and as I always will. I shall try to do my part, as well as I can. It's not perfect, I know..." She bent over and kissed the top of his head. "But please be assured that I'm doing the best I can."

She took a step backwards. The Abbot knew that the enigmatic interview would soon be at an end. He rose to his feet, panic surging through him.

"Most Blessed One!" he cried: "Don't leave us! What are your instructions? Were should I go? What should I do?"

She smiled again. "Oh, Abbot, *really*. What kind of a question is that? I'm tempted to say 'Frankly, my dear, I don't *give* a damn.'" She stretched her arms out wide, from side to side. Small, yellow flames arose in her fingers and coursed along her arms. Within seconds she was wreathed in flames.

"But... but... Holy One..." The Abbot was on his feet, but didn't dare approach the flaming figure.

"I'm sorry — didn't I tell you?" the Goddess said, her face now hidden from view. "Look after the pitheks. I think they're 'it,' or will be, one day. Saviours of the Universe. In fact, I'd put money on it."

There was a rush of heat and light, a flash of sudden flame, and the Goddess was gone, leaving the Abbot standing in the deserted nave. He heard the sounds of people stirring, rising from their seats, coming back to life. He looked round to see Mandergast, next to him. He didn't recognise him for a second, because the pithek was standing straight and tall, a quite different posture from his usual slouch, and was looking straight at him with an expression he could not quite fathom.

Chapter 13: The Last Battle

Earth, August/September, 2054

The cry is still, "They come!"
William Shakespeare—*Macbeth*

For Avi, the Last Battle started when the army Jeep squirled and wheeled to a right-angled stop on the hot tarmac in front of the Technion, temporarily pitching up on the nearside wheels against the kerb before bouncing back to a halt.

"Get in. Now. *Do it*." yelled Rivka, from the driving seat. Avi climbed in beside her.

Or perhaps the Last Battle—the first skirmish, anyway—had come a few days earlier. Oh yes, that was it. In their kitchen, the evening before he'd seen Tom and Shoshana off to Tel Aviv, when Rivka had told him of the latest intelligence intercept—that when the Khalifa invaded Israel, they'd head first for Mount Carmel.

"But why?" asked Avi. "Unless there's some strategic importance, I guess..."

"Oh, for sure, Big Boy," said Rivka, lighting an Alia and resting her broad backside up against the worktop. God, he loved those hips. But why did she have to smoke that Jordanian shitweed? When he'd tried one he felt like his scalp had rotated ninety degrees with respect to the rest of his head and he'd wanted to fall over. "But what they want is *you*."

"*Moi?*" Avi smiled and pointed to himself theatrically, but as he opened his mouth to speak again, his face darkened.

"Aha! The penny dropped!" cackled Rivka, exhaling two streams of pungent smoke through her nostrils. "Professor Schlong doesn't *just* think with his balls, no?"

"No. Perhaps not," he replied. He moved towards her, putting his arms around her, steadying his nerves by earthing himself to the ground through her curvaceous warmth and the magnetic luster of her hair, but his mind was far away. The Buddhas of Bamiyan. The statues at Petra. If there was one thing on which the Khalifa refused to compromise, it was the continued existence of—or even any memorial to—any religion that antedated its own. And there was nothing more ancient than the religion of the Neanderthals.

358

"For sure, they didn't mention anything too specific to begin with," Rivka continued. "I mean, it was all the usual boring shit about 'paving the road to Damascus with the skulls of Jewish children.'" The old ones were the best, thought Avi. They'd been saying things like that since at least the 1967 war. "But buried in all that dismal crap—believe me, baby, I had to listen to hour after dreary hour of it—the words *Malkeinu* and *Muhraka* did come up rather often." Muhraka was the Arabic name for the part of the Carmel massif that stood above the Battle Cave. God, he'd thought that the Battle Cave was a closely guarded secret. This was *precisely* what he'd been afraid of.

Then came that fearful morning of the suicide jet-bomb attacks on Tel Aviv and Masada. But the direct hit on the Great Pyramid was the one that stuck most in Avi's mind as he'd arrived at the Technion, the shocking news still on his car radio. He supposed classes would now be cancelled. Later, when she'd picked him up in the jeep, Rivka tried to reassure him that the suicide attacks were, ironically, far from deliberate. She had known this, because the technoids in her department had hacked the telemetry. Okay, sure, they might have *looked* like suicide attacks, but the crashes had resulted from some kind of pilot error, possibly connected, she said, with this strange new disease called POP, but she hadn't been sure about it. That one of the jets had hit the Pyramid was an utter fluke.

"Accident or not, they'll milk it for all it's worth," insisted Avi, as they bounced along towards Mount Carmel. "They'll say was a deliberate part of their Year-Zero policy, and no pre-Islamic artifact, however ancient or treasured, will stand in its way."

Rivka turned to him. "My thoughts exactly, Big Boy. Exactly," she said. Her coal-black eyes blazed with furious excitement.

The truck was full of equipment and supplies for a last turn round the Battle Cave, an emergency mothballing operation: to seal it against assault in the hope of reopening it later. The idea was to blow up the back end of the SSM-lite, filling the ravine that led downwards to that bone-choked tartarus. They had infra-red night goggles, plastic explosive and all the trimmings, and—just in case—a load of hand-grenades, a bunch of standard issue uzis with plenty of magazines, a few nano-uzi machine pistols and even a couple of RPGs.

"I got thermobaric heads," said Rivka. "Fuel-air explosives. Ka-fucking-*boom*! Never know when you might need 'em, so I signed out as much as I could. If the bastards scored a direct hit on us now, we'd be absolutely, completely, gloriously *fucked!*"

"But Rivka..." Avi gasped. "*Fuel-Air Explosives*? In a *cave*? Full of *bones*?" The noise and shrapnel would be unimaginable.

"Oh poor baby!" she mocked. "If you like I'll go back for face masks and ear defenders! And a change of diapers in case you shit yourself!" And then, more seriously. "But we have no more time. We have to hurry. I didn't tell you when we got up, because what you had *done* to me in *bed* had made me *lose my mind*." Avi knew that Rivka had always found the prospect of warfare and imminent death a huge turn-on. Hence the orgasmic prospect of using FAE-loaded rockets in what was, even in the loosest sense, a confined space. "And also because I heard just now" — she tapped her earbud — "that the Khalifa Tenth Legion has crossed into Israel. Just south of Deganya."

"What?"

"You heard, Big Boy. I know. Crazy. No air superiority. Thirty per cent down because of this POP thing. And our jets will probably pick off a lot more. But I told you what they'd got lined up in the desert. There are so fucking *many* of them — wave after wave — that it probably won't matter. So the plan is for us to dynamite your cave before they do, and get the hell out, yes? We'll go to my office, see what the Boss wants, and take it from there." Avi was too stunned to argue.

The jeep shuddered to a halt between the two prefabs, outside the steel shutter that led to the cave. Avi and Rivka jumped out of the cab. She ran round to the back, jumped under the canvas and busied herself with the equipment. Avi looked around nervously, expecting to see a platoon of Khalifa troops cresting the hillside as he watched. Catching his breath, he realized they'd have forty-five minutes, tops, before they'd have to get back down the mountain and into Haifa. He got a couple of headlights from the machine shop. They'd need them, at least to begin with: he hadn't turned on any of the cave illumination systems.

"Who the fuck keeps filling this vehicle with watermelons?" came Rivka's muffled voice from inside the truck. Moments late she jumped out and handed out kit.

They each had night-vision goggles, a pair of uzis and magazines in easy reach, a rocket launcher and rocket rounds. They tucked nano-uzis into belts or boot tops where they could find spaces. Feeling rather like a walking arms dump, Avi picked a kit bag full of the explosives they'd need to blow up the cave — Rivka took another bag, this one containing hand grenades. Finally, they strapped on their headlights and Avi rolled up the shutter.

Just before crossing the threshold, they paused, and Rivka turned to him. She was wearing an expression of tenderness, of softness, that even he saw only in their most private moments. She reached up to him and kissed him very slowly on the lips. Pulling back, her eyes burned as she said, "this will be a close call, soldier. Let's hope we can get away before the cockroaches arrive.

"And if they catch us in there while we're at it—well, we won't be able to hear ourselves think, so I'll say it now. I love you, Big Boy. And I always will. You're amazing. No... no... no.... don't fucking cry on me, you *schmuck*!" But Avi's tears ran full into the long, glossy hair of his wife of twenty years, this difficult, irascible, foul-mouthed, chain-smoking, argumentative, violent—and yes, he had to admit, very sexy woman. Jadis had started it, but she'd only ever be on a pedestal, a guiding star, like the Statue of Liberty. But it was Rivka who'd been woman enough to make him into a man.

"And I love you," he said—"and let's *go*." So turning on their head-lights, they took each other's free hand and stepped forward to their doom.

A few minutes later they had reached the ravine at the back of the upper cave. Placing the charges was more difficult than they expected. They'd had to use step-ladders to place them on the roof. Avi knew that there were at least two or three long ladders hanging around in the excavation, but finding them took precious minutes. Even then, it was sometimes hard to find a crevice in which a wedge of the putty-like material could stick. Rivka wished she could have got hold of some of the new nanostructural explosive that moved and flowed like quasi-intelligent amoebae, covalently bonding itself into place. However, the explosive they had would be good enough. It had been radio-tuned to detonate by remote control, hopefully when she and Avi were in the jeep and flying back down the mountainside.

It was not to be. Marching feet were already in earshot. Retreat was no longer an option: Avi scrambled down the ladder, doused his head-light and flashed up his night visor. Rivka did the same and, picking up their weapons, they scrambled as quietly as they could down the ravine path and into the Battle Cave.

It was totally dark. At first, his night visor gave Avi nothing to go on, but a process of intelligent adaptation had picked up just enough photons to steer by. As fast as he could, he jogged down the main pathway until, about a thousand yards out, he started to pant and sweat from the weight of the weaponry. Rivka was always one step ahead, fighting fit and hardly breaking sweat despite her forty-a-day *Alia* habit.

What a woman!

Rivka led him along a kind of dodge, a small path that diverged from the main way, between two mounds of shattered bones. Avi followed her as they clambered up the mound so that they faced back the way they'd come. It was hard doing this in the dark, but thankfully some of the bones had been glued together with a thin coat of stalagmite and didn't crumble and clatter as they'd tried to climb them.

Once at the top, they lay flat on their stomachs, laying out their weapons. It was then that Avi realized their mistake. They wouldn't be able to shoot from a single location as they'd be picked off instantly, especially if they used their rockets—the flares would be a dead giveaway. They'd have to dodge and weave. Fire and move, fire and move, hoping to create enough noise and confusion that they'd be able to slip behind enemy lines and escape. Yeah, right, Avi thought—right past dozens, perhaps hundreds of soldiers in a cave mouth not ten feet wide without getting noticed. Like that's really going to happen.

Rivka must have been thinking along these lines. "Are you sure there's no back door to this place?" she whispered.

"We've looked and looked," he replied, "and we've never found anything more than dead ends."

"No way out?" She asked.

"No, none."

"Just making sure." She clasped his hand once more, just as they heard shots ring out. "Fuck it," she said (this time in Arabic). "They must have picked us up. But we can at least take some of the bastards with us." She groped in a pocket for the radio detonator, armed it and pressed the stud. There was a terrific, rolling boom, a flash and a blast wave that almost buried them in fragments of bone and rock. Avi found himself spitting out shards of cannibal Neanderthal and brained human children, forty-odd thousand years dead.

Rivka's detonation had pinched off all but the first few Khalifa troops, successfully sealing the cave against further assault—and all but the remotest chance of their own escape.

He couldn't see her face, but Avi was convinced that his wife was stoked to bursting on adrenaline. He could smell her musky sweat—this gave him a huge hard-on, and he laughed out loud. Her voice became sharp and imperative.

"Fire at will, soldier."

His last words to her were "Yo, *baby*! What a way to *go*!"

The red blobs now popping up in his night visor told of about twenty or thirty Khalifa troops converging on their position. The first shots winged and whizzed past his ears as they each loaded thermobaric rockets into their shoulder launchers. Avi fired first, into a group of soldiers scaling the mound towards them. His view exploded into white-out, a rank smell of petrol and charred flesh. Wow, he thought, good for Rivka: anti-tank weaponry on exposed infantry at close range. Nothing exceeds like excess. Another blast came when Rivka aimed hers at another pair advancing up at them from the other side. He barely heard her demoniac shouts above the racket. More machine-gun rounds pinged at their feet, raising dust and bones from a battle that had raged here more than four hundred centuries before. The Neanderthals would have loved fuel-air explosives, he thought, as a bullet lodged into his shin, fracturing it. He gasped with the pain and sank to his knees, not without letting another rocket whoosh towards his assailant. It skimmed just inches over the cluttered surface of the ground before exploding in a star of white edged with red, dismembering three or four Khalifa troops as he watched. In his night visor he could see their flat red images disaggregate, flying off in all directions, cooling. He had to admit it, his mind groggy, the Khalifa infantry were crap at guerrilla warfare. Perhaps they could afford to waste human lives.

He lobbed a hand grenade down the slope, just to make sure, and then pulled out two uzis and started firing. The more he fired, the slower the firing rate seemed, as if the bullets were moving in slow-mo, like in the movies. He had just managed to eject their spent magazines and re-load when another two bullets slammed into his chest, lifting him clear and dropping him down onto his back, into a bed of bones right by Rivka's feet. The bones danced as more bullets found him. He thought that she hadn't been hit yet, by some miracle.

What a woman!

His last sight before his eyes closed forever was of his wife, blasting away with an uzi in each hand, and a post-coital smile on her face, hair flying.

What a woman!

Lets her uzi do the talking!

Three times a night! *Matinée* on Shabbat!

My Rivka.

Rivka…

Faye. Primrose… Domingo (Domingo always and forever!)…

Jack.

Hair flying. Jadis, behind her hair.

A sharp pain between his eyes and his head was thrown back, breaking his neck. Really, it had always been Jadis.

Shema Israel, Adonai…

And then nothing.

-=0=-

What became known as the War of the Last Days was intense, destructive and short. The suicide air strikes that had hit Tel Aviv, Masada and the Great Pyramid were soon revealed to have been mistakes in an opening salvo that had gone badly wrong. But the Khalifa pressed on with a massive ground invasion, supported sporadically by long-range artillery and missile bombardments. Now wary about using piloted aircraft, Khalifa commanders launched conventional ballistic missiles from silos in Kazakhstan, Dagestan in the North Caucasus and what had once been called Chinese Turkestan.

The temptation to use their more-than-respectable stock of nuclear warheads was restrained by the Imams, who reminded the commanders that the Holy Places would be useless if reduced to radioactive rubble. As for Israel's civilian population, however, they did not care: although given the smallness of Israel, and the proximity of most of it to Holy *Al-Quds*, the commanders were advised to limit the megatonnage. For their part, Israel's commanders knew that to unleash hell from its silos at Dimona would have been to write a suicide note—and that moment had not yet been reached.

And so, on the day that Avi and Rivka fought their last battle, Haifa and Tel Aviv were reduced to smoking ruins that glowed only mildly in the dark. Total countrywide destruction was averted by Israel's own strike forces, which holed several Khalifa warships in the Mediterranean and Red Seas, and by retaliatory missile strikes on Damascus, Amman and Baghdad, capital of the Khalifa.

But the most immediate worry was the wave after wave of hardened Khalifa tanks and ground troops that swarmed into Israel from all sides, destroying everything in their path. They rained by parachute down from Ha-Golan, poured in from Lebanon and Egypt and crossed the Jordan by amphibian into Galilee; they established footholds in despised Palestine—seen as a cowed client of the Zionist Entity, and thus worthy of more thorough despoliation—and they pushed into the coastal plain, and towards Beersheva and the Negev. They absorbed the terrific loss from IDF low-level bombing, to tankbusters armed with depleted uranium shells, and even the mysterious plague, by sheer weight of numbers. They threatened to overwhelm Israel within two days, but the weight of the plague picked up, and from the increasing disorder of Khalifa operations, it became clear that the pestilence had sunk its teeth into its military command structure.

The desire to crush the Zionist Entity, great as it was, had been overtaken by even more pressing problems closer to home. Within weeks, almost sixty per cent of the population of the mighty Khalifa—from Morocco in the west to Indonesia in the east, from Kazakhstan and Bosnia in the North to Sudan and Zanzibar in the south—had succumbed to Postembryonic Oolithic Petrosis.

Not that anyone had any idea of this appalling statistic as the green and black tide broke on heavily defended Jerusalem like a storm surge, before falling back and fading into the dust. News pictures of the scene showed a relentless firestorm, pillars of cloud and of smoke, the only centre of peace and clarity the Mosque of Omar, the Dome on the Rock where Mohammed had ascended to heaven, and arguably the most heart-breakingly beautiful building on the planet. Not a few people compared the scene with the famous photograph of Saint Paul's Cathedral in London, defiant amid the blitzkrieg.

And then everything stopped, as suddenly as it had begun.

Israel pulled itself out of the wreckage, nominally the victor, but in reality, broken and almost inviable. Almost three million people in Israel and Palestine had fallen to the Khalifa: even without this, around forty per cent of the population would have been wiped out by POP in any case. Jerusalem itself, sacred to so many, held its golden head high above the carnage and ashes.

The survivors, including Prime Minister Seamus O'Shaughnessy, did their best to pick up the reins where they'd left off: but within a few weeks it was clear that Israel had been blown back to the days when it had been Palestine under the decadent, unraveling Ottoman Empire: a picturesque and largely unpopulated backwater in which the Holy Places were maintained, as much as possible, by small and largely inoffensive religious groups.

Eight months after the War, O'Shaughnessy was only too pleased to welcome the embassy of the newly crowned Khalif of Baghdad, suing for peace and friendship and access to the Holy Places. The young ruler did not arrive by plane, or even airship, but in a camel caravan that had taken two weeks to traverse the desert.

The luxury hotels atop the Mount of Olives always had the best views of Holy Jerusalem, but they were now bombed-out shells. Instead, the Khalif and his court pitched their tents in the Garden of Gethsemane, letting their camels graze amid the groves of trees so ancient that some could have spoken of Jesus and his disciples. As if from a scene straight from the Old Testament, O'Shaughnessy had come to the Khalif's tent for the ritual pleasantries, in which both parties decided to end one of the longest and cruellest enmities in the history of the human race.

And so, amid the general economic collapse as a once-modern state regressed to the near-medieval, the Rabbis of Safed picked themselves up, dusted themselves off and continued to debate the more obscure passages of the Talmud, much as they had for centuries. The Druzes of Carmel, although depleted, came out of hiding. Monasteries of a wide variety of Holy Orders renewed and resumed their contemplation of the infinite, and many new Houses were founded. The inter-denominational bickering over space in the Church of the Holy Sepulcher continued as much as it always had. And Moslems continued to worship at the *Al-Aqsa* Mosque and within the eternal loveliness of the Mosque of Omar.

Traders in the *suq* sold freshly-pressed orange juice and *halal* meat, carpets and coffee, leatherwork and silver, much as they had done for years beyond count. That fewer sold mass-produced tat to gullible tourists was a testament both to the shortage both of mass-produced tat and of tourists. In short, Levantine life went on much as it had before the twentieth century had arrived to interrupt things, a disorderly conglomerate of religions in one Holy City.

But with one difference. Only a minority of the monks, worshippers and traders would have identified themselves as *Homo sapiens*.

Not that much of this would have been evident to the residents of the farmhouse at Saint-Rogatien in mid-September, 2054, as autumn broke in sheeting thunderstorms. The house, in a spume of constant rain, was a haven of befuddled peace for some of its tenants, and anxiety for others.

The loss of staff at the Institute had been so severe that Jack found it impossible to continue, and he decided to mothball it, laying off most of the remaining staff—many of whom seemed relieved to go. Souris Saint-Michel was also shut up, indefinitely: an inevitable decision given the sudden plunge in tourist visitors. The last act was the removal of the Sigil. This was mounted on a small plinth, sealed in hard vacuum within a transparent cylinder of some acrylic polymer, packed into a crate, and made its way to the barn of the farmhouse, where it now rested under a tarpaulin, wedged between two hay bales.

No administrator likes to be the last to turn off the lights, but Jack faced the additional problem that contacting Merlin Tech's office in New York to discuss the Institute's new financial arrangements was proving impossible. There was as yet no answer from New York, and after the favor he'd asked in August—to rescue Tom and Shoshana—he was reluctant to impose.

But Jack always had a way of putting his own wryly positive spin on things, and as the September rain continued to cascade down the study windows from broken and overloaded guttering, he looked up at Jadis over the pile of teetering paperwork, and reminded her that the absence of new discoveries in the foreseeable future might give her the chance address the formidable backlog of findings yet to be described.

"Think of it as a sabbatical," he'd said, putting his feet up on the desk, his arms behind his head.

Jadis looked up from some mending—she'd given up trying to wrestle with the increasingly erratic cybersphere—and smiled over the rims of her reading glasses. She had now taken to wearing them for close-up work, and they made her eyes look even larger and more owlish. "Now you've *finally* got up to date on the accounts..." Jack continued. She threw a book at him and laughed as he fought off the assault. Unperturbed, he went on: "you might start that big general monograph you've always talked about."

Her expression clouded. "Oh, you're right, as always," she said. "But I've a feeling that whatever I write will be slanted one way or another by the Sigil. So, I need to describe that first—and I daren't. Not yet."

"What's stopping you?" he replied. "The world has many more things on its mind right now. Amid the general brouhaha, some bizarre, possibly alien and definitely indecipherable message written before humanity evolved would hardly register."

Jadis tried not to rise to Jack's gentle taunts, other than to flash a stern glance at him, magnified by her glasses. Hamming it up, he pretended to have been pierced through the heart, but he overdid it and fell backwards off his chair, disappearing below the level of his desk. She climbed out of her own chair and helped him to his feet. There followed the routine succession of near-telepathic reassurances and pleasantries that couples of a certain age always exchange when one suffers some trifling injury. These over, they paused and looked at each other for a long moment, both knowing that before they could publish the Sigil she felt she needed Domingo's approval, though she could not really explain why. Domingo had advised her to keep quiet for the moment, and so quiet she had kept.

Jadis wondered when or if she might hear from Domingo again. The weird message about Micawber and Richards had been the last. As for Avi, she'd given up sending messages and given the short but brutal war, she now feared the worst. The newsfeeds collected by her patient airtab had been increasingly patchy and out-of-date, even on those treasured occasions when she could get a connection, and when there weren't power outages.

However, all sources had all been quite clear that a plague of unknown origin had swept through the Middle-east. There had been speculation that this was the same disease that had carried off the Pope—but without Domingo's input, she was unable to corroborate these suspicions. It did occur to her, though, that the plague that seemed to have brought the War of the Last Days to an abrupt and merciful close might have been the same thing that had afflicted so many of her neighbors. Occam's Razor said that it might, but as always she had as yet too little actual evidence to go on.

Whatever its cause, the plague was slowly forcing her, with everyone else in and around Saint-Rogatien, to fall back on a more restricted, ancient and homely existence. Getting to market was becoming difficult, partly because supplies of fuel were sporadic, and also because the markets themselves were thin. If the traders hadn't disappeared or died, they, like her, had been marooned for lack of fuel. She became more reliant on her own efforts on the *potager* and in the kitchen, and aware that she needed to store or preserve excess produce, or trade some with her neighbors. They'd kept chickens and ducks for as long as they'd been at Saint-Rogatien. Jadis started to advertise eggs for barter at the farmhouse gate. They were beginning to run out of things they could get no other way—things like soap, and salt. Milk was almost impossible to obtain. She decided to get a goat, if she could. Maybe two. And a cow.

Jack, like Jadis, was also thinking ahead, to the coming winter. He had a hunch that the already unreliable electricity supply would get no better, and might even cease altogether. So he commissioned their old electrician friend Laurent Gaspard to upgrade the ageing solar panels on the farmhouse and barn roof, and cram in a few more, if he could. They asked him to install a wind turbine on the western elevation of the house, to catch the prevailing winds. And—oh yes—to wire their jeeps to run on batteries.

Gaspard said that trade in such items was booming and presented Jack with a huge bill — which Jack honored with a credit transfer drawn on the Institute account. He thought it wise to spend as much as he could on capital investment before the world banking system froze permanently for the winter, along with the pond, in (he estimated) early November.

As it turned out, he was only a little too optimistic. The world's banks collapsed on Hallowe'en, from chronic lack of staff to maintain its electronic systems. It picked up again the following spring, but only after incalculable damage, riots, mass looting and millions more lives lost in cities all over the world. But by then, Jadis and Jack had electric vehicles, resupplied by their own generating system, and could at least keep a refrigerator, deep freeze, computers and a few electric lights.

Jack asked Gaspard what would happen when the world supply of light bulbs ran out. Gaspard gave that most expressive of gestures — the Gallic Shrug — before revealing that he was buying up as many candles and matches as he could lay his hands on. Jack made arrangements then and there for a year's supply, managing to talk Gaspard down to a reasonably favorable discount.

That the world of the farmhouse was beginning to contract around them meant a great deal more domesticity for Jadis, who consequently did not make her customary rounds of the village every single day, breaking a habit of more than a quarter of a century.

When she did, she found that the Mairie had failed to reopen after the summer. The boulangerie remained closed (she reminded herself to locate a source of flour), and was soon followed by the *Sanglier D'Or* as Sandrine Pasquier gave up the struggle and left with no forwarding address. The church went through several temporary priests as each succumbed in turn to the plague, and it was eventually abandoned: people had to conduct funerals without clerical supervision, as well as digging the graves for their loved ones. Many fields were left unharvested, many houses abandoned. That so few had burned down or had been looted spoke to a rain that fell as hard on the just as on the unjust.

The nature of the plague itself was still elusive. Families of the victims were dead-eyed with horror and grief so that Jadis felt she could hardly inquire. However, she began to amass scraps of gossip about how victims were locked in tetany and were literally *eaten up* by a wave of blackness that spread across their bodies. The rumors about what happened next were even more unbelievable. But Jadis had noticed that the coffins in the frequent funerals marching to the swelling graveyard at the top of the hill were rather small, even for the corpses of children.

The reason why details were so hard to obtain was, simply, fear. Initially, the houses of victims were as shunned as medieval pest-houses, in case the disease could be contracted by close contact. As a precaution this seemed wise, as nobody knew how the disease was transmitted. But from what Jadis knew of epidemiology, it seemed sporadic, striking everywhere at once, with no sign of any particular pattern of spread. However, it did seem to occur most often within families, and its effects varied enormously from place to place. Even though it had exacted an enormous toll in their corner of the world, Gascony seemed to have emerged from the plague relatively unscarred, at least when compared with many other parts of southern France. She'd heard that the coast in particular had been badly hit, and that Marseilles and Montpellier and many other towns were all but deserted. Toulouse had been much less stricken, and a few places such as Carcassonne had been hardly affected at all. Jadis was at a loss to explain why.

Nevertheless, she thanked whoever-it-was who might be flying around above the clouds that the Angel of Death had yet to point his skeletal finger at the farmhouse itself. But with no clear understanding of its rhyme or reason, the worry was always there, at the back of her mind.

Jack and Jadis had the additional worry of Tom and Shoshana, both of whom remained dazed with shock. In the absence of an easily available physician, Jadis had managed to bandage Shoshana's wounded ankle, and was thankful that there seemed no obvious physical injuries that would have called for hospital treatment. Doctor Makeba was almost never available, and Jadis wondered when her longtime physician would perish from overwork, if not from the plague.

Not that the injuries weren't serious enough. Tom, lacerated and bruised all over, had evidently lost his sight. So much was clear from what Jack and Jadis could infer, because Tom himself had hardly said a word since his arrival. He wandered around the house and garden as sure-footed as ever, but seemingly without comprehension, and was often found curled up like a baby in odd places. Jadis wondered whether she should keep him indoors in case he wandered off and got lost. She hesitated, because whatever part of his mind Tom had lost, he seemed to know that this was his home. He refused to sleep alone, and would either curl up in Shoshana's embrace, or attempt to climb into bed with Jadis and Jack.

Shoshana was neither blind nor mute, and at times appeared quite happy and even chatty, but her mood would lurch without warning into black depression. She'd be with Jack and Jadis before the fire, Tom asleep in her lap, burbling amiably away, but would stop in mid-sentence, eyes staring straight forward, blank and dull.

Jadis was almost beside herself for the first week, until Jack calmed her: Tom and Shoshana were suffering, quite understandably, from some kind of post-traumatic stress reaction, and they would presumably get better, in time. In any case, Jack said, they ought to contact Cambridge to tell them that one student might not be returning for his final year, and another might not be arriving for her first. Getting through to Cambridge was as difficult as it had been to anyone else, and after a while they gave up trying.

Eventually, in the second week of October, when the air was growing chill, they received two postcards from the University — one for Tom, the other for Shoshana — to say that 'owing to circumstances beyond its control' it would be closed until further notice, but that all courses would be resumed when such notice might be given. The postcards had no signatories; were scuffed and battered; and, from the evidence of the postmarks, had taken several weeks to arrive.

Jack and Jadis had no way of knowing that the ancient University city that had brought them together, in which they had first loved and courted, was now almost completely devoid of human inhabitants.

As autumn advanced, Tom and Shoshana slowly began to emerge from beneath their personal rain-clouds. By the beginning of October Tom began to speak complete, intelligible sentences, and confessed — to Jadis' evident delight — that he could see again, though his eyes were playing tricks on him. He'd be happier, he said, if he'd be either blind or sighted, but this kind of in-between state was driving him demented.

Tom struggled to describe what he was seeing, even to himself. His best attempt (so he said) was that his vision was a hybrid between regular, normal vision — though heightened in some way he couldn't begin to address — and the kind of geometrical, kaleidoscopic patterns you see when you close your eyes and rub them. And this was just it: normal objects in the everyday world were accompanied, more or less, by a train of dancing, psychedelic after-images. Jadis could hardly begin to conceive what this might be like, except that it must be like seeing the world through one of Domingo's shirts. In any case, whatever Tom's new conception of the world might be, Jadis felt it orthogonal to her own, and hoped for his sake that Tom would learn to live with it.

What Tom kept to himself—partly, though not wholly through his inability to describe it—was with his new eyes, Shoshana looked even more fascinating than she had before. Every person he saw now seemed to be surrounded by a coruscating, electric aurora, and he soon worked out that this was not some objective view, but deeply conditioned by his own feelings. Jack glowed with green reassurance; Jadis with maternal love, a sparking, purple corona edged with ferocity and possession. But Shoshana's aura blazed brightly enough to eclipse and consume all else, in colors beyond the range of normal human vision. And there was more: he could now sense the flow and pulse of blood beneath her pale skin, alert to every nuance of her mood, arousal or depression. He hardly knew how to begin describing this to Shoshana, so he did what he always had, which was to replace words with demonstrative action. In perfect tune with every beat of her body, he could make love to her in ways that left her gasping for breath. He hardly needed to touch her, let alone penetrate her: it seemed like he only had to wave his hands around her, like a conductor with his baton, describing some pattern in the air, and she would be brought to a state of saffron orgasm that would last for hours.

Not that she did not want him to emphasize his skill more physically, for she loved to be caressed and kissed as much as ever, and the yeasty-buttery texture of her skin, the allspice-cinnamon smell he raised from it when he ran his fingers across it, were powerfully arousing for him. He gloried in the smell and texture and sight and *beyond*-sight of her curves, her aura an excited yellow-bronze around her full hips and golden thighs: he was always amazed by the softness of her neck, her shoulders and her hair, and the richness of her breasts, streaked with rose; and the hugeness of her indigo-velvety nipples. When she climaxed the room was filled with pink and violet streaks of joyful self-annihilation. But he noticed that when he came inside her, her aura darkened to deepest ruby edged with black and lined with lightning bolts. He had no idea what this could mean.

And, just once, her body and the air all around it radiating a playful fur-edged magenta, she insisted that he stop pussyfooting around and penetrate her firmly from behind. He tried to be gentle, but she pushed herself backwards onto him, parting her buttocks so that he was as fully inside her as possible. Kneeling behind her, he dusted his hands lightly across her shoulders, around her breasts and hips. Without his moving inside her at all, she came in glorious waves of deep crimson rapture. Her insides squeezed against him in exhilarated response, forcing him to come. But the instant he did so, she stifled a scream and her aura *switched off*, like a light—just for an instant, before resuming its glow, a subdued, funereal amethyst.

Afterwards, when she was lying in his arms, beads of sweat like bright maroon blood on her brow, her salty hair in disorder, a powerful smell of panic-edged musk from between her legs and her aura more or less recovered, he'd asked her what was wrong. She did not reply, except to kiss him.

No, he'd insisted—there was something *wrong*, he could feel it, he could *see* it.

Don't be so sensitive, she'd responded, perhaps rather too tartly. They'd both been through a hell of a lot together, hadn't they? Perhaps she'd been bruised or something in the explosion, maybe?

C'est possible, he'd said. After all, the effects of the explosion on his own sensory system had been both drastic and alarming. Some as-yet-undetected internal bruising might be expected.

But he remained unconvinced. He wished that she could get herself checked out by a doctor. He didn't say this, however, as even the most basic doctoring was currently very hard to come by.

Shoshana knew more. Since they'd been in Israel—even before the Masada incident—she had been troubled by non-specific, internal pain. At first it went away with a few analgesics, but it was now a constant, nagging, metallic ache. Her periods had never worried her greatly, but now they were titanic in intensity and volume, as if someone had poked a garden hoe up inside her and had been stirring vigorously—and the blood was always very dark. Then came the day that her blood turned black. There were spots of blood in her urine, too. They were black, too, and soon her urine itself was black, like oil from sump.

It was then that she realised what was happening. She had the plague, but instead of consuming her in a single episode of overmounting horror, it was eating her, slowly, slyly, from the inside out.

She dared say nothing to Tom. After all, what *could* she say? But as the weeks passed, she noticed that he became worried, too, fretting in silence at her insistence—which she swore she'd maintain to the end—that it was nothing to worry about.

Chapter 14. Ascension

Gascony, France, Earth, December, 2054

I lingered round them, under that benign sky: watched the moths fluttering among the heath and hare-bells; listened to the soft wind breathing through the grass; and wondered how any one could ever imagine unquiet slumbers for the sleepers in that quiet earth.
Emily Brontë — *Wuthering Heights*

Winter came earlier and was far harsher than it had ever been, ravaging a countryside already weighed down with shortages, tragedy, disorder and death. The residents of the farmhouse were as well prepared as they could be for the blizzards that they knew would strike by the end of November, working hard to lay in as much winter store as possible.

For Tom, working with his hands had proved excellent therapy: he and Jack were out from dawn until dusk, shoring up the roof and filling cracks, stripping down and maintaining the generators, mending frozen pipes and hauling firewood. Shoshana joined Jadis in the domestic department — preserving and bottling, drying and blanching, making and mending. But it was clear to Jadis that the relentless work did not have quite the restorative effect on Shoshana that it evidently had on Tom.

First, Shoshana had lost weight. She was not the round and rosy girl who had first jumped so confidently from the jeep that April, so enchanting Tom. Her cheeks had hollowed, making two great fiery saucers of her eyes, and if Jadis hadn't known better, she could have sworn that Shoshana had aged ten years in as many weeks. Although she tried to hide it — and the effort had been heroic — her pert sassiness had been traded for something mournful, almost spectral. If Jadis had to summarize it in a phrase, as she did to Jack one candlelit evening in the second week of December, when the weeks-long snow storm had subsided leaving a starry, dead-white calm — it was as if the Shoshana had had all the stuffing knocked out of her.

What was so infuriating, Jadis said, was the fact that Shoshana never complained but soldiered on regardless, brushing away any inquiry, spurning any offer of help, wearing a smile and not counting the cost. Jack responded that he recalled another brave and defiantly self-reliant young woman he'd once known who'd been through similarly life-changing events, insisting that nobody should bear the burden but she herself, regardless of her actual capability.

"It's just like you to worry," he said, "but you shouldn't. Shoshana has been through a lot lately, as have we all. She's resilient. She'll get over it, in time."

"But Tom's bounced back," replied Jadis, "so why hasn't she? I do wish she'd talk more. She knows I'm always here. You know, to talk."

"Don't hold it against her," advised Jack. "We all have our ways of coping. And remember, we *know* Tom. Shoshana could be a new person every day, and we'd never know which one was for real."

Jadis made a noise signifying total lack of conviction as she turned once more to her mending, and noticed, as if for the first time, that the saggy old sofa seemed rather a long way from the hearth, and that she missed a hearthrug beneath her feet.

"You know what?" she said. "We could do with another dog."

Jack laughed. "I see—in addition to the menagerie we have already acquired."

Over the past month and a half, Jack and Tom had converted the old field lab in the barn into accommodation for two cows, three goats and a horse, all of which now grazed, weather permitting, in three otherwise abandoned fields close to the house. An outbuilding was full of chickens, and the ducks and geese that now roamed the garden often fought running skirmishes with the Horribles, and, more often than not, winning. The ragged gang of piratical cats soon learned to keep well away from the geese, with their sharp beaks and long, roaming necks that gave them a quite extraordinary reach.

In the absence of anything like silage, locating fodder and bedding for this expanding ark had occupied many scarce daylight hours—though the several abandoned farms round about provided rich stores of maize that could be made into animal feed. Jack thought that one of the fields he was now 'minding' would have to be sown with maize next spring, assuming they could find seed.

"Oh, Jack, I know," she said. "But I still miss Fairbanks. I once thought that to replace him would have been sacrilege, but perhaps ten years might be thought a decent interval."

Jack smiled again. "I get the picture—Fairbanks was therapy for you, so a Mark II version might cheer up Shoshana?"

Jadis pointedly ignored his taunts.

"It's a good idea, though," he said. "For other reasons. A guard dog would be good. A gun dog. Not to mention a gun."

Security was a problem that had loomed large in both their minds of late. The general lack of people had meant the woods were full of boar and deer, which would be useful, if only one could shoot them. But if local gossip were anything to go by, there were also wolves. And there were worse things that Jack had seen for himself.

There had been some odd types roaming around lately — mostly sad and sorry refugees from the cities, trying to sell scavenged items. But some, they was sure, were also looking for places to plunder, to take by force. And a few of these people were very odd indeed: people with long, white, shaggy coats, hammering on the door at all hours and making all sorts of eccentric demands and showing very long teeth if refused.

The clock ticked away a few more seconds, and then, as if on cue, the kitchen door succumbed to a thunderous battering. They both stood up with a start and raced into the kitchen.

"Who is it?" Jadis shouted, lighting a candle on the kitchen table and reaching into the drawer for a long knife.

"A very old friend!" replied a muffled but instantly recognizable voice. Jadis sighed with relief and Jack threw open the door to what looked like a giant snowman. Domingo, unkempt, snow-maned and heavily bearded, swept into the kitchen, sloughing, in one single movement of surprising grace — a vast ankle-length woollen greatcoat, moleskin waistcoat, mittens, scarf, broad-brimmed hat, balaclava and a rucksack the size of a Shetland pony.

Underneath it all was the big, toothy smile that always brought the sunshine — and a Hawai'ian shirt, if rather faded and torn in places, worn over thick corduroy trousers and a pair of boots, each one the size of an amphibious landing craft.

"My dearest friends," he said, shaking a small drift of snow from his beard, "I apologise for the... er... *smell*," (he did indeed smell rather strongly) "but would you mind if I stayed for a night or two?"

Jadis thought Domingo, with his abundance of long, white hair and beard, looked a cross between Santa and a character from *Easy Rider*. Jack asked the visitor if he'd like a glass of whisky, and without waiting for an answer, disappeared into the cellar. Jadis smiled as if she were a little girl and this was the best Christmas present ever.

"Oh, you silly man," she said, "we've missed you like *anything*" — they had had no contact with him since his email from Israel that August — "and you know you can stay here as long as you like." As if willing him to stay forever, she hugged him like a small limpet hugs a vast, black, barnacled boulder. The top of her head hardly managed to brush his chin, and her slim arms wouldn't quite meet round his substantial girth. "Middle-aged spread," he admitted. "Not that you and Jack have been so afflicted."

She looked up at him with shining eyes, which darkened and sharpened as she remembered something. "I've been meaning to ask you, Domingo.... What's all this about 'Mr Micawber'?"

He paused as if he'd suddenly remembered something, reached into his abandoned overcoat and pulled out two objects. One was a sawn-off shotgun wrapped in oilcloth, concerning which Domingo made no comment. The other was bulkier and floppier. Wrapped in sheepskin and fast asleep was a golden retriever puppy, perhaps three months old.

"Jadis, meet Micawber," he said. "Micawber, meet Jadis. Happy Christmas. I rescued him from a house that was abandoned. I'm afraid his mother and littermates had died. He followed me unbidden, walking all this way with me until he tired, so I stowed him in my pack with my socks, until he got cold. Or perhaps the smell revolted him. So I... uh... translated him to my overcoat pocket with my... er... armoury. He is a *gun* dog, after all."

"Domingo... How could you have known? We were only just talking about it..."

"Ah, well, sometimes one... ah... just knows. Goes with the... er... calling. Now, where are the young people? Are they here?"

Jadis explained that Tom and Shoshana were asleep, and, when Jack had returned and had also been introduced to Micawber, for whom accommodation was swiftly found in an old cardboard carton by the kitchen stove, they made tea and filled glasses with whisky. While they drank, Jadis had given a brief account of Tom and Shoshana, their traumatic experiences, dramatic escape and subsequent troubles. Domingo's eyes darkened when he heard that Shoshana had not been well and seemed to be worsening.

"I expect I'll see them in the morning, then," he said.

Jadis suddenly remembered that Domingo would probably be very hungry, but before she could do anything further, the big man shambled over to his up-ended rucksack and (as if it were a sackful of toys) pulled out another parcel, roughly folded in a red-checked tablecloth of summer-picnic *cliché*. He unwrapped it to reveal a vast pork pie; a round of local farmhouse cheese as big as a car tire; and two large loaves.

"Tolerably fresh, relatively unsquashed" he admitted, "and only *slightly* nibbled." Jadis was awed and stunned. She chastised herself for having gotten out of the habit of having Domingo in her life. Domingo took the pause to be of a more active variety. "*Benedic, Domine,*" he said, "*nos et haec tua dona quae de tua largitate sumus sumpturi, per Christum Dominum nostrum. Amen,*" before fetching plates and refreshing the teapot. Jadis was cast back to their very first meeting when this titan (black-haired, then, rather than snowy grey) had barged into her kitchen and had made her lunch before she'd even known who he was.

It wasn't long before Domingo started to flag. His surprise arrival was, he said, the much-wished culmination of a long journey, which he'd be pleased to tell them all about, but only in daylight. "Some of my tale is rather... uh... grim," he said, yawning widely. So Jadis rushed around in a fluster after towels and soap and bedding and warming pans and showed Domingo to a room that had once been his very own quarters, long ago. There was a wash-stand and even the unvarnished oak *prie-dieu* that he'd bought in an antiques market at Seissan—in another world, it seemed. He was asleep and snoring not ten minutes later.

It took Jadis rather longer to find sleep, given the unexpected arrival of their old friend after such a long absence, and not only that, but a friend who had brought Fairbanks resurrected, just as they had been talking about him, and wasn't that a strange coincidence? She tossed and fidgeted next to Jack, who, lying supine, said "well, he did *say* he'd come as soon as he could.

"And given that he presumably had other things to do... and the journey must have been difficult... and it *is* Christmas..." his voice faded, and he yawned, as if in sympathy with Domingo. But she was stirred, jumpy, and wouldn't be quietened so easily. She turned towards him, and nibbled his earlobe. Without a word he responded—not mechanically, nor habitually, but simply because he knew the moods of his wife's body better than he knew his own. Her legs, he reflected, as she wrapped them around him, were as lovely and long and slender and smooth as they had always been, since she had been a young girl, he thought, half in dreams of dells and bluebells.

Across the hall, Tom stirred to find Shoshana's aura blazing in decadent sickly orange splendor. She woke, paused, kissed him with violent intensity, her aura now a migraine fractal swirl of deep orange and magenta, surrounding the bright ultraviolet of her open eyes. She pulled away from him, sighed and looked at him. "I love you, Tom," she said, after a long moment, "and don't you forget it." Her voice was filled with resolution—and also with a keening and regret which spoke to Tom of some imminent, eternal parting.

He lay down again, pulling her next to him. "*Sois gentil,*" he said, "we are young. We have all the time in the world." But her body thrummed with suppressed urgency, as if the very opposite was true, that the world might end at any second.

Tom pulled the covers over them both and cradled her in his arms. As she subsided into sleep, her aura dulled to a filthy orange-brown haze, like street lights seen through an icy smog. Tom stayed awake for a very long time.

The next day, after the family had returned home from their various morning chores, Jadis convened what she called a lunchtime 'house meeting'. Unusually, this was to take place in the sitting room, rather than the kitchen that had traditionally been the venue for all such convocations.

But Domingo had wanted to tell a story, the implication being that it would be a long one, so she wanted everyone to be comfortable. And this is how she saw it as she stepped into the wan, gray shafts of light through the two tall windows that overlooked the snowbound front yard. She bore a tray laden with tea (an increasingly scarce and special treat), new bread, and wedges of Domingo's cheese.

Jack had cleaned and stoked up the fire: Micawber, instantly at home, had settled on the hearth as close to the embers as he dared, imperiously displacing two Horribles, who scowled at him from behind the curtains.

Domingo sat at one end of the sofa, in trademark aloha shirt, his long, graying hair combed and tied at the back with what looked like bailer twine. Jadis thought Domingo looked more than ever like an ageing rock star. She half expected to see a Harley parked outside.

Shoshana rose to help Jadis with the overloaded tray, but she seemed ungainly, awkward, and looked absolutely terrible: her skin was grayish and blotchy, the rose in her cheeks shrunken to two carmine spots beneath her heavy eyelids.

"Shoshana, are you...?"

"Oh, don't worry about *me*, I'm fine," said Shoshana. "Just didn't sleep too well, that's all." She smiled at Jadis but only for an instant, as if she could hardly afford any greater effort: and then, turning her face away, making a great fuss and business of sorting out plates and slices of bread, before sitting—subsiding—on the sofa next to Domingo.

Domingo's much greater size and weight meant that Shoshana couldn't help but collapse on top of him, but his proximity seemed to have an energising effect, so that she now smiled more broadly.

Tom rushed in, late, having caught up with what Jack had self-deprecatingly called 'seeing to the stock'. He murmured an apology and sat down next to Shoshana. Jadis warmed to the infinite and minute concern that her son had for the girl, but it was a pleasure mixed with worry.

As they finished their bread and cheese and topped up their tea mugs, Domingo started his story.

"What I have to tell you will seem somewhat... ah... startling," he began, "but I can make no apologies for that. For I think you should know. And, if I am honest, *I* should know, too."

Domingo paused, as if he were about to launch some great manifesto. "My good friends, we live in a world that has changed. We can no longer hang on to the past. And despite all our discoveries here which, in some ways, have caused people to change their views about things, I had not realized this until fate dealt me a rude blow in Israel this summer. As you know, I was by way of personal assistant to His Holiness, Linus the Second. I say *was*, because His Holiness has now been gathered in. Or so I believe, at least, for all practical purposes."

It was true then, Jadis thought to herself. Or, at least, the ambiguity of the news wires told no more than the truth.

"And, as I suspect you know," Domingo went on, "His Holiness was to give an open-air mass at a large sports stadium near Tel Aviv. The Rolling Stones were going to give a concert there the following night, and I had been hoping to attend, but—ah, well" His eyes misted over in memory of what Jadis now knew was a mildly disreputable folly of his youth.

"His Holiness gave a creditable account of himself, though he had been overtaxed and overtired, or so I thought. I was watching from off-stage, but to my shame, I had got so... er... *carried away* by the proceedings that I did not immediately notice that he had collapsed. Or perhaps my eyes refused to believe what they had seen. Until, that is, a stretcher was wheeled straight past me towards the loading dock. I gave chase and accompanied him in the ambulance to the hospital. His Holiness was alive and barely conscious, but just got grayer and grayer, despite all the heroic efforts of the ambulance crew. Nothing they could do had any effect, and as the body of His Holiness became ever stiller, the crew whirled around him in what seemed like a blur of panic..." Domingo paused to catch his breath, then. "And so it was that without any idea of the precise... er... *nature* of the ills that had befallen my superior, he was placed in an isolation cubicle. I was, I regret, not permitted to administer any last rites, a circumstance which I deeply regret—and which caused me, I have to say, considerable distress—although I can understand why it had to happen."

Domingo now began to choose his words carefully. A dark cloud draped itself over the pale sun, casting the room into drear monochromatic shadow in which all its inhabitants became indistinct blurs.

"The body of His Holiness was at first quite still. But then he started shaking uncontrollably and quite... ah... *violently*, waving his arms all about, so that he had to be restrained with manacles. Then, it appeared as if his muscles contracted into a kind of tetany..."

Jadis started, as if in recognition.

"... throwing his jaw open wide and locking it in place. The isolation cubicle was soundproofed, so I could not hear if he was making any sound, although it looked—I was watching on a TV monitor—like he was screaming. But then—oh, *then*—his body shook with such power, as if he was possessed, that his arms ripped free of the manacles... severing both his hands."

Jadis gasped and paled, her own hands flying to her mouth. Jack embraced her from behind. Tom put his arms round Shoshana who looked up at Domingo, her expression unfathomable until her brow creased minutely, as if she were reacting to some inner pain.

"It was then that the final, awful, transformation started. A small patch of black appeared at his throat. This spread quickly to envelop his whole body in a black shroud, but that was not the last of it. The shroud was active, *alive*. It contracted around him, more and more, until by the time it had stopped, His Holiness was nothing more than a sphere, quite black, of about this size." Domingo brought his hands forward, indicating a sphere about the size of a human head.

The sun now peered from behind the bank of ragged clouds that had obscured it. Although it was late morning, it hung low in the sky, a shaft now piercing the window-glass to illuminate Domingo's hands, as if they were the only things in the room.

"After that, things moved rather... ah... *quickly*," he continued. "The plan was that His Holiness would stay in Israel for two days as a guest of the Prime Minister, an old friend of his. I was going to get time off and perhaps see Avi. Sadly, that was not to be." He stopped, as if looking in the middle distance, and then turned to Jadis, pre-empting her next question: "my dear Jadis, I have no news to report. Our old *confrère* has not answered any messages, and what with the destruction of Haifa and the millions who died in the conflagration, I can only fear for him—*pray* for him." He left unsaid the possibility that Avi, like the Pope, might have succumbed to this dreadful new disease.

How fate has a habit of laying one low, Jadis thought. She recalled how her Dream Team had gathered on the sunny back porch in 2031, twenty-three years before. Of the eight guests at her dinner table, six were now dead. Roger MacLennane, aged seventy, was driving, when he suffered a massive stroke and drove into the back of a petrol tanker, which exploded. Marjorie, unable to live without him, much as she tried, found a bottle of barbiturates and swallowed the lot. Primrose and Faye in Tibet. Avi, almost certainly, in Israel. And Mathilde had once told Jadis how, one day, she had woken up in a bed soaked and dripping with the blood pumping out of her poor Eric's every orifice, the first—and last—symptom of the Naivasha-6 virus. Which left Mathilde herself who, as far as Jadis knew, was still in Cambridge, in a University that had shut down until further notice. And Jadis knew then that she'd had the temerity to have wished them all well, if only in her mind, as if granting such fortune were in her power: the horrible irony being that she and Jack had sailed on regardless, unscathed, apparently unchanged, forced to live with the consequences.

"I had to make several decisions rather quickly," Domingo went on. "I gathered the last remains of His Holiness, including his hands, directed that they be put on ice in a sterilized medivac container, and I left, before anyone could stop me. Exit, pursued by a storm: I had swept out of the Holy Land within three hours, on the Papal hyperjet.

"When I arrived in Rome," he continued, "it was no picnic, either. I found that the plague had struck there, too, with some violence, and the city was close to erupting into anarchy. I did the best I could, holed up in Saint Peter's with what was left of the College of Cardinals, a crowd baying outside, people left and right just… uh… *condensing*, right there, in the square. I saw Cardinal Fratellini, a close and dear friend and colleague, collapse—implode—into blackness, before my eyes.

"As for His Holiness, my colleagues (those that remained) and I could not at first decide what to do for the best. Was His Holiness actually dead? None of us was sure, as there has, of course, been no exact precedent. But even were he alive, we were sure that he would be incapable of office, and after many hours of debate we decided to proceed with the deliberations we'd need to… oh dear, am I boring you?" He looked up at Jadis. She now knelt down in front of him, clasping his hands which were still half in the air, still describing the shape of the absent Pope.

"Domingo, please go on," she said. The man had clearly been brooding over his tale for many lonely hours, lost in a blizzard. It was no surprise that he sometimes appeared to be talking to himself.

"Oh, well," he sighed, "I shall be... er... *brief*. My fellow cardinals appeared to look to me for guidance, because, I suppose, I had had the ear of His Holiness. They asked me what we should do."

Jadis' heart sang towards him: the real reason, she guessed, was because Domingo was intelligent and resourceful, and as he had neither a handsome face nor an elegant frame, he had been forced to become a good listener rather than seek any glory for himself. He had been a friend to her and to Jack, to Tom, to Avi, and presumably to many more.

"... and so my advice was clear," he said. "Given the times, that we should all take some time off for reflection, so naturally I wanted to come here. I apologise for my sudden arrival: as you might appreciate, it is now very difficult to... er... phone ahead. And there was another thing I needed to do. Even though the hyperjet could have had me here within an hour, I decided to take the slower road, for I wanted to see for myself how the land lay.

"You will have a good idea of course, that the world is in a state of some... ah... disorder, but this is hard to appreciate for those of us who spend much of our lives cloistered up in St Peter's. In those rooms we Cardinals shuffle to and fro, admiring the Michaelangelo. But, you know, *ars longa*, and... er... *vita brevis*, or words to that effect. I felt a need — a duty — to stay close to the ground. I set off on the twenty-sixth of September, which just happens to be my birthday."

Jadis was bemused by this, and realized that in all the years she'd known Domingo, she had no idea when his birthday fell, or even how old he was. He had always seemed ageless to her, and he was, of course, an expert in avoiding questions that he thought pried too closely into his origins or early life. He'd dropped hints that he came from Spain: but that was it. That he'd vouchsafed the date of his birth was a revelation.

"I have been travelling ever since," Domingo said. "By bus, by train, but mostly on foot, trudging the highways and watching the world fall to bits around my ears. I was nearly robbed three times, hence the... er... gun. Cities are no place to be, and the countryside is full of anxiety and horror. I have slept under hedges, in barns — following the example of the excellent Dr Corstorphine." Domingo's eyes sparkled. Jack, now standing by the fire, bowed low, pretending to doff a non-existent hat, as if he were in a pantomime. But it had been a long time since Jack had roamed the woods and fields alone.

"Domingo," said Jack: "what's your assessment of the spread of this plague? Jadis and I, well, we've thought about it, and it doesn't seem to be anything normal, you know, contagious."

"That's my feeling exactly," replied Domingo, "but it does vary markedly in severity from place to place. Northern Italy has suffered greatly. People were falling like skittles as I left Rome, and by the time I reached Milan it was quite deserted. Turin was a little better, but as I moved westwards, I met refugees from Liguria who said that Genoa was a ghost town and a haunt of demons and werewolves. An exaggeration, I suspect, but one gets the drift.

"Matters were worse still as I continued my westward course. By the time I reached the Côte D'Azur the plague seemed to have passed, leaving absolutely nothing behind. *Nothing*. I remember a week or so at the end of October when I saw not a living soul, during which I visited Nice. There was nobody there at all—except for a few black spheres, which I took to be the last remains of... er... *people*. I was very tired then, and footsore, and hungry, and I needed a holiday. So I checked in at the Hotel Negresco and availed myself of its elegant hospitality as the only guest, and even then, distinctly self-service, may the Lord forgive me. I ate well and enjoyed two or three tolerable nights' sleep: barricading myself in, of course. On the first night there were sounds that woke me in the small hours I should not like to describe, even here, and in daylight. And so the next day I found a supplier for the *chasse*, not entirely looted and... er... armed myself.

"I am glad I did, for I regret that my shotgun has seen use, and at close-range. For as I continued westwards, across the Rhône, there were more people, and that's when some of them tried to relieve me of such small things I possess. But I am happy to say that there are parts of south-western France that seem hardly to have been affected at all. You will be surprised to learn that Gascony has been only mildly stricken, and in parts of the Languedoc and towards the Pyrenées this *peste* is only a rumor.

"But on the whole the picture is terrible. I am sure it will get better, but it will need help. When I return to Rome, or what's left of it, I shall advise my colleagues that whoever assumes the Throne of Peter should spend as little time in it as possible, but go out and about to see what can be done. Without wishing for a soapbox here, I'll make a case that what we need is a new kind of approach, crossing the papacy with the old Friars Mendicant, a sort of Portable Vatican. I do wish Avi were here to keep me up to scratch on my Hebrew, for he had a wonderful phrase that meant 'mending the world,' as if it were our ordained function, that really said it all."

"*Tikkun olam?*" This from Shoshana, who looked straight up at Domingo as if she were a tiny polar-bear cub seeking approval at the feet of its immense father.

"Yes, Shoshana, that's exactly... er... *it*." Domingo looked down at her proprietorially, and Jadis was pleased and relieved to see how the girl's face changed, as if the sun had fallen on it, or that she'd shed a shabby old raincoat to reveal a shimmering ball-gown beneath.

Having now reached the end of his story, Domingo asked whether anyone might mind were he to take a turn round the village? Footsore he might be, but Micawber needed exercise, after all, and he felt he needed to call in at the church. A professional visit, you might say.

"When you get there, you'll find there's a vacancy," said Jack. "'Mending the World' might start rather close to home, if you've a mind to start right here."

"It is as I feared—and, I confess, for shame, secretly hoped," sighed Domingo. "I shall be the Parish Priest at Saint-Rogatien once again. At least for a little while." He thanked them for their attention, rising to help Jadis with the plates and mugs. Tom and Jack had to hurry outside again for another seemingly endless round of farmyard chores.

Jadis always had plenty of other tasks to keep her busy, so it was Shoshana who asked whether she might accompany Domingo on his short trip up the ancient hillside. A little voice inside her told her that this opportunity must not be wasted, for it would never happen again. She asked the little voice how it could be so certain of this, but it gave no reply.

To begin with, she felt a little embarrassed even talking to him, as if she were undressing in public, or something. Not that this ever embarrassed you *before*, a new voice inside her said, replaying a picture of a school-bus bacchanale. She waved it down: that's ancient history, she insisted. I've changed. And with that, her nervousness ceased. But the new voice persisted. What did she think she was doing, a nice Jewish girl, talking over these things with this strange (*very* strange) man she hardly knew, who, in case she hadn't grasped this fact, was a Catholic priest, *noch*? She interjected that it really rather depended on what one meant by *nice*, and, moreover, whether in the context of her own particular early experience, at least, this bland epithet could ever sit next to *Jewish*, until another voice joined the internal conversation. This was the first voice, the one that had told her to hurry.

And then her own thoughts reigned: she had, if she were honest, no qualms whatsoever about baring her soul to this man. *Not* because he occupied a unique position, in the family circle, but not of it, that afforded both knowledge and objectivity; *not* because he was (she had to admit) far more articulate than Jack, or Jadis, and certainly more than Tom (not that she loved him any less for it); and *not* that he was a man trained and used to keeping secrets. But simply because he was a good listener. She recalled what Tom had said to her, on the shores of the Dead Sea, four months and a million light-years ago, about the comfort of Domingo's very presence, to small, lost souls in distress, even small boys who'd lost their dogs.

There was something else, too. That despite everything, their many superficial differences, she felt that she and Domingo shared a community of experience which, for her part, she had never felt entirely happy discussing with anyone else, at least, not fully.

So, sitting together in the front pew of the freezing church, their breath forming damp clouds in front of them, she told Domingo about the trauma of her early life. How the humanity of religion had been sapped by ritual so rigid that one could no longer see God (yes, she — *she!* — talked about *God*). Of how she'd found greater humanity among those who wore their religion more lightly, or even — she meant no offense — not at all.

So there.

She'd told Domingo everything. *Everything*. About her Mum and Dad, and Howie Levinson. About Avi and her trip to Israel. Most of all, she told him about Tom, and her love for him, and of the pain inside that would soon, she was sure, soon sweep her away from him, and all of them; that it was now so great that she felt she could hardly stand. Yet for all that, she still smiled, for she very much did not want to hurt Tom, or put any stain on Jadis' act of charity and help, in that she had been offered a new home, away from all that *stuff*. And there she sat, still, waiting for Domingo's judgement.

Domingo put his arm round her. She looked up into those inscrutable eyes, and saw that they were — or was she imagining it? — glinting with moisture.

"In return for such candor, I should tell you things, Shoshana, that only my Maker knows," he said, his voice almost inaudibly quiet.

"Domingo?"

"Hmm? Oh. Yes. Despite all external appearances, my dear Shoshana, we two have much in common. Perhaps. Well..." He seemed unsure whether to go on. Looking straight ahead, he began a story which, Shoshana was sure, he'd never told a living soul.

"I never knew my own parents, Shoshana," he said. "I was a foundling, discovered, or so I believe, in the gutter of a small mountain village in southern Spain. I was taken in by the Sisters of Mercy who, while they had undoubtedly saved my life, gave me, as a kind of joke, I think, the ridiculously inflated name under which I now labor. Are you aware of my name, in all its baroque, even rococo glory?"

Shoshana said that she wasn't.

"Wait for it—it's Domingo García Vasquez Santéria Sanchopanza de Orellanzana von Hohenzollern und Taxis." Shoshana tried and failed to suppress a giggle. "But my friends just call me 'Pongo'. Yes, I know. As someone once told me, it's quite a handle."

Shoshana pulled closer to the big, warm man, a buttress against any amount of cold the world might throw at her.

"But—where was I?" Domingo said. "Ah, yes. I throve, and grew, and that was the problem. I kept on *growing*, so that the Sisters, while they looked after my material needs, told me that whatever the Lord might think, I was such an *ugly* child. Yes, I have to say that I was spurned, and kicked, and teased in front of the other wretched children who'd found their ways to the Sisters. But I soon forgave them. Especially as I grew to be a lot bigger than they were, and was able to retaliate in kind. After all," he said, turning to Shoshana, "I was only a child. But as I got older I was generally left alone, until the Sisters found the first opportunity they could to pack me off to a monastery.

"It was just as hard learning to be a monk as it had been to learn to be a... uh... a human being. And, I agree, the strictures of religious observance did sometimes make it hard to see God. And this, my dear Shoshana, is how, in spite of all appearances, we two are so much alike.

"As you know, a long time ago, Avi Malkeinu and I were great friends, working with Jadis, here at Saint-Rogatien. Like you, Avi found it hard to see God, and I remember our having a very similar conversation. That ritual gets in the way. I found it hard to put this into a succinct... ah... *sentence* at the time, but Avi helped me out. It was something he was taught long before, by his grandfather, he said. That there was once a famous rabbi, who said that the ritual is neither here nor there. The important thing was *love*, because—what was it? Ah yes—because 'everything else is commentary'. It was a Rabbi Akiva, I think...?"

"It was Hillel," said Shoshana, finding herself smiling, embracing the big man by her side.

"You see! I *knew* you'd know," he said. "And rabbi... er... Hillel was quite right, and so are you."

But, he noted, looking directly at her: that just because the ritual hides God doesn't mean that God isn't there, or that he doesn't *care*. It was because of this knowledge that despite the abuse he'd suffered all his life, he had embraced the Church, finally, with gladness. And it was because of this same knowledge, he said, that he found Judaism so full of contradictions, which he found fascinating.

"How so?" she asked, her eyes closed, nestling up against his warmth.

"Avi asked just the same questions. I see it like this. That there is more to the Jews than having a covenant with God: they are, in truth... ah... *defined* by it. So how is it, then, that Judaism demands every perfection of ritual with no demand made on the supplicant that he has faith? If he has not faith, how can he be a Jew?"

"I used to have a lot of rows with my stepfather about this," said Shoshana. "My goodness, did *we* have *rows*. But I can see now, that he was only trying to do right by the ritual. He'd say that if you walk the walk for long enough, then you'd learn to talk the talk, and then you'd find yourself believing in God without knowing it. You had to have the ritual to *invoke* God, my stepfather said. Of course, being a stroppy teenager, I said that you had to have all the marching up and down just to convince yourself that God existed."

Domingo was silent for a spell. He could see it was logical, he replied, but to him it was logic, inverted. And yet both views — faith before ritual, and ritual before faith — led to the same place.

She continued: if God exists, if God cares, then how can it be that God tolerates such suffering? The suffering that you — we both — have endured? The suffering of everyone in the war, this plague?

Ah, he replied, he *doesn't*. But the fact remains that although God has a plan and a design for the Universe, he has, nevertheless, granted each one of us the gift of free will. And, yes, our actions are indeed free, because without freedom, we cannot fairly be judged; and without freedom, God's ultimate design might not be revealed, for if it were otherwise, he'd have thrown his own game, in which case everyone's lives would have been lived to no purpose. The Universe would be stripped of meaning.

But, she said, I did not *will* this pain. And your Pope did not *will* himself into that dreadful fate.

This is true, he admitted. Some people would have you believe that all is explicable through belief, that God can be second-guessed: that we can know what God wants. But in reality, faith is not so different from science, properly construed. There are many things that we do not, and perhaps cannot understand.

"God is infinite, Shoshana," he said, "and we are infinitesimally tiny. The deeds of God may seem kind to us, or cruel, but they are, in a formal sense, incomprehensible. The most we can do is strive to improve our world, and if our circumstances box us into a corner, we have to... ah... *accept* them."

"I cannot do that," she said, firmly, her insides gripped as if within the teeth of a black steel vice. She shook, and started to sweat, but Domingo's grasp stopped her falling to the floor.

"My poor, sweet child," said Domingo, partly to her, partly to himself — that she should suffer so. "But you must."

"Why?"

"Because you have no choice."

She looked up at him, questioningly.

"It is the tragedy of our human state, Shoshana" he said. "Animals meet their destiny without being aware of it: acceptance does not come into it. But we — we human beings — *know* what's coming, and so, despite free will, there comes a point where we *cannot* avoid our fate. It is at that point that we exercise the last option we are given, as part of the *privilege* of humanity — that we *choose* to accept our fate. Even though no other option is available."

Shoshana pulled herself up, now sitting on Domingo's lap as if she were a small child.

"And if we don't?" she said, "if we don't accept?"

"There are two things that make us human," he replied. "The first is that we can see God. The second is that we can love. I think that the two are one and the same, and they are both related to acceptance. And I see it in you. You are afflicted with something which, it seems, is like the plague, which you feel will soon claim you for its own. And yet, as far as I know, you have not breathed a word of it to Jack, nor Jadis — nor to Tom. And you have kept your secret because you do not wish to distress them. In other words, for love. Truly, you know more about God than I do."

She said no more. So he picked her up in his arms, called for the dog, and tramped slowly through the snow back to the farmhouse.

She sat in the same place a few days later. It was Christmas Eve, and Domingo, dressed in threadbare vestments he'd found in some cupboard somewhere—over which he wore his greatcoat—was performing the ancient rite of the Midnight Mass. Tom sat to her left, Jadis, and then Jack, to her right.

They were not alone. Horses, carts, bicycles and a few electric vehicles jostled in the Place Etienne Geoffroy Saint Hilaire, and the church was full. People for many miles around had heard that Father Domingo had returned, and that even after all their troubles, the horror of the past year, that Midnight Mass would be celebrated in the church on the ancient hill. Father Domingo had done many good works in his tenure at the church, twenty years before, the village elders had said. It was no surprise, a man like that, that he went on to greater things. But he had been missed. And it was only proper that he had come back. It was as if normal service had resumed.

Before the service, people greeted one another, embracing, crying, for all the world as if they had emerged from some collective nightmare, and that the future would be brighter. The church was washed a honey yellow with the glow from dozens of candles. Perhaps there is something to be said for ritual after all, Shoshana thought to herself, as a first step in *tikkun olam*.

Not that she could repair herself, at least not directly. For as soon as she had stopped fighting, she knew two things.

The first was that knew her sickness, its nature, it moods. On the outside, she was fresh and new, uncorrupted. On the inside, her entire body cavity was stained black. Her heart pounded in a black epicardial soup; her lungs strained within a cavity hardening like brittle charcoal.

The second was that she felt no pain. Only joy.

Jadis and Tom had noticed how much better she'd seemed. To Jadis, Shoshana had stopped shuffling around like a penitent, and had rediscovered the spring in her step. The color had returned to her face: her skin glowed the color of soft summer sunshine. To Tom, this glow extended to a renewal of tenderness instead of ferocity, calmness instead of desperation. The evening before, they had made love as if for the very first time: her love had a sweetness that he would remember for the rest of his life. And through it all, she was cloaked in a bright electric mantle of butter-yellow, fringed with the sienna of cinnamon.

Shoshana, however, looked straight ahead at the fluid movements of the priest, and realized that Domingo had unbarred the gates for her, so that she could now see God, radiant. And God was calling to her—'come'.

Credo in unum deum, her soul replied: *Adonai eloheinu, Adonai echad.*

God knew everything, *patrem omnipotentem, melekh ha'olam*, and all we had to do was to trust him when he said that there was a purpose in being, because all the rest was commentary. She did not know why, or to what end, only that her life had meant something. It had not been for nothing, and because she had lived, the world would be different.

Avinu Malkeinu, aseh imanu tzedakah v'chesed v'hoshiyainu, she begged him: *dona nobis pacem.*

And her prayer was answered.

Tom turned round then. He noticed, first, that her face was radiant as if reflecting the last rays of the setting sun, and filled with utmost peace. And second, that she was dead.

-=0=-

BOOK THREE

SIEGE OF STARS

Chapter 1. Caveman.

Omo River Valley, East Africa, Earth, *c.* 4,000,000 years ago.

Perhaps in this neglected spot is laid
Some heart once pregnant with celestial fire;
Hands, that the rod of empire might have sway'd,
Or waked to ecstasy the living lyre.
Thomas Gray — *Elegy written in a Country Churchyard*

Old Kra looks out of his cave. The land below is his beauty, his glory, everything he knows. Flowing gray, brown and blue, far, far below is the River Omo, mother of life, flowing her milk into Lake Turkana, where live Brother Fish, Brother Turtle and Big Papa Croc. But the land round the Omo is brown now and dry where before it was green, all green, and leaping with Brother Pig and Brother Gazelle. It is now scorched and dead. Brother Pig and Brother Gazelle left this land long ago.

His tribe tells him he's a crazy man.

He tells them no: the land is like this because you have turned your backs on the Goddess. Our Goddess once had five-and-five big fat dugs but her dugs have all dried up, because you kill our Little Brother Pithek, and you mustn't kill him any more.

Old Kra is the Big Man of his tribe. Many sun-rounds since, in the time they now call the Time Of Long Grass, he wrestled Brother Leopard, breaking his jaw; he brought home Brother Pig and Brother Gazelle, he pronged many wives in the long grass and made many blind kits. Old Kra is the Big Man for many sun-rounds. So the bad men of the tribe say nothing.

They say yes, Big Man; they say No, Big Man.

They do what Big Man says.

But many sun-rounds fly by in flash of rainy seasons, a flash of dry seasons, and now Old Kra is a graymuzzle. His back legs don't work right any more. But still they call him Big Man, they do what Big Man says, and many wives keep him warm at night though his prong doesn't work so good any more because he is not a Big Man any more, but Old Man.

But then Old Kra sees rainy seasons hotter than he remembers when he was a young blood hunting Brother Pig and Brother Gazelle and Little Brother Pithek. And rainy seasons are rainy no more, just big clouds riding high and moving on so grass grows long no more and Brother Pig and Brother Gazelle are far away. Only Little Brother Pithek, he likes the dry. Little Brother Pithek makes knives with stones and bones from the dry water.

And Old Kra sees dry seasons colder than he remembers: the wind has teeth that bite at night. Old Kra says all this to his tribe, and says Goddess says do this, do that, but do not kill Little Brother Pithek. This is strange to the tribe because soon there'll be nothing to hunt *except* Little Brother Pithek, that'll be all there'll be, because Brother Pig and Brother Gazelle are now far away.

First they just make jokes behind his back. They wave their prongs after him in village so he can't see, and they laugh. They bide their time. They do nothing until Big Wife Number One dies and goes to Big Sky Water. Then the bad men of the tribe tell Old Kra, you're no good any more, You're not Big Man, but crazy man.

I am no crazy man, says Old Kra, I am with Goddess. I listen to the Goddess.

Who's this Goddess, they say. No Goddess has been round here lately. What does Goddess say to you, Old Kra Crazy Man, eh?

Old Kra now thinks they're listening but it's just a trick to beat him all the more. He sees that now. So Old Kra starts explaining again like he explained before how the Goddess tells him in dreams and visions in the night that the tribe must stop killing Little Brother Pithek and eating him. 'We must look after Little Brother Pithek,' says the Goddess: 'they are Holy People, chosen, as Holy as our tribe'. That's why he's called Little Brother, not Big Brother, like Brother Pig and Brother Gazelle. He now thinks he's making sense because the tribe is listening. So Old Kra says more, saying that the tribe must leave this old land and go where Brother Pig and Brother Gazelle have gone. The tribe must find new land. So the Goddess says.

But they say—dreams and visions, we see no dreams and visions. You're just a crazy old man, you're just missing Big Wife Number One with warm arms and big dugs five-and-five, no harm in it, but no wife want you now because your prong works no more. You are crazy and you can make no kits. So you go now, Old Man. We need a Young Man hunting Little Brother Pithek.

Then the tribe drives Old Kra from the village. They beat him with sticks, they beat him with bones, they bite him with their big teeth, they scratch him with their sharp claws. They took from him the Big Man

Stone. He remembers the shouts. He remembers the screams. They ran him from the village.

Old Kra looks out of his cave at mother Omo below, down slope. It is not his village any more, they took it. He turns from looking down the slope at the Omo. He looks inside the cave now. He looks at his own self. For many days he is getting thinner, he is getting sick. He can't hunt like a young man any more. He scrabbles around in the dirt for snakes and worms and roots. He thinks of Big Wife Number One. He remembers her comfort. The memory makes him cry salt tears down his leathery old face. But he also remembers how Big Wife Number One found roots and special herbs that made all pain go away.

Old Kra makes a fire in the back of the cave, where a smoke hole goes through the roof at the back, so he can breathe easily but no-one can find him, not Brother Jackal, not Brother Leopard. Old Kra drinks tea with roots and herbs like Big Wife Number One taught him, and Old Kra sees shadows dancing on the back wall of the cave.

Crazily they dance, and like all dancers they tell a story. The dance-story is easier to understand than words. But he finds this crazy dance hard to understand at first, because it is more complicated than any dances he's ever seen, about where Brother Pig or Brother Gazelle will be in the rainy season, or how the World was born of the Big Sky Water. There is more to this shadow dance than that. But after many hours, many draughts of the tea that Big Wife Number One taught him to make long ago, the dance begins to make sense. This is what the dance says. That long, long ago, longer than many, many sun-rounds, there was a village bigger than the one below next to the Omo. Many times bigger than Old Kra can imagine, with a ladder leading up to the stars and angels climbing up and down on it from all over the Big Sky Water.

And the dance says more: that Old Kra was more than a Big Man, many times more—a great warrior, maybe even an Emperor. Yes, Old Kra ruled all the stars in the Big Sky Water. But bad things happened and Old Kra is Emperor no more.

"Why are you Emperor no more, Old Kra?"

At first, Old Kra thinks he spoke these words himself. Talking to yourself is a problem of living in a cave with no-one to talk to except the memory of Big Wife Number One in Big Sky Water. But Old Kra looks across the burning fire and sees a figure loom up. It is Big Wife Number One. Now, Old Kra accepts this. When you are old and thrown out of the village, you live with ghosts, live with your dead relations and your ancestors.

"The Empire has gone, many sun-rounds beyond counting," says Old Kra.

"Too true, Old Kra," says Big Wife Number One. "But you are still an Emperor to me, even in Big Sky Water"

"That makes me glad," says Old Kra. "Old Kra has nothing much to be glad about."

"Old Kra..." says Big Wife Number One, standing up and walking across the flames. The flames rise up and dance around Big Wife Number One, but they do not burn her. Old Kra sits back, not daring to move. Maybe ghosts can do that, he thinks.

Big Wife Number One steps through the flames. She stands over him while he sits on the floor of the cave. Big Wife is an old woman. Her dugs hang down, five-and-five, flappy and loose. Her legs and belly are fat and misshapen from the birthing of many kits. But Big Wife Number One still stands tall and proud. Old Kra thinks she looks like a queen. Especially from this angle.

"Big Wife Number One," he says, "always looks like the Empress of all the stars in Big Sky Water."

"Old Kra says the nicest things," says Big Wife Number One. She lies down next to Old Kra and with one mighty breath blows out all the flames in the fire. Old Kra says nothing. Maybe that's another thing ghosts can do, he thinks. But in the darkness of the cave he puts his arms around the big fleshy body of Big Wife Number One and she feels every bit as real as he remembers from the old times long ago when they were young and the grass was tall. Old Kra pulls her close.

"Old Kra is crazy like an old Lion" says Big Wife Number One.

In the night, Old Kra has strange dreams. He is in a place he's never seen before, not in all the dreams the Goddess has shown him. It is a stone place, next to a great water, like Turkana. The waterside is made of stone, and there is stone all around, huge, many times higher than a man, stones with lights in them. Old Kra thinks these stones with lights are the caves of a great village of cliffs, and then it comes to him—this is the Empire. It is night, and there are stars in the sky. A great silver line, like the web of a giant spider, strings straight as bowstring to the Big Sky Water.

Old Kra turns to look across the great water and sees a great moon hovering above it. But he knows that this not the yellow moon with the friendly face of the Hunting Master, but a great building, a cave, made by the Emperor.

Made by his own self.

But not by his own self.

Old Kra is confused.

He turns to look down the long stone edge of the waterside. Many tall poles with lights run along edge of the water. Old Kra sees a woman walking towards him, along the stone edge.

"Look down at yourself, Old Kra," says the woman. He looks down. He is dressed in strange robes. They fit close, in tubes round his arms and legs. Then he looks up at the woman. Old Kra is not scared of any woman, not even Big Wife Number One. But this woman meets his gaze, which he thinks impertinent. He makes a move to slap the woman down. But he cannot move. Not even a finger.

"Down, tiger," says the woman. "Time for some straight talking." The woman points at a seat looking over the water towards the strange moon. Old Kra sits down. He cannot help himself—it is as if he has been commanded. The woman looks him in the eye. The woman is beautiful and fierce like Big Wife Number One was when Big Wife was a young woman with full dugs, five-and-five, and needed taming. But the woman is dressed in strange robes, like those Old Kra is wearing.

The woman says many things with her mouth, and many more things straight into Old Kra's head. The woman says this will save time. Old Kra is frightened now, frightened like he has never been. He pees himself.

The woman becomes angry. "You did *what*? I'm ashamed of you," she says. The woman waves her hand and Old Kra is dry. "After all this time; after all these years; after all we've done together, that you've come to this... this... degeneracy. Yes, I knew it was a risk, to break the continuity of memory. That's something only a non-linear life table can cope with, I'm afraid—for you, it would have driven you mad." The woman cries out: she looks up at the sky, her eyes wet with tears. "Oh, Solomon," she cries, "why didn't you tell me it was so difficult?"

The woman looks directly into Old Kra's eyes: Old Kra thinks he might pee himself again with fright, be tries hard to hold himself in.

"Anyone would think you were stupid," the woman says. "And that's the tragedy, because I know you're not. I chose you. I made you. And despite your dreadful state—*despite* it, mind—you are doing a tolerable job. The Pitheks are fine now, their evolutionary course is set. Our job is almost over, thank goodness.

"But the Pitheks haven't got there yet, and it is vital that they are not killed. Vital. The whole plan depends on their survival. You have another task, now. You must lead the tribe away from the Pitheks as their seer, their prophet. Take them away, far to the east, where a few of your kind still live. Modestly, to be sure, but at least they don't smell quite as badly as you do—you ape, you great shit-stained, piss-soaked oaf."

The woman's eyes are like huge green lakes, and Old Kra is lost in them, so lost he cannot move. The woman takes a deep breath. "I'm sorry to bind you like this," she says. "I've had to make this Xspace in a hurry. You remember it, of course, don't you? *Don't you?*"

The woman paces up and down, up and down, like Brother Leopard. Her voice rises to a scream: Old Kra sees veins like cords on her neck, her fists bunched. Old Kra cannot speak, cannot reply.

"You mean to say you can't remember *this*? Xandarga Station? The Harbor District? This is the bench, the very bench where we first—we did—we *will*—we… oh, what's the bloody point?" The woman storms until she blows herself out. She sits down next to Old Kra, slouching, arms folded like a truculent kit. Old Kra finds that he can move, and he is boiling up with his own rage at this indignity. No woman ever talks to him like that, not even Big Wife Number One. He rises and tells her now, but his voice is different, strange, like he is, suddenly, the Emperor of All the Stars.

"No subordinate of mine, of any gender, of any species, has ever taken that tone with me," he says. "By rights I should have you taken to the brig and flogged." Old Kra puts a hand to his mouth. His head goes funny, blurry: he sits down again and puts his head in his hands. The woman smiles.

"Oh, Ruxie—thank goodness you're still in there, somewhere."

Old Kra doesn't know anyone called Ruxie. Perhaps it's the name of the Emperor.

"We haven't much time," the woman says. "Quick, now, into the shadows, they're coming."

The woman grabs Old Kra by the hand and drags him into the shadow of a giant cave further away from stone edge of the water. Suddenly the whole place is full of people: tall, bright, in strange robes, laughing, drinking from cups made of stone water. The woman points at two people, a man and a woman, walking to the bench where they'd just been, sitting down, and talking, and kissing, and talking some more. It dawns on Old Kra like the rising Sun on a brand new day after an eternity of darkness that this man, this woman, is the two of them, Old Kra himself and Big Wife Number One, but in the old days, or as if in some other guise remembered through a mist.

"I understand now, Xalomé," he hears himself say. "What should I do?"

The woman looks at him, gives one last, bittersweet smile, and vanishes without another word.

He wakes on the floor of the cave, in the morning chill, the fire now a heap of gray ash. Big Wife Number One is gone. Old Kra sees a glint of something shiny in the ash. He scrabbles around in it, still warm, and pulls out—he can't believe it—the Big Man Stone, the one the villagers ripped from his own fingers. He rubs some of the dust and ash from the pattern of the crescents and circles on its face. As he does so he hears a woman's voice in his head.

This is a monument almost as old as the Universe.

A Sigil.

A Talisman.

A Warning.

Look at it. Take it with you. The Pitheks will need to see it one day, still far in your future, to know when their time has come.

Old Kra holds the Big Man Stone up high. He comes out of his cave and walks down the mountain side.

Chapter 2. Pontiff

Gascony, France, Earth, June, 2073

And I say also unto thee, that thou art Peter, and upon this rock I will build
my church; and the gates of hell shall not prevail against it.
Matthew **16**, 18

The church bell clanged noon.

"Class dismissed," said Jack.

In truth, the six youths had begun to gather their things and rise several seconds before Jack had spoken, and had started to file towards the
door of the classroom, what had once been a ground-floor office in the
Mairie. Summer was here, and even if there weren't already plenty to do
on their family farms, teenagers could always find many reasons to bunk
off in the sunshine. Not that they weren't interested, far from it. But education was just one among many things on offer in a bustling farming
community, and was often considered an optional extra.

"Doctor Jack," sandy-haired Serge had asked: "what was it like, here
at Saint-Rogatien, when you first arrived here with Doctor Jadis?" The
whippet-thin, weasel-faced youth had assumed the mantle of unelected
leader of the village school senior class. He was by far the smallest, but
he made up for it in boldness.

"Yeah, Doctor Jack," the other five chorused, each one a hulking,
dark-haired monolith like the others. "What was it like?" It occurred to
Jack that they were all boys. He hadn't seen a girl in his senior class for—
what?—three years, at least. But he never tired of telling them how different things were just half a century before, just as they never tired of
hearing his stories of what they called the Old Days. It was something
they invariably demanded at the end of morning classes, and they listened with absolute fascination, if not in complete silence. It didn't stop
them jumping up as one when the bell went, even if he were in mid-
sentence. But that's just teenagers, Jack reasoned.

So they listened, rapt, as he'd told them how the world was once absolutely heaving with people, who travelled from place to place in trains,
like we do, although their trains weren't always hauled by coal-fired
steam engines, like ours. To this, incomprehension—the closest rail station was Blagnac, a day's fast gallop away, and none of the boys had
ever been more than six or seven miles from where they'd been born. But

they were intrigued that people felt the need to rush around all the time when there was so much to do right here. What interested them more than trains was that people in the Old Days had also driven around in things called *cars* that hadn't needed horses to pull them.

"Or *cattle*," joked Patrice, the butcher's son, pointing to Marcel Lecroix — by far the biggest of the lot — whose even bigger blacksmith father plodded around the district on an enormous cart hauled by four oxen, a vehicle that occupied the entire width of most of the lanes it travelled along at a top speed of two miles per hour. They all laughed, even Marcel, and in the subsequent high-spirited fisticuffs they might have forgotten Jack entirely had Serge not said "but Doctor Jack — tell us again about the *planes*."

So Jack had told them of a *flight* he'd made in a *plane* from a place called *America* that had taken less than three hours, even though it had crossed the *ocean*. Uproar.

Where is 'America'? Is it further than — say — Marciac?

What's an 'ocean'?

Can you really have a machine that *flies*?

How fast did it go? Oh, said Jack, more than a thousand times as fast as Lecroix *père*'s ox-cart. And this was the best part — *it had no pilot*.

The boys were stupefied by all of this. Drone hyperjets (or indeed any aircraft, however humble); any habitation larger than a smallish town; any number more than a couple of dozen; and geography beyond the nearest market square: all might as well have been science-fiction to them. Either that, or a recollection of history so remote as to defy comprehension: of the Romans, say, or the Egyptians, or even the makers of Saint-Rogatien's hillside, or the buried city of Souris Saint-Michel. But if that were the case, Jack reflected, putting on his broad-brimmed hat and picking up his things, he was in their eyes just as much of a fossil as these ancients. A *living* fossil: a holdover from a past age.

And that, Jack reflected, was the real reason that the boys found it all so absorbing — testimony from the horse's mouth. Given that so many people felt so little need to read anything, oral tradition had once more come to the fore. The storytelling urge that had dominated human discourse for most of human history, in which the past few hundred years of literature was, to take the longest possible view, something of an anomaly.

After calling in at the boulangerie as Jadis had asked, he ambled the quarter-mile down the lane to their back gate. The back lane had once been neatly tarmac'd, but the asphalt skin had long since worn away, and the long line of grass and buttercups between the two wheel-made ruts had spread across the entire width of the lane. Erosion had deepened the lane, too, so that for much of its length it was a gully between two high verges, a cool and grassy corridor. In winter, though, it became an impassable, icy torrent, stripping much of the soil and vegetation: this was the only thing that stopped the lane becoming completely overgrown and impassable. Walking with his long, measured strides, Jack remarked to himself with pride that he could still do it, still walk tall. But he missed roaming the countryside, and wondered when it was that he had stopped doing so. Perhaps it would be time to venture abroad and see the world once again — see how the Plague (my! Was it really almost twenty years ago?) had changed things.

Any dispassionate observer would have seen in Jack a neat, distinguished elderly gent, albeit with a lean frame essentially unaltered since youth, if thinner and greyer. Yet apart from Serge, all those boys in his class were taller than he was, and wider, and the eldest was only thirteen. They all had hands like steam-hammers, and a couple of them had rather ferocious-looking teeth. Jack had to confess, it sometimes made him nervous. Taken together, they were of a type fundamentally different from his own: a new breed. In that case, he really *was* a living fossil.

What saved his class — and all the other hulking villagers like them — from a default sense of ominous brooding, was a generally happy-go-lucky demeanor that tended to throw all that suppressed violence into perspective: even if that, too, could go a little overboard. He remembered a few weeks ago at dusk wandering down this same lane to find one of his recent graduates, trousers round his ankles, humping away at a girl dog-fashion, right in the middle of the road. Jack, being a product of a certain era and upbringing, edged carefully past the grunting four-legged mass while pretending not to notice. Just as he was tiptoeing away, and imagining that he'd got past scot-free, both girl and boy offered a cheery greeting — "Hi Doctor Jack, how's it going?" — as casually as if they had been reaping, rather than sowing.

When he'd got home after that incident he'd been irritable and buttoned-up until Jadis had wheedled it out of him, and once she had, she'd teased him unmercifully, that what irked him more than the fact of conspicuous fornication in the street was his own embarrassment at having witnessed it.

"And anyway," she'd said, putting down the chicken she had been plucking and turning to him, a feather-flecked hand on his chest, "we used to like that sort of thing, once upon a time? Didn't we?" Framed by a mass of unkempt hair, her eyes smouldered with memories of long ago. The Spinney. The Nest. And, well, perhaps not so long ago. Maybe a couple of weeks, in fact. In their orchard.

Yes, he'd said, but we wouldn't have done it in public—would we? No, perhaps not, she replied, eyes sparkling—but it was the thrill that one might be discovered that added to the *frisson*.

But that's just it, Jack said—this routine coupling could have no *frisson* if the participants were plainly quite unperturbed about being discovered hard at it, in broad daylight, in the middle of the highway. To this, Jadis had no answer.

Jack laughed as he recalled a joke Avi had once told—that the reason people didn't have sex in the street in Tel Aviv was that people would stop and criticize their technique. This, he reasoned, was a joke made by Jews in self-acknowledgement of a tendency to pry and to gossip. But, replied Jadis, the joke wouldn't be funny at all if people really did have sex in the street. Would it?

If Jack were some kind of relic in the eyes of the villagers: and if this label were meant kindly, as a mark of respect, then Jadis' status was more ambiguous. Busy as she was trying to keep the farmhouse running, she rarely ventured outside: even her ritual morning round had fallen into decay. To the villagers she had become remote, but more than that— a figure unattainable in theory as well as in practice. For as the only woman for miles around who could pretend to any semblance of an education at all, let alone higher learning, Jack suspected that she was increasingly seen as a bearer of occult knowledge, a witch, even: an impression deepened in recent years as she had been called upon to serve as a kind of unofficial village doctor. To many villagers, especially the younger ones, Jadis' name was mentioned rarely, and with awe, as if her name itself bore invocative power, either to heal or to destroy. Only Serge dared refer to her by name, as 'Doctor Jadis'. The others would go to some lengths to avoid intoning these sacerdotal syllables, using some circumlocution as 'Madame Jack' or 'The Farmer's Wife' or just 'The Doctor'.

Jack accompanied her, as often as he could, on late-night mercy missions to tend the dying, or to bring new life into the world. She seemed quite unaware that her careless use of the French that they'd both learned half a century ago was seen as impossibly quaint, ornamented and antique against the increasingly loose local *patois* that Jack had been accustomed to using as a teacher and occasional Mayor—an argot that seemed to have grown up since the Plague. That, together with her piercing eyes, her flying, silvery-white hair and artless, animated manner, rendered her a creature apart, a shaman, a priestess. She seemed not to notice that their neighbors viewed her as some kind of demiurge. Not that Jadis wouldn't be amused by it—no, she'd think it was an enormous joke—but that the knowledge might, in the end, disturb her, make her change her behavior, so that she would become yet more reclusive. And this would only make matters worse.

The irony—that Jadis really *was* the guardian of occult knowledge—had been preying on both their minds of late. This was the Sigil, still wreathed in its transparent vacuum shell, still packed in its crate, still covered by a tarpaulin in the stable, now buried under a stack of hay bales and a writhing disorder of tack, buckets and other farmyard paraphernalia, all but forgotten. But he and Jadis were getting no younger, and they'd have to unearth it someday. Jack had a feeling that their life's work together would never be complete until they had plumbed the Sigil's mysteries. The problem was that now the machinery of high-tech academia had more or less fallen away, all they could possibly do was just look at it, as they had before, with no hope of further progress or insight. Just describing it seemed somehow inadequate. Having therefore no idea of the direction that research into the Sigil should take, they had no notion of where to start, and so, as is often the case with such problems, it was shelved, put aside, in the face of other, everyday concerns.

And then there was the Plague itself.

It had occurred to Jack quite recently how rarely this event was mentioned nowadays, how little it seemed to influence their lives, as catastrophic and cathartic as it had been for anyone who had lived through it. His contact with the younger villagers should have told him, however, that all his students had been born after its passing, and, to them, the Plague was as mythical a part of the Ancient World as cars and planes. And those villagers who had experienced the summer of '54 at first-hand—an ever-decreasing number—tended not to dwell on it, for its reminiscence rekindled memories of agonizing death, multiple bereavement and two or three years of grinding hardship that had claimed many more lives, through epidemics of lesser diseases, violent confrontation and bald starvation. Like veterans returning from the Western Front, they sought solace in living from day to day, piecing together a mundane, quiet life as best they could, and, most of all, not looking back.

He passed the field-gate and pushed it shut behind him, his mind a swirling disorder of all these and other memories and impressions. He thought about those contrivances called *cars,* and that his students were right—they really had been the most unbelievable things. In particular, he thought about a day that he and Jadis had raced off in one of these selfsame contraptions, so he could show her Souris Saint-Michel for the very first time, setting in train a series of events that would lead them to the Sigil. It had been forty-two years ago, to this very day. Then the occasion had been Jadis' Markham's twenty-eighth birthday. And today was her seventieth.

The village baker, Amélie Foucault, had baked a surprise birthday cake for Jadis. Madame Foucault was a shaggy-haired woman who, like most people in the village, was built along the lines of what Jack tended to call a brick shithouse. But why *was* everyone so big these days? It hadn't occurred to him before, but the parishioners of Saint-Rogatien increasingly reminded him of Domingo—in proportion, if not in erudition. Jack suspected that Madame Foucault's cake was less a gift to a regular customer than a ritual offering, to ensure fertility or a good harvest. But he kept these thoughts to himself.

Apart from the inviolate sanctuary of the Spinney, most of the garden had been given over to cultivation, now just beginning to come into fruition. They'd just enjoyed the last of the asparagus—a hard crop in their clayey soil—but one of which they were particularly fond. They were harvesting the first strawberries and gooseberries, making sure that they preserved at least as many as they ate. Shoots of young maize and squashes were just getting into the swing of having been transplanted from the greenhouses, and fresh green cucumber vines were essaying their first trails across the dry ground. The dark masses of potato plants rose knee-high: Jadis had already dug up the first of the earlies, egg-sized and golden, a welcome, succulent freshness that contrasted with the husks of the last of the winter store. It looked like a cornucopia of such easy plenty: but Jack knew (because his own back told him) that it had been the product of a half-century of toil.

The *potager* gave on to the herb garden with its billows of sage, lavender and rosemary, and then the orchard. He passed through the ranks of mature apple and nut trees, each one shading a kinetic retinue of chickens, ducks and geese, all involved in a constantly shifting stand-off with one another, the goats and the ever-present horde of Horribles.

As he rounded the eastern end of the house and walked into the front yard, he saw two horseman making their way up the long drive. One was small and stocky, with a long, grey, hooded travelling cloak, riding a neat palomino mare. The other, in contrast, was as enormous in height as well as in girth, enveloped in a billowing scarlet cloak, and riding an impressive dappled-grey percheron stallion of a size commensurate with its rider. This rider's hood was thrown back to reveal a bushy riot of snowy hair, silver against scarlet: a cross between a medieval knight and Father Christmas. Both riders wore long black boots, bandoliers and carried guns in long, leather saddle holsters.

Jack saw that they were, respectively, his own son Tom; and his old friend Domingo, whom the world of the past two decades would have now recognized as the ineffably remote figure of His Holiness, the Vicar of Christ. And yet here he was, in Jack's front yard. Truly, had the villagers known that Jadis entertained the Pope to tea, their heads would probably have exploded. But at least (Jack laughed inwardly at the thought) she'd never be burned as an agent of the Devil. Not with God on her side.

"Tom, *look!*" the Earthly Representative of the Divine Majesty called to his companion, on seeing Jack, "we are undone! We are caught red handed!" Then, to Jack, "We had meant our visit to be a complete... er... birthday *surprise.*"

Jack smiled. He could hardly imagine a less conspicuous entrance. The two horsemen plodded into the yard: Jack held their horses while they dismounted. Domingo patted the percheron and embraced Jack enthusiastically, before asking if the Lady of the House were At Home. He shambled to the kitchen door without waiting for an answer, his cloak flapping behind him. Presently Jack heard sounds of glad welcome from within, Jadis' sharp, excited voice a counterpoint to the rumbling bonhomie of the ever-welcome guest like summer lightning across a wall of cloud.

Tom, hanging back, took his turn. "*Bonjour,* Papa," he said, his face hard to read. "I'll just get these two settled, may I?"

"Of course," Jack replied, "if you can find room in the stable."

"Thanks"—Tom smiled, weakly. Tom pulled the saddles and panniers off the horses and led the beasts away. Jack followed him, ostensibly to help settle the horses, which would need rubbing down, feeding and watering, but really to reassure his son with his presence. Tom seemed nervous, as if he couldn't decide if the farmhouse really were home for him, and afraid of any conclusion he might reach. As it was, neither said anything.

As Tom had aged, he had assumed a reticence that eventually punctured the easygoing demeanor of his youth. Now an academic, he could be prickly and difficult, and Jack—being a somewhat reserved soul himself—sometimes found it difficult to get on with him. Especially these days, when years might pass between meetings (it had been a decade since Tom had last come home) and they approached each other almost as strangers.

At times like this Jack found it hard to parade the usual clichés that crowded his mind on such occasions—'great to see you,' 'it's been a long time,' and so on—but could think of nothing more imaginative, and so ended up saying nothing. In truth, both men preferred it that way.

They walked towards the house, both smelling very strongly of sweaty horse.

"Papa, I'd like to stay here for a while," said Tom, as if in a flood, long suppressed. "I need a rest. To refocus, and to think about things. Maybe write. Let's call it a 'sabbatical'. The Fellowship has agreed. I have been working too hard, they said. So I am here. I hope you and *Maman* won't mind. But I do not want to spoil things…"

"Tom, you don't need to ask," Jack said. He looked at Tom: his son was still young, but at thirty-nine he hardly seemed to have changed since his twenties. Only his eyes had aged, and the skin around them; and his general mood had become somehow wizened and shrunken.

Not, thought Jack, that this was such a great surprise, in the circumstances.

In the Spring of 2055, Tom got his summons to complete his studies at Cambridge. The Plague had passed, and the University had managed to scrape itself together, if only on a war footing.

It was just what Tom needed. Shoshana's death had floored him completely, pitching him into an active and sometimes violent depression. He had once again become almost completely mute, and would wander off and be found—meditating, it seemed—half-clothed, in the middle of roads, impervious to the curiosity of passers-by. When it was impressed on him that this behaviour was unacceptable, he took to spending long hours sitting in the church: which had been fine while Domingo was still in residence, but the priest had had to leave at Epiphany, to journey back to Rome as quickly as he could.

After that, Tom would sit in the church alone, wordless and still for hours at a time, whence Jadis had to fetch him at sundown, sometimes after long and difficult persuasion. Shoshana had been carried off by what was subsequently found to have been a rare manifestation of the Plague. Tom, however, had blamed himself. After almost three months Jadis had reached the end of her tether.

"And does Tom think it hasn't affected *us*? Affected *me*?" she'd shouted at Jack, venting her frustration at her inability to intervene. So Jadis spent hours with her son cradled in her arms like a broken doll.

The invitation from Cambridge roused Tom from his stupor. The last thing he said when he boarded the train after the long buggy-ride to Blagnac was not a goodbye, but an apology. He was sorry, he said, for all the trouble he'd caused.

His last memory of his mother had been her smile. Don't forget Tom, we'll always love you, no matter what, she'd said. Always her smile, and her dark eyes.

The train journey was long and bitter—the stormy ferry crossing to England even worse—but Tom made the firm decision that it would represent a bridge between the past and the future. That Shoshana wasn't coming with him was a knife in his guts, but he'd just have to get over it. Hanging nauseous over the stern rail of the cross-channel ferry, he realized that since Shoshana had died he had lost the capacity to see the aura of anyone. Looking up, he realized it was not entirely true—*this* passenger was picked out in a faint puce—or was that just his sickly face? No— that passenger *there*, that girl, she has a halo of blue and gold. But it no longer seemed easily to him: he had to work at it. Not that he tried very hard, because he soon had many other things to occupy his time.

Once back in Cambridge, Tom had thrown himself into his work with a ferocity that surprised those of his classmates who'd also escaped the Plague. More surprising was that he no longer joined them in drinking sprees and girl-chasing expeditions, even though these were more muted anyway, given the imposition of a strict and increasingly monastic discipline on all students. Monasticism had initially been a temporary response to the crisis, but like all temporary solutions, it had acquired an inertial permanence, for the survivors derived comfort from strict regulation imposed from above, a haven from the chaos that had recently disrupted their lives. To Tom, cloistered by candlelight in his room, he felt he had to work doubly hard to make amends to his mother, and in memory of Shoshana, who had never got the chance.

He graduated top of his class that summer, but there had been no-one to greet him on the parched Senate House Lawn; nobody to take him for coffee or walk with him along the Backs. The prospect of travelling home was just too exhausting to contemplate, so he started immediately on the college fellowship he'd been offered.

The college was an amalgam of several pre-Plague ones, now re-established on ascetic lines, and known as the Petrine Fellowship. Even though there was no specific religious allegiance or division along gender lines, the head of the college was not called President or Master but 'Abbot' or 'Abbess,' and the Fellows swore vows of silence (at least while not teaching) and celibacy (whether teaching or not).

The reasons and mechanism for the Plague had remained an intractable mystery. However, the view in many quarters was that the Plague had been, if not a punishment for our sins, then a warning against committing any more. Both vows suited Tom, as they relieved him of the responsibility of enforcing them on himself. If he were not travelling for research purposes, he had taken all his meals in college, the only sounds being the minimal susurrus of knives and napkins and the slurps of several species gathered together on common purpose.

He drove himself, often working until dawn and taking only an hour's nap before resuming his daily duties. He hated the thickets on the margins of sleep where he might dream of times past.

The time when they'd made love the day before she'd died.

After a while the sensation dulled until it was more like an abstract painting, or a postcard received from someone else. But he could never quite shake off the reverie into which he was plunged each time he walked to the lab, for his route took him past the open door of the bakery in Bene't Street, where he caught the yeasty smell of new-made loaves.

By the time of his most recent visit home, to celebrate his mother's sixtieth birthday, Professor Tom Markham Corstorphine had become a rising star in the field of comparative anthropology, specializing in hominid religious practice. He had written an influential paper on Sand-Druid coming-of-age ceremonies, the research for which had taken him once again to Jerusalem, a long and wearisome journey by train and steam-packet. He'd hated every minute of it: apart from Jerusalem itself and a few religious enclaves in the Galilee, the Israel he remembered had become a wasteland, either barren yellow desert or stinking salt-marsh, where the sea had encroached on the ruined cities along the coastal plain. And because every time he paused from work, he saw Shoshana's deep purple eyes against the yellow-brown mountains.

He'd taken his frustration and hurt out on his students, who came to see him as a tyrannical martinet, much given to withering sarcasm. Matters had become much worse recently, with the admission to Cambridge of members of a hitherto unrecognized species of hominid, in addition to the eighteen or so already in residence.

People who regarded themselves as broadly belonging to *Homo sapiens* still made up the largest single species group in the student body, comprising just under half the total. But there were sizeable minorities of Tibetan and Mongolian Almai, Afghan Kaptars, Sasquatch, Pendek and the two known species of Sulawesian, to which could be added a smattering of Sand Druids and Menehune and a few others even more obscure, but which Tom made it his business to get to know, at least for background. Almost all the academics, though—the college fellows and the professors—were hominids. For example, he'd become good friends (inasmuch as he was any longer on friendly terms with anyone) with the Lucasian Professor at Trinity, widely regarded as a genius in transfinite hermeneutics, and the first Laotian Annamite to appear in Cambridge. Barely three feet tall and covered in golden hair so thick he never wore clothes, Professor Alexander Beetle ("my little joke," he said, "my birth name is hardly pronounceable by anyone, even me") he looked more like a mobile mop-head than a human being, but had, Tom thought, an unmatched delicacy of spirit.

But these new arrivals were different again, and to a degree that Tom found offensive. He became convinced that they existed for the sole purpose of humiliating him. After many long, lonely hours of meditation in his cell, Tom had distilled three reasons why he found these new creatures so particularly discommoding.

The first was that they were horribly gregarious. You could never get one of them on its own when you could have—say—four or five at once, all shrieking together. This made one-to-one conversation impossible and turned teaching into a circus. Tom had tried to tease them apart for supervisions, but they never let him. He'd remonstrated with their colleges. The colleges cited counter-complaints that Tom's efforts to separate them had infringed on their 'human rights,' so Tom would have to put up with it and teach them, and God help him if his charges felt the slightest whim to complain again.

The second was that these creatures felt that they had the licence to behave any way they chose in his classes. That they were sexually demonstrative was no particular surprise. Many hominids thought public sex no more shocking than, say, kissing, or even shaking hands (indeed, the Taimyri thought shaking hands a much greater solecism). The outright lascivious behaviour of some hominids in public was, if not the norm, then not much frowned on, either. No, it wasn't that—or at least, not very much. It was that these creatures had tried to importune *him*, three or four of them at a time.

At first it was verbal taunts and catcalls that he could ignore. But then came the awful feeling during supervisions that he was being *watched* rather than listened to, as if he were some prey item being stalked by a hungry pack.

Recently, there had been a couple of occasions when he'd been physically jostled and even subject to situations which could reasonably be regarded as sexually compromising, though he knew as yet too little of these creatures to know how much of their behavior had ritual content. This kept him from complaining to the University authorities. He might have done so had he been aware of any other academic similarly exposed — but he was not. So perhaps it was just him.

The third was their name. All hominids had some proud if unpronounceable name denoting their mythic and divine heritage. These creatures had no such thing, or if they did, they obstinately refused to tell anyone. Instead, they insisted on being known by the self-deprecating term of 'Jive Monkeys'. To Tom, this was the last straw, and the fact that finally convinced him that these creatures were here to get at him, personally.

After a while Tom had had enough and had agreed with the Petrine Fellowship that he take a sabbatical. In any case, his mother would be seventy and it was high time he went home for a spell. But still he hesitated. There were memories of home, which, even nineteen years later, had shells so thin that they might be broken.

It so happened that Domingo was passing through Cambridge on one of his occasional visits to the Astrometry Institute, and finally talked him round. Indeed, the priest had said, he, too, deserved a short holiday, as he was about to take a momentous decision and he wanted to meditate on it. The farmhouse was always a good place for reflection, and he had (he said) another reason for visiting the farmhouse in particular, aside from it being Jadis' birthday. Tom knew that Domingo loved to tease about secrets in his keeping, and so decided to let him spin his web without comment. But Domingo suggested that they travel to France together, and this appealed to Tom, for whatever else one might say, Domingo was always good company, talking so freely that it absolved him from most conversational duties. They could go first-class on the *Chemins de Fer de Saint-Christophe* direct from Cambridge to Blagnac via Saint Pancras and the newly re-opened Channel Tunnel, said Domingo, and then hire horses at Blagnac.

"We could creep up on the farmhouse: take it by surprise!" Domingo had said. Really, sighed Tom, Domingo did *love* his dramatic flourishes.

Domingo, for his part, had promised Jack and Jadis that he'd keep watch on Tom as much as he could, to be a kind of guardian angel.

But he had his own reason for ensuring Tom's health, and, where possible, his happiness—and that reason was guilt. It was he who had brought Tom as a baby to Jack and Jadis, a baby who had proved full of unexpected medical surprises that he, Domingo, was only just beginning to fathom. But even then, Tom's insistence that he had been at least in part to blame, left its mark on Domingo's mind. To be sure, Shoshana had perished from a curious inverse of the Plague, something which, when the dust had settled, turned out to have been rare though not unprecedented. But, then, who knew? Medical research had withered in the face of the Plague, as had so much else, so there was no way of falsifying Tom's beliefs. In the end the scientific realities hardly mattered. What mattered was that Tom blamed himself. And so, Domingo felt, he'd had the blood of an innocent life and the thought of another damaged soul on his conscience. Such was the heaviness of his heart when he finally arrived back in Rome in the early spring of 2055.

The Eternal City was in serious danger of belying its name. By the time Domingo reached the Vatican, Rome had been all but abandoned. Substantial parts of it had burned down, and most of the rest had become an eerie ghost town, made more somber by its vast, ancient ruins. By degrees, the remaining members of the College of Cardinals reassembled, and the election to choose a successor to the lamented Linus was a muted affair that passed unnoticed outside the echoing confines of the Sistine Chapel.

It soon became clear that Domingo himself was the leading candidate—perhaps the *only* candidate. His guilt, he felt, would hamper him, so he entered the lists with extreme reluctance, but his colleagues were adamant that he alone had the vision and energy to undertake what would very likely be the most difficult and thankless Pontificate of modern times. The Church had been thrown back to the early Middle Ages, and it would take a churchman of rare devotion to reignite the spark. The Cardinals had liked Domingo's radical ideas, of taking the Church into the world, rather than waiting for the world to journey to the Vatican. Who'd want to come here anyway, they had said, to this grim mausoleum where walked only the shades of death and agony?

His first task was to choose a name. His real name was out: there had never been a Pope called Dominic, and he didn't want to set a precedent. In any case, his birth-name had been wished on him as a kind of mockery, and this was his one chance to select a name that would sit better with his own desires, his own mission. The effort of examining name after name, only to reject each in its turn, prompted a certain frivolity, a personal trait that endeared him to his colleagues, who reasoned that humor would have survival value in the current crisis. So it was in this mood that he had given some thought to Pope Pongo I: a name fitting for a Primate, he thought, cheekily, until decorum intervened.

In his youth, Domingo had been much impressed by the Blessed John Paul II who, like him, had been an outsider with an unwieldy birth-name. But as a name, 'John Paul' didn't seem to suit, not least because he couldn't help feeling that any true successor would have to have been called 'George Ringo'.

Jolting himself back to seriousness, he reasoned that nothing much else grabbed him. 'Benedict' implied a doctrinal conservatism that he didn't much like. To name himself 'Gregory' seemed unhealthily self-glorifying. 'John's, on the other hand, were two-a-penny. He knew it was just vanity, but he thought he needed a name that would signify difference, a new start, and yet with reverence to the Church in its youth, faced with many trials but full of vitality and potential. Something more *encouraging*, he thought.

His fascination with the more ancient byways of Church lore came to his rescue—emboldened by the choice of his predecessor, who had named himself after the second Pope, after Peter himself. He chastised himself for shame for not wanting to be called Linus III, but his feeling of wanting to break with the recent past proved the stronger impulse. In the lists of Popes from antiquity he found Eusebius, an obscure pontiff who ruled for a turbulent summer in 309, or perhaps it was 310, and later sainted. The word meant 'pious,' which was unexceptional enough. The Church at that time, in the dying days of the Roman Empire, had been riven by dispute about the conditions under which lapsed Christians, driven out of the Church following the persecutions of the Abominable Diocletian, should be readmitted.

Eusebius had been all for readmission and forgiveness—the preda-tions of the Roman Eagle were hardly the fault of those persecuted. His opponents had other ideas, and in any case, they had the mob on their side. Faced with imminent anarchy, the Emperor had had little choice but to exile both the mild Eusebius and the agitating antipope. Eusebius was sent to Sicily, and was dead from starvation within a year. When matters had calmed down, a contrite Church brought his bones back to Rome. More than once had Domingo visited the crypt housing the Saint's remains, and had taken to heart the epigraph written by a succes-sor, Damasus, detailing in eight lines virtually everything known about him.

And so it was that Papa Eusebius Secundus, Episcopus Romanus, took up his mission, his status as the first post-Plague Pontiff being his most unwelcome distinction. Like his ancient namesake, Eusebius's first task was to reunite his depleted and dispersed flock, and do so with love, whatever the cost.

He began by issuing an informal edict to his Cardinals — to leave the Vatican behind, to go out into the world, and to heal it. Were anyone to ask him why his own efforts were always that bit more painstaking, more heartfelt than those of his colleagues, he would, of course, have denied it. But his heart told him that he was driven by a need for atonement. He did it, he told his God in long penitent hours, for the sake of a young girl who had been offered the one thing she most needed in the world, the one thing that makes us human, and in her acceptance had been betrayed by it — and yet in the end she had been full of forgiveness.

For the next decade and a half, Pope Eusebius II travelled widely, founding and fostering new monastic orders. In ancient times, he said, monks had kept the flame of civilization alive by copying the works of the ancients. The modern world had more practical needs. So the first order he founded was the Society of Christophorines, whose devotion would be to the power of steam. Their religious duty was to build and operate steam engines to pump much-needed water; as well as locomotives, ensuring that the Iron Horse crisscrossed the continent, keeping trade flowing and maintaining a basic standard of living for what remained of the population.

The next body he created was the Order of Saint Adelard, whose task was to run the great nuclear furnaces of France, to maintain at least a minimum standard of electrical power. Domingo's critics were few, but some said that electricity, let alone nuclear power, was the work of Satan. Such accusations always triggered a mental juke box usually so deeply buried that he had forgotten it was there at all. And so it was that his inevitable response was "So what? The Devil always did have the best tunes," as Mick and Keith serenaded his mind's ear. Their advice was, usually, to Paint It Black.

The Pope travelled much further afield. His first voyage lasted almost two years. It started in May 2059, and after an Atlantic crossing beset by storms and pirates, took him to the ruins of Rio de Janeiro, whence he hopped northwards to the Caribbean and eventually Florida. The Americas in general had suffered greatly from the Plague. Central and South America had been reduced to a thin skin of trading ports around an almost wholly deserted interior, reverting to jungle and wildlife and — if the lurid folk-tales he learned from the one-eyed buccaneer he'd met in a Cayenne bar were to be believed—far worse things. Demons. Monsters. Anthropophagi who carried their heads beneath their shoulders, and who knows what else.

Things worsened as he travelled north. The East Coast of the United States and Maritime Canada had been completely deserted. New York was a ruin as impressive and as lifeless as the Circus Maximus, waves breaking against the stained glass and tarnished steel of the skyscrapers as Manhattan, like Atlantis, slowly sank. He heard that things were slightly better far to westward, and that the largest population centre in North America was Aberdeen, Washington, the administrative capital of the Shasta, a loose federation of Sasquatch tribes that extended from California to Alaska.

Taking ship once more across the Atlantic, he was briefly marooned on Lanzarote when his steam-powered yacht had not only run out of coal, but had lost its mast. A second ship, similar to the first but marginally less decrepit, took him to Dakar and around the Guinea coast to Lagos. He had hoped to see the Bishop of that city, who had been an old friend.

His wish was vain, for Africa was, if anything, far worse than the Americas had been. In truth, his heart had forewarned him of this. The population of Africa had been in decline for decades, suffering the consequences of disease, climate change, shamefully poor governance and general neglect. The Plague had hit Africa with the impact of a wrecking ball on a rotten watermelon. Apart from a very few widely dispersed coaling stations clinging to the fetid and malarial coasts, no human being was known to have survived in sub-Saharan Africa, as far as he could tell. Not one. Africa, once the birthplace of *Homo sapiens*, was now witness to its extinction.

That was not quite the same as saying that there were no *people*, but such hominids that might have existed were too widely scattered to contact. All that Domingo could do was ensure that each coastal station had a contingent of Christophorines before returning, by slow degrees, to Europe.

The steamer limped back up the coast until it reached Mauritania and the first signs of the Khalifa. The Plague had struck the mighty Islamic Empire hard and had ripped out its heart, claiming more victims than anywhere but sub-Saharan Africa. All that was left were sleepy coastal villages, and the rare, languid camel train that would penetrate the nearer oases. Climate change had struck these, too, so that the entire Sahel and Saharan Interior had now been abandoned to the white-hot erg.

It was when the Papal Barque crossed to southern Spain that Domingo noticed how crowded Europe was, at least by comparison with Africa. Andalusia, the region of his birth, had been among the least affected region of any part of the world, with fewer than one in six people falling victim to the Plague. Life continued pretty much as it always had. Still, the Pope easily resisted the temptation of scaling the mountains to the village where he had spent his earliest years. Instead, he embarked once again and crossed to the ancient port of Ostia, arriving in Rome in April, 2061.

Some of his brethren among the Cardinals had travelled even further than he had, and had equally interesting tales to tell, sitting and praying in the hollow remains of St Peter. The Plague had cleaned out a swath of steppe from Russia and Central Asia through to Mongolia and northern China, and had exacted a fearsome toll in India.

But the story was quite different in South-East Asia, from the Yangtze southwards through Indochina and the Malay archipelago to northern Australia, and outwards into the Pacific. The Orient was, according to one roving Cardinal, a necklace of hominid diversity like nowhere else in the world, almost like a world in itself. New species of hominid seemed to be emerging constantly amid the sorry, lingering remnants of *Homo sapiens*.

And so, hardly as he'd disembarked from the last one, Domingo set off on another, even longer expedition, eastwards through the Mediterranean and across the Black Sea to Georgia, the Colchis of the Argonauts where the Caucasus meets the sea. Thence northwards, across the Kazakh steppes until, after many adventures, he passed the Dzungarian Gates and into the vast, windy desert that northern China had become.

Turning south again, he found that the Cardinal had been right. To cross the Yangtze was to enter a different world, a land where hominids ruled. In streets and markets and temples and palaces from Kunming south to Kuala Lumpur he counted at least twenty different kinds of hominid, from the tiny, golden-furred Laotian Annamites to the fearsome Khong, the twelve-foot-tall, black-skinned, red-eyed trolls from the Burmese highlands. In the Indies the hominids mixed freely together in a permanent state of festive riot, a constantly shifting network of alliances made and unmade, with hominids of all kinds and colours parading the crowded streets of the vibrant, revitalized cities in a never-ending array of dazzling finery. But always, at the bottom, was *Homo sapiens*, reduced to a pitiful and servile state: the menials, the sweepers, the untouchables, the unseeables.

The anarchic brilliance of the Indies was such that Domingo wondered if he'd ever be able to form any kind of coherent memory of it. He was thinking along these lines as he leaned on the stern rail of the *S. S. Venture* as it puffed out of Batavia on the first leg of a voyage that would take him to Egypt and thence Europe. He looked round and discovered he had company. It was the Captain, who introduced himself and invited Domingo to dine with him in his cabin.

"The Plague was the best thing that ever happened round here," the Captain said, placing a well-chewed pheasant bone on a silver salver before it was whisked away by a stooping human. The Captain spoke in a kind of pidgin, a mixture of English, Chinese, Bahasa and a dozen other tongues. But despite its rich heritage, it was a remarkably simple language to learn and to pronounce, as it had been lashed together rather quickly to suit a wide variety of tongues and vocal chords. Domingo found it rather euphonious and had picked up the rudiments within a few days.

"How so?" Domingo replied, in a way calculated to invite further confidences.

"Well, look at it this way," the Captain said. "Here we all are, the underdogs, pushed into all kinds of holes and corners, and then — wham! — the tables are turned, are they not?" Domingo had to agree that they had. "And it's good riddance, too," the Captain continued. "Look what a good thing we've got going. *All* of us. The boot is on the other foot, for sure!" The Captain raised a glass to Domingo. "Cheers, Your Holiness!" he said. "Welcome to a brave new world!"

It was then that Domingo noticed the Captain's eyes, set in a broad, brown face. They were large, with yellow-green irises that almost covered the white sclera, and with oval pupils. He remembered seeing another face like that, once. A much smaller face, looking blindly up at him from a swaddle of blankets. Domingo realized with a shock that he hadn't seen Tom since that Christmas when Shoshana had died.

Towards the end of April, 2063, then, Tom returned to his cell to find much of it already occupied by a huge, weatherworn but otherwise familiar figure, long white hair tied back in a bandanna, barrel of a body clothed in a vibrant pattern of hibiscus, white on purple. All of a sudden he was a tiny child gamboling in the farmhouse yard, recognizing Domingo mainly by his smell — it never varied, his smell, and it smelled always of comfort and security and reassurance. Tom smiled — he remembered that he used to smile a lot more often when... when... oh, never mind.

"Domingo..." he said. He hadn't realized how much he'd missed his mentor until he'd said it. It was as if a lost part of his life had returned.

"We have some talking to do, Tom, you and I."

Soon after that meeting, the two of them had turned up at the farmhouse, to toast Jadis on her sixtieth birthday. Now another decade had passed, and they were here again, in the place that both of them would ever call home.

The party was not lavish, but it lasted well into the late evening, with much talk and wine and more talk, as can be understood by people suddenly reunited with long-lost children, parents and dear friends. There was even a cake, which Jack and Jadis had said was a present from the village boulangerie. 'A shamanistic offering,' Jack had joked, although Jadis had responded with no more than a quizzical frown.

The revels eventually came to rest in the sitting room, Jadis curled next to Jack on the same, desperately sagging sofa; Domingo in a cat-ripped easy chair and Tom cross-legged in front of the hearth, looking silently into the flames that were the sole source of illumination. The scent of burning apple-logs filled the room.

"We have been putting two and two together, Tom and I," Domingo explained, his dark shape punctuated only by the two points of light that were his eyes. "But we're not sure what the answer is yet."

Jadis sat up. "Oh, Domingo," she said, "do you have to be quite so mysterious all the time?"

"Not at all!" Domingo protested. "It is hard not to be...er... as you say, *mysterious,* when one is not even sure *which* two and two must be added, or even if they should."

"Jack," Jadis asked, looking up, "please say something to this silly man, would you? He is making absolutely no sense at all."

Jack just smiled, looked down and tousled his wife's hair. "Who'd like some Armagnac?" he asked. "I believe I still have a couple of bottles of the good stuff left."

Jadis sat up and hit him over the head with a cushion, whereupon everyone laughed some more, and Tom rose to help his father find a candle for a trip to the cellar.

After a long pause interrupted by the smoke and crackle of the apple wood, Domingo said with sudden seriousness: "Jadis, I apologise for this long absence..."

"Don't be silly, Domingo," she said, "I'm sure you've had lots to keep you busy." Jadis now lay curled on one side on the sofa, looking at the fire, her eyes bright coals from beneath her hair's shawl.

Speaking almost to himself, Domingo said: "Since I last saw you, all those years ago, you know, with Shoshana…" Jadis did not move. "I have travelled far and seen a great deal of the world," he continued, "and although many lives have been lost, there is still some hope for it. It is, however, a very different world from the one we've all known, those of us who've… er… been in it for any length of time."

"You mean us old *pantoufles*?"

"I speak only for myself, my dear Jadis," said Domingo. "The world is still wonderful, and in a sense it is renewed and we must take heart from that. There are relatively few… er… human beings in it, though. If you went to eastern Asia, you'd think it a different planet entirely. But I have come to love it, despite—no, *because* of—these differences. I find them somehow… uh… invigorating."

"Where is this leading?"

"Well, it's like this, my dear Jadis—" Jack and Tom had now returned, with a dusty bottle and four assorted glasses.

"What's like what, my dear Domingo?" asked Jack, putting down the bottle before turning to riddle the fire. Tom picked up the bottle, poured four measures and handed them round. The sharp, prune-like aroma from the brandy combined with the general ambience of apple wood to make a scent more reminiscent of Christmas than Midsummer. Jadis sat up to allow Jack to resume his seat.

"Well, Jack, what *is* it like?" Domingo challenged, while raising his glass. Tom resumed his perch on the hearth, looking back at his father.

"I know what you mean, Domingo," said Jack. "I see it all the time, when I am teaching—*trying* to teach—some of the village teenagers. They speak a different language…"

Jadis laughed. "Don't they always?"

"But it's not just the language, it's them. Have you noticed,"—this to Jadis—"that people in the village are so huge these days? I thought it was just us getting old, but you know, I'm convinced it isn't."

Jadis closed her eyes.

"I have an idea. An explanation," said Domingo. "Like all such things you have to travel half way round the world to see what's right in front of you at home. The Plague seems to have spared the hominids. In all my travels, I have seen no case of a hominid falling foul of it. Only humans seem to have been affected, and many have still been spared, thank the Lord. Does that answer your question, Jack?"

"I'm not sure," said Jack. "Yes, people here have changed. They're bigger. But why? Perhaps they eat too much. Don't take enough exercise..." He paused, as if he'd been witness to a stunning revelation: "well, I'll be blowed."

"Hmm?" Jadis stirred.

"It's the Plague again. It didn't take all humans indiscriminately," said Jack, "only those without some admixture in their genes of something else, something... older."

"That's precisely it, Jack," said Domingo, "and I only realized it in the Far East when I saw the pitiful state of *Homo sapiens* in that part of the world. Over there, the earliest modern humans displaced the last remnants of *Homo erectus*. There was some admixture, but very little, and — I'd imagine — very little that was... uh... *viable*. But it was enough to get a few *Homo erectus* genes into the gene pool. And, fifty thousand years later, those modern humans with enough of this ancient DNA were spared the Plague. They are rather sorry and few, and easily cowed by the abundance of hominids."

"And here," said Jack, the light of the fire in his eyes, "we have a similar story, but with Neanderthals. How could I have missed it? They were here for an eternity before modern humans, especially in Gascony. Those who survived the Plague must have had a sizeable amount of Neanderthal blood in their veins. That would account for a great deal. The ancestors have come to claim their own."

"It is true," said Domingo: "the builders of Saint-Rogatien live here once again. What our dear friend Avi would have called the *avoteinu v'imoteinu*, the forefathers and foremothers, implying a skein of continuity unbroken into the deep past."

The pause in the conversation lasted longer than ever, as they all gazed into the dying fire, lost in their own thoughts. It was, eventually, Domingo who spoke.

"Might I change the... ah... subject?" he said.

The brooding reverie broke like a bowstring on a hot knife. Jadis sat up.

"Yes... of course," she said.

"Well, as I mentioned, Tom and I still can't make two and two add up," said Domingo, "and we think we know why. It's the Sigil. Neither of us have seen it for almost twenty years. Have you done anything with it? Published?"

"Of course we haven't, Domingo," Jadis said with a sigh. "We couldn't — wouldn't — do it without you, or without Tom. But we have no labs any more. No Institute. And we don't know where to begin."

"Ah, well," said Domingo, "now that Tom and I are here for a while, we might turn our minds to it, mightn't we?"

Jack and Jadis looked stunned.

"Well, yes," said Jadis," but don't you have other duties now? In Rome?"

It was then that Domingo dropped his biggest bombshell, a secret he had not revealed even to Tom.

"It's like this," Domingo explained. "Rome is not what it was, even after twenty years of restoration. My colleagues and I have decided... well, I have decided, and they have kindly agreed... that the Basilica of Saint Peter, while it is a pleasant place to visit, is not really convenient for living. So we've made it into a museum. So people can enjoy visiting it, and offer a welcome stream of...ah... *revenue*. That way, everyone is happy."

"But where will you go?" asked Jadis, anxiously: "Won't you have any kind of base?"

"Of course I shall, my dear Jadis. I should like to move the... er... Holy See to my spiritual home. That's if you'll have me. *Super hanc petram aedificabo ecclesiam meam.* Or words to that effect."

"Oh, Domingo, you really are a very silly man," Jadis replied, closing her eyes once more and leaning against Jack: "you *know* the answer to that." As if hosting the Vatican at her kitchen table were the most natural thing in the world.

Much later still, Jadis rolled over and embraced Jack from behind. "Thank you for a wonderful birthday," she said, sleepily.

"Oh, I think you should thank Tom and Domingo for that," said Jack. "It was as much of a surprise to me as for you."

"No, not *them*," she said. "I wanted to thank you for my *present*."

"Eh? What was that?" They had long ago given up the habit of birthday presents.

"*This*," she said, pulling him round into her arms and kissing him, and when she'd finished, burying her head in his chest. They lay there, like that, for a long time, forging a link with eternity.

In a small room across the hall, Domingo rose and unpacked a leather satchel which until recently had bobbed by his side, on the flanks of the percheron. He spent some minutes in hopeless contemplation, and then knelt at his old oak *prie-dieu*. He prayed, first, for guidance.

Then, for strength.

And finally, with silent fervour, for forgiveness — for forgiveness in advance, for what he would do next.

For withdrawing from the leather satchel a wooden box lined with the deepest blue velvet; for opening it; for removing the brown and weathered skull roof packed within.

For grasping a handful of herbs and dried flowers from inside a pouch of soft cloth; for placing them with great care within the upturned skull.

For taking a lighted candle from his bedside and setting fire to the herbs. And as the smoke rose, for chanting words hardly heard for millennia, far more ancient than *Agnus Dei,* but having much the same intent.

Bless us, Holy One, All High. Who took up the sins of the world, *qui tollis peccata mundi.*

Chapter 3. Child

Lower Egypt, Earth, *c* 45,000 years ago

Something wicked this way comes.
William Shakespeare — *Macbeth*

Clouds don't look like that, Dogfinger thinks. "Green-Eye," he shouts. "Look at the clouds!"

His sister stands up. Green-Eye is taller than Dogfinger. Dogfinger has nine summers. He is still a boy and runs naked. Green-Eye is older than him. She has twelve summers and bleeds with Mother-the-Moon. She has worn clothes for a year. She says she hates her new tunic. She says it is scratchy. Ma says her tunic makes her look grown-up. Green-Eye tells Dogfinger that she doesn't want to grow up. Next year she will be married to Crow-Knees. She will be called Bride of Crow-Knees. The year after that she will have children of her own.

Crow-Knees is the brother of the Chief. Crow-Knees is a very old man, says Dogfinger. He has twenty-four summers. Twenty-four summers is *not* old, says Green-Eye. It *must* be old, says Dogfinger. Dogfinger cannot count as high as that. Twenty-four is more than all the wheatstalks in Pa's field. He knows. He tried counting them once. He lost count after sixteen.

Green-Eye is tall as a reed. She can stand up in the gully where they play. The gully runs from the village between two dry stubble-fields. Green-Eye's feet are in the mud at the bottom of the gully. Her toes dig into the ooze. The ooze is green and brown and squishy and warm. Her toes are dirty but her hands are clean. Green-Eye is so tall that her head is above the rim of the gully. Dogfinger is smaller than Green-Eye. He lies on his belly on the gully slope, peering over the edge. Green-Eye puts her hand to her face. She shields her eyes against Father-the-Sun. Dogfinger gets onto his hands and knees. He stands up on the gully slope. He jumps up and down. He points at the clouds. They are brown and dusty and close to the yellow land. That is not how clouds should be, Dogfinger thinks.

Green-Eye looks at the brown, low clouds. Green-Eye says one word. "Stoners."

"What are Stoners?" asks Dogfinger.

"Stoners are bad men," says Green-Eye. "They come to do bad things."

"How do you know, sister Green-Eye?"

"When we lie in bed," she says," I hear Ma and Pa. They talk of old things. About how Stoners used to come in the old days. Pa says Stoners are coming west again. Coming here, to the Great Delta. The land is dry. Stoners need food and water, like us."

"I remember! Stoners are demons! Grandma says so!"

"Grandma is right. But demons need to eat. We eat cows. Demons eat cows and people and crops and *everything*. Even the Earth itself. Stoners would eat Father-the-Sun and Mother-the-Moon and the stars, too, if they could. Stoners are locusts in the shape of men. Pa says we should move south, away from the Stoners. But Ma wants to stay in the village. Ma says she cannot walk far, because she is going to give us another brother or sister soon. Pa and Ma argue in the night."

"I've never heard them."

"That's because you're asleep. *And* you snore!"

"I don't!"

"*Do!*"

"Don't!"

"Do *too!*"

Green-Eye sticks out her tongue at Dogfinger. Dogfinger jumps down onto his sister. Dogfinger is small but he is strong. A hunting-dog bit off the little-finger on his left hand when he had only five summers. Dogfinger wanted to wrestle the hunting-dog. Before that he was called Eye-Patch, because of the brown birthmark round his left eye. Now he is called Dogfinger. He is very brave.

Dogfinger and Green-Eye roll down into the gully together. The children are covered in mud. They look at each other and point. They laugh. Then Green-Eye sits up. She looks hard at Dogfinger. Dogfinger sees her two eyes. One eye is brown. The other is green.

"Pa is right," she says. "We must leave the village. We must warn the people of the Stoners."

The children help each other to stand in the gully. The gully is slippery. They climb out. Sand sticks to the ooze on their bare feet. They stand on the edge of the gully. The brown cloud on the horizon looks closer now. Dogfinger and Green-Eye stare hard. They stare into the cloud. Dogfinger sees men like tiny gray dots, all moving. Dogfinger and Green-Eye listen hard.

Dogfinger hears the tramp, tramp, tramp of marching feet.

Dogfinger hears the clank, clank, clank of stone armor.

Dogfinger hears singing, in time with the marching feet.

"Green-Eye!" he says, "It sounds like Ma and Grandma and the other ladies. They sing, when they pound the grain." Green-Eye does not laugh. She tells Dogfinger to keep quiet. She tells Dogfinger to hold his breath. Several breaths pass. Dogfinger can feel his own heart beat.

"Stoners," she says. "I was right. This is an end to play, little brother."

"Aww, but you *said*..." he whines. Green-Eye turns and looks down at her brother. Green-Eye is not smiling any more. Green-Eye is not laughing. Green-Eye's face — one green eye, one brown — looks angry.

She looks like a grown-up.

"Dogfinger," she says, "this is important. We must run home, now." She starts to spring, like a young gazelle, long and lean and coltish. Dogfinger thinks she has returned to play. Dogfinger thinks that her angry face was only a game.

"Last one home is a baboon's bottom!" he cries, and launches himself forwards. But try as he might, Green-Eye, with her longer legs, is always in front.

Dogfinger's house is on the edge of the village. It is round. It has walls made of mud. The walls are very thick. Dogfinger helped Pa mend the walls in the spring. He loved the feeling of the mud and cow dung between his fingers as he squished it into the walls. Dogfinger's house has a roof made of reeds. Dogfinger helped Ma cut new reeds to fix the roof. He loved the feel of the pliant stalks between his fingers as he passed them to Ma. The house is warm in the cold winds of winter. It is cool now, in late summer, when Father-the-Sun is high, and the wheat has been cut. It is dry when the first rains of spring flood the land. Dogfinger loves his house. He was born there. He knows nowhere else. Dogfinger's house is the center of his world.

Green-Eye runs to the garden gate. The gate is made of thorn branches, in between two thick thorn hedges. Green-Eye waits for Dogfinger to catch up. Green-Eye bends over. Her hands are on her knees. Her straggly pale hair covers her brown face. She is panting hard for breath.

Green-Eye stands up. "Dogfinger," she says, "I must go into the house. I must tell Ma and Pa and our little brother and sisters that the Stoners are coming."

"What shall I do?" says Dogfinger.

"You must run into the village square," gasps Green-Eye. "Run as fast as you can, Dogfinger. Shout that the Stoners are coming. Shout for people to run away, into the fields. Shout for the Chief. Shout for Crow-Knees. Whatever you do, shout. Shout, as loud as you can!"

Dogfinger does not run. He does not shout. He stands, looking up at his sister. She looks angry again. He is confused. This is not a game any more. Dogfinger starts to cry. Green-Eye crouches down, so that she can look him in the eye. Green-Eye puts her hands on his shoulders. "Little brother," she says. "Now you have to be a big man. Be brave, like you were with the hunting-dog."

"A game?" he asks, "A game of 'Fierce Dogs'? Grrr!" He wrinkles up his nose. She laughs. He bares his teeth, like a fierce dog.

"A game. If you like," she says. "Go on, now." She stands up. "Well, what are you waiting for?" She smiles at him. He turns and runs into the village.

Dogfinger runs. He runs as hard as he can. He reaches the village square. The square is full of people. The people are running about, this way and that. They look frightened. He sees his cousin, Bride of Fish-Skin, carrying her new baby.

"The Stoners are coming!" he shouts. "The Stoners are coming!" Bride of Fish-Skin ignores him. She looks scared. Dogfinger sees Old One-Leg, hobbling on his crutch as fast as he can, a small animal-skin bag across his shoulders.

"The Stoners are coming!" Dogfinger shouts. "The Stoners are coming!" Old One-Leg doesn't notice Dogfinger. Dogfinger's voice dies in his throat. No matter how loudly he shouts, the villagers shout louder. He cannot be heard. He stands still, in the middle of the running people. All around is noise. The shouts of men. The screams of ladies. All around is smell. The smell of fear. The smell of burning straw. The houses beyond the village square are on fire. There is another smell, like roasting meat. Dogfinger is frightened. He starts to whimper. He wets himself with fright. Pee dribbles down the deep mud brown of his leg. It feels hot.

"What are you doing here, Dogfinger?" says a kindly voice. A fat lady looks down at him. It is Bride of Cattle-Egret. Dogfinger knows Bride of Cattle-Egret. She helps Ma pound the grain. Dogfinger looks up at Bride of Cattle-Egret. The lady bends down to him. She has a friendly, round face. Her round eyes look worried. Dogfinger can smell her fat arms and see the swell of her big warm bosoms swinging under her tunic. He thinks of his Ma. He starts to cry. Bride of Cattle-Egret starts to cry, too.

"Why are you crying, Bride of Cattle-Egret?" asks Dogfinger.

"Run home, little Dogfinger," she says.

"But my sister, Green-Eye," he says, "she told me to run here and warn the village. The Stoners are coming!"

"Sweet Dogfinger — you are too late," says Bride of Cattle-Egret. "Run home. Run home now!" Bride of Cattle-Egret squeezes his shoulders. She stands up, turns, and walks away. Dogfinger does not know where she is going. Bride of Cattle-Egret disappears into a haze of smoke. The smoke makes him cough. Dogfinger turns and runs back the way he has come.

The way home is not easy. The road is full of people, running, some this way, others that. He bumps into people.

"Watch where you're going," a man says. It is hard to see through the clouds of thick, gray smoke. Dogfinger trips over things. He stumbles.

He falls onto something soft. He does not know what it is. He struggles to get up, pushing with his hands. His hands slip on something hot and squishy. Dogfinger gets to his feet. He looks down. His hands and arms and the front of his body are covered in sticky red stuff.

It is blood.

He looks down. Dogfinger looks down, where he fell. It is a dead lady. She has no tunic. He does not know who the lady is, because she has no head. Her belly has been split open. He sees a tiny red child in her belly, and lots of gray squishy tubes, and lots of blood. Dogfinger feels giddy and sick. Dogfinger starts to run home, through the smoke. Dogfinger hopes he doesn't fall over again.

Dogfinger reaches the garden gate. He knows something is wrong. The thorn hedge is on fire. Dogfinger sees his house through the flames. The reeds of the roof are on fire. The mud walls are cracking in the heat. Dogfinger sees two big men go into the burning house. They are Stoners. Dogfinger stands in the street. The two Stoners come out again.

Dogfinger cannot move. Dogfinger thinks his feet have been stuck to the ground. Dogfinger cannot take his eyes from the door to his burning house. Dogfinger sees what happens, through a shifting curtain of flame. He hears the sizzle of burning reeds. He hears the crack of burning thorn branches.

The Stoners come out of Dogfinger's house. They wear helmets made of stone plates, sewn onto a kind of bonnet. They wear long tunics of gray, stone plates, like fish scales. They look like giant fish, with legs. They are laughing and shouting.

With one arm, one of the Stoners drags a man from the house. The man is struggling. It is Pa. Dogfinger wants to shout, but his voice has gone. All that comes out of his mouth is a dry rasp. In the crook of the

Stoner's other arm, Dogfinger sees his two baby sisters. They are twins. They have three summers. They are screaming, silently. Dogfinger cannot see his baby brother. The Stoner puts down the twins and hits Pa on the head. Pa goes limp.

The second Stoner comes out of Dogfinger's house. In one arm he holds Dogfinger's baby brother. Dogfinger loves playing with his baby brother. Dogfinger's baby brother is called Hoopoe, because of his crest of crazy hair. Hoopoe has just learned to walk.

In his other arm the second Stoner holds Green-Eye. The second Stoner makes Green-Eye watch as the first Stoner bashes the twins on the head. Blood spouts from their mouths and eyes. The first Stoner throws their bodies into the burning house.

Then the first Stoner makes Pa stand up, pinning his arms back. The first Stoner makes Pa watch as the second Stoner throws Hoopoe into the flames. Then the second Stoner takes a long flint knife and cuts off Green-Eye's tunic. Dogfinger can see her thin legs and the little points of her new bosoms. Dogfinger wonders why his Ma is not here.

The first Stoner makes Pa watch as the second Stoner lifts up his stone tunic, grabs Green-Eye by the hair and makes her bend over. Dogfinger does not understand what the Stoner is doing to Green-Eye. He knows that it is a Bad Thing. Then the second Stoner grabs Pa, so that the first Stoner can do the Bad Thing to Green-Eye.

Then the first Stoner takes some rope and ties Green-Eye's hands together. The first Stoner makes Green-Eye watch as the second Stoner takes a long flint knife in one hand, grabs Pa's tongue with the other, and cuts his tongue off. Then the second Stoner reaches under Pa's tunic and cuts off Pa's willy. The Second Stoner shoves Pa's willy into Pa's mouth. Then the Stoners make Green-Eye watch as the Stoners take turns doing the Bad Thing to Pa. After that, Dogfinger cannot clearly see what the Stoners are doing, because of all the blood, and the flames, and the smoke. But Dogfinger still cannot move. When the smoke clears, Dogfinger's house and his family are gone.

It is night. Dogfinger is lying down in the gully where he plays with Green-Eye. His arms and chest are crusted in blood. The smell of smoke is in his hair. The insides of his legs are slick with his own poo. His eyes and chest ache from breathing smoke. Dogfinger thinks he has woken from a bad dream. He wonders why it is dark.

Dogfinger wonders why Green-Eye does not come.

Chapter 4. Exile

Mount Carmel, Earth, *c.* 125,000 years ago

I have been faithful to thee, Cynara! In my fashion
Ernest Dowson—*Non Sum Qualis Eram Bonae Sub Regno Cynarae*

The party had begun to wind down, and Mr Khorare, suddenly bereft of duties or of need of attendance elsewhere—the Old King having retired to his chambers—took the opportunity offered by an open window onto the terrace to fulfil an urgent need for a lungful of fresh sea air. His most earnest wish, the desire of decades, had at last been granted, at least in principle. But whether it could be realized—ah, well, that was, as ever, a matter of adroit politics, as well as time. Mr Khorare was a master of both media, but that was of scant comfort.

The terrace was a vast expanse of creamy-white travertine fringed with a tastefully colonnaded rampart, jutting from a cliff, a hundred meters sheer over the Mediterranean Sea itself. Tasteful it should be, because he had devised it himself. The waves could be heard, a dim roar from far below. They could not be seen, however, except to one who wished to lean dangerously far out, over the parapet, and into empty space.

The giant castle—the palaces, stores, armories and the city itself, housing a greater part of the population of the Kingdom that Mr Khorare had served, faithfully, for precisely fifty years—towered even higher above the terrace; bastion on bastion, rampart on rampart, and extended eastwards and over and beneath and around the Mount Carmel massif for twenty unbroken square miles. The heart of the Kingdom Under The Mountain, easily the rival in size and sophistication of any city in the world, including—Mr Khorare had to admit—the now-fading memory of the Very Great and Ancient City of Axandragór, now lost, it seemed, beyond any hope of his seeing it again: given that the fulfilment of Mr Khorare's desires now lay in the opposite direction. Mr Khorare crossed the terrace and, resting a richly sleeved arm on the parapet, gazed across the western sea, over which the Moon was now setting, bathing the castle in a magical, pearly light.

I shall be following you soon, Sister Moon, he sang to himself.

It had taken this long, but, despite everything—despite early problems; despite many occasions when he'd narrowly escaped death; despite the frequent brutality of the Stoners themselves—this was a place he had come to love. Even though he must leave it, and soon. Now that he had contrived an interview with the Old King, albeit brief, before his patron abdicated in favor of his arrogant, unfeeling, belligerent son; before the King, may the Goddess forbid—died of old age or, as seemed increasingly likely, by intrigue, as a result of the impatience of the Crown Prince.

But what the King had actually *said*—well, that had been reassuring and breathtaking in like measure, and, Mr Khorare had to admit to himself, entirely characteristic of the wily old monarch he had served for so long.

Mr Khorare tried not to be torn in two—or in three—for in addition to the duties of his current home, and his pressing need to leave it, he still harbored a fond memory of the place whence he came. He was, in truth, the only one of his kind currently living here, and the only one generally known to most of the inhabitants. He longed for company. Even after all this time, he longed for news.

But that in the press of daily round he might occasionally forget his home and origins was brought to him forcefully earlier that very evening when, in his capacity as Chancellor of the Court of the King Under The Mountain, he had been introduced to one of the very rarely seen members of his own race. This was an emissary from his old home city, seeking permits and guarantees to trade in the Kingdom. Mr Khorare had been eager to interview the man who, like him, was—had been—a trader in fine textiles, and was looking for a market for his wares. That such a market now existed there was no doubt, but Mr Khorare found little solace, now, in the fact that there would have been none were it not for his own advice, his own intervention; his own careful work among the courtiers and the royal household over decades. Were Mr Khorare to have boasted that he'd civilized this Kingdom single-handed, he had ample justification for that claim.

Not that the emissary appreciated any of this. In fact, Mr Khorare found the visitor rude and uncouth, and concerned only with prices, tariffs and percentages, of which he talked loudly and brazenly even in the company of the nobility of the Kingdom, as if these grandees—many of them close friends of Mr Khorare—were servants or savages who might conveniently be regarded as invisible. The emissary had been a great disappointment, an embarrassment, even: Mr Khorare hoped that he himself had not been too much like that in his former life, but admitted to himself that perhaps, in some ways, he had. Mr Khorare buried his feelings of revulsion beneath his need to interview the trader and find out as much as he could about his old city. Perhaps, even, his family. His kits. His wife.

"The old place has become a bit of a hole, to be honest with you," the emissary had said, helping himself to more of Mr Khorare's private store of single malt: "the sea floods the Grand Plaza and most of the major thoroughfares at least twice a year. The sewage system can't hack it, so the whole place is slowly sinking in its own shit. Nobody actually *lives* in the City nowadays. Anyone—anyone of *consequence*, that is—has moved inland or into the Archipelago. The city itself is infested with pithekines and other riff-raff from the interior. In fact, just last year..."

Mr Khorare could no longer restrain himself. "Excuse me Sir, but in your... er... particular line of business, did you ever come across the House of Khorare?" The emissary looked at him blankly, at first, as if Mr Khorare had uttered a profanity in an unfamiliar language. But the wheels behind the emissary's blankly acquisitive, selachian eyes began to turn, and a memory stirred. Mr Khorare soon had cause to wonder whether nostalgia really was an emotion that should be indulged very often. Or at all.

"Khorare? Khorare? Ah yes, *Khorare*. I remember now," said the trader. "It was a scandal from my Father's time. Way back when, Khorare was the biggest and richest textile trader in the City. But he just disappeared—on a business trip, maybe, or just after a bit of stuff, *if* you know what I mean"—here the emissary leered and sniggered in a most unattractive fashion—"and was never heard from again. He'd never put his affairs in order, and the legal disputes dragged on for years. Eventually my father picked up the business for a song..."

"What happened to his family?"

"That's the best part of all. His wife was apparently a bit of a goer. Loved nothing more than banging away on a bit of illicit prong-o, and none too discriminating about what it was attached to. Khong, Yettins, Pithekines, even Floresians, if you can believe it: you name it, she opened her legs for it. As bad as her old man had been, or worse, to be honest with you, *if* you get my meaning. Been putting it around for years, she had, or so the stories went, when her old man was away.

"Well, when Khorare disappeared for good she went on a bit of a bender and made a biggish dent in her husband's fortune. Holed it below the waterline. When she was down to her last *zuzim* my Old Man picked up the Khorare palazzo for peanuts. He'd had the business anyway, so why not? She tried to claim tenancy but of course my Old Man was having none of it. He told me once that she came on to him, flashing her dugs at him, but by that time she was just a raddled old slapper, so he told her to sling her hook. Haven't a clue what happened to her after that, or her kits. Quite a brood, apparently, and evidently not all of what you might call provenanced parentage, *if* you take my meaning.

"Of course, what with the way things were going, the Old Man soon had to sell the old heap on—he got out just before the excrement well and truly hit the proverbial ventilator in the property market, *if* you take my meaning—so I expect the old palazzo is crumbling into the or-*dure* even as we speak, with five pithekine families fouling every room and swinging from the rusty old chandeliers. Nice whisky this, I have to say, Your Excellency. Can't say I've tasted better. Cheers!"

Mr Khorare had given the emissary the rest of the bottle, left instructions for him to be accommodated, and returned to the party, keen to assuage his conflicting thoughts and surges of emotion—his frank revulsion—by dint of assiduous and correct adherence to service and protocol. It was not as if he could afford to be on anything other than his best form. The party was, after all, given in his own honor: a half-century of service to the Kingdom was rare, even unprecedented. Not a few palace staffers, however, wondered whether Chancellor Khorare was enjoying himself, however, given the unwonted sharpness of his tongue.

Mr Khorare returned to the Grand Ballroom just in time, mere seconds before the sinus-jarring bray of auroch-horn trumpets that announced the imminent arrival of His Majesty, Hrothgar the Hideous, King Under The Mountain, Hammer of the West, God-Emperor of the Sunset Seas and so on and so forth in like fashion, and Mr Khorare's oldest and best friend. Mr Khorare was at the edge of the crowd when the royal palanquin appeared, a massive cedar-trunk and mammoth-ivory construction, borne by eight huge Yettin eunuchs, upon which was mounted, rather in the manner of a carnival float, the necessarily capacious and reinforced throne bearing the corpulent figure of the Old King himself.

Hrothgar appeared to be clothed in a suit of ill-fitting, ill-tanned leather. Either that, or he was naked, and the crumpled and hairy skin was his own. Mr Khorare was debating the matter with himself when a third option occurred to him—that His Majesty might have been availing himself of the latest Stoner fashion, led by the Crown Prince Hygelak and his circle, namely clothes sewn of the pelts of the people that Stoners called 'Thinskins'.

The Thinskins were a hominin race, primitive and as yet rather rare, that had recently appeared on the south-western, aethiopic fringes of the Kingdom. Taller but more slender than Stoners, the tenderness of Thinskin flesh, it was reputed, more than compensated for their weakness in battle: their skins, being almost hairless, were easy to tan and made marvelously supple leather. The scarcity of Thinskins in general made them highly prized as delicacies and out of reach of all but the wealthiest Stoner nobility. It was the *female* Thinskins, it was again reputed, that were especially succulent, most particularly in the thigh, rump and loin, and gave the best skins, being even smoother than the skins of the males.

At least, after they were dead.

When they were alive, it was said, by those in-the-know, they gave excellent sport, if one could put up with the screaming, but there were — again, it was said — ways round that.

But no, reasoned Mr Khorare — if the King were wearing a Thinskin pelt, it was a singularly bad one, not like the smooth finery of the Crown Prince Hygelak, lately aped by the fashionable. Hrothgar tolerated the current vogue for Thinskin flesh, but without bestowing openly royal favor on it. "Frankly, Khorare," he'd once said, "it's a little too insipid for our taste. Give us a well-hung haunch of bison any day, what?"

When the Crown Prince Hygelak came into his own — well, the Thinskins in the Kingdom and for hundreds of miles around would soon be hunted to extinction. No, Mr Khorare reasoned — the Old King was naked as the day he was born, a fact that became alarmingly apparent when the eight enormous Yettins stooped, lowered the palanquin to the flagged floor of the ballroom, and the King rose from his throne. All eyes were averted, all heads were bowed, all bodies were prostrated on the floor, as the King puffed and wobbled his way through the parting, shuffling crowd, towards where Mr Khorare stood, head bowed.

Mr Khorare's first view of his sovereign was of a pair of very large and hairy feet. A hand under his chin forced him to stand, to raise his gaze, over the knobbly royal knees; the flabby royal thighs; the royal nether regions (happily buried in several folds of the royal spare tire); the gigantic royal belly itself; the floppy-breasted royal barrel-chest; the royal bull-neck; the royal multiple chins; and, finally, the scarred and twisted royal visage itself. "Frankly, Khorare," said the King, in a quiet voice from a grizzled face, whose principal features were the wicked glint of eyes from within a sea of scarred skin and knotted muscle, the bright but tiny sparks separated by a truly monumental nose, "what's the point of wearing anything at all if our subjects don't even dare look at us, eh? Might as well go around in the buff, what?"

"Quite so, Your Majesty," said Mr Khorare.

"Fifty years, what?" The royal grip on Mr Khorare's chin was firm, despite the pudginess of the hand exercising it. "Seems like only yesterday when we picked you up after that little fracas with the Yettins in our Mesopotamian dependencies, what?"

It did seem like only yesterday when the then Crown Prince, dismounting from his coelodont, rounded him up on that remote hillside. Mr Khorare had expected to be spitted on the spot, or, if not then, later. But no—Mr Khorare had been treated as a long-lost friend, or, at least, a visitor long expected. He still remembered riding in the royal column of troopers mounted on coelodonts, rumbling in stately fashion along the ever-more populated westward roads through the seemingly endless savannah that was Mesopotamia, passing column after column of chained Yettins, and slaves and beasts of many other species, until his eyes were greeted by that unforgettable sight, that incredible silhouette—the pinnacles of the Kingdom Under The Mountain itself, raised sharp and shadowy against the sun, setting over the Mediterranean Sea. He remembered, too, his sharp intake of breath at the sight, and the then Crown Prince's voice, so close: "welcome home, Mr Khorare. Welcome home."

Mr Khorare had long puzzled over the nature of his welcome—that the King (as he soon became) had found him and brought him home as a treasured prize, a wise counselor, and not as a slave or—as was so often the case—live meat, on the hoof. He had his suspicions, though, but these were never articulated, the result being that he'd spent five decades watching his back, waiting for the shift in royal politics that would see his inexplicable good fortune evaporate as snow in summer, culminating with the sudden knife in the guts. But it never had, and now, fifty years had passed as if in the wink of an eye, and here his sovereign stood before him, once again.

"Yes, Sire," said Mr Khorare. "It does seem like only yesterday."

"I expect you've wondered, Khorare, about the reason for your singular run of survival," the King continued—not relaxing his iron grip on Khorare's chin for an instant, "when so many of your colleagues have ended up as eyeball-and-testicle soup?"

"Sire?" Mr Khorare felt his knees go numb, and his heart swap places with his stomach. Perhaps his run of luck was now up: he had outlived his usefulness and must accept his fate.

"Take heart, Khorare." Said the King. "We were led to you through some good fortune of our own. The same place where we still get that excellent single malt. Need we say more?" Khorare was flustered, and felt his face redden. The King shook it, and roared with laughter. "*Nice legs*, eh? Nice *Thinskin* legs? With us now?"

And then Khorare remembered the remote reed-cutter's hut, and the remarkable divine being that inhabited it—the same being who had, it seemed, governed his life, his journey. The Genie of the Talisman—the amulet he still wore, close to his chest. She had, it seemed, been looking out for him in more ways than he had suspected. He allowed himself the narrowest of smiles. He did not dare, however, to wink.

"Nice legs. Indeed, Sire," Mr Khorare agreed. "Very nice indeed."

The King released Khorare's chin with a flourish and looked straight into his Chancellor's almond-shaped, yellow-green eyes. The two men were evenly matched in height, for all that the King weighed more than twice as much. The King's voice dropped, so that what he said next could not be heard by anyone except the two figures, standing in the eye of the still-prostrated crowd.

"We should offer you a gift, for your service, Khorare," said the King, "and something—*someone*—tells us that it should be more than the customary removal of non-essential body parts, or speedy passage to the life beyond. What, then, Khorare, is your desire?" The moment had come. Khorare found that his mouth had turned to sandpaper. Somehow, from some deep reserve, he found the words—the resource—to continue. He swallowed.

"Your Majesty is most kind," he said. "Should your Majesty wish to release me from my long service, then my desire—my most *earnest* desire—is to continue on the westward journey in which I was engaged on the occasion of my very first and propitious meeting with Your Majesty. On that day that seems like only yesterday." Mr Khorare bowed his head, hoping that he had not overstepped the mark. Even after all this time, he never really knew quite how he stood with this shrewd, intelligent Stoner emperor. Hrothgar had the knack of keeping everyone guessing, of divide-and-rule, and this had been the key to a long reign, coextensive with Mr Khorare's own position as the King's most trusted advisor. But Khorare had the sense that Hrothgar, too, felt that his time was nearing its end, an instinct that prompted him to be more forthright in his request than he might otherwise have been.

The eyes of the King Under The Mountain, when he chose to loose their gaze from the folds of his face, were huge and round, each one a

deep brown well of unguessable wisdom and sorrow. After a long interval, in which Mr Khorare felt that he might be swallowed in their peaty
depths, the King spoke.

"Your wish is granted, old friend. And if things are going the way
they're going, you'd better get on with it."

Mr Khorare had had many opportunities to review this scene in his
mind in the weeks that followed. He was doing so now, aching with nostalgia and regret, standing on the deck of the small but perfectly formed
sloop *Exile on Main Street*, the boat he'd commissioned with the full
(though discreet) support of the Old King, as it approached the coast of
the country the Captain assured him was Rhoneland.

"Goddess, I wish I was coming with you, but *someone* has to hold the
fort. Literally, what?" the King had laughed, reviewing the final plans
for the boat with Mr Khorare and deciding on its name. *Chantilly Lace*
and *Paint It Black* had been rejected as being too enigmatic; *Lady Jane* and
Ruby Tuesday, too explicit. Mr Khorare had, however, been able to compliment the King on his inventive choice of names, the origin of which
the King had been unable to explain clearly.

The talisman hanging at his chest appeared to throb with life as he
neared his destination. This was sufficient assurance, thought Mr Khorare, that his path was the correct one, though precisely how or why this
should be he was at a loss to articulate, still less, understand. He'd had
many debates with the Captain of the *Exile* about this, now so long ago.
But now, he knew, all arguments were settled, all debates resolved.
There were tears in his eyes as the coast before them resolved from a thin
line into a shore bustling with gulls and small boats. Tears of joy, tears of
gratitude for the generosity of the patron he'd left behind, and whom
he'd never had a proper opportunity to thank. The King had intended to
come down to the dock at Caesarea for a final supper aboard the *Exile*, to
toast it on its way, but he had failed to arrive. Just before they weighed
anchor, a crewman told Mr Khorare that they should make haste: a battle
was raging in the Castle, between the King's guards and those loyal to
the Crown Prince. There was even a rumor that the King had fallen.

A pilot and customs-yacht drew alongside. Formalities were quickly
completed, and the pilot bade Mr Khorare welcome to the Port of Massilia.

Had Mr Khorare had any expectations at all of the port and city of
Massilia, they should easily have been exceeded within the first few minutes of his arrival.

It was stunning.

As the *Exile on Main Street* tip-toed into the yacht basin, Mr Khorare at the prow, all he could do was stare outwards, jaw agape in frank wonderment—outwards, and also upwards. The boat was dwarfed by the vastness of the ships that crowded in around it, so that the little sloop had to bob and tack round the floating behemoths, the pilot and the captain in frequent conclave, leaving Mr Khorare with nothing to do but stand and stare. There were ironclads, four funnels apiece, blue with hugeness in the ocean haze. There were luxury liners, even greater, each one an immense city afloat. There were elegant three-masted clippers and schooners. All were served by bustling quaysides crowded with passengers and baggage offloaded, and loaded again, and gantries, and cranes, and stevedores, and touts, and hawkers, the throng of them all like tiny black ants against the ships they served.

There were paddle-steamers, too, the sight of which drew Mr Khorare to the rail more than once, his hands clenching and unclenching as he forced a memory to emerge, as a bird from a long-dormant egg. He had sailed on some such boat, he thought, from the Great and Ancient City of Axandragór—now more myth than memory, as if it had been a tale told by someone else, a nameless traveler at a roadside inn, lost in the darkness of immeasurable time. But the talisman still throbbed—no, it *ached*—against the skin of his chest.

More impressive than the busy flotilla by far was the city itself that surrounded it: a ring of towers, each a sharp, extended pyramid of stone and metal and glass, twenty—no, thirty, no (Mr Khorare counted the ranks of bronzed windows upwards, with mounting incredulity)—an amazing *forty* stories tall, or even more. Nothing—not the lost memory of decadent Axandragór; not the recent recollection of the sprawling ramparts of the Kingdom Under The Mountain—nothing had prepared him for this. Mr Khorare felt his hands, tight around the rail, go numb.

"Yes, it's quite something, Your Excellency" said the barrel-chested Stoner pilot, urgent at his elbow.

"Yes," Mr Khorare croaked, his throat quite dry. "It is," and went below.

Once in the city itself, Mr Khorare, who had no shortage of funds at his disposal, paid off the *Exile*'s crew and bade them good speed homewards, and set out to find suitable accommodation. His first lodging was a spacious suite in a grand old hotel, two blocks back from the waterfront. He stayed there for more than a month, during which time he found himself up against two momentous questions that had been advancing towards him, like a slow tide, for what seemed like his whole life. They now faced him like a cresting wave. Where was he going? And why?

He suspected that his destination lay somewhere in this country, somewhere in Rhoneland, but the closer he approached the question, the more elusive it seemed. The talisman burned and tugged at his throat, insistent. Clearly, his quarry was near — but what was it? Would he know it when he saw it?

And if he did — what then?

Nights found Mr Khorare in his suite, clothes and the remains of meals scattered around him in uncharacteristic disarray, staring at the talisman, desperate for resolutions to all these questions. But no inspiration came. Days found him in more positive, constructive mood, exploring the environs of the old hotel, during which expeditions he found a real-estate agent keen to show the well-heeled foreigner a wide selection of prestige apartments that might be made available for his use on a long lease. Until he stumbled on the answers to his problems — answers which would no doubt obtrude themselves randomly on his consciousness, in their own time, and which were, therefore, not subject to timetables or schedules — he might as well make himself comfortable in this unendingly marvelous city.

And so an apartment was procured. Once he had moved in, Mr Khorare ascribed the fact that it was the penthouse on the thirty-seventh floor of one of the city's tallest pyramids to some kind of reaction, first, to the often subterrene life of the Kingdom Under The Mountain — and possibly even to the low-rise sprawl of Axandragór before that. But no, he thought. There was more to it than that. The apartment was no mere cave perched high on a cliff. It had all the most modern amenities — flushing water closets; gas-mantles for lighting and even cooking; a speaking-tube to alert the concierge on the ground floor; and even a pneumatic tube port that could be used to direct capsules of mail to the building's mail-room and thence anywhere in Rhoneland — a country, he was to learn, of remarkable cultural refinement, as well as geographic extent. In addition, Mr Khorare was thrilled to discover that a team of servants was at his disposal. Cooks, valets and footmen were there to fulfil his every requirement. There was even a chauffeur to conduct the steam-powered *barouche* housed in the underground garage, on call twenty-four hours a day, at his own, exclusive disposal.

Mr Khorare lost no time having the apartment redecorated to his own, exacting tastes, as well as finding outfitters whose skill and sense of adventure would equal his own. All this activity entailed many trips in the *barouche*, criss-crossing the entire extent of the vast city. In the course of which he made many friends, and thanks to his own diplomatic skill, as well as the exoticism of his race, and (he was not so naïve not to have realized) his seemingly bottomless purse (which he increased still further through shrewd investments directed by a business contact of his tailor), he soon became tolerably well-known among the Stoner cognoscenti of Massilia as a connoisseur, an arbiter of taste.

How different it all seemed from the Kingdom Under The Mountain! Where there was once surly resistance to his esthetic ideas, there was now fascination, followed by acceptance; where there were once conversations conducted in monosyllables, there was voluble intercourse; where there was once the ever-present threat of severe, physical sanction, there was, it seemed, perfect amity and freedom. The clothes, his new friends, his *salon*, his trips to the theater, the opera, to concerts and to galleries—Mr Khorare loved it all. He had many causes to give thanks to the Goddess, or to Fate, and—in those rare moments of dyspeptic discontent—to imagine that after all these years of exile in a barbarous Kingdom, he deserved it.

Being the cosmopolitan soul that he was—and, perhaps, because his mind was forever engaged in the consideration of stuffs, and silks, and fine wallpapers and porcelain, it took him a while to realize that whereas the citizens of Massilia were, beneath their fine words and accoutrements, Stoners little different from the warriors and pirates he'd known for most of his life, their servants (one would never be so *gauche* as to have called them *slaves*) were of a different race entirely—taller than the Stoners, or indeed himself, with relatively flat, hairless ebony-black faces, and a slender carriage of dignified erectness. It took him a long time to realize that he knew this race well, but he made the connection very suddenly, as if from nothing, late one night after a house-party as he was dismissing his butler, Raull, for the night.

By that time—he had been living in his apartment for almost a year—he had come to know Raull very well. Raull had been his companion on many shopping expeditions; his guide to the Massilian social scene; his bulwark against social solecism; his sounding board; his inexhaustible fund of knowledge; and his *confidant*.

"Thinskins!" he found himself uttering—exclaiming, really, entirely without volition. He sat down, confused and embarrassed. Raull was at the door to the grand salon, on his way to his own quarters. He turned.

"Sir? Y'm'tokkin'?"

Mr Khorare had yet to surmount his occasional incomprehension of the fluidity of the Massilian vernacular, so much more freely flowing than what he now realized were the antique cadences of the language spoken in the Kingdom Under The Mountain; clipped and courtly, of a formality that belied the savagery beneath.

"Yes, Raull—I mean, no. Not really. Oh... What *do* I mean?" Raull hovered in the doorway even as his master wavered on the threshold of decision. "No, Raull—think nothing of it. You may go. Good-night!"

"G'night, Sir, m'tank'a." And he was gone.

How different Raull seemed, how they *all* seemed: his stolid cook, his elegant footman, his chauffeur, the pretty young scullery maids, the concierge so many floors below—from the creatures which, in the Kingdom Under The Mountain, were treated as pack animals, as vehicles for the most depraved sport, and thereafter, as the choicest meats, and—he gasped to think of it now—high-fashion leather. For a split second he looked at Raull, his poised, exquisitely mannered, refined and cultured Raull, and saw a flayed and butchered carcass. The thought made him recoil, shuddering. Had his long sojourn in the Kingdom Under The Mountain corrupted his sensibilities to such a hideous degree? Yet Raull was a Thinskin for all that, as were all his other servants. He resolved to discover all he could about Thinskins—their origins, their natural history, their habits, their dreams, their beliefs, their aspirations. He felt, all of a sudden, that this should be something like his mission. But he didn't have a clue where to start, and, somehow, he knew, this wasn't a topic suitable for discussion with one's servants. So, what with one thing and another, he put it out of his mind and carried on much as before.

It wasn't until many more months had passed, and Mr Khorare was returning from the first-night party of an experimental play at his favorite theater—a play that he found only moderately entertaining, for all that he'd partly funded the production and advised on the costumes and set design—that the subject came up again. Having dismissed his chauffeur and the steam-*barouche*, he wafted, slightly intoxicated, kaftan flowing, through the grand doors of the building and nodded a brief (if sincerely meant) greeting to the concierge. Now, normally, he'd have expected no more than a mumbled good-night in return—the hour was late, after all—but the response on this occasion pulled him up sharply.

"Haraddzjin Khorare of the Very Great and Ancient City of Axandragór!" the concierge said. "What are *you* still doing here?" Khorare turned round and stared at the concierge, from whose lips this startlingly stentorian ejaculation seemed to have emerged.

"I beg your pardon?"

"It's a fair question, isn't it?"

"It's... *what*?" The concierge fixed him a round-eyed, Thinskin stare. He noticed that she wasn't the usual concierge, but a much younger person, a female, presumably from the night-staff. He couldn't remember having seen her before. Mr Khorare noticed three further oddities. First, that her skin was pale, like a Stoner's, rather than the usual thinskin black. Second, that whereas custom dictated that all servants, whether male or female, had shaven heads, this duty concierge had an abundance of long, black hair that flowed from her head, down her back, and even over her face, like an impudent waterfall. Third, that she spoke in the same archaic language as he did, himself. Nothing like the protean speech affected by Massilians of all classes. Perhaps she was new in town and hadn't become accustomed to it. Mr Khorare decided that a diplomatic approach was best. It was, after all, what he was good at. He turned towards the concierge's desk and proffered a hand.

"I don't think we've met. I'm Mr Khorare. Penthouse suite. And you are... Miss....?"

"I know perfectly well who you are, thank you," the concierge said. "I've just told you, haven't I? And if you haven't worked out who *I* am by now, it hardly matters. But time is short, Khorare, and yet here you are! Going to plays, having parties, deciding in earnest tones the height of next season's hemlines, and generally fannying about, when evolution waits for no man. Not even you. To be quite honest, I'm disappointed. Yes, *disappointed*." Mr Khorare stared at her, open-mouthed. The concierge looked down, suddenly embarrassed, so that her hair completely covered her face. But, recovering her composure somewhat, she looked up again, raising her arms and pulling the hair away from her face, as if they were theater curtains.

"I'm sorry," she said, flushing and looking at him once again, her eyes full of beseeching sympathy where before they had been all diamond hardness. "Got a bit carried away." She stood up and, deferentially, indicated a door behind her. "Would Sir like to come into my office? What we need," she said, turning, "is a drink."

Of all the surprising things that were to happen that night, perhaps the most surprising of all was the drink he was offered — a malt scotch as medicinally peaty as anything he'd left behind in the Kingdom Under The Mountain. He'd always regretted not bringing any with him on the *Exile* — an abstinence borne of a desire, possibly misplaced, to look only to the future.

He took the drink from the concierge's hand — pale and slim, in which he could feel every knuckle and sinew, but clothed with skin as soft as a pelt — he took just one, tiny sip, and... without really knowing how... the small, cluttered cubbyhole of an office... hardly bigger than a closet... had grown, spread out, *whitened*... into a vast, wood-paneled *salon* with two button-backed leather sofas and a matching chair (in which he was seated) facing a fire in a gray stone fireplace... and a view of snowy mountains, up close... just like... just like he saw... just like he saw when...

He took a longer draught. It seared the back of his throat. He coughed. Laughter came from the sofa ahead of him and to his left, the figure silhouetted by the snow-blinding panorama behind.

"The reed-cutter... you... how?"

"Took you a while to catch on, didn't it?" she said. "Honestly, I've had to deal with some silly men in my time, and you are, without doubt, one of the silliest. But never mind. The project is almost complete, and you have only one more thing to do. Only one. Even if it's taking you several lifetimes." Mr Khorare felt ashamed, and confused, on account of not being quite sure why he should be ashamed, and these emotions together fuelled a mild resentment which he did his consummate best to conceal.

"My apologies," he said, "but I hardly thought of you in years — decades."

"Evidently." She sat back. He still could not see her face.

"The talisman?"

"He shoots — he scores!" She sat up. He could make out a penumbra of loosened hair like a halo, and her questing hands, each trying vainly to rein it in. "At last!"

Silence fell between them. Mr Khorare did not know what, if anything, he should say, and the duty concierge did nothing to help him (he could not help but think of her in this way — what else could he do?) But the wheels of his mind turned, silently, bringing images to him of the naked, wrinkled skin of the King Under The Mountain; the leather suits affected by the Crown Prince; his loyal butler, Raull (who'd be waiting up until his master's return); the abundant, nut-brown cleavages of the scullery-maids as they bent down to tend the fire, or sweep the floor; and, thence, of a resolution — wilfully neglected, he realized, by dint of the constant distractions of a life spent in dedicated pursuit of the superficial. He leaned forwards in his chair, cradling the scotch in both hands. He felt the chill of the heavy tumbler even as the tang of the vapors furled around his nostrils.

"Thinskins..."

"Hmm...?"

"I was to have found out about them. But I'm still not entirely sure how. Let alone why. And perhaps—well, perhaps that's why I... well, I admit it, I wanted to, but never got round to it."

"The road to hell, they say, is paved with good intentions. But your curiosity, Khorare, is commendable. After all, it's only natural for a person to take a keen interest in their creations."

"My... creations?"

"Don't look so surprised, Khorare. Here you are, thinking that your contribution to the well-being of the world has been to clothe it with ever greater refinement and taste, when what you have actually done is create a race of living beings of a beauty and elegance that only someone like you can confer. Being one of them myself—at least, some of the time—I can only offer my humble thanks, my undying, eternal—"

Khorare stood up. Whisky sloshed onto the floor. "Now look here, whoever you are, this is preposterous! What..."

"Sit *down*, Khorare," she said, with commanding firmness. He was gripped by invisible arms, gentle yet immeasurably strong, that pressed him down into his chair. "Time to talk turkey. Don't you remember anything, Khorare? The mouth of that shark that tore you to pieces? And how you woke up in the marshes, miraculously pieced together? All the King's Coelodonts, and all the King's Men?"

Khorare spoke with difficulty. "Yes... I remember."

"Good. That's a start. Well then, what follows, logically, from that wholly remarkable occurrence?" Thoughts swam in Khorare's mind: they bounced and leaped, breaking the hitherto untarnished sheen of his consciousness. Painful thoughts, of his youth, his father, his wife... and thoughts he could have sworn weren't his own, but framed in the minds of his father, and his grandfather, and back, and back, and a long journey, and a cave, and great cities he'd never seen, and hermitages in the desert, and creatures from out of the clouds, and a long, silvery thread stretching, taut, into the sky, and a quayside at night, and a woman walking towards him, a woman who looked remarkably like...

"Well, I'm blowed."

Another pause, longer, while his thoughts settled back into their usual equanimity. While his eyes could re-focus.

"But what have Thinskins got to do with all this?" he asked. "With any of this?" The sun went behind a cloud for a spell, so he could see a shadow of her face, her glinting eyes. She was leaning forwards, now, chin in hands, elbows on knees. She wore faded denim trousers and a huge, shapeless hand-knitted jersey that might once have been a mildly offensive shade of purple. Her feet were bare. He had the impression that she was one of those lucky people who could get away with wearing combinations of clothes that would have looked ridiculous on anyone else. He remembered models like that, in his fashion house. He wondered, idly, what she looked like naked, and wondered—less idly—why such lubricious thoughts had long ceased to cross his mind. It was then, only then, that he appreciated how old he was. Far older, he realized, than people of his race were accustomed to live—and yet he felt in the peak of health. Clearly, he was being kept—maintained—for a purpose. For as long as it took.

"The Thinskins," she said, waving a recalcitrant wisp from her face, "have everything to do with it. You could say that they are what—all this—is all about." She spread her arms wide, to indicate the tastefully spare salon, the furniture, the wooden floor, the panorama beyond.

"You—we—need them for a task, a great task that still lies some way off, in your subjective future. But they might not have existed at all, had you not become, to all intents and purposes, immortal. That's something that distorts the continuum like anything, especially for baryonic matter, just for starters. You wouldn't believe how much thermodynamic finagling I—we—have had to do to achieve that, not to mention the..."

Most of this passed straight over Mr Khorare's head: the one word that remained, reverberating around the inside of his skull, was—

"Immortal? Me?"

"Honestly, Khorare, how much persuasion do you need?"

"Well, I guess... but for how long?"

"How long has this been going on? No time at all. Or about fifty million years, give or take. Does it matter? The fact is, that without the many tiny things you've done in your infinitely extensible life—most so tiny you won't have realized their significance—Thinskins might not have evolved at all. Or turned out differently."

"Things? What kind of things?"

"Random acts of kindness, mostly. It's a brutal world out there. It doesn't need much to make a difference."

Another long pause. Fifty million years? He couldn't conceive of such an interval of time. He certainly couldn't remember having lived through it all. Perhaps that lack of memory was crucial—he wondered if to remember even a tiny fraction of such a long life would weigh one down into a kind of immobility. Such a power of recall—it would, indeed, be disabling. However, even with such desperate rationalizations going on in his head — really, a kind of damage limitation — Mr Khorare had the distinct sensation that he had become disembodied, and was floating among the rafters, looking down at them both. Deep down, he knew — he must have known — that he could not die. The whole shark incident was evidence enough for that. But when evidence is put before your eyes that is at once so stark, and so outrageous, you tend to put it out of your mind, put it beyond thought.

But something else now occurred to him: that perhaps he owed his long life at the court of the Kingdom Under The Mountain to that assumption of immortality, that whatever might befall him in the service of that bloody throne, whatever pains he might be forced to endure, he would always have come back. Looking back at the decisions he made, at their occasional recklessness (cloaked, always, in diplomatic niceties), he wondered whether that security had given him a confidence that he might otherwise have lacked. And that was, he reasoned, a reassuring thought. It was high time, then, to attend to the matter in hand.

"This... task," he began, "this task that the Thinskins have been appointed to perform. What is it?"

"Never mind," she snapped back. "You don't need to know."

"But..." He bit his lip. There was something in her answer, in its harsh alacrity, which troubled him. But if his long life as a courtier had taught him anything, however, it was that there were no such things as problems. There were only... opportunities.

He was in.

"I don't think you know it yourself, do you?" he asked. He smiled, sat back, and took another sip of the whisky, warmed in his hands.

"I do!" she protested, sitting up sharply. "Or... or at least, I *did*. I'm *sure* I did." Her owlish eyes dulled, then, as if she had turned her sight inwards, inquiring of some deep, inner resource. The moment, however, was fleeting. Swiftly, she gathered her composure, so that Mr Khorare was now no longer sure whether he'd really hit on something, or if the concierge was engaging in an elaborate game of double-bluff. "Anyway," she continued, "there's probably a benefit in *not* knowing certain things. Anticipation of some things might throw the game, and that could be disastrous, at this stage. I've this feeling... just a feeling... that when the time comes for this task to be performed, I'll fly right in there, blind, which sounds scary. Heavens, it *is* scary. But there's such a thing as rushing in where angels fear to tread. But in reverse, so to speak. But anyway, where were we?" She looked up at him, staring directly into his eyes, as if all the foregoing had been a soliloquy.

"Whatever the Thinskins are meant to do, *you* have only one more thing you need to achieve. Just one, but it is of crucial importance. You must *not* get it wrong. Now, listen carefully..."

The world swam. Universes collided, coalesced, pulled apart. He awoke on the *chaise-longue* in his own salon. The million tiny lights of a brilliant evening cityscape shone up at him through the picture windows. He must have just dismissed Raull for the night: his peripheral vision caught the sight of a disappearing foot and a closing door. He could remember nothing of how he'd arrived home—nothing at all, after bidding his chauffeur good-night. Perhaps he'd taken that same elevator journey so often, he thought, that it had become no more than a spinal reflex. That, and the well-rehearsed evening pleasantries customary between master and butler, at close of day.

No wonder.

What was more puzzling was that he could not recall the thoughts with which he had evidently been preoccupied, to the exclusion of all else. If he was certain of anything, though, it was of an impending change in the weather. He started to make plans to leave.

He soon became so engrossed in his arrangements that he failed to notice the fading taste of single malt whisky on his tongue.

Chapter 5. Astrometer

Cambridge, England, Earth, Spring, 2073

If the laws of the Universe are kind, they will never be found.
H. P. Lovecraft—*The Shadow Out Of Time*

The Yahoo cruised uncaring above the woes of the world, looking instead upwards, at the stars, as it had done for many years beyond its scheduled expiry date. It mapped, and patiently, it recorded. Doppler wobbles of distant suns, each suggestive of a planetary system. And, by focusing its well-spaced and extraordinarily acute eyes, it took pictures of the planets circling other, closer primaries. Each one vague, suggestive and pixellated, but planets nonetheless: each another, distant Earth.

Twenty years earlier, it had been the capitalized, acromymized YA-HOO, the Yerkes Automatic Heliospheric Optical Observatory. Such is the hubris of scientists that this was now generally unremembered, and the YAHOO was now just Yahoo. It—or rather *they*, being a matched pair of identical spacecraft—had been launched on a pair of giant Ariane XV boosters from French Guiana in 2050. Although a combined NASA-European initiative, most of the mission specialists had been based at the Merlin Technologies Astrometry Institute on the old Madingley Road just outside Cambridge, and received feeds directly from the twin spacecraft, placed at widely separated Lagrange points in the Earth's orbit, coordinated to act as one gigantic interferometer, a single telescope mirror more than a hundred million miles across—capable of detecting planets the size of the Earth around nearby stars.

Four years later the Plague struck, sweeping away most of the engineers who had built the spacecraft and the scientists who had hoped to profit from the resulting data. And yet on the mission as a whole, the Plague had had remarkably little effect. Apart from a blip in the late summer of 2054—the Plague Year itself—data streaming down from the spacecraft were routinely received and managed.

Only the personnel had changed.

Over the years, most of the scientists had been quietly replaced, as they had left or died, by others equally capable, but who were, in addition, members of the Order of Saint Adelard. Long before, the Yahoo had attracted the close personal attention of the man who would one day become Pope Eusebius II. So even had he not wanted to visit Tom in

Cambridge from time to time, Domingo would have had ample reason to have called on his faithful band of astrometers.

He was doing so now. Thanks to the ministrations of the Chief Astrometer and his colleagues, Yahoo's image-enhancement software had been upgraded to allow not just the detection, but the rough mapping of Earthlike planets out to several dozens of light years, together with spectroscopic detection of atmospheric constituents, including — potentially — oxygen and water, the signs of life.

This raised a number of theological problems for the Pope, who suddenly realized that his own staff was in real danger of discovering life elsewhere in the Universe. To document the Lord's Creation was in itself a laudable aim. But Domingo had yet to work out a formal response to the discovery of alien beings, and was as yet unready to answer even the most obvious challenges that his flock would face were alien life actually discovered. Consider:

Would Christ have died for the unknown but possibly repellent residents of (say) Epsilon Eridani Three?

Would death and resurrection mean anything at all to any immortal hive-minds that might dwell on Canopus Six?

Would any evanescent plasma beings that just happened to be floating around Zeta Cancri even *require* salvation?

After many hours of prayer, thought and consultation, Domingo came to realize that the situation was just *Undique humanitas* all over again. It had been hard enough to convince *Homo sapiens* that other hominids were as deserving of Divine love as humans themselves. Now the tables had been turned, and, if anything, the hominids tended to be narrower and more prejudiced than humans had been. So how would the world react were he to stretch *Undique humanitas* to encompass any intelligent life in the cosmos?

He realized, tentatively at first and then with greater enthusiasm, that for all its early trials, *Undique humanitas* had actually worked. He had never shied away from a challenge, and he would not do so now: if Giordano Bruno had been forgiven for positing a plurality of worlds, then there should be no reason why intelligent life on Earth was any more deserving of love than were it to occur anywhere else. Why is the Universe here, he was fond of asking himself, if only so he could laugh at the rejoinder — why, where *else* would it be?

Once he had resolved that particular issue, he became as excited as any schoolboy at the possibility that life might be detected elsewhere in the cosmos, and looked forward keenly to meeting the Chief Astrometer,

Father Tikko Bray, who, he had said, had some potentially interesting news. It concerned the discovery and subsequent characterization of a system of planets around Lacaille 9352, a star in the Solar neighborhood so nondescript that earlier searches had largely ignored it.

"Tell me about your new star—your *Nova Stella*," said Domingo on a warm day early in the spring of 2073. Domingo could hardly resist a joke, especially not one in Latin.

"Hitherto there has been little to tell, Your Holiness," said Father Bray, smiling in response. "Lac 9352 is a dim, red-dwarf star, about half the mass of our Sun but very much dimmer, not quite a dozen light years away from us. Despite some early interest in possible planets, it somehow dropped off the menu, as it were, what with one thing and another. I have another interest, of course, your Holiness…"

"Which is…?"

"I'm sorry to say it concerns the Sin of Pride. The star is too dim to be seen without a telescope, for all that it is relatively close in space. It was not known to the ancients, but instead discovered by one of ours. De La Caille was an eighteenth-century astronomer and Man of God, Your Holiness. I number him among my distant relations."

"In that case, Father Bray," said Domingo, "*ego te absolvo*. Please continue."

"Of course, Your Holiness," said Father Bray, evidently somewhat relieved. "The star has two planets much like our own Earth. One orbits at around the same distance from the star as the Earth from our own Sun. But being as the star is so dim, this planet is frozen and lacks any atmosphere we can detect. The other, however… yes, the other, orbits much closer in, rather like Venus or Mercury. It is—well, it's… *interesting*."

"Interesting? In what way?"

"Well, Your Holiness, it's too early to say precisely, with any confidence. For all that the stellar system is relatively near to us in space and the star itself intrinsically dim, the planet is small and rather close to its primary for us to get a pure signal, untainted by stellar influence. Yet we have signs of an atmosphere rich in hydroxyl radicals. This, as Your Holiness is well aware, means water and oxygen. We think there is appreciable nitrogen, too. We have some rough images—*very* rough, I'm afraid—suggestive of surface features that rotate with the planet. If I may…"

Bray pressed a remote, and a grainy image of a rotating, alien world appeared in the air, just centimeters in front of what had until recently been a portrait of the late, lamented Linus II. In the dimness of the blood-red star, the blues of the ocean were deep purple, almost black: the greens of the continents dark and somber. Scaphes of white ice rode the polar regions.

Even to Domingo's untutored eye, it was clear that these masses moved in tune with the planet's rotation. "So they are not clouds or atmospheric features…" he said.

"That is correct, Your Holiness," said the astrometer. "The planet appears to have separate continents and oceans. But as you can see, in some ways it is not very Earth-like. Lac 9352 isn't our bright, yellow Sun. The planet's year is very short, some fifty-five days, and the proximity to the star means that the planet is almost tidally locked, so that the days are very long indeed. A day on this planet would take more than a month."

"And yet, Father Bray, and yet," said Domingo. "The day is separate from the night, and the water from the land. What price the additional Days of Creation? Or has it stalled? Did this Eden go… ah… *awry*?"

"As to that, Your Holiness, we cannot yet say," Father Bray continued. "However, this is the best candidate for Earthlike life we've yet seen in twenty years of searching. The presence of oxygen speaks greatly towards an atmosphere very far from equilibrium. This suggests the possibility of photosynthetic organisms, perhaps even the presence of some kind of plant life, in which case — if one might speculate — there might be birds of the air, things that crawl, and so forth. But any more than that, well, that would be beyond the evidence."

And so it was that Father Bray and his colleagues continued their work, warmed and encouraged by Papal approval. Further meetings followed, in which the astronomer-priest and his employer reviewed further progress on the Lac 9352 system, such as it was. Images were improved, but not by much; further data came in, adding decimal places to numbers that were already accurate. But there was, as yet, no further news of birds, or fish, or whales, or of things that crawled. Creation had, indeed, stalled.

Domingo was beginning to think he might inquire of Father Bray whether there might have been any progress concerning the several other candidate systems that the Yahoo had been observing. As he himself had reasoned, even in our sleepy corner of the Galaxy, the sky was teeming with stars, brimming over with planets, all furnished by the Creator for our exploration, instruction, and delight.

A few miles away, in the center of the Cambridge, Professor Tom Markham Corstorphine of the Petrine Fellowship was preoccupied with more corporeal concerns.

Morgana had been the first of the Jive Monkeys he'd been able to distinguish from the mocking, menacing collectivity. Perhaps it was because she was slightly taller than the other two, whom she held somewhat in thrall. Other than that, they had all looked identical: very long,
shiny black hair, big, accusing green eyes, and skin the colour of polished teak. Telling them apart had been essential if he were to impose
any kind of order, to ask each questions individually during supervisions that veered crazily to the edge of anarchy. And they did their best
to make that job as difficult as they could.

He did wonder why the three of them bothered to come to supervisions at all—none of them seemed to care a hoot about Sand-Druid religion, or the ceremonies of the Tungusi Kaptars. Except that he *knew* why.
They hung on his every word, like cats ready to pounce on a hapless ro-
dent, for any suggestion of sexual innuendo, at which they would all
screech with laughter and, increasingly, direct unwelcome suggestions at
him personally.

He squirmed when he recalled the disastrous discussion about cir-
cumcision among the Sand Druids. Unlike all other Jews, who circumcised their sons as tiny infants, Tibestians waited until the *Bar Mitzvah* at
thirteen—when they did it in public, using a hot blade of polished obsid-
ian, without any kind of anaesthetic. Now, he just knew that any mention of genitalia would have them in fits so loud that the lecturer in the
class next door would remonstrate with him afterwards, and even as he
opened his mouth to speak he wondered why—*why*—he hadn't skipped
that part of his notes, and gone on to something less controversial.

In the event it had been worse. *Much* worse. After the predictable disarray at the mere mention of penises, Morgana had looked him in the
eye and asked "Have *you* been circumcised, Professor?" And before he
had managed to collect himself sufficiently to respond, the others had
joined in: can we look? Oh, *please*. We must take a *look*… it's *research*…
and before he could do anything, they had pinned him to the desk and
had started to pull off his clothes… I bet he's got a *big* one… *oooh*, he
has… we'd like to get our teeth into *that*… and despite his efforts to fight
them off… they hard started to take off their clothes, too… he was starting to panic, to feel sick… and, despite himself, to become *aroused*… re-
doubling their interest… so that when he screamed for help, the lecturer
from next door arrived with several worried-looking students to witness
what looked like a gang-rape in progress, although it was not, by then,
clear who was raping whom, or if it wasn't just an orgy.

After that Tom flatly refused to teach any Jive Monkey, threatening their colleges with criminal proceedings if they insisted. The colleges responded with counter-charges of racism and breaches of hominid cultural rights, implying that Tom had put them up to it, inflaming them with talk of genital mutilation, *leading them on.*

It was then that the Abbot of the Petrine Fellowship had called him in and very gently suggested that Tom do his best to get to the end of the academic year and then take some time out, a sabbatical. The only reason that he had not lost his fellowship, the Abbot implied, was that Tom had friends in very high places. His parents. And places higher even than that. And, for the moment, he'd have to keep teaching the Jive Monkeys.

That evening, after he had dined alone and disconsolately in Hall and had returned to his cell, he heard a soft knock at his door. It was Morgana.

"Go to hell," he said.

"Look, Professor Corstorphine — Tom — we're... I'm... well, we heard what happened, and..." He was amazed she'd managed to smuggle her way into the college past the Porter's Lodge.

"You heard me," said Tom. "Leave me alone."

"... well, we're sorry," she persisted, ignoring him. "We didn't mean... I want to explain..."

"I'm not hearing any more," he said, and shut the door in her face. But her expression, just a split second before the door closed — somehow sorrowful, contrite, but with a barely controlled inner indignation — gave him pause. And it was more than that. It was her aura. He realized that it pulsed in dark colours indescribable to human vision. And that no aura had blazed brighter than a candle flame for him since Shoshana had died. Without wondering to ask what this might mean, he knew he just had to see it again, to know more. He pulled the door ajar, and within an instant she was inside, and in his arms.

Morgana was a mote at the centre of a great ultraviolet mandala, and it was then he noticed for the first time in his life that he, too, had an aura that matched hers, interlacing, interacting: it was the most glorious sensation imaginable. This must be how Shoshana had felt when he waved his hands through her body field, too... but it was too late now. Too late to turn back, even if he could. For now there was more than radiance: there was communication. He felt that someone had started talking to him in a language that he hadn't heard before, but which he felt he had understood all his life.

Her lips on his were like red hot coals, her tongue a solar flare inside his ready mouth. Each frenziedly unbuttoned the shirt of the other, and it was then that he became conscious of her brazen non-humanity.

And it was beautiful.

Beneath her perfect, brown breasts, each finished with a prominent, ebony nipple, there was another smaller, breast, with its own nipple, and beneath that, a still smaller breast... she had ten in all, paired, five each in two tracks that ran down her front, each path curving outwards towards her hips. It was weird, he knew. But he had never seen anything so exotic, so... lovely. Her green eyes flashed at his, defiant, and he read each nuance of her slit-like pupils as if it were speech.

Now do you see? That's why we made such fun of you. Because you are one of *us*, and you refused to admit it.

Worse, refused to admit your *manhood*.

If you'd only known, you'd have shown us and serviced us all—each one of us in her turn, in front of the others, according to her rank—*before* talking to us. It would only have been polite, to grown women, such as ourselves. *That's* how we acknowledge dominance. *Then* we would have listened to you. We would have been quiet as lambs. But instead you ignored us.

Insulted us.

But I for one, as the senior female, am prepared to forgive, on behalf of us all. If, that is, you observe the *Proper Forms*. And with that she raised the hem of her long skirt.

She wore no underwear. Between her legs, up as far as her navel, and almost from hip to hip, she was extravagantly, outrageously furred. Not the sparse springiness of pubic hair, but *fur*, rich and luxuriant. He hesitated, so she kissed him again, and with one hand unbuckled his belt and reached into his trousers. He had already hardened to beyond the point of pain. She weighed his balls in her hand as dispassionately as if she were judging fruit in a produce show, before running her fingertips along the underside of his shaft and squeezing the end, sharply. The pain was agonizing and wonderful.

"Tom—*please*..." she said, as if any acquiescent girl, but her eyes said something different, imperative: now, you *know* what you must do, to command my respect, and that of my subordinates.

With that she turned away from him and knelt on Tom's narrow bed, flipping her skirt up across her back and pointing her exposed backside at him, in accusation, in challenge. Her hair fell forward around her shoulders, exposing a single raised ridge of sharp, black hairs, running down from the nape of her neck to the small of her back, like the clipped mane of a pony. Even from this angle, he could see the tufts of fur between her legs, and that she was hugely engorged, to an extent far greater than would have been possible for any human female. Her aura now enveloped her like two bright violet wings: he saw that it radiated from within her body, and that her swollen vulva was its bright centre, its conduit, gushing torrents of white-hot radiation towards him. She was like a flower, marked with lines and arrows that only bees can see, arrows pointing to the hidden treasure of nectar.

He climbed onto the bed behind her to do her bidding, and drove into her. He felt himself swell even more to fill her, and her tissues responded, ring-like waves of hot, liquid pressure squeezing him and letting him go, compressing and releasing, and always drawing him inwards. The more he thrust, the more their twin auras danced in the air as one pulsating thing, until he became one tiny point inside her ready to burst. But he found he could not. He became bigger and fuller, tighter and more painful and pulled ever deeper inside her, until he thought he'd pass out, when her aura said

You May

and he exploded in an actinic fury of golden-tinged purple and then velvety blackness.

He had no idea at all whether she too had climaxed. For without a word she rose, dressed herself and left without looking at him, her aura following her like a deep, inky cloak. As the door closed behind her it said

I am content.

Honor has been satisfied.

For the remainder of the academic year, the three Jive Monkeys were as demurely attentive and studious as he could have wished.

That evening, however, Morgana left him eviscerated. For as much as he glowed with sexual satisfaction that crowned anything he had ever experienced, he felt he'd been emptied, *used*. Not only had he betrayed his vows, he'd betrayed the memory of his love for Shoshana, who had loved him too — unlike this creature, whose attentions were solely concerned with the niceties of the etiquette of ritual. Not love, or even lust — but politics.

When, some hours later after he'd bathed and dried and, still unsatisfied, bathed again; when the wash of hormones inside him had passed, he brought back the language of her eyes and her aura, when it had said that he was one of *them*; that he could not deny his origins. His soul rebelled: he was a human being, no more, no less, and not a hominid.

But was he? He knew that he was not Jack and Jadis' biological son, that he had been adopted. He had never sought to investigate his origins—and why should he? The farmhouse had been his world, self-sufficient and bounded by a love he now realized he'd taken for granted. Yet Morgana's argument had still made sense. *Visceral* sense. The instant bond he'd felt; that despite its utterly alien character he had still grasped each precise tic of her body language; and that their auras had actively *interacted*. Even more, the act had seemed so natural, so easy, despite the strangeness of her anatomy. There had been no thought that he might have been too big for her, as there had sometimes been with Shoshana, and all his girlfriends before that. On the contrary, he fitted inside Morgana like a key in a lock.

He remembered that he, too, had a stiff ridge of black hair running down the back of his neck. He recalled, with a pain that now brought ears to his eyes, how Shoshana had loved to run her fingers along it, delighting how each stiff tuft of hair bent under her touch and immediately sprang back.

Shoshana...

No, another part of him protested, more loudly as it knew it was weakening, he could not be one of these *things*, these... *Jive Monkeys*. The thought was horrifying. *Bien sûr*, it's a shock, the rest of him reasoned. But you *liked* it, didn't you? He realized that he had.

To the outside world, however, he would continue to paint himself, resolutely, as a human being, in the hope that he would, one day, convince his soul. After all, there were important parts of him, held with iron affection, that he would not relinquish. A human being he would remain.

The morning after Morgana's cathartic visit, Tom was roused from a miasmic dream in which Shoshana had stood before him like a painted doll in some kind of *dirndl*, and he was shooting at her with a small-caliber pistol. The bullets disappeared into her long skirts and she was yelling at him angrily. "Get yourself an eyeful, mister," she screamed: "where you gonna find knockers like these, eh? *Where?*" squeezing her magnificent, snowy-white breasts over the top of her bodice and thrusting them at him, flaunting them... and not just one pair, but five. Then the Shoshana-*thing* had turned round, lifted her petticoats and thrust purple, monstrously protruberant genitalia at him.

Surfacing to the sound of rain pummeling his small window-pane, Tom knew this could not have been. He had known her every silken surface. What if she'd been tricked out, like Morgana had been, with some kind of baboon's arse? No way—that was a machine optimized for one thing: routine, peremptory, *contractual* copulation, and that was all. No scope there for intimacy, for love. The thought of it revolted him.

A rough shake to his shoulder. The college servant, a Pendek in the robe and cowl of the novitiate who, while utterly silent, was clearly determined that Tom should wake up, and once he'd pressed the letter into Tom's hand and indicated a cup of herbal tea on Tom's nightstand, he left—walking backwards to the door, crossing himself as he did so.

Tom sat up abruptly in bed. He felt terrible. His limbs were sluggish, obeying only with sullen reluctance his commands to stir themselves, as if they were schoolchildren and it was Monday morning. His throat was dry, and his head pounded to what felt like the opening ceremony of the international festival of gong-makers. His eyes focused groggily on the envelope, which bore only his address. The letter inside was from Domingo, in his neat, precise hand and as full of mysteries as ever, but with an uncharacteristic note of urgency that brought Tom instantly to his senses.

My Dear Tom,

he read:

> *It is time that we talked about the Sigil. We have put it off for too long, I fear. Matters have lately progressed in an exciting but possibly unwelcome direction and we are in danger of being overtaken by events. I think it of over-riding importance that you should be fully informed of these new developments. Please come the instant you receive this letter to the Astrometry Institute. A hansom will be waiting for you at the Porter's Lodge. I shall greet you on your arrival. In haste—*

The previous evening at around midnight, about two hours after Morgana had left Tom in a state of anguished and fretful disarray, the Chief Astrometer, Father Tikko Bray received some disturbing news of his own. That Lac 9352, the small, distant object on which weeks of attention had been lovingly lavished, had literally winked out of existence.

Within twenty-five seconds of receiving the paged message, Father Bray had dressed, in the total darkness of his cell in the Institute compound on the Madingley Road. Muttering snatches of Vespers as he ran across the yard to Mission Control, he found that two colleagues had already arrived, and were already busy with the monitoring equipment.

"We first noticed an unusual darkening on the planet's face," said Father Frederick, the older of the two, a tall, grizzled Almai astrometer who had taken Orders late in life.

"But it wasn't our instruments," added Father Jonas—a Sulawesian, barely half the height of his colleague, very thin, red-eyed and covered in jet-black fur—"we were calibrating them against a target star the whole time—the darkening was really happening, as we were watching, and..."

"And yet the darkening wasn't even, the same all over," Frederick's gruff voice interrupted, "there were huge variations on the planet..."

"... like something was casting shadows on it..." said Jonas in counterpoint, counter-tenor.

Father Bray's eyes darted from Frederick to Jonas and back again. "Hold it!" he demanded. "Not so fast! Whatever it was, it's nothing to do with the planet. These shadows, or whatever, came from the star. We already know the star is variable..."

"Yes, Father," interrupted Jonas. "But not all *that* variable. And certainly not so variable that it vanishes altogether. We got that, too. Here, look at these pictures from the wide-field camera."

A wide monitor, integrating images from Yahoo to present a picture of what the Lac 9352 system would look like from a few light-minutes away. Or, rather, two pictures. Yesterday's had the star, a small and sullen disk, the planets as smaller, star-like points. Today's had nothing—nothing at all, apart from the background of stars. If the planets were still there, they could not be seen; but that the star itself had disappeared was unarguable. Bray muttered a profanity too low for the others to hear.

"There's more?" he asked.

"Yes," growled Father Frederick. When we saw that, we looked back at the logged recordings and pinpointed precisely when the star vanished. Then we studied them in closer detail and strung them together to make a kind of time-lapse movie. We think it's extraordinary. We don't know what to make of it at all. That's when we summoned you, Father."

"Thank you," said Father Bray. "You may play the film now."

When it ended, Father Bray sank into his padded Mission Control chair, dark eyes staring from a bloodless face.

"I think I should call His Holiness," he said, before rising hurriedly to find a toilet cubicle, wherein he was violently sick.

Father Bray had composed himself early the next day, when His Holiness arrived, dripping wet from the Spring shower now sheeting down outside, and accompanied by a man who seemed his opposite in every way. Where the Pope was enormous, Professor Tom Corstorphine was compact; where His Holiness was expansive, his companion was quiet. He looked ill, actually, and Father Bray wondered why he was here at all.

"Professor Corstorphine is a good friend of mine," the Pope explained, answering the unasked question. "He might also have an interest in what you are about to reveal, I think."

Father Bray beckoned to Father Jonas, whose lithe, black fingers waved at a holographic panel against one wall of the control room. The room lights and the other monitors dimmed in response, giving the watchers the impression that they were floating in space, looking down on the great red disk of Lac 9352. Although a midget compared with the Sun, it was still a star, and all stars are mighty indeed when seen at close quarters. At first it seemed much as it always did, like a roiling mass of angry tomato soup, with the occasional cluster of dark spots and a few flares and prominences.

"We're seeing it in enhanced visual, with a little of the UV fed into the blue end," noted Father Jonas. "Now, watch closely." A time code and other data flashed by in the bottom right-hand corner of the image. What they were about to see would take less than ninety seconds to elapse.

The first sign of anything odd was an added dullness to the stellar North Pole (to the bottom of the picture) that slowly built up in intensity and definition, until it looked as if the whole north-central sector of the star was in deep shadow. Another, similar shadowing soon followed on the eastern limb (to the left of the picture), joining and fusing with the northern shadowing until it looked as if the entire bottom-left-hand-quadrant of the star had been occulted, or eclipsed. Except that the eclipse only deepened, and was joined by several other spots of darkness on the remaining, unshadowed parts of the star's face.

After a minute the star was completely black. It evidently still existed, from a few remaining, fitful flares, and the fact that it masked any stars behind it. But then it appeared to break up, its black remains fragmenting against the still darker blackness of space, until—after the full ninety seconds—absolutely nothing was left. Lac 9352 had ceased to exist.

-=0=-

The Trans-Europe Express burst from the Sangatte end of the tunnel, dragging streamers of acrid, ashy smoke which it would not shed completely for several miles. In a private compartment near the front of the train ("being the Pope has its privileges,"), Domingo pulled open a vent. Curling scuts of soot flew in, soon replaced by fresh air.

"Steam trains in the Channel Tunnel—what mad pursuit, eh Tom?" Domingo laughed recklessly, offering the basket of croissants to Tom, who refused. "They used to be powered on gasoline. Or was it electricity? But *steam*! It has taken the Christophorines fifteen years to upgrade the ventilation, and *still* it's like pea soup in there. What struggle to escape! What pipes and... er... *tunnels*?"

Tom permitted himself a half-smile and poured coffee for both of them. Since leaving Cambridge they had talked relatively little, and nothing at all of the monstrous revelations at the Astrometry Institute. That a star—a whole star—could disappear before their very eyes, literally dismembered, by—*what*? The whole thing was just too stupefying to contemplate.

And then something stirred in Tom's mind—something that he had forgotten for twenty years. Not surprisingly, as it had been blotted out by the subsequent trauma in which he and Shoshana had narrowly escaped being atomized in the War of the Last Days. A tall, thin, freckled seminary student called Fearon Brimstone, who'd mentioned something about disappearing stars, and the Astrometry Institute, and his theory that there was something Out There ready to 'bite us on the bum'. Haltingly, he explained all this to Domingo.

"So whatever it is," Tom concluded, "this phenomenon has been known about for some time. Why did nobody hear about it?"

"I know the work to which you refer," replied Domingo. "And there has been much of a similar nature published before and since. The first report of a disappearing star—disappearing, that is, in unexplained circumstances, and leaving no trace—was in 2031, I think."

"But..."

"But why has nobody taken any notice?" said Domingo. Tom nodded. "Because," Domingo continued, "there was no way to explain it, no mechanism. And phenomena without mechanisms tend to just lie in the literature as curiosities until someone can come along and tie things together."

"What we saw—what we have just seen" said Tom, hesitantly, "I understand that this is the first close-up, real-time demonstration of this thing—this *phenomenon*—in action?"

Domingo nodded and sipped his coffee, not taking his eyes off Tom. "I believe, Tom, that the star was destroyed by the coordinated action of alien beings. I can think of no other, natural explanation, and neither can the Chief Astrometer."

"So it should get noticed *now*, shouldn't it?"

"I very much doubt it," said Domingo, "because, now we know what's happened to that star, how do we tell anyone? *Should* we tell anyone? And if we did, what then? We should have replaced complete ignorance with something that strains credulity to the limit. If given the choice between ignorance and he whole, pitiless truth, most people go for ignorance."

After that they were silent for a long time, each lost in his own thoughts.

Domingo felt himself chastened. Be careful what you wish for, his thoughts declaimed. He had earnestly hoped that, one day, alien life would be discovered that he might welcome into the Fellowship of Christ. But that such beings could exist whose purpose was to consume stars — well, that would require some modest reflection.

But then, he reasoned, he'd made a fundamental error, of assuming that such alien life that one could detect across the gulf of space must, by virtue of that detection, be intelligent. These star-swarming behemoths had not intellects vast, cool and unsympathetic, because they had not intellect to begin with. They were no more rapacious predators than the ichneumon wasp whose young devour the living meat of their hapless caterpillar hosts from inside.

Tom's mind registered little but shattered amazement. The discovery of vast entities that swallowed stars formed a resonant, gothic backdrop for the newly ignited personal battle over his own nature: a battle fought in sodden marshes of metallic despair that left him cold, cheerless and utterly exhausted.

The Trans-Europe Express thundered across the flatlands of Normandy, the bright Sun climbing above a bank of woolly grey clouds. Tom gazed at it, flying in the eastern sky, as they passed Chartres. He was grateful that it was still there, and wondered if great black shapes might, one day, be converging on it from out of the depths of space. His blood turned to ice: he turned to Domingo, and noticed for the first time how old his mentor looked, how lined his face, and wondered if he, too, felt the same horror.

Suddenly Domingo spoke, breaking Tom's reverie: "You know, Tom," he said, "as I believe I mentioned, we really should have another look at the Sigil."

"I haven't seen it since before the Plague struck," said Tom. "I'd be hard put to it to recall it in detail. So that I could draw it, for example."

"The same goes for me, Tom. And that's why we must see it anew. Too much has happened, in both our lives, and we need our memories... ah... *refreshed*."

Domingo explained that lately he'd been obsessed with the Sigil's three circles, and wondering if they had anything to do with the final fate of the Plague victims.

"It seemed too great a coincidence," he explained, "that the circles in the Sigil are the circles of end-stage Postembryonic Oolithic Petrosis. I started wondering whether the Sigil was some kind of document of this disease striking in early times, or maybe a prophecy."

"But what about the crescents, and the radiating lines?" said Tom.

"I know, Tom, it's futile, but I can't help thinking about it. Mind going round and round in circles, and circles can never be squared. It could simply be... well..."

"Yes, Domingo?"

"You never had the misfortune of watching any human soul succumbing to the Plague, did you, Tom? Even when you—we—were in Israel?"

"No, I did not."

"Well, I'm afraid to say I did. Perhaps I am suffering from nothing more than my own reaction to seeing my superior, a human being of great gentleness and humility, being mercilessly crushed, and crushed again, into that small compass. A circular compass, in what must have been unspeakable agony and mortal terror. So, you see, I tend to imbue circles with a great deal of... ah... significance."

But Tom recalled, as if it had happened to somebody else in a long-vanished age, of a discussion around the farmhouse table. It must have been in '54, just before the Plague, because he remembered Shoshana's pale face and wide purple eyes when she said of the Sigil's makers that:

"They wanted to ward them off, at all costs... to find a way of chasing the dragons away..."

"Tom?"

"It was something she said. That Shoshana said," said Tom, realizing that he'd voiced his thoughts aloud. "We were all at the farmhouse, just before the Plague. We were talking about the Sigil..."

"…and the Chinese legend that eclipses are caused by dragons," Domingo continued, "and how Shoshana said that the Sigil could be an expression of that same impulse. To chase the dragons away."

Domingo looked across at Tom, who, with the mention of her name, felt crushed, the betrayer, still alive, undeservedly, eking out a kind of un-life for so long as he could retain the memory of her. Tom saw that there was a moisture in the old man's eyes, as if he, too, felt some complicity in Shoshana's passing. Tom knew it was deeply uncharitable, but he didn't want Domingo to get away with it, with even a tenth of the anguish that he felt, all day, every day—even now.

"In which case," said Tom, his voice flat to the point of sarcasm, "Shoshana was closer than any of us knew. And that would be *some* small crumb to show that she had not died *utterly* in vain. And again, *in which case*," his eyes flashed at Domingo in reproach that was close to rage, "What would have the Plague to do with it—with any of it?"

"Why—nothing of course!" replied Domingo, as if he'd been slapped. But he then hesitated, as if he had reached a conclusion in undue haste. "But, my dear Tom, please forgive me."

"I know, Domingo. I should apologise." Even so, Tom was determined to allow Domingo no quarter. He would rather focus his pain on somebody else than open up, even to Domingo, because he was convinced that the latter course would expose his being to an overwhelming tide of guilt and shame that would then destroy him.

He was *human*. But if he were human, how had he killed her?

But if he *weren't* human, how could he have loved her?

But, on the other hand, if he *were* human, how could he have found sex with that alien *thing* so horribly magnetic? His mind spun crazily in futile circles of its own.

Domingo looked closely at Tom. "My old friend," he said, "I believe that each of us in his own way, has reached an impasse."

Tom looked dejectedly up at Domingo from the banquette opposite, his eyes vacant. Domingo parted his arms fractionally and without further encouragement, Tom crossed the compartment and sat next to him, burying his form in the older man's enveloping scarlet cloak.

Domingo was cast back to the time when he bore Tom proudly to the arms of his adopted mother. Why? Was his impulse pure? Was it to ease Jadis' burden of childlessness or, more to gain her approval, to bask in her sunshine? If the latter, it would have been a grievous error. Domingo wished more than ever that Tom would take him into his confidence. But perhaps Tom had not experienced enough for him to realize that acceptance is the wisest course. Not like Shoshana, who died untimely and cruelly, but at peace.

Part of the problem — not that it *was* a problem — was that unlike Shoshana, Tom had grown up in an atmosphere of unconditional love, which exacted no tribute. In such a situation he might have felt that no spiritual journey was required of him, because he could live his entire life in Eden. Pity, thought Domingo, that happy lot falls only to creatures without souls, for which the notion of love is meaningless, and for which acceptance requires no struggle.

"But whether the Sigil has anything to do with the Plague or not," Domingo said, more to himself, for Tom had fallen asleep in his lap: "we must go back to the farmhouse and see it again."

For the farmhouse, he continued to himself, is not just a sanctuary for both of us, but contains two of the most nimble minds I have had the fortune to encounter in my long life. Minds that once achieved fame on the remarkable intuition of one, and the penetrating insight of the other.

Like their discovery, Domingo thought, these two minds have been idle for far too long. *That* is the reason why we must go home: to crack the code. For we may not have very much time.

He looked up at the Sun and realized that a dozen light-years is but a mote in the eye of the Creator. No, not very much time at all.

Chapter 6. Hunter

Western Desert, Earth, *c.* 45,000 years ago

He took his vorpal sword in hand
Long time the manxome foe he sought
Lewis Carroll — *Jabberwocky*

Something beyond his senses alerted him to the plain fact that he was not alone.

He kicked out the small fire in the dell beneath the roots of the thorn tree where he'd made his den. He flattened himself on its slope, peering over the edge. He tried not to think of another time — another life, far away — when he'd been in such a position. Now was not the time to count the Father-the-Suns, the Mother-the-Moons, all that had circled since then.

Neither was it the time to count all the things he'd learned in the meantime. How to hunt. How to kill. Beasts, from mice and frogs, to that single coelodont that had fed, housed and clothed him for months. And men too, men much bigger than he was. Stoners. Others. None of his own kind. Well, not unless he was really desperate. People whose brains he'd guzzled, still warm, straight from their skulls.

There was a spike standing proud on the western horizon, small but hard against the setting sun. He squinted into the reddish haze. It was no more than a speck, but it was growing, even as he watched. It was coming his way. There was nowhere to hide, except in the dell itself. His thorn tree was the only one for at least half a day's walk around — and the water-skins hanging from the branches gave the game away. He was suckered. He was caught.

Oh no, he wasn't. The more he watched, the more he was convinced that the speck was alone, not some Stoner scout, not the advance guard of an army he'd soon see stretched from one horizon to the other. He'd been in situations like that, too, many times, and he'd escaped to tell the tale, if only to himself. A single wanderer, however, would be an easy target. Easy meat. And easy other things, too — marrow, bones, teeth, scraps of clothes, pottery, flakes of quartzite — anything and everything, to keep himself a step ahead of death. Half a step, really. That was all he needed. Half a step. The rock-hyrax he'd caught that morning would help. Maybe a whole step, then. Brained with a lucky stone. He hadn't eaten as much for weeks. He slavered at the very thought of eating it later, after dark. Roasted hyrax, turned on a spit.

He loosened the gazelle-horn throwing-knives in his belt. He hoped it wouldn't have to come to that. Still with half an eye on the horizon, he strung his wooden bow with Stoner hair, winding the strands tight. He probed the ground around him for arrows, each with a sharp of Stoner bone for a point. He could only find three, and two had missing fletchings. He'd long since run out of bitumen to fix things, and the last asphalt seep he'd raided was long away.

Oh, well, they'd have to do.

The speck had grown noticeably larger in the time he'd taken to grab his gear. It was still small, but it now had the shape of a man. But the more he watched, the harder it was to see it. One minute it had grown enormously, so that he recoiled, almost dropping his bow and nocked arrow: the next, it had receded almost to the vanishing point. He forced his eyes closed, squeezing out patterns behind his eyelids — opened, and refocused. The speck jounced around, now up, now down, now bigger, now smaller, now gone altogether — now reappearing in a different place.

A mirage. He'd seen plenty of those. The problem was that they made it even harder than usual to shoot straight. And this was the liveliest mirage he'd ever seen. A mirage that played games with the mind as well as the eyes.

"Put the bow down, boy," said the mirage.

The voice was so close that he dropped the bow and arrow with the shock of it. In a reflexive flash he pulled out a horn dagger, turned towards the noise, and bent his knees to spring. He sprang. He hit the ground with a crunch. He tasted blood in his mouth.

"That's the ticket," said the voice, now from above. The voice was deep, but dry, like the boom of the wind ricocheting through the ruins of monuments. A shadow stood over him, blotting out the sunset. "Now, might I trouble you — if you're not too busy, that is — to get an old man a drink of water?" The voice extended a hand. The hand was long and pale, but old and leathery. He grabbed the hand, which pulled him, straight off the ground, and on to his feet. The voice was commanding: the hand, amazingly strong.

Father-the-Sun fell like a stone into the west. He saw nothing more of the visitor than a silhouette.

"No matter," said the deep, dry voice. "You're somewhat surprised, I see." The shadow raised a hand. He saw a deep sleeve fall, exposing a thin, bony arm. "I can get it myself."

The young hunter knew no more.

He woke from a fevered dream in which he was underwater. A girl stood above the surface, wordlessly shrieking, but he could hear nothing. He knew that the girl was older than him. His sister. If only he could remember her name.

He was on the ground, in the dell beneath his thorn tree. His small fire in the roots had been rekindled: in the deep night, it was the only spark of light. The rich smell of roasting hyrax filled the small space. A figure, robed, hooded, crouched over the fire, turning the spit. He sat up.

"Who...?" he asked.

"*Me*?" said the voice. "If only all questions were that easy. My name is M!shay. Some people call me M!shay Ha'Shala/Mal. But plain old M!shay will do." The young hunter had never heard such sounds as these. There were real names here, he was sure, but the sounds within them—clicks, grunts, growls—were like dogs at bay.

"Shay. Shala-mal," he tried.

"Well, it's a start. 'Shay' will do, if that's all you can manage. Here, have some soup." Shay extended a bony hand, bearing a skull bowl filled with a dark liquid. The young hunter could smell the roots he'd collected, mixed with blood and hyrax liver. He gulped at it, spluttering at the heat. No matter—he was starving.

"The real question—the *big* question—the Question of the Age, if you don't mind my saying, is not my name, but yours."

"My... name?" He had not been called by his name since... since... since, well, since his life had ended and his life had begun. In all the Fathers-of-Suns and Mothers-of-Moons since, he had been too busy just surviving, alone in the desert, to ponder matters as inconsequential as his name. And besides, he had not spoken more than two words together, to anyone, for longer than he cared to remember.

"Well, let's try to guess," said Shay, squatting back on his heels. "You have a deep brown birthmark around your left eye. So, according to the traditional nomenclature of your tribe, you might be called... oooh, *I* don't know... something like 'Pop-Eye'? Or maybe 'Eye-Patch'? Perhaps? Mmm? You might help me out here." He paused. "Look, don't all rush at once," he prompted. "I'll be here all week."

Eye-Patch.

Memories, stirring. Honey-sweet scent of a mother's flesh. First steps. The smell of meat drying in the sun.

Hands, hands to put him down, hands to raise him up.

Tall, tall stalks of grain, of reeds, taller than he was.

Threshing, threshing grain, motes in sunlight, women standing in a circle, pounding, singing, always singing.

"No?" said Shay. "Well, you seem to be missing most of the fifth digit on your left hand. Unfortunate. An accident, maybe, in youth? Perhaps a narrow escape from a wild animal? An event worthy of commemoration, surely?"

"Name... my name?" The young hunter raised his left hand before his face, silhouetted it against the bright fire. He saw that his little finger was just a stub. He saw it as if for the first time.

A snarl of teeth across his vision.

Too fast, too fast.

Pain.

The voice, from the shadows to his right, only its long, pale hands visible, as they turned the spit, the voice said:

"I have looked long and hard for you, *Jjadhazev*. Dogfinger."

"Dogfinger..."

A gully between two fields.

Bright sun.

A girl, tall, squinting against the horizon.

She had one green eye, and one brown.

And all the Stoners he'd killed, whose blood he'd drunk, in all the Mothers-of-Moons since, were all in her long-forgotten name.

Green-Eye.

Revenge.

Dogfinger sat up, and looked at his mysterious companion. "How did you know? How? *Why?*"

"Let us say I've had... *help.*"

"Help? Who? Mister Shay, there has only ever been me."

"Yes, Dogfinger. Yes — but not quite. There has always been you, alone. And you have done well. See — you were once a boy, but now look at you! You are a man. But it's not just you, you know. She watches over us. Over us all. *HaShekhna.*"

"You are a riddler," said Dogfinger. "Nothing but a riddler, a riddler and a schemer. I should kill you now, old man, as I have killed all the others. I'd have the hyrax all to myself, and add your eyeballs, too."

"Oh, would you? Really?" said Shay. He put up one finger, a single digit into the air, and Dogfinger felt his arms, legs and tongue go numb. "I shouldn't advise it. And before you ask me where I get such power...? Oh, I see, you are struck dumb. So I can say my piece without interruption, can I? Good. By *Hashekhna*, I have been dying to get this off my chest for years."

And so Shay told his story, about being a wandering conjuror of his tribe, a beggar, a thief, the lowest of the low, kicked along the street. "*Shala/Mal*, in the language of my tribe, it means a beggar," he said. "But to me it means more. Ever since, when I was thrown off the walls of the City on the Heights for buggering a goat, and enjoying it, though not half so well as the goat, I fancy; and thinking that the best thing I could do was die, she was there. *HaShekhna*, that is. Not the goat. That was a 'he'. *HaShekhna* stood over me, pulled me up, scolded me. She became a mother to me, a sister, a lover. She took me to places. Oh, such places..."

Dogfinger recovered his voice. "She? Places? Talk, riddler."

"And there was me, thinking *I* had the speaking part," Shay sighed, turning the spit once more.

"I'm sorry, Mister Shay."

"Thank you. And 'Shay' is quite sufficient, without any spurious adornment. I can remember what she said to me. 'Get up, you silly man.' That's what she said. And then, she said, 'I've probably fucked it up, like I always do, but I cannot always be everywhere at once.' And then, *Jjad-hazev*—ah, and *then*. She entered my very *soul*. She spoke to me from *inside my head*. She told me that I had to find you—*you*—and take you to safety. 'I hope I'm not too late,' was all she said.

"And then she went, just like that—*pouf!* The gap in my soul seemed immense, and I fell onto the ground again. I knew she was *HaShekhna*, the ancient Goddess of my tribe. But when again I woke, I had such powers, such *powers*. No-one will call me *Shala/Mal* again with such... scorn."

"Mister... er... *Shay*... can I ask a question, now?"

"Of course. That's why I'm here. *Hashekhna*, she said—guide this young man. Be his mentor. Be as a father to him. So, please, ask away. Whatever you want."

"What's 'buggering' mean?"

Shay was silent for a spell. "I can see you have still a lot to learn, *Jjad-hazev*" he said. Then he turned his finger in the air, just like *that*.

Dogfinger saw a flash of infinite space.

And then it was morning.

The early chill, just before the dawn. Dogfinger was wet through with the desert dew. Father-the-Sun had yet to crest the eastern horizon. Several bright stars still shone in the blueness of the western vault. Dogfinger panicked. For a moment he forgot where he was. Then he cursed — he'd forgotten to spread skins out, pieces of pottery, anything — to catch the dewfall.

"Don't worry, *Jjadhazev*," came the voice. "I've done it already. Come, drink, enjoy — later, we'll talk."

Dogfinger looked up. And then, for the first time, he saw the face of his strange new companion. The face, framed by a dirty ash-gray hood, of M!Shay Ha'Shala/Mal, unfrocked elder of the Annakhnu of the City on the Heights. It was the strangest face that Dogfinger had ever seen. The face was tall, but narrow, with a lipless mouth surmounted by a tall, narrow nose. The face was parchment-white, ivory-white, as white as his own face was brown as the earth. The face was framed by straggly hair the exact color of ostrich egg-yolk. But strangest of all were the eyes. Large, shaped like almonds, with round irises as egg-yolk yellow as his hair. The face of a ghost. Dogfinger shrank back. As he watched it, the eyes stared back at him, unblinking — all, that is, for the wipe of nictitating membranes that rolled across them, shrowding them for a long, glutinous moment in a chalky caul, before retreating, exposing the eyes once again to full and disconcerting acuity.

"Here, take the cup," Shay said. Dogfinger, too stunned to argue, took the skull-cup from Shay's white hand, and took a draught of cool hyrax stew. "It's time we were on our way."

Dogfinger struggled to his feet. He could feel a light wind blowing over the lip of the dell. It dried the moisture on his body, cooling him.

"Where are we going?" Dogfinger asked.

Shay slung Dogfinger's water skin over his shoulder and walked with deliberation over the lip of the dell and headed towards the west.

"You'll see when we get there," he said.

The journey took only two days, but to Dogfinger it seemed like years. Dogfinger had walked far and wide in the seven years of his exile, but never in this particular direction — straight across the furnace-heart of the Erg. He toiled, struggling to follow Shay up the steep, shifting slopes of the dunes, trying not to topple and slide down the far sides of the great waves of sand.

Dogfinger rarely wore any more clothes than his moccasins and a quiver of arrows, but he was grateful for the broad leather hat that Shay had made him wear against a molten sun, and the rough cloth bandanna across his face that deflected most of the flying shrapnel of sand from his eyes. He was thankful, too, for his own moccasins: the heat of the sand burned into his feet, but the soft leather on his soles made all the difference between pigeon-stepping across the sand and not going anywhere at all. But the sand scored at his calves as he walked; it burned his ankles as his feet sunk in; the sun scorched his shoulders and his back. The muscles in his calves ached and stung as he slid down the farther sides of dunes. His tongue seemed to swell to twice its usual size inside a mouth that seemed to have been coated in red-hot gravel.

Shay was quite unperturbed by any of this. He drew his dirty-gray robe about him and stepped at the same, unvarying pace, loping up hill and down without distinction. It was only at the end of the first day that Dogfinger noticed that Shay's feet were bare. Bare, gnarled as white old roots, disfigured with ancient scars, but completely free of any recent cuts or blisters.

At the end of the first day, they huddled together in a foxhole in a country as bleak and barren as anywhere Dogfinger had ever been. It looked like another world—only the familiar stars barrelling above told him that they were still under the same celestial vault he had known all his life. Only after Shay had squatted on the ground, kindling a small fire with some resinous twigs he'd brought with them; taking out the waterskin and handing out scraps of greasy, day-old hyrax meat, did it occur to Dogfinger to wonder how Shay had found this place so unerringly. They had left the Erg behind several hours earlier, the land grading into an entirely flat surface, free of any mark whatsoever. There were no stones, no trees (nor indeed any plant life of any kind), no skeletons of dead animals. Not even any distant mountains whereby one might orient oneself. The land was utterly flat. And yet Shay had walked to this scrape in a dead straight line, looking neither to right nor left. Dogfinger stopped chewing the rubbery meat long enough to begin to frame a question, but Shay glanced at him from beneath his hood—his eyes catching the last of the sunlight—in a way that told him, as nothing else might, that he should remain silent.

Putting down the remains of his meal, Shay reached into an inside pocket of his robe and drew out a soft leather drawstring bag. He placed the bag carefully on the ground, spreading out the opening with both his long hands. After a few moments he reached in and withdrew a lamp made from the skullcap of a Stoner, the inner surface of which had been charred black and greasy with the passage of years. From another small pouch Shay took a handful of herbs and dried flowers, placing them with great care within the upturned skull. Dogfinger could not be sure—and didn't dare ask—but it looked as if Shay was arranging the herbs and flowers in particular, exacting patterns. Then Shay took a lit twig from the fire and ignited the herbs. As the smoke rose, he chanted words that Dogfinger had never heard before, although he had the impression that they were very ancient.

The syllables that Shay pronounced were indecipherably glottal, guttural and barbarous, as gentle as thunder, as euphonious as an avalanche. But as Shay spoke, Dogfinger had the unsettling sensation that he knew what they meant. Softly, inside his head, was the voice of a woman. It could have been his mother. And seemingly with his mother's voice, the voice said:

Bless us, Holy One, All High. Who took up the sins of the world, *qui tollis peccata mundi.*

Shay did not speak again until the late afternoon of the second day. His words were just as enigmatic then, too. He turned to Dogfinger, grasped his sun-sore shoulders in both hands and looked him straight in the eye.

"*Ijadhazev,* listen to me. *HaShekhna* might think you're some kind of Big Shot, but *I* think she's a soft touch. Me? I'm not so sure. You might think you're the *Moshiach.* But wisdom is more than about killing. Remember that." Shay turned away before Dogfinger could reply.

On the second day of their journey together, Dogfinger and Shay walked westward across the hard-pan until Father-the-Sun had set in a red ball before their feet. And still they kept walking. Dogfinger followed Shay closely and carefully as the last light of day was extinguished and all around was completely dark.

Unable to see anything except the ghostly folds of Shay's robes a yard or so ahead of him, Dogfinger's other senses sharpened. The air became cooler, yes—night in the desert could chill one's bones—but it became moister, too. He could smell the green of growth, burgeoning all around him. And he could hear things, too—more than the careless desert wind, but the rustle of vegetation, the rattle and clack of tall stalks beating on one another. The chirp of crickets.

It felt like he had come full circle, back to his village: he was a boy again, playing with Green-Eye in the irrigation ditch between the fields, and all he needed to do was climb out and walk home to his mother's embrace. But no—he knew that could no longer be. In any case, he could not afford for his mind to wander. It took all his concentration to keep up with Shay's pace, unrelenting even in this utter blackness. If he missed

his footing and fell, he might lose Shay and be abandoned, without any
bearings whatsoever, in this unknown place. Shay's pace did not slacken
until they walked into some darker blackness, Shay pushing Dogfinger's
head downwards so he wouldn't crack it on a lintel—they had walked
into an interior space, a dwelling. How Shay had been able to reckon his
way, without twist or turn or any doubt whatsoever, remained an
enigma.

Shay knelt down on a dry earth floor and took out his small belongings, igniting the herbs and dried flowers in the upturned skull as he'd
done the night before, and chanting the same, ancient ritual obeisance.
By the small, flickering light, Dogfinger—still standing—saw that they
were in a small mud hut, with two sacks of wool on the floor, either side
of the skull-altar fire. Shay looked up at Dogfinger who was aware, for
the first time, of the round reflections at the back of the old man's eyes.
Like a cat. Now he understood how Shay could see where he was going,
even when he—no mean tracker in the dark himself—was almost completely blind.

"Take a pew, *Jjadhazev*," Shay said. And without another word, the
old shaman curled up on one of the wool sacks like a baby and fell
asleep immediately, his face hidden by his hood. Dogfinger tried to follow his example, lying down on the vacant wool sack. At first the softness of it was uncomfortable, and even disconcerting, to one who'd
spent every night, as long as he could remember, curled up in the crook
of a thorn-branch or a scrape in the ground, or stretched out on the hard
desert soil. But the fatigue of the two-day desert march soon claimed
him, and he slept.

Dogfinger awoke to the grayness of early morning and an uncomfortably full bladder. Without thinking, he rose and went outside to relieve himself against the wall of the hut. So desperate was he to urinate
that he failed to notice, at first, that the hut was just one among many,
huddled closely together between thorn-branch stockades of aurochs
and goats, stands of crops and the scattered shade of trees—acacia, palm
and other kinds he did not recognize. There were people, too, going
about the usual early-morning errands of any village, and one stopped to
look at him. It was only when the warm and welcome relief spread
throughout his lower body, and Dogfinger arched his back so that he
could shake the last drops from his penis, that he had the uncomfortable
sensation of being watched.

Now, usually, whenever this happened, his reflexes would spring
into action, and he'd turn to face the perceived threat, antelope-horn

dagger in hand. This time, it felt different. That he was quite naked was nothing unusual, this being Dogfinger's normal state. More worrisome was that he had let himself be caught unarmed. But the feeling of being under surveillance was different from, say, being looked up and down by a prowling leopard: not so much danger, then, as a kind of embarrassment. And yet this was not the shame of being caught doing something naughty, as he'd felt as a boy. Well, not quite. For in this not-quite-shame was something entirely new — fascination. He turned to face his adversary, and as he did so, he felt his balls shrink into his body.

His adversary was a species of human being he'd seen many times, long ago, in his home village, but never yet since. He had not, however, been old enough, as he was now, to appreciate such a creature for what it really was.

Standing before him was a young woman.

The first thing that struck him was the color of her skin. Not deep brown, as he himself was, but almost white. And not, then, the dead parchment-white of Shay, but a smooth lusciousness like a she-goat's new milk. This pure-white skin was freckled all over as if she'd been sprayed with honey. Her hair, though — now, that was *truly* extraordinary, being very long and *bright orange*. Her wide eyes were as brown and as dark as his own. The contrast with the pale face that surrounded them made their stare seem impudently inquisitive.

"Well, take a look at *you*," she said. "And be *careful* with that thing, won't you? It's not just for pissing through, you know." She giggled. Dogfinger looked down and discovered, with equal parts horror and wonder, that his penis was as stiff as a branch and standing away from his body. He turned, to see the woman walking away, a sway to her walk as she balanced an urn on one hip, rucking up one side of her woollen skirt so that he saw the back of one thigh, as white and smooth as the rest of her. The urn must have been very heavy, if full of water, Dogfinger thought, yet she carried it with an elegant ease. He felt heat in his face, and not the heat of the rising morning. He turned, ducked, and entered the small hut which he shared with Shay.

"Some of us are... er... *up*, bright and early," Shay said from his bed, looking up at the slowly shrinking erection of his young *protégé*. Dogfinger sat down sharply on his own woolsack, trying to conceal an expression of mingled confusion, frustration and rage.

"Where are we? Who are these people?" he barked at the old man.

"Easy now," Shay said. "If it's any consolation, which it isn't, I understand how you must feel. You left your village hardly more than a tadpole, and now you are a fine figure of a frog. A bit unkempt—perhaps a little on the scrawny side—but well, you'll do. A lily pad and a few lessons in croaking and you'll cut quite a dash, I fancy. In the meantime, such reactions in the... um... southern regions are only to be expected when one comes face to face with unfamiliar... er... *stimuli*."

"Southern regions?" said Dogfinger, "I thought we were going far more west than south. And you haven't answered my questions. First— where are we?"

Shay sighed. "Would knowledge of the name make any difference?"

"The day before yesterday you seemed to think names were important."

"*Touché*, my lad. We are, as you see, in an oasis. In my language it is called *Baj!ra'adhzt*..."

" 'Ba-yit'? 'Be-reshit?'" Dogfinger rolled the strange, angular syllables around in the mouth. It felt like trying to gargle with knuckle bones. Shay laughed—itself a weird, guttural sound.

"It's a fair start," he said. "But you need to try and say both words simultaneously. In any case, *Baj!ra'adhzt* means both 'home' and 'beginning': which, as you'll see, I hope, is most apposite. A little history, if you will—in ancient times much of the rest of this region was like this— fertile, farmed, tilled—but the desert has slowly swallowed it up, a little more each year, until only a few oases like this remain. My people once roamed far across these lands, made a great empire.

"But hubris comes to us all, even the Annakhnu of ancient days, and the few of us who remain live somewhat farther to the west of here, in huts such as these, in the lee of the far greater mansions our ancestors— the *elda enta geweorc*, to coin a phrase—and whose means of construction most can now only surmise, even were some few to distinguish them at all from natural features."

Shay sat up. Dogfinger heard the old man's bones creak and saw a fleeting grimace across the strange, elongated face. Shay must have registered Dogfinger's concern. "Don't you worry about me, *Jjadhazev*," he said. "Just a bit stiff after our little excursion, that's all. But to the present. *Baj!ra'adhzt* is, as you've seen, somewhat off the beaten track. Stoners don't know it's here, and wouldn't be able to get here even if they did."

"Stoners?"

"Indeed. Need I say more?"

"But who... these people? That woman?"

"That *brazen hussy*, you mean? Her name is Moonrise, and her temper is as fiery as her wholly improbable hair. Just like her to judge a man by his... ah... accoutrements."

"So... you heard?"

"It's only a little hut, *Jjadhazev*. And if you *will* run around as naked as a baby, waving your... er... *advantages* around for all to see, like some crude advertisement, you're going to attract attention, aren't you? Now, help me to my feet, will you?"

Dogfinger obliged.

"Now then," Shay said, stretching, "I'm off to find some clothes for you, and some breakfast for both of us. Don't move from this spot until I return. Agreed?"

Dogfinger nodded. Shay looked unconvinced, and ventured into the gathering heat muttering something about the ingratitude of young people, and how they weren't what they used to be. He had the feeling that he was meant to discover that answer for himself.

At first Dogfinger found his woollen kilt and shirt—the customary clothing worn at the oasis—irritating and constricting. He said little to anyone, and listened only slightly more.

After a while, though, he got used to his clothes, and the regular farmyard chores he was assigned by the others at the oasis. He even began to enjoy them. As life became routine, he found that his mind wandered, more than it ever had, to daydreams of what life might have been like at home, long away, had he reached manhood there, undisturbed by the Stoner raid. He'd have been working alongside Pa, perhaps, tilling and sowing and herding and reaping. And maybe he'd be looking forward to marriage, as Green-Eye had been. Funny, that, he thought—the thought that he himself might be in such a situation had not occurred to him until now.

Perhaps it was no surprise, given what Shay had referred to as 'stimuli'. Virtually all the residents of the oasis were young men and women. There was nobody younger than Dogfinger, and very few older than twenty-two or twenty-three summers or so. The reasons—the tragic, heart-stopping reasons—soon became clear. Everyone at the oasis had a story to tell: of rape, and mutilation, and murder, and of narrow escapes from Stoner raids on their respective villages all across the delta and as far south as the Cataracts of Cush. Of parents forced to watch the slaughter of their children before being slaughtered themselves—or being carried off by the Stoners to some unknown fate. The oasis was a refuge. A very few had found it by accident, but most, it seemed, had been led there by Shay.

Few had any more idea of the world beyond the oasis than Dogfinger did himself. But his mind, ever quick to anger, slower to reason, began to work on new paths. The people at the oasis, he wondered, were probably all that was left of humanity that had not been enslaved or killed by the Stoners. Not that Dogfinger came to that conclusion in such a measured way. Initially, what he felt was rage—intemperate, and volcanic. It was not Dogfinger's fault that many of the other people, especially the men, felt the same way. Tempers were often short, and fights broke out. Dogfinger seemed to be at the center of most of them.

That he won far more often than he lost seemed only to goad his persecutors. To taunt Dogfinger became a kind of sport—the older youths would jibe at his eye-patch, his missing finger, the fact that he was the youngest, until he could no longer contain his fury. His most potent adversary was Kingsnake, a man of twenty-one summers who, by reason of a cunning mind and superior bulk, had accreted a small group of men whose intent, it seemed, was to gather the fruits of the oasis to themselves, deserved or not—the food, the water, and especially the women. No-one dared speak out against Kingsnake and his gang, and when Dogfinger whispered about it to Shay in the depths of the night, the old man's response was that he was too far above such playground squabbles to get involved, and that if Dogfinger didn't like the other tourists at this resort, he should either sort it out himself, or find an hotel more to his liking.

One occasion, an hour before nightfall, about three months after Dogfinger had arrived, was typical—distinguished in Dogfinger's mind only by the cataclysmic event that followed immediately afterwards.

He had been herding the goats, spending the past week camping out with them in the dry pastures on the outer fringes of the oasis. The task was not arduous, but dull. Dogfinger had the distinct sensation that he was given such dead-beat jobs because nobody else wanted them, and because he was the youngest and smallest and never complained. Not that he was displeased: for one whose company had been himself for almost as long as he could remember, solitude was always the best of friends. The trouble began, as it always did, after he'd handed the goats over—on this occasion to Heron-Wing, a tall and very thin youth only a little older than he was—and returned to the village. If asked, he could not have remembered how he'd gotten there through the wide fields, or what he had been thinking about, but when he looked up, there was

Kingsnake and two of his cronies, hardly less bulky, blocking the gate through the village's thorn-bush perimeter. Dogfinger tried to sidle past, and succeeded—but he was not out of trouble, as the gang followed him into the village centre, accreting more members and onlookers as it went, and taunting Dogfinger all the while.

"How's your Ma, Squirt? Butt-fucked by any Stoners lately?"

"Yeah—chinless wonder. Bet your Pa was a Stoner."

"And if not your Ma, maybe *you* like to fuck Stoners, you fingerless fucker?"

"Bugger 'em up their hairy asses, don't you?"

"We all know you think you've got the cock for it."

"Oh, yeah, we've all seen how you love to wave *that* around"

Such taunts might, once, have riled him. But their constancy had worn him down so that now he felt only the mildest irritation. In truth, he was *bored* of being followed around by these idiots.

An image came to his mind, then, of being tracked across the savannah for several days by a leopard. Dogfinger was bored, then, too. Just tired of being followed. So Dogfinger had climbed the tree in which the leopard was lurking and ripped its head off with his bare hands. He couldn't have had more than ten summers, then. Now he had sixteen: and Kingsnake, while formidable, was no leopard. Dogfinger's only worry was that he'd rather not kill Kingsnake. Not straight away. But if he didn't, Kingsnake would only raise his game. So what was to be done?

Well, he thought, he couldn't just do *nothing*.

At the very center of the village, in the open grove of palms that served as the village square, Dogfinger turned to face his adversaries. They were all there, arranged in front of him: Kingsnake, with a bruiser of almost equal bulk on either side, and more of his gang arranged behind. Crowds of people were all around them, among the trees, forming a circle around the impromptu arena. The air was thick with anticipation, with fear. Dogfinger could sense that this was an important moment in the fortunes of the village; a moment of bifurcation, when the community would take either one course, or another. He hadn't asked to be put in this situation, but now that he had, he felt that the fates of the world had converged to this single point, and it was his choice, his privilege, to act.

Quick as thought, Dogfinger sprang forward, burying his head just beneath Kingsnake's ribcage. Kingsnake staggered back, bent double, winded. Before Kingsnake or any of his gang knew what was happening,

Dogfinger had pulled back, clenched his fists together and brought them up, hard, beneath Kingsnake's chin. Kingsnake's head snapped back with unnatural suddenness. The crack of his neck as it broke reverberated around the square. Kingsnake's body slumped, lifeless, before Dogfinger's feet. Dogfinger stood above it, arms spread, knees flexed, hands tingling, blood pounding in his chest and head, waiting for the assault that would inevitably follow.

But none came.

Instead, the crowd of villagers erupted with anger, setting on the rest of Kingsnake's gang before they could make good their escape. A crowd which just a dozen heartbeats earlier had been tense and quiet was now a seething anthill of rage. Amid roars and screams, daggers were drawn, and people started to fall. The sand of the square was soon stained with red.

Dogfinger found himself at the fringes of the melée, trying to engage with one of Kingsnake's gang, who was doing his best to evade him. Dogfinger felt a hand gripping his right forearm, yanking it behind him, painfully. He spun round, loosening the enemy's grip while simultaneously bringing his left hand down hard on his assailant's collarbone — and found that it was Moonrise, the young woman with the remarkably red hair. Her jaw was set with a grimace of pain, her wide, dark eyes afire with determination.

"Let him go, Dogfinger," she screamed above the din. "You must come with me, now." And without another word she gripped his arm again and pulled him away from the square at a run. They did not stop until they had reached a stand of tall rushes above the broad, sandy beach that surrounded one of the many lakes around the oasis. Moonrise pulled Dogfinger down into the rushes — her mouth met his before their bodies hit the dark, wet ground.

At first he struggled, fearing another attack. But if it were an attack, its tactics were like nothing he'd ever encountered before. The more he fought, the more she moaned, and the noises she made seemed more like pleasure than anger. Dimly, he remembered noises like that coming from the part of the hut where his Ma and Pa slept, separated from him and Green-Eye by a rush screen. Before he could work out what to do, Moonrise had gripped his head with both hands, and had plunged her tongue into his open mouth. He let his own tongue explore her mouth in response. He relaxed, and as he did so, Moonrise grabbed his left hand and pulled it up and inside her shirt, folding it around a breast. He had never felt such softness. Not even the freshly exposed internal organs of slaughtered animals, as he plunged his bloodied hands into their carcasses to rip them out—had such lustrous vibrancy, a sensation overtopped only by the dim pulse of her heart's beat.

Moonrise released her mouth from his, moaned once more and threw her head back, exposing her neck, white against the crimson infusion of her cheeks and parted lips. Dogfinger kissed and bit at her neck, took his hand from her breast, feeling it vibrate and recoil as he did so. With the same hand now away from the hot aura of her flesh, he rucked up the cloth of her skirt and ran a hand up a thigh as endlessly smooth as the fabric above was coarse. Her flesh, just above the knee, was at first firm and cool in the pungent afternoon heat of the reed-brake, but became broader, warmer and more yielding as he progressed, curling his fingers around and inward until his palm came across the tight-sprung curls of her sex. Moonrise parted her legs slightly, allowing Dogfinger's hand to come to rest between them. His palm fitted round the inward curve of her body, where he felt his fingers drawn inward, more, and further still, to her moisture, releasing a rich, powerful odor as he did so. An odor to overtop the seething fecundity of the damp, root-choked soil on which they lay. An odor of need; an odor of something lost that will never be found, no matter how feverish the search.

Moonrise groaned softly and bit hard on his earlobe, breathing hard and hot into his ear, and reached downwards to grab onto his penis, which he now noticed had become excruciatingly hard, its tip stinging against the inside of his kilt as it rubbed against it. Moonrise pulled it free. "I want you inside me, boy," she said, her voice dark, quavering and thick. Dogfinger pulled himself above her, lifting the hem of her skirt, as part of the same, sweeping choreography that demanded that she spread her legs apart for him. Kneeling above her in the green nest of rushes, he was entranced by the neatness of her red fur, counterpointed and contrasted by the clarity of the skin that surrounded it, and the marvellous scent that rose from her sex that made him throb with a pleasure so intense it almost frightened him. She reached down with a hand, her fingertips grown ruddy with arousal, and with great gentleness where there had been urgency and force, guided him inside her. He felt a feint of resistance, but no sooner had he thrust further in, to a region of delight beyond any means for him to express it, than he came. Confused, terrified, he pulled back, seeing his own juices spread and spill over her thighs. She pulled him down beside her and sighed, more with resignation than pleasure.

"You've never done this before, have you?" she said. But her voice that could as well have been spiked with frustration and anger was softened with concern. Dogfinger said nothing. "Oh, well. Plenty of time to learn," she said, and lay back among the reeds. He lay down beside her. The noise of crickets as Father-the-Sun descended; the scent and warmth of her flesh, and the soft sound of the breeze in the rushes and wavelets lapping on the shore below; all conspired to lull him into a smooth and even state somewhere between sleeping and waking.

But they didn't sleep.

Instead they began to talk, at first softly and quietly, then with increasing animation. Dogfinger told her of his history, telling her things that he'd never told anyone, not even Shay — the details of his last day in his village before he fled, as clearly as he could recall it. Moonrise then narrated her own tale, different in each grisly detail, but in general terms much the same as his, and of everyone else at the oasis — of the increased Stoner raids; of the arguments about whether they should move; of their helplessness before the brutality of the thick-set, stone-armored warriors.

"Shay found me," she said, "Wandering along the sea-coast, far to the north. He brought me here. At the end my feet were burned so badly that I couldn't walk, so for the last few days he had to carry me. By then, though, I wasn't much of a burden."

"How many summers had you?"

"Twelve. The Stoners raided when the village had turned out for my older sister's wedding feast. I was to have been married the next year. I can remember everything about the man to whom I'd been betrothed — what he looked like, the sound of his voice, everything. Except for his name. Isn't that strange?"

"Shay," said Dogfinger. "He said something to me, just as we came to the oasis."

"Hmm?"

"A warning. That I wasn't the big shot I might think I am. That winning was more than about... killing." Kingsnake's dead face, an expression of shock painted indelibly upon it, rose in his mind. "That I wasn't the... one of his strange words... *Moshiach*?"

"Messiah," she replied. "Shay says that to everybody."

"But... why?"

"I've given up trying to understand Shay," she said. "He seems like this crazy old man, bringing humans to his refuge like a crow obsessed with collecting shiny beetles or sparkly pebbles. Why does he do it? He's *driven*. Something about a goddess, he says."

"*HaShekhna?*"

"That's the one. But the dear old thing, batty though he might be, he's saved our lives, hasn't he?"

"Yes, sure, he's strange," he said. "But isn't there a purpose to it? Are we humans just his toys, or are we free to leave? Take our chances with the world? We can't stay here for ever, can we? Shouldn't we break out, to take the fight to the Stoners? To take back what is ours? For the sakes of our families? Our... our... self-respect? I had more of that when I was a lonely hunter in the desert, living off rats and roots, than I've had here, with food and clothes and other people, with..." Dogfinger stopped, stunned by his own eloquence—he'd said more words together in this one speech than at any other time in his life.

Moonrise sat up, and her expression on her red lips, her burning eyes, was, at first, unreadable. Triumph? Desire? Both? She pulled him closer.

"Shall we have another go?" she said. Within seconds he was inside her, pushing into depths so warm and liquid that at first he could not feel his way, but as he moved, the tissue inside her folded and corrugated so that he could feel its arousing rasp as he moved back and forth. She spread her legs as wide as she could, moving them upwards, canting him forwards above her as she did so; and wrapped her calves across his shoulders, pressing his sides with her thighs, forcing him inside her as deeply as he could go. Her voice rose into a strangled pitch of pleasured sound as he felt her wetness spread across his own thighs and belly. He pushed deeper, now, and harder, and found that he was now in control of her emotions and his. She climaxed in one last spasm, raking his shoulders with her fingernails, and fell back with a whimper.

"Now," she said, through full, red lips, her brown eyes closing with one, last, insouciant sparkle, "*that* was more *like* it."

In the months that followed, Dogfinger found that whereas people had once been dismissive towards him, they were now deferential. Where they had once ignored him, they now sought his advice. Slowly, almost without his being aware of it, his vote was not only registered by the other refugee villagers, but became the decider, the casting vote.

Dogfinger moved out of Shay's hut and in with Moonrise. Their marriage was celebrated for days, crowned in the early spring of the following year by the birth of twins. Nobody objected that Dogfinger named them after the twin siblings he'd so cruelly lost, for everyone had similar memories, and these new births were seen as harbingers of hope unlooked-for.

These children were followed by many others, born of women all over the oasis, and fathered mostly by Dogfinger. It was the tradition of many tribes, including that of Moonrise, for the chief of the village to impregnate as many women as possible, so that the strength of his seed would be spread. Dogfinger was at first startled by this, but was persuaded by Moonrise's acquiescence, if not her overt encouragement. After one such birth, Shay offered Dogfinger a monosyllabic word of congratulation (accompanied by a sly wink that spoke volumes) before setting out on yet another trip of retrieval, to add more stray humans to his collection.

"I shan't need to *schlep* my carcass around for much longer," he said, "now that you've been jumping on all the village girls with such gusto. I must say, they do seem so terribly obliging. But there's no accounting for taste."

Five more years passed. Five years in which the village at *Baj!ra'adhzt* turned from a refugee camp into a prosperous township, whose business was punctuated with the screams and whines and wails of children from what seemed like every house. One day close to the beginning of the dry season, when the cold of the desert at night would creep from across the oasis and into every heart, Shay returned after an absence of almost a year. Dogfinger had wondered where the old Annakhnu had got to, or indeed if he'd see him again, until a knock came on the lintel of his hut, as evening fell.

Dogfinger drew back the cloth curtain to see, silhouetted by the full moon streaming into the house, a man desiccated, sandblasted, as if the winds of the desert had sculpted his very flesh. Across his shoulders he carried a ragged boy of perhaps nine summers, a boy who was in hardly any better state than he was.

"Well-met by moonlight, proud *Ijadhazev*," said Shay, before his knees buckled. Dogfinger caught the boy as he toppled from Shay's shoulders—and Shay, shortly after. He looked into the child's eyes, and all his own history came back to him in a sudden rush. A history much like his own. He had been the same age as this child when disaster had overtaken him and his family. Now was the time, he resolved: *now*. The time had come for action.

Moonrise hurried through from the hut's other room, accompanied by the twins and two smaller children. She took the boy from Dogfinger's arms.

"This child needs feeding," she said, her voice pointed with worry. "I have some broth on the go."

"Chicken soup," said Shay, tottering, resting on Dogfinger's shoulder for support. "It solves everything. Might I beg a cup for my own agèd and unworthy lips, O Fair Bride of *Ijadhazev*?"

Moonrise smiled. "Coming up," she said, before disappearing amid a flock of offspring. Moonrise had ripened: her thighs and hips were broad, her snowy breasts swung loose and full beneath her shirt, and the roundness of her belly indicated continued fecundity. Shay looked up at Dogfinger, who was gazing at his wife with undisguised adoration. "You've done well, young man," he said, "although, personally, I don't think I could put up with the *noise*."

It proved to have been Shay's final trip, but one. More than wind and sand was eating away at his increasingly emaciated frame. Less than a month after Shay had returned with the boy across his shoulders, Dogfinger called on the sage, to find him comatose, sprawled on the floor of his hut, in a pool of his own excrement. Shay didn't seem to know quite where he was, nor the identity of the small but well-knit man with the birthmark round his eye who picked him up, cleaned him, and took him to his own, warm and well-ordered home, where he was cared for by a voluptuous woman with surprisingly orange hair and a lot of noisy children.

Shay's recovery was slow, but steady, and by the time that Moonrise gave birth to her fifth child, he announced that he was ready to move back to his own house. Dogfinger and Moonrise objected, but Shay's response was just as strenuous.

"Are you kidding?" he said. "Look at you. With seven souls in this hut, what you clearly need is an old fart like me cluttering up the place. For sure, like a hole in the head." He would not be gainsaid.

Indeed, once Shay had returned to his old quarters, and Moonrise and several other village women had cleaned it up a bit, Shay returned very much to his old self. After the festival of the vernal equinox, by which time Moonrise had fallen pregnant again, and at which Shay insisted offerings were made to *HaShekhna*, the old man summoned Dogfinger to his hut.

"My last trip into the world, *Ijadhazev*, was most instructive," he began. "If I have been adding fewer new acquisitions to my collection — oh, yes, I know what people say, and I don't mind — it's not just because age has taken its toll. It's because there are fewer souls to save. The Stoners have completely cleared this entire region of humans, as far south as Cush and far to the east, beyond the great delta. There are none left alive. None more to be rescued.

"I fear that the only free humans in the world are here, at *Baj!ra'adhzt*—at least as far as I can tell. If *HaShekhna* had not instructed me, so long ago... well, I dread to think..."

Dogfinger remained silent. He knew Shay well enough to interpret his dramatic pauses as just that, and not invitations to interrupt.

"I tell you that there is hope, *Jjadhazev*," Shay went on. "Yes, *hope*. I have seen and heard about many other kinds of people in the world, on my travels—from giants, twice the height of a man and covered with white fur, to small, sly, dark men with the eyes of cats, who can work great magic, though I have this only by reputation, I might add.

"But no matter what their differences, they all say the same thing— the Stoners are in retreat. It might seem hard to believe, but they, along with all the other kinds of men, are sliding into extinction. All you need to do, *Jjadhazev*, is reach out your hand and take what's yours."

Dogfinger thought of Shay's final acquisition, the small boy. A boy very much like himself, once upon a time.

"The time is now," he muttered. Shay said no more.

The following morning, it was found that Shay had disappeared. A search party was sent to scour the oasis. It was Dogfinger who saw him, a wavering speck, disappearing on the western horizon. Disappearing over the edge of the Earth, a reflection of how he had first come into Dogfinger's life, rising above Earth's rim, so long before. Dogfinger kept this secret to himself.

And so it was that in the refuge of *Baj!ra'adhzt*, which means both 'home' and 'beginning,' a boy once so feral that he could hardly recall his own name grew into a loving husband, a proud father, and a great leader.

But most of all, he grew into a man.

Chapter 7. Witness

Gascony, France, Earth, June, 2073

Then felt I like some watcher of the skies
When a new planet swims into his ken;
John Keats — *On First Looking into Chapman's Homer*

First, they had to work out how they were going to study the Sigil in reasonable comfort. The day after Jadis' birthday party, they opened the doors to the stable to assess the upcoming task. It was greater than any of them had anticipated.

When the Sigil had first taken up residence, the barn was a well-lit laboratory, with clean concrete floors, polished benches and plenty of lighting. The intervening years had not been kind. The concrete floor was still there, of course — scrubbed daily by Jack and whatever help he could get, in the course of mucking out the cows and the pony, and now Tom and Domingo's rented horses. The percheron seemed to occupy about half the space all on its own and looked distinctly cramped and unhappy.

The lighting had lasted as long as they could keep the solar panels and wind turbine in adequate repair, but an accumulation of wear and tear had meant that it worked at best intermittently, when it worked at all. In any case, the scarcity of light bulbs rendered as superfluous any efforts to keep the panels in trim. But light bulbs could now be obtained from the Far East, albeit at great cost, so now the machinery would have to be mended — another job to add to Jack's endless list of Augean tasks. The lab benches had been scavenged when more immediate uses for valuable slabs of hardwood had seemed more pressing.

The Sigil itself, mounted on a sturdy plinth inside its evacuated transparent plastic case, and packed in a crate, was too heavy and too fragile to move without lifting gear they no longer had. In any event it was buried beneath an accumulation of farmyard clutter. Just getting at it would demand an excavation almost as archeological as the one that had brought it to light in the first place.

Even without this impending dig, there was no way they were going to get close to the Sigil unless the livestock were put into one of the fields more or less full-time. Now summer had arrived there was no reason why this could not be done. But it took another week for Jack and Tom to renovate a crumbling storm-shelter for the animals close to the field-gate, where they could be fed and watered, freeing up the barn once more.

Tom reflected that the farm was slowly slipping into general dilapidation as his parents got older. But even a day here at his home had cheered and freshened him, blown away some of the brooding disquiet of Cambridge. Perhaps he could extend his sabbatical more or less indefinitely. Working here alongside his parents, putting the farmhouse to rights, digging in the dirt of this hallowed and ancient place, had always been a source of immense satisfaction for him.

Domingo, on the other hand, seemed to chafe at the delay and added his mighty frame to speed the work as much as he could. But while Jack and Tom were busy, he took the opportunity of a trip to the village to assess the logistics of moving the Vatican to the hilltop. Jack told Domingo that he could probably take over the top two floors of the old Mairie. His own duties as village schoolteacher teacher and sometime ex-officio village headman barely occupied two ground-floor rooms of the cavernous, crumbling, once-handsome pink-stuccoed building.

And so, several mornings later he and Jadis took a turn around the village. The thought of resuming her daily walk in Domingo's company filled Jadis with so much excitement that she practically bounced up and down with the eagerness of a little girl promised a trip to the funfair. It took her back to days of contentment long ago, when the then black-haired Domingo had first appeared in their lives.

Not that there was any chance of a tranquil wander, just the two of them talking, without interruption. The village itself saw to that.

Their first stop was the *Sanglier D'Or*, still a café of sorts, but now more like a tavern from an earlier age, the village's centre for news and gossip. Always bustling with life, its clientèle included a motley assortment of travellers from far and near—from tinkers to mendicant friars—pumped by the regulars for tales and ballads and word of things happening far away. News of Domingo's arrival had reached the *Sanglier* long before he had, so he and Jadis found the bar packed with spectators. Indeed, these now spilled out into the Place Etienne Geoffroy Saint-Hilaire, to make a welcoming committee fit for the return of a conquering hero.

"It's the Pope!" the cry went up. "The Pope and the Doctor! Make room! Make room!"

On hearing this general acclamation, Yvon Rossignol, the latest inn-keeper of the *Sanglier*, made his corpulent way to the front of the throng.

As a relatively recent arrival, Rossignol had hardly ever seen Jadis; and the news of the Pope's arrival had been colored by stories of how, as plain Father Domingo, he had pulled the village together in its moment of crisis almost twenty years before. If the tales he'd heard were to be believed, Jadis was a white witch, a priestess of great power with the uncanny ability to restore life, whose healing arts had touched every family in the village and for many miles around.

"She brought my twin sons into the world," recalled one bright-eyed patron, whose account was typical. "Breech births! My Bernadette nearly died, a goner for certain, but the Doctor brought them into the light and saved her life, too! And all my sons and daughters after that!"

Left unsaid was the general assumption that she had some direct line to the core of the Earth, and was in mysterious communion with the long-dead ancestors of them all.

For some years Jadis had wondered at the source of the eggs, the hams, the produce, the bunches of flowers and especially the small dolls made from wheat stalks left anonymously by her kitchen door. After a while it had dawned on her that these were presents for services rendered. It never once crossed her mind (as it had Jack's) that these were votive offerings. She had turned into her own cave-painting.

And Father Domingo, said the locals — *our* Father Domingo, mind — has become the Pope himself. And he's here, in Saint-Rogatien! Where the Doctor had mended the ills of the village, rumor had been current for some time about how Domingo was doing the same to the rest of the world.

"Truly, he is a master of the fates of us all," a hooded and grizzled Christophorine had said one night, sipping a foaming pint of ale, recounting inflated tales of Domingo's travels to a rapt audience of locals.

"He is that — nothing less," said a colleague bearing the cross and lightning-bolt blazon of the Order of Saint-Adelard, his face scarred with radiation and chemical burns that would have been the signs of sorcery were they not carried by a man not so plainly touched by holiness. "They say he has been to the ends of the Earth... and *beyond*," he declaimed dramatically, raising a *pastis*. "He meets the creatures of Satan head-on, they say, and faces them down!"

Rossignol's first sight of the old friends, as they crested the hill and walked slowly into the cobbled square, did not disappoint. The Pope was a giant of a man, his bearded face framed by a long, snow-white mane, his hood thrown back, his scarlet cloak lifted into a swirling train by the gentle breeze, his chasuble richly decorated with a splendid design of red and green parrots, beautiful dark-haired girls with floral head-dresses, and muscular young men riding great blue waves on yellow planks. If this really was the Pope himself, he knew how to make an entrance.

The woman who walked so confidently next to him, despite being hardly more than half his size, seemed at first a pale shadow, in her long, grubby grey coat, floral skirt, sandals, market bag and floppy straw hat. But he could see that hiding behind her flowing grey hair was a face of all-consuming intelligence, concentrated in two large, penetrating eyes. He would not bear that gaze too long, Rossignol thought. She had the kind of eyes that could see right through you, if you'd let them. Perhaps cast a spell on you. But when she smiled, she seemed like the freshest village girl.

When they found the village all out to greet them, the Pope laughed heartily, and the woman laughed too—but when she saw the extent of the crowd, she took off her hat, lifted her arms and gathered her hair on the top of her head. Rossignol gasped as the lithe slenderness of her figure. This white witch must have been a captivating beauty, perhaps not so long ago. She looked—what—seventy? But she moved? Ah! Like a girl at her first dance.

Rossignol now found himself at the front of the crowd, pushed before the two dignitaries. Standing up to his full height of five-foot-three, he bade them welcome in the gravest voice he could muster, and bowed as low as his globular frame would allow. Domingo bowed even lower in response, his nose almost touching the ground, and the crowd hooted with mirth. Domingo helped the innkeeper to his feet, and fearing he might have made fun of him, embraced him like a brother.

"My good innkeeper, I thank you. And as I have the pleasure of so many ears at once, I have something that might prove of interest to all." The crowd hushed in an instant.

"Now, I would not wish to discommode any of you, my old friends. But although I have traveled to many places, I have always thought of Saint-Rogatien as my true home. Ever since I first arrived here in... er... *when* was it, Jadis?"

Then the woman spoke for the first time. She looked up at the huge man, smiling at the Representative of Christ on Earth if she were indulging a pet dog, and talking in the kind of French that Yvon's grandma would have found quaintly antique.

"Verily, methought 'twas of twenty hundreds of years and of twenty of nine."

"My old friend and colleague Dr Markham is quite... er... *correct*," continued the Pope, whose French, while in the high style, was at least this side of medieval. "I first came here... ah... forty-four years ago. It was different world back then, eh?" General laughter.

"And I love this place so very much that I have chosen to make it my home again: *et que sur cette pierre je bâtirai mon Église!*"

Deafening roars of approval.

"Now, my friends, I would not wish to keep you from your errands. However,"—Domingo looked over the crowds to count several hoods and cowls—"I should very much appreciate the offices of my Christophorine and Adelardian Brethren, and the good Priest of the Parish, if I may..."

And so Domingo was carried off to organize the Vatican in exile. Jadis felt slightly deflated. She did not wish to have coffee alone, so she went to the boulangerie and chatted with Amélie Foucoult's daughter Camille, exchanging a half-dozen fresh duck eggs for two loaves, still hot from the oven. Jadis reflected that Camille, a strapping girl of nineteen, was the first child she'd brought into the world, with inexpert midwifery, that first, bitter winter after the Plague had struck. Jadis complimented Camille on the excellence of the birthday cake she'd made for her.

"Why, *thank you*, Doctor," blushed Camille, as if Jadis had blessed the bakery with a spell for its continued success. She leaned forward conspiratorially and, asked, half-whispering: "Is he really... *you* know... the *Pope*? You know, from *Rome*?"

Jadis confided that he was.

"But Rome must be so *grand* compared with our village, mustn't it Doctor?" gushed Camille. Jadis confessed that she'd never actually been to Rome herself, but for all its reported refulgently grandificent omnipulence (Camille found the Doctor hard to understand sometimes, she used such long words) the Pope had always thought Saint-Rogatien a *much* nicer place. And so they parted in mutual satisfaction, the one with bread for the next day and a feeling that her first patient hadn't turned out so badly; the other with the vague sense that she'd touched the hem of greatness.

Ten days after Domingo and Tom's arrival, the barn was now clear of animals. Jack and Tom fixed the solar panels and turbine as well as they could, but in the end they had to call on professional help. Laurent Gaspard, the farmhouse's regular electrician, had escaped the Plague, but had perished in the dire winter that followed, when, up on a church steeple fixing a lightning conductor, he'd slipped on an icy tile and had fallen to his death. It was his son Pascal who now carried on the family business. A basic electricity supply now existed thanks to the ceaseless efforts of the Adelardians, though its coverage was nothing like as extensive as it had been before '54: so Pascal Gaspard could afford to be only a part-time sparks. These days, he was really only interested in breeding beef. Jack managed to tear him away from his beloved herd of prime Limousin to get the barn lighting at least partly functional again. This meant a great deal of cursing, trying to source components (not just light bulbs) and digging holes in the adjacent field, tracing buried cable and patching the places where it had been gnawed through by dormice.

After that it was only a matter of shifting the detritus of decades to disclose the Sigil. Straw bales that were once stacked ceiling-high were shifted to the other end of the barn, lifting clouds of floury, sour-tasting dust, quantities of owl pellets and the desiccated corpses of unidentifiable small mammals that the Horribles had stored for rainy days that never came. Jadis was amused and delighted at the quantity of *objets trouvés* that were unearthed in the process, including her favourite border fork (mislaid, '68); a basket once used by Micawber, the dog (discarded after his death in a road accident, '61, but which Jadis could never persuade herself to cast onto the bonfire, and now much chewed by mice) and—amazingly—several boxes of very dusty but still functional light bulbs.

The first day of July was scheduled as the day when the tarp would be removed, and the Sigil revealed. The day was fiercely hot from the moment the Sun broke the horizon: the family attended to their chores as quickly as they could and then broke for breakfast at eight o'clock. Then it was to the barn. Not a word was spoken, and the tension rose with every step they took across the egg-fryingly hot yard, the remaining fragments of weathered tarmac already starting to soften and bubble.

For Jadis, the feeling was uncannily like that she'd had when the Sigil had first been discovered, in the shaft beneath the summit of the Great Pyramid at Souris Saint-Michel: that each time she'd covered it up and returned to it, she'd half-hoped that it would not be there, or have turned into something else.

Domingo's feelings could be summed up as an angular disjunction of hypotheses. His mind was so full of the many different ways he'd sought to explain the provenance of this object, and the diverse theological implications implied by each, that he hoped he'd be able to see the Sigil simply as it was, unadorned by his preconceptions.

Jack had thought relatively little about the Sigil until recently. He'd been far too busy with the mundane matters of organizing the farmhouse and the community of Saint-Rogatien to concentrate overmuch on science. Lately he wondered if his avoidance hadn't been deliberate, and, rather despite himself, he was beginning to wonder whether he'd become a little superstitious about the thing.

As if, he thought, it had been the Sigil that had called him to Souris Saint-Michel, or even to France in the first place, even before he'd got his doctorate: the long-sought focus of all his desires, the grounding for all his instincts.

No, that wasn't it, surely? His trip to France had been to give Jadis some space while she completed her finals — hadn't it? But what if it were a mixture of both — moving away from Jadis as he had been drawn into the orbit of the Sigil? He knew that this line of reasoning (if it could be dignified as such) was entirely ridiculous.

But it could have been worse, even than that: that the Sigil that had tugged on his soul from his youth, when he'd walked the hills and valleys of Britain and felt the landscape start beneath him, like the struggles of a caught leveret felt through a poacher's sack. It wasn't the Sigil's fault that he'd started out in England, rather than Gascony. If he'd come from Timbuktu, he'd still have been drawn *here* — pulled by the Sigil in its quest for its own revelation. In which case the Sigil had had nothing in particular to do with Jadis, except inasmuch as she'd also been snared, right from the start, by Jack's unconscious quest. No wonder, then, that he felt his boots drag with each step he took closer to the barn. The distance from the kitchen door was hardly twenty meters, but it could have been twenty miles, or twenty parsecs.

For Tom, inevitably, memories of the Sigil were tied up with those of Shoshana. He had only ever seen it in her company, and she had been party to the last serious discussion that anyone had had about it. As for the Sigil itself — the bald, physical reality of it — he had no particular memory or expectation.

The barn was dark and cool after the yard. Jack pulled the doors open and disappeared into the sharp shadows to switch on the lights. The interior was flooded with a soft yellow radiance more like that of mellow eventide than bright early morning. Jadis imagined she'd turned up for a barn dance a little early, and half expected people to barge in after her, with musical instruments, barrels of beer and strings of bunting and fairy lights.

Under the lights, strung on chains from the gnarled and cracked oak beams high above, the floor was bare except for a trestle table, four chairs of assorted sizes and types, and a few oddments kicked into corners that nobody had got round to clearing up. And, at one end, the Sigil, under its blue tarp.

The four of them stood over the shrouded object, each waiting for the other to make the first move. Jadis could hardly believe that they'd worked themselves up into such a state. She was convinced that they'd been feeding off one another, and that had each of them been alone, they'd have simply marched in and pulled the tarp away.

"Well?" she demanded: "Are we going to wait here all day? Some of us have things to do!" And at that she stepped forward and dragged off the tarp to reveal—a wooden packing crate like any other. The others exhaled at once, as if they had expected a monster rather than some ordinary household object. Released from immobility they crowded round, helping Jadis prise open the lid and remove some of the polystyrene packing chips. In a few moments they'd exposed the surface of the Sigil's hard plastic prison, and in a few more, they'd removed enough packing for the Sigil to be clearly seen.

Jadis peered at it through its casing. No, she thought—it's still there. It hadn't gone away, as she'd secretly hoped. The object was much smaller than she'd imagined, as it had expanded over its unseen years to fill her dreams. It was no more than a gray tablet, maybe twelve by three centimeters, and a centimeter thick. If you looked very carefully indeed, you could just about discern the faintest tracery of engraving on its face. After a minute or two, the whole pattern would become evident, and you'd see the three perfect circles, the crescents, and the fine, straight lines that radiated outwards from the central circle to the corners and edges of the bordered inscription.

Funny, she thought, it was the unnatural smoothness and flatness of the object that had first drawn their attention. The inscription itself had only become apparent a little while later, so fine were the lines in which it had been wrought. Jadis remembered the headaches she'd got whenever she found herself staring at the inscription for more than a minute or two. Silly me, she thought—she'd thought then that the headaches were part of the menopause she'd been going through at around the same time. Nevertheless, she'd got into the habit of looking only at photographs of the Sigil. These were just as good as the real thing, for no matter how they recorded the object—X-rays, UV, infra-red, in the visual, magnetic resonance — the pattern of lines and crescents and circles showed up, just the same.

Domingo bent closely over the transparent casing and found himself tracing the Sigil's lines with mental fingertips. The line's edges looked almost as sharp as those of newly cut paper. He wondered at the remarkable evenness with which the inscription had been drawn, and with that, began to imagine a startling possibility. That what they were looking at was not something individually hand-crafted, but mass-produced. And if so, why stop at just one? For the moment, he kept these thoughts to himself.

For Jack, hanging back, it was the tablet itself, rather than the inscription on it, that resonated most strongly with his sense of what belonged in a landscape, and what didn't. This lump of nameless material most definitely did *not* belong, not in *any* landscape. No matter how hard they'd tried, the Sigil's matrix remained defiantly unidentifiable. He remembered a talk he'd had with a physicist who confessed herself baffled by the way that any gravitational detectors went awry whenever they came close to the Sigil.

"It's *weird*," she'd said.

"How so?"

"Well, it's not just random gravitational anarchy," she said. "Put a detector a few hundred meters away from the object, and you know something's up. The readings get more... well, more *deviant*... the closer you get, until they reach a peak about half a millimeter above the surface of the object. But then... well, it's *weird*, that's all." The physicist had smiled, nervously, revealing an array of perfect teeth, but her gray-blue eyes had shown nothing so much as *fear*.

"But then... what?" Jack had pressed. The physicist had been a rather striking blonde from the University of Uppsala, he remembered, wryly, though he couldn't quite recall her name. Frida? Agnetha? Something like that. He wondered idly what she was doing now. If she'd married. If she'd had kids.

If she'd survived the Plague.

Back then, she'd just looked embarrassed, as if to discuss the Sigil any further would somehow have compromised her professional integrity.

"Well, closer to the object than that, the gravity field plunges to... well, there's no getting away from it. It plunges to zero."

Jack was stunned.

"That's right," she'd said, this time with more confidence. "It's as if there's nothing there at all. This material… well, it's like a *hole*. A hole in space-time."

Jack remembered relaying this information to Jadis later that same day, or perhaps in one of the days following. He felt he had to pick his moment. They were in the kitchen. She had grabbed her mac and market bag for a trip to the village.

"That physicist…" he began.

"The blonde? The rather *good-looking* one?" Jadis had teased. Jack remembered how he'd flushed. Agnetha or Frida or whoever it was had indeed been rather attractive.

"She thinks the inscription basically isn't there," he'd said. "Much ado about nothing."

"Well then," said Jadis. "Nothing for us to worry about, is there? What do you fancy for supper?" And his wife's long legs had carried her out the door with the insouciance of a gazelle.

If only the Sigil *had* been nothing to worry about. Were he to admit as much, it had haunted his thoughts from that day to this. Had the Sigil woven threads through his whole life just to bring him here, only to leave him mystified? Had they avoided studying it simply because of its nature, strange almost beyond conception? Beyond imagining? Jack felt that a dead end was not the answer. It *had* to mean *something*. But what?

"Domingo," asked Tom, in a voice so quiet that it was barely audible, yet which quavered with an emotion hardly controlled: "would you mind stepping back, I…"

"Yes Tom, of course… of course," replied the big man, standing up straight and turning round to look at Tom, whose eyes now blazed with an alien radiance.

"*C'est incroyable. Incroyable!*" Tom fought to catch his breath, his face bathed in wonder and terror. Domingo moved towards him, solicitously. "*Non*, Domingo, I'm sorry, I'm okay, really… I'm okay."

"What is it, Tom?" Jadis asked. "What can you see?"

In truth, Tom could hardly describe precisely what he had seen on the stone, except that it was so completely unexpected that he was temporarily winded with shock. When he'd last seen the rock all those years before, it was just that—a stone, with the feint, elegant lines of the Sigil inscribed on it. But sometime between now and then, either the Sigil had changed, or he had.

Or maybe it was that he'd long ago discarded his iShades habit, and was looking at the inscription with his naked eyes, for the first time. This time, for real.

When his mother had scooped the last of the polystyrene chips from the Sigil's case, it was as if she'd uncovered a bank of bright ultraviolet runway lights that blasted into the backs of his eyes.

Squinting, he saw that the radiance was not general, but coincident with the lines of the Sigil. For him, and him alone, the pattern was etched in lines of purple fire that cast everything else into shadow: the contrast was so strong that this alone was all he saw, freed from its matrix. But, even as he watched, the pattern lifted from the matrix and tilted towards him in space. It grew, unfolding into something altogether more complex, drawing him into a new realm of sensation in which the barn, Domingo, his parents, and even his own body, faded into a ghostly background. The Sigil that evolved before his astonished eyes was to the engraved inscription as the finished mansion is to the architect's floor plan.

The central circle rose from shadow and grew into a violet sphere before his eyes. It seemed to fill his vision. The violet softened to pale blue, and then to yellow, as the sphere contracted to an apparent size of around a meter in diameter. Flares and prominences shot out from its surface into a turbulent, million-degree plasma. The sphere rotated before his eyes, like a giant, hot globe.

It was a star.

Tom could have sworn that he was a disembodied spirit, floating in space above the stellar corona.

And then it was joined by two other spheres, rising from the circles to right and left. Like the central star, they developed from an incandescent violet, although their fates were different. The star on the left condensed to a sullen red, like a pool of magmatic sludge. Tom thought of Lac 9352, the star whose terrifying fate he'd seen for himself. The star on the right also condensed, but the purple turned to an icy blue-white of an almost unbearable brilliance.

For a while all three blazed before him — red, yellow and blue-white — rotating, spitting out sparks, disgorging rivers of plasma into one another's orbits to create a dazzling, multicolored aurora. And then the stars on the right and left turned black: he could see spots on their surfaces that spread like hideous cankers hundreds of thousands of miles across, until the stars were eclipsed, each one giving vent to a final coronal blast of a power that would vaporize planets — before they van-

ished. The spaces they had once occupied were blacker than their surroundings, traversed only by a few stray and lonely photons. Floating
above the voids, Tom thought that if only he were able to glance directly
into them, he'd see dark tunnels that stretched forever. Except that
shapes began to move within the blackness itself, still darker than the
pitchy voids they inhabited, writhing angrily like maggots squirming
over a rotten corpse.

"What do I see, *Maman*?" said Tom. "I can see the pits of hell opening
up beneath my feet."

The dark shapes climbed out of the stagnant pits where stars had
once stood, rising like two horribly fluid, ebony cobras, until they fragmented into smaller, black shapes that moved in formation towards the
central star, from right and left. The shapes were much smaller than the
stars, and their precise forms were hard to make out. But the formations
in which they moved were all too recognizable. They were crescents, like
the two crescents in the Sigil. They fell on the central star like soldier ants
on a tethered goat, diving into its surface, breaking it up into shredded
masses of livid orange fragmented by black fissures that looked hair-
thin, but which could have accommodated the whole Earth millions of
times over. Within minutes the central star had disappeared, and all that
was left was yawning, eternal night.

Disoriented by the sudden and complete blackness, Tom staggered
and fell backwards, bumping into Domingo. Trying to stand, he turned,
vomited on the floor, and, tripping over his own feet, caught his head on
the edge of the table with a crack. He toppled like a falling tree. By the
time he'd reached the floor he was out cold.

He awoke to an intensity of pain that made him wish he were dead.
He was vaguely aware that it was evening.

"Tom—it's me," said Jadis, her voice seeming simultaneously close,
and yet coming from a wintry distance, as if she were calling to him from
across a snowbound field.

"*Maman*? I'm sorry, I don't feel so well." Jadis saw her son's face turn
green and whisked the bowl into place just in time for him to be sick in
it, after which he turned over and slept solidly for thirty hours.

He was still feverish when he awoke two mornings later, but he felt
well enough to sit up on the sofa in the sitting-room, when he told them
all what he had seen. Jadis and Jack were aghast. Only Domingo seemed
to understand, but perhaps that was because he had also witnessed the
destruction of Lac 9352.

Tom could understand why they'd be so shocked, but what puzzled him more than anything else was that none of the others had seen the visions he'd witnessed. When it became clear that all they'd seen was the naked Sigil on the rock, he became irritable, then angry. The last thing he said was that if everything he did prompted people to make fun of him, he wouldn't give them the benefit of his company, and went to his room. In any case, he still had a pounding headache, and wished to lie down with his eyes shut.

Domingo, Jack and Jadis met in worried conclave in the kitchen late that evening. They'd all had very long days, and, much against their better judgment, were forced to leave Tom to his own devices. Jadis had worked hard with the animals and in the garden. Tom felt well enough to do some weeding for an hour or two in the late afternoon, but would exchange no more than a sullen monosyllable and did his best to keep out of Jadis' way—a fact that distressed her more than she was prepared to admit.

Jack had spent the day mostly in the village. He'd had a class to teach, and also to welcome the visiting Mayor of Seissan who had come to bask in reflected Papal glory. There had been a seemingly unending stream of such people over the past couple of days, when Jack's mind had become a helpless, torpid mass with Tom at its centre. His son had seemed so terribly unhappy: the communications they'd had from the Petrine Abbot explained some of it, but the essence of the problem was clothed in characteristically Cantabridgian circumlocution. And as Tom was unwilling to say any more, Jack felt tied, helpless—literally, unable to help.

As for Domingo, he spent much of the time in deep discussion with his expanding retinue of monks, making seemingly endless plans for moving people and equipment to the old Mairie, and yet all the while worrying about Tom. What was to be done, if he wouldn't talk? What *could* be done?

"Jack, Jadis, we must do our best to excuse Tom," Domingo began. "He has been under the most incredible strain at Cambridge. What with all that... ah... business with those East Asian hominids, and the destruction of the star we witnessed together, at the Astrometry Institute, I rather think he has had enough. Our homeward journey together was rather...ah... *fraught*. He is consumed with preoccupation; he will confide in no-one, yet it is plain that coming back here has brought back memories of Shoshana, for whose death he feels responsible."

Jadis's eyes were pools looking into space. "Oh, my poor boy," she said, and hurried from the room. The two men could hear her small, confident steps fading across the hall, and the creak of the treads as she climbed the stairs. Jack and Domingo remained as silent as expectant fathers outside a maternity ward, barred from the secret ministrations of women. Presently, Jadis returned.

"He's locked the room, but all is quiet. He's asleep. I managed to peep through the keyhole. Don't worry, Jack, he's breathing. I'll go up again later and…"

"But what was all that about disappearing stars?" Jack asked Domingo: "Is that… true?"

"Yes, I rather think it is," said Domingo. "This should probably go no further than this room, but I have a strong feeling that Tom's interpretation of the Sigil is the correct one, whatever one might think about the manner of its… ah… communication. He and Shoshana were quite correct — it is a *warning*. There is something in space that consumes stars, and it is not very far away from the Sun. I dread what the next few years might bring. You might as well know, but I am arranging with my more… ah… *technically minded* brethren to wire up the Mairie so that we can be in real-time broadband contact with the Astrometry Institute." He laughed, nervously. "So if we *are* in for the End of the World, we'll hear about it here first. We owe it to ourselves to be prepared spiritually, even if there is nothing practical that can be done.

"And that, my oldest and best friends, is what most worries me about Tom. He is boiling with anxiety, but bottles it up inside, with no… er… *release valve*. Confession has a value that goes beyond the perfunctorily religious, I think."

He paused, weighing words in his mind before speaking further. "Shoshana Levinson was worried about things, too. She'd had a rotten life before coming here, and then it got worse, because of what was… ah… *eating* her inside. She told me about it, too — or as much as she was prepared to — a little while before she died. And I believe that when that moment came, she had achieved some degree of… ah… *equanimity*."

Silence reigned while the ghost of Shoshana Levinson took its place at the table and then, with a sigh, evaporated.

"I never knew…," Jadis said.

"I am sorry, Jadis," Domingo replied, "but I am honor-bound to keep confidences… ah… *confidential*. In any case, were I a doctor, as you seem to be nowadays, I'd recommend that sleep is probably the best medicine for Tom, at least for the present."

"Yes. Let Tom sleep," said Jack. "It's clear that he needs it. Heavens, we *all* need it."

Jadis, unable to sit still, rose again to boil a kettle. "Domingo," she asked amid the flurry of cups and jars and spoons, "did Tom *really* see all that—what he says he did? Was it generated by the Sigil? Or did he imagine it all?"

"It is very hard to say," Domingo replied. "We have, I think, two options. Either Tom's account was brought on by his own mental strain, amplified by having witnessed, with me, the destruction of a star. Believe me, the experience of seeing an entire star dismantled in less than two minutes is every bit as cathartic as you might suppose. The other option is that Tom saw something external and real that we didn't, which, in the end, boils down to much the same thing."

"But we don't always *know* what Tom is seeing, do we?" said Jack: "Remember how we hardly even thought about him being blind, because he seemed to get around without vision?"

Jadis put three mugs of hot tea on the table. "And wasn't he blind again when he came back here?" she added. "After they had escaped from Israel... and then..."

"Jadis?"

Her face lit up with revelation. "Yes! He really *did* see what he says he saw! He *did*!" She leapt up, her hair flowing around her excited face like a wheeling shoal of silvery fish. "Don't you remember, after he and Shoshana came back from Israel and he regained his sight? How he said that everything had what he called an 'aura' about it? Perhaps that's what he saw in the Sigil—an aura that only he had the ability to see, an aura that contained real, encoded information."

"But Jadis.... *how*?"

"How should *I* know, Darling Jack? How *should* I? It's an artifact, perfectly crafted by creatures with advanced technology, goodness only knows how long ago, only somehow—somewhen—it found its way up our pyramid at Souris. We have absolutely no idea who made it. If there are dragons that eat stars, perhaps the Sigil was left here by little green men with three legs. Who knows what it can do? What properties it might have? Honestly, perhaps the Sigil is a dragon's egg! The deeper we get into this, the more glad I am that we never published the thing."

"No, that's not what I meant," said Jack. "Well, only partly. What I *meant* was how *Tom* could see these things, but we couldn't?"

"If the things he saw were real, not just symptoms of stress, well... I..." her brow furrowed, her large eyes crossing slightly in inward concentration. She looked up. "I don't know, Jack—I really don't."

"Well, in any case," said Domingo, perhaps a little too breezily, "it rather puts paid to another idea I discussed with Tom: that the circles in the Sigil somehow represent the end-stage of the Plague."

Jadis shuddered.

"We talked about it on the train," Domingo continued. "Tom was quick to point out that this idea doesn't account for the crescents and... er... *lines*. Especially now we know that the crescents are equivalent to the dragons of Chinese folk-astronomy — if we accept the remarkable evidence of Tom's eyes."

Jack sat up and looked at Domingo with a curious expression of concentration, as if he were reaching for something only just out of mental range. As if he'd had antennae, they would have been humming. "Domingo," he said, "I don't think you should throw that idea away quite so quickly. I know it seems ridiculous, if you'll pardon me, but, you know, it makes a kind of sense."

"How so, my dear Jack?"

"As to that, I have absolutely no idea. None whatsoever." The pieces in Jack's brain clicked into place. "I shall have to sleep on it."

Jadis finished her tea. "Sound like the cue for turning in. Domingo — would you pass me those cups, please?" Domingo stood up, passing the cups to Jadis with deliberate care. He felt drained, worn out, suddenly feeling every minute of his seventy-three years, and yet that he still had one duty to perform before retiring.

"Domingo, are you okay?" Jadis asked.

"Me? I'm remarkably well, thank you, Jadis, when all things are... ah... considered. However, I have some unfinished business with my maker. Good-night!"

Domingo would be kneeling at his *prie-dieu* until the early hours, pleading for guidance. His prayers were becoming increasingly ragged, desperate even, as he tried to solve all the mysteries that crowded his head at once, each clamant for urgent attention and immediate resolution.

What were the dragons? Were they coming this way? What was the Plague? What was the source of Jack's hunch, that the Plague had a connection with the Sigil and the appalling events depicted therein? And, while we were on that subject, were those events history — or prophecy? And who had *composed* the Sigil? How had they come by all that information? What was their purpose of leaving it *here*? Were there others? And why *now*? Why? Why? *Why?*

None of it made any sense at all. At three o'clock in the morning he awoke to find he was still there, kneeling, uncomfortably chill, his hands clasped together, his back aching, his legs full of cramps. His knees were acutely painful, both from the pressure of his weight, and because his blood had pooled around them. He struggled to his feet, crossed himself and hobbled painfully to bed. He had fallen asleep even before the sharp pins-and-needles sensation in his legs had subsided.

Across the hall, Jack and Jadis were under the covers, each one enjoying the familiar warmth of the other, the sanctity of the darkness and their own thoughts, and yet each wishing the other would break the silence. They, too, had unfinished business. It was Jadis whose resistance broke first.

"Jack..." she whispered, "what *are* we going to do about Tom?" He turned towards her and pulled her head into his chest, running his fingers through her hair, caressing her cheek. Her skin was dry, soft and warm, perhaps a little too warm, and he could feel that she was tense. He felt her lashes flicking and flittering against his fingertips as her eyes moved this way and that, searching for reasons, for answers.

"I don't know," said Jack. "Just keep on showing him that we love him, I guess, and by being patient. He seems so, well, I can't think of the word."

"*Alienated?*"

"Yes, *alienated.*" They parted, and Jack sank onto his back, looking up towards where the ceiling would be, were he able to see anything at all. Human eyes naturally crave the light, and faced with gloom, Jack's created a show of tiny auroral sparks that danced before him. Perhaps Tom had seen something similar, albeit grotesquely magnified. But Domingo was right—if it were only Tom who had seen the dramatic display of cosmic carnage, how would the rest of them know if it were real or not?

"I wish I knew how to get to him, Jack, to get my little boy back," said Jadis, "but he's somehow buried himself under a shell."

"But he's not our little boy any more, is he?" Jack whispered to the dark shape of his wife. "He's a grown-up. Maybe he needs space and time to sort it all out by himself."

Jadis continued, as if she hadn't heard. "There was poor Shoshana, no-one knew how or why she died, and he blames himself... I can understand that, but really, dreadful things do happen..."

Jack had felt Shoshana's loss as keenly as Jadis had, mainly by virtue of their own impotence to stop whatever it was that was slowly killing her. Domingo's revelation about her last days had brought it all back.

But that was past, and Jack's emotion was now more empathy for his unreachable son than grief for someone long dead and who could no longer suffer. For Tom, any effort to break with the past, however strenuous, seemed to run into a roadblock.

"He seems to be having such a dreadful time in Cambridge," said Jadis, "with these... these... what are they called? Jive Bunnies?"

"'Jive Monkeys,'" Jack laughed, quietly. "I know, they sound like they should be rather fun, with a name like that." Jack remembered hominids who had seemed 'rather fun' on the surface—quite comical in fact—which on closer questioning turned out to have eaten your friends, but only after torturing them in the most degrading and dehumanizing ways.

"Well, whatever they're called, I think they need teaching some manners," she said.

"But that's the point, Jadis. They said the same thing about him."

"And then watching a star being eaten by *more* aliens. No wonder he needs a rest."

"As do I," said Jack, pointedly. But he could tell that she was in one of her moods in which she was over-tired, still taut as a bowstring, and would remain quite unable to sleep unless she'd resolved some inner conundrum. She sat up. He heard the swish of her hair against her shoulders.

"But I don't understand it, Jack."

"Hmm?"

"*Why* doesn't he understand these... these Monkey thingies? Tom's an expert on hominid cultural differences. An authority. He's practically written the book on it. So why did he fail to understand these ones, in particular?" She sank down again, onto the bed. "I just don't get it."

Jack said nothing. But the cogs and wheels in his mind meshed again, and found purchase. As usual, Jadis was way ahead of him.

"I've always had a feeling about Tom," she said. "Well, more of a niggle than a feeling. You know, that he's one of a kind. More than just all that business with his eyes. He was always so alone at school, quiet, reserved. But he was *happy*, wasn't he? I just wish he'd talk about it more. Let it go. I hope he knows that whoever *he* thinks he is, we'll still love him, no matter what."

And, thus decided, she turned over and fell asleep. Jack was still awake when she had begun to snore.

Jack nodded off a little while later, subsiding into a half-dream in which everyone seemed perfectly ordinary until you saw their green, cat-like eyes.

In another room, Tom woke from sleep to find that the bump on his temple had gone down a bit, and no longer hurt quite so much. He'd made little sense of the dream whose shreds were now dissolving like mist before sunrise, but the last image had been of Shoshana, asleep. She had opened her eyes, which got larger and larger and bored into him accusingly. They turned from blue to purple, blazed like stars, and then became two black holes that covered first her face and then, like an expanding burn in a photograph, the entire scene. No, Tom, *NO*, her eyes said. You're not going any further until you get yourself some *menschkeit*. Pull yourself together!

Tom sat up abruptly and then quickly wished he hadn't. His head started to throb again. *Bien sûr*, he might feel confused, conflicted, angry even, but he had no right to take it out on other people, and especially not here. Part of the problem was that he really did want to talk, but apart from his natural tendency to say as little as possible, he was afraid of exposing too much of what he was convinced was his own guilt, and this itself was conflicting.

Another problem was that he felt, now, that he'd been spoiled: perhaps just a bit too lucky. Shoshana had had to fight to get to the farm-house, the end of a journey that she had almost paid for with her life, several times over: a fare that had been—finally, cruelly—collected. And he had lived his whole life here, cost-free. The Shoshana in his dreams had been right. Even if he revealed to no-one the potentially debilitating anxiety about his own identity, he really did have to pull himself together. To grow up. And as he made that resolution, he imagined Shoshana looking down on him with love, her eyes blue once more, streaked with purple; her wide, full lips parting in a smile to reveal her crazy, loveable teeth, her soft hair falling down over her honey-coloured curves. Yes, he said. Shoshana, I shall do this for you, so I can continue to merit your affection.

So, that was that, then.

But there was also an important, practical aspect to all this. After an absence of a decade, he noticed that his parents had suddenly become elderly. They were as fit as any septuagenarians had a right to be, and probably a whole lot fitter, but he felt that the effort of the farm was becoming too great, and it was beginning to slip away from them. He would prolong his sabbatical indefinitely. The University could hardly complain—he was, after all, right on top of Souris Saint-Michel, for all that nobody had actually visited it for years.

And there was the Sigil. With what he now knew about stellar extinction (his mind was already pacing out the problem in scientific terminology), it was time to write it up. He would ask his mother about it in the morning. He felt that they had to get on with it, in case they were... how did Domingo put it?

Overtaken By Events.

As he slid into sleep, he realized that those three words could describe his whole life. At every turn, he'd been prey to external influence, buffeted around like a rag doll in a hurricane. Shoshana had arrived, blowing him off his feet. She'd departed—likewise. And then they had both been blown off Masada, and then there had been the whole stomach-churning episode with the Jive Monkeys in which he had been a follower, when he should have been a leader. *Tiens*! He was almost forty years old. It was time he took control of his own destiny.

The following evening, Jack and Jadis ambled up the back lane, hand in hand in the sunshine, towards the village square. It felt like years since they'd done this—just to go out, simply for the pleasure of it, with no particular errand in mind or appointment to keep. But Tom had said he'd settle the farm down for the night, so why didn't they take some time off? Jack felt a sensation of relief, of a load slipping off his shoulders, whose weight he'd hardly noticed until it had been removed.

They found the Place Etienne Geoffroy almost deserted. The silent, old buildings under a rich blue sky of almost alien clarity looked like a cityscape by De Chirico. The boulangerie had closed for the day, and most of the *Sanglier* regulars were still hard at work on their own farms. In fact, when they wandered into the shade of its cheerful blue-and-white striped awning, they saw that they were the only customers. Yvon Rossignol was happy to attend to their every need—which was herb tea for the Doctor, and a *pastis* for Jack.

"My pleasure! On the house! We don't see you much these days. Busy on the farm, eh?"

"Ah! But things are going to change, Yvon," said Jack: "my son Tom is back and is showing signs of wanting to take over. Respite for a *vieux pantoufle* like me. I have to say it's welcome."

"*Change*, eh? Let's drink to the younger generation!" beamed Rossignol. The clash and clang of pans within betokened the arrival of Madame Rossignol in the kitchen. The innkeeper's face turned dark and anxious. "Please excuse me," he said, waddling into the shadows — "duty calls!"

The two of them sat there at the round, rust-pocked café table, remembering the first time they'd sat there, on their honeymoon. Each replayed the moment in their mind: Jadis felt her eyes moistening. She'd been pregnant. Funny, she'd almost forgotten that, and how much she'd enjoyed it — the feeling of pride, at a life growing inside her. The irony bit her now, that she spent most of her time away from the farm attending the births of others, and yet she'd never borne a child of her own. She became conscious of an ache in her lower abdomen, a sympathetic echo of times past both sweet and bitter.

Inevitably, her thoughts turned to Tom, who had, it seemed, decided to emerge from beneath his long, black cloud, and who just that morning had volunteered himself to write up the Sigil for publication. Although she felt a rueful pang at this, she was grateful, for she knew now that she'd never get round to it herself. Not any more — it was not just the farm, and village life, but that she'd got out of the habit of thinking along academic lines, and she was easily distracted. *Damn it*, she cursed herself, *it's because I'm an old woman!* The true source of her pang, then, was the recognition and acceptance of her own mortality. As long as she'd kept putting off writing up the Sigil, she'd had a ticket to forever.

"Drink up," said Jack — "I have something to show you." Hand in hand — for they were on their honeymoon, once again — they left the café's shade and ventured into the scorching afternoon heat. They picked their way carefully across the worn, sun-drenched cobbles to the sanctuary of the churchyard gate. She knew where he was leading her. Past the ranks of well-tended graves (so many more than they had been then, almost half a century before); past the welcome, fragrant shadows of the giant yew trees; to the limestone parapet on the other side. The view seemed hardly to have changed. But in those days the vista had been one of morning, and the sun had been at their backs. It now hung before them like a great blood-red ball, bruised on the Earth's western rim.

Jack reached out for her hand, although his eyes were fixed on the far horizon. She could feel the tension running along his fingers like electricity through a cable.

"Somehow," he said, "somehow, we have to make sense of it all. We can't just leave it all to Tom. Not that he couldn't do it, far from it — but because *we* are responsible."

She thought back to that horrific night when they'd seen that yeti, interviewed on the Zenge show, confessing to the murder of Faye and

Primrose and their friends, and when she'd begged Jack to understand what they'd unleashed on the world. If it hadn't been for Saint-Rogatien, the way it changed everyone's understanding of history, the hominids might still be hidden, and Faye and Primrose and many others might have lived to climb other, greater mountains.

And if it hadn't been for Jack's feeling that something unusual stood here, a gigantic monolith from an almost unbelievably remote antiquity, none of that would have happened. Souris Saint-Michel might still have been a dusty footnote to the career of a long-dead cleric.

Domingo might not have come into their lives.

And if it hadn't been for the fact that her dear Jack could never quite articulate his intuitions, her life might have drifted away from his own. Their first date might have been their last. There'd have been no Nest, no accident... no Tom.

Rainstorms. Brainstorms.

Jadis stared straight ahead, at the sinking star. She wondered how many more times she'd see a sunset. Indeed, she wondered how many more times there would be a sun to set. Or to rise. The ancients had spent a great deal of time, thought, ritual and bloody sacrifice in an effort to guarantee that very thing. How we arrogant scientists had laughed at this naïve presumption—that anything humans could do might influence the majestic clockwork of the heavens in any way, or be influenced by it.

And yet the Sigil had been a product of a science which, while indescribably ancient, was presumably far greater than theirs, seemingly designed with that very end in view—to propitiate the Gods, to keep the stars from going out.

Jack had had this insight too, she knew, affirming Domingo's wild surmise that the Sigil and the Plague were connected. But as he had with his sense of the landscape long before, he had no way to constrain or articulate it. Jack had needed her then. And he needed her now.

It could be that the world needed her.

The Plague and the Sigil. The Sigil and the Plague.

Circles, circles.

Let's just look at the facts, she said, and take an appropriately long view. The Sigil, irrespective of its own inherent antiquity, had been buried in the Pyramid more than a hundred thousand years ago, a rough estimate based on the context of the layer in the Pyramid in which it as found.

A hundred thousand years. An interval way beyond our normal experience. But when mapped against the scale of the Universe, an interval as evanescent as a flash, seen through the corner of one eye, of the scarlet hem of a gown disappearing behind a mud hut. Turn round, and it would be gone. On the largest scale, that of the Universe, we and the Sigil exist at what is, for all practical purposes, the same moment.

So far, so good. Now, consider this, she said to herself: human beings evolve at more or less the same time that the Sigil is deposited within the Pyramid and is then uncovered, and again, at around the same time, a Plague arrives. It's funny, she said, nobody has ever found any kind of infectious agent for Postembryonic Oolithic Petrosis. All we know is that it is specific to people who can claim to be *Homo sapiens*, with relatively little genetic introgression from other hominids. In fact, we know so little about the disease that we can't even tell if the victims are 'dead' in any sense we'd understand the term. She voiced this thought to Jack.

"Perhaps they're listening to us talk, right now!" said Jack. Even though the sun was on their faces, they both shivered: the graveyard was full of Plague victims, brooding in their caskets. "'That is not dead which can eternal lie,'" he murmured, "'and with strange aeons even death may die.'"

"Hmm?"

"Just something I remembered from my student days, tramping the hills. An old Lovecraft story..."

"Oh, Jack, you really are a very silly man!" She turned to look at him then, her dark eyes glistening with that mixture of love and exasperation one can only ever find in couples married for so long that each knows and tolerates every wrinkle and foible of the other. The way that she always tolerated Jack's strange fascination for anything Gothick. She could never understand how anyone could derive enjoyment from scaring themselves witless. But he kept half a shelf in the office to indulge what he imagined was his secret vice, and sometimes, when he couldn't sleep, he'd carry a candle to his creaking recliner and, feet up on his desk, take another midnight stroll into what the blurbs of the faded paperbacks would always say were 'eldritch realms of preternatural and chthonic terror' or some such tosh. She smiled. Dear, sweet Jack. The world might need her, but if it weren't for Jack, she'd long since have vaporized and vanished on the wind like smoke.

She still rememberd the first moment they'd met, when she'd breezed in late to his supervision, all a fluster from a bike puncture, trying to brazen out her embarrassment. How could one be late for a supervision?

And a *first* supervision? But he'd only looked at her with those calm, blue eyes, his slightly lopsided smile, and she knew—she just knew, in that moment, with the kind of absolute certainty that is the currency not of science but of faith—that this man would be her rock, would make everything all right. Whatever happened.

They now held each other close in the cooling air: a breeze from the distant Bay of Biscay was making its way across the land, leaching out its warmth. Shaking the hair from her eyes, she looked up at him and said: all we have now is a correlation. No, not even that, a *coincidence*. There's too much we don't know, she said, rehearsing just some of the possible unknowns.

Are the dragons munching their way through this corner of space alone, or are they found more generally?

Does their activity change with time?

Are there more Sigils? Domingo thinks there might be.

And if someone found one in Cretaceous rocks among some tyrannosaur eggs—well, that would seriously weaken the link. And, taking the long view, is the Plague unique to humans? Maybe there's some unknown animal reservoir, or a virus, or something. The trouble is, she said, nobody knows, and since the Plague, nobody has had the means to find out.

"No," he'd said. "You worked that out long ago, don't you remember? The disease didn't seem to spread by any kind of agent."

"Yes. So I did," she replied.

As they watched, the sun sank behind the distant hills, and just as it disappeared, it shot a shimmering curtain of rays upwards, dressing a few shreds of otherwise nondescript clouds in a rich array of pink and gold. Jack and Jadis stayed a little longer to admire the display, then turned and walked homewards.

"I know it's just a coincidence," sighed Jack, as they walked down the lane, their field gate coming into view as darker blur against the deep blue of night, "and, yes, you're right. Perhaps Tom was right, too, to dismiss Domingo's wild surmise. It's just, well..."

Jadis had known him long enough to recognize the signs, or to know that Jack's hunches were always worth following to the end. She turned to him again.

"Jack—*tell* me."

"No, it's probably just daft," he said, "for all that it's been niggling me for years."

"What has?"

"Oh, all right. But it's more to do with the Sigil itself, rather than any connection with the Plague. Funnily enough—well, not *funny* really, but... well, it's all to do with Tom's eyes. You see, I've seen eyes like his before. Just once. It's only in the past few days that I've made the connection."

It was now fully dark and the summer stars had begun to appear. Vega, Deneb, Altair. Jadis looked up at Jack—his head was a silhouette against the wheeling sky.

"Jack...?"

"You remember just after we opened up SSM and I flew off to the States?"

"Yes—you finally got to meet Ruxton Carr."

"Well, it's him. He had eyes like Tom's—big, green, cat-like pupils. And then, when Tom came into our lives, I thought I'd seen eyes like that before, but could never place them. Well, it's all clicked. After all these years! And just think about Carr. You remember when dear old Roger first told us about him, and that he'd set up two institutes?"

Jadis said she had. She remembered that she'd been pregnant at the time. How much had happened when she was pregnant. She missed it. Oh well, too late now. *Far* too late. But she snapped back to the present, and jumped into Jack's argument. But she held his hand more tightly, and warmed to the reassurance of his grip in response. Oh, Jack, I shall forever be just a child in your arms.

"I remember," she said, "one for landscape archaeology—for you, and me, and Roger: the other for astrometry. And how everyone was puzzled by the choices."

"Yet in hindsight," Jack continued, "they shouldn't have been, because Carr had always publicly said that he backed 'The Future'. And what two, precise things are we having to study *now*? Interesting, eh?"

"I see," said Jadis "if it hadn't been for Carr's choices, we'd never have found the Sigil, nor known about stellar extinctions. Jack, that's amazing. It's been in front of us the whole time, all these years. How could we have missed it?"

"But there's something else, too, something that only I could have known about, because he told me at our one meeting. I remember it like it was yesterday. He told me that our work—yours and mine—was of 'the utmost importance,' and—get this—that 'it might even save the planet.'"

Jadis felt that Jack was talking more to himself than to her or anyone else in particular, for in two minutes he'd said more than he usually did in a whole day. This meant that he was really on to something, his mental bloodhound hot on the trail.

"Ever since I've been wondering how digging ever deeper holes underneath France could ever do anything to save the planet," he said. "But now there's the Sigil, and the links with the disappearing stars, and *somehow it all fits in together*. I'm *sure* of it."

"And the Plague too?"

"Yes, that too. God knows how or why, but yes... that too. I'm sure about that. Absolutely."

They were now at the back door that led to the *arrière-cuisine*. In the deep shadows, Jack's eyes sparkled like polished coals.

Chapter 8. Pilgrim

Massilia, Rhoneland, Earth, *c.* 125,000 years ago

The wicked, quaint fruit-merchant men,
Their fruits like honey to the throat
But poison in the blood
Christina Rosetti—*Goblin Market*

The last stage of Mr Khorare's journey—the most wonderful, and the strangest—began in a dawn of mist, when Raull toted what few belongings (just two small bags) Mr Khorare had chosen to take down to the lobby. No concierge was to be seen: the steam-*barouche* waited beyond the bronze-and-glass doors, its fumes adding to the fog, the chauffeur in shadow.

Mr Khorare and Raull embraced in the silence of friends, unsure that either would see the other again. Mr Khorare had reassured his servant that he would indeed return, but his business was such that a precise time of homecoming could not be given. He had entrusted the valet with his keys and his affairs, confident in his abilities to service all such needs with delicacy and discretion even in the extended (and perhaps indefinitely prolonged) absence of his master.

For himself, Mr Khorare knew that there would be no return, and no need, in truth, for any luggage aside from his own self and the talisman he wore in a soft leather drawstring bag, hung on a cord around his neck. To signify such to himself—if not the valet—he wore a grayish silk chemise that might once have been cream, or white, and a pair of faded knee-breeches of indeterminate color and fabric, but which might once have been velvet. He had discovered these at the back of his closet, and, surprised to have seen them at all, pulled them off their hangers to his face, greeting them with the same tears of joy that an owner might lavish on a much-loved pet whose disappearance, long before, is now no longer expected to be followed with prodigal reappearance. Once Mr Khorare had recovered his composure, his expert eye noticed the skill with which these weather-worn garments had been patched and mended: gussets almost invisibly stitched into otherwise irreparably corrupt seams, the near-invisible needlework of matchless quality and refinement. Mr Khorare could not remember having ordered such restoration, nor having paid for it—still less having undertaken it himself (would that he could!)

But that his life was often punctuated with long lapses of memory was a circumstance to which he was now accustomed. So, now, he simply offered an inchoate thanks to whomsoever it was, and took the reappearance of his old, shark-shredded, battle-rent travel garments as a good omen.

The steam-*barouche* took Mr Khorare and his two bags (a small haversack and a smaller, leather belt-pouch) northwards through the morning fog to Massilia's main rail station. As they passed through the near-silent streets of early dawn, the white shrouds concealed the buildings on either side so that Mr Khorare lost all sense of where he was, or when, or how fast they might be going. But at last the twin pyramidal pinnacles, framing the main gate of the rail station like cathedral spires, loomed forth. The steam-*barouche* pulled up outside the gates, puffing gently, and the chauffeur gave a hand to his master as he alighted. Here, only the usual friendly valediction. No heartfelt farewell, as had been with Raull—the chauffeur had no reason to suspect other than that his master would return, the next day or the day after. Any more surprising intelligence could be conveyed to the servants by Raull at a time and convenience of his own choosing.

In any case, Mr Khorare had not the heart for any more good-byes. Those few he had made had drained him, emotionally—and in any case, his mission was now to look forward, not back. His ticket purchased in advance, Mr Khorare had only to find his train and board it. Before another quarter-hour had passed, he was comfortably seated aboard the *Princess of Aquitaine*.

The main concourse of the Massilia rail station was so vast that Mr Khorare could not see the ceiling above him—iron girders and stone pillars teetered upwards to be lost in the steam from the engines and the mist curling in from outside. The marble floor was peppered with people—mainly Stoners, with a few Thinskin servants and porters. Very occasionally, the roughly-maned figures of Yettins could be seen towering above even the tallest Thinskin. Every single one, though—Stoner or Thinskin or Yettin—seemed no larger than a crawling ant when placed against the scale of the station building. Mr Khorare was soon lost amid the crowds, just one brownian particle among hundreds, though his face was turned upwards to find the great black wall of the departures board, steam fuming from small vents as the pneumatically powered destination indicators whirled and flapped, pacing each new departure, each fresh arrival, as if the machine itself were the controller of time, rather than simply a herald of events posted within it.

Within the surging crowd below, Mr Khorare stopped, awed not only by the size of the board but by the wealth of possibilities it offered. In a moment, he could be on the *Northern Lights* that took three days to reach Far Yotunheim, realm of the Ice Giants; or the *Tundra Herald* that tracked the endless forests of Rhús as far as the High Frontier of Altaic Yettinland. He could climb aboard the *Sierra Mountaineer* that would call at the golden city of Carcassonne before traversing the Pyrenees and crossing Iberia to the Guadalquivír. Then again, he might hitch a ride on the *Flying Reindeer* which, arrowing through Rhoneland, would set him down at Calais Station for the boat-train interchange to distant, wild Britain.

In his relatively short time as a resident of Rhoneland, Mr Khorare had — of course — been aware of the Stoner Civilization at its apogee, the culmination of the best part of a million years of slow acculturation from nameless progenitor species. Such, though, was dry intellection. Not until he'd seen the great departure board had he been truly aware of its scale, which humbled even the extensive realms tributary to the Great and Ancient City of Axandragór, and made an impudent wart of the barbarous Kingdom Under The Mountain.

But more was to come. Amid the departure board was a notice advertising the imminent departure from Track 29 of the *Princess of Aquitaine*, headed for Bordeaux with connections for Poitiers and Rennes, but calling at a number of places in between, including the one now engraved on Mr Khorare's mind — the Great Pyramid of Xxántroghátrem.

The train itself, resting at Track 29 and fuming like a dragon but lightly at rest, was an awesome sight in itself. Starting from the immense, cylindrical engine nearest the barrier, fuming with brutal, barely concealed power, a chain of sleek, silvery carriages stretched into the blue distance, farther than Mr Khorare could clearly see. Each carriage was as tall as a house, as long as a street, and there were, according to Mr Khorare's own squinting count, at least thirty of them (a steward later confirmed that there were thirty-six, culminating in a traction locomotive of a similar impressive order to the one he'd already seen). Mr Khorare reached inside the leather pouch strung around his neck, and, warm from the talisman next to it, retrieved his ticket. His assigned berth was in Coach Fifteen, he read, somewhere in the hazy distance. He hastened to reach it before the train departed: indeed, he heard the guard's whistle as he stepped, winded and panting, onto the footplate. He followed the directions to his seat—a small cabin, in truth—up a winding *escalier*, deeply carpeted in rich crimson and with reassuringly thick brass-work handrails.

As he climbed, he was reminded of the stairs to the box in his favorite theater, the box reserved for distinguished personages, and patrons such as himself. But the time had long departed for memories of past glories — Mr Khorare's mind was canted resolutely forward. He found his perch on the third and topmost level of the carriage, and had had barely time to register the small but luxurious washing facilities; the roll-top *escritoire* with its lamps and pens and inkstands; the carved walnut side table bearing a bone-china platter loaded with fresh bread and ripe fruit, and, next to it, a neat stack of polished skull-bowls; the elegant *fauteuil* and *chaise-longue* before great crystalline picture windows on both sides — before the leviathantine monster he now inhabited jerked and lurched into wakefulness beneath his feet and all around him, and, with a boom and a roar and a clang, the glooming vastness of the station building began to slide smoothly back, away into history, revealing a landscape of pearly white light.

The next revelation to assault the bruised senses of Mr Khorare was the extent of the city of Massilia itself. The great train slid slowly through crowded suburbs, punctuated by the clipped spaces of parkland, dissected by streets, rail lines and long-tamed rivers and canals crossed by well-maintained bridges, and the frequent exclamations of pyramids. These were of various shapes and sizes, some four-sided, others three, or five; some as small as shacks, others towering far above the houses all around; some as gently sloping and voluminous as hills whose gentle slopes belie their height; others, like spires, steeply raked and needle-sharp.

Such was the townscape with which Mr Khorare had become familiar during his sojourn in Massilia. What, however, defied his expectation was that the landscape did not soon thin out into farmland or wilderness, in the same way that the massif of the Kingdom Under The Mountain soon gave way to cedar forests, tamarisk scrub and the open savannah of Mesopotamia. No — it continued, unchanging and yet endlessly varied. After an hour and a half, Mr Khorare realized that the entire country of Rhoneland was nothing more than a greatly extended city, a region that had been subdued by the Stoners for many hundreds of thousands of years. After an hour more, it came home to him that the course of every river had been altered, the better to suit its usage; the very hills themselves had been leveled, remodeled, even moved. The entire continent of Europe had been shaped by the massive collectivity of

Stoner effort, muscle and will for time out of mind. Mr Khorare, awed, scooped some bread and fruit into a skull-bowl and subsided onto the *chaise-longue*.

He knew that he could not afford to get too comfortable as his station stop was no more than an hour away, so, with the tamed town-lands passing by below, he gave thought to his destination.

Mr Khorare had had no clear thought as to this, nor what he was to do once he'd got there. He had learned to let the whims of the world guide his fate. Hence it was—or so he imagined—no more than mere chance that had led him to pronounce the name of Xxántroghátrem when his wayward feet had guided him to a travel agent a few days before. The travel agent had suggested the present date, being one of pilgrimage to that greatest and most ancient of pyramids. Mr Khorare confessed, however, that he'd seen precious few other passengers on this train that might have passed for pilgrims—but then, he reasoned, he was late boarding, and his cabin was a private one.

In the days before his departure, Mr Khorare had made several trips to the municipal library, where he'd read—in very old books, themselves translated from still more archaic records—that the Great Pyramid of Xxántroghátrem was one of the oldest structures in Rhoneland, if not *the* oldest. The problem was that nobody really knew *how* old it was, nor the identity of the builders. The Xxántroghátrem of the title referred to *Róghadhr*, a mythical Stoner chieftain who had lived (if indeed he had existed at all) many millennia earlier, and whose name had become attached to the structure by virtue of several legendary exploits when the structure to which his name had accreted already labored under a toll of years beyond count.

The original name for the structure had been lost in remotest antiquity, and it was likely that the creators of the Pyramid had not themselves been Stoners. Despite their manifold achievements in subduing the very earth to their will, the Stoners regarded the long-lost builders of the Great Pyramid with nothing short of religious reverence. For not only was the Great Pyramid extremely old, it was also extremely large, dwarfing any comparable structure the Stoners had erected. The structure covered sixteen square miles, and its apex rode a full two and a half miles above the plain. Even the hardiest pilgrims took more than a week to climb its thousands of steep and teetering stairs, and only the fittest of that select group would find enough air at the summit to satisfy a ragged gasp.

And the Great Pyramid of Xxántroghátrem was just the start—a barbican, a gatehouse, to still further wonders. From the southern face of the Pyramid a wide road shot due southwards, the Great South Way, dead straight for ten miles, connecting the massive structure with something equally wondrous, underground. He could find no hint of what that something might be. When asked, the travel agent simply turned away as if Mr Khorare had suddenly become inaudible, and no book he could find so much as mentioned the matter. It was clear that whatever it was, Mr Khorare had to find out for himself. As if he had been drawn to it. As if it were his destination, the culmination of his existence.

Mr Khorare was pondering on this and related subjects when he felt a slight shift in the tenor of the vehicle in whose belly he was traveling. The note of the engine seemed to weaken and drop by no more than a quarter tone, but this was enough to alert Mr Khorare that he would soon be reaching the station that served the Great Pyramid of Xxántroghátrem. Hastily, he finished his meal and placed the skull-bowl on the table next to the (depleted) bowl of fruit. Picking up his baggage, he half-walked, half-swung down the tight, spiraling staircase until he reached the ground-floor footplate. Once there, he found the way barred by a clot of other passengers, mainly dressed in flowing robes of purple. There were men, and women, and small children, and much luggage, and a great confusion of noise. But it was only when the train had finally shuddered to a halt, the hydraulic rams of its brakes shrieking, and the doors had opened to admit a clear northern light, that Mr Khorare noticed. Every single one of the pilgrims was a Thinskin.

The secrets of Xxántroghátrem were beginning to reveal themselves.

The sun of summer climbed steeply into the blue vault. Mr Khorare alighted onto the platform and was immediately assaulted with heat and humidity, as if someone had dropped a sodden blanket on his head. He had not noticed, before, that his cabin had been climate-controlled, responding—perhaps—to the automatic sensation of his own warmth and boldily moisture, so that he would reside in comfort at all times. He had had a closely similar arrangement fitted to his own apartment in Massilia, and, having framed that thought, felt a stab of regret. But no, a second thought came—the time for regrets was past. Things were moving to a head. Shouldering his meager haversack, he walked briskly into the stream of people surging through the station building and into the small town clustered before the eastern face of the Pyramid.

The town of Xxántroghátrem was small. But then, reasoned Mr Khorare, any town not cowed into insignificance by the vastness of the Pyramid would have to have been extensive indeed. Even so, the conurbation, such as it was, was hemmed by the press and noise of humanity, almost all of whom were Thinskins. Mr Khorare had no choice but to dive into the crowd in the wide street outside the station, whereupon his vision became instantly restricted to the bright robes and animated people within touching distance of himself. His senses were soon all but overwhelmed by the acrid musk of Thinskin bodies, and the constant chatter and boom and shriek of Thinskin voices (Stoners being, as a rule, much quieter in all situations except the extremis of battle).

It was plain that Mr Khorare had arrived on market day. From glimpses between the tall, brightly-clad people he saw gaily decorated stalls on each side of the great street, selling all manner of things—fruit, meat, and cloth, and house wares, and cheap souvenirs. All such orientation as he could contrive was to be made by viewing at a steep angle, which view afforded Mr Khorare a clutter of pyramidal rooftops, and, behind them all, a vast canted wall, bright white in the late-morning sunshine, which occupied most of the sky.

The Great Pyramid itself.

No amount of reading or preparation had prepared Mr Khorare for the sight of the Pyramid, close up. He stopped, where he was, amid the crowd, transfixed. The crowd surged and flowed about him as were he were no greater an obstacle than a pebble on the bed of a great river. Occasionally he would be buffeted by a glance or a jolt from a passer-by, but nothing could tear his eyes away.

The Pyramid was so incomparably huge that it seemed to tower into the sky and overtop him, so that, at first, Mr Khorare had trouble retaining a secure footing. Mr Khorare's eyes scanned the bright face of the structure for some detail—anything—that would bring some ordinary sense of scale and proportion to his rescue. But as his eyes accommodated to the assault of blank, reflective whiteness, he noticed a line of black dots trailing up the median line, from base to apex. The dots were scattered, clumped, with more towards the base, and thinning out towards the summit. From where he stood, Mr Khorare could discern no movement, but that, he realized, was an artifact of distance. The dots he saw were people—pilgrims—ascending and descending the Pyramid's morning-side face.

Having recovered himself, Mr Khorare looked down and brought to mind that his travel agent had made him a booking in a small *pension* in a small side street just off the main thoroughfare. Reasoning that the latter was the great street in which he found himself, he let the crowd push

him on once more, further away from the railway station, and deeper
into the town. The names of the streets were, fortunately, inscribed in
large signs at a high level, in the clear, angular characters of the Stoner
language current in Massilia, so it wasn't long before he found the street
whose name accorded with that in his memory. The problem now was
how he should make his way orthogonal to the movement of the crowd,
without, first, being carried straight past. However, the observation of
the pell-mell movements of small children, weaving in and out of the
adults as small creatures amid great trees on the forest floor, gave Mr
Khorare an idea. Already almost a head shorter than most of the Thinskins, even the women, he ducked down and made his way in a kind of
crouching lope, dodging bodies and legs, and soon found himself in the
shade between two market stalls, and, in rapid progression, in the street
of his desire.

The shade here was welcome, as was the quiet: the sidewalks were
populated by relatively few pedestrians, and just one steam-*barouche* — a
taxi-cab — had stopped kerbside, allowing a small party of richly attired
pilgrims to alight. How such a conveyance could advance in this town at
any greater speed than a pedestrian was a mystery. But when he looked
up, the Pyramid appeared to close the end of the street like a great white
wall. This closeness must have been an illusion, for Mr Khorare knew for
a fact that it was at least half a mile away.

The party of pilgrims from the steam-*barouche* was headed, as chance
would have it, to the *pension* in which Mr Khorare had been booked, so,
hurrying to catch up with them, he joined the knot of people as they entered the building. He waited, patiently, as the pilgrims completed their
transaction with the receptionist, with much shouting and waving of
arms and jostling of what seemed like a quite inordinate amount of luggage. When they had dispersed to the elevator, their luggage before
them on a heaving trolley pushed by a harassed-looking bellhop, Mr
Khorare found himself at the front of the queue. The receptionist looked
up. She was a Stoner female of middle years and quite unprepossessing
appearance, but her dour face was quite transformed by the smile with
which she greeted Mr Khorare, as if responding to a welcome quietness
following the rumbustious fuss of the Thinskin pilgrims. Mr Khorare's
immediate business was completed with polite expedition. But Mr Khorare, responding to the receptionist's welcoming smile, and perhaps a
shared solidarity of reticence, felt prompted to start a conversation. To
answer the question that nobody seemed willing to address.

"Madam," he started, tentatively, "I wonder if I might inquire...?" She looked up from her tickets and documents.

"Sir?" Her accent was polite and clipped, as something she wore as part of her job, conversing with tourists from all over Europe. Mr Khorare imagined that as soon as she went off-shift, she'd resort to the ever-changing fluidity that was the argot of Rhoneland.

"I'm not a regular... uh... pilgrim here..."

"Yes, Sir. I thought you weren't, but I didn't like to say."

"Where do they go—the pilgrims—after they have ascended the Pyramid, and come down again?" She looked straight at him, eyes wide.

"You mean, you don't know?"

"No, Madam, I'm afraid I don't," he said, "I've tried to find out, but no text I can find, no tourist guide, says anything about what lies underground, buried at the end of the Great South Way. Not so much as a name. When I ask, people turn away, or change the subject, as if I had made some impolite personal remark. It really is most perplexing. Might you shed any light on the matter? I do apologise if to do so might prove inconvenient or embarrassing. I should not want to cause you any discomfort." The receptionist flushed.

"Sir, I should have to explain something that visitors to the Pyramid usually know without anyone having to tell them, something to which they have become accustomed since childhood." She lowered her voice and leaned forward, as if about to vouchsafe a confidence. "It's a taboo, you see, and... well, really, I don't think I should say anything more. It's something that only Thinskins ever discuss, and then only between themselves. Do you plan to head that way?"

"Yes, I do." The affirmation just popped into his head, where only a vague cloud of possibility existed before. The talisman burned like a brand against his chest, its heat only slightly dulled by the leather pouch in which it hung.

"You have no plans to ascend the Pyramid, then?"

"No," he said. "The Great South Way is my course."

"In that case," she said, "we serve breakfast at 4 a.m. sharp, after which you should check out and follow the guests who've just checked in. They are going that way tomorrow. I'm sure they wouldn't mind an addition to their party."

"Do you think they'd be willing to... uh... take me into their confidence?"

"Really, it's impossible to say. But at least they'll know the way, and what to do, and perhaps furnish you with some assistance. Oh—before I forget — here's your room key," she handed over a thick metal disc like a large coin, engraved with complex, labyrinthine patterns on both faces. "It's room two-oh-five, take the elevator to the second floor. Is that all your luggage?" She gave a winsome smirk.

"Yes, Madam. It's just me."

"Well, have a nice day, now." She turned and disappeared into a back room. Mr Khorare was left quite alone.

-=0=-

It was not until the fifth mile of the Great South Way had passed that anything changed in its remorseless monotony. Mr Khorare had break-fasted in the dining room of the *pension* at a table for one, a discreet dis-tance away from the loudly chattering party of Thinskins, before check-ing out. The morning receptionist was a Stoner woman, younger than the one with whom, the day before, he'd shared such confidences: so his un-easy loneliness was heightened, rather than eased, by any sense of con-spiracy, however ill-merited.

He left the *pension* in the dawn's chill, trailing the colorful party of Thinskins as it draggled and honked like herded geese — heedless of the tranquility of a town as yet only slowly waking — through a warren of nameless streets, sometimes broad and well paved, but mostly narrow alleys of dirt in which the party was obliged to walk in single file, step-ping gingerly over puddles and piles of refuse. The Great Pyramid of Xxántroghátrem was ever their guide, and, as they walked, its aspect, above crowded tenements and elegant public buildings alike, slowly changed: the blank eastern face, bright in the dawning sun, gave onto the southern face, with a promise yet brighter — the two gigantic facets sepa-rated by the razor-edged line of the south-east ridge. The journey was so bafflingly tortuous, and the turnings so unexpected despite the universal signpost that was the pyramid, towering above everything, that Mr Kho-rare found himself repeatedly grateful for having had the fortune to be following a party that was at the same time so well-informed about the route (which he should not have been able to have found himself) and so noisy in their prosecution of it (so that even if they passed out of sight behind some building or obstacle, he could still hear them, and so fol-low).

After almost an hour of walking through the mazy ways of the town, the south-eastern ridge faded behind them and the bright southern face of the Great Pyramid now presented its way to them, entire. Before long the party found itself at a small cluster of modest stone huts at the end of the broadest and straightest road Mr Khorare had ever seen. Standing at some distance from the Thinskin party while its members gathered in conclave, apparently in prayer (to whom, or for what, Mr Khorare remained frustratingly in ignorance), Mr Khorare could only wait. Wait, that is, until the party moved off down the immense thoroughfare, with himself trailing at a respectful distance. No chance of losing them here: this, the Great South Way, arrowed southwards with diamond-hard straightness, its surface a perfect jigsaw of dressed slabs, pristine, for mile after mile, and a full twenty yards wide. The town of the Pyramid ended abruptly here, just as the road started, giving way to a featureless emptiness of gently sloping countryside, with not a farm or a building in sight on either side of the road, as far as the eye could see. It occurred to Mr Khorare that this was the only part of Rhoneland he'd seen that could count as in any way deserted. Which meant, he reflected further, that this desolation was entirely deliberate. A wilderness, cultivated for a purpose.

That purpose was soon to become apparent. To step with deliberation along a straight road without distraction is, as Mr Khorare discovered, to set up a rhythm in which one's steps soon become entrained with one's breathing, and, before long, with the beat of one's heart. Although the heat of the day increased — there being no shade of any kind — Mr Khorare soon found himself bowling along with a welcome serenity of spirit and determination of purpose, even though he was as yet still ignorant of what that purpose was. The way, the way — that was all that mattered.

To step, first once, and then again.

To breathe, first in, then out.

Systole, diastole.

A small fragment of Mr Khorare's mind, detached from the rest, observed his generally calm and meditative mood, and speculated that were all pilgrims to have achieved that same, trance-like state by journey's end, then it was no wonder that definite reports from that destination were hard to come by.

As he walked, the knot of Thinskin pilgrims ahead of him faded into a colorful mirage-like blot, their chatter subsiding and, finally, dying, as distance and meditative purpose sucked it dry. The pilgrims were always at a fixed distance ahead of him, pursued, but never attained. At first, Mr Khorare paid little heed to the impression that the knot had broken apart; that a small piece of it had become detached, and was growing larger. As he paced, though, a disturbance clouded his mind.

Had this fragment stopped, or had it reversed its direction, and was now approaching him? He was helpless to investigate, though, as his arms swung relentlessly back and forth, his legs and feet moved like mindless machinery, pacing the way.

Mr Khorare drew level with the fragment at the five-mile marker — the halfway point of the Great South Way — when the fragment spoke.

"We thought it meet that one of our number should accompany you, Excellency Khorare," it said. "We should be honored if you would join us."

Mr Khorare was less startled by the content of the Thinskin's message, and that he knew Mr Khorare's name and former office in the Kingdom, than the sound of the voice in which these words were articulated. It was quite unlike that of a Rhonelander, and had every cadence of the Kingdom Under The Mountain. At first, Mr Khorare found any answer at all hard to produce, in any accent at all.

"Did you...? Might I...?"

"Don't be alarmed, Sir, please. My name is Vortigern. Like you, I am a former resident of the Kingdom Under The Mountain." The Thinskin whose name was Vortigern put out his hand for Mr Khorare to shake. Mr Khorare, his diplomatic poise recovered, took the proffered hand and shook it, and responded with the most courtly greeting he could muster in the language of the Kingdom.

"Well met on the road, Friend Vortigern," he said. Vortigern bowed, rose, and the two men fell into step together, trailing the still-moving blot of pilgrims now on the horizon.

Chapter 9. Jester

Mount Carmel, Earth, *c.* 45,000 years ago

Not to go on all-fours. *That* is the Law.
Are we not Men?
H. G. Wells — *The Island of Dr Moreau*

"There was a Yettin, a Stoner and a Thinskin, and…"

"Crusher? *Crusher*! Put *down* the Royal Convenience and listen to this!"

"Your Most Exothermic Majesty is too kind. As I was saying, there was a Yettin, a Stoner, and a Thinskin, and…"

The big Stoner pulled his still-dripping penis from the Thinskin female tethered on its arms and knees, spat on its haunches, and took another bite from the bone he was gnawing.

"Hnnn?"

"We said, listen to this. It's a good one. Fucking get on with it, Catshit."

"My most panegyric obeisances, Majesty." Catshit, the motleyed jester, bowed low. "I shall continue, at the orgiastic pleasure of Your Egregious Tremendousness." He stood up to his full height, barely half that of the Stoner bodyguards in the hall. There were six of them. Add the Royal Convenience, and he himself, Catshit thought, and you'd have all that was left of the Court of the King. And only two — he and the King — still had tongues. The King had had a brutal way with dissent, in his time. But that time was rapidly fading, and there was no dissent left. Just a lot of very, very old jokes.

"There was a Yettin, a Stoner and a Thinskin…"

"We've already heard that part, Catshit."

"I crave the bounteous mercy of Your Most Meretricious and Ordovician Majesty."

"And you can get up off the floor, too." Hengest, King Under the Mountain, adjusted his bloated frame on a throne much too small for him. His belly sagged over its arms. Skeins of drool ran from the corners of his mouth as he chewed on morsels he'd picked from a nearby platter. Streaks of piss and shit ran down his legs, smearing the seat and plinth, and running across the dais. His blotched and bloated hands scrabbled blindly for the last few scraps of meat as his blank eyes, almost buried in the folds of his face, twitched this way and that, gazing around his hall. Catshit the Jester chose not to refer to his employer's mistake. An easy mistake to make, in his condition. But it was never good—never *safe*—to second-guess the King.

"There was a Yettin, a Stoner and a Thinskin..." The King sighed. The jester continued, quickly, his voice quavering. That it had come to this. "... and they were travelling across the savannah. After many days, and all sorts of exciting adventures with which I shall not tax Your Vertiginously Anechoic Majesty's patience..."

"We told you to get to the fucking point, Catshit."

"I am ever delighted to serve Your Most Thunderously Thanatogenic Majesty. As I was saying, the three companions—the Yettin, the Stoner and the Thinskin..."

A bone, with scraps of meat still attached, whizzed past his left ear. The King was blind, but his aim was still pretty much near the mark.

"... they found a vast palace, in the shape of a pyramid. They entered without resistance, and found that it was equipped for their every whim. Mountains of food—haunches of aurochs, sand-baked coelodont, mammoth steaks, succulent fatted Thinskin, offered live and fresh for the slaughter, and the choicest cuts; vats of mead and beer; flagons of testicle-and-eyeball soup; as much fresh, young, willing Thinskin cunt as they could fuck in a lifetime, before sampling that exquisite savor that only just-fucked Thinskin flesh can provide..."

"Huh. *We* like our Thinskin cunt *un*willing. More resistance. It's the *fear*, you know. Brings out the flavor. *Oi*! Ripper! Gnasher! Slasher! Pay *attention*. And Crusher, we told you to leave the Royal Convenience *alone*. We should like another go at it before we retire. We should not like it *spoiled*." Grunts of flat assent echoed around the hall.

"Get the fuck on with it, Catshit, will you? We haven't got all day. Empires to rule. Cunts to fuck. You know how it is. The endless duty of government."

"As your Most Euxinic and Palindromic Majesty requests," continued Catshit the jester. "Anyway, after a gargantuan banquet, at which their every wish was fulfilled, the Yettin, the Stoner and the Thinskin retired."

"Oh, we *bet* they did."

"The next day, after further debauchery on their couches, they availed themselves of such further pleasures that the Pyramid Palace could offer."

"More fucking? We do hope there was more *fucking*. We *like* fucking." Three or four of the bodyguards laughed. The sound was ugly, like flints smashing together. Another of the bodyguards shambled over to the Royal Convenience, pulled up his stone-embroidered kilt, and rammed his cock hard into its anus. The Royal Convenience, bound as it was by its elbows and knees to a raised platform, emitted no more than the tiniest whine. The knees of the Royal Convenience were splayed somewhat further apart than its elbows, for ease of access, particularly for the immense bulk of the King. That, and stability, given the punishment to which it was repeatedly subjected.

"Your Psychotropically Tendentious Majesty will be pleased to learn that the fucking was free and abandoned," continued the jester, "involving various species of man and beast in as many ingenious positions as even the boundless imagination of Your Most Mandragorously Cumbrous Majesty might surely contrive."

"Tell us the one about the Thinskin baby buggered to bits by a bull mammoth in *musth*. We *like* that one."

The jester told him. The laughter that rang around the cave was sustained and appreciative. The bodyguard currently using the Royal Convenience used the cover of noise to drive harder into it. Its meager dugs flapped back and forth in time with the assault. Rivulets of blood and shit ran down the backs of its scrawny thighs. The bodyguard climaxed and withdrew, turning his attention away from the Royal Convenience as if it did not exist.

"Get on with the joke, Catshit," bellowed the King, as the laughter subsided. "The one about the Yettin and so on. The Pyramid Palace."

"I prostrate myself before even the most fleeting desires of Your Most Mendacious and Zymurgic Majesty," said the jester, kicking aside a few of the bones scattered across the filthy floor of the throne room. Just to make some space. "As I was saying, the three companions availed themselves of such abundant further pleasures that the Pyramid Palace could offer.

"The Yettin left early to track down a herd of coelodonts across the plain. The Thinskin left early to find others of his kind, and sailed off on some ridiculous pilgrimage to the west, seeking the Fabled Port of Massilia and the Pyramid of the Goddess..." The jester's voice turned a darker shade then, as if he were talking more to himself than the King. As if he'd been on such a pilgrimage himself, once. Certainly, that was the part of the story he loved to tell most. So much, that he often ran the risk of losing himself in detail that came to his mind far more easily than his other inventions.

Thankfully, the King Under the Mountain failed to notice his jester's reverie, being convulsed up with mirth. "Port of Massilia!" he guffawed. "*Pyramid of the Goddess!*" Tears of laughter spurted from his porcine eyes. His bloated belly shuddered and heaved. A further stream of piss dribbled from between his massive thighs, down his calves and over the scabbed, rotting stumps of his feet. "Go on, Catshit, go on! What happened to the Stoner? What happened to *him*, we wonder?"

"As Your Most Bohemian and... er... *Rhapsodic* Majesty commands," the jester said. "The Stoner chose to remain in the Pyramid Palace that day. There was always another dainty to try, another drink to sup, and the Thinskin cunt just kept on lining up for his attention."

"Go on, Catshit! Go on! Don't Stop! What happened next? We do so *enjoy* this part."

"As Your Most Corpulent and Hemispheric Majesty commands. Well, as the Stoner was just finishing off fucking his thirty-fifth or thirty-sixth Thinskin cunt, and just wondering whether he should stagger off for lunch, or simply rip the latest cunt's tongue and eyeballs out, then and there, for a snack to keep him going until teatime..."

"Yes? *YES?*" the King bellowed, his swollen breasts and sagging arms vibrating with the promise of yet further entertainment.

"Certainly, as Your Most Feculent and Necrotic Majesty pleases. Well, at that very moment..."

There was a scuffle in the shadows near the door to the throne-room. The jester had his back to it, so he could not see it. Neither could the King, being blind. Two of the bodyguards moved off to investigate.

"At that very moment..."

"*YES?*"

"... there was an earthquake. It was so violent that the Pyramid Palace collapsed instantly, and..."

"*YES?* What the fuck happened to the Stoner?"

"... and the Stoner? He was *crushed to death.*" The jester finished with a flourish of his multicolored, tricorn cap. The King laughed so hard that his guffaws turned to wracking coughs. "Catshit, you have excelled yourself," he spluttered, before wretching, red in the face, and wiping dribble from his beard.

The jester bowed low. "One endeavours to give satisfaction, Your Majesty," he said.

"Oh, you do. You *do*. But now we need satisfaction of another kind. The Royal Cock stands to attention. Guards? *Guards!* You know what is required of you."

Four of the guards clustered around the King. Two hoisted him up by his armpits, their beefy hands disappearing into folds of fat. The two others bent down and wrapped their own well-muscled arms around the King's flabby thighs. Despite the hugeness of the bodyguards and the lengths of their arms, each one could only just barely encircle a royal thigh with both his arms, and even then not without burying his face in the enveloping mass of the royal gut.

With no sound apart from the occasional grunt of effort, and the shuffling of feet across the rubbish-strewn floor, the bodyguards lifted the King into position behind the Royal Convenience, lowering him gently on to his well-cushioned knees, so that at no time did the decaying stumps of his feet touch the ground. The Royal Cock emerged from between the mounds of fat. It was enormous, by any standards, but compared with the surrounding bulk, it seemed no more than a seedling sprouting from a cracked fissure between mountains of blancmange.

With a bodyguard supporting each of his shoulders, the King thrust himself into the Royal Convenience like a pile-driver. His belly spilled around the haunches of the tethered Thinskin female so that the jester could not really see what was going on. Nevertheless, the force of the King's movement drove the creature forwards, so that its knees and elbows strained against its tethers. Catshit the jester noticed how blistered the Royal Convenience's limbs had become, squeezed taut by the knotted leather thongs that held it in place, permitting only a limited range of movement.

The throne room was silent. Silent, but for the wheezy gurgles of the King *in copulo*, and for scuffles from the back of the room, where two of the Stoner bodyguards held a third, smaller Stoner, who was struggling against their grip. It was a Royal Messenger.

"Your Majesty! I have news of clear and present danger! The army of the Hated Usurper!" he shrieked, before one of the bodyguards smacked it hard across the side of the head. The messenger fell silent, head to one side at a crazy angle, eyes now lifeless, tongue lolling.

One of the two bodyguards swiftly decapitated the messenger, while the other chopped and jointed its arms and legs. The first then took a long knife and slit the messenger's belly open. Guts spilled out onto the floor. The bodyguard plunged in, ripping the messenger's ribcage apart like the pages of a book. When the second bodyguard tried to intervene, to take the messenger's still-beating heart for himself, a scuffle broke out.

Hengest, the Two Hundred and Forty-Fourth of that name, and the Twelve Thousand, Four Hundred and Seventy-First and Final King Under the Mountain, took no notice, but continued to take his evening's pleasure as he had always demanded it—in contemplative silence, and uninterrupted.

-=0=-

Zagrond lifted his muzzle to the air, nostrils flaring, and sniffed. Pale mucus slid from his cavernous nostrils. His long, prehensile tongue caught it before it fell. "The wind is before us," he grunted. "The time is now."

Horsa the Stoner, astride an armoured coelodont which, while gigantic, was a dwarf beside the mighty steed of Zagrond the Yettin, looked down from the bluff at the long, westernmost slopes of the Zagros as they fell away towards Mesopotamia, lost in the sunset haze. As far as he could see—in front, and from side to side—the land was carpeted with the signs of an army, poised to spring. Stoners and Yettins, arming, sharpening flint knives and hefting bone shamboks; repairing long coats of flint-scaled fish-mail; stringing horn bows with the precious guts of Thinskins.

Stoners and Yettins together, tending the vast corrals of armoured coelodonts, the ranks upon ranks of assault-mammoths and the teams of aurochs that would make up a supply train at least five miles long. Had Horsa but known it, it was an army the like of which the world hadn't seen for millions upon millions of years. The warm wind was in his face.

"You are right, friend Zagrond," he replied. "We move out in the hour before dawn tomorrow."

"You're no friend of *mine*, Stoner," came the gruff response. "You are only my *customer*. When the service is rendered, so shall the payment be due. Remember *that*, Stoner."

"I shall," said Horsa, wondering whether, even with a division of the spoils, that there would be enough to satisfy an army even a hundredth the size of the one arrayed before him. His scouts had told him that the slender assets the Kingdom Under the Mountain had controlled in his youth had long since been squandered by King Hengest—the dissolute elder brother he now intended to overthrow. There was little tribute, and less crops, the scouts had said. All the forests had been cut down or burned; the wells had become too salty to use, or had run dry; and desert had spread over once-verdant grazing land. Raids for the few wild Thinskins that evaded extinction had gone so far afield that they had become uneconomic to pursue, the supply-lines stretched to beyond breaking point. The only prize left was the broodstock of Thinskins lately bred in captivity in the Citadel of the Kingdom itself, at Mount Carmel—a smart move by his brother, Horsa had to admit, which had bought the ancient Kingdom a little more time.

But that might be a prize that his Yettin allies might not need, or appreciate. Or perhaps they would—and fight his own, better-trained but wildly outnumbered Stoner force for access to it. In his heart, Horsa knew that Zagrond's scouts would have given the Yettin warlord precisely the same information.

"Very good, Stoner," Zagrond said. "We meet on this spot, an hour before sunrise." The Yettin swung his coelodont around, plodding uphill to his own camp. Horsa heard the mercenary's long white braids, beaded with Afghan lapis, clink and chime in the cooling air. The coelodont, each leg the size of a man, its immense horn like a shard cut from a mountainside, snorted its response. Horsa, on his own, lesser beast, remained motionless, alone with the clamor of his thoughts.

Strategy, on the hoof.

He could, of course, let the Yettins take the Thinskins, herding them all the long, rocky miles to the Pamirs and the far Altai, allowing him to keep the Kingdom, even if all its cupboards were bare. But what if the Yettins couldn't be bought off so easily? After all, Horsa had heard that plenty of manflesh existed beyond the Yettins' eastern mountains. Pithecanthropines—smaller and scrawnier than Thinskins, but far more abundant and easier to herd. Gigantopiths, too, and many other creatures he'd only heard about in travellers' tales: from the ruby-eyed, coal-black giant Khong of the jungle, to small, lithe monkey-dancers with the clever eyes of cats, whose females had five pairs of breasts. Fancy that! He smiled—perhaps he should change his plans utterly, abandoning the bankrupt west, and make his way to the mammiferous east?

No. The time for such idle speculations had passed. He had an injustice to avenge, and an army at his command, an army that had taken many years to assemble. West was his course, for good or ill.

But then—now *here* was a thought—what about *beyond* west, to Europe, the heartland of the Stoner civilization of old? Travellers from that region were scarce, and his own scouts rarely ventured that far. Europe was a desert of ice, some said, and the ancient pyramids of fabled Rhoneland stood in ruins. But there were hints—only *hints*—of great Stoner cities that still survived, deep in the Earth. Cities surrounded by herds of mammoth and bison and reindeer that stretched unbroken from horizon to horizon. Yes—he could let the Yettins take the Kingdom and everything in it, and he would go further, to Europe.

The trick then, of course, would be trying to convince his own commanders that any payment they might receive would be deferred indefinitely in the cause of a prize that was nebulous, if it existed at all. His plan, spun from delicate webs of wishful thinking, dissolved before his eyes. No, he sighed—the Kingdom Under the Mountain was where his future lay. Such as it was.

-=0=-

Hengest had retired, taking his coterie of guards with him, and the throne room was quite deserted. All, that is, for Catshit the Jester, and the Royal Convenience, still pinioned to its dais. Catshit—who wasn't *really* called Catshit, but had been so for so long that he could recall his true name only with difficulty—now performed a less public but still-necessary duty. His old, wiry frame scampered onto the dais, scattering the putrid litter of bones and other refuse. His slender fingers teased apart the thongs that bound the Royal Convenience's elbows and knees. The poor creature could not have untied anything itself, except, perhaps, with its teeth—for it had neither hands, nor feet.

Catshit still remembered that day—it couldn't have been any more recently than fourteen years ago—when it had been brought in, screaming with fear, the sinews in its neck knotted with hatred, after a long raid into the Nile Delta. It had been a 'she,' then, a defiant young woman. "I like my cunt with *spirit*," Hengest had said. He still had his feet and his sight, then, before the Sweetwater Disease claimed them. "I'll have *her*."

The removal of her extremities, along with her tongue, had been peremptory and swift. But they had gouged out her eyes, too. Catshit always remembered eyes. Partly because people kept reminding him of the oddities of his own—yellow-green, almond-slitted, like a cat's. But that young woman's eyes were equally distinctive. Distinctive, for their asymmetry.

For one had been brown; the other, a bright, emerald green.

But when she lost her hands, her feet, her tongue—and especially her eyes—she lost her being, in the fading eyes of the King. She was just the Royal Convenience, forever poised on knees and elbows at His Majesty's pleasure, and that of his courtiers and guests. A tool to be used, as neutral and neuter as a spear or a drinking cup.

Having untied her, Catshit braced himself beneath her and lifted her, as gently as he could. He stopped for a moment to re-balance himself: a *pietà*, crouched in the Throne-room's shadows, of a little dark man, the round tapeta of his eyes reflecting moonlight from the open doors onto the terrace, cradling the maimed, emaciated form of a royal servant even lowlier than he was. Its arms and legs were still flexed, stiff, frozen from having held themselves that way for at least ten hours each day, every day, for fourteen years. Catshit could see the scars, the scabs, the sores, the open wounds; the corrugations of its ribs, the pitiful flaps of its dugs, and its face—its poor, dear face; the sore, chapped lips; the sunken pits where its eyes had been; the masses of its hair, once full and rich and the color of the desert sand, now thin and lank and gray.

It looked up at him, then, as if it could see, somehow—see, even without its eyes. It stretched its arms towards him, knobbled stumps of wrists prodding the sides of his face. It forced a weak smile in its lined and sunken face: its thin lips moved, ever so slightly, as if it were trying to say something. This had happened every night, night after night, beyond count, beyond recall. Yet Catshit could never understand what it meant, until now. For now, his job was done.

He stood up, this human wreck lightly in his arms, and walked out onto the white travertine terrace. He could feel the patched motley of his pathetic jester's costume grow stained and warm from the fluids of abuse emanating from between the sticks of the Royal Convenience's legs. The wind from the terrace came straight off the sea. He could hear the waves crashing to shore, hundreds of feet below.

The terrace was no less a worn-out ruin than everywhere else in this dilapidated husk of a Kingdom, but he felt that it was somehow special, somehow *his*, and it was here, against the worn marble rail that teetered farthest out over the waves, that he had made his home—a heap of tattered blankets and those few trinkets that had somehow remained unlooted by the King's dwindling number of ever more brutish bodyguards.

Catshit the Jester felt, though, that he could forgive them such intrusions, for he had made greater thefts by far. For it was he who had arranged for all the wells of the Kingdom to be poisoned with rotten bodies, of which there had always been a plentiful supply. It was he who had commanded, pretending to be acting on orders for the King, to burn the remaining forests, and to irrigate the fields with seawater. This process of sabotage had to be so slow that nobody would see it coming, nobody would notice. It had taken at least three of his own lifetimes. Final notice had come in the form of the messenger, slain before the full importance of his message could be appreciated by the ailing King. The Kingdom that had lasted for more than two hundred thousand years was now no more than a rotten husk, hanging on a high branch by a slender thread. The slightest gust, and it would fall. And fall it must, if the stratagems of the Goddess were to be fulfilled.

Not that he planned to be there when the final blow fell. His task was complete, and he understood, at last, the message on those mute, ragged lips, a message broadcast with such silent yearning for more than a decade.

"I understand, Green-Eye," he said. "I understand."

He walked straight past the nest of rags that had constituted his home—and hers—and climbed up onto the parapet, still holding her mutilated form to his chest. He launched them both into space, and as they fell, he fancied that he could almost hear her whisper of thanks.

Chapter 10. Paramedic

Cambridge, England, and Gascony, France, Earth,
May, 2025 and November, 2075

Shortly before I left the Other Earth a geologist discovered a fossil diagram of a very complicated radio set. It appeared to be a lithographic plate which had been made some ten million years earlier. The highly developed society which produced it had left no other trace.
Olaf Stapledon—*Star Maker*

Her face showed nothing but blissful peace within the halo of her long, dark hair. Lying flat on her back, her neck was in a brace, her body rigid in a frame. The paramedic had seen many accidents worse than this, but it always distressed her to see victims so young. Worse still, pregnant. She thought of her own two young children, both at school and happily ignorant of the abandoned carnage that occasionally troubled their mother's working day.

Escaping from the reek of the burning car, the police, the fire engines, the crowds of people and the general mess attendant on all road traffic accidents, the paramedic and her colleagues wheeled the gurney into the relative peace of the ambulance. The driver switched on the sirens and the blue-and-yellow-check van screamed southwards towards Addenbrooke's hospital.

Once inside the vehicle, the patient was briefly jolted into consciousness and emitted a small, urgent sigh, as if she were asking for something. The paramedic turned to look at the patient's face, barred with blue from the flashing lamp reflected through the window. She was amazed, having been convinced that the girl was dead. But then, as she looked, the patient opened two large, dark brown eyes, which looked directly at her, just for an instant, but with frightening penetration. A moment later, the gaze softened, looked inward: the patient mouthed just one word before grimacing with pain and retreating once again into a coma.

"Solomon..."

The paramedic had not wanted to look again at the bruised and bloody mess between the patient's breastbone and thighs, a field of destruction against which her face made an even more poignant contrast.

Later, in the operating theatre, the surgeons had done their best. Dilatation and curettage is upsetting enough even when the mother is healthy. When the mother has suffered from multiple ruptures to her spleen, pancreas, liver and intestines, and is clinging to the slender web-strings of life, it is more like emergency field medicine. The uterus looked like it had been shredded, like a basketball run down by a combine harvester. Stitching it up took some hours. Luckily for the patient, one of the surgeons was currently on sabbatical from Los Angeles and arguably the world's leading expert in the treatment of gunshot wounds to the abdomen.

It is possible that he saved her life.

Her baby was already dead, however, having taken the full force of the impact as the patient belly-flopped onto the bonnet of the car. During the course of this very complex procedure the third-trimester fetus was removed, one piece at a time, its remains swabbed out and discarded.

One would not have expected the surgeons to have removed every scrap of misplaced tissue, every particle of detritus that had penetrated the patient's body, and they did not. They can hardly be blamed for that, given the circumstances. Indeed, they were as overjoyed as anyone else when the patient went on to make a good recovery from her injuries.

But some damage, while it seems invisible, can be long-lasting.

Cells from the lining of the ripped placenta had buried themselves in the uterine wall, beyond immediate detection. In the course of time, most of these were flushed out by the patient's immune system. A few, however — possibly not more than one or two — fused with host cells, making tiny inocula of chimaeric tissue, each an intimate ikon of grieving mother and dying child, sculpted on a subcellular level.

It is now known now that women, as they get older, often become chimaeras, each one bearing patchworks of cells in unconscious memory of each one of the children they have borne. Although scientists continue to see this as a conundrum in itself, theologians have come to regard it as evidence for God's compassion. This phenomenon was hardly known in those days, when the patient was recovering from her trauma. So she never knew that some tiny protoplasmic scraps of her never-to-be born child lived on inside her.

Try as they might, chimaeras cannot always obey the rules, and after fifty years of effort a small colony of the descendants of what had once been fetal cells finally broke free. Eluding the ever more placid sentries of an ageing body, they declared independence, and, finding no resistance, they started to send out new colonies throughout the harlequinade that was the re-patched, re-healed and re-sealed endometrium.

They meant no harm.

That's just what they did.

And so it was that in November, 2075, when Jadis was in her kitchen pickling the last of that year's cucumber crop, she felt a sudden stabbing sensation in her belly. It felt as if someone had kicked her. Hard.

Her mind went into a sudden giddy swirl, and just for an instant, she thought she was outside, in a walled garden. Instinctively she glanced down and saw her frayed jeans where she had expected to witness a thin, viscid trickle of cherry-red blood running in a determined line across the snowy field of her inner thigh. Pulling herself together, she put down, with great deliberation, the pan of hot vinegar she was holding, and sat carefully at the kitchen table until the pain had gone away.

She had been conscious of a dull pain there for—what?—it could have been a couple of years, even. But she had dismissed it as a sign of ageing, and paid it no further attention. Only now had it intruded into her life and mind with such force. But she would dismiss this pain, too, as a symptom of the same incurable disease. Who was it who once said that the most you can expect in advancing age was to wake to a day free from pain? "Well, whoever it was," she said to herself, "they were right." She continued with her task, despite the fact that her mind kept wandering, so much so that she frequently came to senses to find that she had stopped, motionless, gazing at everything and again, at nothing.

The rogue cells inside her continued to breed.

She reflected on the pain as she continued her work. It dawned on her that it had grown steadily alongside the increased tensions in the farmhouse that had surrounded the seemingly endless, futilely circular arguments about the publication of the Sigil. That the pain had finally broken out to stand before her explicit, conscious scrutiny mirrored the plain fact that matters had now reached an *impasse*, in which the three men in her life wanted her consent to publish the paper that Tom had diligently drafted. But she had refused, without compromise. The more they pleaded, the more they pestered, the more she hardened her heart. But *why*, a part of her asked?

Two years earlier, when they had revealed the Sigil with such ceremony, she had happily consented to Tom writing it up for publication. No, her soul cried in response—not 'happily'. Her acceptance had, in fact, been both provisional and grudging, and something that had troubled her, being a tacit admission of mortality, of declining powers, of *failure*. Such an admission, tacit or otherwise, would have represented a violation of her very nature, for inside she felt she was still a young woman. It had never horrified her to see her hands and face as brown and lined, because she had always assumed they'd belonged to someone else. Furthermore, she had never allowed herself to fail at anything, for, to her, failure was an abnegation of the self, and on that point she would never give any ground at all.

Not that she would ever have couched her attitude in these precise, formal terms, either to herself, or to the outside world. On the contrary, she had focussed her anger and frustration into the sharp beams of logic. She could not just drop the news of the Sigil onto the world free from context, as she kept on saying to Tom during a period of what had seemed like several weeks over the summer, in which he had harried her constantly. No, she said, it would look ridiculous, as if they had arrived from nowhere to say they had discovered Atlantis. The Sigil could not be published, because they had no idea who could have made it, and why it was there—and that was that.

Tom's habitual response was that the chances of answering either question were utterly remote, as she well knew: and therefore that he might as well not have bothered drafting his report. In which case she might have had the grace to have made this clear before he'd even started. Tom would often finish this line of argument by stalking out of the room in search of some hard physical activity on which to vent his frustration.

At this point Jadis had always bitten her lip, as if wanting to say something more. Tom (if still in the room) always pressed her to spit it out, whatever it was, and have done.

Matters had come to a head when the three of them were sitting down to supper—it had been in September, just a couple of months earlier—and Jadis and Tom had started to circle each other in the same weary dogfight.

Jack simply pretended it wasn't happening. He had told Tom quietly, many times, to back off, that Jadis would come round eventually, in her own time. But Tom seemed compelled to harass his mother, the compulsion growing as Jadis became more entrenched.

"But why, *Maman*, why?" Tom had said. "Why can't we just publish it, get it done, move on?" Tom had said.

"You know very well, why, Tom, and please don't whine." She pulled herself up abruptly. She had never talked to Tom like this, not even when he was small.

"I just don't understand," said Tom, "I really don't. It's such a simple thing. Describe the artifact. That it *is* an artefact nobody can doubt. We put our doubts about the age on the table: that it seems to be older than any dating technique we know can measure. We put our doubts about its composition, likewise, on the table: that the cursed thing has resisted every known means of penetration. If nothing else, to show how hard we've worked. We need not even speculate about what it all means, if you don't want to. But we could show the world what we've found. Maybe invite comment. Invite help."

"No, Tom, *no*," she'd insisted. "And why don't you understand? All those years ago, she…"

This was the point.

"'She'? Who?"

Jadis hid her eyes beneath the gray shroud of her hair. She felt that she had crossed a line that had forever been there, for all that nobody had mentioned it. Inviolate, violated. Her answer came slowly, through her frustration, her embarrassment.

"It was… well, it was Shoshana, if you must know. In the first week she was here, I asked her, and she…"

"*Maman*…" Tom was a picture of a cold rage.

Jadis couldn't pull back now. Sensing a weakness in the cordon that surrounded her, she went for the kill.

"Yes, Tom, *Shoshana*. It was *Shoshana*. Remember her? Shoshana said that before going public, we needed to know more about who made it. It was plain enough to her, and she was a schoolgirl with nothing more than native common sense. Something that some people seem to have lost. *Some people who should know better.*"

"This really is the limit," said Tom. His face was white with anger, his green eyes flashing. "You know," he said, in a tone plainly calculated to wound, "I think I might as well just publish the thing under my own name and have done."

"You will do no such thing!"

"All right! I'll publish it with your name on it! The lead author!"

"Tom, the answer is still no." She gripped her belly and drew a long, anxious breath. "We *have* to know more about its makers before we can legitimately say anything. Otherwise it looks like a joke… a very, very sick joke. And do you want to make fun of us—of *me*?" She had wanted to apologise for raising an old ghost, but the argument had now gone too far. Tom pushed away his plate, snorted contemptuously and went for the door.

"If you want me," said Tom, looking pointedly at Jack, "I'll be in the shelter, settling the horses." The Sigil, now effectively abandoned once more and with winter approaching, the barn had returned to its accustomed use.

Jack helped Jadis clear and wash the dishes in absolute silence. Even from a few feet away, he could feel the pain and rage envelop her like a fetid cloud. To an extent, he agreed with Tom. They should just write it up and have done. After all, he and Jadis were getting old; it was important unfinished business; and, resignedly, he just wanted to clear his desk.

At first—years ago—he had felt that Jadis had been quite right in her insistence that one could not publish the Sigil without any idea of how it got there, or why. But as the years passed with that question still unresolved, and perhaps without any realistic hope that it ever would be resolved, he was coming round to the view that they should simply publish the Sigil, be candid about the problems with dating and provenance, and leave it at that, just as Tom suggested.

A datum for others to explore in the future. A mystery for others to solve.

So Jack screwed up his courage and just told her—maybe Tom's right, publish the inscription, be candid about its provenance, nothing more.

"Jack—I can't do it," she said. "I—I just can't."

"Sure, of course," he said. "But it's not an ideal world and we won't be here forever. We should really put our spin on it before anyone else comes along when we're dead and gone and does a hatchet job. You were there when it was uncovered. You deserve the credit."

"Jack…"

"In any case," he continued. "Tom's right. What does it matter who made it? You can't have all the answers at once."

"Oh really! There's no need to be quite so patronizing," she replied with some asperity, not looking at him, concentrating on the dirty dishes in the sink. Jack ignored her barb and tried another tack.

"Anyway, I think we owe it to Ruxton Carr and his people and the confidence they always had in us. Roger, too."

"Jack, that's not fair. It really isn't."

Jack decided to say no more, because he knew he'd hit home. In the last analysis, he felt, the Sigil could have been what the whole story had all been about, from the very beginning: the Institute, perhaps even their being together. And he knew that Jadis, in her heart, knew this too.

They said nothing further about it until they had gone to bed, and they'd heard Tom come back inside and lock up. In the darkness, Jadis felt that it didn't matter whether she met anyone's eyes or not.

"Jack, I'm sorry about what I said to Tom," she said.

Jack said nothing for several seconds.

"Jack?"

"Well, I rather think you should apologise to Tom... not me."

Silence.

"Jack, really," she said, "I know you and Tom are both right. Publish the thing as an announcement and, as Tom says, move on."

"Hurrah." Jack's tone was quietly sarcastic. It did not suit him—never had—but he was getting better at it as he got older.

"Jack, don't. Please don't make this any worse. It's just... well..."

"Hmm?"

Slowly she tried to explain what had been haunting her, the reason for her reluctance. She might—*might*—be prepared to live without having to identify the makers if the message of the Sigil could somehow be decoded, in a way independent of its origins. They'd had Domingo's eclipse theory, and then Tom and Shoshana's suggestion that it was a warning, and, finally, when they had unveiled the Sigil, Tom's shattering, apocalyptic vision. And then there was Jack's quiet insistence that the Plague had something to do with it. The problem, she said, was two-fold.

First, which option should they choose?

Second, how could their choice—any choice—be substantiated?

"But why don't we just lay out all the possibilities and leave it for someone else to worry about?" Jack asked. "As Tom says, just put it all on the table?"

More silence.

"We could do that, of course," said Jadis. "But..."

"But?"

"Oh, hell: it's all about Tom. It all comes back to Tom and what he saw in the Sigil. That's the most graphic evidence any one of us has ever had, but only Tom was capable of gaining it. Nobody else has—or, perhaps, can. We really need to put it in, but how on Earth can we? Tom's account can't be substantiated, replicated. And, apart from that, how do we—I—ask him about it? After everything that's happened?"

Jack turned to wrap her in his arms. She squirmed slightly, finding it hard to get comfortable. These days, she felt like she was no more than a loosely aggregated bag of bones, all sharp corners and unwieldy angles.

"So, Jadis, really, what you're really worried about," Jack said, "what it all boils down to is… is reproducibility."

"Darling Jack — what would I do without you?"

"Much the same as you'd have done otherwise, I suspect."

He noticed that her laugh had faded to a kind of gasping pant.

"But I wish Tom wouldn't keep on at me all the time," she said. "It's making me tired, Jack. So very tired. And…"

"Jadis?"

But Jadis had fallen asleep.

-=0=-

After two years of hard work, Pope Eusebius II had made the top two floors of the old Mairie into his Portable Vatican. The upper floor contained a very small flat for himself (what he called his 'Official Residence,' given that he also spent many nights in his old quarters in the farmhouse), and a chapel for the use of his staff.

The floor below contained two small offices, staffed by Christophorines, and what he liked to call his 'laboratory,' a chamber really no bigger than a large cupboard. This room contained, thanks to the diligence of Adelardian engineers, direct qWave links with the Astrometry Institute in Cambridge. It was as far from the glories of Rome as possible, but that's the way Domingo liked it. He could keep in touch with his Cardinals and Bishops remotely in a constantly convened virtual consistory. It was, he thought, an excellent and efficient way of working. And what he spent an increasing amount of time doing was watching the stars, as more and more of them winked out.

"News is not good, Your Holiness," Father Tikko Bray had said by qWave one afternoon in the early Summer of 2075. "Ross 248 and 154 have gone, Your Holiness. But you already know about those. But Wolf 359 seems to have dropped off our screens, too. These… *things*… appear to be converging on us, from all points in the Heavens."

"I understand, Father Bray," replied Domingo, thoughtfully. "However, I believe that Lac 9352 remains the only star we've had the misfortune to have watched actually in the act of disappearing."

"Yes, Your Holiness," replied Father Bray. "But that was two years ago, and several light-years further out."

There was a long pause.

"But now you have so much more data, Father Bray," Domingo went on, "and the case of Lac 9352 needs to be set in… ah… *context*. You understand that I can hardly put my name on a paper, much as though I'd like to. But let's look on the bright side. By not being directly associated, I can remain free to establish context in a manner that can be construed by those sufficiently charitable as... er... *independent.*"

"Your Holiness?"

"Yes, I think it high time that *you* and your colleagues wrote something up. I really do. I think it might prove extremely helpful."

The world carried on in general ignorance of a note that appeared in October on an Adelardian-run astronomy preprint engine by T. Bray and colleagues entitled 'Systematic stellar extinction in the Solar Neighbourhood'. Domingo had a printout sent down to the farmhouse, marked for Jadis' attention. Having not had a reply for some weeks, he called round himself.

He found Jadis far from her usual state of animated business. Instead, she was seated at the table, gazing into space, surrounded by pans and jars and half-pickled cucumbers and the tang of vinegar. There was a seam of pain in her face. She was clearly miles away, and before she knew it, Domingo was pushing a mug of tea into her hands.

"Domingo?" she said.

"The same," he said. "Now, Jadis, what's the matter?"

"Oh, you know, everything and nothing, much as usual," she said. "And especially Tom. And what to do about the Sigil."

"Publish it, of course." The words slipped out fractionally faster than he had intended.

"Oh not you, too." She stood up and turned away. She seemed about to launch into a tirade, but stopped herself, turned back and sat down again.

"Jadis," said Domingo, "I passed you a preprint from the astrometrists in Cambridge. About how more stars have been disappearing, and how the... er... *dragons* appear to be approaching our particular corner of Creation."

"I know. I read it — thank you, Domingo," she said. "I'm sorry for not thanking you earlier. It's just..."

"It is hard to take in, I admit," he said. "I prayed long and hard about it, to overcome what I felt was a feeling of utter denial. But it is useless to resist, I feel. We can only pray for equanimity and... uh... acceptance."

"Acceptance? Of what?" She looked at him, wide-eyed, reproachful, as if he were a villager who'd had the gall to interrupt her mid-sentence. He read anguish in her face. Domingo took her hands in his.

"Acceptance that the world is about to end," he said. "There. I've said it." Jadis sat motionless, seemingly unable to comprehend what her friend had just told her. "This is why you—we—really should publish the Sigil. Don't you see? The pattern we see in space is recorded in the Sigil. Documented."

She smiled weakly. He wasn't sure whether she had taken any of this in.

"Tom…" she began.

"Jadis," Domingo said, "you need not worry about the… er… *eschato-logical* aspects of Tom's vision. Not now… now that we have proof."

"No? What? No, that's not what I meant at all," she said. "It's just that I… it's… I don't feel particularly well, Domingo. Do you mind? I am not sure I can really talk or think about all… well, all *this*, just now. Is that all right?"

Domingo noticed that her movements were hunched, uncertain, like an eggbound chicken, whereas before she'd always been so easy and carefree. And she looked so pale, her skin like beige parchment stretched over prominent cheekbones, making her brown eyes stand out all the more. Strange: until now, he'd never noticed that she'd aged, and quite considerably so in the past year.

As he tramped back up the hill to the Mairie in the teeth of a strong autumnal westerly, bringing with it the detritus of leaves and maize stalks, rain, and the faraway smell of the sea, he wondered whether acceptance would come fast enough before an end which he felt was inevitable. He'd have to summon his Cardinals here, to Saint-Rogatien, in person, for what in his mind he was already calling the Council of the Last Days.

To an extent, he felt, it was a moment for which all clergymen prepare throughout their ministries. From the Pope down to the humblest shaman (and there were many times when Domingo felt more akin to the latter than the former) the function of any priest is to guide his flock through the great transitions of life: birth, marriage, death.

The imminent death of the whole world should be the same thing, only on a greater canvas. Really, just a matter of administration and logistics. He felt he ought to be comforted, that his own religion had detailed prescriptions for this very eventuality. And yet, and yet, no novice, no seminarian ever feels that it will be *they* who has to preside over the millennium, the rapture, the Last Days. He felt that if he didn't keep moving, keep busy, the responsibility would crush him.

That, and the terror of utter helplessness.

How similar he was to Jadis, he thought. Perhaps that's why Jadis looked so distracted. When he finally crested the hill, musing on Jadis' condition, he was met by an anxious monk in the hooded robe of the Adelardian novitiate, hurrying across the rain-slicked cobbles.

"Your Holiness," the novice said, bowing low. "I am requested to ask you to qWave Father Bray immediately. He has some urgent news."

-=0=-

Later that same evening, Jack saw the compost bucket in the corner of the kitchen full to overflowing. Tom had been busy with the stock all day. Jadis would normally have emptied it, but this evening she'd seemed more than usually absent, lost in thought. When asked what was wrong, she'd bitten her lip and turned away, shrugging off his glances, the touch of his hand.

It concerned him, but the immediate problem was hefting the bucket of peelings and other kitchen detritus down to the far end of the garden. He was astonished by the weight of it, and relieved when, after much puffing and heaving through the chill of the evening air, he'd upended the contents onto the compost heap. Placing the bucket carefully on the ground, he stretched himself upwards. He could almost feel his strained back muscles and bones clicking back into place. That, initially, was not the cause of his delight. For, looking up at the cold, high northern sky beyond the spinney, the night now washed by the rain into an un-matched clarity — he saw a shooting star. The briefest flash at the corner of his eye, and it was gone.

Now, he thought to himself: *that's* interesting.

It occurred to him that in all their years at Saint-Rogatien he'd never seen a single shooting star, not one. As he paused to consider this, he saw two more, much brighter this time, and then a whole shower. For several seconds, the whole sky was streaked with the silent trails of in-candescent interplanetary debris, before fading quickly to nothing. Jack's eyes had by now accommodated to the bright show, so now he was plunged into darkness. This in itself did not unnerve him. He stood quite still, staring at the sky, waiting for the stars to come back into view, one by one.

Jack loved the stars. In his youth and early manhood they had been his constant companions as he tramped the hills and vales. Now, in his old age, living in a village in which artificial light was a rarity, they had become his friends once more. He turned to face the south, and saw the familiar figure of Orion march high above the roof of the farmhouse. White Rigel; Betelgeuese, baleful red; Bellatrix; the remarkably bright haze of the Nebula where new stars were, even now, being born. Further up he saw orange Aldebaran, and the exquisite ice-blue points of the Pleiades.

Looking downwards once more across the belt of the Hunter he found a bald patch of sky that looked like it shouldn't have been there. Perhaps he was a little rusty? But no, Orion was in the same place, and the other constellations, and all the stars shining evenly from a sky so clear that he could pick out the Milky Way from horizon to horizon. He was worried, disoriented, and fought to quell a tiny tendril of panic.

No. Start again.

That old stargazer's trick. He traced Orion's belt downwards and left-wards... but it was true.

The Great Dog had closed its Eye.

Sirius, the brightest star in the night sky, had vanished. Jack felt his legs go numb. He sat down abruptly on the upturned compost bucket.

-=0=-

Domingo walked to the qWave set, his mind sparking premonitions of disaster even as an Adelardian technician spoke briefly into the hand-set, passed it to him, and left the room, bowing. Domingo waited until the oak door had shut with a click before speaking. He sat a plain bent-wood chair at a desk before the curtained window, three small qWave monitors on standby in front of him, each one a shimmer of light, no more than a coherent arrangement of air molecules. The only other light was the golden glow from a pair of candles in a sconce on the wall be-hind him, throwing his own face into shadow. Yet this simple room was qWired directly into the Astrometry Institute in Cambridge, and through that, the Yahoo spacecraft. From his Portable Vatican, Domingo had eyes in the sky.

"Father Bray?" he began. He was surprised at the nervous tremor in his voice.

"Your Holiness." The Chief Astrometer's voice seemed crackly and distant. Domingo became conscious of how warm the small room was, how oppressive.

"You have... er... *news*?"

"Yes, Your Holiness," the Chief Astrometer cleared his throat. Per-haps he was as nervous as Domingo. Or maybe it was just bad quantization on the line. "I pray, first, that Your Holiness is seated?" Domingo assured him that he was, and that he was anxious to hear the latest information from Cambridge. He hoped his demand did not sound too hoarse, too peremptory.

"Very well, Your Holiness," said Father Bray. "It's like this... the star Alpha Canis Majoris disappeared sometime in the early hours of the morning, Greenwich time. The latest Yahoo plate should be on your leftmost monitor." Silence on the line. Domingo looked through a porthole into the blackness of space where once a giant star had raged. All that was left was a set of superimposed crosshairs and a squirl of numbers against a field of faint, distant stars. He was absolutely stunned.

"Your Holiness?"

"Yes, thank you Father Bray, I heard you. Sirius."

"It is the first naked-eye star to have been, affected, as far as we know." To call Sirius a naked-eye star was, Domingo thought, typical astrometric understatement. Just nine light-years away, it was—*had been*—the most splendid jewel of the night sky and the fourth brightest object in the heavens, after the Sun, the Moon and Venus.

"Did you... ah... *capture* the process in action?" Domingo wondered how much more disturbing the destruction of a large, blue-white star such as Sirius would be, compared with the disaggregation of the red dwarf Lac 9352 that he had witnessed.

"I'm afraid not, Your Holiness. But it's definitely not there *now*, and neither is the neutron-star companion, Sirius B, and... oh, Your Holiness, something's just come in. Please allow me a second..."

"Of course, Father Bray." Domingo heard, faintly in the background, the exchange of sharp, excited voices. He could not make out what they were saying. Father Bray came back on the line.

"Your Holiness—I have just now heard from Cardinal Signorelli." Domingo knew that this indomitable Cardinal and his airship-borne expeditionary team were in northern Australia, searching for an unusual and very secretive tribe of hominids called the Potkurok. "The Cardinal's news is extraordinary," the Chief Astrometer continued. "He says that Alpha Centauri has disappeared." Domingo felt that no further surprises were possible.

"What—*all* of it?"

"It seems so, Your Holiness... and I must apologise once more for a short delay while I...?"

"Of course." More hurried exchanges in the background. Pops and clicks. Domingo waited for almost a minute until Father Bray returned.

"Your Holiness—I apologise once again for the delay—yet I have now managed to corroborate Cardinal Signorelli's observation with real-time data from Yahoo. The central pair of stars—Alpha Centauri A and B—well, they've definitely gone. You can see the latest Yahoo image in your central monitor." Domingo looked through a second porthole into space, opening next to the first, the two hanging ominously over his desk. "We cannot see Proxima, either," Father Bray continued, "and have to assume the worst."

Proxima is—was—the lonely outlier of the Alpha Centauri triple-star system. It had another distinction, too. At just over four light-years away, it was the closest star to the Sun. Domingo could hear his heart pounding: he steadied himself against the edge of the desk in case he fell.

"Father Bray," he said, "I guess that it is fair to assume that we are... er... *next*." Domingo did not want to see what might open up in the third monitor—still blandly showing the default screen of the crossed keys of the Holy See—and, for the first time, began to appreciate the utter terror that Tom had felt when he first saw the Sigil, in all its hellish splendor.

"Pray for us, Your Holiness," said Father Bray. "Pray for us all."

"Yes, of course. I understand. And please convey my deepest thanks to your redoubtable colleagues, for continuing in such circumstances." He took a deep breath, gulping for air. "But before you go, Father Bray, I should like to know one further thing."

"Your Holiness?"

"I suspect you have a fair idea of the distribution of these... er... *dragons*, in space, no?

"Possibly, Your Holiness, but they are very hard to see. They can be detected from very slight gravitational effects, and lucky occultations of background stars, so one assumes that they are made of a very dense and dark material. There have been some reports of cometary activity in the Oort Cloud, which suggests that they are quite close, and..."

"Please, Father Bray, I do not wish to halt your disquisition, which is most... ah... *interesting*. But can you estimate when these... er... *entities* will be in the vicinity of the Sun?"

"My sincere apologies, Your Holiness. We have been discussing this very thing in some depth..."

"And?"

"Our best guess is that the path of the closest group of these... ah... gravitational anomalies... will intersect the Sun in five months time. If we were pressed, and strictly off the record at the present time, we'd say between the 17th and the 19th of April next." Domingo could hardly believe his ears.

"You know, that date..." he said.

"Yes, Your Holiness. I do."

"May God bless you, Father Bray. You may go." The Chief Astrometer offered the customary response and the line went dead.

Domingo sat quite still for a very long time, quite unable, at first, to assimilate what Father Bray had told him. The nearest and brightest stars to the Sun had all gone, and the dragons were now nibbling the outer reaches of the Solar System itself. But what struck him more forcibly than anything, even more than these cataclysms, was the timing. No, surely not. This had to be a coincidence. *Had* to be.

He looked up towards the curtained window, and even though his face was entirely shadowed by the candelabra, he felt the warmth of light on his face. Escape from bondage. Plagues. Angels, passing over. Hope.

Resurrection.

Slowly at first, and then with increasing conviction, he pieced it all together.

-=0=-

Tom dreamed that he was looking at the Sigil again. He was tiny and it was huge, like a vast sculpture, a monolith. The pattern of circles and lines was picked out in oxyacetylene flame against a charcoal-black background. As he watched, the flames burned down into the underlying matrix as precisely as any laser cutter and it fell to bits, a crazy three-dimensional jigsaw of angular blocks. Tom tried to spread his arms around them all, to stop them tumbling to the floor, but they just kept falling, falling with a regular rhythm, *knock, knock, knock,* and more and more, until he pulled himself through the surface tension of wakefulness to hear a gentle rap on his door.

It was his mother, with a cup of tea.

"*Maman...*" He sprang from his bed to take the teacup from her: it looked like it had become somehow awkward for her to carry. Tom was struck that she looked terribly old, and ill.

"Thank you, Tom," she said. "Thank you so much." She sat down on the edge of the bed, a small sigh escaping like the wheeze of an ancient accordion. "Tom, I apologize. For everything. Of course you can publish the Sigil. I won't stand in your way. No longer." Tom sat down next to her.

"*Maman* — why? After all this time, you..."

"Please, let's not have a post-mortem. Suffice it to say that Jack has convinced me. And Domingo, too. They are both of them very silly, much as I love them."

The rest came out in a confusing tumble about disappearing stars, bringing Tom smartly back to his disquieting experience at the Astrometry Institute, of watching the death of Lac 9352, echoed by his vision of the Sigil. Even so, he found it hard to take in that Sirius had disappeared. Yes, Jadis had said, Jack had appeared wild and breathless at her side in bed last night, having seen it — or rather *not* seen it — and could hardly get the words out. She had to cling to him, she said, to calm him: she had never — never in her whole life, their long marriage — seen him as agitated.

But anyway, Jadis said, she would need no further convincing, and so perhaps she was being small — petty, even — to hold things up any more.

"*Maman*, surely not."

"You know, it's not that I don't still have serious reservations about the whole thing." She looked straight ahead, as if Tom were not there.

"Hmm?" Tom sipped his tea.

"Yes. For, you see, it resolves nothing." She looked round at Tom: "we are still no closer than we ever were to understanding who made the Sigil, or why. Not really. It might as well have dropped from the sky. Although I have some ideas. Guesses, really." She coughed. It was a hollow, dry sound.

"Jack has been on and on at me about coincidences," she said. "How odd it is that Ruxton Carr funded two things that seemed as disparate as an archeology institute and an astrometry institute and, my goodness, what should we find? *Quelle surprise*, but the Sigil, and disappearing stars, and that they are somehow tied up together. What a coincidence it seems! But Jack has an idea that the Plague is all mixed up in it too, which I'm not sure about and..." She looked directly at him, into his eyes, unflinchingly, as if he were not her son, but a zoological specimen. Tom suddenly felt cold and pressed his hands round the tea mug.

"*Maman*? What is it?"

"Look, Tom," she said. "I know we haven't always got on recently, and I desperately don't want you to take what I have to say the wrong way. Really, I don't." Tom was silent. He felt that whatever was coming next would be another shattering blow, and that his mother had backed him into a corner with some species of emotional blackmail.

"Tom," she continued, "you never met Ruxton Carr, did you? Not even in all your time in Cambridge? And even though you were our son, associated with one of his largest and most long-term projects?"

"No, *Maman*, I didn't..."

"Well, I never met him either — but Jack did, just once, long ago, and he said something very odd to me, just the other day. That he reminded him of you. That you and Ruxton Carr had the same eyes.

"And, Tom — please don't mind this — everything has come down to your eyes, and how you see things, ever since you were a little boy, when you couldn't see anything. I remember the first time you saw, as clear as day. It was Fairbanks who... ah, well." Her voice petered out as she paused to draw breath in a jagged gasp, but in that instant, Tom saw a whirl of blinding light, and felt the comforting, furred bulk of his first and, perhaps, his truest friend. The one who said nothing, but somehow always knew.

"*Maman*..."

"And now, with what you and *only* you saw in the Sigil," Jadis continued, her eyes looking inward, as if Tom weren't really there. She paused again, and then turned the twin spotlights of her gaze upon him. "You have a gift, you see — a gift that I think Ruxton Carr had, too, which is why we — that's Jack and me — set this whole thing up in the first place. But you weren't related to him, were you?" The question seemed rhetorical.

Tom thought of auras, and how, despite himself, his own aura had meshed so compellingly with Morgana's. He shuddered, and his voice was strained and sharp.

"*Maman*, where is all this leading?"

"I'm sorry Tom, I don't really know. Everything these days seems so... well, mixed up, beyond my grasp." Her eyes lost their sparkle for an instant. "You may as well know. Well, I'm just getting old, I suppose." Tom put down his cup and moved forward on the bed to embrace her. He was shocked at how little there was to hold. The warmth and softness — the maternal *hugeness* he remembered, as if he were no more than a babe — had turned into nothing more than a starved sparrow. It comes as a shock, he thought, to know that one's parents are mortals. That they will get old and die.

"The fact is, Tom, someone made the Sigil," she said, softly, "and we haven't really thought much about them. We've always had the excuse that because the Sigil was the only sign that its makers existed, that we couldn't possibly make any headway. But that's not true. We can say something, even if we cannot prove it. Which is frustrating, but there it is." He felt the tremors of agitation course through her suddenly fragile body.

"If we can say one thing about the Makers," she continued, "it's that they already had a very advanced technology, far in advance of anything we could ever match. That gravitational business: that it seems to be some kind of hole in space-time. That it seems to be made of a material that nobody has ever been able to identify, though, once... one of the physicists thought it might be some form of metallic ice. He was laughed off the podium, I seem to remember..." Tom thought her mind was beginning to wander, to fade.

"*Maman?*" he prompted.

"Oh... sorry Tom... where was I?" she answered, pulling herself up. "Oh yes. So either the Makers were people of this Earth — hominids, presumably — or they weren't. Something from elsewhere. Little green men. So which is it? What would you choose, Tom?" She turned directly to look at him.

"I... well, I'd have to say that a hominid would be the most likely option," he said, nervous in the spotlight beams of his mother's eyes, "given that we have plenty of evidence for the existence of hominids stretching back millions of years... the early Sand Druids and so on... and that we have never detected any intelligent life elsewhere in the Universe."

"Go on, Tom."

"But if the Sigil's makers were hominids — *if* — they must have raced ahead of their fellows." He said. "We've always thought that the latest common ancestor of all the hominids we know about — including the Sand Druids, Almai, *Homo sapiens* and so on — lived no earlier than eight million years ago, around when the chimp lineage diverged, and..."

The penny dropped.

You see, Tom, you *see*?" said Jadis, picking up on Tom's argument. "That whenever people say we've 'always thought' something, I always suspect that we've 'always thought' wrong — made the wrong assumptions. Now, this'll be ancient history to you, but I still remember Jack's conviction that the landscape of Europe had been tamed and shaped for a million years, a fact that was as plain as day to Jack despite the fact that everyone had 'always thought' it was a wilderness. So, that's one thing.

There might have been hominids with truly, breathtakingly advanced technology, living far longer ago than we've assumed possible..."

"But, *Maman*," Tom interrupted, "there's absolutely no evidence of that. Technology like that would have left a trace in the fossil record, surely?"

"Oh, Tom, you know better than that!" She smiled and bowed her head, her eyes, huge, peeping through the skeins of gray. "The fossil record leaves us virtually nothing. Who knows what might have existed, that we'll never know about? If it hadn't been the Sigil, we'd not even have suspected that its makers even existed. Why should we?"

"Yes, *Maman*, of course..."

"All right then," she said, with animation. "Absence of evidence isn't evidence of absence, but I'd concede that given that we have no evidence of technologically advanced hominids maybe, oh, ten or twenty or, damn it, fifty million years ago, we have to look at the other possibility." She drew breath, slowly, laboriously. "What if the Sigil-makers weren't hominids, but something else?"

"*Aliens?*" Tom was incredulous. "You mean to say that they really were little green men? *Maman*, you've always pooh-poohed that idea."

"Well, yes, but think about it. We finally—finally!—have evidence that we're not alone, don't we? We know nothing of ancient, advanced hominids, but we *do* now have *proof* that some kind of alien life exists."

"The dragons..." Doors flew open in Tom's mind. "Maman, you're right. So if there is one alien species, there might be others, and... and..."

"Tom, whoever the Sigil's makers were, and whenever they lived, I think that its makers were trying to speak—to send messages—using signs that we humans can interpret. Just as you... just as Shoshana said they had."

It had been Shoshana all along. Shoshana, dead for twenty years, still lived in the fact that she had brought reconciliation between Tom and his mother.

"Shoshana..." whispered Tom.

Jadis turned, creaking, to look at her son. "You loved her very much, didn't you?" She paused. Tom felt that her emaciated form was bracing itself for a final spurt, as if in the teeth of a gale that might blow her fragile form apart. He held her closer, to steady her.

"*Maman*, don't worry, I'm here."

"Tom, I must say this while I still have the chance. That you are my son, and you always will be, no matter what; and that I have always loved you since Domingo brought you the path through the snow on

Christmas Day, no less, wrapped in swaddling clothes just like the baby Jesus. And I love you now, despite everything. And I love you because you loved that poor, lost girl. And I'll love you until the day I die, which I fear will not be long."

"Oh, *Maman*..."

"Tom, hear me out." She said. "Domingo is always droning on about 'acceptance'. He told me something about the end of the world being nigh or some such, which I did not accept until Jack told me about Sirius. The dragon-things—the aliens—are coming this way. Just as the Sigil-makers said they would, whoever they were, or whenever they lived. So now I accept it. The world will end sometime sooner or later, because the dragons are coming to eat the Sun. The Sigil was a warning about the dragons. A vision that Shoshana *imagined*, and you *saw*.

"No matter that you thought we were making fun of you, we—me, your father, Domingo—we never doubted the truth of that vision for an instant. So, really, you are the very best person to describe the Sigil. So now it's *your* turn to accept something, Tom—that the Sigil's makers might have something to do with *you*, though I can't imagine what. Whatever species you belong to, Tom, I suspect—only *suspect*, mind—it has a history longer than any known hominid. Did you ever get your DNA tested?"

"No, I..."

"Of course you didn't," Jadis said. "There was no reason to have done so."

Tom thought, with a shock, about Morgana and her crew of Jive Monkeys, and brought to mind a paper he'd seen in an obscure journal saying that a preliminary analysis of their DNA looked more like that of lemurs or tarsiers—not like that of higher primates at all—his assuming that the researchers must have got it wrong. Assumptions. How frail they were, and how fickle.

"There, that's all," Jadis croaked. "I don't think I can say any more." She collapsed into his arms, gasping for breath.

Tom saw a fleck of blood on his sleeve. It was the tiniest spot imaginable. But it was there.

Acceptance.

Shoshana.

Himself.

Chapter 11. Saviour

Rhoneland, Earth, *c.* 125,000 years ago

'The time has come,' the Walrus said,
'To talk of many things'
Lewis Carroll — *The Walrus and the Carpenter*

Mr Khorare seized the moment, as a warm wind rose and brushed against his face. "Please, friend Vortigern," he asked, "as we are both heading that way, would it be possible for you to tell me something of our destination?"

Vortigern smiled, but his eyes, which were disconcertingly blue-green in his ebony black face, looked straight ahead, as if wistfully, to the end of a road which might be attained only in physical fact, but not in spirit. His robe, a deep purple, billowed and flapped in the light breeze. It was a long time — at least a dozen paces — before he replied.

"As we are, as you say, both going that way, I think I might be able to tell you something of it," he said. "However, you should know, Excellency Khorare, that to say anything about the... the destination... is... how should I say? Unusual. My friends and I have talked long and hard about what we should say to you, should the opportunity present itself."

"You knew it was me? All along? How so?"

"Excellency Khorare — you are aware from our speech that we come from the Kingdom Under The Mountain, just as you do. When we saw you in the *pension*, we were thunderstruck. We debated the implications of your apparition well into the night." Mr Khorare could imagine the raised voices and extravagant gesticulations that constituted debates among Thinskins. Vortigern sighed, and continued.

"Your appearance — here, now — could hardly be a coincidence. There must be a purpose to it, and we hardly dare to presume what that might be, though we can guess it. But irrespective of that, the fact remains, Excellency, that your name is one of infinite respect and reverence to my people, the Inheritors."

"It is?" Mr Khorare's surprise was piqued with curiosity about the name that Vortigern had used. The *Inheritors*.

"Look back at the Kingdom, Excellency," Vortigern said. "Its rule. Its customs. At the indignities my people have suffered, and continue to suffer, and will, no doubt suffer, long after you and I have turned to dust on the wind." Mr Khorare did indeed look back, and it was as if peering through a keyhole into a country of distant memory. What he saw was most unpleasant. People hunted and kept as cattle, used for sport and all manner of depraved pastimes by the Court of the King, before being flayed, butchered for meat, their skulls used as drinking-cups, their fat rendered for lamp-grease, their skins tanned and made into lampshades or fire-screens or clothing for the wealthy and the fashionable, their guts made into ropes or bowstrings, their bones carved into toys for children, their teeth into gaming pieces. Mr Khorare flushed with his shame at his easy compliance with such atrocities, over so many years.

"I know, friend Vortigern," said Khorare. "I am deeply ashamed. I'm sorry that I..."

"Don't be. Sorry, that is," said Vortigern. "But for your steadying hand on King Hrothgar, matters would have been very much worse. Because of your civilizing influence, many thousands of our people managed to escape the Kingdom, to disperse both west and east, to more civilized countries—or make their way south, back to the High Simien, our ancient homeland in Aethiopia. Without you, we fear that our very species would have been diminished, even to the point of extinction."

"I had no idea that I..."

"If anything, Excellency, your influence is proven in the breach. Since you departed these past two years, matters have deteriorated alarmingly. The Old King was assassinated by the Crown Prince Hygelak on the very eve of your own departure, and the slaughter since has been... well, I need hardly describe it. My wife, my children..." Vortigern's eyes began to water, but his bearing remained otherwise poised and erect. "Suffice it to say that as many of us as could manage it escaped to come on pilgrimage."

"I'm sorry, Vortigern. Truly, I am."

"What's past is past, Excellency Khorare. But please, before I tell you of our destination, might you honor me with some account of your own adventures? And of how we come to be treading the Great South Way, both together?"

Mr Khorare told Vortigern something of his history; of his upbringing in the Great and Ancient City of Axandragór now far away; of his ill-fated voyage to Dilmun, and his subsequent meeting with the Stoner Prince in whose service he'd spent most of his life; and his wish, on retirement, given that everyone he'd known in Axandragór would have died, to move instead westward, rather than east, and see something of the wonders of the world before he died himself.

He knew that it sounded unconvincing, but if Vortigern thought the same, he gave no hint of it. To be sure, had he been attending closely, any percipient listener might have read a great deal between the lines. For Mr Khorare was careful to omit all mention of his curious meetings with the reed-cutter and her avatar, the concierge; the seeming fact of his own immortality; and the existence of the talisman in the leather drawstring bag hung about his neck—the talisman whose safe delivery to their mysterious destination seemed so inexplicably important.

Mr Khorare, his story having finished, paced onwards, the Thinskin at his side, his own fellow pilgrims still a blur a few hundred yards in the distance. Vortigern was silent, and Mr Khorare guessed—rightly, as it turned out—that he was measuring his words, assaying the weight of what he was about to say, and what he could judiciously omit. Mr Khorare was, of course, a businessman at heart, and recognized that information has its price, just as much as any bale of stuff.

"The destination—*our* destination—is, in many ways, a mystery," the Thinskin said, at length. "I have not been there myself, you understand, but from what I know, it is a kind of mirror to the Great Pyramid and the town around it."

"A mirror?"

"Yes, I know: the analogy is not a very good one," Vortigern said. "Suffice it to say that the destination is a city that lies under the Earth. A city dominated by a pyramid."

"So much is suggested from what I had learned, friend Vortigern, although I had not known of the underground pyramid. Am I given to understand that the destination is much like the Kingdom Under The Mountain?"

"In some ways, yes—in that both are subterranean. But the destination is greater, by far: it stands to the Kingdom as a lion to a lentil."

"Who created this underground city?" Khorare asked.

"That's part of the mystery—nobody really knows, not even the Stoners. Their tradition has it that it was built by their predecessors, much as we, the Inheritors, will be their successors. Thanks to you."

"*Me?*"

Vortigern slackened his pace. He was clearly uncomfortable about what he was about to say next.

"The Stoners have many legends about the underground city," he said. "Legends about its past. We, on the other hand, have legends about its *future*."

"But—friend Vortigern—you mean prophecies, don't you? Not legends? Legends are necessarily about things in the far past, which, while once real, have been obscured and made fanciful by the dimming effect of time, by the…"

"Excellency Khorare—*friend* Khorare—please bear with me on this. It is a concept that I find very hard to convey, and a great secret of our race. Were you a Stoner, you'd not have heard even as much as I have told you. But I assure you that I am cognizant of the distinction between prophecies and legends. *Quite* cognizant."

"And what, then, are your… *legends?*"

"Friend Khorare, there stands at the center of the underground city, a great pyramid, as I have mentioned. It is—of course—nowhere near as great as the Pyramid standing at our backs." Both men knew that the passage of several miles had hardly reduced the loftiness of the Great Pyramid behind them, even though the city surrounding it had sunk below the horizon.

"It is, however, far less accessible. Whereas hundreds of people ascend and descend the Great Pyramid of Xxántroghátrem every day, the summit—and even the slopes—of the underground pyramid are barred to us. We do not know what lies at the summit, but we suspect that something—or someone—lives there. We Inheritors precess around the pyramid in torchlight parades, cementing our legends, our traditions, our hopes, but we never set foot on its slopes. We *never* ascend it."

"Because it is sacred, a taboo?"

"That is what it has become. But to set foot on the pyramid is death. Real, physical death. At least for us. But the legends speak of a visitor, a traveller from the farthest east, a man who is neither Stoner nor Inheritor—a man with the eyes of a cat. A man, in short, like you. The legend says that this man will ascend the pyramid, with an *offering*, to… to *placate* whatever it is that lives at the nameless summit."

"And what then?"

"That, friend Khorare, is not known. But our interpretation of the legend is that the visitor from the east will, once at the nameless summit, make the appropriate offering, or obeisance, or at any rate do *something*—something momentous—to ensure that the Inheritors really will come into their own."

"Something…?"

"That's all I know, friend Khorare. That's all anyone knows."

The two men continued to pace southward. The Sun had passed its zenith point, shining directly into their eyes, and was now slowly edging towards the southwest. Mr Khorare was, by now, very hot, very sweaty, and footsore. The leather of his sandals was beginning to chafe. His discomfort perhaps explained why his initial reaction to Vortigern's story might have been one of waspish dismissal, even disdain, though he knew better than to give voice to his misgivings. Yes, he did have eyes like a cat, he supposed. And he did have what might be called an offering, which even now fretted in its leather pouch: Mr Khorare felt at times that the talisman was alive, like a mouse, squirming and struggling within its narrow cage. But legends of the future? That really was too much to credit.

As if reading his mind, Vortigern spoke. "I can appreciate your skepticism, friend Khorare," he said. "It must sound most exotic to one who confronts such matters for the first time, matters with which every Inheritor is familiar from early childhood. If it will help, I might let you in on another secret."

"Yes?"

"It is our scripture, the Book of the Goddess, a text so ancient that its origin is utterly obscure—a fact which, to us, only magnifies its holiness. Despite its antiquity, friend Khorare, you will never find a copy written down, for among the Stoners, the possession of this book means instant death. I myself have never seen it written down, and neither have any of my fellows. So children are taught it, by rote, line by line. Every Inheritor knows it off by heart."

The mention of the word 'goddess' triggered something in Mr Khorare. He felt it as a kind of analogy, a small red flower, blooming in the desert.

"Can you—are you permitted—to recite any of it to me, friend Vortigern? Anything concerning the Goddess of whom you speak?"

"Yes, I shall try. I cannot think it would do any harm, given that I am convinced that you, friend Khorare, represent the fulfilment of our legend, even if you are not so persuaded yourself."

Without breaking step, Vortigern began to intone, in a sing-song voice, a beautiful, keening song like a lullaby, full of unexpected if melodious intervals, and mellifluous ornament. For a moment, Mr Khorare felt that he'd been transported to the opera house back in Massilia.

The song told of a bright young goddess robed in red, who appeared among a nameless people, blessing them, hallowing them, and chiding them as both brave as lions, and yet as foolish as newborn lambs. Her countenance then became stern, warning her people to beware of imposters. Her discourse then, according to the song, concluded, as far as Mr Khorare could tell, in this wise:

> *For I am a Jealous Goddess, apparently,*
> *And even though I've probably fucked it up*
> *For everyone, as I usually do,*
> *I'm not going just to lie back with my legs open*
> *And be two-timed by a load of silly old men like you,*
> *Lovely though you are, each and every one.*
> *So you guys had better watch out. Grrr!*

Vortigern finished his song with a keening ululation. He turned his face away from Mr Khorare, as if he'd just confessed some appalling misdemeanor, and was embarrassed at having done so. Turning to face straight ahead, and pointedly not looking at Mr Khorare, Vortigern cleared his throat.

"I'm afraid that I do not know precisely what it means," he said. "The language is ancient and—if I might say so—somewhat barbarous. But in its obscurity lies its holiness, I think, or so we Inheritors interpret it. For while it is recondite, it has the ring of authenticity held only by the most ancient, arcane things. I do not think that anyone could have made it up."

"No, friend Vortigern, I agree," said Mr Khorare. Indeed, Mr Khorare could hardly contain his shock. For beneath a veneer of what he hoped was interested, if detached, appreciation, Mr Khorare felt his emotions rip through him like a scimitar, a sensation of *deja-vu* of such disabling intensity that he almost crumpled to the ground where he stood.

For he had heard those words before—those words, *exactly.*

It was in another life, and in another time, but the words evoked for him a ruined temple, and a young goddess in red fading into golden flame: a young goddess subsiding into his arms. And a small creature by his side, hardly more than a pet, but standing tall for the first time, like the inheritor his descendants would, one day, become.

It was then that Mr Khorare's whole life coalesced about him, the hitherto vague clouds condensing to a needle-point, a finality of purpose. It took no more than a second, but he felt a new steeliness come into his eyes. He turned those eyes ahead to see, beyond the fuzzy knot of pilgrims, a cluster of monumental stone buildings rising on the horizon, in the middle of which was a great, yawning gate, giving on to a void of blackness.

The nameless destination, at last.

-=0=-

Torch in hand he climbed, leaving the bright round of pilgrims far below, marching round the pyramid in concentric circles, in alternating directions. From this height he could see only the points of their torches and the patterns they made, as whole things that would have been invisible from ground level. Magical mandalas of flame they made, circling the pyramid. But he could spend no more time or energy marveling at the allure of these patterns. For time was running out, now, and in any case, the slope of the pyramid was steep and stony, deserving of his full concentration, the slope increasing in pitch as he climbed. The soles of his sandals slipped on the steepening scree, until he was crawling like a spider on hands and feet, the talisman in its bag swinging out, past the neckline of his worn chemise, dragging along the pyramid's stony surface. The entrancing songs of the pilgrims that had filled his ears on the lower slopes were now drowned by the rasps of his own breath and the beating of his heart.

The crawl turned into a climb, and the final ascent was as of a cliff, demanding that every step he took, every crevice and every handhold, was as considered as a move in a game of chess. But, finally, after an age, and when the palms of his hands were scratched, the soles of his sandals scored, its straps and buckles and the knees of his crushed-velvet pantaloons almost worn through, his face became level with the summit. Not a pinnacle, but a perfectly flat, featureless square no more than five or six yards on a side.

Featureless, that is, except for a plain door of wood, in a frame, standing in the center of the platform, hanging teasingly ajar. Through the crack, Mr Khorare could just make out a room whose windows looked out over a landscape of dazzling whiteness, punctuated by the jagged forms of conifers, with a range of mountains in the distance.

Mr Khorare scrambled onto the surface of the platform, dusted himself down as well as he could, and without a second thought, walked across the threshold.

The talisman sat on the coffee table between them, a trinket surrounded by tumblers and bottles and the remains of a meal. Mr Khorare looked down at it, the strange, gray object, perhaps stone, perhaps metal (for he had never thought, before, to inquire of its substance), at its finely drawn cartouche of circles, crescents and radiating lines. He had never

studied it for long, for whenever he did, he'd always had the most un-
pleasantly vertiginous sensation of somehow being sucked into it, and
the effort of tearing his eyes away always gave him a headache that lingered for several hours. He ripped his gaze from it now, refocusing on
the hazy figure in the chesterfield opposite.

"No, Khorare," she continued. "Nobody really knows who made this
city. Well, *almost* nobody." She gave a teasing smile, and tossed her head.
"It was here before the Stoners came and built Rhoneland. When they
are gone, it'll be here still."

"And the Thinskins? The Inheritors?"

"Oh, they'll be gone too, for a while," she said. "Despite all appearances, the Stoner civilization you have known is long past its prime, and
will soon collapse into barbarism once again, taking the Thinskins with
it—as the pleasantly tropical climate you have known all your life breaks
up into deserts, whether cold, dry, or both.

"But before they fade out altogether, the Stoners will reoccupy this
hidden city, and fastnesses like it, as refuges, both against the weather
outside, and being fearful of what is to come. They'll take their model
from something—somewhere—you know well, Khorare."

"The Kingdom? The Kingdom Under The Mountain?"

"Yes. Thanks to you, Khorare, the Inheritors will indeed inherit. But
the matter will be decided in your old adopted home.

"Why, then, have I come here? So far westward?"

"Because, Khorare, there are only so many plates I can keep spinning
in the air at once."

Khorare wondered why he could not see her face as anything more
than a blur. That quick glance at the talisman must have done something
to his vision. He felt himself growing fuzzy, fading. Perhaps he'd had
too much scotch. He was aware that as she spoke she had risen from her
chesterfield, and then, wending her way round the sofa, come to stand
before him.

"Because, Khorare," she said, "the talisman had to be delivered here.
At the top of this pyramid. And you've delivered it. So now your work is
done."

She bent down, then, and Mr Khorare was dimly aware of the graded
curves of her breasts pendant beneath her blouse, of loosened strands of
hair across his face, a warm, welcoming scent of musk; her small, delicate hands on his cheeks, and the impression of her lips on the top of his
head. The world, already distinctly vague, faded out, and when it came

back into focus, Mr Khorare found that he was in a different body and in another country whose dry scent he thought he recognized.

Oh no, he thought — not again.

His second thought, once he'd risen, resignedly, from the rock on which he was seated, was that he should really do something about his clothes. This harlequinade of diamond motley. This three-pointed cap. *With bells on.*

Honestly!

What was the world coming to?

Chapter 12. Convergence

Gascony, France, Earth, Easter, 2076

Fortunately this early philosopher left descendants; and from these arose, in due course and by means of a series of happy mutations, a race of large-brained and non-simian creatures whose scanty remains your geologists have yet to unearth, and catalogue as an offshoot of the main line of evolution.

Olaf Stapledon—*Last Men in London*

The drove moved on through space. Most of the time it grazed on stars that were rich in carbon and other complex atoms, but which were otherwise small and dim. On the other hand, the recent consumption of several powerful energy sources had stimulated rather than sated—radiation in abundance, but these young, bright stars had been of relatively low metallicity. The white-dwarf star orbiting the biggest and brightest of the young blue-hot stars had, however, been a real treat for those of the drove that had got there first.

But what the drove wanted most were stars that had both size and reasonable metallicity, somewhere in between the abundant but small M and K-class dwarfs, all brewing elements for billions of years, yet each with its own savor, like stationed salt-licks for migrating cattle; and the O and A-class giants, too young and hot to have acquired much in the way of complex elements. Main-sequence F- and G-class suns were most prized—neither too hot nor cold, neither too rich nor too poor. As if they were some galactic Goldilocks, they drew the drove like a magnet.

The drove sensed a suitable star in the path of its current somewhat haphazard migratory route and converged on it from all corners of space. By the time it reached the star's Oort Cloud, the drove numbered approximately thirty thousand individuals.

Not that any member of the drove would have thought this way, or even thought at all. Although some of the inhabitants of an aluminosilicate pebble orbiting close to the star had named them 'dragons,' they were more like sheep, cattle, or even whales, grazing mindlessly on the fruits of galaxies and nebulae, as indolently as were they plucking berries from bushes, or sifting krill from the sea.

Perhaps even to have thought of them as living organisms might have stretched a point. Generated during the inflation phase of the Big Bang, each member of the drove was a dimensionally complex knot of space-time whose size and shape in 3-space was consequently hard to estimate. But whatever its exact size, a dragon (for want of a better word) exerted a disproportionately large gravitational field, while radiating no discernible energy. Had astronomers but known it, the dragons of space made up a small but appreciable fraction of the non-visible mass from which the Universe was thought to have been constituted. In practice, a dragon was a mobile black hole with a hunger that could never be assuaged.

By January, 2076, the dragons were observed to have sucked star-like Saturn and Jupiter dry. Uranus had disappeared, too, by way of collateral damage. Now so close, the aliens were discernible (against a luminous background) as individuals, in the way they had not been during the remote observation of Lac 9352. Domingo would never forget the image of a swarm of black specks swirling around the King of Planets like a mockery of a shrouded gossamer ring, before a column of them plummeted like a spearhead into the Great Red Spot. It only took a few moments for the rich russets and browns of the Jupiter's cloudscape to be drained of all color; only a few more for the giant planet to implode and disappear into nothingness, as if it had never been.

By the early Spring of 2076, rumors of the end of the world were in general currency. The great cities of south-east Asia erupted in flames before settling down to sullen acquiescence. Hominids in isolated corners of the world worked themselves up into a frenzy of sacrifice. In a small community in the Negev Desert, a Sand Druid called Bob looked up at the sky, sighed, and closed his egg-yolk eyes for the last time.

The people of Europe, after south-east Asia the next most populous part of the planet, were suddenly on the move, even though there was no chance of escape, as all parts of the Earth were doomed equally. It is likely that they were spurred on by the meteor showers of extraordinary frequency and intensity—now, as they ever were, harbingers of doom.

As the rumors spread from house to house, from refugee to monastic hospitaller to mendicant friar, it became clear that the last of all harvests would be gathered in at Easter, and as time passed, the rumors became firmer and more consistent. The world would end some time mid-afternoon (Greenwich time) on Easter Sunday.

Messages came from the Holy See at Saint-Rogatien that this was in fact a sign not of despair but of *hope*, given that Good Friday coincided with the ancient Jewish festival of *Pesach*, celebrated with a ritual meal. Among Christians this would always be indelibly associated with The Last Supper: the last meal Jesus took with all his disciples before his death, and now the last meal that the peoples of the Earth would take with their families and friends before — before, well, who knew what?

The end now seemed certain, but the messages emanating from the ancient hilltop at Saint-Rogatien were of expectation, not resignation.

Throughout the winter, clergy had been gathering at Saint-Rogatien and finding accommodation where it could. Their number was swelled by people from many miles around — people who wanted to hear the words of His Holiness, Pope Eusebius, some time before the end. A tent city sprung up in still-snowbound fields; carts and caravans congregated in corrals under snow-laden trees. More and still more arrived as the land thawed in late March, until the farmhouse was an isolated eye of peace in the maelstrom of people. The early sowing season was disrupted — but if the crop was never to be gathered in, what did it matter?

Only a very few were agitated. Soapbox cranks and false prophets were far less frequent than one might have imagined, given the imminent apocalypse. Indeed, most of the migrants seemed to be at peace, and all were waiting for the promised outdoor mass on the morning of Easter Day itself, when the Pope, it was said, would address the crowd from the roof of the old Mairie opposite the church on the hill. In the meantime, there was a mess of people, all clothed in the slick brown of muddy slush; the screams of babies; the whimpers of children realizing that they would never go home; the press of beasts; the wild parties and bacchanalian festivals of people who had nothing more to lose; the queues for scarce food and stinking, hastily dug latrines amid the mired ground.

A harbinger of doom came on the very last day of March. The destruction of most of the outer planets had scattered moons and other small bodies like grapeshot all across the Solar System. Although much of the débris was yet too far from the Earth to have reached it since the dragons had laid the outer Solar System to waste, the gravitational ripples were felt much closer in, disrupting the courses of several Earth-crossing asteroids. Meteor showers were a nightly occurrence. Several objects had already made close approaches to the Earth, although none had actually made contact.

The first object to hit the planet was Mnemosyne, hitherto an utterly insignificant fly-speck of an asteroid, which struck the wide and empty North Pacific at a relatively shallow angle. The sea boiled, and the consequent tsunami inundated the coastlands from the Philippines to California.

The second impact, later the same day, was closer to home. This was another tiny Earth-grazing asteroid that had long troubled the Astrometry Institute on account of a long series of projected near-misses: the object was extremely small, but regularly approached the Earth within a few tens of thousands of kilometers. The gravitational disturbances from the outer Solar System had tipped its orbit just enough to raise the probability of its striking the Earth into the red zone.

As sunset on 31 March, Minor Planet 100039 Ziemelis streaked southwestwards across southern France and made landfall at the ancient Episcopal seat of Urgell, in Catalonia, just across the Pyrenées. The impact had the explosive yield of a small nuclear bomb. Urgell itself was obliterated in an instant.

Within seconds, the superheated blast wave had scoured the valleys of Andorra, atomizing everything in its path. The mountain wall shook and crumbled, but in the main stood firm, protecting Saint-Rogatien from the worst effects of the blast and the subsequent shower of white-hot rocks: yet an incandescent wake had been painted across the vault of a sky that looked like it had been split in two. The southern horizon was utterly black, a field against which the mountains could be picked out in ominous relief, making them look unusually close.

There were other changes, too. The strange gravitational eddies, slip-streams and wakes created by the passage of the dragons through the Solar System set up tidal stresses in the fabric of the Earth itself. The ground seemed to grumble from constant low-level earthquakes. Over the past two or three months the unquiet Earth had increasingly erupted into cataclysm. The Pacific Circle of Fire was alight: the last remnants of Tokyo and San Francisco had tumbled. The Sasquatch Confederation of Shasta was devastated by the resurgence of Mount St Helens; Yellowstone was a lava lake of boiling fury; the San Andreas Fault opened like a wound. Iceland had burst into flames and split asunder. Mount Tiede in Tenerife had slid into the Atlantic, dousing the already sodden Eastern seaboard of North America with a twenty-meter tsunami. What with the dust raised by the bolide impacts, the exhalations of the world's volcanoes forged a livid spectacle of the final sunsets.

Those with sharp eyes had noticed that the Moon, too, had changed. It had begun to vary in size through its cycle, as well as in phase. And those with sharper eyes still noticed craters and rills never before seen from the Earth, riding on the Moon's eastern and western limbs. The Moon had been shaken in its orbit: the lunar dark side would not be dark for much longer.

Comets, earthquakes, volcanoes and impacts. Heralds of doom, scrawled across the face of the deep.

The evening of 18th April was the Last Supper, celebrated both quietly and loudly, gladly and sadly, with acquiescence and with terror, in a thousand campfires around Saint-Rogatien, and in homes and hovels and caves and towers across the writhen world, as the Sun set for the last time. The final sunset was, fittingly, the most spectacular yet. The bloated orange ball of the solar disk, magnified by the richly refractive horizon, sank through palatial ranks of deep red and purple clouds and, as it finally vanished, launched penetrating streamers of saffron yellow above it to the zenith, painting in gold the undersides of the cinnamon cloud-banks.

Jadis watched from the door of the *arrière-cuisine*, propped on Tom's arm. When the Sun disappeared behind the church, she sighed and looked at her son. His own expression was hard to read: Jadis thought it might have been awe. But what Tom actually saw was always impossible to know — like trying to describe color to a cat.

"Let's lay the table," she said.

Very little further was said as Jadis, Jack, Tom and Domingo ate their simple, final meal, of bread and cheese with some of last year's pickles and the very first stems from the year's asparagus.

Domingo had blessed the meal as he had done many times before, in happier and less contemplative times. He had spent the day at the Mairie and alongside the parish priest, assisting at several services in which the congregation had spilled out of the church, into the square and down the adjacent streets; ministering, comforting and blessing a constant stream of supplicants, and helping as much as he could.

He should have been exhausted.

Instead, he was fired up with a potent mixture of eager anticipation and uttermost terror, as if he were a small child invited to dive into the pool from the high board. He couldn't sit still, and his chair creaked with a thousand tiny squeaks as he shifted his bulk this way and that. He kept stealing glances at Tom, as if in solicitation for a friend who had to reach an uncomfortable decision; and also at Jadis, who now seemed very sick indeed.

Jadis didn't know what to think. The pain in her insides was now so great that connected thought was very difficult in any case, but those thoughts she did actually manage mostly left her angry and frustrated.

The world coming to an end? What was one meant to think of that?

How ought one to react? Regret? Happiness? Horror?

She was even less prepared to give any quarter whatsoever to the illness that was now plainly eating away at her. On his many visits to her bedside in recent weeks, Domingo had blithered on about 'acceptance'. She thanked him for his kindness, but said that his visits were cheering in themselves, whatever he said: and that she wouldn't know what to do with such abstract concepts anyway.

Her one spark of hope came from Jack, who said very little, but who was always *there*, especially in the long and increasingly interrupted nights of the past two or three months; who would hold her close and stroke her hair, combing it with her ancient tortoise-shell plastic comb, rekindling half-buried thoughts of matters long past when her flesh had been young and full and incorrupt, to the extent that she had been quite capable of engendering more life within it. Had she any tears left to shed, she would have cried for that, for her childlessness was now her single greatest regret. In idle moments she found herself blaming Tom for this—and this shamed and horrified her. So she clung to Jack all the harder. Were Jack to die or disappear, she thought, there really would be no need to go on living, were she in an infinity of pain, or none.

Really, she thought, nothing had changed—for it came back to her as clearly as it had been yesterday, when she had been revising for her finals while Jack had made his first visit to Saint-Rogatien, and the pain of his absence then had been a bitter hunger. Rather like the pain she felt now, except that not even Jack's arms could ease it.

Jack was mostly worried about Jadis, against which the end of the world would always come a poor second. At dinner, he would reach over to her and squeeze her hand—small, bony and hot, like the body of a goldfinch—just to reassure himself that she hadn't vanished—or died. Whenever he touched her she seemed energized, becoming the center of the occasion, as she always had been—bright-eyed, excited, animated, the long, leggy girl he'd first met, with the wild, dark hair and matching eyes of quite disconcerting ferocity. The eyes—well, they were still there, large and round in her pinched, lined face, and as fierce as ever. But he was distressed that there was no means of easing her pain, and even if there were some palliative, he was not sure she'd have done anything more than ignore it. To have acknowledged help would have been to admit that she was gravely, even terminally ill, and this might have made matters worse, not better. As with all things, it was usually best to let Jadis achieve equanimity on her own.

However, he did wonder, trying to bury the shame of even thinking along such lines, that were she to die, what then? He suspected that the farmhouse would revert to being a place like any other, and not the center of his world as it had been for half a century. And once his heart had been torn out, he imagined himself an ant from a colony whose queen had died, wandering hither and thither without direction until he met his own random fate.

Tom had completed his paper on the Sigil a few weeks earlier and had sent it to *Nature*, courtesy of one of Domingo's qWave transmitters. He had received an acknowledgement, but nothing more, not even a polite yet curt notice of rejection. Not even the offices of that august journal were immune to the death of the Solar System. Tom viewed all this with resignation. He was glad to have got the thing off his desk—off all their desks—and in any case it didn't much matter now. If the world were to end, he was glad that he'd meet it here.

He reflected that his world had ended so many times already, and his reaction to each event had never been a credit to his own soul. His world ended first when he'd gained the gift of sight, and he had had to adapt, painfully, to the new world of light. Yet he had never trusted it fully, so that when Shoshana had arrived, ending his world for a second time, he had had to adapt all over again. And then there was Masada. And Morgana. And the first viewing of the Sigil.

And then—*then*—there had been Shoshana's death, for which he felt himself responsible though he could not work out precisely why this should be, even though he flagellated himself constantly in an inexhaustible (if now tolerably well-hidden) black pit of remorse. Oh, yes—Tom felt that he had already died a thousand deaths, like the coward he felt himself to be.

Yet, from all this, it seemed clear that ends were never as final as they first seemed, but were in the great scheme of things better regarded as transitions. In which case, perhaps the end of the world would not be such. But no, he thought, he had seen what had happened to Lac 9352: his only course was to compose himself with as much dignity as he could muster.

For *Menschkeit*.

For her sake.

Amid all this, Tom was still trying to make a further accommodation, to the conversation he'd had with Domingo earlier that same day, in which wave followed thundering wave of revelation, so that Tom had felt as bleached as a plank of driftwood washed up on a tropical shore. So much, he had thought, for taking back the reins of his life.

He had just bedded the horses into the stable, locking the door carefully behind him. What with the volume and press of people in the district recently, one couldn't be too careful. He looked up from the padlock and was startled to see Domingo's great bulk close by. Domingo apologised for making him jump.

"We have long tried to put two and two together, Tom, you and I," he said.

Tom looked into the older man's face, questioningly. It was richly lined, where one could see past the thick white beard and moustache, but the brown eyes were as deep and as wise as the bones of the Earth. The eyes lit up again as he continued: "I have a problem which I cannot solve alone, Tom," he said. "I'd value your help."

Tom was torn. On the one hand, he loved and trusted Domingo as a father. On the other, as sons and fathers might, he felt himself in constant danger of being trapped by the older man's guile, his greater experience, especially if he, as the younger and greener, were approached on the pretext of needing help, as if he were the wiser of the two. Domingo had done it again—here was an occasion when Tom could hardly have denied him.

So Tom suggested that they talk it over, whatever it was, in the Spinney, where they could be quiet, and enjoy the slanting rays of the afternoon sun through the branches of the trees. They sat on an old split-log bench of Jack's ancient devising, cracked, worn to a silver-gray smoothness after the ravages of many winters and summers.

"Domingo?"

"Yes. Tom." Domingo swallowed, as if—Tom imagined—he were going to ask a favor from a superior that he didn't expect to have granted. "I wish to... er... *solicit* your understanding, and also, possibly, your forgiveness. Concerning your origins and circumstances, and my part in them."

Tom was shocked, but not—if he were honest—entirely surprised. He thought he knew what was coming, particularly after his recent conversations with Jadis, and imagined that Domingo had cooked up whatever-it-was with his mother, perhaps as a last wish, a last attempt at final reconciliation, before the end. He thought he'd get his retaliation in first.

"Domingo," he said, "I'm sorry, but I have been through all this with *Maman*. How I have something to do with whoever-it-was that made the Sigil. I understand that you wish to make it up to me, but really, there's no need." He rose to go. Domingo placed a restraining arm of Tom's elbow as he did so.

"Please, Tom," he said, "indulge an old man in the last days of his life—of *all* our lives." His voice was stern. "I do not think you should have anything to lose by listening, and by listening, my heart would be eased somewhat." Tom sat down again and tried not to look like a sulking teenager. Guiltily, he remembered other times when Domingo had contrived to ease his pain. A boy standing next to a man in an aloha shirt, before the new grave of a dog.

"I offer no more excuses for the following," Domingo began. "If it pleases you, just think of it as a... er... well, a *story*. Some of it comes from the evidence of my own eyes. Rather more comes from my own travels in the Far East, together with the recollections of some of my colleagues. And some, my dear Tom, comes from *you*."

"Yes, Domingo. Of course." Again, Tom tried not to sound as if he were humoring his old mentor. He rather thought he had failed. Domingo cleared his throat.

There was, once, a species of people raised on this Earth (said Domingo), who were neither hominids nor aliens. Their own origins lay back during the Eocene epoch more than fifty million years ago. In that remote period, the Earth was as warm and lush as it had been during the reign of the dinosaurs. The Eocene world was an Eden, a jungle of riotous life from pole to pole. Indeed, the subsequent history of the world could be read simply as a tale of steady yet inexorable environmental decline.

If the Eocene marked the high fortunes of any particular group of animals, it was the primates, which evolved rapidly from small squirrel-like forms into a range of creatures like nothing seen since. Palaeontologists had long appreciated the diversity of Eocene primates, while acknowledging that only a tiny fraction of all those species that had ever lived had been preserved in the fossil record. Eocene primates colonized every niche that forests had to offer.

Some even colonized that most evanescent of niches: intelligence.

These creatures were remotely akin to what would become the nocturnal tarsiers of Borneo, although they gradually evolved an appearance almost indistinguishable from that of modern humans. This was no more than the well-known phenomenon of convergence, in which unrelated creatures, through the adoption of similar lifestyles, come to look similar to an uncanny degree.

Over a relatively short period several more-or-less related species of these primates had appeared, flowered and become extinct, until one species alone survived. This species erupted into a massive, world-girdling civilization that tamed the Earth to an extent that dwarfed the greatest achievements of *Homo sapiens*. In short, it transformed the world beyond recognition. This civilization and its *sequelae* ruled the Earth for the next several million years, against which the span of humankind looks trifling indeed.

Tom thought about the wilder and grislier excesses of Avi Malkeinu's tall tales, but chose not to draw that comparison aloud. Instead, he wondered aloud, as he had with his mother, how evidence for such a great and temporally extensive civilization could have remained unknown, even given the well-known roulette of fossilization, in which most species on Earth evolve, live out their spans and die without ever once troubling posterity with even a single scrap of bone or tooth robust enough to stand the test of deep time.

Ah, said Domingo, but these creatures *did* leave their mark—in the very face of the Earth, in its denudation and wholesale alteration. It was this civilization that was responsible for the climate change that withered the Eocene jungle. Had it not been for this mighty civilization, the Earth's climate would not have declined as severely as it did.

"It is ironic, is it not," said Domingo, "that Jack's recognition of the Neanderthal civilization that shaped Europe a million years ago was itself but a reshaping of a world that had been civilized for almost fifty times as long? Because, without these Eocene primates, there might have been no Ice Ages. This was what nearly derailed what I think—I guess—was their greatest plan."

"Their... greatest plan?"

"*Homo sapiens*. Yes, Tom, you looked shocked. And I apologise for my small dramatic... er... *flourish*." Domingo explained that nearly everything he had to say was pure guesswork, for all that it fitted the evidence. "A civilization that lasted as long as I suspect this one did must—*must*—have ventured into space. So if these creatures weren't aliens themselves, they probably encountered several extraterrestrial forms, over a very long period."

It was during this star-faring phase, Domingo suggested, that these creatures learned of the dragons from other species, or even discovered them for themselves. It became apparent from their researches that a biological solution might be engineered to combat the dragons, and that this would take a very long time indeed. But millions of years are easy to a civilization as ancient and stable as that of the Eocene primates. The task was to select a strain of primates and set in train a course of evolution that would produce a species that could combat the dragons in some unspecified way when they next arrived in this sector of space.

"Don't ask me how, Tom—I really *am* on... er... thin ice, here. And, unfortunately, as so often happens, even the best-laid plans gang aft agley at the last minute."

"Like mice and monkeys, maybe?"

Domingo laughed, chose to ignore Tom's attempt at gentle skepticism, and went on. Listen carefully, he said: this is the interesting part.

By around twenty million years ago or so, the final civilization of these once Galaxy-spanning creatures was on its last legs, fragmenting into smaller and mutually hostile factions. Their experiment had been going well for some time, but as a result of internecine strife and discord, they had created not one clear lineage of dragon-slayer but many—the hominids—and it was not at all clear, even to them, which if any of their several biological *protégés* would be of any use. So, knowing that they might not survive long enough to oversee their *Grand Projet*, they engineered the Sigil. It was, indeed, a warning—a prompt—for any hominids that might survive.

"Of course," said Domingo, "if we have learned anything from your mother and father's researches here at Saint-Rogatien, and later at Souris Saint-Michel, it's very hard indeed—even, perhaps, impossible—to pin the tool on to the toolmaker. So these primates whose existence I have... er... hypothesized might not have made the Sigil, but appropriated it from some even older civilization, perhaps even one elsewhere in the Galaxy. The strange... uh... *nature* of the artifact certainly suggests that might be a more likely explanation. In any case," he continued. "It hardly matters. Not now. That the Sigil exists is enough, I think, for us to discern its purpose."

Tom recalled an argument from long ago, an argument since suffused with a keening longing, loss, pain, and regret.

"A warning," he said. And then, after a pause, he whispered one more word: Shoshana.

Domingo grasped Tom's hand, then, and the two men sat in silence for some time, listening to the birdsong and the wind in the trees, and watching the sun in its stately fall towards the world's edge.

At length Domingo continued his story, painting a picture of a civilization now so decayed that its products, perhaps once the rulers of the Solar System, or of more than one, came to live humbly among the hominids, the products of their own technology, mingling with their own creations and writing themselves out of history.

Tom sat up straight and looked back at his mentor. For the first time he saw the lines of care, of worry – of age – in Domingo's face.

"And who are these remnants?" Tom asked. "Who are they?" In his heart Tom felt that he probably knew the answer, as his mother had done. Yet he had to hear it from Domingo's mouth, as much as he dreaded it.

"They are the creatures that now call themselves 'Jive Monkeys,' Tom – no, now, don't start, I suspect that this is not a complete surprise to you given what you already know, and your... ah... recent *experiences.*"

Tom sat back, trying to drive from his mind the horrible yet fascinating image of Morgana, and more than that, of him and Morgana together. But why *should* he continue this futile denial? Why not just accept it as a fact of life and move on? His mother, with her penetratingly logical mind, had worked it out. If Domingo had worked it out too, whose insights into human desires and motivations were perhaps more profound than anyone alive, Tom knew that it must be correct.

"And, Tom," the old man continued, "this is why I have asked you for your time this evening, and have been so rudely... ah... *insistent.* For I have felt your pain over many long years. It seems that you are of a greater lineage than any of us, and we've forced you to... er... *slum* it."

"Domingo, don't..." The memory of Shoshana's purple eyes filled his mind's sky, as soon as he had taken off his iShades to see.

"But I'm afraid I must, if only – selfishly – to ease my own mind, my own heart, before the end. For it was I, as you know, who brought you to this hearth and home, to comfort the childlessness of a good friend who'd had an accident that meant she could no longer bear children – your mother. And know this, Tom, she loves you with the tenacity of a lioness. That is why the past few months – years – have been such a trial for her. And you too, I suspect."

Tom nodded.

"The fact is, Tom, that you are a... ah... 'Jive Monkey,' and neither you, nor I, knew it. Just like, I suppose, those with whom you've had such problems in Cambridge. I must apologise for that, too, for it's my fault. I didn't know it when I rescued you from that massacred village in Borneo forty-odd years ago. I could have – *should* have – made more inquiries, I know, but Jadis was desperate, and... well... we didn't really know anything about hominids in those days. In retrospect, I guess, we should have seen it.

"But it is, perhaps, the curse of a species that has inherited the Earth to assume that it is alone and has always been so, and will therefore see in every face, no matter how different it looks, a reflection of itself—because it can conceive of no other. Had we known your true nature, Tom, it would have explained many things that perplexed your parents, and, I have to say, me."

"Such as...?"

"Well, Tom, in short, it's your eyes." Tom heard his mother speaking, but Domingo's voice carried a greater authority and knowledge than hers. For Domingo had been aware of his own perceived failure and had been engaged on a long and penitential research effort, if not in atonement, then at least to understand. "One thing I have discovered is that Jive Monkeys are habitually born blind, and a certain altriciality of development means that they cannot see at all until they are around five or six years old. At this stage the Jive-Monkey visual system is remarkably similar to that of a human, apart from an unusually shaped pupil. But the visual capacity increases with age as new banks of rods and cone cells develop in the retina, permitting a fair degree of sensation in the infrared and ultraviolet..."

"Domingo, please, stop, please... I... understand," Tom begged. "And I forgive you." Domingo put his great bear-paw of a hand on Tom's slender brown fingers.

"Thank you, Tom," he said. "Thank you."

"But there is more, isn't there, Domingo? Shouldn't you be telling me more? If I am a... a... one of these creatures, then aren't there consequences—from any liaison with a human?"

Domingo paused for a long time as if he—even he—had not the words sufficient to say what he wished. "I expect that there might be, Tom," he said. "There might. But, I... honestly, I do not think I can say any more."

Tom could have sworn he saw a single tear well up in a wrinkle in Domingo's left eye, overspill the lid, and run down a line in his weathered cheek before disappearing into the eaves of his coniferously forested moustache.

The time for raging was long over. Shoshana's eyes, starred and flecked with violet, looked at Tom from out of the setting sun and, with a sudden flash of hardness, demanded that he be a *mensch*. This father-and-son game was not over. Not just yet. So Tom placed his free hand on top of Domingo's.

"Domingo, my forgiveness still stands." He smiled. Domingo nodded his thanks like a penitent. "But there is a question I must ask you, too."

"Tom, name it."

"Your stirring tale was of humans and other hominids as potential dragon-slayers. Did you mean that the long quest of the ancestors of the Jive Monkeys was to produce a species that could kill these things? The same creatures that we two, with our own eyes, saw destroy Lac 9352? Even when they could not?"

"Yes, Tom, but that was where the ice was at its thinnest... I didn't..."

Tom interrupted, his voice spiky and sharp as if chasing down a logical quarry before a roomful of hesitant, frightened undergraduates. "But that's just *it*, isn't it?" he said. "The whole business with the Jive Monkeys, though it concerns us closely, is a side-show. But if their ancestors were star-farers, why couldn't they have just blasted the dragons out of space with... oh, I don't know... ray guns?"

"Tom, I'm afraid I don't know..."

"... and yet you mentioned humans and other hominids as dragon-slayers," Tom continued. "You were quite specific about it. But no species on Earth today can launch anything more than a firework, and the dragons eat stars for breakfast and kick planets around like footballs. So where are these valiant *Saints-Georges*, when we need them?"

Tom rose to go, muttering that he'd promised to help his mother with the supper. That thought, too, struck him with a pang—she looked so frail, and yet defiantly denied the very suggestion of infirmity. Almost as a parting, Parthian shot, he turned again to the older man, still seated.

"And what's more, Domingo, *Homo sapiens*, which I expect was what you were getting at, has only just avoided extinction, and that by the narrowest of margins, effectively ruling them out of contention..." Tom stopped, quite still. He felt the blood drain from his face, and his knees weaken. He sat down again next to his old—his oldest friend. "Domingo—I must apologise," he said. "It's the Plague, isn't it? There is a connection, and..."

"I believe so, Tom. Or, rather, I *hope* so. I know you shot down that idea long ago, and you were right to have done so, given the evidence, or lack of it. But Jack thought there was a connection, somehow, and if it weren't for Jack's iron whims, neither of us would be here discussing all this, here, now."

"But... *how*?"

"I have no idea, Tom. None whatsoever," he said. "All we can do now is hope. And pray."

-=O=-

As he had done on so many nights of late, Domingo stayed up all night, praying and thinking. If not kneeling at his *prie-dieu* — in which his knees had now worn two great craters — he was pacing the confines of his narrow room in the farmhouse. On this night, he consoled himself with thoughts of the ancient midnight antiphon, on this, at the very darkest hour before the dawn.

cum rex gloriae Christus infernum debellaturus intraret

He thought again of the transitions that marked men's lives, and how he and his fellow priests were only the gatekeepers. Did they have a responsibility to be reliable guides to the world beyond?

qui tenebatur in morte captivus

His teaching insisted that they had, for scripture was quite clear on the nature of the next world and the terms under which it could be entered. He remembered how Avi had often needled him about this: the Jewish conception of the after-life, he had said, was necessarily vague, for who could say anything about a country whence none had returned? And yet, Domingo had countered, the Jews did not deny the conception of afterlife outright — and there was, after all, one who had come back from Heaven, to show everyone else what it was like.

advenisti desiderabilis quem expectabamus in tenebris

In that he had complete faith. But attendant on the incarnation and resurrection there had been salvation, too, and for that he prayed his hardest.

te nostra vocabant suspiria te large requirebant lamenta

Even then, he could not entirely dispel Avi's teasing empiricism, for it had resonated with him, too. After all, had he not been a scientist in his younger days? A cleric, certainly, and yet one who had been taught, even encouraged, to question received wisdom? In his thirst for more knowledge from the Astrometry Institute, despite its dreadful implications — was he not a scientist now? In that spirit, he had felt his mind increasingly drawn to the images of blood-spattered horror twenty years earlier when he had stepped into the isolation ward, deaf to the pleading of poor benighted Dr Al Hajj, to scoop the spherical remnant of Pope Linus the Second from beneath the gurney, and to insist on an appropriate container.

tu factus est spes desperatis magna consolatio in tormentis

The flight time of the Papal hyperjet from Israel to Rome had been less than an hour, and yet Domingo recalled it having been the longest hour of his life. Running from the storm as the fury of the Khalifa broke on the Mediterranean shore, he had sat in air-conditioned peace, with the sealed box at his side.

He recalled the *touch* of the erstwhile pontiff. The sphere had been hard and smooth—smooth enough to be slippery, almost as if it were alive. Handling it, he felt as if he were trying to restrain a wet and writhing otter, or a newly caught fish. When he had finally got a grip—with an awkward combination of hands and sleeves and forearms—he noticed that the sphere was noticeably warm. This was, perhaps, to be expected, in a corpse which until moments before had been alive. But not after several hours and days had elapsed, when, still just as warm, the corpse was buried with due ceremony. At the time, Domingo had been puzzled by this: but many other concerns had pressed on his time and his mind and he had put his perplexity aside.

It was only lately that Domingo had begun to think that the Plague represented a very strange kind of death indeed, perhaps much less final than the phenomenon usually associated with that stygian scythe: more, then, of a transition.

Billions had been swept away in the Plague.

Billions of agonized finality, each one initially in circumstances all its own, and yet ultimately all exactly like Linus the Second, in that the final product was always the same—the black spheres, each featureless and identical in size and colour with every other.

He'd seen clusters of them on his travels. A dusty square in deserted Nice with these ominous matt-black Plague spheres instead of the smaller, graven chrome pieces of *petanque*. Banyan trees in the East Indies, with collections of black spheres rolled calmly against their bases. Whole towns in China, utterly deserted but for the spheres, lying in the streets, in shops, in homes.

In recent weeks he had often cause to recall a curious line of Jack's whose derivation he could not place, and which Jack, skittishly, wouldn't reveal:

> *that is not dead which can eternal lie,*
> *and with strange aeons even death may die.*

All over the world, these black spheres were brooding. Waiting. But for what? Domingo earnestly hoped that if his intuition—and Jack's—

was correct, that their condition was transitional, not final. And that they would not take much longer in choosing their moment.

-=0=-

Tom, like Domingo, could not sleep, either. Curiously, he felt, his insomnia had nothing to do with the promised cataclysm. The end of the world was far too stupefying a concept for him to even begin to imagine. He supposed that most other people felt the same, which was why there had been so few disturbances in the tents and campsites around the village. If one had no idea what to expect, not even in one's worst nightmares, it was pointless even to worry.

So why insomnia? Reason urged that he be at peace, finally, having scrambled after many hazards to a high, clear summit of equanimity, long desired, often denied. After all, he had achieved some kind of reconciliation with his mother, with Domingo, with the memory of Shoshana, and even with his own identity. And, as he always was these days, he had been running the physical side of the farm more or less single-handedly, and always went to bed in a state of welcome exhaustion.

At about four o'clock he gave up even pretending to sleep. Perhaps he'd go downstairs and make himself a cup of tea, and take it into the garden. It had been his traditional routine in Cambridge when the cramped confines of his cell closed in on him — to take a midnight stroll around the cloisters, the rhythm of his steps resonating with the waves of sleep. That is, until the pressure of work and other matters had become too much for him. But that was then. He rose, dressed and went downstairs.

He put the kettle on the range and, while it was heating, walked through the *arrière-cuisine* to the back door. He did all of this in darkness, as he always had, without thinking: against the pitch interior of the shuttered house, the night sky was a brighter curtain of slate-blue. He walked out on to the terrace — the same, had he known it, where Jack had first announced Souris Saint-Michel to the Dream Team.

The Earth grumbled and groaned beneath his feet, as it had done for several weeks. The constant infrasonic rumble had become an accompaniment to their lives so persistent that most now chose to ignore it, despite the threat it represented: that their small, fragile planet was trying to hold its course despite being tossed on a sea of unexpected and occasionally violent gravitational cross-currents.

But there was something else, too—something that only Tom could see. That the planet seemed to be generating its own aura, an aura that pulsed to the rhythms of the titanic forces now stressing the crust.

He saw it first on the edge of the *potager* as a faint blue-white glow against the near horizon, and traced it towards him as an illuminated network of thin lines that criss-crossed the terrace beneath his feet, as if they were phosphorescent sea-worms, and he were standing on glass. His eyes followed the glowing lines back to the *potager*, where they met other networks and formed greater branches and boles across the garden, through the field gate, and up the back lane to the village square. Picked out against the yellowish haze of the western horizon, he saw the luminous trunk join others moving in from other directions, and they all converged on the graveyard behind the church where the trunks fused into something like ball lightning, making strange dancing shadows and silhouettes of the looming yews and cypresses that shaded that part of the cemetery, on the very peak of the ancient hill.

And then there was an almighty crack like thunder, followed by a sustained roar, as the graveyard buckled and erupted. A shaft of white light, almost unbearably bright against the night, stabbed upwards from behind the trees, broad and straight, like the blade of a broadsword, fading only by virtue of its increasing distance. Tom saw it taper to a point and vanish above his head, at the zenith.

From the kitchen, the kettle whistled like a cock-crow.

Chapter 13. Usurper

Mesopotamia, Lower Egypt and Mount Carmel, Earth, c, 45,000 years ago; Souris Saint-Michel, France, Earth, c. 45,000 years ago and 1866 AD

Someone had blundered.
Alfred, Lord Tennyson— *The Charge of the Light Brigade*

Dust, dust.

The Yettin champion Zagrond wheeled, turning in the high saddle of his coelodont in a whirl of white fur, gray flint and blue lapis, as the gigantic, snow-maned animal reared, turned in mid-air and thundered to the ground in a yellow-brown cloud. Zagrond charged at Horsa again, head down, its vicious two-meter horn pointed straight at him.

For an instant, Horsa — his long shambok flailing in his right hand from its leather strap, reins grasped in his left — saw nothing but the point of his enemy's horn barreling towards him, surmounted by the fanged, bloody yell of defiance in Zagrond's face. At the very last moment, Horsa willed his own mount to step aside. His rhino, clanking, like he was, in flint fishmail, was huge, yet still puny compared with the might of the Yettin's mount.

Zagrond, startled by Horsa's feint, surged in a rage of spume and fur through a gap he did not expect. The ring of Stoners cheered, but their triumph was short-lived. As Zagrond passed by, his momentum too great for him to pull up without injury, he gave an almighty swipe at Horsa with his three-branched bone flail, smashing it towards the Stoner's head. Had Horsa not blocked the blow with his shambok, he would have lost half his face, ripped clear from his skull.

Bone flail met bone shambok with an impact that jarred Horsa's right arm so violently that the sinews in his shoulder strained and tore. The force of the blow instantly shivered both weapons into flying shrapnel. Blasted in Zagrond's wake, Horsa felt several fragments bury themselves in his hands and face. The Yettin whirled past like a hot wind. Horsa felt a stab of agony in his left eye. His vision was stained with red. His right arm was numb.

In the yellow distance, Zagrond slowed and turned once more in a screech and a fog of dirt, pulling out more weapons for another assault on the renegade Stoner chieftain. Horsa drew a narwhal-horn javelin from a saddle holster, and, transferring the reins to his weakened right hand, resting them in a knot on the pommel, hefted the weapon uncertainly in his left, waiting for the Yettin to return.

It was an outcome that Horsa had not expected, for all his contingencies and stratagems, and one he could not, now, afford to lose.

-=0=-

He had met the Yettin leader as they had agreed, at dawn after the evening of their last parley. With a wave of his hand, the Stoner army and the larger force of its Yettin allies moved off. Horsa could not help but gasp at its immensity. It seemed that the entire surface of the hill-slope, all the way down to the valley bottom far to the westward, had moved at once on his command, as if the Earth itself had adjusted its blankets over the ground beneath.

The deep-cloven Tigris had been the first obstacle, revealing the first signs of strain between the always fragile alliance between Stoners and Yettins. They had come up against the lip of a steep-sided canyon where they had expected an easy ford. Several assault-mammoths, always in the vanguard, had slipped and fallen over the rim before anyone realized what was happening.

The regrouping of such a vast army had taken three days, until scouts had had the chance to discover a ford some miles to the northward. More days lost, but worse was to come. The ford had been held against Horsa's scouts by a small contingent of Stoners from the Kingdom Under The Mountain itself. Lightly armed and easily cowed, this distant outpost was easily beaten.

Too easily.

By the time the main host had reached the ford and was halfway across—a maneuver that Horsa reckoned would take an entire day—they were ambushed by a sizeable force of Stoners. They appeared from nowhere, as if the rocks in the water and the banks on either side had simply melted into men.

The Battle of the Fords of Tigris was fierce and desperate. Arrows rained down, slashing beasts and men. Mammoths, their legs cut from beneath them, toppled into the river, unbalancing more mammoths and troopers on coelodonts, raising great waves that swamped Horsa's contingent and Yettins alike.

Despite its cost, the ambush had been routed by sunset. The Yettins, impatient for the joys of battle, had come into their own: each of the huge, furred man-beasts had picked up a Kingdom Stoner in each huge hand and had ripped out throats with impressive fangs. But all surprise was lost, and all momentum.

The subsequent passage across Mesopotamia, between Tigris and Euphrates, was ominously quiet, but this time it was the land itself that conspired against them. Horsa's childhood memory of this land had been of lushness and ease, of homesteads amid rushes and fields of wheat taller than a man; lakes full of fish and fluttering with spoonbills; the shade of frequent, bountiful palms. Such was the picture of this country he'd painted for Yettins more used to the enclosed world of mountainsides than this open, flat land. A country of plenty, with supplies to be found wherever needed, and grazing for the enormous contingent of beasts. Even if he knew in his heart that such a rosy image was unlikely to be borne out in reality.

But this land of plenty was now a pitiless, brown desert, utterly lifeless and uninhabited, with hardly a dry blade of grass for fodder—let alone palms, lakes, waterfowl and the rest. The only water revealed itself slyly, as quicksands, where the lakes must once have been, that mired yet more assault mammoths and troopers on coelodonts, weighed down with armor. Horsa realized with sickening shock how long ago his boyhood must have been, when he with his mother and her loyal courtiers had fled the rapine of the young Hengest. Whether this evil transition in the landscape had been the result of the depredations of the Kingdom, or the slowly worsening weather which, in the past twenty years, had led to six months per years of snowfall on the higher ground where his boyhood remembered hardly any at all—was not, at the moment, at the forefront of Horsa's mind.

Of more concern was the friability of his Yettin alliance. The Yettins were clearly beginning to suspect that Horsa had lied to them, deliberately: had led them into a trap. The worst thing, Horsa reflected, was that he had allowed *himself* to be fooled by his own childish expectations. That the innocence of childhood would have survived the ghastly betrayals of adulthood.

It was on the marshy banks of the sluggish Euphrates that matters had come to a head.

The Euphrates and the Tigris could hardly have been more different. Whereas the Tigris had ambushed them with sudden canyons, the Euphrates was slothful and meandering, and crept up on them by stealth. As they approached it, the flat land on which they had been traveling dipped so gently that they were unaware of it, until they found themselves in a country of tussock and tall reeds. Platoons became cut off from one another as their vision was obscured.

Horsa, at the head, found that he could no longer see his lieutenants to his right and left. He rode in a debatable land of pools and reedbeds, unable to see over the tops of the reeds, even mounted on a coelodont. The rhino, for its part, was swaddled girth-deep in mud and water, and was making heavy weather of it, snorting, and bucking its huge head. By the time Horsa had calmed it and looked up, he realized that he was quite alone. The world was eerily silent. Even Zagrond had disappeared.

He rode on, looking for what remnants of his army might still exist in this treacherous country, until his coelodont breasted a wave, scattering a clatter of ibises that flew up right in front of him. Now the last reedbeds had gone, and the Euphrates stood before him, wide, flat and blue. It was a relief, to be honest, to see a horizon uninterrupted by reeds. But this river was no mountain stream to be hopped at a bound: it was almost as broad as the sea. The farther bank could just be seen as a thin silver line ahead, parched under the westering sun before him.

As his rhino began to wade across, he began to pick out the motes of troops on rhinos, the smaller specks of footsoldiers, and the larger images of mammoths, all making their way across, in front of him and to either side, as far as the eye could see. The reeds had spread the army out, refracted it, so that it must have been five miles wide. The reeds had also slowed some parts of the army more than others — he, for example, had been at its head before they had strayed into the land of reeds, but now he was some way behind the leaders.

No choice now, thought Horsa, but to ride the shallow river to the other bank, and regroup. Horsa took some solace from this. Like all military men, he found comfort in being able, now and then, to subsume himself blindly to external constraint, absolving himself of all responsibility, all thought.

As it happened, their crossing point had been at the farthest extent of a vast meander, so whereas the eastern bank had been flat almost to the point of inexistence, the western bank was high. The final stretch of river was treacherous, with deep, fast-moving currents, and the farther bank was a broad, shelving beach. When Horsa's coelodont finally made landfall, shedding braids of water from its armor, Horsa looked down to see a motley selection of his own troops. They were in a sorry state. Many appeared to have lost their armor. Some were injured, a few gravely — bodies lay in disarray up and down the beach. Several were disposed in crazy angles. The stench of death lay thickly on the ground like a poisonous vapor. Only one man rose to greet him. It was his esquire. He took the coelodont's reins from Horsa and helped him dismount.

"What news?" asked Horsa, wondering how the army was to re-group.

"Very bad, Sir," the esquire said. "As you see, we had to fight our way across."

The story that the esquire told was grim.

-=0=-

Zagrond pounded towards him, bright white and blue against a rising plume of yellow-brown dust. Almost at the last minute, the Yettin let go the reins of his charging coelodont, raising both arms wide. He held a long, broad-bladed scimitar in each hand, poised to bring each one down at an angle and slice Horsa's head off with two diagonal cuts. Horsa weighed the twisted spike of narwhal horn in his left hand. It was heavy, reassuring. He tensed himself for the throw. The last thing he saw before the final strike was the inside of the Yettin's mouth, his array of teeth, the huge tongue, lolling, trailing gobbets of saliva. With one final heave, Horsa launched the dense ivory javelin at his adversary.

-=0=-

"It was the Yettins, Sir," the esquire said. "As we entered the reed forest, they doubled back. Some of us gave chase. We found them in rear, looting the supply train and making off back East."

"And what then?"

"We gave battle, Sir. The battle went back and forth, and the last tongues of it licked us across the river itself."

"You did well, it seems."

"Yes Sir, most of the Yettins will go no further. But, I regret, neither will most of our army. I've sent scouts up and down the banks to start a regroup. I took the liberty…"

"You are to be commended."

"Thank you, Sir. But we brought one just Yettin to account. A Yettin who killed many of us before he could demand to be brought to you for… for justice."

"Look up, Stoner," came a voice from ahead and above. On the grassy ridge above the beach was Zagrond, still mounted, silhouetted by the descending sun, surrounded by a crowd of nervous-looking Stoner spearmen, plainly afraid of being trampled by the Yettin's monstrous steed. Horsa shaded his eyes but said nothing.

"It is as your servant has said," Zagrond said. "We Yettins suspected treachery, Stoner. So we took our payment on account."

"But the contract has yet to be fulfilled, Zagrond," said Horsa. "The Kingdom still stands."

"The Kingdom, Stoner, as you well know, is rotten. It is poised to fall. Just one gentle push and all will collapse. A baby could do it. Even *you* could do it." The Yettin laughed. It was a horrible sound, like skeletons being crushed inside a giant fist. "Such prizes as there'd be would not satisfy our Yettin hunger: our Yettin thirst."

"You are without honor, Yettin. Be gone," said Horsa.

"Honor?" the Yettin cackled. "Honor? You are a beggar and a thief, Stoner, as you have been all the days of your life, cowering from a bully of a brother who dwells like a great fat maggot inside a rotten fruit, long bereft of value, with nothing but the other maggots for company. All entirely satisfactory, I dare say, if you are a maggot, and rotten fruit is to your taste. I, on the other hand, am a contractor, taking his due. Really, it is you who should read the small print."

"I cannot let such a slur passed unmarked," said Horsa, his temper rising sluggishly to the surface. A duel was the last thing he needed. He was uninjured, to be sure, but he was soaked through and weighed down by his armor; and he was exhausted. But the worst thing was that everything the Yettin said was true. He, Horsa, was nothing but a vagabond trading on the glories of a Kingdom that had in reality faded long ago, and which was now hardly worth the effort of claiming. He knew in his heart that he had deceived the Yettins—and his own men. But he could hardly admit as much in front of the remnants of his troops, who'd traveled so loyally and so far. Rank has its obligations, as well as its privileges.

"I thought as much, Stoner," replied Zagrond. "I suggest a joust. Shall we do it here on this dreary beach, or go slightly inland, where there is more room for a decent run-up?"

-=0=-

The narwhal-horn javelin left his hand with what he thought was agonizing slowness, compared with the breakneck speed of the approaching Yettin. The ground shook. So violent was Zagrond's final approach that Horsa could feel his own teeth rattle in their sockets. Horsa had aimed the javelin at Zagrond, but his left arm had not the strength of his right, and the javelin fell short. So rather than strike the Yettin, it pierced his coelodont through its right eye. The forelimbs of the gigantic animal buckled beneath it, pitching Zagrond forwards, through the air. The animal ploughed on through the dirt, carried by its momentum, its rider arcing above it.

As the animal came to a stop, half buried in dirt, Zagrond belly-flopped onto its huge, sharp nose-horn, which impaled him. Gray-brown innards streaked with blood dripped from the Yettin's wound, ran over the coelodont's head and dripped in viscous gouts onto the grass. Blood ran from the Yettin's mouth, frozen in an expression of horror, and dripped from the ends of his fangs.

It was only then that Horsa realized he'd been holding his breath. He exhaled — a hideous, gasping rasp of relief. There was nothing before him now but the Kingdom, his birthright. He'd take it alone, if he had to.

-=0=-

Dogfinger's eyes flashed open and he was suddenly awake. Father-the-Sun had yet to rise above the rim of the world, but he could still see — or, rather, sense — the body of Moonrise, his Bride, asleep with her back towards him. Hitching himself up on his right elbow, he traced the fingertips of his left hand over the sweeping curve of her hip, enjoying the contrast between the underlying hardness of her hipbone and the luxuriant fleshiness of her buttocks and thighs; feeling her skin yield to his touch, smelling its fragrance, released, as he did so.

"The time is now," he said, as much to himself as to her. "The men have gathered," he whispered to the darkness. "The scouts have plotted our course. We shall make our way north to the sea, and walk along the shore with the sea to our left. Then we shall meet the Stoner city, and take it."

"And I suppose you expect me to stay here with the other women and the children, waiting for your triumphant return? Hmm?" Her voice in the dark came suddenly.

"I thought you were asleep, Bride," said Dogfinger.

"Evidently."

"I wanted to leave without fuss, and... well, you are with child, as are many of the other women."

"Whose fault is that, may I ask? And yet you thought you'd leave me... us... behind?" She turned over to face him. He caught the twin glints in her eyes, fierce and hard. "You've had a sheltered life, Dogfinger," she said. She sat up. Dogfinger could just make out the fullness of her gravid body as she did so, the sway of her huge breasts; the swish of her long hair.

"Husband," she said, "I was older than you when I came to the oasis. I am older than you still. I know the world better than you do. It's bigger than you imagine. When—if—you finally get to the Stoner city, you're not going to come back, all this way, to fetch us, and then go all the way there again? Three journeys, when just one would do? Are you?"

"Well, I... I confess..."

"So you are taking us with you? Good. I think you'll find us all... prepared." She lay down again, but closer this time. Dogfinger could feel the velvet skin of her belly and breasts rub against him. Her nipples, now coarsened and baby-chewed, were hard against his ribcage. "However," she continued, "I think we might have to put off our departure for a day or two. It's not as if we have to keep an appointment, is it?" She bit his earlobe. "I mean, after all," she continued, "the Kingdom will still be there, when we get there." She ran her fingers down across his belly. He stiffened. "And after we've taken it," she said, "it will, presumably, need populating."

She heaved her bulk on top of him, her distended belly resting just under his ribcage. She braced her mighty thighs on either side of his hips. Dogfinger felt himself slide into the cosseting warmth between. Yes, perhaps, his expedition against the Kingdom Under The Mountain could wait another day.

Maybe two.

But no longer.

-=0=-

By the time it reached the Sea of Galilee, the greatest army ever seen on the surface of the Earth, or near it, for tens of millions of years, had been winnowed to fewer than a hundred Stoner footsoldiers, ragged and hungry. Horsa and his men paused by the shores of the lake to recuperate.

The passage across the steppe had been relatively simple. Horsa's band had met no further resistance, but hunger and thirst had begun to take their toll. When the soldiers reached the shores of the Sea of Galilee, they broke ranks, some running—others limping and hobbling—into its healing waters, ripping off their armor and diving in. Horsa hadn't the heart to stop them, and indeed raised morale considerably by ordering the slaughter and consumption of the last of their animals—his own coelodont. The land all about was barren, and they'd had nothing to eat for two days. There was time, now, for hurts to heal. The redness in his vision faded, the inflammation receded. Healthful swims in the lake and a rich diet of broiled coelodont liver prompted his strained shoulder to knit together.

In truth, Horsa felt happier as a leader of a band of brigands (for that was what they were) than a massive army. They could move more quickly, and perhaps penetrate the heart of the Mountain even before its inhabitants knew that they had been invaded. Burglary, then, rather than full-on assault. It was in that spirit that Horsa and his band, refreshed, crept up on the Eastern Gate of the Kingdom one evening about a half-moon later.

Horsa remembered the splendor of the Eastern Gate as it had been in his childhood. He remembered the gigantic seated statue of Hrothgar the Great, the near-legendary King Under The Mountain who had ruled the known world perhaps eighty millennia earlier, towering above: the Gate itself opening between the statue's knees.

He remembered the immense stones, painted in gay colors, the flags and the banners cracking in the breeze; the perpetual market in the lee of the gate, the busy traders and throngs of people made as small as ants by the giant statue, people buying goods of every kind.

He remembered gawping beneath the awnings of the tannery market, at the richly furred Yettin pelts, piled high, contrasting with the darker hides of Thinskins.

He remembered running errands for his mother to the apothecary stall, to fetch Thinskin bone paste (a guaranteed cure for all known ills).

But most of all he remembered the delicatessen, with its jars of sweet-meats designed for the epicure—and with fabulous prices to match—for wild-caught Thinskins were scarce, even then. Bunches of Thinskin tongues, pickled and dried; deep-fried Thinskin ears and noses; pretty displays of crystallized Thinskin fingers and toes, almost irresistible to any five-year-old Stoner princeling; translucently-thin slices of ham from Thinskin heifers, freshly caught in the Nile Delta and 'newly violated' (he'd asked his mother what 'newly violated' meant, but she'd changed the subject); and, most of all, great, richly decorated stone jars of Thinskin eyeball-and-testicle soup, seasoned and prepared for the discerning palate.

He remembered his mother allowing him just a small spoonful of this most magnificent of all delicacies at a banquet. He remembered it as being insipid and tasting of nothing more than salt, and told his mother so. She laughed—how he remembered her laugh—and had said that it was something called an 'acquired taste,' which he'd appreciate when he was older. He'd never had the opportunity: his mother and her court took him into exile just a few weeks later.

Horsa had imagined the scene of his return for decades.

He had imagined himself a conquering hero, walking into the bustling market with his men, garlanded with Thinskin body parts by the oppressed citizens of the Kingdom, who would flock to his banner and overthrow the hated Hengest.

He had been bracing himself for the impact of what he suspected— *knew*—was the reality for several days, as his band passed through deserted villages, barren fields and homesteads laid waste, where once had been light and life. Nevertheless, the sight that greeted him as he and his band crested a knoll about half a mile from the Gate was heartbreaking. The Gate itself was unguarded, deserted, its stones drab and broken. Of the statue of Hrothgar, just the legs were left, trunkless, standing either side of the Gate. The head lay some distance away, on its side, its writhen expression half-sunk in piles of rubble and refuse.

Horsa decided to camp in the modest cave formed by Hrothgar's left nostril, and strike at the Kingdom the next day. He wondered, with resignation, if he was preparing to burgle a ruin whose treasures had long since been looted by others: that he was nothing but a vulture, a graverobber.

The final day of Horsa's long-planned, long-desired mission of revenge dawned bright and cold. Leaving a small detachment of Stoners to guard the Gate, Horsa led his remaining men through the Gate itself and into the heart of the Kingdom.

Where once had been elegant halls, full of life and gaiety and business, were now dark caverns that reeked of decay and neglect. Piles of refuse lay everywhere; bodies, and parts of bodies, and skeletons, of Stoners and Thinskins alike, were scattered all across the floor. Remains of food, dried and furred with mold; shattered flints, broken weapons, plates, flagons. Horsa's heart sank with every step. The trail of desolation went on for hall after hall, for hour after hour. His men, who had awoken in good heart, fell into brooding silence. They had expected at least some sign of battle, token resistance, even a feint. If one is to lead fighting men on such an expedition with a promise of a battle at the end of it, Horsa reflected, that promise really ought to be fulfilled.

He was heartened, then, by a ghost of a sound, coming from a passage ahead. Some of the men had heard it too, and Horsa felt the spark of spirits reviving all around him. He rushed ahead to a passage leading sharply downwards from one of the seemingly interminable series of once-grand but now-deserted and gloomy staterooms, and signaled for his men to gather round him and be silent. He heard his own breath and the beating of his own heart punctuating — what? It sounded like screams of agony and rage, one merging into another, without cease. He remembered that sound from his youth, again from the market at the Great Eastern Gate.

It was the sound of herded Thinskins at bay.

This, if anything, was the prize, the spoils of conquest. Horsa beckoned his men to follow, stealthily, down the broad passage. They needed no further encouragement. A few minutes later Horsa found himself on the threshold of a golden opportunity.

A later commentator might have recognized it as the jaws of Hell.

The passage opened out into a broad cavern, the roughness of its walls thrown into relief by the guttering flames of torchlight. Before him was a moving mass of pale color, in shades from ivory white to a kind of livid pink. It took a moment for him to realize that the mass was a press of bodies, jostling, shifting — and screaming. This had been the source of the noise he'd heard from the stateroom above. Screaming not in words, because the screamers, having been raised in strict captivity, had no language, even had they tongues to frame words.

This, then, was the prize domestic Thinskin herd raised by his brother Hengest, bred in captivity in caverns deep beneath the Kingdom. It was his brother's last attempt to prolong the life of a Kingdom which, Horsa now realized with a feeling of wrenching emptiness, had been no more than a grinning death's head of contempt, existing on borrowed time — perhaps for millennia before he himself had been born.

As he looked more closely, first at one Thinskin and then another, he realized that this herd was hardly a prize worth fighting for. These creatures were no more than oversized, bloated maggots. Whimpering within rolls of fat, heads shaved, dead eyes staring, lips slack and drooling, Horsa saw gelded cattle where once had been men; creatures without ears, without noses, without eyes, without fingers, without hands. And all, without exception, howling without cease.

In that moment Horsa felt a sensation he'd never felt in his life—pity. Not just for these wrecked and wretched specimens, bred for their meat and their pelts, but for himself, and even for Hengest. They were, every one of them, prisoners, witnesses to the fall of a once-great civilization. The Thinskin herd filled the great cavern from wall to wall, and Horsa could just make out, in the distance, the figures of Stoners assigned to guard and protect this last pitiful vestige of a Kingdom's wealth. A cry went up from the guards—Horsa's band had been spotted. Arrows flew: one of his men went down. Several Thinskins in front of him collapsed, pierced by flint-tipped shafts.

Horsa's men broke ranks, then. This, they realized, was the last throw. There was no Kingdom here, just booty to be swagged before a hasty retreat. He saw his men, to his right and left, diving in, grabbing at Thinskin arms and legs, slashing with their bone daggers, slaying, and then raping before slaying, and then eating. Thinskin heifers were down on the ground, each pinned by two or three of his own men at a time. Stoner heads came up, faces grinning, blood running down their faces.

Horsa saw the Kingdom's guards barge and trample their way through the crowds, but not, he saw, to fight his men directly. No, Hengest's men had also realized that the game was up, and were now trying to corral Thinskins for themselves. Fights broke out over Thinskins between the guards, between his men, and between his men and the guards, as if no distinction were now to be found between one Stoner and another, between guard and invader. He saw one young Thinskin heifer pulled in two, her guts slopping onto the cave floor and lapping up the legs of her assailants. Some of these stooped to gather the offal, but did not get up again, for they, too, were slain in their turn by Stoners jealous of these dubious prizes. In another place, he saw Stoners—guards and invaders together—sitting down for an impromptu banquet of raw, tender Thinskin flesh.

Horsa could watch no more. Not because he was especially disgusted by the actions of his troops. Thinskins were legitimate spoil, after all, and he could hardly deny his men their booty after such a long and costly campaign. But because he had business of his own. He picked his way through the growing carnage in search of his elder brother Hengest, the last King Under The Mountain.

Horsa scurried like a ferret through a maze of passages, all the while trying to dredge the memory of the Kingdom when, as a small boy, he'd run along these same alleys. But that was then, and whereas there had once been light, and kindly servants of whom to ask directions, now there was drear, lone darkness.

At length, however, he came across a broad way that he would once have recognized from its contents. This had once been the Way of Trophies, a hall lined with prizes from ancient campaigns; lapis armor from ancient battles on the Yettin frontier; weapons, armor and banners from even further afield; the Cush, the High Simien. As a child, he remembered the Court Jester, Kraator, taking him by the hand and explaining where it had all come from and why it was there.

He remembered being particularly frightened by an image of a black, red-eyed troll which the Jester had explained was called a Khong, from lands far to the East and South. Horsa remembered looking up, then, into Kraator's curious yellow eyes and seeing an expression which he did not then understand, but now realized was an picture of loss, of longing for something only just now brought to mind after a long lapse of memory.

"I saw one of these, once, long ago," the Jester had said, "a Khong."

"Did you? What was its name?" lisped the infant Horsa.

"Its name was Axaxaxas Mlö," replied the Jester.

Horsa laughed. "What a funny name!" he said.

"Yes, Highness," the Jester said. "Perhaps that's why I remember it! Come on, it's time for your bedtime story."

These memories now crisped and bleached like shreds of gibbeted skin before the sun, and Horsa found himself once again in the Way of Trophies as it had now become. It was as black as night, the way now lit by the sullen glow of torches in sparse wall-sconces, burning low and guttering with soot. If any trophies remained unlooted, they were impossible to see in the mirk. The gloom deepened as Horsa went on, towards what he now realized was the Great Chamber of the Kings — so dark, now, that he could no longer see the ground beneath his feet. This was awkward, he soon realized, as he kept tripping up on refuse scattered in his path.

A greater darkness loomed up before him, which he reasoned must have been the doorway to the Great Chamber itself. There seemed to be no trace of a door: the monumental, square-topped arch grinned dark and open, like the nasal cavity of a skull. Night must now have fallen outside. Had this not been the case, the Chamber would have been lit by the great windows giving directly onto an ancient terrace that looked directly over the sea. But all was as black as charcoal: Horsa was amazed to think that he'd been underground for almost a whole day.

Horsa paused on this, the last threshold, and drew breath. The stink of the place was overwhelming—of rancid grease, and rotten meat, and feces, and desperate decay, and corpses that should have been buried centuries ago still walking impudently beneath an astonished sky. He took one step forward into darkness.

Then another.

On the third, he brought his boot down with a crunch onto some hard, knobbly object. As he raised his foot, the object came with it, grasping weakly at his calves. He suppressed a spike of panic, realizing that he'd stepped in the chest cavity of a desiccated corpse, his boot caught in its ribcage. He shook the obstacle free, cursing, and in the next moment knew that all surprise had been lost—and also that he'd reached his quarry.

"I knew you'd get off your pimply little arse and come here eventually, baby brother," boomed a voice from the shadows ahead of him, "but you're a little late for the party, don't you think?"

"You have squandered the last vestiges of honor in our house," replied Horsa. "All pride... all... self-respect. Come out of the darkness and fight, Hengest." To have replied at all was Horsa's greatest error, for his voice allowed the blind King to get an accurate fix on the new intruder.

"Ever the insufferably pompous little shit, I see," sighed the King. "A snot-nosed little wanker you were then, and a snot-nosed little-wanker you remain. Do us a favor, please, and fuck off." Horsa hefted a narwhal-horn javelin, aiming at what he imagined was the source of the voice. He pulled his arm back and launched the missile into space. He heard a kind of wet crunching noise in the distance, followed by a gasp and a gurgle. But before he could learn whether his javelin had hit home, a heavy object whistled through the darkness and cracked him smartly between the eyes. Stars flashed before his vision, and then—nothing.

-=0=-

Dogfinger's first view of the Kingdom Under The Mountain was from the south, as its topmost pinnacles were picked out by the first rays of a new rising sun.

Unable to sleep, he'd crawled from the bison-hide bivouac he'd shared with Moonrise, untangling himself from her snoring form. The air was fresh: a cool wind was coming off the sea. His people were spread out, with careless lack of vigilance, in small supine mounds all along the beach, almost as far as the eye could see. He heard the mewling of a newborn baby, somewhere in the distance, away south.

The exodus from the refuge of *Baj!ra'adhzt* had been relatively uneventful, and they had met no resistance whatsoever along the way. The first push, across the erg, had been brutal, but they had overcome it, even with the long trail of women and a seemingly endless parade of children, and things had become much easier once they'd reached the coast. After that, it was simply a matter of walking with the sea to their left, until they reached the Kingdom.

But journeys are uneventful only in retrospect. Dogfinger had expected a Stoner ambush at any moment, and spent long hours planning contingencies with his immediate circle of lieutenants. Even after he'd retired, he'd lie awake for hours, despite the gentle chidings of Moonrise (who was, by that time, nursing another baby, born on the journey) that he really should turn off his brain and get some sleep.

"The country is quiet, Bride," he'd say, "*too* quiet."

"It's not like *you* to be suspicious, Husband," she said, her voice punctuated by the soft slurping noises of the nuzzling infant. "It doesn't suit you. Do you not think that this silence is nothing but the absence it seems to be, and not some cunning Stoner stratagem? Do you not remember what Shay said before he left? That the day of the Stoners had passed, and that all we had to do, now, was reach out and take what was ours?"

But Dogfinger only grunted in acknowledgement, turned over and stared at the wall of the tent.

As soon as he had left the tent on that new morning, Dogfinger stretched to his full height, and spread his arms. It felt good to be free, and to be doing something. He walked straight to the shore, bent down in the surf and splashed the cool foam on his face. Then he turned to face the north, and saw the city for the first time. He'd seen nothing like it in his whole life. Its scale simply defied description. An entire mountain, rising from the sea, fortified with gates, and ramparts, and towers. He was seized with panic—here they were, no more than a mile or two from the Kingdom, which they'd stumbled on almost without knowing it (having camped under cover of night the day before), and presumably within sight of any sentry that might choose to peer from its battlements.

His people were sitting ducks.

The men, the women, the children, the last hope of humanity against the Stoners. *His* children. *His* wife. But as he thought of Moonrise, he reflected that she'd been right. Yes, they were probably almost within bowshot of the Kingdom—but if that were true, they'd have been dead by now, or taken prisoner. He squinted in the new dawn, looking more closely at the mountain. It was perhaps a little far to be sure, of course, but his sight was keen, and he could see no movement either on the Mountain or anywhere near it.

There were no brown clouds on the horizon.

There were no men like tiny gray dots, all moving.

There was no tramp, tramp, tramp of marching feet.

There was no clank, clank, clank of stone armor.

There was no singing, in time with the marching feet.

"Green-Eye!" he'd said, "It sounds like Ma and Granma and the other ladies. They sing, when they pound the grain."

Green-Eye had not laughed. But she had, at last, been avenged. Dog-finger looked again at the Kingdom, but to his eyes it was just a mountain again, a relic of a distant past he had no wish to revisit. He looked past the mountain now, at the waiting world. It lay open and ready before him, for him to take at his leisure.

-=0=-

It was time to rest, Dogfinger thought, putting down his flints and awls and sucking at the tiny cuts in his gnarled hands. He stood up, stretching the curled and tightened sinews in his legs, stamping out a sudden cramp.

The day was darkening, now, or it might have been the strain in his eyes beginning to tell, he wasn't sure. But the forests he used to see from this rock-shelter, down to the lakeshore where their winter camp now thronged with his children and grandchildren, seemed thinner than they had been when they had first come here, so many years before. The herds of bison now marched further to the south in the winter, and rein-deer, once scarce, were seen every winter, in enormous herds. Dogfinger breathed the rapidly cooling air and pulled the bear-fur jerkin tighter around him.

Yes, he was sure that Father-the-Sun didn't come as far north as he once remembered, or rise so high in the sky. But yes—he remembered now—he had come from a distant land, where Father-the-Sun had been fierce and vigorous. But perhaps Father-the-Sun was old, like him. And, in truth, Father-the-Sun had died for him the previous winter, when Moonrise had been taken from him—from them all—just as they'd looked into the eyes of their first great-grandchild.

It had been a girl, whose eyes opened defiantly and stared hard at him. Dogfinger smiled at the memory: for one eye was as brown as the earth, and the other as green as the sea.

Dogfinger opened his hand, where he stood in the evening chill, and looked down at the lump of mammoth ivory resting on his palm. To anyone else, it would have seemed no more than a roughly-shaped blob, and Dogfinger knew that many hours more work yet remained before the ivory in his hand matched the picture as yet fresh in his memory. Of Moonrise when they were young. Of white skin in the reed-brakes; of fecund and fleshy curves; and of impossibly red hair.

-=0=-

The old man wheezed his way down the slope from the *abri* at Souris Saint-Michel. The crew had retired for the day, but as evening fell, the man couldn't help have one last look around. The field season of '66 was drawing to a close, and he knew, in his heart, that it might be his last, despite the promise of that enigmatic back wall. Something lay behind it, he just knew it, but any investigation would now have to wait. Besides, he'd promised to help Marc de Chetalier in his orchard.

Negotiating the steep, rock-strewn slope would have been difficult for anyone, let alone an old man with a cane. As he descended the last slope he slipped, and nearly fell. Righting himself, he saw that the end of his cane had dislodged an interesting pebble from the spoil-heap. He stooped, creaking, and picked it up. It was a sculpture in ivory, no bigger than a brooch.

A sculpture of a woman, idealized.

Her thighs were fat, tapering to tiny feet. Her belly was grossly distended, and surmounted by improbably vast breasts. The face was blank, but was framed by scratch-marks that might have represented hair. Squinting more closely, he thought he could make out traces of red ocher.

He smiled, the kind of rueful smile gifted only to those who have lived long and eventful lives, and have only just accommodated themselves to the sad fact that all such lives are finite. For sure, he thought to himself, he'd seen sculptures like this before, and scholars were inclined to regard them as no more than sympathetic magic; votive offerings to fickle gods, pleading for fertility in a pitiless world.

Some went further, seeing in the abundant curves of these sculptures the first stirrings of organized religion.

Such vanity, he thought. Such vain castles of speculation.

Because, were one to take the time to look more closely, and closer even than that, past one's predjudices and assumptions about the unknowable spiritual lives of our ancestors, you could be sure that whoever made these sculptures were human beings, with the normal complement of human urges, dreams, and memories. This tiny image, he was sure, was a portrait of a real person. No, more than that—a portrait of the sculptor's *love* for a real person.

The names of the sculptor and his model were irretrievably lost. But the love—ah, the *love*. That had lasted not months, or years, but millennia, transcending death itself.

The Abbé Gaston de Bonnard pocketed the sculpture and tottered down the slope.

Chapter 14. Apotheosis

Gascony, France, Earth, Easter Sunday, 2076

For the growing good of the world is partly dependent on unhistoric acts, and that things are not so ill with you and me as they might have been is half owing to the number who lived faithfully a hidden life, and rest in unvisited tombs.

George Eliot — *Middlemarch*

Disturbed by the stresses in the Earth in which many of them had been interred, the spheres stirred into renewed life. Not that they were really dead, for Domingo's intuition had been correct, as had been the suspicions of the massed ranks of scientists in the Khalifa who had tried to probe their secrets and failed. Were anyone left to appreciate it, it had been ironic that every one of those scientists had ended up as a sphere himself, united with their former enemies in a single, headlong rush to the zenith, as insistent as the migration of glass-eels from the Sargasso Sea.

Had the scientists managed to break open a sphere, they'd have been disappointed. For beneath the thick shell was nothing more than a gluey, protoplasm-like substance, its monotony broken by a few roving amoebocytes. This should not really have been a surprise, for the insides of a pupating caterpillar are similarly featureless, with no immediate, visible clue to the glorious transformation about to take place, when the cells within grow and divide, and something emerges as perfect as a butterfly.

Such clues as there might have been would have been genetic. It was indeed a wonder to the genetic pioneers of the twentieth century that the same genes that create a caterpillar also produce a butterfly. But there was a greater wonder still, unknown to all: that the genes of those human scientists held the key to a similar but quantitatively more profound transformation.

The genetic code is often seen as a language. The words that scientists use to express the manipulation of DNA — words like 'translation' and 'transcription,' and even 'code' — are evidence enough that this analogy is deeply rooted. If the genetic code *is* a language, however, it is one of a subtlety greater than any invented by human beings. Nature has transcended the apparent simplicity of the genetic code, written in an alphabet of only four letters, to create a means of communication of almost infinite nuance, in which meaning is almost wholly dependent on the context in which the DNA is transcribed by the microscopic machinery that reads it—and which is in turn created by that selfsame DNA.

Who can read the meaning of any given string of DNA, just by looking at it? Without the infinite recursion of context, it might contain the memories of trees, the autobiographies of the archangels, the key to all mythologies, a complete history of the future, or all of these things—or have no meaning whatsoever. In this ambiguity lies flexibility, for the DNA might be the instructions to make either a caterpillar or a human being—or anything in between. All living organisms contain genes that are substantially the same as in any other given organism. In the great scheme of things, relatively little separates the genetic complexions of humans and butterflies. It is the *context* that matters. Fragments of the same genes can be shuffled, placed against new neighbors, forced to form new and unexpected interactions—and generate new meanings.

So had human DNA been shuffled and tended, pruned and tweaked, over tens of millions of years, such that when the time was right, the human form might rearrange itself into a new shape. A sphere, black as space, a metaphor for the end of the Universe.

Or its beginning.

Although the spherical shells were resistant to anything the Khalifa could throw at them, they were not uniformly unquestioning barriers. For there was one, further signal, just one, that could penetrate them.

That signal had now been received.

The genes within the spheres rearranged themselves for one last throw, in a way analogous to the gavotte in which the genes in the human immune system rearrange themselves to create antibodies, customized to fight any conceivable infectious agent. The analogy was, however, remote, for this rearrangement manipulated the shape of matter itself, puncturing the fabric of time and space, opening tiny doors into the heart of the cosmos,

All across the world, the spheres responded to the call. As Tom saw it in the early hours of Easter Day, the spheres engaged in their own spectacular resurrection, hurling their brilliance towards the zenith point. And so it was elsewhere, from the deserted villages of China to the abandoned game of *petanque* that Domingo had visited in Nice. The radiance split the sky above the smoking ruins of Los Angeles, half-drowned New York, and the desert oases of Africa. The shade of Linus the Second broke free from his tomb and joined the downed hyperjet pilots of the Khalifa in one, final flight.

After the destruction of Jupiter, the plague of dragons had jarred the Yahoo from its focus. Had it been able to have turned its fantastic binocular gaze on the Earth at that moment, it would not have seen a quiet, blue-green planet, but a star: the center of innumerable incandescent shafts radiating into space. Once out in space, the rays gathered, as if they were so many geese finding their bearings before the long voyage home; swayed, and turned at last towards the beleaguered Sun.

-=0=-

Just before sunrise, Domingo realized, once again, that he had fallen asleep where he had been kneeling. Struggling to his feet, pins and needles shooting up and down his legs, he shook his head clear, padded across the hall to the bathroom and washed his face clear of the last shreds of night.

Haec dies.

This is the day.

He felt he should be rejoicing, but his heart was overwhelmed with dread. Have faith, he told himself.

Faith.

He swallowed, and calmed himself with a series of long, deep breaths. How peculiar, he thought—he had never before considered the matter, but for the first time in his life he actually felt *old*, as if his usually boundless energy were ebbing away into the ground. *Faith*, he told himself.

He shuffled downstairs, praying that each creak of the polished wooden staircase wouldn't wake the other inhabitants of the farmhouse, and left the house by the back door. He drove wet swathes in the long, dewy grass, yet to be warmed by the dawn. Pausing to unlatch the field gate onto the back lane, he looked anxiously up at the sky. It was a deep blue, like the velvety interior of a wooden case one might use to keep, for example, silverware. Or, perhaps, an upturned skull roof slicked with the millennial deposits of burned herbs. His eyes darkened. Hope, he felt, really *ought* to spring eternal.

A few stars could still be seen in the west, but they were fading rapidly. He turned now to the east, looking across the fields, and saw the Sun crest the horizon. He was about to sigh with relief—but caught his breath. For the sky did not lighten. It remained the same, deep, saturated blue of the late hours of night, as if he were viewing it through a polarizing filter. The Sun seemed larger than normal, and was clearly visible as a disk against the darkened sky. He had the briefly vertiginous sense that he had woken up on another planet and now surveyed an entirely alien scene. Reassurance, such as it was, came in the form of a few high, red cirrus clouds, the only blemish on the clear lapis bowl of the heavens. If not another planet, then, he felt he'd walked into a fresco by Giotto, the hagiography of Saint Francis, or some such. He decided to take heart from this comparison.

Haec dies quam fecit Dominus exultemus.

Today would be the day he would meet his Maker. One way or another. He set his face against the Sun, turned westwards once more and hurried up the hill to the square.

-=0=-

Jadis awoke with a start just before sunrise, imagining she'd heard a creak on the stairs. She was immediately assaulted with a pain so overwhelming as to be almost unbearable. It was not just her insides, this time, but every single joint, every nerve in her body.

"Jack... Jack?"

"Mmm?" Jack stirred.

"Would you be a love... and make some tea?"

Without a word Jack swung out of bed and padded out of the room. The dawn was just peeping through the southward window in the hall, the window that looked over the courtyard. It struck him, first, that no birds sang, because although the Sun had clearly risen, it still felt dark. Not that any thoughts of apocalypse entered his head, for his mind was now wholly occupied with Jadis and, he was almost certain, her terminal illness. Frankly, she was slipping away from him, a little further each day. With each new dawn she was thinner and more fragile, and he felt helpless to intervene. The first step in curing an illness is always to admit that something is the matter, and Jadis simply refused to do this, or even discuss it. But perhaps it was now too late for that.

In the kitchen, he found a half-filled kettle, still warm. He was not the only person in the house who'd had a troubled night, then — but it was Easter Sunday, and Domingo would presumably have left early, and Tom would have gone out to tend to the stock. Jack brought the kettle to the boil and filled two mugs.

As they cooled, he ventured just outside the back door to cut some mint for their tea. *Real* tea was a rare treat, saved for visitors. While he was in the back yard, he cut a sprig from the abundant hemp that had seeded itself just outside the back door a few years before, and now formed a curiously twining vine up the wall. Funny, he never knew hemp could climb like that. Neither he nor Jadis had ever been enthused by recreational drugs, and neither of them had ever smoked: but it was an attractive plant, so they just left it. But if Jack put some in Jadis' tea and added enough sugar, perhaps she wouldn't notice. At the very least, it would stop her constantly wanting to throw up, not that she ate very much these days, anyway.

The great ball of the Sun was now a degree or two above the eastern field, but the sky was as deeply blue as ever, the colour of cornflowers, or a child's painting. He felt, rather than heard, a crack like a distant gunshot, but coming from beneath his feet: the Earth, too was waking up to greet the new and final day.

Haec dies.

This is the day.

Having cut the mint and marijuana, and with the leaves in hand, Jack stretched in the new warmth. The night had been no worse than usual. Jadis had talked a great deal in her sleep and had woken up twice, disoriented, sweat beading on her brow, her eyes huge and frightened in her thin face. He could have sworn that once, when, tossing and turning in her dreams, when she had meant to chide him for being 'such a silly man,' the words had come out as 'Solomon'. No, *more* than once: the biblical name was repeated several times until she had willed herself back into deeper sleep.

Jack allowed himself a wry smile. 'Solomon,' eh? Fancy that. A name of proverbial wisdom. He rather liked that, he thought. He resolved not to tease Jadis with it in the morning. It would, he thought, only distress her.

The kitchen welcomed him again with the cool dark of waning night. He stirred the leaves into the hot water and added some sugar.

He really ought to have felt aggrieved about the whole thing, he felt, that Jadis could let herself die with no consideration for his feelings in the matter. But that was just it. Jadis had this over-inflated sense of duty that extended to not being a burden on anyone else, taking self-sufficiency to an extreme. As far as Jadis was concerned, either she wasn't ill—or she *was* ill, but she would get better if the symptoms were ignored for long enough. It never crossed her mind that this course of action might—would—destroy her in the end.

He smiled again, but this time with great sadness, because it was this relentless self-reliance in the face of all advice or evidence that led to the car crash that led to Tom, to…

For many years he wondered whether, had Jadis reached Addenbrooke's, their baby might have been saved, or if she'd have miscarried anyway. He recalled Marjorie MacLennane having made the same point, not long after the accident. Great heavens! This was more than fifty years ago, so why brood on it now? Well, it was something to do with the Plague, and something to do with Domingo, too, but he couldn't work out what. And then there was the farmhouse, where he stood, a place that had always seemed utterly changeless. Even when the world rushed and swirled around it, as it had lately, the farmhouse always remained inviolate.

A magic space.

But the Plague had honored no such boundaries. When they realized that the Plague struck *Homo sapiens* exclusively, he started to wonder. The Plague might well have claimed poor Shoshana—albeit in a form that had been extremely unusual.

Tom, they knew about.

Domingo? Jack wasn't so sure.

Jadis? Well, not all humans got the Plague, so perhaps she was in the lucky minority.

And himself? Ah, himself. Who knew? Perhaps, like many people these days, a smidgeon of Neanderthal blood ran in his veins, enabling him to recognize the landscapes of his longfathers where others could not.

He gathered up the mugs and headed upstairs. As he climbed, he was seized with an awful premonition, that he would push open their bedroom door to find that she had died. He stopped to catch his breath, putting the mugs down on a bookshelf in the upstairs hall.

-=0=-

Domingo arrived in the square to find it already full to overflowing with people. The press of supplicants, the hands thrust out to him, the pleas—demands—for blessings, for absolution; he heard them all, but after a short while they merged into a constant stream, like the sound of the sea in his ears. He made his way, slowly, to the church, where he'd assist the priest in some of the Easter offices. He made a point of not looking back at the slowly rising Sun, although he felt its welcome heat on the back of his head. Every other person, however, was gazing at its saffron disk riding in the unnaturally blue sky. Watching, open-mouthed, and wondering.

The rituals of Easter were usually of great joy to him. He realized, now, before the church heaving with a sea of people, that his previous comfort had been little more than the smugness of children who enjoyed a bedtime story they had heard already a dozen times—because they knew the ending. In which case, the solemnity of the antiphons and psalms seemed hardly more than a sham. In this unnervingly detached frame of mind, he wondered what the first Easter had been like, when Christ's disciples were convinced that their Lord was going to die a nasty, slow and, above all, certain death: and the genuine joy when the Resurrection, beyond hope or expectation, was made plain, even to the doubters.

That first Resurrection morning, he thought, has less in common with the way we came to celebrate Easter, with its ending already known, than with the rituals of the ancients, who made bloody sacrifices to en-sure that the Sun would rise the next day: because they were gripped with a terrifying certainty that this would not happen were the proper forms not maintained. The Easter they were celebrating right now had that same *frisson* of terror, of uncertainty.

Part of him knew that the world would end today, in a few hours. But another, the greater, still hoped for some form of Divine deliverance. Easter was so close to Passover, as he and Avi had often discussed. We were slaves in Egypt, as Christ had explained to his fellow Jews at their own Last Supper, but the Lord saved us, with his mighty hand, with his outstretched arm. Although Domingo found it hard to engage in the of-fices themselves, his prayers were as heartfelt as ever.

-=0=-

After Jack had left the room, Jadis slowly and painfully sat up in bed, swinging her legs very carefully over the side. When the giddiness had ceased and the spots before her eyes had cleared, she looked down at her knees, and all of a sudden she realized how bony and blotched they looked. Her arms, too. Indeed, every part of her. She felt truly, utterly, horrible.

Trying very hard not to be sick, she rose, very carefully, to look for her comb. This had always been an important part of life—sitting on the edge of her bed and combing her long hair—especially when Jack helped, even as her black hair had turned to gray. She'd be damned if she were to stop it now, just because she felt ill. The oversized faux-tortoiseshell comb was the same she'd had, for as long as she could remember. Remarkably, it had not lost a single tooth despite the daily punishment to which it had been subjected. She thought she'd left it on the bedside table, because this was where she'd *always* left it. But if so, she could no longer see it. Perhaps it had fallen on the floor. She slipped to her knees on the floor beside the bed. The twin impacts on her knees shot up her thighs like lightning bolts, and she just stopped herself from crying out. Gingerly, she lay down full length on the floor to look under the bed, but her comb was not there, either. Where had it got to? It was then that she realized that she was immobile, quite unable to get up. She started to cry with the frustration of it.

-=0=-

The procession made its way out of the packed church and into the square. The Sun rode high before it from its deep blue vault. The crowd parted, inasmuch as it could, for Domingo, the parish priest and the lines of Christophorines and Adelardians as they made their way across the square to the Mairie. The crowd surged forward once again, right to the building's iron railings.

Once inside the cool of the building, Domingo thanked the parish priest and his brethren. He believed that the time of judgment was imminent — and whatever happened, he said, he prayed that God would be with them all. They bowed, and left, taking up stations in the well-kept front yard of the Mairie, just inside the railings, a peaceful haven of ordered paths, box hedges and bay trees.

Domingo was alone again. He was relieved, but also frightened. Loneliness is a not a natural state for human beings, which is why enduring it had always been a test for people of faith. It was appropriate that in this last office — the last one of all — that he was not only alone, but that all eyes should be upon him. He thanked God for the opportunity that had been presented to him, that he should be in this position of command. He saw himself at that moment against the cosmos, and was humbled. Just one old man, alone, to present the eulogy for the world.

Painfully, he climbed the stairs to his private apartment on the top floor. Painfully, because despite the almost proverbial strength he'd enjoyed throughout his long life, he felt at last — as he had this morning — that age was beginning to tell. He was seventy-six, and his weight was a considerable strain on his knees, already bruised from his frequent vigils. He sat down to catch his breath and offered one last, small prayer for strength.

It was his favourite psalm, which he murmured under his breath, over and over like a mantra, as he went back into the hall and found the small winding stair that led to the parapet on the roof of the building.

nam et si ambulavero in medio umbrae mortis

he gasped with deep and unsteady breaths as he negotiated the steep and tightly curving staircase:

non timebo mala

as he reached the parapet and looked down — how far it was!

quoniam tu mecum es

Domingo was no stranger to making speeches — indeed, he had always quite enjoyed it — but now his mouth was dry, and nothing seemed to come out. The crowd below saw him, a robed figure on the parapet, and fell silent. There was no wind, even the birds of springtime were silent. It was as if the world waited on Domingo's next words. But all he could say was what was in his mind at that moment.

"My friends," he said, "although we walk together in the valley of the shadow of Death, we shall fear no evil, for the Lord is with us."

And then the sky boiled.

-=0=-

She must have blacked out, for the next thing she remembered she was in bed again, beneath the sheets, with Jack looking down at her, his brow furrowed.

"Darling Jack, it's me... I couldn't find my comb, and..."

"Hmm? It's right there, on your bedside table. Where you left it."

"Oh, really? I thought... Perhaps I was confused... I thought..."

"Let's prop you up," he said, "and I shall comb your hair. Would you like that?"

"Oh you silly man! Of course I would!"

So he gently lifted her into a sitting position on the side of the bed, propping her up with pillows so she wouldn't fall back, or sideways. He took the comb and began to tease her hair with long, easy strokes.

She closed her eyes and, at first, she saw all those combings past, all together, at once. And as he combed, she relaxed and began to make out each event separately. When they were younger, it had all been terribly erotic, and they had often ended up back in bed, which only made her hair all the more disordered. She laughed at that now. These days—and for many days before that—it was simply one of those silly rituals that bonded them together. Something they liked to do because... well, *because*.

Part of the reason Jack liked to comb her hair, he had said once (well, actually, a lot *more* than once) was because it was an inherently futile act, which tickled his sense of humor. She had the kind of hair that would never stay in one place for long, and that, said Jack, was one of things that had first turned him on when they'd first met. And after that, it seemed, her home had always been with him.

-=0=-

The spheres formed a cohort of billions, but in the dimension they now inhabited, they were but one vast, linked entity, as if each sphere had been a macroscopic quantum object, an instantiation of a single thing, a crystal with innumerable facets. From the human perspective, they were no longer spherical, but formed a shape impossible to describe except in purely formal terms, and even then only with mathematics not yet discovered by human beings.

In words, the description could only have been a mess of contradictions. In one sense, they united to form a point of infinitesimal size but infinite density. In another, they linked up to form a new, larger spherical shell, this one large enough to surround the Sun and the entire volume of space out beyond the orbit of Venus.

In yet a third sense, the effect of the spheres was to twist time and space into a series of knots of infinite curvature, linking every instant with all the others that had ever been, or would be; uniting every point in the cosmos with every other. In this way they recreated, in solar orbit, the moment of the Big Bang in the instant of inflation that had expanded it from a singularity to the size of a human fist. The dragons were sucked into this vortex and translated to the very beginning of time. But even in such exotic circumstances, matter and energy had to remain conserved.

In destroying the dragons, the spheres had only ensured their regeneration.

-=0=-

She leaned back against him, and made her way to the very edge of sleep. How odd—she no longer felt any pain. None at all. She had to admit it was a blessed relief, and she now realized quite how uncomfortable she'd been for the past year, or more. Oh dear, she must have been most disagreeable to everyone around her. Especially poor Tom. She hoped they'd all forgive her.

Ah, but her mind was wandering again, and she was a cloud floating over a calm landscape before the foothills of a range of high mountains. How far it stretched, in all directions, with the yellow sun shining down on the snowy peaks from a deep blue sky. She wondered when or where she'd touch down, as she knew she would, and, thus distracted, she was only vaguely aware that the sky had changed color, from blue, to gold, and then to blue once more. This time it was the clear blue of any other spring day. She idly wondered whether they should get the early potatoes planted.

But what was this? The wintry ground came up to meet her, and she landed, gently as a snowflake, on the bottom of a high mountain valley. She got to her feet, looked up, and was only mildly surprised to see, on the ridge to her right, what looked like a hunting lodge, built on a monumental platform of dressed stone. There was a floor-to-ceiling window the entire width of the building, which was flooded with a welcoming yellow light. She looked up, then, and it was night, and the stars had begun to come out.

-=0=-

At the very moment that Domingo finished speaking, the dark blue sky fell to pieces. Fractal lines like lightning bolts split the heavens from horizon to horizon. More lines joined them, until, after a few moments, the entire sky had turned a uniform golden colour. Domingo looked up and gasped—as did every person in the square below. All thought was lost at the wonder of it. When Domingo had recovered his senses, he felt that they really had been transported into a fresco by Giotto, to a time when art was just waking from the Middle Ages. A moment before perspective had been achieved, when there was in effect no distance at all between any object in the Universe, when Man and God were at one and at peace, and all skies were golden.

The phase of gold lasted for a minute or two, just long enough for everyone in the crowd to have turned round to gaze in astonished awe, before it faded, to be replaced by the clear, pale sky of springtime, the yellow Sun gazing down as it had for billions of years, and as it would for billions of years to come. The birds sang again, as if they had experienced no more than a momentary interruption. Domingo's spirit soared—his God had heard his cry in the wilderness. His prayers had been answered.

Tears coursed unasked down his lined face. He stretched out his arms once again, to the sky and to the crowds.

"*Et misericordia tua subsequetur me, omnibus diebus vitae meae,*" he roared: "*Et ut inhabitem in domo Domini in longitudinem dierum.*"

I shall enjoy your mercy for all my days, and I shall dwell in your mansions of glory for ever.

And the crowd roared back: "*Amen!*"

Epilogue

Gascony, France, Earth, February, 2096

We wonder,—and some Hunter may express
Wonder like ours, when thro' the wilderness
Where London stood, holding the Wolf in chace,
He meets some fragments huge, and stops to guess
What powerful but unrecorded race
Once dwelt in that annihilated place.
Horace Smith—*Ozymandias*

From the Private Journals of Eusebius Secundus, Episcopus Romanus.

This might well be my final entry in these journals before I leave, finally, to take up my long-vacant throne.

I have been reluctant to do this for many years, having formed a strong attachment to this old place, but the College of Cardinals has become more insistent of late. The Eternal City thrives once more, they say, but cannot truly live without its 'Supreme Arch-Episcopal Adornment' (their words, not mine).

In any case, I might not be long for this world, having almost matched the impressive longevity of the great Gaston de Bonnard, in which case I really should move back to Rome while I still can, so that my succession might be managed without too much fuss and bother: and in case I am tempted to climb one of the magnificent apple trees that Jack planted long ago, in search of riper fruit that hangs yet, only just beyond my grasp. Even so, once in Rome after so long a spell at Saint-Rogatien, I'll feel like an exile on Main Street. Perhaps, then, it might be appropriate to reflect on some larger matters, before I go.

The world changed irrevocably, in the Spring of '76, as everyone is now aware. However, just as a new generation grew up in ignorance of the Plague, a further has risen to maturity that would gasp in disbelief were one to say that the Solar System once had many more planets than it has now. Once we had assessed the damage, as it were, we found that Mercury had vanished, in addition to the giant planets consumed by the dragons.

Venus moved closer to the Sun: its clouds boiled, and its hellish surface was once again exposed. Mars, also, moved slightly closer, and was devastated by asteroid impacts. Its great volcanoes surged into life after perhaps a billion years of sleep. That, and the additional impact of two comets, shrouded that Harbinger of War in the mantle that Venus had shed, and its surface is now hidden from us. Some say that when the clouds part—in one year or in a million—Mars will look like another Earth, with blue skies and open oceans, and, perhaps, the blessing of life. Apart from that there are a lot of rocks about, until one reaches lonely, blue Neptune.

We should be fools to cry. Our Earth has been spared major devastation, although her orbital parameters have changed a little. My old friends the astrometers in Cambridge tell me that the shape of the Earth's orbit is a shade more eccentric, the tilt of the axis a few shavings of a degree greater, and the Moon is marginally further away from us. This might explain why the Moon is now to be seen fully in rotation, and why the summer weather is in general hotter and more oppressive than it has been for many a long year, and why the winters, while mercifully brief, are very cold indeed. But that could an old man talking: an old man often tempted to take his winter holidays at Nice, where is he once more a guest (albeit now one who settles his accounts) at the Hotel Negresco.

What has been the cause of much perplexity is that the year has lengthened by about two and a half days, which—what with the antics of the Moon—has made calculating the date of Easter a matter of some contention, still unresolved. Cardinal Bray implores me with some urgency that my first task when I get to Rome must be to convene a conference on this very issue. Probably before I have a chance to unpack, if he has his way.

Whereas I acknowledge that a return to Rome will be a blessing, in the end, it shall tear my heart to leave the house in which I now reside. I well remember my first visit, when I had the good fortune to have met Dr Jadis Markham, who became my closest friend and, I have to say, my confessor. Jadis died at the very moment of God's victory, and I am confident that she sits close to the throne of the Almighty.

After her death, many people wished to view her body and pay their respects, for there are many in Saint-Rogatien and the adjacent communes who would not have lived but for her ministrations. She lay in state, as it were, at the church, before Jack, Tom and I buried her in the Spinney, which was her favorite place on this Earth. I still sit there by her grave, on Jack's old bench, on occasion, when I wish to think through some particularly knotty point of theology, and I can still hear her voice whispering through the trees—'oh you silly man, it's like this'. And the problem will have been resolved.

Jack's mortal remains now rest beside her in this quiet spot. After
Jadis died, he felt he could no longer continue, as he said he saw Jadis in
every tree and every hillside, in every country lane and on every horizon. His confession to me was perhaps a little unguarded, for he spoke
with feeling and at length of Jadis as a young woman, full of vivacity
and charm, and of their early days together. This is how we all should
like to remember her, for that is when I first met her, too. Jack went back
to Cambridge, with Tom, and spent two more years as an Emeritus Professor before he died, and his body came back here. Tom resides in
Cambridge still, himself now a distinguished Emeritus Professor.

Jadis told me once, that her devotion to the health of her neighbors
was a kind of penance for what she had unleashed on the world. She
said that she knew it was ridiculous—if not presumptious to an outrageous degree—but she felt that had she and Jack not unearthed the Sigil,
then none of this would have happened: the Plague, the dragons and so
on and so forth. I confess that I had been inclined to dismiss this, until a
curious incident not long after her death, when Jack and Tom were making the house ready for my installation. I happened to be a witness to the
event, for I was helping them to arrange matters, as they had kindly
made over the house to my stewardship.

We had assembled in the barn to essay a general clear-up, and found
the Sigil, where it had been for so many years, concealed under its tarpaulin, since Tom had described it and drafted his paper for *Nature*
which—thankfully, in the light of what happened next—was not yet
published. The three of us discussed what might be done with the ancient artifact, and soon reached the decision that it should be transported
back to Souris Saint-Michel, and stored in the old Museum there. In the
course of this discussion we removed the tarpaulin and unpacked the
crate, more for old times' sake (and in spite of Tom's initial reluctance),
to look at the curious inscription. You may imagine our surprise when
what greeted us was the bare, smooth surface of the matrix. No trace of
the Sigil could be seen. It had vanished, as if it had never been.

Tom's immediate task was to withdraw the paper from consideration,
and this was swiftly done. Without the publicity that would have then
ensued, the existence of the Sigil was known to remarkably few people,
of whom only Tom and myself are now alive.

Perhaps it is better that way.

Nevertheless, in the weeks following that peculiar event, Tom, Jack
and I spent many evenings discussing its significance. First: was the Sigil
real, or had we imagined the whole thing? The latter choice implied

some kind of collective delusion, which did not strike us as likely, even taking Tom's peculiar experience of the Sigil into consideration. But if the Sigil had been a real object, then Jack and Jadis' ideas that the Plague and the visitation of the dragons were not coincidental, but connected, must have had some bearing in fact. The Sigil had been a warning—just as Tom and Shoshana had thought—and it had done its work, specific to the times in which we then lived, and not for all times or circumstances.

Several rather unpleasant implications might follow from this idea. First, that the Sigil was more than a simple notice of the approaching dragons, but that its providential uncovering had somehow triggered the Plague. After all, the Plague had no known, proximate mechanism, and even today, none has been identified.

In addition, it is salutary to note that the event that swept billions away, but which in the end saved the Earth, was sparked by the slenderest chain of events. I was not aware quite how slender they had been until Jack had explained them to me. Were it not for the excavations at Souris Saint-Michel, the Sigil might never have been found. But before Souris, there had to be *Le Dig* at Saint-Rogatien in which I was a participant, and that would not have been possible had not the work been funded by the prescience of one Ruxton Carr; and, in turn, had it not been for a morning in Cambridge long ago when a teenaged Jadis had walked into Jack's class five minutes late, with her hair (as Jack put it) in a state of disorder which he found pleasing, to the extent that he married her. But for a nail in a horseshoe, it is said, the kingdom might fall. Were it not for the long hair of a lovely young girl, the same fate might have befallen an entire planet.

It occurred to Tom that there was another even more chilling possibility. That the Sigil was more than a warning, and more, even, than the trigger for the Plague—that it had been an interstellar beacon that actually drew the dragons towards us. For millions of years, the Sigil's mysterious makers and the dragons had played a great and shadowy game. *Homo sapiens* had not been the sacrifice—it had been the bait.

Another issue which occurred to none of us at the time was this: given that the Sigil had been physically inscribed, how had the inscription then been removed? This is the least explicable of all these thorny issues, and so I shall not attempt to discuss it further.

In consideration of all these matters, I must own—despite my earlier shameful insistence to the contrary—that Jadis was right to have held out against the publication of the Sigil, and for this and many other reasons to which I have alluded, I pledge myself to her memory. I have given instructions to my successors that her grave, and that of Jack, too, be maintained and revered in an appropriate manner. It has already perforce become a shrine, and a place of pilgrimage, for her reputation as a healer and worker of miracles is widespread. I am not so sure that any of these miracles can be substantiated. And yet, and yet: there was, I confess, always something a little unearthly about Jadis. She seemed to touch the earth but lightly, and held it lightly in her grasp, as if she could see inside — beyond — mere corporeal matter. Should the Lord preserve me long enough, I shall set up a commission for her beatification.

Despite the mysteries surrounding the Sigil itself, more can perhaps be said concerning the role of *Homo sapiens* in the Plague and the subsequent apotheosis. I am fond of considering this by way of an analogy. It has long been known that species can exist happily in one form until transformed into something quite other by the threat of a predator. For example, I have observed, in the garden here, how aphids persist in a wingless state for many generations, until a predatory ladybird appears. Then, a most remarkable change happens — the aphids suddenly develop wings, where none had been before, and fly from danger. My Adelardian colleagues tell me that this phenomenon has long been known to ecologists, and that the chemical stimulant secreted by the ladybird has been identified that effects this startling transformation.

In the same way, it was the approach of the dragons — whether mediated by the Sigil or not — that caused the Plague, transforming the human race into a form that could effectively neutralize the threat. *Fiat voluntas tua, sicut in caelo et in terra*, and quite right, too. *Libera nos a malo*, we asked, and you answered our prayers, sending, through long eons of evolution, through the careful pruning of natural selection, a savior who would, indeed, deliver us from evil. How could anyone ever have doubted it?

I shall close this entry with two confessions.

The first relates to the reason why I did not succumb to the Plague. To explain that, I must needs sketch some details of my origins which have hitherto remained unrecorded. It is known that Neanderthal Man lived in Europe until at least twenty-one thousand years ago, and that his last redoubts were in southern France and Spain. It is a fact universally acknowledged that it is never possible to isolate the last ever occurrence of a vanishing species — particularly if the species concerned does not, in fact, vanish. For the Neanderthals survived in the high Sierra Nevada of Andalusia, albeit latterly as a despised and rarely seen minority in remote and almost inaccessible villages. It occurred to no-one that they were anything other than human beings, even if of a primitive and peculiar kind.

The Neanderthals hung on through the Roman occupation and the barbarian invasions, and were tolerated – and even prospered – under the first Khalifa. It was then, in the Kingdom of Granada, assailed by Ferdinand and Isabella of Castile, that the last references were made to Neanderthals as something other – as inhuman. It came to the ears of their Catholic Majesties that the Emir Muhammad employed 'Demons' as bodyguards, and this was used as a pretext for invading the Kingdom in 1492. What with the persecution of the Jews in Spain at the same time, and the sensitivity of the Inquisition to anything at all that smelled of the alien, the retribution was both swift and terrible. After that date, no further reference is made to the Neanderthals, and it was therefore assumed that they had become extinct.

But as my old friend Jadis often said, it is the things that everyone assumes to be true that tend to be the most egregiously erroneous, and this was certainly the case in this instance. For I now believe that I am one of these Neanderthals, of almost pure stock. I was long unsure of this, but thanks to the progress of medical testing, I am now absolutely certain. In which case, it is a nice irony, is it not, that one of a race deliberately persecuted by the upholders of the Holy Church should rise to become its Earthly representative?

It is of some passing interest to me why nobody throughout my long life has suspected my origins, even those closest to me, and whose daily occupation was the study of Neanderthal bones and artifacts. In my childhood, of course, nobody suspected anything other than that the only extant hominid was *Homo sapiens* itself. In which case, as a child I was seen not as a member of an ancient race but a deformed example of humanity, to be reviled. After that, ecclesiastical vestments tended to distract attention from the Man within. That, and if I might say so in the confines of these pages, a fondness for leisurewear that maintained in vividness what some might say it lacked in style.

Finally, to my last confession, a matter which, even after all these years, I have some difficulty in setting down on the page. It concerns Tom, who was not a human being, but a scion of that most ancient pre-hominid race that created, if not the Sigil, then, perhaps, *Homo sapiens* and incidentally all the other hominids as a way to rid the cosmos of the scourge and pestilence that were the dragons. This in itself is not as well known as it might be, primarily for lack of direct evidence. Tom, to his great credit, accepted his nature after a long and difficult struggle. So much so that he married, at length, one of his own kind. His wife Morgana is herself a distinguished anthropologist, and their house in Cambridge bustles with several children—or, as Tom calls them, 'kits'—shepherded round the house by what must be a very patient golden retriever.

But it was my fault alone that I did not see any of this in advance, and that because of my sole negligence—a deficiency made worse given my suspicions of my own non-human origins—I made a grave mistake. That is, to have allowed him to have been raised as a human being, and for him to have thought of himself as one.

For shame, I know now a great deal that is both fascinating and unusual about Tom's race, the people that call themselves 'Jive Monkeys'. Much of it I found in my journey to south-east Asia long ago, that region bursting with hominid life, in which the Jive Monkeys number among the least conspicuous for all that they—or, rather, their ancestors—created it all. Very few of these facts were ever revealed to me directly, but only as shabby hints and innuendo, in bars and hotels and rickshaws from Singapore to Manila. However, ignorance is in itself no excuse.

The clearest answers I obtained from the Jive Monkey whom I knew best, second only to Tom, an individual of great character whose table I shared over a long journey from Batavia to Port-Said, namely the Captain of the *S. S. Venture*. It is better, they say, to be hung for a sheep as a lamb, so I shall be as frank as allowed by my memory; the likely brevity of my remaining life on Earth; and the fact that these diaries will, I trust, remain private.

This is what the Captain said—that Jive Monkeys have a secret weapon against their human oppressors, those who sought to exploit them in every bar and backstreet hovel throughout the Indies. '*Na misis make pushim wantaim me monyet minari*' he said, '*air mani racun kilim!*'

Even now I am reluctant to translate these words directly, so repellant are they, and so deep my shame. Together with other clues gleaned over the years, I can nonetheless summarise, in a relatively dispassionate way, their implications, if not their meaning.

As a consequence of their own biology, that through the remorseless logic of natural selection, the promiscuous mating habits of Jive Monkeys led to a phenomenon in which semen slowly poisons the females, shortening their lives, reducing their capacity to produce offspring from too many competing males. Jive-Monkey females have to an extent evolved defenses against this. Females of other species, in general, have not. To be brief, for a human female to have sexual relations with a Jive

Monkey over any sustained interval will condemn her to an agonizing death. Shoshana Levinson, who was the love of Tom's life, was definitely human, and it is Tom's tragedy that he thought he was, too. And it is my great sin that I did not realize this until far too late.

Fiat misericordia tua, Domine, super nos. Humanity as a group billions strong was sacrificed that we all might live. But I suspect that few of them demonstrated the love, generosity of spirit and acceptance shown by just one young girl. I pray earnestly and constantly for peace on her soul, and hope that she can forgive me.

This is the final entry in the journal. A later hand reports that His Holiness died peacefully in his sleep on the journey to Rome, on Ascension Day (Old Style), 2096.

-=0=-

ACKNOWLEDGMENTS

The germ of this story—or, rather, two germs—can be found in two SF vignettes I wrote in *Nature*, one pseudonymously. One, called *Et in articulo mortis* (*Nature* **405**, 21; 2000) describes Post-Embryonic Petrosis as an evolutionary response to star-hungry dragons. The other, *Are We Not Men?* (*Nature* **435**, 1286; 2005) reported the emergence of many hitherto-mythical hominids onto the world stage, including Sand Druids and Jive Monkeys. Perhaps ill-advisedly, I thought I'd put the two ideas together in a box and see what came out. The result is as you see.

I offer my thanks to Karl Ziemelis, Andrew Burt, Vonda McIntyre, Ian Watson, Jack Cohen, Brian Clegg, Bruce Goatly, John Gilbey, Richard P. Grant, Heather Corbett Etchevers, Jennifer Rohn, Chris Surridge, Peter Watts and all the residents of the LabLit community forums, and the many others who read various drafts of this book, for their continuing encouragement and comments. David Doughan and Adam Rutherford helped me with my Latin, and Tony Kerstein with my Hebrew.

ABOUT THE AUTHOR

Author Photo by John Gilbey

Henry Gee was born in London in 1962. He received his B.Sc. in Zoology and Genetics from the University of Leeds, and his Ph.D. in Zoology from the University of Cambridge. Since 1987 he has been on the editorial staff of *Nature*, the international weekly science magazine, where he is now Senior Editor of Biological Sciences, and was the founding editor of *Futures*, *Nature*'s award-winning SF column.

He is the author of several works of nonfiction including *The Science of Middle-earth*, *In Search of Deep Time* and *Jacob's Ladder*, and a novel, *By The Sea*.

He lives in Cromer, Norfolk, England, with his family and numerous pets.

ReAnimus Press

Breathing Life into Great Books

If you enjoyed this book we hope you'll tell others or write a review! We also invite you to subscribe to our newsletter to learn about our new releases and join our affiliate program (where you earn 12% of sales you recommend) at www.ReAnimus.com.

Here are some ebooks you'll enjoy from ReAnimus Press, available from Re-Animus Press's web site, Amazon.com, bn.com, etc.:

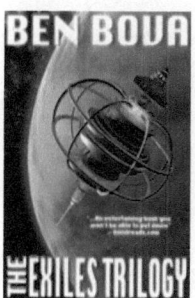

The Exiles Trilogy, by Ben Bova

The Star Conquerors, by Ben Bova
(Standard Edition and
Special Collector's Edition)

Test of Fire, by Ben Bova

The Kinsman Saga, by Ben Bova

The Craft of Writing Science Fiction that Sells, by Ben Bova

Staying Alive - A Writer's Guide,
by Norman Spinrad

Space Travel — A Guide for Writers,
by Ben Bova

Shadrach in the Furnace,
by Robert Silverberg

The Transcendent Man, by Jerry Sohl

Night Slaves, by Jerry Sohl

Bloom, by Wil McCarthy

Aggressor Six, by Wil McCarthy

Murder in the Solid State,
by Wil McCarthy

Flies from the Amber, by Wil McCarthy

Side Effects, by Harvey Jacobs

American Goliath, by Harvey Jacobs

"An inspired novel" – *TIME Magazine*
"A masterpiece…arguably this year's best novel" – *Kirkus Reviews*